KNIGHTS MAGI

Book 4 of the Spellmonger Series

Second Edition

Copyright © 2014, 2018 Terry Mancour

This is a work of fiction. Any resemblance to any person, living or dead, is purely coincidental.

The Spellmonger Series

(In chronological order)

Spellmonger

"The River Mists of Talry"

Warmage

"Victory Soup

"The Spellmonger's Wedding"

"The Spellmonger's Honeymoon"

Magelord

The Road To Sevendor *(Anthology)*

Knights Magi

High Mage

Journeymage

Enchanter

Court Wizard

Shadowmage

"The Spellmonger's Yule"

Necromancer

Spellmonger Cadet Series

(Young Adult)

Hawkmaiden

Hawklady

Sky Rider

Dedication:

To my boys, Owen and Hayden.

They aren't Tyndal and Rondal,

But I have no doubt they will be legendary

Knights Magi in their own right, some day.

And a father could not be more proud of his sons.

Opposites Attack!

When the Magelord Minalan the Spellmonger's two apprentices, Tyndal and Rondal, were knighted after the battle of Timberwatch, they were dubbed *Knights Magi*: a new class of nobility for distinguished High Magi. Designed to combine the pursuit of arcane knowledge with the noble aspirations of chivalry, it elevated them above common warmage . . . in theory. The problem was they had *no idea* how to be a Knight Mage . . . because no one had ever been one before. And as a couple of half-trained rustic apprentices from the Mindens they did not feel up to the task or the high ideals of their title.

But Master Minalan the Spellmonger decided to cure that ignorance. He arranges for Tyndal and Rondal to be tutored and trained together in their new vocation, learning the arts of magic, the craft of warfare and the subtleties of chivalry from the finest masters in the kingdom.

If they didn't kill each other, first.

Fate, circumstance, and the whims of the gods have forced them together, but the raw emotions of adolescence and the trauma of war put them at each others' throats with depressing frequency. Master Minalan can't have that, especially not in his fragile new domain with another baby on the way . . . so he sends them on the road.

Jealousy, anxiety, passion and frustration conspire to make them rivals - but if they don't figure out a way to learn to work together, and quickly, then their stubborn feud could end up affecting the fate of the entire war. Along the way they pick up some enemies, gain a few allies, master a few new skills, and attempt to learn the laws of love. But as they stumble through their lessons and learn to master their tempers they discover that the strongest bonds between men are forged by the most difficult of trials. For after they become proficient at magic, war, and errantry they are put to the test in the field, the most difficult of circumstances . . . a mission where the strength of their friendship and the quality of their honor may be what defines them best as

Knights Magi!

Prologue

Sevendor Castle, Winter

"I," I pronounced forcefully, my finger stabbing the air in front of my two older apprentices, "am about to throw *both* of you off of the tallest mountain in Sevendor!"

Tyndal snorted. *Asshole,* I thought to myself. His defiance and open contempt for authority - when he wasn't being obsequiously charming - was irritating me beyond belief, these days. We were sitting in my workshop in my tower, with both of them sprawled on stools while I paced back and forth. Tyndal had started a fight that I felt obligated to finish. I *hoped* he had enough sense to keep his mouth shut.

"That wouldn't be much of a fall, compared to back home," he laughed, contemptuously. I could feel my nostrils flare.

I growled. "This *is* 'back home', as far as you are concerned," I reminded him, harshly. "At least Sevendor is *my* home, a home I've spent a thousand hours and thousands more ounces of gold than it was worth to restore. The home my son was born in. The home my daughter will be born in. The home my wife seeks comfort and security in while she is bearing our second child. The home . . . *you two seem hell-bent on destroying!*"

They both blanched at my rebuke – no one likes being reminded of their dependence on other people's generosity, and in truth I disliked using such tactics on (generally) good boys like Rondal and Tyndal, but today's little tussle justified it.

I don't know where or how the argument started, but they'd been at each other's throats for days. In fact, they had been skirmishing beyond the bounds of healthy rivalry since we'd returned from Barrowbell last month.

Mostly I had ignored it, dismissing it at first as the them just going a bit "castle crazy" in the winter - you put too many people in a castle around the same fire for long enough, and they start to lose their composure. The weather had been cold and wet lately, and we were all starting to get a little rough.

But this morning had been bad. They had been using *magic* against each other — not deadly, not even particularly offensive, but when two talented apprentices start lobbing arcane power around your dining room because of some girl or some chore or whatever it was, it was time to put my boot down. On their necks, if need be. My castle already made it easier to do magic here than any place on Callidore. I didn't need a full-scale magical duel to entertain the folk with through the winter blahs.

I continued in a slightly calmer tone. "Every day it seems I hear of another dig, another scrap. You can't seem to be in the same domain without sniping at each other, and I blame you both. Tyndal, you go out of your way to provoke Rondal."

"Master!" he protested. "I do *not!*"

"You call him names, you boss him around, and you challenge his mastery of magic regularly. Rondal you sneer at his abilities, call him ignorant, and undermine his success and achievement just as regularly. And I'm *sick* of it.

"You are both High Magi, magelords, and knights magi . . . but you are still my apprentices! And this is my home!" I said. "At first I thought this was about Dara," I said, naming my new thirteen-year-old female apprentice, "but this isn't about her at all. It's about the two of *you.*"

"Master, he tried to talk to Maid Hilma when it's *clear* she's not—" Tyndal began.

"Master, he told Hilma that I enjoyed the virtue of *maiden goats*—!" Rondal shouted back, angrily.

Maid Hilma was a year older than they were; she was the niece of one of my Yeomen, Jurlor, whom I had taken into service as a boon. She was a pretty girl who enjoyed attention, and my two young idiots were eager to compete for it -- as eager as she was to play them off against each other.

Hilma was a problem. I'd have to assign her some duties far away from them until I could get her safely married off to some farmer in the spring. She was a distraction they didn't need. It seemed an opportune time for a fatherly rant, and as neither had fathers of their own, as their master it was my duty to beat them into manhood.

"ENOUGH!" I bellowed. "I don't want to hear it from either one of you! You are both intelligent, competent, and loyal . . . *so why can't I get you two blockheads to bloody well get along?!"* I demanded angrily. As they both opened their mouths again I interrupted. "That is *not* an invitation for comment!"

I sighed and paced back and forth in my workshop. Pacing is one of my favorite ways to think, and I'd become accustomed to walking back and forth in front of my workbench. I've even started to wear a bit of a path in the wooden floor. I had gotten into a pattern where I could think and focus best when I was pacing.

But it also meant trouble, if you were the subject of my attention. The boys knew they were in trouble. They were a study in contrasts, but both of them were on the cusp of manhood and wearing my patience threadbare. I studied them severely for a moment.

Rondal, the older of the two, was actually – *technically* – the junior apprentice, as I had inherited him from his former master and he had been with me six months less than Tyndal. Rondal was a wide-shouldered lad, shorter than Tyndal by four inches, and his hair was nondescript brown, flat, and cut with a bowl. He was just a bit nearsighted and had to correct his vision magically. He had the broad face and wide nose of the Wilderlands peasants and dark green eyes.

Rondal was smart. He was also better educated than Tyndal, as he had spent more than a year under the mediocre instruction and sub-standard care of Garkesku the Great. I could fault my former professional rival for a host of things, but insisting his apprentices have a good grounding in basic Imperial magic theory and practice was not one of them. Rondal was a sponge when it came to learning – math, magic, masonry, you name it.

Tyndal, by contrast, was taller, skinnier, and only a few months junior than Rondal. He had a strong Talent and a dislike of hard studying. That made him powerful but haphazard in his spellcraft. He had a shock of dirty blond hair that never quite seemed to stay put, and blue eyes that the village girls found dreamy. He was well-muscled for his frame, the result of countless hours spent on the practice field. If Rondal was an arcane scholar, Tyndal was a warmage by vocation. He loved swordplay, horses, and the trappings of nobility, too.

Tyndal had initiative and ambition in spades. He also had just a bit more Talent than Rondal, and he was more willing to use magic than his fellow. But he rarely thought things through, and we'd had at least two or three incidents since we'd returned from Barrowbell that were due almost entirely to his lack of thinking before he acted. The madcap Yule we'd had a few days ago was merely the most recent occasion.

They were good boys – but that was the problem. They were boys, and at the moment I desperately needed them to be men. *My* men.

"I have a castle overfull of guests for Yule," I enumerated on my fingers. "I have an encampment of rowdy Stone Folk out back, I have two or three Tree Folk dropping by every week to check on construction of their precious spire or ask me about snowstone, I have a subject domain on the brink of insurrection, I have three magical orders already fighting about their prerogatives, I have a teething baby and a pregnant wife, and I have a King who thinks I should be doing a lot more than I am about the . . . what was it? Ah, yes, the genocidal ball of magical evil that has invaded the Wilderlands and Gilmora and is *trying to kill us all!*"

They blanched again. Unfair of me, I know. After all, the undead goblin head who had launched this invasion had taken their home first. Reminding them of that wasn't sensitive.

But it was necessary. They weren't children anymore. But they were still boys. And that would have to change. That was precisely why they were in my workshop. I felt obligated to explain why.

"Neither one of you have fathers," I observed – Tyndal's (supposed) father, or at least the man who'd married his mother, had died in the south, after the Bovali were rescued. His mother had disappeared soon after. "And as your lawful master, it is my place to usher you into the realm of manhood. I've never done that before. Maybe there is some subtle art or magic to it. But until I discover that wondrous spell, it is my *duty* to ensure that you become men."

"I'm already sixteen," Rondal boasted. "I doubt I have much more growing to do, Master."

8

"This isn't about your boot-size, Ron," I said, disparagingly. "The fact is the two of you are full of piss and vinegar and boyish energy . . . and you're getting on everyone's nerves. Poor Dara barely survived that lesson you gave her on thermomantics. You are boys, but you are boys in the bodies of men. Age does not bring manhood," I explained.

"But Master," Tyndal beseeched, "we're both old enough to marry or fight in a war. We *have* fought in war," he boasted. He was proud of his military service and the lauds it had brought him. That was not the emotion I wanted him to feel.

"And you did so *as boys*," I said, sternly. "Under *ample* adult supervision. The problem is I don't have time or energy to supervise you both anymore, or even the one of you. As much as I would like to devote the time to turning you into men, and men I can use, I do not currently have that capacity."

"But Master, we're still learning plenty from you!" protested Rondal.

"Couldn't we study with Lady Pentandra instead?" asked Tyndal eagerly.

"She cannot teach you what you need to know. Women become women by Trygg's grace. It *takes* a man to *make* a man."

I remembered my own influences as I went from boy to man: my father, of course, but after he had raised me, the teachers at Inrion, the instructors at Relan Cor, and the veterans on the warmage circuit had filled in the gaps in my education. They had taught me the essentials of manhood, inclusive of so much more than choosing the proper barber and the best wife.

I didn't even understand properly what they had done until I had returned from the war in Farise. But they had given me guidance and taught me what I needed to know, not just about my profession, but about how to be a man. What it was to *be* a man.

And *I* turned out pretty well.

So I was going to try to re-create the experience with Rondal and Tyndal. They didn't look committed yet, though. Time to *scare* them.

"Show me your stones," I said, after a long pause.

Their eyes shot open, and they looked frightened. They had cause to be. Under the oaths they'd been among the first to swear, I had the authority to demand the return of their stones at any time. They were

9

honor-bound to surrender them to me, if asked. And they were sworn to retrieve a stone from any other High Mage who refused to return their stone upon command.

They slowly removed them from the tiny silk bags around their neck and held them out for me. I stared at the two small pieces of green amber and shook my head.

"You have in your hands more power than the Mad Mage of Farise, gentlemen," I said, looking at their stones. "More power than any mage since the Imperial Magocracy. You've destroyed *castles* with those stones. You've slain hundreds of foes.

"But you are both still boys, as much as Urik was a boy when he went mad. And I cannot have a boy who cannot control himself in charge of irionite.

"So you're both going to Sendaria Port in the morning, thence downriver to Inrion in the south. You're both familiar with the place," I reminded them – it was the destination we had chosen to rescue them and a few thousand of their fellow Bovali from a certain death. "Put your stones away. You are to report to the headmaster and then spend the next several weeks of winter being tested and examined by the faculty. I want to know just how much you know about magic."

Tyndal, especially, had large deficits in his knowledge, due in part to my poor library and in part to the goblin invasion. Inrion Academy was one of only two magic academies in the Kingdom, now, and they were in the process of kissing my arse devoutly. I'd used their greed for irionite to get a few concessions, such as this special tutoring for my apprentices.

Tyndal wasn't stupid, he was actually very bright. But he lacked education. Inrion should repair that, at least enough for the time being. And Rondal, who was advanced even for a normal apprentice, would love the opportunity to dive into their libraries and learn from the very best academic magi.

"Then you're both going to the War College at Relan Cor this spring," I continued. "Tyndal, you will improve your mastery of swordplay and take formal classes for warmagic. You've mastered the basics of combat, but you need polishing to become a truly impressive warmage. And Rondal, I've arranged for you to be initiated into the Mysteries of Duin."

I heard them both suck in their breath, again with good reason.

The Mysteries were legendary. Legendary for their brutality and rigor. Duin the Destroyer, war god of my ancestors, had stolen them from Gobarba, the old Imperial war god, and now all the gods seemed to prefer them. I'd endured them myself, in abbreviated form, when I was drafted. To my knowledge there was no better way to turn a man into a soldier than the Mysteries. That didn't make them comfortable or pleasant, however.

But Rondal needed it. Tyndal was a bit of a bully, I knew, and while Rondal was fairly good-natured, he needed to learn how to fight back. *Without* involving me. Rondal was smart, but he wasn't strong. Tyndal was strong but he wasn't smart. Rondal whined. Tyndal bitched.

"Aw!" complained Tyndal, looking at Rondal for the first time. "You're *lucky!* Why him and not me?"

"Because *you're* going to be spending the first two weeks he's there on additional study at Inrion," I explained. "And because you don't really need them, not the way he does."

"*He* gets advanced training?" protested Rondal. "That's unfair! Master, of the two of us I am—"

"—going to be enjoying a *lovely* spring in southern Castal, learning the ancient and honorable trade of the infantryman," I said, dreamily. "But that's not all. When your terms at Relan Cor are up, you will return *here* . . . and spend some time learning what it means to be a knight mage."

"What *does* it mean to be a knight mage?" asked Rondal. As both the term and the institution were new, he had a fair point.

"That's what we're going to find out," I promised. "I understand your confusion – I have no more idea how to be a . . . whatever it is *I* am than you do how to be a knight mage. Fair enough. But you're going to figure it out. You're going to learn warcraft. You're going to learn spellcraft. And you're going to learn chivalry."

That earned a grin from Tyndal and a scowl from Rondal. I ignored both.

"Master, whatever I did, I'm sorry—" Rondal began, sullenly.

"I'm not doing this because I want to punish you, torture you or send

11

you away."

"So why *are* you doing it, then?" Tyndal asked. I considered. That was a fair question.

"So that you will be more useful to me," I explained. "I have six jobs for every one of me in this clockwork of magic, military, and bureaucracy I've built, and I need men I can trust to keep it working right. Whatever other problems you give me, I know I can *trust* you two.

"You need to learn chivalry because if we are going to see the profession of magic elevated to the nobility, we damn sure need to establish some boundaries for it. Knights magi will someday, I hope, be the tool we need to strike back at the Dead God. But without the structure and discipline implicit in chivalry, that tool may well turn back on the people who it is supposed to protect."

"I don't much like jousting," Rondal pointed out.

"And I don't much like reading," Tyndal shot back.

"And I don't much like *idiocy*," I said, rolling my eyes. "I'm going to need you both for a number of missions by the end of the summer. Things I *can't* trust anyone else with, frankly. I need you as competent and as trained as possible . . . with all of this boyish rivalry safely buried. You need to learn how to work together, despite your differences . . . because you're going to be working together, like it or not."

That wasn't an understatement. I *did* need them. The problem was Gilmora.

Last summer the goblins had rushed an invasion of the north-central Riverlands, pouring about a hundred-thousand gurvani warriors, trolls, and the occasional dragon into one of the most fertile and productive regions in the Duchies. Gilmora grew just about everything, but the region's major crop was cotton. Gilmora grew the finest cotton in the world, and the land had become ridiculously wealthy on its export to Merwyn, Remere, and Vore.

Gilmora was also full of people. It took a lot of people to deliver cotton to market, and Gilmora had a lot of people. Or at least it used to.

Now the goblins occupied the northern and western third of the

12

region. They had not assembled in one nice, neat, easy-to-defeat army, of course. They went after the smaller human settlements piecemeal, mostly looking for slaves, driving the survivors to flee south and east, consolidating them in the larger cities. The invasion had played havoc with unsuspecting Gilmora last year. The folk there were used to civilized feuds between cotton dynasties, not the savage attacks of genocidal non-humans. The Dead God had even sent dragons out of legend there to destroy the armed strength protecting the land.

That hadn't worked out so well, after the initial shock wore off. My warmagi and I had slain the last one he'd sent. Barely. Tyndal and Rondal had both been involved in that fight.

So now the goblins had stopped advancing. They were just . . . *waiting*. Waiting and rounding up every human they could find to feed the sacrifice pits at Boval Castle.

This had been a fell winter for Gilmora's normally-mild climate. The daily dispatches I received from Knight Commander Terleman were grisly tales of gurvani raids that had driven thousands into flight and had seen thousands more captured, coffled, tormented, and force-marched north into the Penumbra and beyond.

As horrific as the reports were, the focus of the nascent kingdom had been on stopping the advance, not reclaiming lost territory. The resistance behind the loosely-defined "front line" was strong in some areas, extinct in others. Gilmora was not a bellicose land – *"make cotton, not war"* was the motto of one prominent family. Most of those who had chosen to flee from the region were now castled or still moving away from the front lines in long columns of refugees. Those who stayed to try to protect their property were often left alone . . . at first.

The goblins weren't advancing. But they wouldn't stay in such a playful mood for long. Soon they would be on the march again. South, west, east, any direction they picked to march didn't bode well for the kingdom. If they persisted in an aggressive attack the kingdom's resources would be required to repel it.

Like it or not, these two half-grown half-men who had resorted to exploding chamberpots and itching spells were some of the best potential resources we had. As I watched Tyndal cut sidelong looks at his rival, and Rondal's eyes narrow in boyish derision, I wondered whether or not we were already doomed.

"I have no choice but to train you into the men that I need," I said, almost apologetically. "Our fate is rarely our own to choose, but we can make the best of what the gods have gifted us with. You both have tremendous potential. For harm as well as good. You're both reasonably intelligent," I understated. "You generally have sound judgment. You're loyal. You both can read. You're both fit and hale. The only thing you lack is . . ."

"Experience?" asked Tyndal, hopefully.

"Seasoning?" asked Rondal, warily.

"*Instruction,*" I replied, flatly. "You are both ignorant children, rustic rubes up-jumped far beyond your station and given power far beyond your capabilities or worth."

They both looked at me with a mixture of embarrassment, shock, and anger.

"Stings, doesn't it boys? But that's what everyone will be saying about you based entirely on what they've heard and your accents. They say that because while you are both, in your ways, brave, intelligent, and energetic, you also both know *nothing* of the world beyond your little mountain vale. You do not understand the social position into which you have been thrust, and you do not have the upbringing that your social peers did.

"But ignorance can be cured with instruction. And yes, experience. 'Seasoning,' although considering the dietary habits of our foes that might not be the best term," I chuckled. The gurvani didn't mind eating human flesh, and the priests of the Dead God encouraged the practice to inspire terror and dread in us. It was quite successful.

"But beyond knowing how to address a count or seduce a countess, there are a thousand thousands of other things you *just do not know*. And I *need* you to know them."

"Like what, Master?" asked Rondal, a little obsequiously.

"Like swordplay and warmagic, idiot!" snorted Tyndal derisively.

"Like military intelligence and observation," I began, "how to tie knots, how to read Perwynese with fluency, the proper way to bribe a rich man or a poor man without offending their dignity, how to lie to a woman and persuade a man, how to read a map, how to dance a pavane, how to stop an assassin, how to sail a boat, how to fight in the dark, how to hire a thief, how to run an estate, how to command men in battle, how to use your authority, how to use your wits, how to ford a river, how to climb a mountain, how to explore a cave, how to survive in the wilderness, how to survive at court, how to tilt with gentlemen and brawl with cutthroats, how to inspire loyalty and deliver honorable service, how to kneel to the gods and influence the priesthood, how to order a drink, how to deliver an insult, how to flatter a man or spit in his eye, how to choose a wife, how to duel a jealous husband, knowing when a woman is considering a tumble with you and when she is *not* – and whether it is worth the trouble. How to make money, spend money, lose money, and yet not let it command you. How to know the law enough to avoid it or use it on your behalf. How to spot a traitor, cultivate an asset, tell if a man is lying, know when he's telling the truth, and when cutting his godsdamned *throat* will solve a multitude of your problems.

"And that, gentlemen, is just where we will *begin.* There is more. Much more. Experience? Seasoning? You'll have more of both than you are comfortable with. That is what you two 'knights magi' are going to learn, if I have to knock your fool heads together three times a day to motivate you!"

Their eyes had gotten wider and wider during my recitation, and I'd gotten closer and closer to them with every item.

"Master?" Tyndal began, hesitantly, "I don't know if I'm . . . I'm *capable* of all of that."

"I'm having reservations myself," agreed Rondal, his eyes wide. He's not a violent soul – not that Tyndal is, but my younger apprentice is more comfortable with violence. Perhaps overmuch. "I do not know if I am the man for the job."

"You *aren't,*" I agreed. "You're still a boy. That's precisely my point. You won't be a man for a while yet. And the process," I admitted, "*might* just kill you. That's a fact. Every man who's worth a damn risks his life to achieve who he is, one way or another."

"We survived goblins," Tyndal agreed, bravely. "We can handle this!"

"You both have faced death before. This is worse. This is *adulthood* you are facing. While both are inevitable, the big difference is *you cannot screw up dying.* Adulthood, and manhood in particular, on the other hand, is all too easy to bungle. Dying is *easy,*" I summarized.

15

"Being a man is *hard*."

"I, for one, look forward to the challenge," Tyndal said, arrogantly.

"Then you're an *idiot*," I pronounced. He winced, but I'd called him worse. You couldn't use silk gloves when dealing with adolescent boys. "This is going to be the hardest thing you've ever done, if I've planned it correctly. The boys I see before me *will* be dead, metaphorically speaking. I can only hope that they will be replaced by men worthy of the investment I'm making."

"I will not fail you, Master!" Rondal assured me, trying to prove his loyalty through enthusiasm. I groaned. He'd missed my point.

"Yes, yes you will," I insisted. "That's fine. I *expect* you to fail me. *That's how you will learn.* I don't expect perfection, I don't expect excellence, and I don't expect miracles. I *do* expect you to try your damnedest and use your heads, honorably and intelligently. We'll have to see what kind of men you turn out to be to determine *how* you're useful, but . . ."

"Master," Rondal said, suddenly, "speaking philosophically, shouldn't *we* have some say in this? What if we don't want to be knights magi?"

"Interesting position," I agreed, thoughtfully. "Let's put aside the fact that – legally – you are both still my apprentices and subject to my mastership. Beyond that, looking at it purely philosophically . . . the fact is, *you don't get a vote*."

"That doesn't seem very fair," Rondal said, sullenly.

"And when did the gods promise you a fair life?" I demanded. "It *isn't* fair. But it isn't about 'fair'." They stared at me, a couple of browbeaten boys. Time to explain some of the facts of life to them.

"Don't you two clods realize that our society sees you as nothing more than strong bodies to use up, until you've proven yourselves?
Behind a spear or behind a plow, free or bonded, you're *young men*: if it wasn't for your strength and tireless energy, you'd be more trouble than you're worth.

"So you don't get a vote because among men you have to *earn* that vote. And you earn it by your sweat, your wit, your ingenuity, your competency and your luck. But *mostly* by your sweat," I admitted.
"You have little value, apart from your stones and your strength.

16

That's part of being young men. To women you're rapacious wolves barely able to speak coherently. To men you are pretentious, ignorant upstarts who have yet to earn the right to their respect. A young girl can be fair, she can be plain, but either way she is *youthful*. She has value. You . . . until you have been through the forge of manhood, you're a bar of iron. Dull, thick, blunt and apt to rust, if not put to use."

"That isn't very fair," agreed Tyndal, gloomily. "We're not *that* bad."

"It's not a matter of being 'bad'," I sighed. "It's a matter of being *useful*. And you are not terribly useful if you are ignorant. Untrained. Unschooled, unskilled, and uncultured.

"But that, thankfully, can be remedied. I have done my best to arrange for it to be. All that it will take," I grinned, "is your enthusiastic participation."

That earned a pair of groans.

"This is your fault," muttered Tyndal. "If you hadn't made that chamberpot—"

"It's not his fault and it's not your fault," I said, patiently. "Blame it on the gods, if it pleases you. It would be more appropriate to blame me. But it is something every man must face, regardless of his station. A man is not molded from clay . . . he is pounded like hot iron on an anvil. There is *no* substitute for that. It's painful, uncomfortable, and exhausting. But that's the price you must pay to earn the respect of your fellow men.

"And that, gentlemen, is worth more than gold and titles and lands combined."

I looked at them as they stared off into space, guiltily. They did not look convinced. "Try to think of it as an adventure," I suggested. "One with lots of danger, excitement . . . and reading lists."

Another pair of groans.

The pronouncement didn't gain me any gleeful looks. They both looked like I'd beaten them. Time for the reward. I handed them each a purse I'd prepared.

"Here's enough for expenses for your trip to Inrion, and then some. Let me know if you need more, but *don't* need more." Those they took eagerly. I knew they both had a little money tucked away, the results of ransoms or odd magical jobs they didn't think I knew about. But travel is expensive, and I was feeling generous.

"Pack up tonight, and in the morning saddle your horses and be on your way. And," I added, as I turned my back on them, "I expect you two to sort out this . . . animosity you have toward each other without my guidance or assistance. I have enough to do without untangling your feud every five minutes. So keep the distress calls to a minimum, please."

"Yes, Master," they both said, glumly.

"Now get down there and clean up that mess before my wife sees it and asks me to re-install the stocks in the village. You should know by now how hard it is to keep an all-white castle clean."

They skittered out like the boys they were. I sighed. Even after my lecture, they still had no inkling of what lay ahead of them. I don't suppose any amount of lecturing could, nor, I decided, would it be helpful if it did. Like all Mysteries, manhood was something that had to be experienced as much as taught. And it was rarely a pleasant experience, I knew.

I felt bad about it, a bit, but I also knew it was necessary. I *couldn't* coddle them. Not with assassins and goblins and enemies and rogue Censors hiding behind every bush. My court was now filled with flattering magi and exotic adventurers from several races, but the words of each one concealed hidden agendas and obscure loyalties.

It was unfortunate, but I *needed* them to grow up, and fast. I needed good men I could trust. I hoped that's what I'd get back.

And I might just get some peace while they were gone. A man can dream.

Part One:

Inrion Academy, Winter

Tyndal

The tests never seem to end, Tyndal thought with a despairing groan as he surveyed the table outside Master Secul's study. It was filled with scrolls, books, and folios the Remeran Master of Magical Philosophy had suggested should be read in preparation for yet *more* tests. Tyndal found the process hellish. But the torture of study in his prison of parchment was almost peaceful, compared to the rigor of the actual examinations.

The tests lasted for two solid weeks, day in and day out, within the august and dusty confines of the Inrion Academy of Imperial Magic. And they weren't just tests; they were *examinations*, in the literal sense.

He and Rondal were examined by some of the greatest magical scholars in the land. He should be honored – Rondal told him so often enough. His fellow apprentice was glorying in the opportunity to test his magical skills and knowledge with adepts of great lore and deep subtlety.

That didn't mollify Sir Tyndal of Sevendor, sixteen-year-old knight mage, one bit. Sir Tyndal was a man of *action*. After two weeks on the dreary old campus, he felt the fetters of fine education frustrating

19

his every thought. And that had worked against him today when he was examined for his knowledge of the Philosophy of Magic.

Examined, evaluated, measured, questioned, interrogated, assessed, and – worst of all – *tutored*. After every master had an opportunity to figuratively crawl around inside his head to see how ignorant he was, Tyndal was given a list of texts – mostly remedial – they recommended to repair the deficiencies in his education.

Therefore, he spent most of his time outside of examinations *reading*. The vast wooden table he and Rondal were given in the Main Library was filled with thick books and scrolls. The table and their studies seemed as menacing as armies of foes. When he looked at all of the texts he was supposed to consume, he devoutly wished that he was about to go into battle against a legion of bloodthirsty goblins instead.

Goblins he understood. Reading was *hard*.

It wasn't that Tyndal couldn't read; it wasn't even that he couldn't read *well* – he even understood *why* he needed to read, as some lessons were just far better relayed through the written word, and he had come to appreciate it. He just felt that there was usually something more exciting to be doing when he was reading . . . and usually he was correct.

But he had promised his master to lay aside his mageblade for the next several weeks and diligently focus on his studies. He was being assessed by the prestigious Inrion Imperial Academy of Magic to see how close he was to having a chance at taking his journeyman examination, and he did not want to fail or embarrass Master Minalan.

He was supposed to be getting educated as one of the first Knights Magi, the ennobled and augmented warrior-wizards who were being trained to fight the goblin invasion. It had sounded so exciting, when Master Min had proposed it. Unfortunately his master had decided that he was to do so here, in this dusty old dump that smelled like age, old parchment, and rotting fish, instead of someplace more comfortable with someone bribable.

As bad as reading was, he reserved his real despair for the examinations, each one an exercise in humility and humiliation. The tests came in many forms, and in different fashions, administered by different masters. But they came relentlessly. For two long winter weeks the two knights magi were shuffled from room to room in the labyrinthine campus and had their knowledge of magic tested by the acknowledged masters of the land.

Not their *powers* – both had power far beyond the lot of masters put together – but what they *knew* about their power, and how to efficiently manifest it.

Power, as Master Secul, the esteemed lecturer in the Philosophy of Magic, had told them repeatedly, was pointless without *control*, and control could only come through *understanding*. And understanding could only come through *knowledge*. And knowledge could only come through *study*.

Long, tedious, *odious* hours of study.

Tyndal thought that was bullshit, of course – he'd *seen* just how useful raw power could be. But he humored the magical adepts because, in truth, the young mage was intimidated by the sheer age and gravity of the men and women who were examining and tutoring him.

He was a mage, a warmage-in-training, and a nascent Knight Mage. The folk of Inrion Academy were true *wizards*, adepts who had devoted their lives to the study of the Art he had just begun to tame. The sixteen-year old could not help but feel intimidated. And respectful.

So he answered their questions, as best he could, even when – regrettably – he had to answer *"I don't know"* to whole areas of study his master had neglected to explain to him – or, if he was honest, he had neglected to recall because he was distracted at the time. He could read, and did, but *remembering* what he'd read – especially now, when he had so *much* to read – was a trial.

Master Secul said as much, when he walked Tyndal down to the dining hall after his particularly exhausting morning of examinations in Magical Philosophy and History. The old wizard was almost apologetic about his findings.

"Lad, I cannot fault your master for his instruction. The education an apprentice undertakes is by its nature a different experience than Imperial Academy training," he explained, sympathetically. *"Far* more emphasis on practical magic, far less on theory – it's to be expected. But," he added, with a kind twinkle in his eye, "it does help if the student is willing to remember the *boring* parts, not just the parts he's interested in. Your friend Rondal seems to have more of a knack for that," he added. That didn't help matters.

"Rondal is my junior apprentice, *not* my friend," Tyndal snapped back automatically. That was about all he could correct of the man's assessment, however. He couldn't argue with the rest. Rondal seemed to have a facility for remembering the most obscure and occult aspects of magic, and had a genuine understanding of its workings.

Tyndal guessed a lot.

That put the two boys at odds frequently in matters arcane. They had different Talents, in addition to different magical educations, so there were often gaps in their spellcasting abilities, gaps Master Min had tried to repair, but . . . he had been busy of late. But it didn't help that Rondal's superior, smug attitude about his abilities and knowledge had made an already tense situation almost unbearable.

It had been hard, living with Rondal. Since they had embarked together downriver from Sevendor a few days after Yule, they traveled in stony silence or conducted gruff arguments of mutual antipathy, each finding fault in everything the other did. Rondal was a devious know-it-all, in Tyndal's opinion, always ready to kiss an arse or cite a rule. He never wanted to actually *do* anything.

Tyndal, on the other hand, considered himself a man of action. He loved magic, of course, but he loved it for its power and utility, not for its subtlety. The difference in approach infected their styles. It also fueled their rivalry. Rondal had a nasty habit of adhering to the letter of the rules, even when it was clear a little improvisation was called for. Tyndal could only imagine how far advanced he might be if he didn't have Rondal's cautious nature constantly slowing things down.

As fervently as he felt that, Master Secul had not thought it legitimate to blame his fellow for his own failures.

"Junior or not, academically speaking he's about *three years* ahead of you," Master Secul said, frankly. "He's nearly ready to take his journeyman exams. You, on the other hand . . ."

"I know," Tyndal sighed, defeated. "I'm still . . . *learning.*"

The old wizard laughed. "Oh, we're *all* still learning, lad. Myself more than anyone. But there is a definite need for some remedial work on your part. And it's not a lack of intelligence. I think it's more a lack of exposure. Do you know how many books Rondal has read?" he asked, his voice challenging him a little.

"Thousands?" Tyndal asked, sarcastically.

"Closer to two hundred," Master Secul smiled. "His first master apparently had a decent library, and your current master has made a point of giving him more of the basic texts to read. And he's made a point of borrowing books or reading them when they are available. From what I've seen you . . . haven't."

"What? He's been reading books he didn't *have* to read?" he asked in disbelief. That sounded like signing up for extra bonus torture. It was just like a miserable little snot like Rondal to kiss ass at that level.

"Oh, my, yes. He's made a point of it. He's read some rather obscure works in the libraries of Castabriel, for instance. Weren't *you* there, for King Rard's coronation?" the wizard prompted.

Tyndal suppressed a frustrated sigh. Yes, he had been there when Duke Rard had become King Rard, but he had been too busy attending receptions and running errands and standing around in his tabard looking Mage Knight-ly to waste his time with mere *reading.*

And there had been the girls . . . plenty of city girls were curious about the war stories a dashing young knight mage from the deepest Wilderlands, in service to the Spellmonger himself, could tell them in private. Soft, sweet-smelling girls who had sweet voices and gentle hands and a *terrible* curiosity about his many adventures. He'd done his best to entertain them when he was at the capital. Rondal, on the other hand, had studiously avoided girls in the capital and had kept to the libraries when not required to be elsewhere.

Tyndal had thought he was an idiot, at the time. He was reconsidering that estimation now, despite his reluctance to do so. But a choice between girls and books . . . well, he never had considered the latter more important than the former. Until now.

"And how many books have you read?" prompted Master Secul.

"Fourteen," he said, proudly. And he had. From the first primers Master Minalan had used to teach him *how* to read to the basic texts on magical theory and practice he'd copied in his own crude hand, to more specific books on various areas of magic. He'd even read a book of poetry, once, but he hadn't enjoyed it. "That was all we had, back up in the Mindens," he said, defensively as he watched the master's face. "And since then my time to read has been . . . limited."

He almost felt justified reminding the old man just *why* it had been limited – he had been fighting goblins and protecting the people and other useful stuff instead of becoming a bookworm.

"So you can see my point," Secul said, ignoring the lad's sarcasm. "You've read fourteen books, and Sir Rondal has read a hundred and eighty or so. It's not that he's more *intelligent*," Secul added in a quieter, more conspiratorial voice, "it's that he's just read *more*. He's educated himself. That's all the journeyman exams are for – to see if you have the knowledge you need to practice magic at the professional level."

"But that takes years!" Tyndal exploded, angrily. "We haven't *got* years!"

"It does take time," agreed the teacher, as he opened the door to the dining hall, "but it also takes *opportunity*. And here you have a small measure of both," he reminded him, as the noise of the assembled students forced him to raise his voice. "Inrion Academy has an excellent library, more than one, free to all students – save some restricted texts. All may make use of it. And you are to be here at least another five weeks, if not more. Your master has asked that you stay and study until you can pass at least the first two forms."

Tyndal's heart fell, but he knew there was no arguing the point. When Master Minalan made up his mind on something, there was just no budging the most powerful mage in the world.

"But I'll be here *forever!*" Tyndal whined, dejectedly, as he considered the prospect. "I'll grow old and gray while I struggle through all of . . . *that!*"

"Just play to your strength, lad," the old sage advised him, kindly. "Every mage has *rajira*," he said, referring to the magical Talent that allowed them to work their will upon the universe through their spells. "And every mage has a varied measure . . . but every mage has strong points he can often use to compensate for the weak ones."

"I'm a warmage," Tyndal said, as he stared out across the sea of tables where his fellow students were dining. "Unless I can hack and slash my way through the library . . ."

"Please *don't*," the wizard said, sharply. "It took five centuries to assemble, and I don't think I could restrain the faculty from slaying you on the spot if you did so. What would you say your greatest strength is?"

"Swordplay," Tyndal said, knowing it was not the answer Master Secul was looking for. To his surprise, the old mage did not reject it as an analogy.

"Then you might consider that learning swordplay is but another discipline you have studied. Approach the others as you approach swordplay, and you may find your studies bearing riper fruit. Mistress Selvedine will be examining you for your knowledge of the Lesser Elements after lunch in the Monk's Study," he reminded him. "Good day, Sir Tyndal, and good luck." With that he left the depressed young mage staring at the door of the crowded dining room, looking for a spot.

All of the regular tables were filled, of course – seating assignments had been handed down at the beginning of the term, and were rigorously enforced. He had to eat at the "special" tables, the ones designated for guests and visiting dignitaries. They were at the front of the room, on the dais just below the Master's Table . . . where everyone could stare at him.

Worse, Rondal was already there. And he had a *book* sitting open next to his trencher. Could he not even *eat* without reading?

Tyndal was starting to resent Rondal, resent him mightily, as the examination process continued. The reminders of Rondal's successes and his failures seemed to come hourly. The scrawny, brown-headed apprentice had zoomed through the basic First Form examinations quickly, and had done most of the Second Form the second week, earning passing grades in biology, natural science, symbology, basic elemental theory, physics, magic theory and philosophy, mathematics and practical cantrips.

Now he was into the beginning stages of the Third Form: high elemental magic, alchemy, thermomantics, photomantics, magical history, thaumaturgy, spellcraft, geometry. Every master they'd had in common had mentioned how impressive Rondal was, before learning just how poorly trained Tyndal was.

Worse even than that humiliation was Rondal's *attitude*. He was rarely prideful and almost never boasted about his more advanced education. Instead he was humble, displaying a pronounced humility in the face of his opportunity. In fact, he was frequently apologetic and tried to be helpful to Tyndal as he struggled through the sea of parchment. It was perhaps his most annoying trait.

There was no avoiding him, however. He had to eat. And they had been quartered in the same room, upon their master's request. That didn't mean they had to talk overmuch, he reasoned.

Sighing and steeling himself for the encounter, he pulled a trencher from the great basket at the serving table, added a few sausages, beans and some vegetables, sliced off a wedge of cheese, and poured an earthenware mug of the weak ale they served before he made his way to the spot directly across from Rondal. Tyndal was not one to avoid a confrontation, even when he was not eager for it.

"How did you fare?" Rondal asked quietly, as he sipped his ale.

"Beastly," Tyndal admitted, despite his inclination not to discuss it. "I know as much about the Philosophy of Magic as I do necromancy, now." Since neither boy had studied that obscure branch of their Art, Rondal nodded his head.

"Don't worry," his fellow soothed, "Philosophy of Magic isn't that important. Not *really*," he added, unconvincingly as Tyndal drank.

"Do you really think Master Min is going to *share* that opinion?" he asked, cocking an eyebrow as he put down his mug. The ale was terrible here. Watery, like it was brewed in a mop bucket. He swallowed half of his mug in his first pull.

"No," Rondal admitted. "But I can—"

"Don't," Tyndal said, sharply, setting down his mug with a thud. "If I can't do it, I *can't do it.* I don't need you to make my excuses for me!"

"I wasn't going to suggest I do," Rondal said, indignantly. "I was just going to try to explain that you hadn't had the time to immerse yourself in the proper texts on Philosophy of Magic. It's First Form stuff. Hells, the only reason I know so much about it is because Garky kept throwing *The Mirror Beckons* at me, instead of teaching me anything *useful.* I've read that monstrosity *four* times," he said, disgustedly.

"I haven't even read it *once*," Tyndal snapped.

"There are three copies in the library," Rondal suggested. "It's only about a hundred, a hundred and twenty pages."

"That would take me *days!*" Tyndal said, frustrated. "And I wouldn't

26

know half of the words in it! It's mostly in High Perwynese. I can barely read Narasi."

"Just relax and read it," Rondal urged. "It's really not that hard. I can help you with the—"

"I don't need your help!" Tyndal said, angrily. "I will fail on my own, thank you!"

Rondal blinked. "Ishi's tits, Tyn. *Calm down.* I'm not trying to make you feel like an idiot. I just want to help."

"I don't see what the point of all of this is, anyway," he said, sourly, as he started in on the sausage. "We're High Magi – hells, we're *Knights* Magi. All of this remedial crap is just insulting, after what we've done!"

"It's not about what we have done," Rondal said, patiently, "it's about what we *know*. This isn't a punishment, Tyn. This is to help us get more out of our witchstones. Make us more *useful*. Think of it that way."

Rondal let Tyndal finish his meal in silence, as he went back to the book he was reading. Tyndal noted with annoyance from the script that it was entirely in the flowing script of High Perwynese – a language he barely recognized, let alone could read fluently.

Unfortunately, most of the classic texts on magic that he was expected to know were in the ancient tongue of the Archmagi, not the barbaric, runic script of the Narasi he knew . . . sort of. His frustration almost palpable, he finished his meal as quickly as possible and stood up.

Rondal's eyes followed him. "Where are you going?"

"To the one place here where I know what I'm doing," Tyndal shot back. "The practice yard."

*   *   *

Since the first time Tyndal had held a blade in earnest – his master's long Farisi "knife," a prize of war from the Farisian campaign he had given him the night the goblins had invaded – Tyndal had found a sense of power and control in swordplay that eluded him otherwise.

While he loved magic, the song of steel and footwork and sweat was what drew him when he needed to *think*.

He had taken every opportunity to practice with the blade. From the long days during the siege of Boval Castle, to the few weeks spent at this very academy as a refugee, to the brutally active Battle of Timberwatch, where he had been able to spar with some of the finest blade masters he knew, he had learned all he could to become a better swordsman.

He had even spent hours and hours with Sire Cei and Sir Forondo, back at Sevendor Castle, working on the finer points of his technique. And of course his master had made a point of passing along all the wisdom of steel he possessed when he had begun training his apprentice as a warmage.

Inrion Academy was in a peaceful village, and its new Royal Charter affirming its rights and prerogatives under the new Kingdom ensured that it could not be attacked by its neighbors the way most feudal domains could be.

But that didn't mean that the school lacked guards. A full guardhouse, with nine veterans enjoying the easy duty, stood at the entrance of the school. Most students passed by without even noticing the burly men who guarded their peaceful studies. Tyndal could not pass by with*out* watching.

He wasn't entirely alone in his interest. Most of the students at the Academy were from noble families, and until the emergence of their *rajira*, their Talent for magic, they had trained to be knights and warriors. To those who found an affinity with arms, the prospect of a life of books instead of steel was as appalling as Tyndal found them. Every day one or two of the students would sneak down to the practice yard out behind the guardhouse and work out with the guardsmen.

Tyndal had acquaintance of them since the first time he had come to Inrion – through the magical portal of the *molopor* from Boval, a refugee fleeing an invasion. The weeks he had spent here while the authorities sorted out what to do with the *four thousand* Bovali suddenly appearing in the courtyard had introduced the apprentice to the guard captain, Ancient Galdan, a grizzled old mercenary with a limp and a strange accent.

Galdan had been in dozens of campaigns and hundreds of fights, but age and weariness had convinced him to apply for an easy position guarding snotty magical students.

He'd liked Tyndal from the first, partially because he *wasn't* a student, and partially because Galdan was Wilderlands-born himself, he said, from just south of Vorone, and he liked Tyndal's enthusiastic approach to swordplay. He'd started working with the lad back then, in his off time, right up until Tyndal departed for Talry-on-Burine with his master's pregnant intended bride. Now that he was back, a year older and a few campaigns more experienced, the old soldier enjoyed working with him even more.

Unfortunately, Galdan wasn't alone in the yard today. Apart from the two guardsmen who were working on shield technique, there were two noble students Tyndal had gotten to know in the week he'd been here. Stanal of Arcwyn and Kaffin of Gyre.

They had been hanging around watching him for a few days now, and Tyndal had learned a little about them without actually speaking to them.

Stanal was a beefy boy Tyndal's age, and would have been knighted by now with his own domain to rule if his Talent hadn't emerged. Under the old Bans of Magic, he couldn't own property or be ennobled if he had Talent. Under Master Minalan's new system, he could now inherit from his father's estate, and even keep his noble title.

Unfortunately his bulk did not deter his intelligence, which was canny, or his arrogance, which he had in abundance. His father was Baron Sargal of the southern Riverlands region of Arcwyn Dales. He was Sargal's third son, and not a favorite, from what Tyndal had learned. The Baron had apparently been more than happy to ship the brutish-looking, arrogant boy off to a cloister of magi, rather than deal with his powers at home.

Kaffin of Gyre was also of noble stock, but was the second son of a knight from the coastland domain of Gyre Shore. The Sea Knights of Gyre, as Tyndal had learned six times in the two weeks he'd been here, were descended from Farisian pirates who'd sworn fealty to the Dukes of Castal, in return for keeping their brethren at bay . . . and engaging in a little lucrative piracy against Merwyn and Alshar themselves.

Kaffin reveled in his family legacy of honorable cutthroats and their skill with the blade. Becoming Talented was, from what Tyndal could see, a crushing blow to the enthusiastic heir of the Sea Knights of

Gyre. He did not let that stop him from learning how to use the slightly-curved blade his family preferred.

"Where's Ancient Galdan?" he asked the corporal on duty. "I was going to see if he was up to sparring for a bit."

"He's gone to town with the manciple to collect a debt," answered the corporal. "But have at it, *Sir* Tyndal," he said with a smile.

Tyndal *really* wished he hadn't said that – as one of the few knights magi to have been created, he was one of the very few amongst the largely-aristocratic population of Academy students to actually be ennobled . . . and that was a sore point among many of them, who had been forced to give up their titles when they entered the trade. Under the Bans that was law. Now, many of them would be appealing their status, but until it was confirmed by the Crown they remained . . . *common.*

Except for him. The horse-shit-on-his-boots ignorant Wilderlands apprentice was *a knight.* They had been respectful about it, but he could tell they resented it. And him. Tyndal sighed and chose a wooden sword from the rack and began to warm up. Without Galdan here, it seemed pointless, but . . .

"You want a bout . . . *Sir* Tyndal?" smirked Kaffin, arrogantly. "I've been fencing since I was six," bragged the son of a seaknight. "I've had three swordmasters . . . before my Talent emerged. I'd like to think I've kept it up since then," he sniffed.

"Ever . . . *kill* a man?" Tyndal asked, casually, as he selected his wooden sword from the rack. That took the young aristocrat aback.

"I haven't had the need to," the boy replied. "Have you?"

"I *have* had the need to," Tyndal admitted. "You first, or the big guy?"

"The 'big guy' is Stanal of Arcwyn, and his ears are way up here at the top," the larger boy said, snidely. "I'll get what's left of you after Kaf has warmed you up."

"Suit yourself," Tyndal shrugged, giving his blade a few more practice swings. He didn't care who he fought when, really, he just wanted to sweat. And hit something. "Ready?" he asked Kaffin. When the man nodded, Stanal signaled for the bout to begin. And Tyndal immediately relaxed, feeling at home for the first time in two weeks.

This was Tyndal's element: a single opponent, a single sword in front of him, a single sword in his hand. He noted both of the other boys had chosen long cavalry-length wooden swords, no doubt due to their knightly instruction.

Tyndal had chosen a somewhat shorter sword. Not as short as an infantryman's, but the approximate length of his mageblade, Slasher. It was the sword he was most used to, and the mock blade was close enough in length and balance to make him confident in its use.

Kaffin began by circling him to the left, which Tyndal expected, and countered with a quick step-and-reverse pivot that put him on the boy's other side within moments. Footwork, Sire Cei had always drilled into him, was the key to swordplay. He was borne out when Tyndal reached out and tapped Kaffin's unprotected shoulder just hard enough to sting.

"Hey!" protested the student, whirling and striking back. Three fairly-standard blows at head, arm, and neck. Tyndal parried all three easily, and then crouched well-below the usual position one expects from a dueler.

"Come on," Tyndal encouraged. "That was almost *good.*"

Kaffin grunted before flinging a flurry of blows that proved to drive Tyndal back two steps before he pivoted once again and re-directed the fight elsewhere. They crossed the sand pit quickly, forcing the other combatants to get out of the way. Tyndal grinned when he realized that Kaffin had failed to control his momentum . . . so he side-stepped and tripped the boy. When he fell to the ground Tyndal's wooden blade was on the back of his neck.

"I yield!" groaned the young scion of pirates, weakly.

"Your turn, Big Guy," Tyndal said, encouraging Stanal to attack. The larger boy snorted derisively as he watched his friend crawl to his feet, then hefted his greatsword-sized wooden blade in a mock salute and advanced.

Tyndal actually enjoyed fighting Stanal more than Kaffin, for the simple reason that Stanal was indeed a bigger opponent. That gave him far more area to target, and the big guy was by nature slower than the wiry former stableboy. While Stanal was wise enough not to charge headlong into him, he did swing with exaggerated arcs, and his

31

balance was atrocious. Sire Cei would have scolded him into the Void for that kind of sloppiness, no matter his size.

Another pivot, and a backhand strike at the student's thigh, giving a satisfyingly meaty thwack.

"*Duin's dong!*" he swore. "Don't hit so hard! It's *sparring!*"

"My apologies," Tyndal said with a bow. "I'll try to be gentler in the future."

"Asshole," spat Stanal, who lunged at him again.

Tyndal saw his way through the big sword was through using Stanal's bulk against him. Even a sword that big could only be in one place at a time. Tyndal took two pivots and a side-step, and laid his fake mageblade across Stanal's shoulders.

"You cheated!"

"I *won*," Tyndal corrected. "I'll win again next time, too, if you keep lumbering around the ring like an ox."

"I, Sir, do not 'lumber'," Stanal said, self-consciously. "I . . . *amble.*"

"You're going to amble yourself into a blade, if that's how you fight. Don't *ever* let an opponent get behind you like that. A big sword doesn't make any difference if you have a slit throat."

"I still think you used warmagic," Stanal said, sullenly.

Tyndal laughed. "If I had used warmagic, I could have slaughtered both of you in an instant. I don't practice with augmented senses. It defeats the purpose." He spoke authoritatively on the subject . . . because he had been lectured about it dozens of times by his various sword masters, Master Minalan, included.

"Why wouldn't you?" Kaffin asked.

"The point of sparring isn't to show how deadly you are, it's to work on your technique and reflexes. Using warmagic to win doesn't help your technique and reflexes."

"But . . . you *do* know warmagic, right?" Kaffin asked. Tyndal put down his sword.

"Yes, some," he admitted. "It's . . . useful."

"I might become a warmage," Stanal said, thoughtfully. "They say that's about the only way to get irionite."

"Even then, it's no guarantee," Tyndal agreed. "There are hundreds of professional warmagi in line for them. There are less than a hundred High Magi."

"But *you're* one," Stanal pointed out, as if Tyndal didn't deserve to be.

"I was in the wrong place at the right time, or something like that. But if you want one now you have to get it the hard way . . ."

"You are so *lucky!*" Kaffin fumed, enviously.

Tyndal stopped and whirled around to face the boy from the coast.

"Lucky? Do you know what it's like to have your home ripped away and destroyed? Half the people you ever knew dead, some of them . . . *eaten?* Your home turned into an abomination and a home for abomination? Do you have any idea what it's like to know that that . . . that *thing* is out there, and he won't rest until every man, woman and child in the Duchies is dead? *And he doesn't even sleep!*"

Both of the boys looked at Tyndal, shocked by his reaction. Tyndal was shocked a bit himself. He realized he was clenching the practice sword as hard as he possibly could. Hard enough to hurt his hand.

With a sudden spark of reason he realized that if he lost control, he could inadvertently tap into his stone and unintentionally do something regrettable. Like kill a couple of students who probably didn't deserve it.

"Sorry," he whispered. "Long day." He tossed the wooden sword back at the rack. It missed, clattering to the ground. He didn't pick it up. "That's enough relaxation for one day. I've got to go face Lesser Elemental Theory, now."

*   *   *

Tyndal returned to his quarters he shared with Rondal in the North Tower after his long and intense session with Mistress Selvedine.

It had not gone well.

The tyrannical old bag had questioned him thoroughly and relentlessly . . . and gotten *"I don't know, Mistress"* for her trouble more times than not. She had grown increasingly impatient with his ignorance, and as each new question arose Tyndal became more and more intimidated. After the first twelve or thirteen lesser elements he had had to confess his ignorance of the others. He even confused the Sacred Number of Carbon with that of Silicon. That had caused an eye-roll and a snort of disgust.

By the end of the examination, there was no doubt what the venerable mistress of magic thought about Tyndal's education. Whatever else he would do in his professional future, alchemy and enchantment were unlikely to be major elements of it.

The fact that he had spent almost a year fighting goblins, running for his life from the Censorate, and helping re-organize the way magic was administered in the new kingdom impressed her not at all. Not even his witchstone impressed her – in fact, he thought she found it insulting. At least that's how she sounded when she lectured him: power without knowledge, she had said at least five times during the interview, was as useful as being in a boat in a storm without a sail.

But even that insult wasn't the worst of it. She had ended the examination by writing him out a list of *thirty-two* books and scrolls she advised him to read . . . before he left Inrion. Some of them, she pointed out, were the only copies in the world, and should be savored for their rarity. Most were odiously boring, judging by their titles. *Introduction to Alchemy. The Meaning And Purpose Of Lesser Elemental Theory. Yrentia's Gift: A Practical Tour Of The Elements.* And more. Many, *many* more.

When he got back to the visitors' room in the North Tower they'd been given to share late that afternoon, Rondal was also back from his afternoon exams, sitting at the big, highly-polished wooden table in the double room. But he seemed far more pleased with himself than Tyndal was.

"So how'd you do?" he asked, eagerly. Without waiting for a response, he continued to prattle: "Master Indan and Master Trondel were both impressed with my knowledge of practical thaumaturgy and magical materials – they said I had the makings of a first-rate enchanter, should I choose to specialize! Or even a thaumaturge, if I felt like going an academic route. They're going to pass me on the thaumaturgy part of the exam for certain!"

"That's . . . *great*," Tyndal said, without enthusiasm as he flopped into the other chair in the room. "Mistress Selvedine was less charitable. I, apparently, am a *young idiot*."

"Well, she could have just asked *me*, and I would have saved her some time," teased Rondal, uncharacteristically.

That surprised Tyndal. *So Rondal wasn't above that sort of thing.* It was perhaps the most interesting thing he'd said in months, in Tyndal's estimation. And the most telling.

"I kind of wish she had," admitted the disheartened "senior" apprentice. "She said I had almost no understanding of rudimentary lesser elemental theory, thaumaturgy, magical theory, or anything beyond . . . *cantrip* magic. She hinted I might make a good market-day conjurer, if it wasn't for my glass."

"That seems a bit . . . harsh," Rondal said, putting down his book. "I mean, that would take you a couple of *years* of practice, and you don't really have 'showmanship' down, exactly. Maybe if you studied with my friend Baston—"

"I'm a bloody *Knight Mage*, not a market stall conjurer!" exploded Tyndal, annoyed. "Why in six hells do I need to know *how* magic bloody *works?* All I need to know is how to work *it!*"

"It's actually a lot easier when you understand the theory," soothed Rondal. "But I agree, some of the concepts are a bit . . . obtuse."

"I know! I'm struggling, here!"

"For example, we know energy cannot be created or destroyed . . . but when we do magic, we're 'borrowing' energy from the cosmos, the Magosphere, or 'returning' it. With our *brains*."

"But it feels like it is just coming out of nowhere!"

"'*Magic is the arcane art of intertwining of thought and reality, perception and matter, order and chaos into beauty, truth, wisdom and light,*' quoted Rondal from some important book Tyndal probably should be able to recall. "Magic is essentially powered thought. And it's hard to put a thought into a measuring cup."

"That's *exactly* the kind of bullshit I'm talking about," sighed Tyndal wearily. "Why would I *need* to know that?"

"Because it helps to know how it works if you're trying to do a really complicated spell," Rondal reasoned. "Look, I'm sure Mistress

Selvedine suggested a book or two—"

"Actually," Tyndal said, unfurling the parchment she had sent him along with, "I have *over thirty* here. Apparently our master did not include some elementary texts on the subject in the six months he was teaching me about curing warts on cow udders and other useful crap."

"Ouch!" Rondal said, wincing. *"Thirty* books?"

"Thirty-*two*, actually," groaned Tyndal. "And all in one subject! I haven't read that many books in my *life!"*

"And she wants them read . . . ?"

"Before I leave," groaned the boy again. "Sometime when I'm an old man."

"Oh, c'mon, Tyn," Rondal said, trying to rally his fellow apprentice as he took a look at the list. "It isn't *that* bad. The first six are pretty short scrolls, and then – oh. I mean . . . *oh*. Never mind. Yeah, it *is* pretty bad. These two are *only* in High Perwynese."

"See what I mean?" Tyndal declared in frustration. "It might as well be in gurvani pictographs! It's like they're determined to fail me!"

"We're already High Magi," Rondal said dismissively. "Brave warriors of the Penumbra, and all that. And we have irionite. They can't take *that* away from you. Only Master Min can."

"I know, I know," he sighed. "That's part of the problem. *You* know what kind of stock he places in formal academics. When he got you as an apprentice I'm sure he wept tears of joy. When he finds out just how bloody awful I am . . ."

"Relax. Look, if you read . . . *these* five here . . . then that will cover most of the basics," suggested Rondal. "I mean, these others are useful, but when it comes to understanding lesser elemental theory, these are the five that will cover almost everything you need to know."

"And the other . . . twenty-seven?" he asked, after figuring out the remainder in his head. "Why those?"

"Because they each cover a specific element or class of elements in lesser elemental theory that these first five don't. Not in any depth, at least. But they can be useful, especially . . . this one, this one and – oh, yeah, that one is brilliant," he said, reverently, as he finished reading the list.

"You've *read* all of these?" Tyndal asked, incredulously.

"No, just . . . well, nine of them. But I've read the summaries of the others. Useful reference texts for the professional alchemist or enchanter, no doubt, but they don't really cover basic theory as well as these others."

"Where did you find the bloody time?" Tyndal said, irritated. "It takes me weeks to get through a book. You finish one in a day!"

"It's just practice," Rondal said, a little defensively. "You've been reading for only two years or so. I've been reading for eight. You get faster, the more you do it."

"All those words make my head hurt!"

Rondal shrugged. "Just think how hard it would be if you had to find a living authority on each of those subjects," he reminded him. "Those books are invaluable. And once you've *read* them, you'll *know* them. Lesser elemental theory is the essential building block to alchemy," he reminded, "not to mention enchantment."

Tyndal groaned a third time, even more expressively. "*Don't* mention enchantment! Tomorrow I have to face the enchantment masters. I don't know *anything* about enchantment, outside of warwands and such. I'm doomed!"

"You aren't doomed," Rondal said, patiently, "you're *ignorant.* Doomed can't be solved. Ignorance can," he said, tapping the book Tyndal was supposed to be reading – *Loray of Bannerbane's Introduction To Thaumaturgy*, one of the five his "junior" apprentice had recommended before his thaumaturgy examination with Master Indan tomorrow. "If you start on it tonight, maybe you can get a good lead into it by the time you see him. And then you can study before you see Mistress Selvedine again."

"Where I can explain to her, proudly, that I am now slightly less ignorant of the Lesser Elements," Tyndal said, dejectedly. Rondal looked at him with an amused smirk.

"Well, it beats admitting that you are slightly *more* ignorant, doesn't it? Start with Thaumaturgy. Master Indan is a good scholar. He'll be fair."

Tyndal groaned yet again and picked up the book. He opened it to the first page and began reading aloud.

" *'When approaching the delicate art and discipline of Thaumaturgy, that most noble of pursuits for the mage, one must be aware that you are beginning to understand the very nature of magic; for Thaumaturgy is but the Science of magic, just as Medicine is the Science of the body. The ability to impart one's Will on the universe and see it resolve to your satisfaction is, of course, the very essence of magic, yet it is practiced by many, understood by few. The basics of this sublime science are easy to fathom, in general, but when it comes to the practical application of thaumaturgy to the dissection and analysis of a spell, putting those basics into practice can become one of the most difficult tasks any mage ever does. Beginning with the assumption that magic flows from—"*

Rondal dropped his book on the table in disgust.

"What?" Tyndal asked, alarmed.

"DO you mind?" Rondal asked, annoyed.

"Do I mind what? Thaumaturgy? Hell *yes,* I mind it! It's—"

"Not that," Rondal said, through clenched teeth. "Do you mind not reading *out loud?* I find it distracting.

Tyndal's eyes bulged. "You mean . . . read without . . . without *saying* it?" he asked.

"I do it all the time," demurred Rondal. "You don't *have* to speak the words to hear them in your head."

Tyndal looked at him skeptically. "You *don't?*"

Rondal rolled his eyes. "No, you mud-brained pud! You read with your eyes. You just don't . . . *talk.* You *think.* Just like mind-to-mind communication, only you're talking to yourself. It makes things move much faster when your mouth isn't involved."

"That's not been my experience," Tyndal quipped with a snicker. His humor was wasted on Rondal. "But I'll try it."

And he did. To his surprise, he found that *not* vocalizing the words as he read them increased his pace. Enough so that he wasted precious minutes mentally kicking himself for not thinking of this *ages* ago. If he just relaxed, and let his eyes move as fast as they needed to . . .

"Hey!" he said, sitting up, suddenly, and forgetting that Rondal wasn't hearing what he was reading. "Is this *true?*"

"What?" groaned Rondal. He hated to be interrupted. That was one of his more annoying traits, as Tyndal had no compunctions about interrupting, and being upbraided about it was irritating. Indeed, Tyndal had to admit he enjoyed interrupting Rondal because it annoyed him.

"That the first magi each made up their own *personal* systems of magic?"

"That's what the text says. I wasn't there."

"So . . . Wild magic . . . that's just what the first magi were doing?"

Rondal sighed, realizing that his brother apprentice wouldn't leave him to his book unless he explained. "Right. Before the Alka Alon stepped in and taught us Imperial magic. Only that was before the Magocracy, really, so it wasn't exactly Imperial magic. It was just . . . *human* magic."

"So what did the Alka Alon do that was so important if we were already practicing magic?" Tyndal continued to dig.

"They – you know, you *could* just read the text!"

"I'm just looking for context," Tyndal insisted. "If the first magi were all wild magi, why did the Alka Alon teach them to be . . . well, civilized about it?"

"It wasn't a matter of *civilization*," Rondal explained. "It was a matter of *standardization*. If each mage used their personal system of magic then working together – or even teaching magic to anyone else properly – would be hard. The Alka Alon gave us the means by which to measure the *nature* of magic. Like figuring out just how much energy it takes to raise one cubic centimeter of water one degree in temperature. Or to force an empty sphere of space to illuminate. The Alka Alon gave us a . . . a common language. Like theirs, only . . . dumber."

"That . . . that makes complete sense. How come when you tell me stuff like that I remember it, but when I read it, it just . . . *evaporates?*"

"I don't know! Memory spells are Blue Magic, and I haven't studied that yet!" Rondal was annoyed – which he didn't mind – but that caught Tyndal's attention like a flipped skirt.

"Wait, there are *memory spells?*"

Rondal groaned and slammed his book shut. "Yes! Blue Magic!

The magic of the mind and the consciousness! You are the loudest silent reader I've ever seen. I think I'll go read in the courtyard!"

"Memory spells," Tyndal said, thoughtfully, as he ignored Rondal's huffy retreat. "I had no *idea . . .*"

*   *   *

Tyndal spent the rest of the day in the library, only he wasn't reading any of the books on Mistress Selvedine's list. Instead he was doing something he'd never imagined himself doing in a dozen lifetimes.

He was doing magical research. On his own.

It had never occurred to him that there might be spells that could help him *learn* magic. But the somewhat obscure branch of the Art known as Psychomantics, or more commonly Blue Magic, had a solid and dependable history. Blue Magic was the sorcery associated with the human mind.

Tyndal quickly discovered that the most elementary texts on the subject were not even found in the Main Library of Inrion Academy. Most of the discussions on it were in books on other subjects, though the assistant archivist informed him that there was a small but in-depth collection in one of the reserve libraries. That surprised Tyndal. He had never suspected the school would even *have* more than one library, but it did. Indeed, it had six.

There was the distinguished and stately Main Library, which Tyndal admitted, upon reflection, *did* imply that there were *non*-main libraries. He'd just never thought of it that way. He even recalled Master Secul mentioning more than one library. But upon inquiry with the helpful advanced student on duty at the main reference area, he learned that there were in fact *six* libraries at Inrion Academy.

The student librarian told him of the others: the Master's Library (off-limits to all but faculty and reputed to be a vast repository of old examinations) and the Scriptorium Library, where commonly-used texts were kept (and where all advanced students could – and were required to, as a condition of their graduation – copy the books for their own use. And at their own expense, the student explained with disgust). There was the Enchanter's Reference Library, a vast technical archive specific to the art, and the Student's Reserve Library in the basement of the East Tower, where nonmagical works were kept.

And then there was the Manciple's Library.

Stuck in an out-of-the-way chamber, the Manciple's Library was where the more rare works on the more obscure branches of magic were kept. It was kept under the care and authority of the manciple, not the principle archivist, for reasons of tradition and academic feudal obligation that Tyndal didn't quite understand.

But he tracked the man's student assistant down in his closet-sized office just off the school's large buttery and begged the key from him, after confirming that it was the campus's only repository of Blue Magic texts. The library was located in a spare tower that didn't look useful, nor particularly decorative, a chamber built for some forgotten purpose and then re-purposed repeatedly over the years.

Now it was the dusty home to hundreds of volumes unlikely to be regularly consulted by the normal students. Advanced students would sometimes find their way here, but the place was almost unused.

Tyndal surveyed the scrolls and books around him after floating a bright magelight in the air, and he was suddenly glad that the place was warded against insects and pests. It was creepy enough as it was without spider webs. He pushed a pile of scrolls off of the main table in the small library and created a space in the dust, pulling a rickety stool into place.

Then he got to work. The Main Library archivist had given him the names of a few books or monographs on Psychomancy he could start with, including the helpfully-named *Primer On Psychomancy*, by Master Loden, whoever he was. Tyndal found the book after ten minutes of searching, and then pounced on it like a free meal.

Quite against his nature he learned he was *fascinated* by the magic of a man's mind. He learned how many common spells had a psychomantic component, but that the discipline as such was rarely taught, due to its obscure nature and dubious use. The well-trained Psychomancer, Master Loden frequently pointed out, could be a menace to society if he lacked good moral character.

Tyndal hoped they weren't too specific about that.

Blue Magic was the study of the conscious, the subconscious, the dreamworld, the Other World, and of course such basic factors as

41

memory, recollection, learning and knowledge. Tyndal was in awe of the idea of the mind being an objective thing for study, like carbon or pinecones.

Tyndal found himself staring off into wonder as he appreciated the scope of the discipline. Master Loden wrote that human consciousness is merely the *accumulated aggregate of experience and memory.* And that made sense to Tyndal. *We begin life as an empty sack,* he reasoned, *and along the way our mind picks up what it needs.* He could relate to an empty sack.

The art of Psychomancy was how to put things into – or take them out of – that sack. And it was, he discovered quickly, much, *much* harder than merely producing flame out of thin air or manifesting a light in the darkness. Compared to the human mind, the mechanics of the basic magic of manipulating mass and energy were children's games.

Part of the problem, as Loden explained, was that the Alka Alon, the masters of magic on Callidore, had no cognate for the discipline; the human mind worked differently than the Alka Alon mind, and so outside of some basics in common with both cognitions, they had little to give the *humani* in that regard. What had evolved into Psychomancy was largely of human invention.

As was (it was pointed out repeatedly in the text) the science of Theurgy: the magic of the Gods. The gods of the humani were the aggregate subconscious expressions of humanity clustered around a psychomantic architecture of abstract symbols, based on the needs of humanity. The human gods could take material form on Callidore, when conditions were ripe and the need was great. Some had even played a role in history.

The gods of the Alka Alon or the gurvani, by comparison, were more hallowed ancestors or culture heroes. The gods of humanity, when they manifested in reality, were magically strange expressions of pure ideals crammed through the combined sources of thousands of minds over hundreds of years. They could appear or fade from existence as individual entities, reforming later in different form for different needs.

But they responded, theurgists theorized, primarily to the primal needs of the human mind. The gods existed because humanity willed them to exist, *needed* them to exist, and Callidore gave them shape.

But it all began in the mind.

Beyond basic theory, which Tyndal was surprised to find fascinating but difficult to accept, Loden also gave some examples of spells of special utility . . . including one that allowed the mage to theoretically remember *every word* of *everything he read* under its influence.

It was built on the third series of Antodine glyphs most Imperial-style magi used, one of the less-common sets dealing with abstract concepts rarely useful for warding away insects or making fire dance on your palm. Tyndal had never seen much use for the set of glyphs, even as he learned it by rote back in Boval his very first year.

But once he saw them in the light of Psychomancy, suddenly many of the glyphs and sigils began to make a new kind of sense to him. When viewed in the context of the human mind, then understanding how to invoke a man's memory or rouse his emotions might, indeed, require a sigil designed to *suggest* or *imply,* for example, as opposed to *command.*

When he figured out the spell's architecture, he cast it on himself.

And he remembered every word of the book he'd just read.

Remembered it *as if it was floating there in front of him.*

Luin's liver! Why the hell don't the masters teach that one the first day? he swore silently.

Then he got started in earnest, with *Bannerbane's Introduction To Thaumaturgy* and a big grin on his face. Maybe this wouldn't be as bad as he thought.

*   *   *

After that, Tyndal's exams got a little easier.

When he met with Master Indan the next morning, he was able to rattle off – nearly by rote – the complex interplay between *Will, Desire,* and *Intent,* and how they differed, according to orthodox magical theory. By using the Blue Magic spell, he was quoting almost word-for-word from *Bannerbane's Introduction.*

The words just kept spilling out, as they appeared in front of him, and he interjected just a few *"If I recall correctly,"* and *"I believe Master*

Minalan said . . . " variables in each recitation to keep it from sounding . . . *too* scholarly.

Master Indan was impressed. "I knew Minalan was a thaumaturge, but from what Mistress Selvedine told me about you, I had . . . well, lower expectations," the old mage admitted.

"My master is enamored of thaumaturgy, Master," Tyndal pointed out. "He has often given me lessons framed in terms of a thaumaturgical, as opposed to practical approach." Considering that's precisely what *Bannerbane's Introduction* recommended, he figured it was the answer Master Indan was looking for.

"Why yes, that is the way it *should* be approached," he agreed, stroking his gray beard. "But too often the pragmatic approach is preferred, simply because it is more immediately useful, particularly in an apprenticeship. An *academic* student, of course, usually comes to a more enlightened understanding of the science of magic. You are a credit to your master's instruction. Let us explore your knowledge of the theory of systems, then . . ."

At the conclusion of the examination, without revealing his official notes, the venerable Master Indan indicated that he approved of Tyndal's impressive basic understanding of the discipline, and would report as much to his master.

That pleased the lad so much he skipped the study session in the Manciple's Library he'd planned for the early afternoon and worked out for a few hours with Galdan in the guard's yard, practicing footwork and combinations of blows until after lunch, when he went directly to Master Trondel for his next test on Elementary Enchantment.

This one was a little more difficult, as his knowledge of the elements of enchanting physical objects was very limited. But he had discovered a tightly-written monograph on the subject in the Main Library that covered many common materials, and he was able to rattle them off as if he was reading the scroll.

"More study," the taciturn old master insisted, "but you seem to know your knot coral from your knuckleweed," he agreed. "And your understanding of the role of thaumaturgic glass in placing a permanent enchantment is noteworthy. I only wish my other students were as canny with that."

Tyndal was elated. With only his Thermomantics, Photomantics, Geometry and Symbology exams to get through next, he started to regain some of his confidence. And since the next two days were feast days (Briga's Day, specifically) with no regular classes he had some time to study. The lousy weather helped: Inrion had a wet, cool winter without even the benefit of snow. That lent to studying, instead of swordplay. No one liked to spar in the mud.

Tyndal was discovering that despite himself he was beginning to appreciate magic as an academic subject, now that his challenges with reading were abated. In some ways that made the task harder. As easy as it was to recall a text with a spell, that didn't automatically bring understanding of the subject to the apprentice. He realized that Rondal's perspective of the value of knowing why a spell works was, indeed, important.

Being able to recite the five kinds of knot coral, for instance, didn't give him any true understanding of how it worked. Or how its properties could be best used. He could rattle off one symbol after another from the *Symbolography of Master Mires*, but that didn't tell him how or why they were *useful*.

Rondal, on the other hand, seemed to be absorbing knowledge like a sponge . . . without the secret benefit of Psychomancy. Despite his new studying regimen Tyndal found him even more resentful of his fellow's easy understanding of magic. Especially when he seemed to prefer it to all other pursuits – feminine companionship, for example. Tyndal didn't hesitate to use his ability to easily talk to girls against Rondal when Rondal started showing off his impressive brain.

When Tyndal had returned from his final exam before the festival holiday, Rondal was finishing a book he had started in the morning. The rain made an almost hypnotic sound on the slate roof of their gable, and that encouraged the exhaustion they were both feeling. The warm fire in the grate did not help their languor. Rondal stretched tiredly.

"I *love* this place," he admitted, after they had both agreed to get some sleep. "I could *live* in that library."

"You practically *do* live in the library," Tyndal grumbled as he slipped off his day clothes. "Really, you *should* go meet some girls. You . . . you do *like* girls, don't you?" Tyndal asked, feigning a sudden uncertainty. "If you *don't*, I understand, I just—"

"Of *course* I like girls, you idiot," sighed Rondal. "I'm not an Andrusine. But I have my whole life to chase skirts. I've only got a short time here at Inrion to chase parchment."

"You need to carefully re-evaluate your personal priorities, Sir Rondal," observed Tyndal, thoughtfully.

"Says the mage who spent *three days* trying to encapsulate his own farts last fall," remarked Rondal, amusedly.

"It was an interesting personal course of study," Tyndal defended. "And if I recall you did want to learn the spell, after I figured it out."

"Tyndal, you have access to more books on magic than most magi get in a lifetime," Rondal reminded, "you really *should* take advantage of that."

"But we're only here for a few more weeks!" Tyndal protested, as he collapsed into his bed. "Even if I read constantly, I could only manage a few!"

"Then read *faster*," Rondal insisted. "And quit letting a little female tail-wagging distract you. Yes, there are girls here. No, they will not make you a better knight mage."

"But they would make me a *happier* one," he groaned. "Perhaps if you aren't an Andrusine, you should have considered the life of a celibate monk," Tyndal said, sourly.

"Perhaps you should have considered life as a stableboy, if magic is too cumbersome for you!" Rondal shot back with a bit of venom that surprised Tyndal.

"The gods didn't really give me much choice in the matter!" snapped Tyndal in return. "Suddenly, I'm not so tired. I'm going to the library!"

"That," Rondal said, "is the single most *unlikely* thing I think I've ever heard you say!"

Tyndal suppressed the urge to throw his fellow apprentice out of a window and escaped, instead.

The Manciple's Library was usually locked when not in use, but Tyndal had made friends with the Manciple's assistant by letting him see his witchstone, and now he had open access to the place. At this time of night it should be deserted, and he could study without distraction.

Only along the way he spied a distraction: one of the female students.

The Bovali boys had not mixed much with the regular students at the Academy, since they were there under special provision, so other than meal times or the occasional lecture they were directed to attend they had not gotten to know very many of the two-hundred or so nascent professional magi enrolled at the prestigious Inrion Academy.

While the students were overwhelmingly male, there were a number of bright young women whose position, Talent or the whims of fate had brought to the institution. Some chose to spend their afternoons and their evenings outdoors, studying among the many scattered benches that littered the campus. The benches weren't quite reserved for the girls, but they seemed to flock to them like crows to a fencepost.

This one, if Tyndal was any judge, was at least sixteen or seventeen. She had the longest, *darkest* hair he had ever seen, and when she looked up from the book she was reading, her brown eyes glistened like well-polished jewels. An Imperial girl. Like Lady Pentandra.

And she was *absolutely gorgeous*. He didn't care who she was, he suddenly had an inclination to start a conversation with this girl.

"Why, hello," he said, automatically. "Is it interesting?"

"What?" the girl asked, taken off-guard and alarmed at the interruption.

"The book. Is it interesting?"

She glanced at the book and then back at him – big, *gorgeous* brown eyes. "It's advanced biological alchemy, so *no*."

"I *hate* alchemy," Tyndal agreed. In truth he had barely studied it, not much more than the parts of it that led from lesser elemental theory. But he did not mind the deception: it wasn't untrue. He *did* hate alchemy, what little he knew of it. But he had to give her something to respond to. "Although I'm getting better at it here," he admitted.

"I just seem to get worse," she admitted. "Give me pure physical alchemy any day, over the maddening complications of life!" she added, fervently, as she closed the book. "Your name, my lord? I haven't seen you in class . . ."

"Sir Tyndal of Sevendor, apprenticed to the Spellmonger, Magelord Minalan. I happen to be a special student," Tyndal said, shrugging nonchalantly. "My master sent me . . . and another fellow . . . here for *special* evaluation."

"Oh. That explains it then." She went back to her book, as if he wasn't there.

Tyndal blinked. He wasn't used to being so casually dismissed by girls. He *knew* he was handsome and charming, because dozens of girls had told him so. Hells, plenty of grown and *married women* had told him so. Add in his title, position, and who he was apprenticed to, and he realized that the girl might just not realize who he was.

Of course, he didn't know who *she* was, either. That didn't deter him.

"I'm *Tyndal*," he repeated, making her look up again. "Sir Tyndal of Sevendor. Knight Mage of the Realm," he added, with a bit of relish.

"I'm Estasia," she said, politely. "It's been a pleasure meeting you." And went back to her book without further comment.

Tyndal wasn't about to be rebuffed. Persistence, he decided, was the hallmark of a knight mage. "Hello, Estasia. So what do you want to specialize in when you graduate?" he asked, taking a seat next to her on the bench. It was the most thoughtful question he could think of. Estasia didn't seem to agree.

"*Silence* spells," she said, sourly, looking at him pointedly.

"I'm partial to love spells, myself," he said, inching closer to her.

She looked him up and down appraisingly with her pretty dark eyes. *Now I've got her!* he thought to himself.

"No doubt you'd *need* to be," she concluded.

"Hey!" he objected. "What do you mean by *that?*"

"I *mean* that it is my intention to become a professional mage in my own right," she answered, matter-of-factly, "and that does *not* include becoming the doting wife and brood mare of some puffed-up magelord."

"Hey! I'm *not* puffed-up!" He flexed his bicep. "That's all solid!" he teased, knocking on it with his other hand like it was made of wood.

"That is a delightful relief to hear," she said, flatly. "And *I'm* not going to be your wife. So we've reached an understanding." She bent back to her book.

Despite her objection, Tyndal could tell that she wasn't *entirely* uninterested . . . otherwise she would not have insulted him. Quite the contrary. The opposite of attraction isn't disgust, Lady Pentandra had told him one time, it is *disinterest.* And the way she kept cutting her pretty eyes toward him indicated that she was, at least at some level, intrigued by him.

It wasn't rejection. It was riposte.

He considered what to do while he stared at those pretty eyes darting across the page. He could have pressed the issue and forced her to make a decision on the matter – and if she had been a peasant girl, he might have considered doing just that. Plenty of village girls developed round heels and generous natures with just a hint of potential in a man.

But an educated woman pursuing her own career was a different type of girl altogether, and called for a different approach, he reasoned. Lady Pentandra had been coaching him in such things, mind-to-mind, as a kind of unofficial project of hers. They were lessons he did not discuss with anyone, but the wisdom she'd led him to regarding affairs of the heart had been invaluable.

"Just as well," he said, nodding sagely. "I would insist upon a far, *far* friendlier woman to be my bride. And I would have to carefully consider the value of pursuing a mere sporting relationship with just . . . *anyone*," he dismissed. "Fair *or* plain," he added, innocently, suggesting the pretty girl was in the latter class.

Lady Pentandra had been clear about that: *beautiful women get told they are beautiful all the time. They only take notice of a man if he voices a flaw in their beauty. As soon as a woman feels a man has rejected her,* Pentandra had repeatedly told him, *she finds him more attractive.* It seemed counterintuitive to Tyndal, but – once again – Pentandra's instruction bore fruit.

She looked up sharply. "Oh, *really?*" she asked, her delicate nostrils flaring a bit. "And why is *that?* Am I so ugly to your sight, Sir?"

"You are, without a doubt," he said, slowly and solemnly, "possibly the third or fourth prettiest girl I've seen today," he said, sincerely. He considered a moment. "*Fourth*," he said, decisively.

Estasia gave him a startled and not terribly charitable look.

"But pretty face is no assurance of a warm and friendly disposition," he continued, airily, "and in affairs of the heart I prize such a thing beyond mere transitory comeliness. Why, one might as well dally with a fishwife or a barmaid, for the satisfaction it would give. Well, I'll let you get back to your studies, then," he said with an exaggerated yawn.

"I would be happy if you would!" Estasia said, her eyes flashing angrily at him.

"You know," he added, "if you smiled once in a while then folks might get the *idea* that you were friendly." With that he got up and jaunted off. She had her lips pursed out hard in a pout.

"I don't *want* to be friendly!" she insisted, shaking her head.

"I didn't say you *were*," he shot back over his shoulder as he left. "And I'd never mistake you as such. But you might want to *fool* someone, sometime, into thinking you *might* be friendly. Before you offered them a poisoned pie, or something. You'd have to smile to do that. And I'm afraid there is no class at this prestigious institution to teach you to smile. You'd have to conjure one for yourself."

He only glanced back over his shoulder for a moment – *but she was smiling*.

Now that's how you do real *magic,* he thought to himself with a smirk as he headed for the library.

As helpful as Pentandra's coaching had been, he had to credit his recent interest in Psychomancy for the idea. There was much in the obscure texts about how to prompt a woman to react in a desirable fashion, a science as complex as alchemical biology, in its way. Indeed, it was a serious subject of study in Psychomancy. Once he realized that the discipline could be used in love as well as war, he found it even more alluring.

He knew from his studies that to let Estasia assume that she was not all *that* terribly interesting to him would flatter her sense of self while at the same time challenging the value of her heart. It was a maddeningly sophisticated and subtle approach to what should, properly, be a straightforward discussion . . . but it was also (apparently) *highly* effective. By the time he arrived at the Manciple's Library, he had committed himself to mastering the art from the ancient books therein.

There were entire treatises on persuasion, argument, discussion and seduction in the Blue Magic archives. He began to devour them. A few were quite revealing on the subject, and he committed them to memory for later study even if he did not understand them.

Seduction was an art, he discovered. There were many masters in antiquity who had left the results of their work buried in the corners of obscure lectures and discussions of Psychomancy.

Every maiden aunt and tipsy priestess had hours of advice about how a young man should pay court to a lady. He had listened to all of them with a healthy dose of skepticism. The men who wrote about the way to a woman's heart seemed far more practical than the women who discussed the same matter, he quickly noted.

Tyndal was wise enough to know when he did not have mastery of a subject, and astute enough to enlist the aid of those that did, so when it came to learning how to court and woo a woman, he had appealed to his best living authority on the subject: Lady Pentandra Benuvrial, one of the few living masters – mistresses – of sex magic.

Pentandra, of course, had given him far more useful instruction than he'd received from the other women who had offered their counsel. Indeed, her approach seemed as practical as the other female guides were whimsical. Lady Alya and Lady Estret, for instance, had been *replete* with advice about women. But their counsel relied heavily on flattery and proper treatment, and that was easily learned.

What Tyndal had needed help with was navigating the dangerous territory of introduction and seduction – preferably without involving jealous husbands or irate fathers disturbing his work.

At first, he felt a little deceitful applying base science to what, according to poets, minstrels and the priestesses of Ishi, should properly be a matter of fate, fortune or divine will (depending upon which theory one favored). But in matters of the heart, Tyndal had learned, one could not go into conflict with your mind unprepared any more than one could go into battle unarmed.

He had often solicited Pentandra's advice on seduction, after he'd gotten to know her better before Master Minalan's wedding. He did not hesitate to call her now, mind-to-mind, and explain his goals to her. In truth, he expected a lengthy lecture on magical ethics from the beautiful wizard, but Lady Pentandra did not judge him. She helped him out.

Amused, she took the challenge of instructing the eager and naïve lad and pointed him toward the proper texts he needed among the groaning wooden shelves of the Manciple's Library. Her guidance was a gift from Ishi, he quickly realized. She did not steer him first to a ponderous tome of impossible jargon. She played to his strengths, one of which was brevity. Among the scrolls on the nature of seduction, Lady Pentandra informed him, one was known to be short but highly informative for a young man.

She'd even told him where he might find it in the library.

Penned by some obscure courtier or rogue in the Later Magocracy, under the ridiculous pseudonym of Sire Rose, Master of Castle Heart, the *Meditations on the Sixteen Laws of Love* were purported to be a divine revelation from Tharis, Ishi's illegitimate son with the god Luin. Hailed as the harbinger of summer and the master of seduction, rustic dance and casual dalliance, Tharis was known in the myths for his lusty and capricious nature. He was a divinity after Tyndal's own heart.

Tyndal read the scroll eagerly. It's concise "laws" resonated with great humor, as well as much insight. Over and over he recalled proofs of the assertions they provided within the realm of his own limited experience. It amused and awed him, how astutely Sire Rose seemed to understand the complex dance of hearts and loins. He found the Meditations to be wonderfully practical and applicable in such matters, if not always entirely . . . appropriate for polite society. Or even common society.

The Tenth Law, for instance, affirmed his decision to verbally spurn the beautiful Wenshari girl: *If she be truly fair, ignore thee her beauty and treat her as a common-looking woman; treat her not as a great beauty, or she will despise you for it.*

If he'd told Estasia she was the prettiest girl he'd seen, according to the venerable Sire Rose in the commentaries of the Tenth Law, it was unlikely she would be as interested. *Pretty girls hear how pretty they are often,* said the Sage of Castle Heart, agreeing with Pentandra's advice. *Acting as if they are not impressive to your senses challenges their sense of self.*

Of course, that was difficult. Estasia was, indeed, gorgeous. And while Estasia might be fuming and fussing about the slightly rude remark all night . . . she'd be fuming and fussing about *Tyndal's* slightly rude remark all night.

And interest, as Pentandra would say, is *far* more valuable than apathy in the arena of love.

Perhaps he had been too aggressive, too forward; but then the Thirteenth Law stated *Boldness, not timidity, clears the path to a maiden's heart.* He was confident that she'd remember him, now, and remember him with some interest for his boldness.

He didn't know why, but his interaction with her had somehow relaxed him. By the time he got to the darkened Manciple's Library, he was actually whistling. It might have been a bit irrational of him to feel so confident about Estasia, but that was recommended, too: Law Eleven said *Stride the Path of Love confidently and without apology, acting as with the assurance as a king though you be but the lowliest villein. Confidence, to the point of madness, is a surer key to a lady's skirts than garb or coin.*

Tyndal had irrational confidence in wagonloads.

*   *   *

Even with two feast days to study, his appearance for his Symbology examination was problematic. Not because he hadn't read the texts – thanks to the memory spell, he now knew the technical descriptions and invocations for *hundreds* of common arcane symbols – but because he hadn't actually used a tithe of them in his short career. Symbology was one area in which the masters expected a practical knowledge, no matter how erudite the student.

Still, Tyndal struggled through, and when asked he was able to produce eight basic glyphs to his examiner's satisfaction. And six that were utter failures.

"You have a good knowledge of the academics," admitted Master Donrain, after the final failure, "but you need to work on the practical side."

"If you'd like to quiz me on warmagic symbols," Tyndal offered, "I could show you a few . . ."

"No, no, not what we're here for," the man dismissed. "You have demonstrated your abilities, young man. I have a proper appreciation for your level of knowledge. You are dis*missed*."

Master Donrain's even tone told Tyndal nothing of how well or poorly he'd done, but he'd given as complete answers as he could. Indeed, he had rattled of dozens of symbols. So many that he was feeling unusually cocky when he got to his afternoon examination, the one on Thermomantics and Photomantics.

He was prepared for that one – the ability to manipulate matter with energy to produce heat and light were pretty basic fundamentals. And just to be sure, he had read Alstod's short but thorough treatise on the subject, as close to a reference manual as one could ask.

But when he had quietly called it into memory to answer a question about thermodynamics, Master Yndrain gave a casual wave with a wand . . . and the spell failed.

"Let's try it *without* the memory charm, shall we?" he asked, amused. "Young man, do you think this is the first time someone has tried to evade a fair and proper examination of their abilities? Perhaps some of the *other* instructors are willing to let you depend upon that sort of thing, but I am *not* that lenient. Pray, tell me again, what is the Second Sacred Law Of Thermodynamics?"

Tyndal paled, swallowed hard, but he answered the question from memory. After that, his sessions with the masters got a lot more difficult again.

"Serves you right for trying to cheat," Rondal chuckled, when Tyndal confessed his discovery that night after dinner.

"I wasn't cheating! I was just . . . using a resource!" he said, defensively.

"Well, now you *won't* be able to use it. Still, that wasn't a bad idea. I'd love to learn the spell," he said, almost grudgingly.

"It is handy," agreed Tyndal, reluctantly. "In fact, there's a lot of interesting things in Blue Magic I never thought of. Most of the theory is way beyond me, but the some of the spells are quite practical."

"Like what?" Rondal asked, absently.

Tyndal enjoyed being an authority for once. "Well, did you know you can compel someone to tell the truth? Or to forget a day of their lives? Or forget they ever even knew you?"

"Sounds dangerous," Rondal said, after considering it a moment.

"The Censorate thought so," Tyndal agreed. "They almost banned it. Except for *their* use, when they were hunting down unregistered footwizards and prophesying hedgewitches. *Immoral Use of Psychomancy* is a serious crime. Or it used to be."

"It should still be," Rondal said, quickly. "Spells of forgetfulness are one thing. What about a spell of compulsion?"

Tyndal thought about the possibilities. "Ethically? I don't know . . . but that *could* be a lot of fun . . ."

". . . until someone used it on *you*. Like that innkeeper's daughter who wants to get married so badly?" Rondal reminded him.

Tyndal blushed, despite himself. Before he was even knighted, back in Master Minalan's home village of Talry-on-Burine, he had been stalked and nearly captured by a husband-hungry young innkeeper's daughter. While he still had fond memories of the girl, she was not the sort Tyndal found truly appealing, much less a fit wife for a knight mage, should he ever desire one.

Still, he felt a bit defensive about her – she'd helped him out, she'd been very sweet, and she'd been one of the first girls to kiss him properly.

"She's not a mage," Tyndal pointed out, quickly. "And she wasn't so bad. If I was still a stableboy, she'd be quite a catch." He had a fond spot for the girl, he decided, and suddenly determined to pay a call on her again one day, should he have the chance.

"Just an example," Rondal shrugged. "Besides, I've always heard that Psychomancy was highly unpredictable. The human mind just isn't as neat and tidy as the Sacred Periodic Table."

"I'm just saying it could be useful. Hells, a third of the warmagic combat spells are psychomantic."

"Do you recall what Lady Pentandra did to those two Censors at Master Min's wedding?" Rondal reminded him. "That was Pscyhomancy. Had to be. They didn't even know their own names, after Pentandra was done with them. Those Imperials all have all sorts of forbidden magic, they say," he said, a little suspiciously.

"Well," dismissed Tyndal, "You know what kinds of things *they* say. Lady Pentandra was acting to protect Master Min," Tyndal reminded him, defensively.

"Sure, sure," Rondal dismissed. "I'm not criticizing. It was just likely illegal. But about that spell . . ."

Tyndal looked at Rondal searchingly. After all the acrimony the two had indulged in during their rivalry, to have his better-educated junior apprentice actually *ask* for him to teach him a spell touched Tyndal's pride.

"All right," he sighed, as he took a seat. "It's actually not that hard . . ."

*   *   *

Eventually, after the holiday, the two apprentices were called into the presence of the highest ranking faculty for a report on their findings – thus far. Tyndal found himself anxiously biting his lip while he stood in front of the long table in the faculty hall and listened.

"My lords," Head Master Alwyn of Terone began in his creaky old voice, "it gives me a certain degree of pleasure to be able to inform your master that your skills are . . . *adequate* for your age and experience." He made the pronouncement almost reluctantly. Or it could just be his great age, Tyndal reasoned. He tried not to take it personally. Master Alwyn continued.

"We were asked to evaluate your areas of weakness, identify your strengths, give what remedial instruction it was felt was necessary, and prepare a course of individual study for each of you, in preparation for eventually taking the traditional journeyman examinations. Here, then, are our specific findings.

"Sir Rondal of Sevendor," he continued, glancing at a scroll – and obviously using magesight to correct his vision to read it. "You have demonstrated an admirable grasp of Philosophy of Magic, Thaumaturgy, a decided competence in Greater Elemental practice, an understanding of Lesser Elemental theory and Alchemy, an impressive knowledge of magical history, and a talent for mathematics, natural science, pyromancy and enchantment. Well done, young man," the old

56

wizard added, his eyes cutting to the bookworm. "If you had been properly enrolled here, no doubt you would have been ready for your exams a year ago. Or perhaps some advanced study."

"Thank you, Head Master," Rondal said, bowing humbly. Tyndal's face burned. At least he could have the good grace to gloat a little.

"Sir Tyndal of Sevendor," Master Alwyn continued, as a second scroll was brought to his attention by an aide, "your scores were . . . *less* impressive, but in consideration of your unique circumstances, it is felt that your wit is sufficient to absorb some remedial education in certain subjects to bring you up to level.

"You do have an excellent grasp of basic cantrips," he said, almost apologetically, "and a talent for woodbending – I saw the chair you put together, that was quite striking – a good basic knowledge of Greater Elemental practice, and a bit of a knack for sigils and runes. But there are many, many gaps in your education, gaps that I cannot in good conscience allow you to leave here unfilled. Not if we are to fulfill your master's request."

"Thank you, Head Master," Tyndal said, almost choking on the words.

"So, my lords," the wizard continued, flopping the scroll onto the table, "I am recommending that young Sir Rondal, here, be given two more weeks of advanced study with the lecturers in Thaumaturgy, Enchantment, and Lesser Elemental Theory.

"Sir Tyndal shall spend the next *four* weeks in training. When he has satisfied the faculty of his basic competence in his deficient areas, then he will be sent after you to Relan Cor."

"*Four* weeks?" Tyndal almost shrieked. "I'm going to be—"

"*Studying,* my lord," Alwyn said, sharply. "Studying *every waking moment.* Taking every opportunity to improve your knowledge of our Art."

"*That's not fair!*" Tyndal almost shouted. He struggled to keep himself under control. "It's not *my* fault that I didn't get started until a few years ago!"

"And this is not a punishment, young man," Alwyn riposted, without offense. "It is an *opportunity*. An opportunity hundreds of magi across the Duchies would give a limb for, and you should keep that in mind."

Tyndal opened his mouth to speak, and then closed it. He knew the old wizard was right. Inrion Academy was the largest and most renowned school of magic in the western Duchies. And one of only two in the new Kingdom.

"I understand, Head Master Alwyn," Tyndal sighed. "I'm just not used to such . . . inactivity."

"Nor should you be," Alwyn chuckled. "I was a young man once – even did a stint as a warmage, believe it or not, before I caught a flux on campaign. Nothing wrong with brisk activity, young man, it encourages an active mind. I have heard that you occasionally practice in the guard's yard – I encourage you to continue. It will help keep you focused and your mind on your studies if you exercise an hour a day.

"Both of you can count on a full courseload for the next few weeks. I suggest you take full advantage of it. From what I understand, your opportunities to study will likely be limited in the future." The old wizard stared off into space a moment, reflecting a bit, before he concluded. "This is an uncertain new world your Master has forged for the magi, and it appears you are destined to become his agents in it. Whether that is a good thing or a bad thing remains to be seen . . . there are many of us who are suspicious of the consequences of overturning the Bans.

"But regardless of what happens, you are to be ennobled warmagi . . . Knights Magi, they're calling it. A blend of chivalry and sorcery – the very idea is novel. And dangerous," he added, warningly. "Particularly when irionite is involved."

"But Master," Rondal objected, politely, "we are faithful servants of the Spellmonger, and loyal to the King! How could our service be dangerous?"

"It isn't your loyalty – or your dedication – that is at issue, Sir Rondal," Head Master Alwyn sighed. "Young men are by nature hot-headed and foolish. Such power in young hands is inherently dangerous." The old man looked out the window wistfully. "Part of me dreads the trials ahead of us in this new world, as wizards. For good or ill, your master has smashed the old way of doing things."

Then he looked back at them sharply, his eyes fierce under his bushy eyebrows. "And part of me is envious that I am not myself young

58

enough to enjoy the changes. I do not blame you for your enthusiasm and eagerness, gentlemen," he said, amused, "Nor do I resent such power as you have in hands so young. I merely urge you to temper it with education, caution . . . and wisdom."

*   *   *

"I bet you're *elated!*" Tyndal said accusingly as they left the Master's Hall. "Two more *endless* weeks of studying everything you want!"

"Are you kidding? *You're* the one who should be thrilled," Rondal said, angrily. "You get to read in peace for four weeks! I've got to go to bloody *military school* in a fortnight!"

"How is *that* fair?" Tyndal agreed, disgusted. "Why should you get to go first?"

"*Get* to go?" Rondal shrieked. "I feel like I've been condemned . . . for being *better* than you!"

"What?" Tyndal whirled around to face his fellow apprentice. "*Better* than me?"

"You know what I mean!" Rondal said, sourly. "I know more than you. I'm a better wizard than you. I—"

Tyndal stared at him in disbelief. "*Better* wizard? Just how do you figure *that?* You may know more than I do . . . *on parchment*. But did *you* defeat two Censorate warmagi on your own?"

"If you remember correctly, Lady Pentandra and I *were* there to help out!"

"I was doing fine without you!"

"You were about to get *blasted* without us!"

"Without *her*, maybe. *You* were pretty much useless!" Tyndal snorted.

"I was *following her orders!*" Rondal said, his nostrils flaring.

"*I* was saving Master Min's family!" Tyndal stated triumphantly.

"And that makes you a better wizard?" Rondal asked in amazement. "That speaks to your motivations, not to your skill. Someday maybe we'll settle who the better wizard is . . . but based on those marks, you'd better hope it's not any time soon!" his fellow apprentice nearly bellowed as he stomped away.

Tyndal seethed as he watched him go, but he didn't have a ready retort. Mostly because he couldn't really argue with Rondal's reasoning. Tyndal had outstanding motivations . . . but even in the scrap he'd just bragged about he hadn't used anything much classier than a cantrip.

Rondal was, indeed, Tyndal realized, the *better* wizard. And for some reason that *infuriated* him.

Tyndal considered heading to the library to study, as he had been bidden . . . but his mind was not on scholarship, after his argument. Instead he sought out the gatehouse guards and managed to work out some of his emotions with wooden swords and padded armor.

He'd been fortunate enough to arrive just as the duty shifts were changing, so he was able to spar with four guards each in turn. One after the other they fell to his blade – or at least gave him a challenging fight. Only Ancient Galdan had any success in keeping the lad's swift strikes and well-delivered blows from bruising him.

"What's gotten into you today, boy?" the older man said, after their third pass with the wooden practice swords. "You seem driven by demons!"

"Just working out some tension," Tyndal said, tight-lipped.

"That's more than mere examination stress," the old veteran noted, quietly. "I've seen enough students come through here to tell. Nay, lad . . . someone's *gotten* to you."

"I'm just not nearly as good a mage as I am a warmage," snorted Tyndal as he strapped on the practice armor.

Galdan shrugged as he traded his steel sword for a wooden one. "That's to be expected. Takes years to become a good mage."

"Well, I didn't *get* years," Tyndal complained, sourly as he came into guard. "I got *months*. And now everyone is expecting everything from me!"

Galdan chuckled as he returned Tyndal's off-handed salute. "Lay on! Welcome to manhood, boy. You're going to spend the rest of your life chasing after your own inadequacies, no matter if you're a mage or a miller." He rocked back and forth as he and Tyndal circled around a common axis, seeking advantage of their opponent.

"That's hardly a comforting thought," Tyndal said acidly as he threw a vicious combination of blows to head, torso and leg.

"Nor was it meant to be," the soldier said, philosophically, after neatly blocking them. "There's damn little comforting in manhood. First we fail the expectations of our fathers," he said, striking quickly each new point, "then of our masters, then our wives, and then our children."

"So why even bother?" the younger man asked as he spun and struck at the man's opposite shoulder.

"That's what *you* have to figure out," Galdan said, parrying the strike. "Every man gets a different answer. For some it's duty," he said, breaking away and resuming the fight, "or honor, or the pursuit of a craft or a vision. For some it's a woman . . . or *all* women. For some they struggle and seek their entire lives and die before they figure it out. For you?" he continued, looking at the apprentice with an appraising eye before rushing to attack. "For you, I'd suggest you figure it out *quickly*. Before it burns a passionate lad like you to cinders," he said, as Tyndal blocked his blows.

"What if all I can come up with is 'disappointment'?" asked Tyndal. "That's hardly a worthy aspiration."

"Then you'd be doing as well as many a man," the old Ancient agreed, stepping away and saluting after the rigorous session. "Although I doubt you'll do anything so uninteresting, Sir Tyndal. I'd offer you another bout, but I think I see fresher victims approaching . . . "

He was not mistaken – a small group of students was approaching, four or five of the seniors, boys about his own age – Kaffin and Stanal, leading them. He recognized a few, from brief introductions here and there and the occasional lecture. Bandran of Gars was one, one of those boys who talked far too much, and the shifty-eyed Daris of Hoden's Mead was there, too, a lad from the Castali Wilderlands whose reputation for being an asshole was greater than Tyndal's.

"We heard you were practicing, Sir Tyndal" Kaffin said with a broad grin, when he got to the edge of the yard. "Some of the lads wanted to watch . . . mayhap get in a little sparring, if you're agreeable," he added, casually. "And not too winded."

Tyndal surveyed the group and grinned. "As long as you don't accuse me of cheating again," he agreed.

"Of course not," Stanal said, hurriedly. "You're just . . . anyway, you said you weren't even *using* warmagic."

"I wasn't, I swear," Tyndal said, adjusting his helmet.

"So . . . what if you did?"

"What?" Tyndal asked, not understanding what the boy was asking.

"What if you used warmagic when you fought," Kaffin explained. "How many of us could you fight? At one time?"

"And *win?*" Tyndal asked. "You know, I have no idea."

And so it was decided that Tyndal would try to fight four of the boys at the same time, much to the amusement of the guards and their captain. They scraped together enough armor – with Tyndal promising not to hit any exposed bits – and outfitted four of the boys enough for the bout. While they were armoring, another half-dozen had gathered from across the campus.

"I really haven't tried this before," Tyndal said, almost apologetically. He suddenly realized that just beating them without a lesson wasn't exactly . . . chivalrous. He felt obligated to turn it into a demonstration, to remove the dishonor.

"The spell I'm about to use is a standard warmagi perception augmentation. It burns power like cheap wood. But it speeds your perceptions, as if time were slowing down around you. A *psychomantic* charm," he added, proudly displaying his new knowledge as he strapped his helmet on. "It acts only on yourself, on your own mind . . . but it can make seconds seem to pass like minutes."

He tapped into his witchstone around his neck and invoked the proper symbols in his mind, whispering the mnemonic that triggered the spell. It had become second nature by now. He had it hung almost all the time, now, thanks to the possibility of sudden attack by Censors or goblins or angry fathers and it got easier and easier with each use. "Lay on!" he shouted, and encouraged his fellow students to attack him as the spell took hold.

Suddenly everything around him was moving as if through a cloud of thick, cold honey.

It was during moments like this that Tyndal's mind was the clearest. When he could stop and consider his options and their consequences, carefully weigh his best course of action, and then proceed with confidence and commitment. Augmented, he commanded his universe. It was when he got rushed that he made clumsy mistakes.

Within the first few seconds in his augmented state he had evaluated the strengths and weaknesses of each boy facing him. None of them were particularly noteworthy – of them all, only Kaffin seemed to understand how to hold and wield a sword. The rest had a litany of problems, from shoddy footwork to poor posture to embarrassingly weak grips. They may have studied arms in their youth, but these scions of nobility hadn't held a sword in earnest in years.

It was almost too easy. Taking his wooden mageblade in hand, he carefully moved between his first two opponents while they were still lunging clumsily at him, and without otherwise touching them he smacked them both solidly in their helmets. Bandran of Gars and Daris of Holden's Mead fell like toy soldiers. Not enough to injure, but enough to ring their chimes and knock them off-balance.

Stanal was being more cautious in his approach this time, but Tyndal couldn't help but note how loosely he held his blade as he tried to direct the attack. Smirking to himself at incredible speed, he plucked the wooden greatsword out of the big student's hands, reversed it, and used the hilt to clunk the boy in the back of his helmet. Once he was sure Stanal was going to end up face-down in the sand, Tyndal could turn his attention to the last boy, Kaffin.

The son of a seaknight was wild-eyed as he frantically looked around for his opponent. His body had yet to catch up to his reflexes, and while he swung his blade in a passable strike, Tyndal was far beyond its reach. Instead he put his body in line with Kaffin's, extending his leg so that the boy tripped over his thigh.

His practice sword was flung away – and to his horror, Tyndal realized its trajectory would carry it directly into the unprotected crowd.

Cursing to himself, Tyndal realized what he had to do to avoid catastrophe. He leapt over Kaffin's stumbling body and made an effort to get to the sword before it landed. He made it with little time to spare, even in his augmented state. He grabbed the wooden blade just before it collided . . . with the very pretty face of Estasia, the Imperial student he'd met the day before.

She must have come at the commotion, he realized, not knowing it was he who was creating it. Her pretty eyes flashed at him over the top of the wooden blade.

Grinning broadly, he couldn't resist showing off. He continued to hold the wooden sword in one hand, but tucked his own under his arm before leaning casually on the fence that surrounded the yard. He also took a moment to thoroughly smell the tantalizingly girlish scent of the dusky lass and appreciate her pretty features up close and in the daylight. Only then did he drop the combat augmentation.

"I just *knew* you couldn't stay away from me," he said to her, casually, while the four boys behind him tumbled into the sand, their helmets ringing.

"EEP!" Estasia squealed in surprise, startled. When she realized who the speeding warrior was, she blushed, and then frowned. *"You!"*

"Me," Tyndal admitted, charmingly, as he lowered the carelessly flung sword. "Just saving the day."

"You!" she repeated.

"Me," Tyndal said, with feigned humility. "And my big sword. And your face," Tyndal added. "Completely unblemished by splinters and contusions."

"You . . . I . . ." the pretty girl sputtered.

"Excuse me, won't you?" he asked, sweetly, then turned to face his opponents and address their performance.

His tone changed dramatically, as he critiqued their performance. "Kaffin, you were bloody awful, and you were the best of the lot! If you don't keep your feet under you, why have them? Do you just like shoes? Stanal, if you don't hang on to your sword, don't expect to keep it. And you two? *Bloody* pathetic. If your sires paid for swordmasters, by Duin's hairy sack I hope they got refunds. Daris, I could have handed you your head, you were so slow, and Bandran, you . . . you just need help," he said, sadly.

The crowd burst into applause and cheers. Tyndal felt a little foolish accepting them – this wasn't difficult magic to do, just obscure. Who taught warmagic at a scholarly Imperial academy? Why would they need to?

But he didn't mind the attention. Even Estasia had to admit she was impressed, although she spun it into a technical vein that meant she didn't have to admit she was impressed with *him* – just his magic.

Tyndal was no fool. He took the compliment. Law Twelve of the Meditations instructed the young man to *maximize his strengths and minimize his weaknesses when under a maiden's thoughtful gaze.* Magic and swordplay were both strengths for him. She might be a cool academic, but Estasia couldn't ignore his performance.

He did the stunt twice more, the third time besting six opponents to the amazement of an ever-more growing crowd.

"That third time would have been beyond the ability of all but adept warmagi," he instructed his opponants, panting from the exertion. "*Without* irionite, it's difficult for a mage to raise enough power to manage that for more than a few seconds. *With* a witchstone . . . well, I could go all day," he said, earning some naughty chuckles and girlish giggles from the crowd.

He grinned at the girls, and made a point of speaking with a few who *weren't* Estasia, particularly the plainer-looking ones who were openly doting or overly expressive about their admirations. He didn't even look at her, while he did so.

Law Two was quite clear on the utility of that move: *Seek favor and attention from those maids whose interest you enjoy, but do not care for; for in jealousy oft has a maiden found a man more appealing than when he suffers from attention's lack.*

Ancient Galdan broke up the gathering after that – it was almost time for the evening meal, he reminded everyone, and there wasn't a student there that didn't have a mountain of studying to do. Tyndal most of all.

"Good work, lad," the old soldier confided as he helped him remove his practice armor. "That was as neat a spell as I've seen – and I've seen some warmagi," he added, appreciatively. "Your swordplay is really quite good."

"Thank you," Tyndal shrugged. "It really didn't need to be, against that lot. I just wish *all* of my studies came to me as easily as swordplay."

"It's all just studying," Galdan pointed out, philosophically. "The flash of a blade or the turn of a page, you're doing the same work . . .

just focused on a different part of the mind."

"The pages seem to outnumber me," Tyndal said morosely, shaking his head.

"You just have to find their weakness," chuckled the older man. "Every opponent has one. Play to your strengths, lad. That's my best advice," he said, inadvertently quoting Sire Rose of Castle Heart as Tyndal stripped off his practice armor. The remark caught his attention, and he wondered if that was a coincidence.

Tyndal felt better as he walked back across the campus to his quarters in the North Tower. His arms and legs ached a bit, and his chest thudded with the exertion, but he hadn't felt this alive in days. *Weeks.* Warmagic was something he was good at – not the only thing, thank Ishi, but one of the things he was better at. At least better than Rondal. *That* was his strength, he knew in his heart.

But how could he use that to tame the dragon-sized pile of books and scrolls he was supposed to get through?

Every step closer to his room seemed to bring him closer to that doom . . . when he spied Estasia lurking near-by, trying hard not to look like she was lurking.

Tyndal grinned to himself. He might despair of learning the secrets of an untamed universe, but some things he *could* predict – like the effect a deft display of swordplay could have on a girl.

"Well, that was . . . *interesting*," she admitted, as she caught up with him.

"Just a little exercise," he dismissed. "It keeps me from going crazy here."

"Why would you go crazy *here?*" she asked, confused. "This is about the most wonderful place there is!"

"Wonderful? If you're a bookworm, perhaps. After three hours of reading I'm ready to claw at the inside of my own skull. I prefer a more active life."

"I prefer to understand the secrets of the universe," she riposted, flirtatiously.

"You'd get along well with my fellow apprentice then. Rondal of Sevendor. *Sir* Rondal," he corrected. "Also one of the Spellmonger's apprentices. The better one, to hear him tell it."

"Then I take it your master doesn't put a premium on swordplay?" she asked with a shy smile.

"Oh, he does," Tyndal admitted with a smile, enjoying her company, "but he's even more concerned with our academics. He trained here," he reminded her. "Apparently slaughtering legions of goblins and the odd troll just isn't enough for the old man, these days," he said, philosophically. "He wants us to get good marks, too."

Estasia laughed, her dimples dancing across her cheek. "You haven't really slaughtered a troll . . . *have* you?" she asked, her face turning cloudy as she realized the possibility was genuine.

"Close enough," Tyndal said, glumly. "Really, it's not as glamorous as it sounds. Trolls *stink.* Like an uncleansed cess pit. So do goblins, for that matter. But Master Minalan is right: I *do* need to learn this stuff. More of this stuff. It's amazing what I can do, but I'm starting to . . . "

". . . recognize the limits of your education?" she finished, diplomatically, smiling at his admission.

"'. . . *realize what an idiot I am*', is what I *was* going to say," he admitted. "But I admit that I like your version better." He expected her to gloat over that, but Estasia's delicate face looked sympathetic, surprisingly enough.

With a start he realized he was inadvertently following Sire Rose's advice again, this time Law number Nine: *For best effect, the youth should demonstrate to a maid that their hearts can find connection, should he desire to proceed further on the Road to Love.*

"You just have to relax," she advised, thoughtfully. "Quit worrying about the exam and learn the material. As Mistress Quentine says, *'no one who has mastered the subject should ever have to worry about a test'.*"

"Oh. *Perfect.* All I have to do is wake up as an adept tomorrow, then . . ." he moaned. "I can't master one discipline, much less all this . . . this . . . this arcane stuff!"

"Just relax!" she repeated. "You'll get it. We all do, eventually."

He stared up at the tower he had to climb to begin his fight against the book dragon. "I hope you're right. Otherwise . . . well, I hope someone somewhere needs a good stableboy. Apparently, I'm not cut out for the life of a market conjurer."

*   *   *

"I heard you were busy on campus after our meeting today," Rondal remarked, looking up from his book at the room's lone table.

"You mean the practice yard?" Tyndal asked, casually. "Why, were *you* there?" he asked, skeptically. If he had one criticism of Rondal – one legitimate criticism – it was how quickly he found other things to do than work with his muscles and improve his swordplay.

"Me? No! I've had enough of that madness for a while. I was studying. Magic. And my point, oh senior apprentice, was that *you* should have been, too."

"Hey! They *told* me I could practice a little! It keeps my head from exploding from the pressure!" Tyndal shot back, defensively.

"Practice, yes. Put on a bloody *entertainment?* Did you do the dance of the warmagi, or just blast someone with a wand? I don't think that's what they had in mind."

"I was just demonstrating some warmagic to the students who'd never seen it before," Tyndal explained, defensively. "Isn't that what this place is supposed to be about? A chance to share our education? And no, I didn't use any warwands. Just a little combat augmentation," he added, sullenly.

Rondal snorted. "You were trying to impress a skirt again, weren't you?" he demanded.

"No!" Tyndal said, sourly. Then he considered. "Well, I may have anyway, though, without really trying. You know a girl named . . . what was it . . . Est . . . Estra . . . Estasia?" he said, finally recalling it by how her lips moved when she said her own name. "Estasia, looks like an Imperial, a senior student . . ."

Rondal's eyes bulged. "You mean *Estasia of Mistalagan?*"

"I don't know where she came from. But wherever it is, they grow big—"

"She's from House Devarina, descended from one of the great Wenshari magical families," Rondal explained. "Her grandfather was Remeran Ducal court mage for twenty years. I heard about her from Lady Pentandra as someone I should try to meet, if I got the chance. She's considered something of a genius. I hear she's almost legendary for her alchemical skills. Why would a scholar like her be hanging around the practice yard? With *you?*" Rondal asked, his nostril's flaring.

"She likes the way I swing a sword," Tyndal shrugged, pleased with how impressed Rondal was with the attention he was getting. And from whom. He decided to add another dig. "She was giving me advice about my study load," he added, nonchalantly.

"Estasia of Mistalagan . . . *spoke* to you?" Rondal repeated, his eyes wide. "She probably showed up here knowing more magic than you and I will ever learn. Ishi's tits! Was she pretty?"

"*Gorgeous,*" sighed Tyndal. "Brown eyes that glistened like black walnut. Hair as black as night. A smile you could watch forever. And smart. Too smart. Smart enough to see what an idiot I am."

"Well, that's doesn't take much," Rondal dismissed. "And it's hardly newsworthy. But she actually came up and *talked* to you?"

"Yes," Tyndal said, enjoying his fellow apprentice's envy. "She told me I just needed to relax. Just another bit of useless advice I've been getting. *'Relax'. 'Master the subject.' 'Play to your strengths'.*"

"*'Don't be such an asshole',*" Rondal added in the same instructive tone. "All brilliant bits of advice that you should really carefully consider, I agree. But Estasia of Mistalagan . . . that's *impressive,*" he admitted.

"She's comely," Tyndal shrugged, "but I doubt if she's going to spoon-feed me Alchemy."

"Not when you haven't managed basic lesser elemental theory," agreed Rondal. "Estasia of Mistalagan . . . she *must* have been impressed by your sword work. It certainly wasn't your magic."

"Not necessarily," Tyndal protested. "I was doing a warmagic demonstration. Combat augmentations, perception enhancement, that sort of thing. I took out *six* student opponents at the same time," he bragged, weakly.

"I'm sure they were *stunning* examples of manliness," Rondal said, rolling his eyes. "And you were using warmagic. Perhaps she was intrigued by the novelty."

"She said as much." Tyndal looked away, guiltily. "Ron, uh, I'm worried about my studying."

"You're chatting up *Estasia of Mistalagan* and you're worried about your studies?" he asked, incredulously. "Relax, your exams are over, for the most part," he pointed out, turning the page in the book he was reading. "Everything now is just absorbing information and learning new spells."

"That's what I *mean*," he sighed, heavily. "You've seen my reading list. It's only gotten longer, now. Even with the memory spells, so I can review it later in my mind, I'm . . . well, I'm only hitting the surface."

"Well, Estasia was right about one thing: you *do* need to relax. I know you want to do well, but there's no substitute for turning pages. And no time like now to get back to it." Rondal pushed the thaumaturgy book Tyndal had been reading across the desk they shared toward him.

"I know," Tyndal sighed, as he picked up the book. "Four more weeks of this hell of parchment."

"Just think of the bright side – you only have to put up with me for *two* more," Rondal observed. "That has to lift a burden."

"You aren't so bad," Tyndal admitted. "Even if—"

"Let's end your sentence *there*, shall we?" Rondal interrupted, suddenly. "I'm already irritated you've met Estasia and I haven't, and any further discussion isn't going to get the pages read. It's just another distraction waiting to happen. Tyn, you've *got* to ignore everything else and just . . . *read*. Study. Ask questions. You have a great opportunity here, and not nearly enough time to take advantage of it," he finished, annoyed. "That's what Master Min wants you to do."

"Yeah," Tyndal said, returning to his book with a sigh. "I guess I've got to get committed."

*   *   *

The next few days were awful, for Tyndal.

While his exams might be, technically over, the ocean of reading recommendations and practical exercises kept flowing in from the masters of Inrion Academy. His list grew to over forty books and scrolls, and nearly everyone wanted to meet with him for remedial training in their subjects. The Head Master had made it clear he would not be allowed to attend Relan Cor until it was done. The only way to manage that as by pouring himself into studying, as lackluster as his performance was.

It didn't help that Rondal was flourishing, asking questions and trading ideas with some of the best minds in the duchies while Tyndal was slowly making his way through his reading list, struggling through tutoring sessions, attending the odd lecture, and falling more and more behind where the masters thought he should be. It was maddening, to hear the broad-faced boy discourse at length on obscure subjects Tyndal was just being introduced to.

The only time he felt relief from the oppression of academics was when he took a break – no more than an hour, he promised himself – to go spar in the practice yard in the afternoon. Apart from that, he was in his room, reading. Or in the Main Library, reading. Or sitting in the dining hall. *Reading.*

"It hurts less if you don't move your lips," a pleasantly amused female voice interrupted, as he was struggling through a Philosophy of Magic text in the library one afternoon. Tyndal looked up to see Estasia grinning at him, clad in a simple scholar's smock. With the light behind her she looked adorable. The same Imperial features as Pentandra, but younger and much more rounded, Tyndal decided.

"I just learned I didn't have to say the words," Tyndal complained. "I still have to sound them out. Especially the Perwynese."

"Those are always hard," she agreed, sympathetically. "Even if you grew up with it, like I did. I suppose the question is, are you *mastering* the subject?"

"Are you jesting?" he asked in frustration. "I'm barely keeping my head from rolling off of my shoulders. I've read two monographs on Thaumaturgy that I didn't understand, and I keep forgetting the noble gasses in lesser elemental theory! It's just too much to take in! Especially in the time I've got left!"

"What? You're *leaving?*" she asked, surprised and concerned.

71

"Relan Cor War College," he explained. "That will be fun . . . but my master is paying a lot more attention to how I do here. Four weeks. Just over three, now."

"I suppose the life of a Knight Mage is full and abundant with such tasks," she observed, amused, as she sat beside him on the bench unbidden. Tyndal became intensely aware of just how close. She smelled lovely.

"This one certainly is," agreed Tyndal, scooting over to give her room . . . mostly. That left her side nearly pressed against his own. He found he did not mind. Their shoulders touched, now, and he could stare at her pretty face.

"Your master is Minalan the Spellmonger? The Magelord?" she asked, curiously.

"Yes. And no, I can't get you a witchstone," he told her. "Don't even ask."

"I wasn't going to," she said, shaking her head. "In Alchemy there isn't much use for them, anyway. It's not a power-oriented discipline."

"And you would know – you're the greatest Alchemist of your generation, I hear," Tyndal said, closing his book with a snap. He was merely teasing, but he struck a nerve, he found.

Estasia made a sour face and looked away guiltily. "Blow up *one barn* and suddenly you're an evil sorceress!" she snorted in disgust.

"You *blew up a barn?*" Tyndal asked, intrigued. He couldn't help but laugh.

"What, you didn't know that?" she chuckled, covering her mouth behind a dainty hand. "I thought *everyone* here knew that," she said, blushing slightly. "I've been waiting for you to ask about it, but you never did."

"We weren't appraised of the gossip, before we arrived," he reminded her. "Not the minor stuff, anyway."

"I'm here in Inrion because Alar Academy wouldn't have me any more after what I did."

"What did you do?" Tyndal asked, suddenly desperate to know the entire story. "Before I was even accepted to Alar, another student and I were experimenting with nitrates in one of my father's barns and . . .

72

well, things got out of control," she said, blushing. "No one was hurt –
not *seriously* – but . . ." she shook her head. "There was hay . . .
everywhere! The horses were terrified! And the sides of the barn were
blown half-way to the next estate!"

"Now *that's* impressive!" Tyndal said, laughing approvingly.

"How is blowing up a barn in the slightest impressive?" she
demanded, getting angry at his response.

"I used to be a stableboy," he explained to her. "Before my *rajira*
came. Believe me, I can see the appeal of blowing up a barn perhaps
more than you do."

"You're . . . *impressed* that I let a spell go all-futzy?" she asked,
surprised.

"Let's just say that as a novice warmage I can appreciate a powerfully
destructive spell. For purely professional reasons," he said, still
chuckling at the thought of . Establishing a common connection was
highly recommended by the Master of Castle Heart.

"Well, it was the talk of Wenshar for months. It was a *horrible*
scandal. People started to talk about me being a Wild Mage! My
father finally imposed on some friends at court to get me sent here – as
far away from Wenshar as he could. Until the embarrassment dies
down," she said, unhappily. "No one in my family likes a reckless
mage."

"What happened?"

"I don't know, exactly – the other student was the one mixing the
compound, and that's where the blast started. She was burnt. Not
badly but . . . we're no longer friends."

"So, you *aren't* just the brilliant Wenshari witch who knows more
Alchemy than a master . . . you're just in exile because you're an
embarrassment!" Tyndal snorted, as the girl blushed prettily.

"I think I like the former description better," she said, biting her lip in
irritation. Or was that interest?

"Who wouldn't?" he asked, sympathetically. "Just as I would prefer
to be known as the dashing young knight mage, not the stumbling half-
trained apprentice who doesn't deserve his witchstone."

The admission was a bit of vulnerability, true, but Tyndal felt
confident in making it. Sire Rose counseled a man to lead a woman by

inviting her to share his feelings on something simple. According to the sage of love, it would soften her, and make her more attracted to him. Sympathy could be a sword in the duel of hearts.

"So, you have a few more weeks here?" she asked hesitantly, her eyes darting from side to side. "Maybe I'll see you from time to time."

Tyndal was almost startled. He hadn't expected the bold move to work so well – but that was *clearly* an invitation to share her company. Tyndal decided on the spot that Sire Rose was not, as some claimed, merely a cynical courtier. The man was a genius.

"Not unless you live at the library," he moaned, exaggeratedly, counting on the common complaint of students everywhere to strengthen the bond. "That's where I get most of my sleep these days."

She smiled again. "I nearly do. So, I guess I'll *definitely* see you, Sir Tyndal," she said, with a toss of her hair, and made her way across the campus.

As warm and pleasant as the exchange was, Tyndal realized after the girl left that she was one more distraction from the books he *had* to get through. He redoubled his efforts and read voraciously all morning and through luncheon until it was time for his "afternoon stretch" at the practice yard.

This time the students were absent due to some pointless lecture, so he got to work out with the guards, which he found far more satisfying. They knew how to fight, the importance of footwork, and the subtleties of swordplay. None of them were outstanding, but each of them could give him a good run. And he even picked up a few tricks from the new opponents, as a good swordsman will do.

Finally, huffing and puffing with the day's effort, he was stripping his armor off regretfully at the end of the hour he'd allotted himself when Ancient Galdan said something off-hand.

"Too bad you can't use warmagic on that pile of books," he said approvingly. Tyndal had just defeated three of his guards using combat enhancements, as a special demonstration of his abilities. "I expect it would be nice if you could slow down time enough to get through them all."

"Yeah, it would," Tyndal said, automatically, before he started discussing his critique of the Ancient's men. The comment stuck in his brain, however, as he walked back across the campus to the North Tower. *Slow down time.*

Well, why couldn't it? he finally asked himself, as the comment lingered in his mind.

The combat augmentation spells, he reasoned, were designed to slow your perception of time to allow you the opportunity to choose your options. The other elements of the enhancement – the increased speed, strength, and agility that magic's power could borrow for the warmage – weren't exactly necessary, if one wasn't going to fight. They were the elements that consumed magical energy with such abundance.

In fact, if one was merely going to *read*, from what Tyndal understood, many of the drawbacks to the spell faded from importance.

Why couldn't he use warmagic to study? There had to be some good reason why people didn't do it.

He found his feet walking past the great wooden entrance to the North Tower and back into the kitchens and storerooms while his mind contemplated. Then he found them bounding up the stairs to the Manciple's Library, where he immersed himself in answering that question with a passion he'd rarely felt for academic work.

His familiarity with the library and its collection on Psychomancy led him precisely to the references he needed, and soon he was sitting at the table, surrounded by books and scrolls. The more he read, the more reasons he found to consider the matter. Tyndal found it fascinating – without the physical augmentations, the perception element of the spell was almost purely Psychomantic, he discovered. It was a simple trick of the mind. A magically-fueled trick, but it didn't use much power on its own.

Psychomantic spells had been around since the earliest days, and some – like the instant-recall spell he'd relied upon so frequently of late – had become a staple in most adepts' grimoires. Eventually.

But warmagic? At least the perception alteration elements of the spells? Those, he found, were rarely employed outside of the discipline. Most magic just didn't require that kind of fast-paced action or necessity for increased perception. Most wizards were content to stumble around like normal people.

He found the core element of the spell eventually, of course, in an old Merwyni scroll on the subject, the author long lost to history. It was considered a minor curiosity, a spell of dubious value for most occasions. But one could speed perceptions alone, without the power-consuming enhancements of warmagic. The spell was actually quite simple, once you grasped the concept, he was pleased to learn.

He tried it out. A scroll he was to read – a monograph on sigils – lay before him. Tyndal summoned power, formed the necessary symbols in his head, and cast the spell . . . but nothing seemed to happen.

He thought he had futzed it, until he noted how slowly a moth flew through his magelight. He could see the individual dust motes tumble from its wings as it challenged the light in slow motion.

Grinning, he began reading the monograph, doing his best to absorb the material as he normally would. It wasn't a huge scroll – only eight feet of parchment – but he was done before the moth had finished flying through his magelight.

He let the spell fail, and his perceptions returned to normal. His retention of the information, he found, was completely intact.

Delighted, he then cast the memory spell, and began to chew through the stack of scrolls and books with blinding speed.

*   *   *

The next day passed in a daze. While Tyndal's discovery had allowed him to read four entire books in one night, as well as a dozen scrolls from his list, his mind could only understand a limited part of them. As it was, his dreams were filled with the writings of obscure magi and perturbations in the Otherworld.

But he remembered what he'd read. Despite waking up feeling barely refreshed, his mind was filled with magic as he followed his assigned tutoring for the day as best he could.

After a disappointing morning working on Photomantics theory with Master Honreed, instead of practicing in the yard Tyndal went back to the Manciple's Library, where he wouldn't be disturbed, and began the process of stuffing his brain anew. With dedication and devotion, he managed to read another six books before dinner. That was more than he'd read in his first six months' apprenticeship.

Even though the spell took little power, the mental energy required was immense, and his mind still needed time to absorb and appreciate all the new information. He ate voraciously that evening, heading back to the serving table for seconds and thirds to replenish his arcane reserves. He was so engrossed in his meat that he did not see his other experiment, the lovely alchemist, come up behind him.

"I didn't see you fighting today," Estasia said, shyly, approaching him as everyone was finishing their meal. There was a note of disappointment in her voice. Tyndal looked up. She looked very attractive today, he noted. Her hair was perfectly combed under her wimple, her dress a simple but elegant Remeran style in dark red velvet. It suited her complexion. And her figure. Clearly, not a gown she usually wore to class.

But he was too wise to note it to her – the remark may have flattered her, but it also might reveal too plainly Tyndal's interest in her. He didn't mind being interested in her, but the moment she knew he was interested in her, according to the Laws of Love, she would actually become *less* interested in him. While it might be confusing, he could see Sire Rose's point.

"Too busy studying," Tyndal said, looking at her with his mouth full.

She looked like she was about to deliver a witty response, to which he could repay a wittier reply, thus escalating into more and more when they were suddenly interrupted – by the person he wanted to see the least, at the moment, barring the Dead God.

That idiot Rondal.

"I find that *incredibly* difficult to believe," Rondal said, setting down his trencher next to Tyndal's and bowing far too low for the occasion. *Moron.* "Hello, milady, I'm Sir Rondal of Sevendor, this brutish thug's junior apprentice." He was trying to sound interesting and important and playful, all at the same time – which was what Sire Rose and his commentators recommended – but his delivery was *embarrassingly* bad.

"I'm Estasia," the pretty student replied to the boy, without visible enthusiasm. She ignored him and kept talking to Tyndal – a minor victory. "So why didn't you *really* fight today?"

"It's not fighting, it's sparring," Tyndal explained, swallowing. "Whole different thing. I'm just practicing when I'm out there. Working on technique. Working up a sweat."

Estasia wrinkled her nose at the thought, but she didn't seem to mind the image it invoked. "Well, if you plan on *sparring* tomorrow, let me know," she asked. "I find it entertaining to watch. Like a cockfight."

"I'll see if I can oblige," he said with a spare smile. Her beautiful brown eyes caught his, and she caught her breath and looked away.

"I'm a knight mage, too," Rondal said, in a lame attempt to elicit her interest.

"I know," Estasia said, absently. "I heard. I'll see you anon, Tyndal!"

"So it's 'Tyndal', not 'Sir Tyndal'?" Rondal groused, as the shapely mage left the hall with grace and a backward glance over her shoulder. "And she's *far* more beautiful than you gave her credit for!"

"I didn't think you were interested in her looks," taunted Tyndal, feeling cocky. "I thought you lusted for her mind?"

"Well, if her mind happens to have . . . a couple of *heavy thoughts* like that associated with it, all the better!" Rondal blushed.

"She's pretty," conceded Tyndal. "But I wouldn't spend any coin on it, if I was in your boots. She seems to have eyes for me, not you."

"But *I'm* the smart one!" Rondal protested. "She's supposed to *like* the smart ones!"

Tyndal laughed and shook his head. "You sure don't know much about girls, do you, Ron?"

"Does anyone?" asked Rondal, miserably.

"If I said 'yes', would you believe me?" asked Tyndal, studying his fellow apprentice seriously for once. Rondal's lack of grace around girls was legendary. Perhaps if he gave him some actual, useful advice about girls he'd quit being so . . . painfully awkward. Certainly, it made Tyndal look that much better in comparison – a girl was always more receptive to a confident introduction, after rejecting a stammering, stumbling suitor. But he didn't need the help.

Rondal studied him back, warily. "Mayhap," he admitted, grudgingly, just loud enough for Tyndal to hear it. He looked around nervously. "I'm . . . kind of bad at it. So bad that Lady Alya and Lady Estret tried to help me," he lamented

Tyndal scowled good-naturedly and rolled his eyes. "I thought as much," he sighed. "I know not what our fair mistress told you, but . . . well, she's mistaken.

"They all *say* they like smart ones," he explained to his friend, philosophically. "Or *funny* ones. Or *rich* ones. Or *good* ones. But . . . well, Ishi has her own ideas about that.

"Girls . . . girls tend to like a certain *kind* of man. And if you are *not* that kind of man – or can't portray him effectively – then you will be, at best, a lady's *second* choice. A lady for whom you are the second choice, well, she is less likely to share your feelings. Therefore," he reasoned, "you need to learn how to *be* that kind of man . . . or fake it convincingly," he added, as he saw his fellow's face grow more ashen.

"Lady Alya told me all I needed was to be true to my pleasant character and treat ladies with courtesy and deference, and I would soon have their attention in abundance," he said defensively. Tyndal could tell that he doubted the words even as he said them.

"And she's seduced *how* many girls?" snorted Tyndal. "I may not know a lot about women, Ron, but one thing I do know is that they rarely tell you what you *really* need to know about courting one. Indeed, their advice often is *worse* than your own pathetic bumbling. And you wouldn't think that possible."

Rondal did not contest his assessment, but he brooded about it. While Tyndal did not have much familiarity with girls – or at least not as much as he would have preferred – what he had far outweighed the older boy's experience. He hoped that gave his words some additional heft in Rondal's ear.

"So tell me, oh wise master, where lies the key to Estasia's heart? Purely as an academic exercise," he added, dismissively.

"Estasia? I'd say with that one, for all of her pretensions of academics you would likely catch her attention more by flexing your muscles than showing off your knowledge."

"A lady of *her* renowned intellect?" asked Rondal, surprised.

"She might *respect* intelligence," Tyndal reasoned, "but it's not her mind that controls her heart. This much is no secret: girls like muscles. Estasia likes big muscles as much as any other girl."

"Gods be praised," Rondal said, sourly, as he studied his own spare physique. "Now all I have to do is learn to conjure some muscles!"

"Muscles would be a start, but they wouldn't be enough," Tyndal said, sagely, as he considered his courting from an academic perspective. "Estasia isn't that dumb. What arouses her interest, in my opinion, is confidence and competence. Not achievement, exactly," he said, appraisingly, "she's not the type to be allured by position or title. Or even academic prowess. Nor, alas for you, pure intellect. She admires spirit, character and confidence, more than anything else, I'd say. And that's good news for you," he added.

"Why?" Rondal asked, suddenly interested.

"Because confidence is easier to conjure than muscles," he pointed out, stabbing the last bit of meat on his trencher with his knife and flipping it into his mouth with a sigh. "And *far* easier to fake."

"*Pretend* to be confident?" Rondal asked, bitterly amused.

"Essentially," agreed Tyndal, finally pushing himself away from his plate. "It's actually not that hard. You just have to practice. And Estasia is a good girl to practice on."

"Why?" asked Rondal, surprised and hopeful. "Do you really think I have an opportunity to catch her eye?"

"Oh, Ishi's left nip, *no!*" Tyndal laughed at the prospect. "Not with me around. She's already decided that she likes me."

"Well, maybe I can get her to change her mind!" Ron said, standing from the table defiantly.

Tyndal studied him. "Do you really think so? *Really?* Honestly?"

Rondal continued to look defiant, but then doubt stole his attention. "No, probably not," he finally admitted through clenched teeth. "So why are you helping me, then? Just to witness the humiliation of my inevitable failure?"

"No," shrugged Tyndal, realizing that he didn't, indeed, wish to see his fellow suffer. "Not at all. I said Estasia would be good practice, and I was genuine. It *is* good practice, and not without design. Because around every girl like Estasia, there's *another* girl hiding behind her skirts, coveting what she has. *That* girl will strive to change the stars in their courses if it would mean she gains the prize."

"And *you're* that prize?" Rondal asked, skeptically.

"I didn't say it was a good prize," Tyndal smirked. "But there's almost always a girl on the lookout for the boy who can't get the girl he wants, which keeps the boy that girl likes too busy fighting her off to pursue that girl properly, hence she has recourse to that boy as a consolation. And that boy is *you*," Tyndal said, confidently.

"It is? There is? She is?" he asked, confused.

"I'd stake my life on it," boasted Tyndal. "Now, before you go looking for her and making an ass of yourself, there's a certain scroll you need to read . . ."

^   ^   ^

^   ^   ^

Tyndal continued his studies late into the night, long after the campus was silent. With judicious use of his newly-learned spells he was able to make significant progress on his list, doing days worth of reading in hours. And thanks to Blue Magic, every work he read he could recall at need, word for word.

Much to his own amazement, he was starting to understand it, too. Even thaumaturgy, his nemesis. Things began making sense.

How Callidore's etheric field, the Magosphere, interacted with sapient thought, allowing willful direction of its energies, for example – that mystery revealed itself with incredible clarity in his mind that night. How the same magical architecture that allowed elementals to mimic the movements of life could be adapted to influence any inert system, if properly understood. How *photoni,* the bricks of light that ricocheted around the universe, acted as both matter *and* energy – all of it started to make sense. Slowly, sometimes, or in great leaps of understanding, some obscure and darkened area of his education lit-up.

He found it startling, when it happened. Sometimes it occurred when something he read in an apparently unrelated topic triggered a thought, and then another, and then whole new areas of understanding would open like a sudden avalanche.

His instructors began to notice a difference, as well. The next day's lessons went much easier, and he was able to manifest some far more complicated spells than he'd previously dared, earning some grudging praise from the dour photomantics instructor before lunch.

He was feeling in a generous mood while he ate, and for once he was happy to be discussing academics with his fellow apprentice. Not about magic – he was nearly sick of it – but a subject he was far more comfortable and conversant with: girls. Rondal had found the reading he'd recommended and devoured the short treatise in one sitting.

But where Tyndal had seen the beautiful pragmatism of Sire Rose's discourse, Rondal was skeptical, and troubled about the ethics of the matter. That led to a debate in which Tyndal tried to answer questions for Rondal, who had brought the elegant scroll containing Sire Rose's Sixteen Laws with him. Among his difficulties with it was the nature of its very existence.

"It just seems scandalous to take what should rightly be left up to Ishi's Will and turn it into a base trade," Rondal complained, not for the first time.

"But why not?" Tyndal countered. "If we study magic, and warfare, and all of the other things we must to master them, why would *not* a man apply the principles of science and magic to the realm of the heart? It is no dishonor to Ishi – on the contrary, by knowing the Laws we pay her homage."

"There are some things that should remain a mystery!" Rondal insisted.

"That mystery can lead to misery, if a man is unschooled and unprepared!" Tyndal riposted. "The Laws are as fundamental to Ishi as the Lesser Table is to Yrentia. Do you think that the maids you court are not preparing themselves against the day they find their love? What about them causes you such discomfort?"

"Well, let's begin with the very first of the Laws: *'Pray ne'er to a maiden profess thy love lest she hath first declared her heart to thee; to do else is to invite her scorn.'* Why should a man not tell a woman he holds affections for her?" he demanded.

"Because it shows weakness of the heart, and women cannot *abide* weakness in a man," Tyndal explained, matter-of-factly. He knew this one. "A man who forces her to declare her heart first holds his hand above hers in the affair. It proves his strength, and therefore vindicates the risk she takes in such a revelation."

"And the second Law? *'Seek ye always to inspire jealousy within the castle of her heart by her vision of your flirtations and enjoyments with other maids.'* Such an action is cruel to her, and dishonorable to the other maids!" Rondal pointed out.

"Is it?" countered Tyndal, breaking a loaf of soft bread. He was eating naught but bread today so that he would have energy for sparring later. "Would you not say that maids contest among themselves for the attention of men the way men contest amongst themselves for feminine attention?"

"Well . . . yes . . ." Rondal admitted.

"The world condemns a woman, not of her temple, who too freely grants Ishi's Blessing, does it not?"

"Yes, of course!" blushed Rondal.

"Yet *you* would encourage a man to just declare his affections before he knows a maiden's heart. Then *you* would urge him to spend his commitment to her favor so cheaply, without knowing if she shares his feelings . . . or even the worthiness of the maid in question."

"What's wrong with that?"

"Should he value his own company so little, so soon will she. When she sees that other maids are eager to share your affections, she naturally seeks to guard her mate. Or mate presumptive."

"The third law is easy enough to understand," he continued, before Rondal had time to regroup his thoughts. That was *"Forever shall the errant make the mission, not the maid, the target of his desire, and thus shall the maid come to desire him whose eye lights elsewhere."* It was one of Tyndal's favorites.

"You wouldn't want a knight throwing a mission over a girl – that would be stupid," Rondal conceded. "But this one, the Sixth Law, *'Certainty in the mind of a maiden about your thoughts is Love's festering foe. Instead in conversation challenge her assumptions, evade her inquiries, tease her for her motivations, and obfuscate your mind from her. Thus she preoccupies herself with your heart as an initiate ponders a mystery, '"* Rondal said, triumphantly.

"What about it?" It seems clear enough."

"Well . . . its saying *don't* tell a girl what you're thinking!"

"Yes," Tyndal agreed, flatly. "You read it very well. Even the big words."

"Even if she *asks*," Rondal continued, ignoring the jibe.

"Yes," Tyndal agreed, pouring a mug of the weak campus ale for himself from the common pitcher.

"But . . . isn't that . . . *cruel?* Mean-spirited, at least, and certainly unfair."

"Rondal," Tyndal said, catching his fellow's eye, "think back, carefully: have you ever *once* had something *good* happen when you told a girl what she wanted to know? Or did it somehow turn in your hand like a rusty knife?"

The question hung in the air for a few moments, as Rondal searched his memory. Apparently, he could not suggest a counter argument.

Then the boy sighed. "The Eighth Law, then, *'Apologize unto a Maid only at great need, for such sorrows professed smell of weakness in a Maiden's nose. To be strong in word and deed and character draws a maid's attention even as needless apologies repel it'.* I can sort of see this one, I guess, but . . . shouldn't you be sorry for something? That's just basic politeness."

"That took a while for me to understand, too, until I remembered that awful woman at Yule, the one from the new domains? Before things got . . . crazy," he said with a grin, "do you remember how her husband kept apologizing to her? It was *'I'm sorry we were late, my wife,'* and *'you were right, my love, I'm sorry I ever doubted you'* . . . do you remember?"

"Yule is a bit . . . hazy," Rondal admitted, shooting Tyndal a nasty look.

"Oh. Right. Sorry. Uh . . . anyway, first you felt sorry for that man, but then you realized that he was doing it to himself. She had grown so used to his little apologies, like a cat to milk in the morning, that she stopped hearing him altogether. She . . . *despised* him. And everyone *else* despised him for allowing it to happen."

"I'll have to take your word for it," Rondal said, without expression.

"Sorry," Tyndal repeated. "A legitimate apology for a specific wrong is one thing, but to have one fall from your lips with every breath . . . well, it's just damn annoying. To a man or woman. But particularly to a woman. If the man she's with admits he's wrong over and over again, she'll quickly start to wonder *why* she's with him."

"I . . . can see that point," Rondal conceded.

"The key is strength," Tyndal summed up, as he gathered his belongings together before his next session. "You have to *appear* strong, even if you aren't. Confident even if you're scared. Bold, not timid."

"You're not really helping my case," Rondal said, dejectedly.

"It's not a mountain you can climb in a day," Tyndal said, standing. "It's like magic. You have to understand the theory, and then practice the drills until you reach mastery."

"Seems an awful lot of trouble to go through for love."

Tyndal grinned. "The best horses are usually also the hardest to break. Besides," he said, nodding towards the table where a knot of female students still lingered, "you never cast a net to catch just one kind of fish." Rondal turned his head just long enough to catch their attention. They giggled and looked away predictably.

One young student in particular - Lindra, he thought her name was, one of the pullets in Estasia's circle - seemed quite intent on them. Far less comely than the Wenshari alchemist, Lindra had a thirsty look about her when she gazed at them. At him, in particular, he realized, but she seemed the type of girl to be more than willing to accept second prize . . . but make her rival work like nine hells for first.

Just the sort of girl to throw at Rondal to keep him busy . . . and away from Estasia. He had served his purpose there – providing an excellent poor alternative to Tyndal in Estasia's eyes. Now he just had to keep him out of the way. And Lindra might be an easier answer than finding someplace to hide his body.

Ron looked at him thoughtfully. "You might be right," Rondal conceded. "But leave the pronouncements of wisdom to the scholars. The way you mix metaphors makes me weep inside."

*   *   *

Tyndal flew through his afternoon session, thanks to his new-found perfect recall of formulas mathematical, magical, and alchemical. It was amazing how easy things became when you could always see the Sacred Periodic Table with perfect accuracy.

Since he completed the assessment so quickly, most of his day was free, so afterward he celebrated with a double-length workout. He was eager to push himself on the cold, dreary day, using muscles that felt cramped after what had seemed like weeks of reading.

Much to his pleasure, Estasia came out to watch him and flirt with him as he sparred, along with a half-dozen other students.

Much to his annoyance, so did Rondal. He stuck to Estasia's side while Tyndal and the guardsmen went through drills and sparred together.

Much to Tyndal's annoyance, Rondal seemed to have understood enough of the Laws of Love so that Estasia was giggling at his jokes by the time rain called an end to the practice. That was fine with Tyndal. Rondal had called out criticisms of his style during the entire bout, and he hadn't been kind about it.

The small crowd broke up. Estasia did not stay to speak to him. Rondal stayed, though.

"*Ishi's tits!* Why did you have to linger like an oozing sore?" Tyndal asked his fellow apprentice, crossly, as he tossed his wooden sword carelessly in the direction of the rack after the robust session. He had waited until after the pretty alchemy student had left to attend her afternoon lecture in the company of two other girls – one of them Lindra. One of the boys he'd dueled brought him a tankard of water from the well while he stripped off his practice armor.

"What do you mean?" Rondal asked, innocently from behind the fence. "I thought you'd appreciate the support!"

"*What* support? You criticized virtually everything I did!" Tyndal said, angrily, after taking another drink. "You kept talking about my sloppy footwork – which was flawless, by the way – when meanwhile *you* can't draw a blade without tripping over your feet!"

"*I'm* not the one trying to show off for the girls," Rondal pointed out. "Besides, I had to find something to talk about . . . you were handy," he reasoned.

It was a bullshit answer. They both knew it. Still, Rondal looked at him stubbornly.

"You were supposed to be focusing on Lindra," Tyndal reminded, through clenched teeth.

"I'm not interested in Lindra," Rondal said, flatly. "I'm interested in Estasia. And you told me to practice on Estasia. So I did." He folded his arms defiantly.

"And what was all that giggling about? What did you say to her?" he demanded.

"Why?" Rondal challenged. "Afraid I'd mention your predilection for maiden goats? Or just worried about your sloppy footwork?"

"She's an alchemist," Tyndal said, his nostrils flaring. "You couldn't find any *matter or energy* sitting around to discuss?"

"I just wanted to *talk* to her!" Rondal said, defensively.

"She doesn't *like* you like that!" Tyndal shot back, angrily. Wasn't that clear to Ron? It was clear to him – Estasia didn't notice the junior apprentice romantically, despite what Rondal desired. He was just making a fool of himself by continuing to try. How could a boy so smart be so stupid about something so basic?

"Maybe she *would*, if you didn't eclipse everything I do!" Rondal shouted back, and changed direction before Tyndal could think of a witty retort. "I'm going to the library to study," he snapped. "Perhaps you've heard of it?" He stomped off.

Feeling angry, irritated, and almost as tired as he'd been when he'd started, Tyndal decided against another night in the Manciple's Library, feeding his brain on arcane matters. He considered going to find something to eat – it was a few hours until dinner but you could always scrounge something if you knew which kitchen drudges to speak to – but his stomach was upset after the fight.

In fact, he was *exhausted*. He didn't know if it was Rondal's asinine behavior, the long hours of study, or the accumulated effects of using magic so frequently, but instead of feeling refreshed after his sparring he felt lethargic. He could barely drag himself across the campus back to the North Tower, and the seven flights of stairs to his room were brutal.

He was tired – beyond tired. The Blue Magic spells he was using may not have tapped his physical condition, but they drained his mental energy faster than a three-mile run. He stumbled to his room barely conscious, and then fell into bed without even taking off his boots. He was asleep before his head hit the pillow, the sun still in the sky.

If he sought peace in slumber, he sought in vain. His dreams were anxious and vivid, filled with danger and sorrow, terror and despair, the product of too much magic and too little sleep.

In the midst of chaotic dreams featuring Estasia, Rondal, and Master Minalan, with appearances by Lady Pentandra, Lady Alya, a cast of his friends in Sevendor and a host of ugly goblins, Tyndal restlessly endured his long, restless nap. Eventually his busy mind quieted, but not before his own subconscious featured some distressing scenes to torment him. But he did not wake.

Later in the night, he wasn't certain how long, Tyndal's sleep was interrupted by a sudden sharp, stabbing pain in his mid-section. He thought it was a cramp, the moment he opened his eyes, but then he realized that someone was poking him in the abdomen with something hard. He felt a flood of energy, magical energy, pass through him.

Confused, he tried to get up – *but he couldn't move.*

Instantly terrified, he tried to move his arms and legs in the darkness, to no avail. Whatever had poked his stomach had paralyzed him, he realized. He could not move a muscle beyond his eyelids. All of his voluntary muscles were dead to his control. Only his eyes could move.

It was not a complicated spell, the part of his mind that wasn't panicking told him. There were five or six methods of casting it, and it was used for everything from warmagic to surgery. He took some solace that it was likely not permanent. His breathing wasn't affected, nor his heartbeat.

But why would anyone do it?

For one brief instant, he thought it was Rondal, vengefully taking action in his failing suit for Estasia. He discarded the thought almost immediately. This was not Rondal's style. So who? And why?

He felt a shadow loom over him in the darkness, and with sudden, frustrated horror he realized what was happening.

Someone was stealing his witchstone.

It was almost unthinkable – that shard of irionite had been around his neck or on his person constantly since he'd received it two years ago. Having anyone else handle it felt like the deepest violation – to have them handle it *against his will* was appalling. He struggled in vain against the spell while his assailant searched around his neck for the bag. Then he relaxed, and calmed himself. He did not have much time, he knew.

His muscles may have been restrained by magic, but his mind was not. Almost subconsciously he tapped into the power of his stone and cast the perception-altering spell he'd employed so frequently of late. Suddenly his assailant slowed down significantly in front of him.

Thinking furiously, Tyndal tried to remember other spells he could do silently, without involving his body in their casting or his mouth with a mnemonic. Most of the most useful spells in this situation were useless, as they had mnemonic components that had to be vocalized, for safety reasons. But there were a few.

The first thing he did was cast a magelight over his bed. He'd cast them so often that it took little more than a thought. The Cat's Eye spell required a word, but magelights were easy. The blue light was small, no larger than an egg, but he made it as brilliant as possible to expose – and possibly startle – his attacker.

Unfortunately, whomever the thief who had the temerity to steal his stone also had the foresight to mask his face for the occasion. More, a haze of indistinct perception hovered around the thief like a cloud of blurred vision. An obfuscation spell.

Whoever they were, Tyndal realized as he studied them, they were schooled in some shadowmagic. Trying to determine the shape of their face, the feeling of their Shroud, even their height was almost impossible under the spell – and he did not know enough shadowmagic to cast a counterspell. He barely knew any.

As the indistinct thief's fingers slowly searched his person, Tyndal realized there was one more thing he could do before the thief found what he was looking for. A marker spell. He'd done them plenty of times before, of course, but usually they were done on an object, not a person. Like the one he'd done on the saddle of those Censors in Talry.

The thief's obscuring field kept him from casting it directly on him – or her – which kept him from hooking the spell on him – or her – but he did note the thief was wearing cunningly-crafted leather gloves that were not thus obscured. Tyndal extended his awareness, chose the proper rune, and affixed a 'hook' on the right-hand glove, just as it found the bag with his witchstone and triumphantly tore it off of his paralyzed neck.

The perception spell turned the quick theft into a long, agonizing ordeal to live through, but Tyndal tried to use his time wisely. He noted, for instance, that while the direct image of the thief was obscured by shadowmagic, he or she hadn't thought to alter their actual shadow – and in the light of the magelight, the thief's shadow stretched across the wall. Tyndal made a mental note of how long it extended and marked the spot in his mind.

Then his perception spell came down, as did his other spells. His irionite shard had been taken from his control as the thief slowly slid the silken pouch into a small stone box. He could feel his link with it dim as it shut, and the thief moved further away from him. Suddenly everything was moving fast again.

As the thief bolted for the open window, Tyndal tried one last-ditch maneuver: he used the continued if fading proximity of the witchstone for one last spell: a mind-to-mind link with the only other High Mage in town. Rondal.

What? the other apprentice asked, annoyed. *Want to shout at me some more? Too bad. I'm studying.*

I don't want to shout at you, idiot, someone is stealing my witchstone!

What? repeated Rondal. *You mean—*

I mean someone crept into our room, and threw a paralyzing spell on me while I was asleep, then took my stone from around my neck. Right now they are fleeing from the North Tower over the rooftop. I'm still paralyzed.

I'm on my way! Rondal said. From the way he said it, Tyndal knew the other boy was already in motion.

That didn't leave him a lot to do. In fact, that left him with exactly *nothing* to do – once his link with his stone was gone, so was his ability to speak mind-to-mind. Even his magelight flickered as its power faded.

In vain he tried to fuel it with what power he could generate on his own . . . but he had become so accustomed to using irionite that he was unable to keep it alight for more than a few moments. Then darkness.

Darkness and paralyzation were insidious foes in his mind.

An indeterminable amount of time later, the door to his room was thrown open, and a magelight blazed again. This time it was Rondal's . . . and out of the corner of his eye, he could see his fellow knight had managed to arm himself with a sword from somewhere.

Rondal rushed over, dropping the sword with a clatter as he began to conjure the beginning of a counterspell.

"Who the hell did *you* piss off?" Rondal demanded angrily, as his spell began to sap the strength of the paralysis spell.

It was several moments before Tyndal could make his mouth move properly again, but he tried his best to answer. "Why . . . think . . . *me?*"

"Because you piss *everyone* off, eventually," reasoned Rondal. "That's the only reason why I can think that someone might steal your stone!"

Tyndal looked at him, rolling his eyes. While that might be true, it was hardly the time or place to bring it up, not when there were better motivations close at hand. He hated to waste energy on pointing out the obvious, but he felt compelled.

"Greed?" he managed. He could feel tingling in his fingers and toes.

"Well, yes, I suppose we *are* both walking around with a barony's ransom around our neck," conceded Rondal, "but why you and not me?"

"Oppor . . . tunity," struggled Tyndal.

"Right," agreed Rondal. "But . . . never mind, we can deal with that later. Let me go alert the hall steward while you recover." Before Tyndal could voice an objection, Rondal was gone.

While Rondal was away, Tyndal could feel the spell ebb and feeling rush back into his body, from his core out to his extremities. Soon he was able to move his limbs and speak more clearly.

By the time Rondal returned with the hall steward, an older student already in his nightdress, a panicked look in his eye, Tyndal was sitting upright. At least the paralysis wasn't more severe, he thought, though it was a minor comfort in the face of losing his irionite. But it was a comfort. He couldn't imagine spending any length of time like that and not going mad.

"A theft? In the *North* Tower?" the steward was saying in disbelief. "Never in all the years—"

"I'm not *blaming* you," Rondal said, quickly, "or faulting your security. I just need your help. Care for him while I try to track the thief!" he ordered. He gave one more assessing look at Tyndal, apparently decided he would be fine, and went out the window after the thief.

Tyndal's stomach leapt as he watched, anticipating disaster. While not precisely clumsy, Rondal was far from the sturdiest when it came to footwork in the yard, and the centuries-old slate roof outside of their rooms was a treacherous landscape of broken ankles awaiting their debut.

Idiot, Tyndal thought to himself. He would have told him that mind-to-mind, had he his stone. He could still almost feel it but the sensation and awareness was already gone.

Thankfully, so was his paralysis. He could stand, now, and his speech was back completely. He needed it to calm the senior student who was supposed to take care of him. The hall steward was beside himself with emotion – the two young knights magi were the most important guests his hall had had during his tenure, and the man was certain this incident would end his career.

Tyndal tried to sooth him, as he felt the feeling come completely back to his limbs and joints, and finally persuaded him that he was sufficiently recovered that the man could summon the guard without his guest keeling over.

When he was gone, Tyndal examined the room as carefully as he could.

Summoning magesight was *hard* – as hard as it had been before he'd gotten his witchstone. He found himself calling upon basic spell elements that he'd been able to do automatically just this morning. And while there was a thrill of success when the spell allowed him to see the traceries of magic in the room, the effort had also demonstrated to him just how diminished in potency he was.

The thief had come in through the window he'd left by, Tyndal could tell at once – there were remnants of a silence spell that had blocked the noise of the shutters opening. That suggested the thief had come in already garbed in shadowmagic. There was no signature associated with the spellwork, or at least none that Tyndal could see, but then he wasn't a thaumaturge.

There was also no sign of a paralysis spell being cast. That concerned him, as any spell will leave minute traces of arcane energy when it was cast . . . until he realized that the effect must have come from an artifact, not a living mage. A wand or other device had arrested his muscles.

He was examining the wall, where he'd mentally noted the height of the shadow, when Rondal came back in through the window, a tragic look on his face.

"I followed his trail across the roof," he explained apologetically, "but then he obscured his route and disappeared into the shadows between the towers. I think he slid down a rope or climbed down into the courtyard. I couldn't even see him with magesight," he lamented.

"He was cloaked, I think," Tyndal said, slowly. "Shadowmagic. I've never seen it before, but I've heard of it. Whoever it was, it was like my eyes couldn't focus on them at all."

"Shadowmagic? Are you sure?" Rondal asked, alarmed.

"It had to be," Tyndal insisted. "Who do you know who does Shadowmagic?"

"No one," Rondal admitted. "I suppose . . . spies and thieves and assassins would use it," he reasoned.

"Exactly," Tyndal agreed. "Lady Isily, one of Princess Rardine's ladies-in-waiting, is a shadowmage," he revealed. "I . . . met her a few times. At Timberwatch."

"I remember her," Rondal nodded, "the night we got knighted. Uh, do you think she . . .?"

"No," Tyndal dismissed. "She was given a witchstone—"

"She *was?*" Rondal asked, surprised.

"Yes, she was. I don't think Master Min was happy about it, but it was part of the deal he cobbled together to get the army formed in Wilderhall. But I haven't seen her since. Besides, she was an adept – whoever did this was sloppy. An amateur. An amateur who doesn't already have a witchstone," he reasoned.

"How do you figure? I'm not disputing," he added, when he saw Tyndal's face. "I just want to hear your reasoning."

"That's fair," Tyndal sighed. "Whoever stole my stone didn't have their own because they used a wand to paralyze me. If they had their own stone, they could have just cast the spell."

"It would have left a signature," Rondal pointed out.

"Not necessarily with Shadowmagic," Tyndal said. "But even so, they were sloppy. They obscured their appearance magically, but they did not obscure their *shadow*. I was able to cast a magelight – about all I could do – but when I did, the thief's shadow went up to . . . *here*," he said, indicating a spot on the stone wall. "Here, cast a light over the bed – egg-sized, about six candles worth," he requested.

Rondal did so in a moment. "Now," Tyndal continued, standing where his assailant had stood, next to the bed, "if he was standing here . . . and that light – bring it down a bit lower . . . *there*. That light cast the shadow over *there* . . . which makes the thief no taller than five feet and a half," he said.

"That's a short thief," Rondal said, sagely. "And that's . . . Tyndal, you just did *math*. Geometry, even. *Correctly*." The other apprentice looked impressed.

"Thanks, I've been reading," he dismissed, crossly. "It also rules out an awful lot of suspects," Tyndal pointed out. "Now, if I can manage to cast the recall spell, maybe I can track the trace I placed on his gloves."

"Wait – you cast a *trace spell* on him? Why didn't you say so?"

"I cast it on his *gloves*. It wasn't subtle. If he's got a brain in his head and even a modicum of training, he would have recognized it and discarded them. But perhaps we have a stupid thief. Uh . . . can you, uh, lend me some power? Otherwise this might take a while," he said, apologetically.

"What? Oh, sure," Rondal said, realizing how weakened Tyndal was without his stone. He closed his eyes and quickly created two *kabas* full of power, and an *apis* to transfer it.

The surge of power was intoxicating, after being bereft of his stone even for a short time. He took a moment to enjoy it before putting it to use. The tracking spell worked, he was gratified to see, and in a moment he had the distance and proximate direction of the gloves.

"They're about six-hundred feet . . . *that* way," he decided, pointing. "What's over there?"

"The courtyard, the East Tower, the kitchens, the stable – quite a lot, actually," Rondal said, apologetically. "Six *hundred* feet? That would put it . . . in the courtyard!" he said, excitedly. The both rose and bolted at once, Tyndal stumbling a bit as his legs tried to get used to their role again.

The boys raced outside following the magical trail, following the line into a tiny garden near the edge of the courtyard.

"That planter thing," Rondal indicated, pointing to one of the raised beds that littered the campus. They both fell to searching it at once until they found the gloves . . . along with a mottled black cloak, an empty glass vial, and a discarded wand.

"He did abandon them," Tyndal said, dismayed. "Crap!"

"He was sloppy, remember?" Rondal pointed out. "But not stupid. Let me check them out thaumaturgically – don't touch them!" he cautioned. "I don't want to confuse your signatures."

"You can do *thaumaturgy*? Practically?"

"Thanks, I've been reading. I know enough to know where to start," admitted Rondal. "Beyond that . . . well, let me see what I can see," he said, getting on his knees in front of the discarded equipment. He closed his eyes, and Tyndal experienced a tinge of resentment as the other apprentice began casting.

While he waited, Tyndal explained the theft to Ancient Galdan, who arrived soon after upon the summons of the steward. And then again to Head Master Alwyn. Both looked profoundly disturbed and upset by the matter – with Master Minalan suddenly so important in the profession, a theft of a witchstone from his oldest apprentice reflected very poorly on the school, and they knew it.

Of course it reflected poorly on him, too. He was happy for them not to point that out. To him or his master.

The guards, a few more masters, and even a few students came out of their rooms and out into the courtyard to investigate the small commotion. Soon a crowd gathered around Rondal, who was still deep in his spellcraft. Tyndal did his best to shoo-away anyone he could but there were a few of such rank that his dismissal would not do. But he didn't mention the theft, specifically, unless he had to. He confided only in faculty, knowing he took a risk in doing so. They were all appropriately shocked.

"Whoever it was," Tyndal explained to them, "they were between five foot three and five foot five. Talented, but un-augmented by irionite. Until *now*," he added, sourly.

"That describes about a hundred different people in the school," Galdan said, disturbed. He was fully dressed, unlike most of the others gathered. Likely he slept in those clothes, as many guardsmen did.

Estasia, dressed in her nightclothes but with her mantle over them against the chill of the night and the season, was among those who would not disperse. She could tell there was something wrong, and with a look of concern she asked him.

Tyndal found himself telling her everything, almost guiltily. He drank in her looks of sympathy like a thirsty man in the desert. His witchstone was lost . . . *what would he tell his master?*

"Oh, Tyndal," she sighed, sadly. "I can't believe that would happen! Not here, not to you . . . well, whoever did it, they must be *mad!*"

"No, they're not," Tyndal decided. "They're very, *very* smart. Smart enough to track me and my movements, get me alone, wait until I was asleep, make sure Rondal wasn't around, slip into my room through the window . . ."

"I could try to do a thaumaturgical essay," she offered, helpfully. "I *might* be able to pick up a signature."

"Rondal's already working on it," Tyndal nodded toward his fellow, whose brow was knit with concentration as he tracked the stone. "Besides . . . how tall are *you?*"

Estasia looked confused at first, and then upset and then angry. "What? Are you accusing *me?*"

"I'm not accusing *anyone*," Tyndal said, easily, "I'm just asking for your height. And I don't want anyone looking at that stuff until Rondal does."

Her nostrils flared. "You think you can't trust me?"

"I *know* I can trust him," Tyndal said, throwing his thumb toward the other apprentice. "He might be a . . . I know I can trust him. Everyone else . . . well, I just met you good folk," he said, apologetically.

"I understand, lad," Master Alwyn said, shaking his head. Alwyn leaned heavily on his staff. He did not look offended, he looked distraught.

"*I* don't!" Estasia said, offended. "Do you take me for a thief?"

"Don't worry," Rondal said, opening his eyes suddenly. "It *wasn't* her."

"How do you know?" asked Tyndal excitedly. "Did you get the thief's signature?"

"No," groaned Rondal, standing up and brushing the cold dirt of the courtyard off of his butt. "They weren't *that* sloppy, unfortunately. But I did establish a few things. For instance, the thief was male. He was also younger," he said, which seemed to relieve the shorter masters in the crowd. "Someone else can check behind me, if they like. See if they can find anything else out about him."

There were several volunteers, and the Head Master Alwyn chose Master Secul to do the tracing. A few minutes later he had to concur with Rondal . . . and commended the boy on his thorough job.

"Younger, male and magically gifted," Ancient Galdan repeated. "That narrows the suspects down to . . . say sixty? Seventy?"

"That's assuming that he is a student," Estasia said, darkly. "Who knows what enemies these two have attracted?"

"This wasn't done because of *hate*," Tyndal pointed out. "Otherwise my throat would be slit. This was a thief, not an assassin. This was done out of greed. Greed for power."

"Then who is *that* greedy for power?" asked Rondal.

"That could be anyone here," Master Secul admitted. "Ambition for power is always a hazard for a mage. I, myself, am not above it," he admitted.

"Why can't you scry for it?" asked Estasia. "Irionite is magically expressive. I would think it would show up—"

"It would," Rondal agreed. "I tried. The thief used some sort of shadowmagic spell to conceal it soon after he stole it, otherwise it would have. It can be done," he added. "It's not too complicated. The gurvani shamans try to mask themselves from our scrying that way."

"Then how *do* we find it? Assuming the thief isn't halfway upriver by now," Master Trondel asked. "Or riding for his life over the horizon?"

"Sir Tyndal," Master Alwen said, doubtfully, "While I understand the magnitude of this incident, do you not think it better if older and wiser heads were to conduct an investigation?"

"With respect, Head Master," Rondal said, formally, "as this involves irionite, which is held under oath to the Spellmonger, and since we are unsure of exactly who is involved, my colleague and I would prefer to run the investigation. I still have my witchstone, and that will be of immense benefit in finding the first. Perhaps even instrumental."

"Master, the young ones seem to have this in hand," Ancient Galdan said, respectfully, "I'll work with them and ensure they don't go too far astray, but . . . where exactly would you start?"

The old wizard looked thoughtful. "In truth, I have no liking for this theft. Irionite is too volatile and too powerful to be in sinister hands."

"Just how powerful is it?" asked Estasia, looking alarmed.

"I destroyed a castle with it last summer," Tyndal said.

"It was a small castle," Rondal said apologetically. "I helped."

"My point is, Head Master, that I don't think that you and your staff are quite equipped to handle this. Without irionite, and without a better idea of who the thief is, you'll be as much in the dark as a non-mage, I'm afraid."

"I see your point, lad," the old wizard said. "Of course we'll help in any way you can, but . . ."

"We will keep you apprised of our investigation, Head Master," Rondal assured him. "For now, simply keep the theft quiet, please. If we need specific assistance, we'll request it."

"So how *are* you planning to find it?" Galdan asked, curious.

Tyndal suppressed a groan. Wasn't that obvious? "We can find it if we play to our strengths," Tyndal said, instantly. "If we have the most advanced—"

Tyndal stopped, as his stomach started to churn. Before he could say another word, he vomited profusely into the shrubbery. Everyone else stepped back quickly.

"Sorry," he moaned, when he was finished. "That must have been an after-effect of the paralysis spell . . ."

Estasia looked at him, disgusted, and he suddenly felt ashamed of losing control like that. Vomiting in front of girls you liked was almost never a good idea . . .

"No it's not! That smell!" she said, wrinkling her nose. "I know that smell! *Bardain!*"

"Who?"

"Not who, *what*," she corrected. "Bardain is a common hypnotic sedative, made from a particular kind of sea kelp. It's odorless, colorless, and tasteless. Until it hits your stomach, that is, where it converts into other chemicals. Some of them smell like green apples – of which your vomit," she said, distastefully indicating the disgusting puddle, "*reeks*. Vomiting later is also common as your stomach rejects the toxin. Someone *poisoned* you, Tyndal!" she declared, angrily. "*That's* how they snuck into your room so easily. They wanted you dead asleep for the theft. Then they paralyzed you to be sure."

"Who could have poisoned me?" he asked, confused.

"Bardain is subtle, it could have happened anytime in the previous six, seven hours," agreed Master Secul. "*Excellent* identification, young lady!" Estasia beamed and blushed at the praise at the same time.

"I ate in the Dining Hall at lunch," Tyndal recalled, "but I served myself from the common table, just like everyone else. I missed dinner. Slept through it."

"It wouldn't have to be dinner," she decided. "Mixed with some other compounds, Bardain can even be absorbed through the skin. Physicians often administer it in water or broth. But *someone* had to have done it." She picked up the glass vial the thief had left behind gingerly, using a handkerchief to protect her fingers. "With your permission, Head Master, I'd like to investigate to confirm."

"As long as someone you trust verifies her work, Head Master, we have no objection," Rondal said, quickly. "No offense, my lady, but . . ."

"None taken," she dismissed. "I . . . I'd be mistrustful, too, after something like this, with something that powerful. That's the sort of thing that inspires people to do . . . well, anything. I'm sure your master is *not* going to be pleased," she said, looking at Tyndal sympathetically.

Tyndal did not look forward to that conversation.

"That is likely the biggest understatement of your life," Tyndal said, shaking his head quietly in misery. "Master Min will think of something particularly nasty to torment me with in punishment." That was probably an overstatement – it hadn't truly been his fault – but would his master see it that way?

"We'll find it," Rondal assured him. "*Before* we have to report it to Master Min. It can't have gone far. No one was moving within two miles of the campus, and I'll know if anyone does."

"So let's go over what we know: we have a five-foot-five male with Talent, a knowledge of shadowmagic, and a knowledge of herbalism," Rondal said, ticking off the clues. "How many students fit that description?"

"Herbalism is a common class, a prerequisite for most advanced Alchemy classes," Estasia said. "And just about anyone could look up Bardain. It's not hard to find, this close to the coast. Surgeons use it when they operate, sometimes."

"But Shadowmagic," Secul said, shaking his head, "that's a different story. *No one* teaches Shadowmagic . . . anywhere."

"Anywhere *legitimate*," Galdan reminded him.

"It is an obscure discipline," Alwyn agreed in his creaky old voice. "Hardly respectable, for all of its utility . . . to *some* folk. If Shadowmagic is taught these days, it is usually taught secretly. Someone who has a secret patron, perhaps. Or someone who learned it within their family. Some families have their own grimoires," he reminded them. "Secret spells they only pass down from generation to generation."

Tyndal recalled that Lady Pentandra had a store of those herself, 'special' spells that had been proscribed by the Bans . . . but that she had learned from her father. Master Min had a few books he wouldn't let anyone else look in. Secrecy was the prerogative of the mage.

"Then whoever the thief was comes from a magical *family*," he reasoned. "How many does that narrow your list down to, Ancient Galdan?" He watched the man figure in his head.

"Twenty. No, nineteen. Maybe eighteen, depending on whether or not . . ."

"So twenty," Rondal repeated. "Twenty suspects. Progress. That's not too many to question."

"If they know Shadowmagic, they will likely be able to conceal themselves from detection, even in an interrogation," Master Secul observed.

"But they aren't *adept* at Shadowmagic," Rondal pointed out, "or Tyndal would never have guessed their height as he did. Someone who has an imperfect understanding of the discipline might be vulnerable, if we're subtle enough."

"Or they might just get nervous enough to reveal themselves under pressure," Tyndal agreed. He began to walk back to his room, resolutely.

"Where are you going?" Secul called after him.

"To get my mageblade, Slasher," Tyndal growled. "It's time to play to my strengths."

*   *   *

The boys stayed up all night, working with Galdan, Estasia, and Master Secul to manage the crisis. Rondal suggested that they spread the rumor that someone had tried to steal Tyndal's mageblade as a prank. That was plausible enough - pranks at magical academies were legendary. Tyndal displaying the allegedly-stolen- and-recovered blade was enough to put an end to the rumor. No one outside of the investigation knew the true scope of the crime. If the thief didn't remember stealing the stone, then it was best not to alert him prematurely.

They came up with the best possible plan, under the circumstances. The next morning at dawn, twenty boys were summoned to the rarely-used Enchanter's Hall for "special examination".

Rondal thought that this would make the thief suspicious, but he was assured by Master Secul that such sudden and unexpected tests were a common thing at Inrion. Students could be summoned for all sorts of reasons, and often were gathered together without being told why, to avoid any chance of impropriety.

The twenty boys who milled around the old hall, the fire smoldering in the fireplace, were a little nervous but mostly bored, Tyndal could see from the convenient peep-hole in the next room. The ones who were supposed to be in class seemed happy to have been called away, while the ones who were out of class were grumbling about disturbing their sleep.

"I was up all night studying thaumaturgic theory!" complained Kaffin of Gyre, tiredly to no one in particular while they were waiting. "I have a test this afternoon! Making me stay awake on my morning off is cruel!"

"You think *you* have it bad?" moaned another boy – Taris of Dardendal, Master Secul whispered to Tyndal as he watched through the peep-hole – "You're a good student, you'll do fine! I've got a test in Practical Spellcraft this morning I'm missing, and I still haven't read the last third of the text! Now I'm going to have to skip lunch to make it up!"

"You should have prepared more, then," taunted another one – a bookish lad who reminded Tyndal more of Rondal than anyone else. Jesden of somewhere. "That test has been on the calendar for weeks!"

"I just want to know why we're here," complained another – Bandran of Gars, Secul supplied, though Tyndal remembered the boy.

"We all know why we're here," Daris of Holden's Mead said, gravely. "Someone was clearly caught cheating. I trust each of you will exercise due restraint," he added, warningly.

"We *don't* know why we're here," Kaffin said in disgust. There was a murmur of agreement. "If it was cheating, then I'm not even in the same level classes as most of you," he pointed out.

"I think we're getting drafted," Jesden said, suddenly terrified. "There's that war, and those two warmagi—"

"*Knights* Magi," Kaffin said, earnestly. "And don't you forget it!"

Tyndal was surprised to hear such a defense coming from a boy he'd beaten so soundly. Maybe these academic magi weren't so bad after all.

"We *could* be getting conscripted," Daris agreed, his eyes darting back and forth in a calculating manner. "I heard the Knights Magi were headed to Relan Cor after this. They *might* be recruiting."

"Oh, *shit!*" moaned Jesden.

"Oh, *relax*," Bandran of Gars insisted, leaning back and closing his eyes. "Just appreciate the fact you're not in class right now."

"That just means more reading later!" someone else moaned.

"What a bunch of whiny little girls!" Tyndal whispered to Master Secul in amused disgust.

"Do you recognize any of them?" the master asked.

"Well, yes, I've seen most of them around campus. But can I tell who did it by looking at them? No. He wore gloves and a mask. He didn't speak. He was enshadowed."

"Did any of them seem suspiciously guilty?" offered Secul.

"No," shrugged Tyndal. "But they're in their teens. You don't feel guilty about *anything* in your teens," he grinned, sheepishly.

Master Secul rolled his eyes. "Very well," he whispered. "I had hoped to spot the miscreant before we addressed them, but . . . that, young man, gave me an idea."

A few moments later Secul and Tyndal walked into the room, each of them holding a roll of parchment. Tyndal did his best to appear his normal self. He liked this idea.

"Gentlemen," he began. "As you are aware, there is a war on. The King has requested that the Arcane Orders identify young, talented magi still in academy for potential military training." There were gasps and oaths from around the room. "To this end," Tyndal continued, pleasantly, "we'd like you to write down in your own words what kind of service you could foresee yourselves doing, based on your own assessment of your Talents and skills."

"Are we getting graded on this?" moaned Kaffin.

"*Ishi's tits!* Are we going *tonight?*" Bandran said, anxiously.

"I'm too young to die!" Jesden squealed.

"Calm down, gentlemen," Tyndal continued, "there are no immediate plans to conscript you – we're merely preparing for the possibility. And hearing from yourselves how you think you would best serve your King and country is the place to start. If you *don't* think you'd make a good warmage, tell us why."

"I'm going to need more parchment!" wailed Jesden.

He passed out the sheaf of parchment and provided ink and quills to the students, then . . . then sat back and watched.

"What are you watching for?" Master Secul whispered.

"I have no idea," Tyndal said, confidently, his voice hushed. "But the Psychomantic grimoires I've read have stressed the importance of keen observation of human behavior. Since that's about what I'm left with . . ."

Master Secul nodded. But as Tyndal sat and watched the boys struggle through their military assessment, his heart sank. If any of them were guilty of the crime, they were hiding it splendidly.

One by one they blew their parchments dry – or used magic to dry them, if they were skilled enough – and then put them in Tyndal's hand.

"I don't want to die," Jesden said, in a daze as he handed in his short assessment.

"That's an outstanding attitude for a warrior to have," Tyndal nodded, sagely, as he took the bookish boy's parchment.

"*I'm* not afraid," Kaffin of Gyre said, boldly, handing his in next. "I fear nothing!"

"That can *also* be an asset, for certain missions," Tyndal admitted. Not the kind of missions Tyndal liked.

Bandran scowled as he turned his in. "I've a lucrative prospect as a resident adept, if the war doesn't get in the way," he said, angrily.

"No one has asked you to do anything but write," Master Secul pointed out.

"It's not that bad," Daris of Holden's Mead said, trying to appear casual. "But I'm not cut out for army life. My uncle was killed in the battles last year. Torchwood? Torchmont? Someplace like that?"

"Timberwatch," Tyndal corrected. "I'm sorry. I was there."

"Never liked my uncle much," shrugged Daris, handing Tyndal his sheet.

"So," Master Secul said, as the last boy reluctantly turned in his paper and then filed out of the Enchanter's Hall. "That seemed a waste of time."

"Not necessarily," Tyndal said as he rifled through the parchment scraps. "If the thief is among them, then they saw me here acting as if nothing was wrong, not acting in the panic I *really* want to indulge in right now. That has to be confusing. And if not . . ."

"Yes?"

"Then think how happy the warmagi at Relan Cor will be that I got these self-assessments from the rising class at Inrion," he said, smiling weakly.

"Yes, one never tires of the prospect of hearing of some bright young mind you've nurtured and instructed for years go off and get slaughtered," the master said, sarcastically.

*   *   *

"Any luck?" Tyndal asked hopefully, when he returned to his room.

"The thief did not leave the premises with the stone," Rondal declared. "Of that I am certain. And if he tries to move it away from here, I'll know about it, since I warded every possible travel route. Apart from that, I can't tell you anything."

"What?" Tyndal asked, his eyes wide. "It's still *here?"*

"It hasn't been removed from within a mile, I should say," Rondal said, stretching out on his bed. "So it's still close-by. But shielded. It took all morning to figure out that much."

"But if it's here, then . . . well, *someone* is hiding it!"

"Yes, when you cannot find something that someone took," he reasoned with exaggerated patience, "it's usually because *someone is hiding it*. Damn clever of them, too."

"All right, enough abuse," complained Tyndal. "Of *course* they're going to hide it—"

"No," Rondal interrupted. "I mean they really *were* damn clever. Wherever they stashed it, it's hidden from simple scrying. And it's hidden from intensive scrying. In fact, I can't even find it in the Otherworld. It's cloaked."

"You can't?" Tyndal asked, confused. "But . . ."

"Yes, I know," sighed the other apprentice. "More shadowmagic. I hate shadowmagic. That stuff complicates everything."

"You don't say," Tyndal said, dryly.

"You don't still think it was one of the students? Or one of the staff?"

"I haven't ruled out anyone but you . . . and it wouldn't be fair to the others if I didn't consider you a suspect, too."

"I've already got a witchstone, why would I want another?"

"I didn't say you were a *good* suspect, I just said it wouldn't be fair," Tyndal said, a little annoyed.

"Am I interrupting?" came an amused female voice from the door. Estasia. As much as he enjoyed her company, he was a bit annoyed she was there. He liked to present his best side to a girl, and that was hard to do when you were half-mad with rage and magically crippled.

But she was more than just a sympathetic ear. She was a good mage, a brilliant mage, by all accounts. She was helpful.

"Just my slow descent into madness," groaned Tyndal. "What do you want?"

"That's no way to treat a guest, Sir Tyndal!" Rondal complained, quickly standing. "Sire Cei would be ashamed! What can we help you with, my lady?" he asked. "You have news?"

She snorted at Tyndal's display. "I just thought you'd be interested to know that the remnants in the glass vial found in the courtyard were *not*, in fact, Bardain."

"Ah!" Tyndal said, triumphantly. "Then you were wrong!"

"No," the comely alchemy student said, patiently, "there was plenty of Bardain in your vomit, that part I got exactly right. I just said that the residue in the *glass* in the yard wasn't Bardain. But it was even more intriguing. It was Lanlinyeir."

"What . . . is Lanlinyeir?" asked Rondal, sparing Tyndal the task.

"It's a highly exotic, *extremely rare* herbal extract from some island somewhere," she said. "I spent hours tracking it down. It's only mentioned a handful of times anywhere."

"So what does it do?" Tyndal asked. "Shadowmagic?"

"No. It makes you *forget*."

"What?" Tyndal asked confused.

"Like that, exactly," Estasia teased. "It makes you forget everything that has happened in the last twelve to fourteen hours. Essentially everything that you experienced from the time you woke up that morning," she explained.

"But I remember everything about the theft!" Tyndal protested. "What kind of stupid herbal extract is that?"

"It's actually quite useful, hence the 'rare and exotic' nature of the substance. But you're right – you *do* remember everything from that night. So it wasn't used on you."

"Then who?" Rondal frowned.

"The thief used it on *himself*," Estasia proclaimed, entering their room unbidden. "It takes fifteen or twenty minutes to take effect, but after that, you won't remember *anything* that happened after sunrise."

"Why would the thief use it on himself? That's even more confusing!" Tyndal said, angrily. He had a thick warwand in his hand he continuously smacked into his palm. The young woman watched with a mixture of horror and fascination.

"Stop, slow down, *relax*," Estasia said, soothingly, closing her hand over his to still his wand. "You aren't thinking this through. It was actually very clever – very clever indeed."

"Why is it clever to steal a witchstone and then forget where you put it?"

"I was perplexed about that myself, until I figured it out. The thief didn't take the potion to forget where they put it," Estasia reasoned. "The thief took it so that he would *forget he was a thief*."

"I . . . *what?*" Rondal asked. Tyndal was gratified that he wasn't the only one confused. If his brainy fellow apprentice didn't follow the bewitching student's reasoning, he didn't feel so bad about his own failure.

"Look at it from *his* perspective," the pretty alchemist said, taking a seat on the one chair the boys shared. "You want to steal a witchstone, but you know – with absolute certainty – that the moment you do, you're going to be a suspect. Possibly subjected to torture or execution if you're exposed. How do you steal the stone and then avoid revealing that you stole it under heavy questioning? How do you even avoid suspicion?"

"By . . . not having a guilty conscience," Rondal said, finally understanding. "If you don't *remember* the crime, you can't feel guilty about it!"

"Exactly," she smiled. "You're smarter than you look," she tossed at Rondal. The idiot beamed like a puppy who was patted on the head. Then she ignored him and spoke directly to Tyndal.

"Let's go back over what we know about the crime. When the thief stole the witchstone, they had to know *where* Tyndal was, when he would be alone in his room, and that he would not be disturbed long enough to complete the theft."

"Then they had to poison me," Tyndal reminded her.

"Right," she agreed. "And that could have happened at any time yesterday. Bardain can take a few hours to work. But it works slower on some than others. So they had to keep watch on you, somehow, and then wait until it had taken effect enough to get you back to your room."

"That wouldn't be too hard," reasoned Rondal, staring at the alchemist. "He's not exactly . . . subtle."

"No, he is not," Estasia agreed, amused. "So someone was watching you. Did anyone seem to be following you around or watching you more than usual yesterday?"

"That's not exactly the kind of thing I keep track of," Tyndal said, annoyed. "I may have an ego, but I'm not in love with myself that much."

"Let's assume they watched you from afar. They saw you head back to your room. They had to know that you would not be joined. What were you doing when he was being robbed?" she asked Rondal, suddenly.

"Me?" he asked, surprised. "I was in the Scriptorium, copying a scroll on Thaumaturgy. Why?"

"Who was with you?"

"No one," Rondal said, his lips pursed. "There were other people there, but no one was really with me."

"So you could have been watched," she nodded. "But . . . not by the same person who was watching Tyndal, I expect. Not if they had to know where both of you were at the same time.

"He had to be alone. He had to be in his room. He had to be drugged. They had to have a means of getting into his room without being spotted. Once those conditions were met, all he had to do was scale the roof, cast his shadowmagic spells to conceal his identity, paralyze Tyndal with the wand, take the stone, escape through the window, and then down a rope or something into the courtyard. So whoever it was is good with heights."

"Not really the sort of thing you can test for," Rondal mumbled.

"But they also were canny enough to plan this thing, and then have the resources to do it. They had Talent," she recited as she paced the scene of the crime. "They had some education, so that leaves out the first year students, perhaps the second years. And they weren't idiots. They were good enough to realize you had put a trace on the gloves," she reasoned, "so they abandoned them."

"Wouldn't they have hidden the stone near to where they dropped the gloves?" asked Rondal.

"Nowhere near where they hid the stone," Tyndal said, shaking his head.

"You're right," she nodded. "They would not have taken the chance. So they hid the stone first, abandoned the empty wand, marked gloves and incriminating cloak, wandered away . . . and *then* they took the potion. They were gone by the time you two arrived in the courtyard.

"That means they only had fifteen minutes to stash the stone – *somewhere* – and get back to wherever he was *supposed* to be . . . in time to forget everything and not end up wandering around the campus aimlessly."

"That would arouse suspicion," agreed Rondal. "So where could they have hidden the stone?"

"Pretty much anywhere," admitted Estasia. "And there are a dozen different entrances to the various towers as well as balconies and such. Whoever this thief is, he's nimble. They could have easily gotten back inside without notice. Or hidden in one of the outbuildings."

"So that helps us . . . not at all," groaned Tyndal.

"No," Rondal said, evenly, "it actually tells us quite a bit about our thief. Look at the specialized equipment he had. That wand isn't something you can buy at the student canteen! And those gloves are lightly enchanted, too, for grip, and they're specially made. Far beyond the scope of a student. Someone else would have to provide them."

"So he was unlikely to be working alone, if he was a student," Tyndal said, nodding. It made sense.

"He wasn't poor, or his backer wasn't. And he was smart and sophisticated enough to anticipate us using some psychomantic method of avoiding even a truth-telling. If you don't *remember* doing something, you can't *lie* about it."

"So he has knowledge of shadowmagic, alchemy – herbalism – and warmagic—the paralysis spell, remember?"

"That was a wand of undetermined origins," Tyndal reminded her. "And not, strictly-speaking, a warmagic spell. It does have other uses. Unless you *learned* its origins," he added hopefully.

"No," she said, sadly. "I examined it with Master Indan. It was a basic one-use spell. Whoever did it didn't leave enough of a trace to get a signature. Professional."

"But that still indicates a lot of resources – consider how much such a thing must cost, if they didn't make it? Add that to this expensive forgetting potion. And the expensive sedative that lured me to sleep. And the enchanted cloak that must have taken someone a year to make. That is someone who has a lot of coin in their purse. But yeah, I guess this thief has a clever brain, too. Or his partner does."

"That's actually likely. I doubt any of the boys here would have the skills, much less the brains, to undertake such an enterprise on their own."

"I beg to differ, milady," Rondal said, shaking his head. "These are some of the smartest—"

"Smart," she interrupted, "but *unsophisticated*. If *you* were a half-trained student mage, would you consider trying to imperil your future, not to mention your life, by daring to steal the witchstone of one of the first and greatest knights magi?"

"I am a half-trained student mage," Rondal countered, a little sourly. "And no, I wouldn't try to steal a witchstone . . . unless I knew what it was really capable of."

"No, of course—hey, you think I'm *great?*" Tyndal asked, confused. That was unexpected. And welcome. He made note of the interest, as the Laws of Love suggested he do.

"Enough *other* people do so that you have that reputation," Estasia said, coolly. "It's what people *believe*, not what actually *is*, that matters in a case like this."

"Ouch!" Rondal said, wincing on his fellow apprentice's behalf. Tyndal ignored the jab. He knew she liked him.

"She's right," Tyndal sighed. "On parchment, I'm not a guy you'd want to mess with unless you were very good."

"On *parchment,*" conceded Rondal. "But there was a lot of forethought here. Someone had to give you the Bardain. Someone had to watch where you went. Someone had to prepare to rob you. And it's possible – if not likely – that the thief handed off the prize to the confederate before taking the Lanlinyeir. Or stashed it along the way."

"That would save a lot of time," agreed Tyndal. "If the thief didn't have to worry about holding the stone, then they'd have ample time to get back to . . . wherever they were supposed to be."

"Have we accounted for everyone's whereabouts?" asked Estasia.

"Close enough," reported Rondal. "The Head Master spoke casually to each boy and got his alibi without him realizing it. Almost all of them were studying or doing their assigned chores, and the ones who weren't had witnesses."

"That's annoying," Tyndal said, disgustedly.

"That doesn't mean that we can rule them all out, though," Rondal reminded him. "With the thief not remembering committing the crime, he could have been lying, truthfully, when he spoke with the Head Master."

"And the confederate doesn't have to be another boy, either," observed Tyndal, his eyes opening a little wider. "It could be . . . *anyone.*" Involuntarily his eyes flicked to Estasia.

"Hey!" she protested, "I was in front of witnesses when I heard the commotion! And I'm the one who agreed to test the vial," she pointed out. "I even consented to have my work double-checked by Mistress Quentine! Flawless," she added, casually.

"That *could* just mean you're cleverer than you look," Tyndal said, helpfully.

"Hey!" Estasia protested again. "If I *wanted* your stupid stone, I'm sure I would have had other ways to get it than to climb through your window!"

"Is that a flirtation, milady?" Tyndal asked. Estasia's face darkened.

"That's *enough*, you two," Rondal said, disgusted. "Let's save our energies for the problem at hand. We're going to need them. Every moment we waste puts that stone further out of reach."

"Agreed," Tyndal said. Then he thought of something. "Estasia, just why *are* you helping us?"

"What do you mean?" she asked, suspiciously.

"I mean, why devote your time to this, when you're just making yourself a bigger suspect by your interest?"

He expected an outburst, but instead got a curt nod. "I can see your point. All right, let's just say that I've been here two years now, and I'm bored to tears. Tracking down a lost—"

"Stolen!" Tyndal reminded her.

"—*stolen* witchstone is actually a practical challenge. A lot different than slashing my way through theory or working in tubes and jars in a laboratory. Besides," she said, her blush returning, "I know the political tides are turning, and it's raising both of your ships. I figure if you knew my name and my face, it might prove beneficial in the future."

"We've been hounded for less reason," Tyndal said. "Back in Castabriel during the Coronation there were these—"

"Every moment we waste!" Rondal reminded them sharply. "I'm going to assume Estasia isn't either of our criminals, because . . . well, because I just do, and she's proven an asset in the search," he said, hurriedly. "Besides, if she is one of them, then being close to her will help trip her up and reveal herself."

"Oh, thank you, Sir Knight," the alchemist said, curtsying sarcastically.

"To continue, we have to find out two things: who the thief is, and where the witchstone is. The thief can lead us to the confederate – I hope – and the confederate can lead us to the witchstone. So let us find the thief."

"Yes, let's," Tyndal grumbled. "Only we've been searching for hours, and we have little sign on the trail. Where do we go from here?"

There was a pregnant silence in the tower chamber as the three thought furiously. It stretched and stretched long beyond the point of comfortabilty. Several times the glimmer of an ideal would – almost – compel someone to speak, but as time wound on, nothing sprang to mind.

"I'm beat," Tyndal finally admitted. "I feel lost without my stone, but my body just can't keep my mind thinking anymore."

"We've been up for thirty hours or more," agreed Rondal with a yawn. "If we're going to think properly, we're going to need to rest. I'll set the wards," he offered.

Estasia smiled apologetically. "I was hoping I could think of something, but . . . not without alerting everyone to the theft. Maybe I'll dream up something tonight."

"I'd offer to help," Tyndal teased, "but I'm just not up to it."

"I don't need your help," she assured. "Just get some sleep. We'll think of something. And if we don't . . ."

"If we don't," finished Rondal, "I'm going to have to call on our master . . . and I don't think anyone wants *that* to happen."

*   *   *

"The question becomes," Rondal said as they walked to lunch, "how do we flush out this thief when he has no memory of stealing?"

"He couldn't have been an unwilling dupe," pointed out Tyndal, who had been disappointed the dawn had brought no further insight into his problem. "He had to have known enough magic and had enough ambition to make the attempt."

"Or he was coerced into it," Rondal observed. "His help could have been extorted."

113

"I don't think he was," Tyndal said. "No good reason – I don't know, he seemed kind of . . . eager. And he was definitely triumphant when he left."

"You got that with him in the dark? Paralyzed? In a mask? Cloaked by shadowmagic?"

"I can be a pretty subtle guy," Tyndal bragged.

"All right, assume he was a willing accomplice," conceded Rondal, "why would you take that kind of risk and then just . . . forget about it?"

"Apart from the obvious advantages? You wouldn't. Maybe that drug's effect was meant to be temporary. Maybe the accomplice will alert the thief to what he did after the fact—"

"Would you?" asked Rondal.

"Uh . . . no," admitted Tyndal. "Assuming I'm a murderous cutthroat who wanted a witchstone, no, I'd never let the idiot I got to steal it for me remember if I'd gone to all the trouble to make him forget."

"Exactly," sighed Rondal, as they passed by a work crew hauling the cart that emptied the garderobes and chamberpots – it was not one of the better student jobs, and usually given out as a severe punishment. To their surprise, Stanal of Arcwyn and Kaffin of Gyre, his sparring comrades from the yard, were the ones pushing the cart.

"Trygg's holy cramps, who did *you* piss off?" asked Tyndal, partially amused by and partially sympathetic to the boys' plight.

"Mistress Selvedine didn't like a comment I made about . . . a classmate," Stanal said, blushing. "She thought some time pushing the honey cart might make me more respectful."

"Must have been some comment," whistled Rondal. "And you?"

"I failed an exam," Kaffin said, miserably. "Thaumaturgic Theory. *Utterly* failed it. I got *one question* out of thirty correct. It was like it just went in my eyes and leaked back out again." He shook his head. "So I get to do *this*, instead of studying. Master Secul reamed me out – *verbally*," he clarified, "and then decided I wasn't taking my studies seriously enough. This experience is supposed to help focus my attention." He made a face.

"Ouch," Tyndal winced. "I'm suddenly terribly glad I'm an

apprentice, and not a student."

"You should be," Stanal nodded. "See you at the yard, later?"

"I'm . . . working on a special project," Tyndal said, reluctantly. "I might not be there."

Stanal looked disappointed. "Damn. You're the only one around here who can challenge me, apart from the guards . . . and Kaf."

"Challenge you? I kick your ass three times out of four!" the son of a seaknight boasted. Kaffin was the better swordsman of the two, Tyndal had to admit. But he could never say so.

"I don't think either one of you should be bragging much," Tyndal confided, quietly. "You're both decent fighters, but . . . well, you need seasoning. It's clear you've never fought for your life – *really* fought for your life before."

Stanal looked pale. "I'd rather not, if I could help it. I just like swordplay."

"And I've never fought for my life," Kaffin pointed out, "but when I do, I want to know what I'm doing."

"Then keep practicing," assured Tyndal. "Besides, with a war on, you never know when knowing how to fight will come in handy. And you're more fun to beat up than Rondal, here."

The boys both made faces, but they nodded and pushed on, their cart sloshing evilly as they moved it.

"Gods, I'd rather suffer one of Master Min's lectures!" Tyndal said, shaking his head as the stinking cart rolled by.

"With Garky I only had one chamberpot to empty," agreed Rondal. "And a junior apprentice to delegate that to. I'm starting to see the advantages of our situation," he admitted.

Just then a door opened allowing six or seven female students to stream out toward the dining hall after noon service in the chapel, carefully avoiding Kaffin and Stanal's wagon as it lurched across the campus. The boys stopped and allowed them to go ahead of them.

"On the other hand, there are some unique advantages to student life, too," Rondal observed, watching the giggling mass of young femininity pass by, leaving a perfumed cloud in their wake.

"I see your point," Tyndal said, then shook his head to clear his mind.

"And here I thought you were considering celibate holy orders . . ."

"Look, I am a little shy," Rondal said, annoyed, "that doesn't mean I'm uninterested! When Ishi decides the time is right—"

"If you wait around for divine intervention to find you a woman," snorted Tyndal, "you're wasting your time. Ishi doesn't tie our hearts together just because she fancies it. You have to go out there and make yourself vulnerable with a girl," he counseled. "Really *connect* with her."

"I thought I was *doing* that with Estasia," his fellow apprentice said through clenched teeth. "But she seems strangely distracted . . ."

"Let's get back to my . . . problem," Tyndal said, quietly, realizing he was getting distracted. "Two accomplices and they haven't left the area with it yet. How do we draw them out?"

"They've got what they want," grumbled Tyndal. "All they have to do is not get caught."

"If Master Minalan comes here to search, they're not going to get away with it. They have to realize that."

"They need to not get away with it *before* he comes," Tyndal complained. "I can't believe I lost my stone! I—"

"Hey!" called a familiar female voice from the line into the Dining Hall, ahead. "You two mage knights!" Estasia broke through the crowd, a book in her hand. Her mantle was thrown back, and her shapely form distracted him pleasantly for a moment. "I think I have the answer."

"Answer to what?" Rondal asked.

"The answer to the question of which of the two of you is the dimmer," she said, sarcastically. "But what I really have the answer to is your problem."

"You do?" Tyndal asked, skeptically.

"Believe it or not, I do!" she said, excitedly. "Do you have a moment?"

Rondal looked at the large line in front of the Dining Hall, and how slowly it moved. "It appears we have several," he nodded. "What do you have?"

"Before I show you," she said, biting her lip, "let me tell you how I arrived at the solution. Firstly, why can't you scry for the stone?"

"Because someone is cloaking it," Tyndal answered. Rondal nodded.

"Exactly," the alchemist nodded, eagerly. "So . . . what would you see if you looked for it?"

"Nothing," Rondal said, confused. "Why?"

"So what happens if you light up the *area* with magic?" she asked. "Like . . . like . . . imagine if we made it rain. Rain *magic*."

"All right," agreed Tyndal, slowly. "It's raining magic. Now what?"

"If it is, indeed, raining magic – that is, we cast spells or sigils or whatever all over the campus, we should be able to scry out pretty much everything—"

"Except for the places that are cloaked!" Rondal agreed, excitedly. "Oh, sweet Briga's bum, that's brilliant! That's what we did when we were looking for that tree in Alshar, remember Tyn? We look for what *isn't* there, not what *is!*"

"That . . . that might work," conceded Tyndal, who was hardening his heart against the idea that he'd lost his stone.

"It *will* work," she declared. "I'm so sure, I even looked up the right spell for it," she said, shoving her book under their noses. "It's a little obscure, and about as useless as . . . nipples on a man," she giggled, "but I found it!"

The boys both read the spell, a mere three or four pages worth. It was surprisingly simple, if one had the power for it. A mage, it declared, could fill a space half a rod in diameter with low-level power, should he need to, with the spell.

"We can't search this place one half-rod at a time," Tyndal said, discouraged.

"We don't have to," corrected Estasia. "With Rondal's stone, he would have the power so that he could conceivably fill every part of the campus at once. Then one of us does the scrying while he's working . . ."

"And my stone shows up because of what's *not* there," Tyndal concluded. "All right, what do we need?"

"Some time, some quiet space, and . . . well, a map of campus."

"We can find all of that in the Manciple's Library, after closing hour," Tyndal suggested."

"Tonight after classes, then," Rondal decided. "Meet us up there. How long will it take to cast the spell?"

"For me? Three or four hours. For you? Unknown," she conceded. "But it takes about an hour to fade into effect, and then it only lasts about fifteen minutes."

"That doesn't give us very much time," Tyndal frowned.

"That gives us plenty of time . . . if we're prepared," pointed out Estasia. "I'll scry while Rondal does the summoning. You can mark spots on the map as we encounter them, and then . . . "

"Then we'll find my stone – and punish whoever took it!" Tyndal said, resolutely.

"One step at a time, Sir Knight," she said, amused. "Where do we cast it? The library? Or check out a student laboratory?"

"We can do the spell in our room," Rondal said, flatly. "We don't need all the symbolic stuff for this," he decided as he studied the spell. "The essence of the work is pretty straightforward."

"You want to do high level magic . . . in your *bedroom?*" she asked, scandalized.

"That's where I do my best work," quipped Tyndal, smugly. "But we should do it in the Manciple's Library. Believe me, no one will disturb us there."

"It sounds like an intriguing place," Estasia said, an eyebrow arching.

"We should study together there sometime," Tyndal said, with a smirk. "We could—"

"Oh, shut *up!*" Rondal moaned. "Yes, she likes you, you like her, you're going to get married and have twenty fat babies and live in a pretty little castle surrounded by happy peasants but *let's do this.* Now. If I have to keep hearing him whine about his stone . . ."

"Not now," pleaded Tyndal. "As much as I want my stone back, I want food more. I haven't eaten in forever. And I vomited, don't forget!"

"I really wish I could," Rondal said, mildly.

"We can do it this evening, assuming the thief doesn't try to get away. And Ancient Galdan is inspecting everyone and everything leaving the campus. What do we need, then?" Tyndal asked, ignoring Rondal. He knew he'd been complaining about the theft. He wondered how Rondal would have reacted to it.

"It's fairly straight-forward," she said, referring to the text. "From the Cylomancian scrolls on thaumaturgy. The good news is that this spell can carry another, and I think I have just the spell to restore the criminal's memory too, while we're at it. But that will take yet more time to build yet more power."

"No, it won't," Rondal said, digging out his own shard of irionite. "I can build a couple of *apises* and feed the power to you two. You can do the inauguration, Lady Estasia, and Tyndal can do the scrying, which takes far less power. Then at the end you can do the memory restoration."

"That could work," agreed Tyndal, a little more annoyed with his competent rival. "But it means we're going to be . . ."

"Intimate, I know," Rondal swallowed. They'd only combined their efforts in the traditional Imperial manner during instruction, never for any real work. Irionite gave them plenty of power, reducing the need for such techniques. It made them both uncomfortable – being pressed up mind-to-mind with someone put you very close to them.

"I'm game," Estasia said, giggling. "I've done very little group work like that. Alchemy rarely requires that sort of work. I'd love to try, though. And . . . I don't mind being intimate," she added, softly.

*　　　*　　　*

Tyndal wasn't particularly hopeful, but he was willing to give the scheme a try. He was desperate, feeling as if he had betrayed all of the people in his life who had invested in him. This idea wasn't his style, but he didn't have a better idea. There was no harm in it, he supposed. It wasn't the sort of thing that would alert the thief, say, if he had warded the stone somehow.

They timed the spell for late evening on the premise that less movement and a still campus would make tracking the results easier. Tyndal arrived first, as he had the key, and he brought his mageblade, a warwand, and a waterbottle. Then he stood in the dark for ten minutes while he tried to cast a magelight. The result was so mockingly impotent that he banished it, preferring the darkness to the mockery.

"I don't know why you did that," Estasia said, as the globe of pale illumination faded. "I've only been able to do that spell once. In the lab. One candlepower for three whole minutes."

"It gets easier with practice," Tyndal said. "But it takes too much power and concentration, without irionite. I'm just used to doing it." Instead he found a taper from a cluster in a sconce and used a cantrip to make it light. He could do that much, at least. "I suppose I could still have a career as a marketplace performer. Cantrips are still relatively easy."

"Let's not be pessimistic, shall we?" Estasia said in an overly-casual voice. "I know this has been hard for you, but you have a lot of really good people helping you find it. You'll have it by dawn, I promise." Before Tyndal could protest that she had no real assurance of that, she swept him into an unexpected – but not unwelcome – kiss.

He had known that the pretty alchemist liked him, and was certainly flirting with him, but this was the first tangible sign that she had feelings beyond professional respect and admiration.

As her softer-than-dew lips pressed against him, her tongue playfully dueled with his. The effect was erotic and mind-stopping - for a few moments he forgot about all of his other troubles and just enjoyed kissing the sweet-smelling girl.

When they finally, reluctantly broke the kiss, Tyndal had found himself possessed of a new optimism about his situation. Estasia's kiss gave him the validation he needed that he was on the right track, like a sign from Ishi. He also understood that it was a feeling born more of desperation than reason, but that very desperation allowed him to ignore that fact.

"Why did you do that?" he asked, curious. "Not that I'm objecting . . . it just seems . . . a little out of character."

She smiled in the candlelight. "What, taking advantage of a powerless, incredibly handsome hero whom I've lured into a dark, deserted library? Considering the folks back home who believe I'm destined to become an evil sorceress, that's *completely* in character."

"No, I meant . . . why kiss me, when it's clear you're set on a career in magic, not a husband? I mean, you remind me of Lady Pentandra, and despite her discipline—"

"Sex magic?" Estasia asked wickedly, delighting in the scandal of the controversial field of study.

"Uh, yeah. She'll screw a maiden goat, if that's what her studies demand, but she doesn't go around. . cultivating romances," he finished, lamely.

"Maybe a girl just likes you, Sir Tyndal," Estasia said softly, with humor. "Maybe she's just taken by your charm – or lack thereof – your wit, your bravery, your, your . . . *muscles*," she said, reaching out and feeling his bicep. "Dear Ishi's dewy- well," she said, dropping her hand and regaining her composure. "Can't a girl just *like* a boy, and want to be intimate with him?"

"Sure," Tyndal said, not entirely displeased by her commentary. "I'm fond of the practice. You have to understand, though, why I'm cautious. My master has enemies—"

"And apparently you do as well," she pointed out. "I don't know much about your master, but I imagine he also has allies?"

He thought of Lady Pentandra, Lady Alya, Sire Cei, Baron Arathanial and all of the other good folk Master Min had surrounded himself with,

"Well, yes," he admitted.

"And now, so do you," she concluded. "It's a wizard's prerogative to cultivate allies. That's essentially what I'm doing with you and Rondal. Good, dependable, powerful, well-placed allies."

"So you aren't trying to just get me drunk and drag me to a priestess?" he asked, only half joking.

"Ishi's *twat!*" she swore, unexpectedly. "Get over yourself! You might be Sir Tyndal the great Knight Mage, but I *do* have a career to think about. You might be cute, but you aren't cute enough to convince me to give up magic!"

"My wife would never have to give up magic," Tyndal said, absently. "But I'm not looking for a wife!" he added, desperately.

"Nor do I aspire to being one," she said, coolly. "But it's good to know your feelings on the matter."

For once Rondal arrived in a timely-enough manner to cut short the conversation's uncomfortable direction. If he suspected the two had been kissing, he showed no signs.

"It's way too dark in here," he said, as he took his bag off of his shoulder and casually cast a bright magelight. Tyndal suppressed a surge of envy, as well as a twinge of regret. He liked being in the dark with Estasia.

"Let's get this started," Tyndal agreed in a businesslike manner. "I don't want to wait one second longer than necessary."

"I'll spellbind the door so we won't be disturbed," Rondal offered. "You get ready."

They took positions on the floor after Rondal warded the door. Tyndal sat down and tried to make himself as comfortable as possible. He was pretty good with action-based spells, like combat magic or spellmongering. These more contemplative workings were the stuff of academics and scholars, not warmagi. He glanced at Estasia and vowed to cultivate such disciplines more in the future.

The process of forming an *apis* was incredibly difficult without the crutch of his witchstone, Tyndal realized. But once it had manifested, he connected it with Rondal's matching spell and suddenly he had a surge of power at his disposal like he had not felt in days. Not nearly as much as if he'd had his own irionite, but more than enough to do the job at hand.

But Rondal had been right to be concerned about the intimacy of the working, Tyndal realized as they settled into the first big spell they'd done together. After making the connection with the other two magi, he suddenly knew and felt things about Estasia he never would have known. Just how much she liked him, for one. The strength and intensity of the feeling was potent. She, too, suddenly recognized some things about him, things that made him uncomfortable.

And his fellow apprentice, too, had some residual feelings that bridged the connection along with the power. The longing, the loneliness, the envy, the disappointment, the self-deprecation, the . . . the whole long sad litany of things that made Rondal who he was inflicted itself on Tyndal with an understated sadness. Tyndal felt sorry for him and was irritated by it at the same time.

Then he realized just what feelings he might be projecting, and he resolved to focus his mind and emotions more tightly. He felt the emotions of the other two pull away as they made their own adjustments.

They said very little while they worked. Rondal provided the power until Estasia was able to cast her portion of the spell. The moment she nodded her head, Tyndal turned his attention to scrying.

The results came in much more slowly than if he'd had his witchstone, but even so their combined efforts yielded a number of "blank" spots in their scrying. More than Estasia had figured upon. But luckily there were but a few within the area they had decided would be the only possible places the thief could have stashed the stone.

"Time to let the thief remember what he did," Anastasia said, "Casting the recall spell . . . now!"

Without a means of knowing whether or not the spell had worked, they let the working fall and discussed the results over the map.

Soon they had narrowed the field significantly, and were excited by the spell's success – excited enough that they didn't feel the need to speak about the unaccustomed intimacy. They had gotten plenty of data, enough so that they were able to make some astute guesses about just which, exactly, of the "blank spaces" might be hiding the stone. They narrowed it down to a list of the most likely, and decided what order they would explore their options.

They trudged up the stairs to the North Tower, where their first target field lay. It lay outside of their room.

"Let's go get it," Tyndal said, at once, as he looked out the window that had allowed the thief to come in.

"No!" Rondal insisted. "He's got to have it warded. Spellbound, even. With shadowmagic we could spend days searching for it and never see it. We have to get the thief to lead us to precisely where it is, and then get him to dispel the cloaking and protection spells."

"Which I'm certain he'll do out of a sense of contrition," Tyndal said, dismissively.

"No, you'll threaten to stab him if he doesn't," Rondal pointed out.

"That is my plan," agreed Tyndal.

"Well, don't," argued Rondal. "At least not yet."

"You have a better suggestion?" Tyndal asked, skeptically. Stabbing sounded terribly effective.

"I do. We need to flush him and his confederate out. We've narrowed the list of prospective thieves, we've re-constructed the crime, and we have some good guesses about who it is . . . and who their confederate is."

"We do?" Tyndal asked.

"Don't we?" Rondal responded. He named a few suspects who fitted the facts. Tyndal considered each one, and then added another. Estasia chimed in with two more possibilities, and then they argued until they had discarded some of their suspects. She left soon after they had concocted a plan that might flush the thief out, the boys thanking her profusely for her help.

"So do we really think we can flush this guy out?" Tyndal grumbled. "Can't we use your witchstone as bait?"

"Hells, no!" Rondal said, appalled. "No, we're using *your* stone as bait. And our story to motivate him. Just keep calm and let the magic work," he encouraged. "We spread the rumor that Master Min is coming here for a surprise visit, let it be known off-hand that it amounts to an inspection, and the only people who will be troubled are the guilty ones." He sighed, expressively. "You know, that was . . . that was *amazing!*"

"What was?" Tyndal asked, still staring out of the window.

"That spell. The way we were connected. It was like . . . like watching her breathe. From the *inside.*"

He chuckled despite himself – it was an apt description of the experience. "So if you got *that* much," reasoned Tyndal, "then you also realize . . . ?"

"Yes, she doesn't like me," groaned the boy. "At least not like she likes you. Yes, point conceded. You are her heart's temptation. I'm not. That doesn't make me hate you less."

"'*Fault not the victorious for their achievements, but instead fault the rules of the contest,*'" quoted Tyndal. "I cannot help how she feels."

"No, but you don't have to feel that way back!" Rondal accused.

"As if I had any say over Ishi's whim!" he snorted. "Look, I *do* like her. She's pretty. She's smart. She's . . . funny, even. But I don't like her nearly as much as she likes *me*. And part of why she likes me is I *don't let her know* I like her that much. That's one of the Laws of Love."

Rondal made a face. "You can't study love like you study physics!"

Tyndal shrugged. "Why can't you? Just because love is Ishi's domain does not mean it's forbidden to study as you would any other subject."

"It's . . . it's dishonest!" blurted Rondal. "You should let it happen naturally, and not try to force it!"

"And how is that strategy succeeding for you?" Tyndal shot back. The question hung in the air, defying Rondal to defend his position.

"It's just wrong," Rondal said, sullenly, at last. "Love just *happens*. There *are* no rules."

"Why are those who know the least about love those most insistent they know all about it? There are *too* rules," Tyndal assured him. "You can deny it, but you might as well deny gravity. It will be as effective. Men and women," he stated, matter-of-factly, "*mate*. And they do so according to easily-observed rules of behavior. A wise man does so consciously, if not conscientiously, according to Sire Rose."

"Sire Rose!" sneered Rondal. "He's a self-absorbed, cynical boob!"

"You've read him," Tyndal countered, evenly, "and he has a lot of excellent and pragmatic advice on love. And no, he does not advise fawning all over a woman. Quite the contrary. He counsels strength and silence."

"And they just walk into your arms when you do that!" Rondal said, skeptically.

"Well, you keep doing what you think best," Tyndal said with a sigh. "And I'll follow Sire Rose's advice, and we'll see who fares better," proposed Tyndal.

"My romantic life is not here to amuse you!"

"Your romantic life isn't amusing *anyone*," Tyndal pointed out. "Take my advice or keep doing this idiot-waiting-for-attention act you've perfected, either way is fine by me. But eventually you're going to get tired of being lonely and realize that being nice and friendly to girls makes you seem harmless."

"I am harmless!" Rondal declared.

"And that's why you fail," Tyndal snapped. "*Quit* being so harmless. Girls *don't desire* harmless men. They want dangerous men who have decided to lay aside their danger on their behalf."

"That's . . . that's . . ."

"That's a *testable hypothesis*," Tyndal finished. "I'm not saying that to be hurtful, Ron, I'm telling you this because the longer you spend playing the rabbit when you should be playing the hound, the more you will resent it when you do realize this."

"I think you're just trying to get me in trouble," dismissed his fellow apprentice. Then something suddenly dawned on him, from his expression. "But . . . that actually gives me an idea! I think I know who the thief is. *And* his confederate!"

"You do?" Tyndal asked, almost speechless.

"I think so," Rondal agreed, smugly, and explained his reasoning.

"That . . . that actually makes a lot of sense," Tyndal agreed. "How do we . . . ?"

"We get them to move it," answered the other boy with a nod. "Then you wait here to nab the thief while I contend with his friend."

"You think you're up to that?" asked Tyndal, surprised.

"I'm a knight mage," reminded Rondal. "And right now, I'm the most powerful one on campus," he added, boldly.

Tyndal rolled his eyes and handed him the wand he had been toying with. "Take this anyway," he advised. "If your great and powerful sorceries cannot bring him to bear . . . poke him in the eye or something."

*   *   *

They started the next morning at breakfast, after reporting to the Head Master, where they all quietly spread the whispered rumor that Magelord Minalan the Spellmonger was due to make a surprise visit . . . and inspection. They left the details of his arrival and its purpose open to speculation, but the word spread like milk across a table. Both boys were alert for any signs that their prospective thieves would give themselves away, but there were no confessions forthcoming.

But the rumor did have the required effect. They let it brew all day, until the entire campus was abuzz.

"There's no way he'll let that stone just sit there and be discovered," Rondal promised, when they met up after lunch.

"Let's just stick to the plan," Tyndal said, worriedly. "I still think it's a long-shot."

After dinner Tyndal collected Ancient Galdan, the captain of the guard, to sit with him at the darkened window and await the thief while Rondal shadowed his partner elsewhere. Estasia had insisted on waiting with Tyndal, and in truth he did not mind her company. She smelled much better than Ancient Galdan.

Now . . . if everything they'd figured was correct . . .

Their patience was rewarded when a dark figure crossed the rooftops, swathed in black and shadow. With a single glance toward their window the thief went to a chimney leading from the bowels of the school below . . . and triggered the wards Rondal had set there.

The spell wasn't highly focused or dangerous - that might have been noticed with magesight – merely something to foil a quick getaway and indicate where the trespasser had touched.

With a growl Tyndal sprang out onto the roof through the window, Slasher in hand, the Ancient right behind him as they moved cautiously but quickly across the slate tiles. As they came nearer, the thief overcame the effects of the spell and whirled to meet them. His hood had been thrown back, confirming their suspicions.

"Kaffin!" Tyndal said, sighing sadly. "I thought it was you!"

"Really? How? What gave me away?" he asked in a friendly voice.

"The test," Tyndal decided. "You *utterly* failed that test. You're a good student. I checked. But you were supposed to be studying all night. That was your alibi."

"But other people testified that they saw me studying!" he protested.

"Exactly! You *had* studied. You're even a quick study, if you're familiar with the material. But you weren't. Even though you read it. *Because you were under the influence of a memory agent.* You read the material, but you didn't recall it any more than you recalled poisoning me, paralyzing me or stealing my stone. Not until the restoration spell we cast last night!"

Kaffin smirked. "Then why didn't you come after me?"

"Because I wanted to be *sure*," Tyndal said, walking carefully toward the boy. The Ancient drew his sword behind him. "It made sense, but I wanted you to reveal yourself. I restored your memory—"

"Actually, *I* restored his memory," reminded Estasia. "Remember?"

"It was my idea," Tyndal defended. "When you remembered you committed the crime, you also remembered where you had stashed the stone. You didn't need to retrieve it until you left the school at the end of term, so you didn't need to remember where you left it until then - when your partner would remind you when it was safe to do so.

"By that time either it would have been discovered or we would have given up the search. We could have questioned you a hundred times, but if you didn't remember stealing it, you couldn't confess it. Without remembering you did it, you wasn't couldn't remember where you put it.

"But then we made you remember," Estasia said. "We let it be known that the stone's hiding place was in danger. You might be able to hide it from us, but the Spellmonger? You couldn't take that chance. So you had to check and make sure that it hadn't actually been found, and move it, once you remembered you stole it."

"So I made you come to me," Tyndal picked up. "Or at least back to where you hid my stone. Once you had your memory back and heard that my Master was coming to Inrion, you had to act."

"And how did you know where that was?" he asked, conversationally.

"I saturated the entire campus with a low-level magical field," explained Estasia. "The same time we did the memory restoration spell. It was visible by scrying . . . every place it being absorbed or countered. Once we knew where the cloaking spells were – and there were a lot more than we anticipated – narrowing it down to the most likely spots, the ones near to the path between the tower and where we found the cloak, wasn't difficult."

"We knew you couldn't have had it on you, and you wouldn't have stashed it in your room. So you put it up here, on the way of your escape. You met your accomplice – but didn't hand off the stone. He gave you the drug, instead, and stashed your cloak and gloves. You had just enough time to get back to your room, slip in without notice, and return to studying without anyone suspecting you got out. Shadowmagic," Tyndal said.

"Very good, Sir Tyndal!" laughed the other boy, drawing his own blade. Not a mageblade, but a long, slender scimitar. "You had almost all of it."

"Except your accomplice, Kaffin," Tyndal said, carefully. "Rondal is heading toward him now."

"I don't believe you," Kaffin said with a sneer, testing the air with his blade. "And the name is not Kaffin of Gyre. Oh, it is my name – in Narasi. In Farisian, though, my name is Relin Pratt. Lord Relin Pratt, of the House of Pratt. My mother's side," he explained with a self-satisfied grin.

"Pratt?" Estasia asked, confused. "Like—"

"Orril Pratt," agreed Tyndal, grimly. "The Made Mage of Farise."

"Do not call him that!" screamed Kaffin, suddenly angry. "My uncle was a great man!"

"Your *uncle?*"

"My mother is his younger sister, Dorilia," he explained, proudly. "The House of Pratt has been producing great magi since before Perwyn sank. She married my father, in Castal, but she never lost her allegiance to Farise. When I was a child, when the war started, I was hidden in the north, in Gyre, under my father's name. The Seaknights of Gyre have ever looked south for their brides . . . and their loyalties are *notoriously* tenuous," he added, with a chuckle. "That's what comes when pirates serve the landborn."

"You are no pirate," spat Tyndal.

"You're right," he agreed. "Nor a seaknight. But I was my mother's pupil long before my full Talent emerged – she knew it was going to come. I've been learning Shadowmagic for as long as I could read. All in preparation for the day when I could act to avenge my uncle!"

"By stealing my stone?" Tyndal asked, incredulously. "I never even fought in that war! I was a kid!"

129

"*This* isn't our revenge, idiot!" Kaffin scoffed, leaping from one side of the roof to the other and landing as nimbly as a cat. "The stone is just the first step. It needn't have been you who donated to our cause, but my captain needed a stone, any stone, and yours was at hand." He straightened, facing them while effortlessly balancing on a ridge.

"I'd originally planned on stealing Rondal's but you gave me the best opportunity. Yours was just too easy to take. Besides," he snorted, "I hated having to lose to you on the field that badly on purpose. But if I'd fought you the way I wanted, you would have started asking questions. That also gave me the opportunity to slip the Bardain into your water after the bout."

"That was you!"

"Your attention was so fixed on the lovely lady," he said, laughing nastily as he walked across the beam, his sword steadily in hand, "that you never looked to see which of your fawning admirers was giving you a drink. A couple of hours later you were easy enough to find in your room."

He stopped at the end of the beam and slashed the scimitar through the air a few times. "Shadowmagic. I could have walked in through your door, but the window was actually easier, for a man who's spent time in the rigging. Shadowmagic and swordplay, I've studied both. That's what will give me a crew of my own some day."

"Crew? You *want* to be a pirate?" Tyndal asked, skeptically.

"Fool! My legacy lies both with the Stormfather and the arcane! I aim to become a captain within the Brotherhood. With this stone, I *will* be. And then I will help lead my House in its revenge against the Duchies – your so-called King Rard, most of all!"

"The Brotherhood?" asked Estasia, confused.

But Tyndal knew. They were a vague, sinister criminal organization in Alshar and southern Castal. They had even infiltrated the Alshari court, he knew from what his master had told him, and had been implicated in the murder of the Alshari duchess. He wasn't the only one who had heard of them.

"The Brotherhood of the Rat," Ancient Galdan supplied, matter-of-factly. "They were pirates themselves once, back during the Magocracy. Then they ruled the night on the docks in ports from

Alshar to Remere. Only the Iris is larger . . . but the Brotherhood is far more sinister, by reputation. Their guile and treachery is legendary," he said, warningly. "Their plots and schemes as tangled as anchor chain, it is said."

"Cutthroats and assassins!" spat Tyndal.

"Princes of the Waves!" corrected Kaffin. "The Seaborne are the elite of the Brotherhood. Our families have guided it for centuries. We swear allegiance to whichever Landborn lord we need to, but our hearts and souls belong to the Brotherhood. I aim to claim my rightful place on the council. A stone will secure that right."

"But you lost your chance at a stone," reminded Tyndal. "You're caught, or did you forget?"

"Am I?" Kaffin laughed. "I don't see a stone in your hand, Sir Tyndal. 'Sir'!" he sneered in disgust. "I can't *believe* the likes of you acquired a witchstone when my uncle was besieged and slaughtered for the crime. You're a bastard stableboy from some godsforsaken pissant mountain village who got power beyond his wits. I am the scion of a family of magi who can trace its lineage back to the third Archmage! I've been trained for command and leadership my entire life. You've been trained to shovel shit and kiss some baker's ass!"

"Baker's *son*," he reminded. "And I've picked up a few other things along the way," Tyndal said, leaping lightly to the top of a chimney opposite Kaffin, Slasher in his hand. The blade his master had carried to fight Kaffin's uncle.

"Your swordplay? It might impress a stupid cunt like Estasia, but I've been better than you since I was ten."

"Hey!" the alchemist said, angrily. "You little—!"

"You know she's been moon-eyed over you since the day you got here, Sir Tyndal? I heard her say that she'd bed you or wed you before the next full moon – that was the term you and Lindra agreed upon, wasn't it?"

"How in seven hells did *you* know?" she demanded. "We were alone!"

"Shadowmagic," he reminded her. "Do you know how many times you've walked right past me and not realized I was there? I've seen you and the other sluts in the South Tower naked a dozen times each. I've heard your secrets, listened to you plot against each other, and heard the awful things you say when you think no one else is listening.

"It's true, Tyndal. She and those other cunts were conspiring against you the moment you arrived. It seems you're quite the catch – handsome, healthy, and the squire to a powerful magelord. And . . . what else did you call him, Estasia? *'Just stupid enough'?"*

"That's not what—" she fumbled, blushing in the darkness.

"It bloody *was*! You two were just as brazen as whores discussing their clients. They knew all about you fellows before you even got here. Knights Magi – what an *absurd* term! And of course there were your witchstones."

"Duin curse you, Kaffin!" Estasia cried, angrily. "That's not what I meant! Oh, I'll have your head for this!" she fumed.

"You should have heard them, Tyn," he said, in a friendly tone of voice, as he shook his head sadly. "It *sickened* me to hear them talk about you like that. Like you were a pair of shoes she could purchase from the cobbler by batting her eyes and shaking her melons at you. But you were just a step up for them," he added, sinisterly.

"It wasn't *like* that, Tyndal!" Estasia insisted. "It wasn't! We were just joking! You have to believe me, I—"

"Let's finish this business between you and me," Tyndal said to Kaffin, evenly. "Leave Estasia out of it. I'm far more concerned with the man who stole my stone than what a girl said about me.

"Hand over your sword and we'll go back to the guardhouse. Rondal is about to take your big lug of an accomplice into custody, and then you can start considering your legal defense. There's no way he's going to hang for your crime. He'll testify against you," he warned, as he settled his footing in.

"There will be no trial, idiot! I'm not surrendering my sword. Haven't you figured it out yet? I am going to get away with it. *Because that big moron isn't my accomplice."*

"He isn't?" Tyndal asked, confused. "Then who is?"

"*I* am," Galdan said, from behind him. Before Tyndal could react to that unexpected news, the head guard sprang to the spot next to Estasia . . . and pushed the girl over the side of the roof with a firm shove.

Tyndal tried in vain to reach out to catch her, magically, but without his stone he didn't have close to the power he needed to use on such a spell. To his horror the young woman bounced once off of the roof five stories below, a terrified expression on her face, and then her body tumbled to the darkened courtyard.

"Sorry, lad," the Ancient said, unconvincingly. "She was a pretty one, but too smart. You can't trust a woman who's that smart. She would have figured it out eventually. She had to go."

"Galdan!" Tyndal said, his blood running cold as rage overtook him. There was no way that she could have survived that fall, not without magic. Without his stone, he'd been powerless to save her.

He whirled and faced the ancient, Twilight in his hand. "*You* betrayed us? But . . . but . . . you're no Rat Brother! You were born south of Vorone!"

"*Seven hundred leagues* south of Vorone," the older man chuckled. "I've sold my sword to a hundred men, but my heart belongs to the Brotherhood. I'm Seaborne. I've been here . . . *watching* things for the Brotherhood. When the young master was sent here to study, I was looking after him.

"Then you two came here without a thought in your head. But you had those witchstones. We saw an opportunity, and we took it."

"I'll kill you both," Tyndal promised, realizing he was between the two of them. He could not fight one without giving his back to the other. From all he'd heard about the Brotherhood of the Rat, that didn't sound like a target one of them would pass up.

He peered into the darkness quickly, pivoting to face first one opponent, then the other. He thought he saw a way to at least change his untenable position. All he had to do was a little warmagic.

He called upon the augmentation that gave superior strength. Always an important thing in battle, it was nearly as useful as speeding perceptions and actions. Instead of swinging his sword, however, Tyndal focused on his legs. Without his stone he couldn't power the spell for more than a fraction of a moment, but that was all he needed.

He leaped, far greater than he could have normally. Enough to allow him to reach another perch, at least fifteen feet away. He came down with a rattle of slates and struggled to keep his footing. But he was out of immediate danger of being surrounded.

Both of his foes looked at him in disbelief.

133

"Warmagic," he reminded them. "Not as sneaky as Shadowmagic, but it has its uses."

"That's not going to save you," warned Galdan. "I'm no stranger to heights . . . or is the young rat over there."

"I rather enjoy them," Kaffin said, making a leap almost as impressive as Tyndal's had been. Without magic. "And to answer your question, earlier? Yes, I have killed a man. In fact, I looked him in the eye while the rat tail in my hand stole his life away."

He produced the assassin's knife, a thin nine-inch long tapered steel blade that was all point, no edge, in his other hand. "It's required, a part of the initiation ritual when you join the Brotherhood. It was an amazing feeling. One I've been eager to repeat. Seeing the life in those pretty blue eyes die will be an especial treat."

"You need your elder's help to do it?" asked Tyndal disdainfully, taking Slasher in both hands.

"Oh, I'm just here to watch," Galdan assured him, lowering his sword. "And make sure things go the way they're supposed to. And testify to the Head Master afterwards. About how it was the *girl* who was the thief, and how we fought her hard, but she tragically killed you before I heroically pushed her off. And the stone was never recovered . . ." he added, mournfully.

"Then let's see how good you are, Pratt!" Tyndal said, jumping to the end of another ridge in the complicated roof of the tower. It was thirty feet long, but only ten inches wide at the top – narrow enough so that it would be hard for the old mercenary to join the fight. He tapped the stone in front of him with the point of his sword invitingly.

"I thought you'd never ask!" Kaffin said, leaping to the opposite end of the beam.

The two boys squared off, taking a moment to be sure of their footing and sizing up each other as opponents. Kaffin slashed the air artfully a few times. Tyndal swung Slasher in slow, deliberate circles. The moon was just peaking overhead, its spare crescent bathing the duel in a soft glow.

Tyndal was employing a Cat's Eye charm, and assumed that the Rat he faced was doing likewise. That allowed the scant light to reveal all it. Both boys wore good boots, and Tyndal was fairly certain he wouldn't slip on the beam . . . but at eight inches wide that didn't give him a lot of room for error. He tried to remember how Kaffin had fought him before in the yard, and he remembered how clunky and clumsy he'd been.

In retrospect, however, Tyndal realized that the poor showing was due to mummery, not lack of skill. Times when Tyndal had thought Kaffin had just hesitated too long to strike, he realized, were instead devoted to observing how Tyndal responded. Kaffin probably had a pretty good idea about how Tyndal fought.

And Tyndal suddenly realized that he really didn't know how Kaffin really fought at all.

The Rat Tail in his left hand would be a problem – he'd never liked fighting two weapons with one. But the slim blade was all offense, no defense. The scimitar, on the other hand, was short and elegant, but the steel looked sturdy enough to take a powerful blow, and the edge promised to be razor sharp.

So ignore all of that, he told himself, *and forget you ever fought the man before.*

"Begin," called Galdan helpfully, just as he had done so many times for him in the guards' practice yard. Apparently he'd done it for Kaffin far more. The scion of pirate lords advanced quickly, and threw a wickedly fast combination of blows at his head, torso, and legs.

Slasher caught them all, and Tyndal was quick to twist away when that Rat Tail came sailing toward his left kidney. It forced him to spin completely, but he was still sure of his footing. He hoped he looked artful. Then he remembered there wasn't pretty girl around to look artful for, and a cold, deadly hate fell over his heart

The next combination was even faster, and cut more at his legs than his head. A feint, Tyndal reasoned, and once again avoided the Rat Tail. Annoyed at being forced to play to his defense, he rushed against the boy with Slasher weaving a series of stop-cuts that changed direction twice before landing. A tricky move he'd learned at Timberwatch, but that he had never tried out in the yard.

It worked, to some extent. Kaffin was surprised by the charge and change in direction and was forced back a pace. He was able to block Slasher's path until the final change of direction, which put a three-inch shallow slice on his right thigh, above the knee.

135

"First blood," Tyndal called, grinning. It wasn't just bravado. He might win this battle if he could get Kaffin to lose his temper and make a mistake.

"Savor it," mocked the boy, who spun and advanced with his own furious combination of strikes, the scimitar weaving a web of moonlit steel in front of him.

This time it was Tyndal who was forced to retreat. He did so rapidly, getting far out of the range of that Rat Tail. As the end of the beam made further retreat difficult, Tyndal risked a moment of augmentation and spun in time with Kaffin's own turn . . . to end up behind him. Facing away from him, but on the other side of the beam.

They both spun again to face each other.

"Clever," Kaffin admitted.

"Just lucky, remember?" mocked Tyndal. "Are you going to dance all day, or are you going to fight?"

Kaffin didn't reply – a sure sign that he was losing his focus. Tyndal had sparred with a fair amount of men . . . when they stopped taunting, they started thinking. That was almost never a good thing for them.

Tyndal started to get a little more confidence, and with the long expanse behind him to retreat to, he decided to press his advantage as much as he could. He put on his best savage grin and began a long combination of blows that increased in speed and direction until he was at the limits of his ability. Kaffin did an admirable job blocking, but received two more minor cuts for his trouble.

Kaffin was losing focus, that much was apparent. Tyndal pressed even harder, dodging two more strikes from the Rat Tail until he had pressed Kaffin to the limits of the beam. One more push, and he'd tumble back . . .

That's when Tyndal's sight went murky, and Kaffin suddenly was *not there* anymore. Tyndal whirled around, confused, Slasher protectively in front of him, and Kaffin re-appeared at the opposite end of the beam.

"Shadowmagic," he reminded. Tyndal noted how hard he was breathing, and the blood from the lacerations he'd inflicted. He was starting to breathe hard himself, but he'd suffered no wound yet. And he was feeling powerfully motivated.

Suddenly this wasn't a sparring, anymore. These men had robbed him of something precious, and killed an innocent woman out of hand. He might not understand politics or murky underground organizations, but he understood the evil in that. It was time to end this duel, and begin the battle.

"It must devour your resources," Tyndal observed. That level of Photomantics was energy-intensive. Shadowmagic, from what he understood, was largely devoted to improving the efficiency of such spells, but it could only do so much.

"I have a sufficiency," Kaffin assured. To prove the point, he flashed a flare cantrip in his hand that lit up the rooftop. Intended to blind Tyndal, he anticipated it and forestalled the worst of its effects. In any regard, he did not lose his guard, and when Kaffin closed the flare had given him little advantage. He met the barrage of attacks as skillfully as he could.

Tyndal couldn't fault the boy's ferocity, or deny that there was a certain elegant dance-like grace to his style. But he wasn't taking full advantage of the blade or the two-weapon fighting style. In fact, his balance was compromised by having to deal with both weapons.

That was his weakness, Tyndal realized. If he could find a way to exploit that . . .

"Finish him, Rat!" barked the Ancient below them. "This isn't a dance recital!"

"I can understand why you'd make that mistake," Tyndal grinned, at the next pause in the action. "He's so dainty, it's *adorable!*"

"*Shut up!*" fumed Kaffin. He reversed the Rat Tail in his left hand and whirled into a fresh advance.

It was a dramatic gesture, and would give Kaffin more leverage with which to power a strike – but it also limited how he could strike. As he came out of the whirl, Tyndal decided to do something stupidly rash. He tossed his blade into the air . . . and engaged his strength augmentation again, plundering the last of his personal reserves to power the spell.

But for that moment he was twenty times as fast and powerful, and a moment was all it took.

Instantly after he tossed Slasher flamboyantly into the air, he lowered his shoulder and bull-rushed the other boy, just as he found his footing again. With two weapons, Kaffin had to fling his arms out to stop the spin to catch himself. Tyndal's charge caught Kaffin with both arms spread wide, and his momentum pushed the other boy over the side of the beam.

The fall was nearly thirty feet, but Kaffin slowed his descent and landed without serious injury. Both of his blades clattered off into the shadows.

"Warmagic," Tyndal heaved as he caught Slasher. Only then did he realize what a stupid, rash, idiotic move it had been. He was glad that Master Min or Sire Cei weren't here to witness it. On the other hand, it had worked, and it was hard to argue with success.

"Enough of this," growled Galdan, bringing his heavy cavalry sword into guard. "Do you want to come down here, or shall I come up there?" he offered.

"Actually, I don't think you could haul your fat arse up here, old man," Tyndal spat. "Not without a strong hand."

"Oh, you think I can't make it up there? Kaffin, grab the box with the stone in it and be on your way. I'll handle this stableboy and we'll meet at the usual place and time."

"But I can—"

"*Do it*, rat pup!" Galdan snarled as he began to climb the roof. Tyndal spared the student a glance, and saw him head toward the chimney top on the other side of the peak, a hateful look on his face.

So that's where it was.

"I'm growing old up here waiting, old man," taunted Tyndal. "I don't even have a stone. My powers are exhausted," he embellished. "It's just steel on steel, if you have the strength for it."

"Oh, I suppose I'll manage," grinned the wrinkled face of the Ancient. Despite his taunts, Tyndal could see little sign that age had dimmed the man's fighting skill. And he'd dueled Tyndal in sparring matches often enough so that he understood just how outclassed he was. As much as he'd boasted of skill with steel, Tyndal knew he would have to use magic to get out of this.

"Just keep him busy," called Kaffin as he climbed nimbly up the chimney. "I want to finish him."

"You do as your told, pup!" Galdan called, irritated. "You almost wrecked us. Let the *real* crew finish the work, now!"

"Asshole," spat Kaffin, sullenly.

Tyndal went into a much more conservative guard, facing the more experienced man. He couldn't count on him losing his temper, he'd have to find some advantage to take and pray to Ifnia that he was lucky.

They closed on the beam, a much more even match, as Galdan gave up the flamboyance of a second weapon in favor of finishing the job with the one he was most familiar with. From the first pass of their blades, Tyndal finally understood the difference between sparring and a man trying to kill him.

Galdan's sword was a war sword of many battles, heavy, thick, designed for chopping heads from the back of a horse. Each stroke he blocked or parried felt like a hammer-strike on an anvil, compared to Kaffin's precise blows. It wasn't particularly well-suited for this venue, Tyndal thought, but then again it was hard to judge what appropriate weaponry was for a midnight rooftop duel. Slasher was lighter, thinner and shorter by two handspans.

And it was a mageblade, Tyndal suddenly remembered. He'd been so focused on not getting killed, he'd forgotten that the tool of his adopted trade was not mere steel – it had a few tricks in it as well. He squared his shoulders, bringing his hilt low, hip-high, in a two-handed grip. Not at all what a warmage about to use a spell

Tyndal threw a cut that, if not blocked, would have parted the Ancient's nose from his face. But it was easy enough to block, and Galdan effortlessly stopped it a good five inches from his face, which was wearing a smug grin. Tyndal whispered the mnemonic, and Slasher threw the spell. A flare cantrip, much as Kaffin's had, illuminated the rooftop for a split-second, right at the point of his blade – directly in front of Galdan's unsuspecting eyes.

The Ancient was blinded by the spell, and threw himself backward, his sword flailing directionless in defense. Tyndal pressed his advantage, beating the heavier blade out of line again and again, and each time he nearly had the man.

But Galdan was good – too good. He recovered quickly, and all too soon it was Tyndal who was on the defense again.

"Got it!" Tyndal heard Kaffin call . . . and then there was sounds of a scuffle, very interesting sounds that Tyndal would have been happy to watch had he not been fighting for his life.

Cursing, Ancient Galdan drew a heavy dagger from his belt . . . but unlike Kaffin, he did not use his arms to balance himself in a wide stance. He kept the dagger in front of him, his left arm shielding while that blade circled behind him like a scorpion's tail, ready to strike.

He advanced. A feint, then another, with the dagger, and then that big sword was swinging for Tyndal's head. Galdan had stopped toying with him. He was making for a kill with deadly determination.

Just as he had slashed at Tyndal's right arm with the dagger successfully enough to open up a four-inch slice in his upper arm, Slasher slipped the tiniest bit in his grip – but enough to let him know that the next strike would push right through his guard and likely take off his head.

A thrill like lightning soared through him as he anticipated the blow . . . but it never came. Instead Galdan's right shoulder was being jerked back, and suddenly his knife-arm had swung wide to counterbalance.

Tyndal didn't stop to think. He drove Slasher's point through the center of the man's unarmored chest using every bit of strength and leverage he could marshal. He could feel the slender blade pierce through his sternum and bury itself eight inches into his chest, right through his heart, and feel the man shudder his death throes, his sword and dagger clattering from his fingers. Tyndal nearly lost Slasher's hilt as the old Ancient tumbled from the roof.

Only then did Tyndal whirl around to the other side of the beam, where Kaffin was fighting furiously, his scimitar recovered. Who he was fighting was the surprise – Rondal had arrived, his crappy mageblade in hand. He was barely holding on against the vicious, well-tutored student. One reason was the box he held under his left arm, which left him only one to defend against Kaffin's onslaught.

"I've got the box!" Rondal screamed.

Tyndal didn't think, once again – he launched himself off of the beam and collided shoulder-to-shoulder with Kaffin, sending him sprawling. He rolled and came up on one knee, scimitar in hand, ready to strike, but he was a dozen feet away. And now he was facing two knights magi, not one.

140

His ally dead, his scheme revealed, his real identity unmasked, Kaffin scowled and with a wordless shout of defiance he activated a Shadowmagic spell that obscured the area with a thick smoke. When the boys could see again, he was gone.

"Track him," Tyndal said, breathlessly.

"I'll . . . try," Rondal agreed, pushing the small stone box at Tyndal. The boy tried to open it, but it wouldn't budge. He searched for a latch.

"It's spellbound," Rondal said, weakly, as he prepared a tracking spell.

"So how do I open it?"

"It's going to be tricky," Rondal said. "I think it's best if –"

Tyndal didn't wait for his fellow apprentice's advice. He hurled the box against the side of the chimney with all of his might. It smashed and shattered, the hinges wrecked by the impact. A small black silk bag was inside.

"Or you could just do that," Rondal finished.

"I'm going after him," Tyndal said, as he felt the surge of power from his stone. It was a heady feeling, like drinking a quart of spirits all at once. He didn't enjoy it, though – he had other priorities. He wanted Kaffin's head, and was willing to chase him all the way back to Farise to get it.

Both boys cast tracking spells, but between the two of them they had not the knowledge to counter Kaffin's Shadowmagic. As the minutes dragged on, they became more and more convinced that the other boy was fleeing.

"He's got to be beyond the campus walls, now," Rondal finally said. "But which direction?"

"Trygg alone knows. Trygg and Herus," he said, referring to the god of thieves and travelers. "How did you know?"

Rondal looked guilty. "I didn't . . . I just knew that big idiot wasn't his accomplice. I was wrong," he confessed, looking at his feet. "It was clear in the first five minutes that he wasn't aware of anything that Kaffin was doing apart from regular dormitory foolishness. I didn't know who the accomplice was, so I figured you'd need my help."

"Estasia—" Tyndal began.

"She's dead," Rondal pronounced, mournfully. "I passed her body on the way over – it was quicker walking through the courtyard than through the towers. Her . . . her neck was broken," he said, in a whisper. "She didn't survive."

"She . . . *damn them*," Tyndal said, realizing that his friend was gone. "Damn them! Damn that rat to nine hells and more!"

"You got your stone back," reminded Rondal.

"So? Estasia's dead!" Tyndal shouted. "They *killed* her! That godsdamned rat pushed her right off the building, as easy as breaking a dove's neck!"

"I know," Rondal said, crouching on the rooftop.

"Damn it!" fumed Tyndal, his blood filled with rage. "Damn them!"

"She's dead," Rondal repeated.

"Damn them!" Tyndal shouted, his voice filling the night.

"She was so . . . so nice," Rondal said, tears in his eyes.

"She was a brilliant mage," Tyndal said, "and they just . . . killed her!"

"I know!" Rondal shouted. "I had my stone and all the power in the world, but I wasn't there, and I couldn't have saved her from that – not like that. I'm not that good."

"Damn them!" Tyndal said, walking to the edge of the roof. With magesight the courtyard was as clear as day. He could only see her legs, but they weren't arrayed as human legs should properly work. He felt sick. "Damn them!" he whispered, tears in his own eyes.

"It's not your fault," Rondal said, helpfully.

"I know!" snarled Tyndal. "You're the one who thought it was Stanal! You sent her up here with me and that murderer, instead of coming yourself!"

"I know!" Rondal said, miserably.

"You were the one who put her up here!"

"I know!" Rondal howled, angrily. "You think I don't know that?"

Tyndal stopped, realizing how unfair he was being to his fellow apprentice. "Rondal, I'm—"

"Just leave me alone!" he shouted, his voice breaking harshly through the tears. "I *know* what I did!" He fled the roof, his mageblade falling limply from his hand as he ran.

Tyndal knelt to retrieve the blade, and noted the glint of something else. He summoned a magelight and looked more carefully.

Kaffin's Rat Tail, fallen and lost in shadow. He picked it up and turned the evil little blade over in his hands. It was long, nine inches, a third of it hilt, in the shape of a stylized rat. The point was sharp to the touch. It would have eviscerated him, had it landed.

Tyndal stared at the blade a long time before he left the roof. He was feeling a lot of things – the loss of his friend, the sting of betrayal, the guilt over rubbing Rondal's nose in their mutual error.

But then they hadn't realized what they were facing – who they were facing. Orril Pratt's nephew, hidden in plain sight. Studying to take his uncle's place, and wage war on the Duchies. On the Kingdom – that was the only reasonable way one would take revenge.

"They want a war of vengence?" Tyndal said, softly to himself and the gods. "By Duin's axe and Briga's Hearth, they will *get* a war of vengeance!"

*   *   *

The night was filled with reports and briefings s they filled in the Head Master about the plot, and the staff disposed of the two dead bodies. A search was made for Kaffin of Gyre at once, but the student had not returned to his room.

The next morning, after a precious few hours of sleep, they told the entire tale to the Head Master and the faculty council in chambers. Tyndal thought the Masters were more mortified about the theft and the death of a student than about its ramifications. To have such a crime in Inrion's sacred halls . . . and against such a powerful lord . . . they were beside themselves with apologies.

Master Minalan had been more thoughtful, and more appreciative of the meaning of the attack. The Brotherhood of the Rat had been an unknown factor in the new kingdom, he'd told Tyndal the previous night, after he'd reported the events to him mind-to-mind. Now they knew where they stood, and against whom they stood.

Their master had been particularly intrigued over the idea that Orril Pratt had relatives. The way he responded, however, it didn't bode well.

Tyndal and Rondal were excused from examinations for the day, as the bodies of Estasia and Ancient Galdan were dealt with. They ran into each other at lunch, however, both of them sitting at the same table, listlessly picking at their food. The 'girls' table' was nearly empty, the few female students there weeping openly.

"Kaffin said that they were talking about marrying us," Tyndal said, eventually, just to break the silence. "When we got here, they were all talking about what good prospects we'd be."

"I'm sure Estasia wasn't—"

"She was," Tyndal said, dully. "I thought she'd be above that sort of thing, too, but . . . she all but admitted it."

"Well," Rondal said, which is what Tyndal noticed he said when he couldn't think of anything else to say. "I guess I couldn't blame her. She didn't know us yet."

"I know," Tyndal dismissed. "It's just interesting, I guess. I didn't think she really liked me all that much. More your type of girl."

"I don't *have* a type of girl," Rondal said, dejected.

"You will," Tyndal nodded. "And when you do, she'll be a lot like Estasia," he predicted.

"You think so? Truly?" Rondal asked, hopefully.

"I do," he nodded, sipping his wine. He had pulled rank on the house steward and gotten a bottle, instead of pouring the weak ale the students were usually served. The man didn't argue when he saw the look in Tyndal's eyes. "Here," he said, dumping out the water Rondal had poured and filling the cup with wine. "Let's drink to her memory. And then drink to avenging her, someday."

"And then?" Rondal asked, cautiously accepting the cup.

"And then we'll keep drinking until it doesn't hurt anymore," he said,

144

darkly.

Part Two:

RELAN COR

Relan Cor War College, Early Spring

Rondal

Rondal looked up at the foreboding fortress and a chill went up his spine.

He suppressed the feeling of dread the edifice inspired, partially because he knew the place had been designed to inspire that feeling, and partially because he felt he deserved whatever horrors lay within.

The guilt over Estasia's death had been a burden he could not escape. The six-day journey from Inrion upriver and across country to the War College had given him far too much time to dwell on his failure, and he arrived at the War College with a dark and heavy heart.

He was no stranger to death - no one who had walked out of Boval Vale could be. He had seen dozens of the people he knew slaughtered by the gurvani.

Estasia's death was different. Even though he had known her only a few weeks, he had become very attached to her, his feelings far in excess of reason, considering the nature of their relationship. But her death hurt more, somehow, than most he'd lost at Boval.

He was emotionally numb over the event. He knew people died in war, and he'd seen it. He'd participated, even. But to have someone that young, someone he knew and liked suddenly just be . . . not there, and have another human, and someone else he'd known, be the cause, that had been a grim novelty. One he wasn't certain of how to recover from.

He'd brooded about the tragedy for the entire journey, on barge and from the back of a rented horse. He'd barely spoken on the way to Relan Cor. He knew, intellectually, that it wasn't his fault. The sinister Brotherhood of the Rat had seen her as an obstacle, so they had removed her. This was Relin Pratt's fault, or Kaffin of Gyre as he styled himself.

He cursed the name, every time it sprang to mind. Even though it wasn't his hand who'd pushed her, it was the young shadowmage's ambition that had motivated the hand that had. Intellectually, he knew he was not at fault for her tragic, untimely death.

Emotionally . . . that was a different story. He'd been given power beyond his years, yet he hadn't the wisdom or insight to see the Brotherhood of the Rat's plot for what it was . . . and Estasia had paid the price.

He had barely eaten, and his sleep was restless and fitful. He felt numb, all the time, and was growing more resentful of his fellow apprentice, Tyndal, every day. Tyndal's accusations afterward hadn't helped – Rondal was more than willing to blame himself for the tragedy at Inrion Academy. But then to see how the haystack-headed moron dealt with it made him sick.

The young idiot had gotten blind drunk the day after Estasia's death, and the next day he barely mentioned it. He had plunged into his studies with an eagerness and determination that Rondal would have welcomed to see just days before. After Estasia's death, such devotion to mere academics just seemed disrespectful. There was a plot afoot, and reading parchment when he should be seeking vengeance just seemed petty.

He felt he owed her that, after he'd been that unexpectedly intimate with her. The spell the three had done together to locate Tyndal's witchstone had been the first time he had worked closely with another mage one-on-one, outside of training. It had been an intimacy he hadn't expected, and the shock of suddenly losing that connection had stunned his psyche terribly.

Rondal found he couldn't study at Inrion anymore. Every time he passed the spot where her body had fallen, outside of the North Tower under his window, he shuddered. The endless feast of learning he had been so enthusiastic about devouring at Inrion had grown stale. He could barely look at a book or scroll without thinking about Estasia. And she had barely even acknowledged his presence.

Rondal imposed on the Head Master to release him early from his courses, and after making the proper arrangements he headed upriver a week early. He didn't speed, didn't offer to assist the barge with a water elemental, he just sat curled up next to a bag of potatoes and a barrel of tar and immersed himself in gloom.

By the time he'd arrived at Relan Cor, he was inconsolable. Whatever hell awaited him there he welcomed. The fortress looked like the kind of place fit for tortured souls.

Relan Cor once had been the greatest fortress in the western world. A relic of the Magocracy, it was the last, largest permanent Imperial presence before the frontier their Narasi conquerors had expanded. Relan Cor wasn't a castle, it was a nine-story quadrangle of granite and limestone put together by the best Imperial warmagi at the height of the Later Magocracy. Magi with witchstones and a centuries-old tradition of magically-augmented defensive architecture. Relan Cor was as strong as a mountain.

It was perched atop a low, flat hill that overlooked the original Castali Riverlands, in the middle of a mage-made lake a hundred yards across. It was surrounded by rough territory, swamps and brambles and dark forests, briar-filled meads and marshy wetlands.

When the first Dukes of Castal arrived to take possession of their new fief, they resided and ruled from Relan Cor for fifty years, before relocating to their new castle at the capital city, Castabriel.

Rondal could see why they relocated. Relan Cor was *miserable*.

Designed for defense, not comfort, the fortress was a work of efficiency and Imperial thoroughness. Six thousand men could live in Relan Cor, and had, at the height of its use as an Imperil outpost. But they had done so living four to a room in dark little cells not much better than a dungeon, eating and sleeping in tightly-controlled shifts. The fortress had less than a quarter of that number living there, now, but it must have been a sight to see during the Magocracy, Rondal decided.

When the great keep at Castabriel was built, Relan Cor became an expensive unnecessary fortress guarding a frontier that had shifted hundreds of leagues west. Yet its might and impregnability were too great to ignore. The Dukes had made it the official residence of the Warlord of Castal, for a century or so, the seat of the kernel of the Ducal Army. After the Warlord's residence was transferred to the capital, it became the Castali War College.

Rondal remembered reading about it in Forard's *Histories of Castal And Remere*. The vision to create an institution specifically for the purpose of teaching skills of warfare was not new – but it was foreign to the Narasi horsemen, who dealt with such matters by squiring. The ancestors of the modern Castali had usually ignored infantry in favor of cavalry, but after the Conquest it became clear that, especially for the Western Duchies, infantry was an important consideration.

Conscripting large numbers of peasants to throw at each other was an adequate, if wasteful strategy. That worked for dynastic wars, and inter-domain disputes, but against an organized force such troops, untrained and untutored, were mere walking corpses.

But the Dukes of Castal had seen the wisdom of more advanced training, even if it meant arming their nobles with military wisdom that could threaten their own possessions. Regardless of who was on the throne, the idea was, the Duchy needed soldiers who knew what they were doing to protect it. They created the War College for that purpose, that and to conserve the mighty library of ancient works on warfare that Relan Cor boasted.

149

Now it was the multipurpose home of hundreds of masters in the arts of destruction and death. The Dukes hired experts in every aspect of warfare, from siege engines to field fortifications to basic infantry training to warmagic, and it was all taught at Relan Cor. It was the main staging area for the army that had invaded Farise, and since then it had collected plenty of veterans eager to pass on the wisdom of their bloody trade between wars.

He showed his credentials at the gate and was quickly directed inside by a steely-eyed sentry. Others were arriving, too, he saw, as he passed three or four worried-looking boys on the way into the imposing main fortress. The commandant, Marshal Lagoran, welcomed him stiffly in his office, his one good eye peering at him appraisingly. The other hid under a silken band. He moved like a man who was more scar tissue than muscle. He quickly wrote down Sir Rondal's name on a scroll.

"Someone kill your dog, soldier?"

Rondal looked confused. "I'm not—"

"As of this moment, you are," the old veteran said, grinning grimly. "From the moment your name was written on the parchment, you've become a Neophyte of the Sacred Mysteries of Duin. That makes you a soldier even if you've never marched a mile.

'And Rondal – sorry, you temporarily lost your title when you were inducted – but I've got *special* orders for you . . . report to the Warmagic Master Valwyn. You still have a few days before the beginning of training, but he wants to work with you some on your own, see what you're made of."

Rondal let the opportunity for a witty retort pass. He *knew* what he was made of. He wasn't fond of it, at the moment. Indeed, he desperately wanted to become something else – someone else.

"Where can I find Master . . . ?"

"Master Valwyn," the commandant supplied. "Third floor, south side, all the way to the back. And whatever pains you at the moment, soldier, realize that the Mysteries sand all that away from your soul. In seven weeks, you won't even remember what it was that disturbs you now."

Rondal was surprisingly open to that possibility. If there was as way to destroy the boy he was, and put something . . . *better* in its place, he had to try. Magic or Mystery, Warfare or Scholarship, he desperately wanted to drown the pain of Inrion.

It took Rondal almost an hour to wind his way through the narrow corridors and staircases that led him back to the Office of the Warmagic Master. The man who worked within was older than the Commandant, though less scarred, and had the confident bearing of one who is a master of his craft. He was known widely by reputation. Rondal had sought out some insight on the man, when he'd queried other magi mind-to-mind. He had yet to hear anything but praise.

Rondal introduced himself to the warmagic master and learned that Master Minalan had, indeed, set forth very specific instructions for him, regarding his inclusion the Mysteries. The idea seemed to amuse the Warmagic master, too.

The man bade him to sit in the single uncomfortable chair that was the signature of any military office, and Master Valwyn produced a pipe and a pouch, offering it to the young recruit. Rondal declined.

"You are to be initiated into the Sacred Mysteries of the Imperial Infantry," he revealed, as if Rondal had won a prize. "Or the Mysteries of Duin, as they are called now, though the Destroyer had little to do with their crafting.

"We hold them three times a year, spring, summer, and autumn, according to the rites, and I will not deny, they *are* brutal. Many neophytes have died before completion – although, if it is any solace, Duin is supposed to reserve a special place in the afterlife for those whose hearts were valiant enough to undertake the Mysteries, but whose bodies or fortunes were, alas, not strong enough to meet the challenge."

"Is this really necessary for warmagic training?" Rondal asked, confused.

"Initiates come out far stronger candidates for more warmagic training," agreed Valwyn, stroking his bears. "Not to mention far more effective on the battlefield, since they understand the perspective of the grunt, and not just the spark.

"But more importantly, they make you what you need to be – a soldier – before you add in magic. It makes a difference," he insisted. "If we hadn't done that with the Farisian conscripts, we would have lost to Orril Pratt no matter how many troops we threw at him.

Rondal quickly tried to change the subject from Orril Pratt. That was a name he did not want to hear.

"I'm already schooled in some warmagic, Master," Rondal pointed out. Valwyn chuckled.

"You just *think* you are, son. And I hope you do know some – it is not forbidden to use warmagic in the Mysteries. Indeed, there are dozens of bright young warmagi gathering for their initiation.

"But Master Minalan did not want you to have undue advantage."

"What?" Rondal asked, confused. "What do you mean? Master?"

"He was very specific about this: you are to secure your witchstone in my office for the duration of the Mysteries and rely on whatever native skills and abilities you might have, un-augmented by irionite. Yes, I'm aware of the recent difficulties," he said, understandingly, when Rondal's face went pale. "I realize what I'm asking of you. Master Minalan suggested you contact him directly, if you had any questions."

That sounded like his master. "I . . . I can see the wisdom in that," he conceded. "But there is the matter of security . . ."

"Of which you are naturally concerned. I assure you, it will be concealed and spellbound; no one will know where it is but you and me, and I'm in line for my own stone, soon enough," he said. "I won't so much as touch it, I swear by Duin, Luin and Huin."

Of course Rondal was concerned – he was loath to let his stone leave his possession. But a quick conversation with Master Minalan, mind-to-mind, convinced him of the necessity. When his master insisted, he had little choice. Master Valwyn provided a small stone box in which he could secure it – one alarmingly similar to the one in which Tyndal's witchstone had been hidden.

The moment the insulating lid was shut, he felt his contact with the precious green amber fade.

"Now we both spellbind it," Valwyn instructed. "That way it can't be opened until we *both* release it."

When they were done, Rondal felt naked. It was tortuous. Yet it suited his mood. He wanted to feel something, *anything*, but relentless remorse and guilt.

He'd gotten his wish. Suddenly, he just felt *weak*.

"Just relax, son," Valwyn soothed him, as he tucked the box in a chest under a shelf of books and scrolls. "It won't go anywhere. You need to learn warmagic the hard way. Once you pick it up again," he promised, "you'll be a different person entirely."

"I find myself anticipating the prospect, Master," Rondal said, formally.

"Good," nodded the warmage. "I'll assign you quarters for the next few days. You'll have the run of the commissary, practice yard and library until the Mysteries begin."

"Um, is it prohibited for me to ask what to expect, Master?"

"You'd be an idiot not to. There are three days of ritual purification and cleansing and examination by the Warbrothers of Duin, as well as a few other war gods, in the shrine encampment in the main field. Once you are deemed a sound neophyte, then you'll be assigned to a troop and squad, and for the next six weeks after that, you'll find out what hell looks like: Army life."

*   *   *

The introduction to the routine at Elementary Training Camp was an initiation as brutal as promised.

He had passed the purification rituals – a series of fasts and vigils, interrogations physical examinations and spiritual explorations, anointings and cleansings, until his head spun. By the third day Rondal barely remembered his own name, so confused was he by the whirlwind of procedure.

On the third day, he and every other Neophyte gathered (and there were slightly over three hundred) were given a rich honeycake, the kind baked for funerals, and a full glass of robust, blood-like red wine. The wine was drugged, and he and his nameless companions felt a sense of intoxication and anticipation as they were driven to dance by bonfire light, to the vocal encouragement of the Warbrothers.

Then he collapsed. And slept. And when he awoke the next morning, cold and wet with the early spring dew, his neophyte shift providing no protection, he struggled awake through the lingering fog of the drug. When he was noticed, a tall Warbrother with a horned headdress came by and examined his eyes.

"Duin has accepted you," he confirmed, with a smile. "Get up, go to the far end of the field, and there you will find a warbrother with a large cauldron. Take no more than a swallow of the brew, and reach into the bag and draw forth your token. You will understand from there," the monk assured him.

Rondal stumbled groggily to comply, stepping around sleeping young men as far as the eye could see. There were seven or eight Warbrothers surveying the field, and apparently the quickness with which one recovered was propitious in their rites, somehow. Rondal took a sip of the sour-tasting, lukewarm brew and almost gagged. But he kept it down.

"Good lad," the scar-faced Warbrother grinned, displaying broken teeth. "Just reach in here and see where you're bunking, now . . ."

He made a point of shuffling around the tokens within the sack, praying absently to Ifnia to guide his hand. He pulled out a black stone with a stylized picture of a mammal on it.

"Ah, the racquiel," nodded the Warbrother, approvingly. "Night fighters, they are. Nocturnal. Vicious, too, when cornered. And clever!"

Rondal had never seen one - they were not native to his Mindens home, nor to Sevendor. But he had to admit the toothy-looking predator carved into the token had some style.

"Now find your way to your squad. That's a stone, not a slate, tile, or chip, so you're in Second Company, on the right. You'll see your encampment soon enough, it has a pole with that device on it. Your duty officer, and the warbrother assigned to your company will be there shortly to provide you further instruction."

"Then what?" Rondal asked, dumbly.

"Use the time until then to get to know your squadmates – you're going to have to start depending on them, and if you're smart you'll figure out which ones are dependable. And that's going to be important, once you get to the Right Foot. Good luck, and may Duin's Blessing go with you, Soldier!"

His camp, like the others was in a lobe of meadow, one of many off the main training field. It was a relatively dry patch of grass that was nearly surrounded by marshlands. The camps on the northern side all faced stony patches and brier fields. Only the vast green practice field between the sides seemed to offer any respite from the nasty terrain around the fortress.

Even with the directions it still seemed to take forever for Rondal to find the right little alcove in the brush, but eventually he saw a tall pole of pine with a stylized racquiel symbol matching his stone affixed to the top. There were already a few boys there, and more were showing up every moment. Rondal set about learning who his squadmates were while they waited as the warbrother had advised him.

They all seemed just as exhausted and emotionally challenged as

Rondal, after the previous night's purification ceremony. Some looked ill.

There was the usual cautious exchange of names, titles and origins, they quickly lost all respect for such things. No one cared if he was a warmage. No one cared if he was a knight. No one seemed to care about anything but clearing their drug-fogged brains and sour stomachs. But Rondal learned a fair amount about his new comrades while he waited.

There were ten of them in the squad. Closest to his own rank, there were three young squires whose masters had felt they would benefit from some intensive training.

Jofard, Handol, and Verd, the squires, seemed overly eager, like young boys camping out overnight for the first time. They did not seem to appreciate the gravity of the Mysteries, though they were clearly strong, healthy, and used to practicing with arms.

Two of the common men, Rax and Dolwyn, were both sons of professional men-at-arms whose fathers had not been able to secure a squirehood for them. This was a far faster means to a career in arms than patiently holding a spear for years – a Relan Cor certificate would earn them a place as a petty officer at any mercenary outfit in the Duchies. It was well worth the bounty their sires had paid. Both boys seemed to take the Mysteries fairly seriously.

The other two commoners seemed worthy enough. Orphil was the bastard son of someone of high rank who wanted to do right by the boy. The other, Walven, was a sly-looking Imperial from Remere who kept his motivations and plans to himself.

He had a keen eye for everything around him, which Rondal appreciated, but he also had a bit of aloofness that made him seem a bit intimidating.

There were also, to Rondal's surprise, two other prospective warmagi. One, Gurandor, was a tall lad with a cock-eyed smile who had failed out of Alar Academy, but had passed his examinations anyway. He sought a viable career as a warmage, and wanted to hear all about Rondal's experience

The other, Yeatin, was even more bookish than Rondal. He was the smallest lad in the squad, and seemingly the weakest.

His frail arms and legs seemed like brittle sticks, and his shoulders hunched over in an almost debilitating way. His lifeless shock of brown hair refused to leave his eyes, and his voice grated in everyone's ears like rusty anchor chains from the moment he opened his mouth. Rondal could almost hear the sour thoughts in his squadmates' heads as Yeatin introduced himself.

Just what was he doing here at the Mysteries? He did not look up to being an infantryman. In fact, he seemed completely unsuited to any profession where strength might play a role. Even more so than Gareth, back in Sevendor. Yeatin was a mystery at the Mysteries, one everyone speculated upon when he was not around.

As the sun climbed the sky, their duty officer arrived with a wheelbarrow full of gear, Ancient Feslyn. He was a large fellow, a veteran of several campaigns and (as all of their instructors were) an initiate of the advanced third degree of the Mysteries.

"Good morning, gentlemen!" he greeted them. Ron could not tell from his tone if he was being genuine or mocking, but Feslyn seemed enthusiastic about the Mysteries. "In this kettle is enough grits and bacon to get you started, but we can have that after the rest of the gear is unloaded. *Get moving!*" he barked.

Some of the boys were reluctant, and the three squires seemed to think such work was beneath them. Ancient Feslyn soon corrected that notion in a small but intense private conference. After that they seemed quite willing to pitch in.

The supplies were scant, Rondal could see as they were unloaded. They found one piece of sailcloth, ten blankets, a kettle, a clay urn of water, a knife, ten bowls, ten spoons, and a hamper of food. Rondal started dressing as soon as he could. The tunics they wore for that day's Opening Rite were long, un-dyed hempen affairs over their trousers and camp-issued boots. Compared to Rondal's riding boots, purchased on a whim in Castabriel, the heavy infantry boots seemed to be made of lead.

They each got one stick of firewood. That was it.

"Where's the flint?" asked Jofard, annoyed at the lack. "How are we supposed to lay a fire without flint?"

"That's *your* problem, Soldier," Ancient Feslyn, said as he came by to check on them. "The first of many. That hamper that seems so full is the *only* food you will be issued . . . for this *week*. Use it wisely. That water jar is the *only* one you will be issued. As are all of the other pieces of equipment."

"That hardly seems fair!" Jofard complained.

"Did someone tell you that our sacred lord Duin valued fairness?" the Ancient chuckled. "Because they *lied to you*. War is not about fairness. It's about survival under adversity. I'm certain you'll think of something. Or you're going to have a very cold night.

"And that goes for the rest of you!" he called out to the squad as they struggled into their new fatigues. "This is *not* a fair contest. It is not a contest at all. This is not some pretty tournament. It is a *sacred mystery* with no lesser end than turning you into a *real* soldier. Or kill you trying. If you are not careful, it *will* kill you. In fact, it can kill you in a hundred different ways if you are not cautious and careful . . . and even *then* it can still kill you. "

"Surely one of you churls can manage a fire," Verd called out, a bit contemptuously, as he scowled at the empty fire pit.

"I would be more cautious of treating your squadmates like that, Verd," Feslyn admonished. "Because if they can, they have very little reason to share that skill with a squadmate who calls them such things. There are no churls here, no commoners, and no nobles. There are only your fellow Neophytes. Your sacred squadmates. Piss them off, and the Mysteries can get pretty rough. Work together, and you might just survive. "

"Well, how *are* we supposed to start a fire?" demanded Verd, who didn't seem particularly bright.

"Any way you like," the Ancient said, unhelpfully. "If you want additional fuel, you may scavenge the swamps around you at your leisure. But I wouldn't recommend leaving your camp unguarded. Keep in mind that all of the other squads are likewise provisioned. And if they run short . . . well, it isn't unheard of for raiding to occur."

"Raiding?" asked Yeatin, his eyes wide. His voice came out like a braying donkey.

"It can get vicious," admitted the veteran soldier as he surveyed the boys. "Not usually the first few nights . . . but toward the end of the first week, when the hamper starts to run empty . . ."

"So we had better set a watch," suggested Walven. "A good watch, too. I don't aim to go hungry this week."

"You will have a full week's worth of work ahead of you whether you eat or not. But protecting your supplies is *your* responsibility. Tomorrow you'll be issued your squad banner. Your banner is the symbol of your troop. To let it fall into someone else's hands is highly dishonorable. It should be protected as if it were your sister's virtue. "

"You haven't met my sister," remarked Gurandor.

"Opening ceremonies in an hour, Gentlemen," Feslyn grinned, ignoring the quip. "I would *really* encourage you not to be late. Duin dislikes the tardy."

"Well, I still don't see how that's going to get a fire lit," snorted Verd.

"You have *magi* with you," he reminded the boy, rolling his eyes. "Try rubbing a few together and you might get sparks."

"What did he mean by that?" demanded the boy, after the Ancient left.

"Watch," Rondal said, with a sigh, as he bent to lay the fire properly. When he had tinder and kindling, gathered from twigs in the brush, he whispered a mnemonic and summoned a very little bit of power. . and the fire ignited.

"That was handy!" said Handol, grinning.

"That was *easy*," boasted Yeatin.

"It is," Rondal admitted. "If you know how."

The boys sat around the small fire and tried to make plans about how to contend with the sudden threat to their sustenance.

"We should divide the food evenly now," suggested Gurandor. "Make each man responsible for his own portion."

"And see each man lose and prove a drain on his squad mates," dismissed Rax. "No, we eat as a squad, we fight as a squad."

"Still, I see the benefit of hiding at least a portion of it," Handol proposed. "Maybe in two separate caches. We can keep a third out at a time."

"That seems awfully complicated," grunted Verd, poking at the fire with a stick.

"It's a sensible precaution," argued Handol.

"So is setting a watch – who is first?" asked Walven.

That's when the arguing began, and it became clear that something needed to be done. Part of the squad wanted the boys to each take a short shift, while the other part wanted half the boys to take longer shifts on alternating nights. The merits of both were discussed, and neither party wanted to yield to the other.

"We've wasted an hour debating," said Walven, sourly. "One thing is clear: we need a leader."

"And that should be you, should it?" asked Verd, suspiciously.

"I offer myself as a candidate," said Yeatin, officiously. Everyone ignored him. Almost.

"He's got as much right as any," pointed out Handol.

"So who *do* we want to lead us?" asked Gurandor, the first time the mage had spoken since the monk left them to themselves. He picked a few twigs out of the fire and began breaking them up. "I say we leave it to the gods to decide. Whoever gets the burnt twig leads until this time tomorrow, then we'll pick again."

No reasonable argument could be made against the plan, so it was adopted, and soon Handol was chosen as the leader of the squad. He set the watch on alternating shifts, giving half of them at least one full night of rest every other day. Rondal was satisfied with the plan and even volunteered to take one of the mid-night shifts.

Then the horn rang for their assembly. Opening Ceremonies, the beginning of their long, dark journey toward the realization of the Mystery.

*   *   *

No one disturbed them that night, as the other camps were as excited and eager as theirs to train. The next morning, an hour before dawn, they were less eager. The chill had been more than the thin blankets we made for. The Ancients and warbrothers began rousing the squads while the stars were still in the sky, using drums and trumpets and whatever else they cared to make noise with.

Ancient Feslyn's grinning face informed them that this was the Week of the Left Foot, in which they were to learn the intricacies of a formal unit formation. He taught them how to stand, how to walk, and how to march within short order and soon the cold was forgotten as they marched to their place on the Practice Field.

That's where the real fun began. As the sun was just lightening the eastern sky, the sweaty boys were taught the basic exercises of Imperial Infantry calisthenics, an essential part of the Mysteries.

At first Rondal found the exercise a pointless waste of time. Then he found them boring. But soon, as his muscles began to ache and the Ancients screamed at everyone indiscriminately, the vigorous, repetitive movements became a challenge. Rondal was no weakling, but he quickly learned just how untrained and weak he was. And if he chanced to forget, Ancient Feslyn made certain to remind him in

161

excruciating and voluminous detail.

Every moment Rondal expected them to end the exercise, certain that they'd pushed them all to their limits. But them more exercises came. His chest began heaving with exertion, his rough tunic became soaked with sweat, and his arms and legs began to quiver under the strain. A few boys dropped out early . . . and were subjected to such brutal humiliations as a result that the rest resolved to move faster. Rondal merely kept his body doing what it was supposed to, as long as he physically could . . . and then some.

Finally, collapsed in a heap, the cadets were allowed to rest for a few moments while a warbrother read morning prayers. Then they were forced to get up and run the three long miles up to the gates of Relan Cor, proper, and then back. They arrived just as the light was bright enough for Rondal to see Yeatin's acne. They would have collapsed in a heap had Ancient Feslyn not told them they had but twenty minutes until the first bell of the day to prepare and eat breakfast.

They spent the morning learning how to march. Rondal always thought such a thing was pretty straightforward – after all, it was just walking. But it didn't take long for Rondal to discover the painful difference between walking and marching. All morning long they marched, from one end of the field to the other and back again. Nothing more complicated – and nothing he had ever done seemed harder, after the first three hours.

When the horn called for lunch, they sprinted back to their camp to gobble down a few morsels, drink some water and tend to their personal needs. All too soon the drum summoning them to parade sounded. Rondal made it back in time, still chewing a brutally hard piece of journeybread, but not everyone was so lucky. Yeatin and Orphil were both late to formation. After he saw what they went through as a result, Rondal vowed never to be late for formation.

"This is your squad banner!" the Captain of Neophytes announced as the Ancients handed out long poles with small green flags on the end of them to every tenth man. "Each banner has an animal, your squad number, and your company number." Rondal stole a quick glance at theirs, clasped in Verd's meaty fist. It had a large 2, a smaller 3, and a racquiel embroidered upon it. He'd never seen one of the nocturnal mammals himself, but the goofy nose and the big eyes didn't seem particularly terror-inspiring, despite the beast's reputation.

"For a cadet squad to lose its banner is the supreme dishonor. A squad without their banner at morning call is subject to restrictions and punishments. A squad who loses their banner and does not recover it . . . does not pass the Mystery. Protect and guard your banner. And remember how great the honor is in capturing the banner of an enemy."

He said nothing further on the subject, but the intent was clear. Rondal immediately began to feel anxiety about the stupid pole.

"This morning, you learned how to walk in a straight line. That's the essence of the Left Foot, and you'll master that this week." There were loud groans. That's how the rest of the Week of the Left Foot went. Just when they thought there could be no more nuance to the art, they learned even more about marching.

After a week, they were, indeed, masters of the art. That's when they learned about the Week of the Right Foot.

"Last week you learned how to walk a straight line," their warbrother informed them. "This week you will learn to walk in a straight line . . . carrying a spear." There were even louder groans. "But since none of you can be trusted with proper weapons yet, we shall use these poles, instead," he said, gesturing to two great piles of staves on either side of his horse. Each one was far thicker than any spear shaft.

For the next seven hours, until long past twilight, they learned how to march bearing a spear, and then learned the rudiments of presenting and shouldering the weapons. When Rondal could have sworn he'd marched his feet off, they were summoned into formation for the warbrother's vespers and a sermon. At last, when the moon was rising, they were dismissed, their overlarge spears over their shoulders, back to their camps to eat and sleep.

"Sweet Mother Trygg, are they trying to kill us?" complained Yeatin, his voice twisted into a torturous whine. "This is just week two! I can't properly feel my legs anymore!"

"Oh, shut up!" growled Verd as he savagely tore into his ration of journeybread. The soup was not hot yet, but some were gulping it down anyway, clumps and all. "All you did today was bitch and moan and I'm *sick* of it!"

"If they would just be *reasonable*—" Yeatin insisted, rubbing his aching, bone-thin calves.

"They don't *have* to be reasonable," Orphil said, philosophically. "In

fact, being reasonable doesn't make good soldiers. They're just
following the same book every other Imperially-trained infantry has,
for the last thousand years. The original Mystery is said to have come
from Perwyn, a gift of the primal god of war to the ancient warriors of
Novaminos. The Mystery has been completed by hundreds of
thousands of soldiers. It *works*."

"It didn't work against the Narasi," argued Jofard, his mouth full.
"We rolled right over them!"

"I don't believe *you* were there," the Remeran, whose ancestors had
fought against them, shot back. "And the Imperial Army was still
better trained than your barbarian cavalry – you just had more, and
could move them faster.

"But your ancestors never won an infantry engagement against the
Magocracy. On horseback, by surprise and stealth, your ancestors
excelled. On foot, they died in droves. Kamalkavan conquered from
horseback, but he could not rule until the infantry surrendered."

"Why the hells are you *talking?*" moaned Handol, his head between
his knees. "Let's pick a leader, post a guard, and *go to sleep!* Do you
know how *soon* dawn is?"

"Is that an order, petty-captain?" asked Dolwyn with a hint of
sarcasm.

"Damn right it is. Do it now. My last order."

Walven drew the burnt twig. He set the watch, finished his stew and
rolled into a blanket. Rondal followed suit, the cold, hard ground
beckoning him like the softest feather bed. He was asleep the moment
his head touched the ground.

Once again Ancient Feslyn awakened them before dawn for
calisthenics, and thence to their mastery of the Right Foot. That day
they learned not only how to march with a spear, but how to move a
spear while marching. After a long morning marching, another run up
to the gate and a surprise additional ration of bitter bread, they fell in
for a surprise inspection.

Rondal swung his over-sized spear haft as deftly as possible, but
nothing seemed to please Ancient Feslyn. He hurled insults at him,
berating him for a coward and the son of a whore. Rondal took it in
stride – he'd accused Dolwyn of abusing sheep.

When he came to Yeatin, however, the Ancient was *really* harsh. He virtually devoured the lad, who quivered uncontrollably with fear as the iron-jawed Ancient bellowed out his deficiencies in colorful terms. It didn't help his cause that Yeatin could barely handle the three-inch thick pole in his slender fingers or lift it with his frail arms, as the Ancient proved by knocking it out of his hand repeatedly.

Disgusted, Ancient Feslyn ordered the entire squad punished. Their three-inch poles were replaced by *five*-inch poles, almost unbearably heavy. Then they practiced marching in formation again until the evening stars rose.

And so it went, and even the beginning of the Left Hand Week was starting to be anticipated – *anything* had to be better than marching with a stupid pole for hours on end. While everyone was furious at Yeatin, they had not the strength to even bully him much once they slumped back to camp. They half-heartedly drew lots, ate a few mouthfuls, drank, and passed out. Rondal had been assigned the first watch, and he could barely keep his eyes open.

The next week, the Week of the Left Hand, went much the same . . . only to their burden was added a bulky twenty-five-pound wooden shield. The strap was cumbersome and fit unevenly. The weight and made their shoulders ache within the first hour. By the end of the week they were exhausted, ready to collapse into dust every night . . . that's when they were forced on a scenic march through the bog to the south of the fortress. They went to sleep that week often unable to even prepare a proper meal.

The next week was the Week of the Right Hand. They were finally issued heavy wooden swords, portraying short infantryman's' blades. They did not use them to practice fighting . . . they simply marched with them. On and on they marched. That first Right Hand afternoon they also received backpacks, each containing a few extra rations and a bottle of water. It also contained three heavy sticks of firewood. They marched to the gate and back again. Rondal was starting to hate the sight of the bloody gate.

The bruises and blisters on his feet were nearly unbearable. He and the other magi used what spells they could to tend the squad's wounds at night, but none were medically-gifted. Only with his witchstone could he have summoned the power needed to do a proper job. At most he stopped the pain enough to allow them to sleep. Most hadn't even stripped off their packs, falling asleep the moment they returned to camp, their poles and shields cast aside.

That was the night of the first raid. One of the other squads had exhausted their food supply, and decided the Third's squads could make up for it. Luckily, their watchman had better sight than the racquiel that was their totem – Gurandor had employed a Cat's Eye spell during his watch, and was able to rouse his mates quietly just before the first of them entered the camp.

What ensued was a confused melee with wooden swords and poles, where friend could only barely discern friend in the darkness. Rondal roused himself quickly enough – he'd learned that trick back in Boval, during the siege. He was challenged almost immediately.

Wooden sword in hand, he faced his opponent, his magesight coming to him automatically. Despite days of exhausting toil, little food and little sleep, he didn't feel his muscles ache or his bones protest as he gave a savage cry and defended his territory.

He was surprised how quickly he responded, and how viscerally. He wasn't the only one. The Racquiel Squad responded with a punishing defense, letting their desperation and frustrations fuel their response. It only took a few hard strokes to speed the other cadets on their way.

Rondal fared well, in that attack. He'd faced two different boys and bested them both in their contests, forcing them to withdraw. Most of his fellows were victorious, as well, with only a few nursing bruises.

Rondal screamed triumphantly over the victory. Someone stirred the fire to life and they spent a few moments ensuring neither the flag nor the dwindling food supply had been touched. After congratulating each other and doubling the watch, they crawled back into their blankets sore and tired, but feeling victorious.

Two more days they marched and marched and *marched*, until the Mystery mandated two days of rest and instruction. Rondal had stopped being able to feel his feet days before and his back only ached miserably, not intolerably now. He was shocked, as he sat at morning prayer, that his legs *felt* like marching now.

He marveled at the sadistic whim of the war god in the irony of that.

The day of rest included little actual rest. Instead it involved instruction in rudimentary swordplay and a whole *new* regimen of calisthenics designed to strengthen the muscles of the infantry swordsman.

They learned the Rite of the Sword, the ancient basis for all swordplay, according to legend. They practiced with their wooden blades for hours, not sparring, just exercising against each other in predetermined patterns. There were sacred chants associated with each exercise to help time them. It became an elaborate dance, one he strove to master, else he attract the ire of the Ancients and the scorn of his fellows. Like a magical exercise, he abandoned his mind and body to performing the moves as flawlessly as possible.

To his horror, Rondal realized what the purpose of the rite was – *he was learning swordplay*, learning it at a fundamental level, at his bones.

He'd always swung his sword inelegantly before, but the rhythms and the pattern of strikes against his partner's blade were teaching his body and his mind to respond as one, like a magic spell. He even caught himself humming the cadence of some of the rites to himself, and imagining his positioning as he did so.

Rondal wasn't a natural swordsman. The swordmaster assigned to the squad repeated every criticism Sire Cei had ever made of his swordplay, but without the restraint of chivalry or propriety.

But for the first time he recognized swordplay as a subject to be studied, not just a practiced reflex or a desperate means of self-preservation. Instead he began to see it as expressions of leverage and force, not pointless exercise. It was like lining up all of the proper sigils in the correct positions in a spell, he discovered, you first had to learn the fundamentals. With every dull impact on his wooden blade, his body and his mind began cooperating a little more, instead of working at odds.

And much to his surprise, he got better.

Not much, at first, but he began avoiding mistakes he had been making for months, so that when the first few real sparring matches came along during the Feast of the Crown, he was able to hold his own against his opponents. Most of his squadmates were likewise acquiring proficiency.

Yeatin, on the other hand, was hopeless. He couldn't push his lanky frame into the proper position, so his blade was always at the wrong place at the wrong time. His arms and legs and ribs were striped with bruises that night. He persisted in moaning his pain until one of his squadmates offered to knock him unconscious.

The second day to their surprise, they were actually allowed to rest. They slept until the sun was in the sky, their bodies grateful. That morning they were given a bonus ration of sweetened oatmeal with nuts and raisins and half a mug of watery ale, far worse than what they served in the dining hall at Inrion.

It was the most delicious ale Rondal ever tasted.

Then the Warbrothers began their rites. There were sermons on Life and Death and Duty and Honor, the four blessings of the war god, no matter his name. The power to defend and to attack. The power to destroy and obey. Unity in purpose led to the greater honor and glory. The solemn lectures went on and on. Only the fact that he wasn't marching kept Rondal from squirming out of boredom half of the time.

Rondal paid attention mostly because there was nothing better to do.

It *was* even kind of interesting, the philosophical side of the Mysteries. The nature of the soul was discussed. The legality and moral propriety of taking life in battle was discussed. The warrior monks of Duin and the other war gods elicited them each to testify of their own experiences in battle.

There were few boys among them who had any experience in combat, due to their age or class, and most of what was spoken of were simple skirmishes between feuding families or, in one case, a raid on a farmstead during a boundary dispute.

When the warbrother called him out, unexpectedly, as a veteran of battle and invited him to speak, Rondal surprised himself by discussing the worst moments of the Boval siege in front of everyone.

While his squadmates and rivals alike listened, he told them about the sudden attack on his homeland, the slaughter of his neighbors and friends, the unexpected siege, the abject fear he'd felt from a threat that wanted to kill him.

He spoke of how he was given a blade and a wand and a witchstone and not much else, and how he was forced to fight for his life. He spoke of the first time he had faced a screaming, fanatical goblin face-to-face and had stuck his sword into his throat until it stopped moving. He spoke of the dozens he'd killed since, and the other horrors he'd faced – trolls, hobgoblins, and even the dragon at Cambrian Castle.

168

That last admission brought a newfound respect from his squadmates. He downplayed his role in the contests as desperate affairs. He'd followed orders, he fought as hard as he could, but he dismissed his deeds as minor, compared to the others who'd fought with him in the war.

There were other tales, some no doubt embellished. But Rondal's testimony captivated them all. There were plenty of un-blooded warriors among them who immediately wanted more details, eager for that kind of glory.

Rondal envied their innocence – if he'd had his preference, he would have stayed at Inrion Academy until he'd read every book and mastered every spell his Talent could bear. And then retired there.

Just before vespers, they were unexpectedly given a few free hours to themselves. Many of his squadmates used it to sleep. Others foraged through the bogs for berries and roots to add to the last of their diminishing supply of food – although after vespers they were each given a honey cake and another half-measure of ale.

The next morning they were issued fresh rations . . . but a third less than the previous week.

*   *   *

"How do they expect us to survive on this?" Yeatin wailed as he looked at the diminished supplies in the hamper. "We'll starve to death!"

"That's the point," groaned Walven. "They feed us less, we get . . . *hungry*."

"I'm *already* hungry!" complained Yeatin.

"So is every other boy out there," Dolwyn reminded them. "That's going to make the competition for resources far more difficult."

"Not if we're dead of starvation!" Yeatin moaned.

"You barely eat enough to keep a squirrel alive, anyway," Orphil dismissed. "Some of us have man-sized stomachs to fill!"

Walven looked uneasy, his eyes already peering at the other camps around the field. "Everyone is going to be hungry. We'd better do a *very* good job of hiding this," he warned. "And be particularly careful with the watch.

The boys did what they could with the little food they'd been issued, splitting it into three small caches around the campsite. As careful as they were, however, upon their return from a class on close-quarters infantry swordplay, they discovered that their preparations had not kept them secure. Their camp had been raided while they were away.

The Racquiel Squad stood around and stared in disbelief at the chaos. Their camp had been torn apart, their blankets torn, scattered, and muddied. The little food that had been out was gone, and one of the two other caches had been raided. What was left could take them two days, perhaps three, but no more.

"I want their *heads!*" Rax, the leader for the day, howled, his eyes blazing. "I don't know who they are, but—"

"*Stop!*" ordered Walven, as the boys began to converge on the camp. "Nobody move! If we're going to find out who did this, we need to read the signs!"

Gurandor nodded, and started waving his hands around to summon magesight.

"I'm reviewing the area," he reported. "No one get in the way." Rondal wondered why he bothered with all of that hand-waving stuff – it was an easy enough spell to do without it. He summoned magesight himself and began scanning, and assumed Yeatin had, as well.

"We *know* who did it!" Dolwyn said, bitterly.

"Actually, we don't," Orphil pointed out. "It could be *anyone.* Trying to throw blame and suspicion on anyone else would be basic strategy."

"But those assholes in—"

"*Exactly,*" Walven agreed. "Those are *just* the assholes we'd suspect. This makes it possible, if not probable, that we were targeted *because* they'd be suspected."

"And whoever did this is trying to get us to go after them," Rondal agreed. "That's as good as theory as any."

"Let's see if the evidence fits it," Yeatin said, airily. "I see . . . five sets of footprints," he reported.

"Agreed," Gurandor nodded. "Two smaller boys, three bigger, almost adults. Same crappy boots as we all wear."

"But," Rondal observed, "one of them carried a staff or spear and just stood there . . . his prints are still there, deep in the mud. All he did was . . . break our water jar," he finished sourly.

"Falor's Flaming Asshole!" Orphil swore, colorfully. "I can see stealing the food, but breaking our water jar? What pricks!"

"That's what makes me think that it was a raid designed to lure us into attacking the wrong troop," agreed Gurandor, sagely. "If they just wanted food that would be reasonable enough. We had our banner with us. So the only reason to do that was to piss us off," he reasoned.

"Done!" Rax said, swinging his wooden sword angrily at the air. "Just tell me which assholes to kill!"

"We're *working* on it!" Yeatin whined, irritated. "Gods! All right . . . look for distinctions in their prints," he suggested. Not only were the magi looking, but Jofard, who fancied himself a hunter, was examining the prints in the mud.

"I've got something," he said, quietly, as he knelt near the edge of the ruined camp. "Look at this . . ." Rondal came over to examine the spot himself. "See this kneeprint in the mud? It's as wide as my cock; whoever knelt here was a chubby little bugger! And deep. Look for a fat muddy knee, and you're in the right domain."

"Can you magi do anything with spit?" Rax asked. "I think someone spat over here. At least it looks fresh."

"Let me take a look," Yeatin said, curious.

"That's *disgusting!*" Handol said, making a face.

"We didn't do any spit-spells at Alar," conceded Gurandor.

"Let the man work," Walven ordered.

"Every drop of sweat contains a man's essence," Yeatin said, matter-of-factly, as he knelt next to the glob of sputum on a leaf of an evergreen shrub. "Every drop of blood, piss, shit . . . and spit," he said, almost reverently. "If you know how to draw forth that essence . . ." he closed his eyes and began a spell.

"No one disturb him," Rondal ordered. He hated when someone did that to him while he was trying to cast a spell. Especially now that he

171

had to raise power the old-fashioned way. "But assuming he's successful, what are we going to do about it?" he asked, quietly.

"What do you mean?" Rax asked, confused. "I want their *heads!*"

"That seems like a lot, for a little raid," Orphil pointed out. "I'm pissed, too, but . . . what can we really do?"

"Steal it back!" answered Handol.

"Maybe," Walven conceded. "Or maybe we get our asses kicked, because that's what they're expecting."

"But . . . that's what *I'm* expecting, too!" Rax said, angrily.

"But that's not *winning*," Walven pointed out. "That's revenge, not victory. We need to *eat*. That's our first priority. It would be lovely to punish who did this so that no one else will be tempted, but if we spend all of our energy on that, we'll starve in the meantime. Getting ourselves messed up and injured on our own time won't help us be victorious."

"Then what will?" demanded Orphil.

"*Eating,*" Handol supplied. "Eating a lot would be, in my mind, a point of victory."

"Exactly," agreed Walven. "We need to eat. We also need a new water jar. We can waste a lot of time running around figuring out who did this, coming up with some brilliant scheme to get back at them and get ourselves beat up, too . . . or we can focus on the problem instead."

"So how do we eat?" asked Orphil. "Rob someone else?"

"That would be one way," conceded Handol. "But let's face it: no one else got more food than we did."

"So we go outside of our supplies and forage," reasoned Walven. "Ancient Feslyn always said that was allowed. These are swamps. Even this early in the spring there are fish and frogs and . . . other things," he said, looking a little grim. "We can hunt."

"I can hunt, with proper equipment," Jofard offered.

"You can hunt *without* the proper equipment," ordered Walven. "See what you can put together. In fact, everyone should start hunting. Any kind of protein would work. Does anyone know what kind of tubers and such are edible from a swamp?"

"Don't pick any fungus," suggested Yeatin. "There are thousands of deadly poisonous ones. Especially in swamps."

"There are birds, too," agreed Orphil, suddenly looking up. "Maybe use a spear?"

"Or sling," suggested Handol. "I used to be good with a sling."

"Get good again," Walven said, "quick. The faster we pile up protein, the better off we'll be. That goes for everyone." He looked thoughtful for a moment. "All right, who has cooking duty? Cook the rest of the food – *all* of it. Tonight."

"Why?" asked Yeatin. "Are you that confident that we'll be successful hunting?"

"I'm that confident that knowing there isn't any food left back at camp will motivate you better," Walven replied. "Besides, what's in your belly can't be stolen."

Even though he was not the official leader, Walven's calmly-delivered and well-reasoned plan was what they needed. The effort to identify the raiders was abandoned for scavenging duties.

Most of the boys headed into the swamp to forage while the others prepared the two soup-cakes and the pound of grits left in their larder. Rondal followed after the foragers, unsure about what he could do. But he knew from personal experience just how powerful a motivation hunger could be.

He had little native energy for magic, outside of a few cantrips, but magesight revealed a number of creatures in the marshes. He discovered a nest of some kind of mammal he'd never seen before, one that bore a striking resemblance to a giant rat, and called it to the other boys' attention. As they trooped off to hunt down their prey, he turned his focus toward the water.

Water was the abode of all life, his masters had told him frequently enough. These swamps were beginning to teem with it, now that winter's harsh edge was past. Though he felt handicapped without the resources of his stone, Rondal was not useless. With a little searching he found two big tubers he knew were edible, and dug them out of the mud with his bare hands. Enough to feed the squad for a day.

The rest of the hunters had varying degrees of success. When the last of them dragged back to camp at twilight, there were three small mammals, six tubers, four decent-sized fish, and two birds – Gurandor had fashioned a bolo from a few thongs and had plucked them both off of the same branch. There were also some winterberries, herbs, marshnuts, and other fare they had managed to gather in the dying light.

It wasn't quite a feast, but there was a feeling of triumph as they sat around their fire that night. Even Yeatin, who had found some wild garlic and some rosemary, was in a good mood. They roasted the meat over the fire before adding it to the soup, and then devoured the whole kettle. Before bed, Walven detailed two boys to fetch water in the empty kettle. The pared-down tubers were boiled until the fire died.

"Wasn't this a better outcome than plotting revenge?" Walven asked, just after they chose lots for leadership. Orphil was chosen this time, which made the boy nervous.

"I *still* want their heads," muttered Rax.

"They wouldn't taste as good as this . . . whatever it is," Handol assured him, gesturing with a roasted limb of some creature. "If we'd gone after our raiders, we would have gone to bed with bruises and empty bellies. I prefer this outcome."

"That doesn't mean we can't keep our eyes open," Jofard nodded. "If we can figure out who did this, we wait for a shot, and then we take it. *Hard.*"

"Agreed," Walven nodded. "But let's wait for the gods to give us the opportunity."

The next morning, the beginning of the Week of the Head, hey began learning small-unit tactics on the practice field, participating in squad-by-squad sorties to demonstrate each valuable point.

The ancient, proven Imperial system of infantry triads, in which two shieldmen side-by-side protected a polearm or spearman, was hammered into their brains until they all began to re-form that way every time their line was crushed. The Ancients yelled at them with renewed purpose as they forced the boys to learn to work together in a coordinated manner. Ancient Feslyn heatedly defamed their ancestry, their personal habits, and their likely sexual proclivities as they struggled.

Like the rest of the Mysteries, it was a brutal exercise. For three days they skirmished and learned and drilled and practiced. Rondal found the weight of his shield less bothersome, and was more focused on his stance and his guard than his misery.

It helped that every infraction against their orderly deployment was punished harshly. He quickly learned not to mess up more than once, else his whole squad suffered. Yeatin was responsible for several painful exercises, but even *he* learned. They learned so thoroughly that they had dreams of formations and maneuvers that night, after chocking down their scavenged dinner.

Along with the physical practice they were lectured on the theory of unit tactics, and schooled in the horn calls and drum beats that were code for the professional infantry battalion. The pace was merciless, but when problems arose with a squad there seemed to be no shortage of Warbrothers and Ancients willing to take a squad in hand and work with the remedially.

The fourth day, after reprising all that they had learned, they were given an opportunity to demonstrate it. Three caches of food were placed atop three wooden pillars, along with a cask of ale, bread, and other luxuries. The short rations had been telling on everyone – it wasn't unusual to hear bellies grumbling in combat. So when the bounty was displayed before the squadrons, there was a tremendous interest.

"The rules are simple," Ancient Feslyn said with a wolfish grin. "The squad who can capture and hang on to the food, gets it." The horn call to prepare for action sounded.

"I want that food!" Rax declared.

"We all do," muttered Walven. "What are your orders, Squadleader?"

Jofard had drawn the previous night. He quickly looked around. "Orphil, Handol, see if the squads to each side of us are interested in teaming up and splitting the loot," he said, quickly. "When the horn call sounds, whoever gets there first is going to have a very brief advantage. Then they're going to be defending against everyone else who gets there. Some will wait for the victors to emerge and pounce."

"So how do we get around that?" asked Rax, exasperated.

"The magi," Jofard decided. "Can you lot do something to discourage anyone from getting too close?"

The three magi conferred quickly. They had few spells hung between the three of them, but they managed to figure out some ways to keep other squads at bay. They discussed it with Jofard, who agreed with them.

Their fellows in the Second and Fourth squads of Third Company were willing to go along with them. Jofard suggested they protect the flanks of the pole while the Third Squad took care of the retrieval and removal. A hasty two-minute conversation between the three squad leaders ensued, and with surprisingly little debate (Second Squad insisted on first crack at the ale, should they prevail) they hammered out a quick battle plan.

Just as they finished, the horn call to action sounded.

"Let's go!" bellowed Jofard, pushing Yeatin, the designated banner bearer that day, forward. The rest of the squad formed up with shields at the ready behind him and charged across the field, the other two squads flanking them.

It only took seconds for their plan to fall apart.

The Fourth Squad became entangled with elements of the First Squad of Fourth Company, and half of them got left behind to hold the others at bay. The Second Squad arrived at the base of the pillar first, thanks to some good sprinters in their ranks, but was immediately set upon by others. The bottom of the pillar churned into a general brawl as the desperate boys smote each other with their wooden swords. They had all been cautioned against excessive force in such trials, but the desperation and competitive spirit in them had been aroused.

Jofard stared at the mess in dismay, the pile of supplies sitting alluringly out of reach of the fray below.

"This is stupid," he said, shaking his head. "We'll *never* get to the base of the pillar!"

"Then let's come at it from another way," Rondal suggested, his brain churning with options. He thought of a plan.

Jofard looked at him thoughtfully. "What do you have in mind?"

Rondal explained to the young squire, who started to grin.

"That is a completely and utterly dangerous feat that has such a small chance of working that it wouldn't be fair not to try it," he decided. "Let's get organized . . ."

It didn't take as long as Rondal feared. Soon his squad, along with the remnants of the Fourth Squad who had been able to break away, formed up in a wedge and charged into the fray, getting as close to the base of the pillar as possible. The sudden force of their attack pushed the mob to the side, but it quickly reformed and started hammering against them.

They didn't have to remain there long, however. The boys in the middle of the wedge raised their shields overhead, creating a rough ramp for Verd, the lightest of them, to climb. He was still more than five feet away from the platform, but a risky leap brought him scrambling to the top. Grinning, once he found his footing, he began chucking the food to his mates.

That only increased the intensity of the fighting below. To distract some of them, he took a bag of beans and flung it as far from the pillar as he could. Nearly a third of the hungry crowd went after it, allowing the rest of the squad to hold their formation long enough for the majority of the food to be retrieved.

But getting it and keeping it were two different things. Once they were burdened by the supplies, it became much harder to fight. Jofard ended up detailing Orphil and Verd to hold the food between their shields, carried like a stretcher, the rest of the squad huddled protectively around it. Skirmishers from the other squads who managed to disengage flanked them, but there were no end to those who would challenge their victory.

"Now would be a good time!" Jofard cried, as he laid into a brace of would-be raiders with his wooden sword. The beefy boy pushed them back, but there were more lined up behind.

Rondal nodded and began to access his spell.

It was a much, much abbreviated version of a warmagic spell Peremundra's Horn, and only produced an earsplitting shriek . . . but it rang in the helms of the unprepared painfully, while the boys of the Third Squad had been able to steel themselves for the aural assault. While the irritating spell didn't quite clear a path in front of them, it did reduce the number of stragglers willing to confront the well-organized effort.

"That," Jofard said, as the spell faded and the losers began to fall in behind them, "was a satisfying display of warfare, gentlemen!"

"Bah!" snorted Walven. "It was a mob, nothing more. Good work

177

getting us organized," he conceded.

"Good work to the magi who cleared the field," called Orphil, who was struggling with the load. "If we had to face one more angry band I would have dropped this!"

"Who has the ale?" asked Rax, sounding desperate.

That night it was a true celebration. The boys of the Third Squad had no issue with splitting the bounty fairly, as they had promised. There were general congratulations offered to all that night as the small barrel of ale was drained, and in the morning the squad had a worthy replacement for their broken water jar.

They finished out their week on small unit tactics with some advanced work, specifically how to prepare for a cavalry charge, and then they had two more days of instruction.

This time the Warbrothers preached to them about rank and obedience, duty and honor. The divine rules of warfare were read and discussed, giving every man a clearer sense of his duty on and off the field, in and out of camp.

The laws of war were many and varied, covering how to deal with civilians, a soldier's duty to his lord and commander, the right to demand fair payment for services and risk, and what targets were restricted from attack or, conversely, what targets were expected to be attacked.

The boys enjoyed the lighter duty, after weeks of warfare drills. The food improved somewhat, too – twice they were given honey biscuits and weak ale, in addition to boiled eggs and beans.

Rondal expected another week of combat tactics after the rest days, as the Week of the Heart was next, but instead the next morning they were issued fresh packs, complete with new blankets, socks, bandages and other gear, in addition to their armor, shields, helms, and weapons.

And then they marched.

Not merely back and forth across the practice yard, as they had been doing. After a brief luncheon they re-formed into one giant line and marched completely out of the Relan Cor complex and into the southern Castali countryside. All afternoon they tromped down the dusty dirt road north of the fortress. Along the way they learned a number of marching songs to keep their cadence, some of ancient source and some more recent, but all obscene and entertaining.

The plod of boot after boot, one foot in front of the other for mile after mile soon turned every boy's feet into numb stumps inside their boots. The Ancients and Warbrothers escorting them on horseback seemed to delight in finding fault with their marching. Only once before dark did they allow the boys to rest before they returned them to the road.

When twilight fell, Rondal was sure that they would stop . . . but they didn't.

On and on they marched as twilight gave way to darkness, until the muttered complaints from all began to swarm. Ancient Feslyn heard them and just smiled. They kept marching. Eventually, when it was clear that no amount of complaining would stop the march, things quieted down. Only then did the Ancients halt the column and allow the boys to fall out of formation. Most fell asleep beside the road still in armor, wrapped in their mantles with their heads on their packs.

Rondal was tempted, but he had been chosen as squad commander that day, the first time he'd gotten the honor. So it was to him that his squad complained bitterly, those who still had breath to do so. He took their concerns to Ancient Feslyn, who did not even try to look sympathetic.

But he did issue rations: a stack of ten flats of journeybread and a sack of tough dried sausages. Rondal happily distributed the food and oversaw the election of Dolwyn as the next day's leader as they at the rations cold. Then Rondal passed out.

The next day the march continued – in the *wrong* direction.

"Aren't we headed back to camp?" Dolwyn asked Ancient Feslyn. "Sir?"

"Today you're to discover the wonder that is the Forced March," the old veteran explained. "We stop at dusk. No sooner."

As appalling as it sounded, the marching was worse. It became a monotonous trial of pain and endurance. Every boy pushed themselves, and each other, when they failed to find their own stock of initiative. Talking was discouraged, beyond singing cadences, and that left them all alone with their thoughts and their tired feet.

"How long do you think we've covered?" asked Rax, anxiously, around noon.

"Thirty miles," suggested Handol.

"More like twenty, since yesterday," Orphil disagreed.

"Quiet!" called a passing Warbrother. *"Quiet in the ranks!"*

Rondal used the time at first to go over spells in his head, but even that grew boring after a while. He recited the Sacred Periodic Table and the Laws of Magic and even Sire Rose's silly Sixteen Laws Of Love, but his brain inevitably brought his mind back to the darkness he was circling.

While he tried to avoid it as long as he could, the plodding pace, mental exercise and enforced activity soon compelled him to think about that awful night once again, the betrayal of Kaffin of Gyre and the death of Estasia. He hadn't thought about the poor girl in weeks, he realized guiltily. But then, he recalled, that was what he wanted to find here, in Relan Cor.

After weeks of avoiding the matter, suddenly his mind became obsessed with it. Over and over the tragic night played out in his mind, and he found himself growing angry, then resentful, then wracked with despair.

And still his feet marched on.

At one point, he found himself crying, tears rolling down his face as his exhausted body trudged on. At first he thought they were merely tears of misery, but soon his frustrated mind began throwing every awful memory and horrible mistake he'd ever made against itself.

Inside his head he savagely recriminated himself over his many, many errors and losses, and tallied the lives lost because of him, from his mother to Estasia. He even thought about poor Urik, the younger apprentice to Garkesku, back in Boval before the invasion, whose abuse by the oldest apprentice had driven him mad. Rondal had silently allowed him to be abused rather than disrupt the way things were established in the tense professional household. Both his fellow apprentices had died as an indirect result.

That did his peace of mind no favors.

He saw himself as a miserable excuse for a human being, and he didn't see why anyone – Master Min, Lady Alya, Sire Cei, anyone – would want to associate with him. His head hung low as he marched, his spear on one shoulder, his shield on the other, his pack trying to drag him to the ground.

But his feet marched on. Tears rolled down his face in his anguish, and yet still his feet kept marching. The pain in his arms and shoulders and tortured legs screamed as agonizing as any he'd ever felt but he kept on marching. Perhaps, he reasoned, if he wore his feet off and died of exhaustion, then the unremitting emotional pain would come to an end.

A warbrother, swathed in a bull skin mantle and an elaborate headdress, rode apace on a rouncey with his section of the column awhile, and noted Rondal's misery.

"Leave it on the road, son," he called after him kindly. "Whatever it is, it's behind you now. March *away* from it and leave it on the road." He urged his horse forward to dress the line before Rondal could respond.

So he just marched. And he tried to leave it on the road.

His anger at the Dead God and the loss of his beloved mountain home . . . on the road.

His grief over the Bovali dead in the aftermath of the invasion . . . on the road.

The fear he'd disappoint his kind new master, who had given him so much and had asked so little in return . . . on the road. His terror of death in battle . . . on the road.

The self-loathing he felt for his role in Estasia's death . . . on the road.

The resentment he felt for Tyndal and for his role in her death . . . on the road.

One by one he recalled his follies and foolishness and he vowed to leave them behind, taking only the lessons learned. That, his mind told his exhausted body, was the only productive thing to do. Cull the wisdom from the chaff of pain and move on another step. And the insights began to occur.

Vengeance and retribution, he realized, were tiring and tireless pursuits. They rarely served a higher purpose, or lent themselves to anything constructive, he reasoned. Fear was a childish conceit he could no longer afford, he finally understood.

Fear of failure, even, he had to leave behind. It did not matter if he failed, he realized. It only mattered that he tried his hardest. It was acceptable for a knight to die valiantly in pursuit of his quest. It was not acceptable for him to die before he even tried to complete it.

The worst of his struggles was with his own self-doubt and self-confidence, he realized, the one sniping eternally at the other. As the column began ascending a steep-graded hill, Rondal reviewed his short life and dwelt on the times when his lack of confidence had undercut him. While it hurt to consider, he recalled that magical evening when he and Estasia (and Tyndal, his mind reminded him) had woven that complicated, sophisticated spell together, and he wondered what would have happened had he been bold enough to chance to steal a kiss from the beautiful girl.

But fear had stayed him. Fear of rejection, fear of competition, fear of being found unworthy in Estasia's eyes. It all came back to fear. Fear, he realized, had been the core of his failure in almost every case.

He remembered the reams of advice he'd been given about the subject of his confidence, everything from swordplay to spellcraft, and he tried to take it all to heart. They all seemed to come back to giving up his fear. Once you gave up fear, he realized, the rest really wasn't that hard.

Rondal realized that he had just discovered a powerful insight into Tyndal's character – the boy just wasn't really afraid of much. That might be a factor of his stupidity but it also accounted for his boldness. And his success.

Of all of his demons, Rondal had the hardest time leaving his feelings for Tyndal on the road. His maddening fellow apprentice had inadvertently humiliated Rondal too many times for him to lightly forgive. It would have been a different thing entirely had he done it on purpose, but mostly Tyndal blundered into his insults and humiliations accidentally. He wasn't trying to be a bully. That was just how he was. It was hard to be angry at that.

But it also made it harder to forgive and forget.

As his chest heaved like a bellows and his knees threatened to give out with every step, he followed the boy in front of him, whose helm and hair he had memorized down to the finest fiber and scratch, up that laborious hill. Every step felt as if he was stepping angrily on Tyndal's face. Every bit of pain was worth the feeling of satisfaction he got from it.

By the time his part of the column crested the summit, Rondal's steps had lightened. He no longer cared if he was grinding his senior apprentice's face with his boot; indeed, it seemed like a silly pursuit. He took a deep breath and felt the weight of his pack ease and even his shield felt lighter. His achingly numb legs continued to carry him onward, but the burden he'd been bearing until then seemed gone, or at least forgotten.

When he stumbled to a halt late that evening, after nearly fourteen hours of marching, he wasn't as tired as he'd thought he'd be. In fact, he lingered before sleep, volunteering for the first watch. As he sat around the fire between patrols the bull-hided Warbrother who'd encouraged him on the march wandered by, apparently in search of him.

"I was hoping I'd run into you, Soldier," he said, gently. "At ease. I wanted to see how you fared, after today."

"It was . . . I'm all right, Warbrother," he decided. "I just had a lot of thoughts to work out."

"Marching away your cares is a fine old army tradition," the monk said, approvingly. "We've been watching you. You've shown a lot of poise in the field. And a lot of fortitude. A lot more than we'd expected."

"A lot more than I expected, too, if you want the truth," Rondal admitted. "I don't feel like I'm the same person who started this march."

"Ah! Then it's working!" the Warbrother said, smiling indulgently. "That's the point of The Mystery, son. It must be *experienced*, it cannot be taught. And it changes you . . . irrevocably."

"My legs, if nothing else," he quipped, rubbing his sore thighs.

"Far more than your legs," the monk said, pulling a flask from his mantle and offering it to Rondal.

"When you lose your identity in the uniformity of the unit," he explained, "you gain the opportunity to remake yourself. Your legs, of course, and the rest of your body are being remade; your instincts and reflexes are remade, and your understanding of honor and obedience are being remade.

"But most of all," he said, solemnly, as Rondal sipped the fiery liquor, "you remake your *soul*. When you learn the rites of the soldier,

183

and feel them in your bones with every step you take, you open yourself to new reserves of power, fortitude, endurance . . . you find you can achieve things you never thought possible, as a civilian. Even as a warrior-monk," he smiled.

"Or a Knight Mage," Rondal chuckled. "I've learned how to study, Warbrother. I've learned how learn. I've even learned how to fight. But soldiering . . . that's an art to itself."

"Any idiot can pick up a sword and learn to swing it hard enough to kill," the monk agreed. "Any tribe can train its men to be warriors – fierce warriors. But the difference between a warrior and a soldier is the difference between honor and duty. And with duty comes obedience. Learning to subject yourself to the orders of those above and contribute to the battle to the best of your ability, that is the art of the soldier."

"I never wanted to be a soldier," Rondal warned the monk. "I only vaguely wanted to be a mage."

"What did you want to be?" the old monk asked.

Rondal considered the unexpected question. No one had ever really asked him before.

"Wise," he finally said. "I guess I wanted to be the one who knew everything all the time."

"Well, now you've learned the Mysteries of Duin, the art of the soldier," reasoned the monk, taking a sip from the flask. "And in learning that art, you've already harvested one of the main benefits The Mystery has to offer the initiate."

"What's that?" Rondal asked, curious.

"Pride," the monk grunted. "You have learned pride in yourself. You came here a boy, and while that boy was unmade in the struggle to survive, you found the pride in yourself you needed to succeed – to thrive, even. As I said, we've been watching you. You've done better than expected. And that shall please your master immensely."

That pleased Rondal immensely. After the monk left he basked in the afterglow of the praise, reflecting on his time at Relan Cor.

He really had cultivated some pride in himself, he realized. He had learned the craft of sword and shield, of command and order, of attack and defense. Just as thousands upon thousands before him had. When he had completed the Mysteries, he would be as fit as any soldier in the Duchies.

Regardless of what else he was –mage, knight, lord, scholar – he would always have this. The skills and knowledge of a soldier. The training and understanding of soldiery. The pride of that accomplishment. No one gave that to him, he had earned it with his sweat and blood and pain. It hadn't been his magical talent, his sophisticated brain, or his title that had gotten him through the Mysteries – it had been he, and he alone.

He slept fitfully that night, and the next morning awoke emotionally and physically refreshed, almost eager to begin the day.

He was in the minority. Most of his squadmates were exhausted.

*   *   *

"Today we're going to head back to Relan Cor," Warfather Dorith, the high priest who had led the march announced to everyone at dawn formation with a wicked grin. "But we're not going in one large column.

"Starting every fifteen minutes after this assembly, one squad will be sent back . . . *overland.* The Ancients and Warbrothers will be patrolling the road and enforcing the rules – you may cross it, but do not travel upon it.

"The purpose of this training is this: often a unit gets broken off from its supply and has to forage on its own. It is a test of any Neophyte's temper, and any squad's effectiveness, to be able to survive in hostile territory and navigate back to your command. Today you need to find your way back to the fortress without our help."

There was a loud groan at the news, but it perked up a lot of the young men. Moving in small groups had to be better than marching in formation.

"To make things *interesting,*" the commandant added, over the cadets' murmur, "we have seven teams of 'foes' betwixt here and Relan Cor, either guarding strategic points or searching for cadets to engage. They will be wearing yellow and red tabards with the arms of

Relan Cor upon them. They will be armed with wooden swords. They eager to keep each of you away from your camp as long as possible. Engage or evade them as you see fit, but if they capture you, your role in the competition is over.

"Oh, yes . . . there is a grand feast awaiting to reward the first full squadron who returns," the sage old Warfather grinned.

That was plenty of incentive for every Neophyte there.

The Third Squad, Second Company did not depart until midmorning, with a young monk, Warbrother Thurgar, accompanying them for the first half-day to ensure they did not blunder too far off of the path. But the monk got less and less helpful as they went, until he had gone completely silent. It was up to them, he indicated, to find their way. He would merely follow them.

"If we just keep heading south, we're bound to run into the road eventually," reasoned Rax.

"And run into the foe as well," Walven pointed out. "Not to mention every other squad who can't think of a better plan than that." Brother Thurgar smirked.

"South, then bear east for a while," suggested Gurandor. "We can range wide of the opposition and then head south."

"That would take too long," complained Handol. "We've been marching for *two days* with little to eat – I don't want to march three or four more with less!"

"Then use your heads before you use your feet!" counseled the Warbrother, when some of the boys beseeched him with their eyes. "The solution is there."

Something dawned on Rondal. "Uh, fellows? Why use our feet at all?" he asked. The others looked at him strangely.

"You have a spell that can fly us all the way back, Sparky?" asked Walven. Rondal ignored the jibe. Walven didn't mean anything by it.

"No," Rondal admitted. "But we might be able to *float* back."

He recalled the map of the region he had committed to magical memory, in his days leading up to the opening of the Mysteries at Relan Cor. He thought it might be useful, and it was. He took a few moments to sketch it out in the dirt with a stick.

"According to the map," he said, slowly, "we're in this forest *here*. So if we bear east and north we can come to the Partoline River. That flows south and west – remember that great bridge we crossed? It comes within six miles of Relan Cor," he pointed out. "By-passing most of the defenders, and most of our opponent squads."

"And you're going to turn our shields into dainty little sailboats, I expect?" asked Dolwyn with a smirk.

"We'll deal with that when we get to the river," decided Verd, the chosen leader for the day. "We can steal a boat or make a raft, but that sounds like a better course than marching again."

The warbrother did not comment, but Rondal could tell he seemed pleased.

"There is one more thing," Brother Thurgar said, as they prepared to depart, "at the end of this journey your unit will chose your War Name for you. That name you will keep with you for the rest of your life, and will be known to your brothers as such. Try not to make it one you're embarrassed to carry. Good luck, and may Duin guide your path!" he said, adding a blessing before he headed back toward the road.

"Herus would be a better guide," grumbled Rax.

"And the Goblin King better company," griped Yeatin.

"Let's make for the river," Verd ordered. "The faster we get there, the faster we can decide what a horrible mistake we've made."

They made it through the woods surprisingly fast and crossed the few miles of fields and pastures until they got to the sluggish Partoline. It wasn't particularly wide, the magi informed their mates, after a little scrying, but it was deep.

They found a small punt nearby, large enough for only one man, and sent Yeatin (who claimed some familiarity with boats) upriver in it to scout while the rest of them stood around and speculated just how quickly the weak mage would get himself drowned.

Surprisingly, he returned on the punt with a small rowboat in tow. A similar journey downriver secured two more small craft, and before long a flotilla of stolen boats made their way down the deep stream.

"This is *much* better than marching!" Rax sighed, pleasantly, as he paddled along.

"So far," agreed Walven. "But don't get complacent. And don't be lazy on the paddle. If we get back first . . ."

They hadn't discussed that prospect, but the idea of a feast was alluring. So much so that the three magi, after consultation began enchanting their journey.

Only in small ways – Rondal lacked the power to conjure a proper water elemental – but they did manage to arcanely reduce the friction of the boats somewhat. The banks slipped past them at a goodly pace for miles as they skipped the long, painful road full of fake "enemies" who would beat them up.

Along the way they discussed everything from girls to their futures to girls to their hopes and plans after graduation to girls. Twice they saw fellow cadets on the banks as they floated by, fellows who had figured out the expediency of river travel late, but the Racquiel Squad passed them in good order, without challenge.

They found themselves at one point facing a bridge toll, and had to convince the bridgekeeper to let them pass without paying. That took a fair amount of intimidation from the boys, but eventually the man relented, and opened the river gate to let their craft through while Dolwyn stood menacingly behind him. Their journey continued.

"I'm getting hungry," complained Rax, late in the afternoon.

"I've been hungry for *days*," agreed Dolwyn. "What are we going to do about that?"

"We could steal food?" Handol suggested, anxiously.

"We could buy it, if we had money," agreed Orphil, dejectedly. "But I seem to have forgotten my coinpurse. My belly is dancing with my backbone!"

"Why can't one of you idiots *fish?*" demanded Yeatin from his punt.

"It would take too long to stop and cook it," Walven decided. "Sparky, you've got that magical map in your head. What is the next village we come to?"

"Uh . . . Grynwyn Estate. Domain of Clairberry," Rondal supplied. He really hoped his new War Name was *not* going to be "Sparky". It was a common term for warmagi, the way you could always call the camp cook "cookie", or the company medic as "doc", but still . . .

"Do they have an inn there?"

"The map I studied didn't specify," Rondal said, dryly. "And we have no money, besides."

"My father," Dolwyn said, slowly, "always said that gold might not get you good swords, but good swords will always get you gold."

"Our swords are wooden," Rax pointed out, unhelpfully. "Does that get us wood? I've got enough wood already," he joked.

No one laughed. The novelty of penis jokes had faded weeks ago.

"No one else knows our swords are wooden," Walven pointed out. "In fact, apart from that we look like any mercenary troop."

"Of *children!*" snorted Rax.

"Of *young recruits*," corrected Walven, evenly. "Plenty of lads our age enter military service. And with helmets on it's hard to tell our ages. Especially in the darkness, of which we should soon have an abundance."

"So . . . we're going to steal someone's food at the point of a wooden sword?"

"No," Walven said, smiling. "We're going to convince them to *give* it to us."

The village of Grynwyn was on the edge of its domain, the river acting as the border of the land. There was no bridge there, but there was a decent ford, and the boys were able to drag their boats onto the bank without discovery.

Under Walven's guidance the squad formed up under their thin cloaks, spears in hand, and marched not toward a village inn, but toward the manor hall of Grynwyn Estate. It was a squat, one-story affair at least a century old, but there was a three-story refuge tower there for defense (empty, the magi declared, upon inspection) and no less than five grain silos.

Walven, who acted as leader by acclamation, pulled his helmet down over his eyes until they were barely visible, and encouraged the rest of them to follow suit.

They marched in good order to the unguarded gate of the well-kept manor, where they rang the bell. The gatekeeper shuffled out of his shed to see them, lifting a lantern high and peering into the shadows.

Everyone kept their shields up. In the darkness it was hard to see the wooden points of the practice weapons they bore.

"What is this?" demanded the rustic watchman.

"We've come to arrest the lord of the manor!" Walven said, authoritatively.

"What? *Sir Andras?* Why?" the man cried in alarm.

"Because those are our *orders!*" Walven insisted. "Open this door at once or we will storm the manor!" To emphasize his point, the rest of the squad brandished their spears menacingly.

"All right, all right!" agreed the man in panic, as he opened the latch. "By whose authority are you—?"

Rondal touched the man and whispered a word, and he fell instantly asleep.

"I *like* that!" Rax smiled, as they helped the guard to the ground. "It's much neater than slitting his throat!"

"Spread out," ordered Walven, gesturing. "Secure the stable, the front door, and the side door. Gurandor, you and Handol take the rear."

The boys scattered out as commanded without questioning Walven's orders. They had learned the importance of obedience on the drill field. In moments, they had effective control of the manor.

"If I'd known conquest was this easy . . ." Jofard grinned.

"It helps when they don't know you're coming," said Walven. "But you fellows just back up what I say, stand around and look menacing, and we'll be fed before you know it."

He led the rest of the squad to the door of the manor where he pounded until someone came. As soon as the door opened, he pushed his way in.

"Where is Sir Andras?" he demanded of the confused old woman.

"What? Trygg take you, the master is at board!" she insisted, angrily.

190

Walven put his hand dangerously on the hilt of his wooden sword.

"Then lead us to him," the boy said, his eyes narrow. "We would have *words* with him. And be sharp about it!" he insisted. The woman wailed and led the cadets back to the great hall of the manor. Three men and two women sat at a trestle table.

"*Seize* him!" Walven ordered. Rondal was surprised at the command, but marched forward to where the oldest man was sitting, and grabbed his left arm as Dolwyn grabbed his right. They dragged the old man to Walven, who was looking at him appraisingly.

"Sir Andras of Devas, you are hereby bound by law by the rightful—"

"*Wait,* wait!" the old man squealed. "You have the wrong man! You have the *wrong man!*"

"What?" Walven said, scornfully. "I think *not!* Sir Andras of Devas, you have—"

"But I'm *not* Sir Andras of Devas!" the old knight insisted, shaking the boys' hands off. "I'm Sir Andras of *Culwen!* I've never even *heard* of Devas!"

"What?" Walven said, feigning surprise.

"I said I've never even heard of Devas! Ishi's itchy bum, I've never even left the *county!"*

"So . . . your liege lord is not Arscot, Baron of Drune?" Walven asked, confused.

"No! Never heard of the man!" the knight insisted.

"That's *just* what a fugitive might say, Captain," Rondal offered, helpfully.

"So it is," Walven agreed, his eyes narrowing. "Can you *prove* that you are not, indeed, Sir Andras of Devas?"

"Fetch my patent! Roquilly, fetch my patent of nobility!" he shouted, apparently to his maidservant. "Quickly!" he insisted, terrified.

"This is *highly* irregular, Captain," Rondal pointed out to Walven, playing the part of the officious clerk.

"If he's not Sir Andras of Devas," Walven said, just loudly enough for the man to overhear, "then what will we do? This is *most* embarrassing!"

"Slaughter them all, Captain?" Rondal suggested, evilly.

"We'll see," shrugged the cadet.

The fat little maid brought a sheaf of parchment bearing many seals attesting that the man was, indeed, Sir Andras of Culwen, not the miscreant Sir Andras of Devas.

Walven appeared reluctant to accept his story, and even ordered his men to prepare to burn the manor down, when Andras finally broke down and pleaded for his life and livelihood.

"Well, I hate to report a failure," murmured Walven. "And I was ordered to arrest Sir Andras, and I don't think my commander really cares *which* Sir Andras is supplied . . . yet . . ."

"Sir," Rondal said, respectfully. "Perhaps if the men were fed and rested while we sort this out? It might keep them from getting . . . *anxious*," he said, casting his eyes toward his squadmates.

"Yes, yes, by all means, Captain!" Sir Andras said, his eyes wide. "Have a seat, let us feed you – you must be weary!"

"Well," Walven said, appearing to waver. "If this is the wrong manor . . . and you are the wrong Sir Andras . . ."

"I am, my lords, I *am!*" he insisted. "Please! There's been a mistake! Let's talk about this like reasonable gentlemen!"

The entire squad ate well that night, raiding the manor's pantry for food and drink, and then stuffing their pockets with more, all at the urging of the frightened manor staff. When Walven was satisfied, he finally agreed to leave without further attempts to arrest Sir Andras.

"And that, gentlemen," the squad leader said as he led them back to the boat in darkness, "is how you rob a manor house."

"I've done it before," Rondal dismissed. "But we didn't even really use magic on this one. Impressive," he admitted.

"I'm happy with the results," agreed Rax, picking his teeth with a twig. "Now let's see just how far downstream we can make it tonight."

The boys almost missed their landing the next morning, as they made better time than they expected. But Rondal, alert with his magemap, got them to stop and haul their boats ashore just before they arrived at the bridge closest to Relan Cor. As restive as their journey downriver had been, they were eager to be underway.

"Only six miles?" scoffed Verd, as they began to march. "That's *nothing!*" Even Yeatin seemed eager to get going.

They moved quietly through the countryside, along side the road to Relan Cor, and were nearly there . . . when they ran into a knot of yellow-and-red-clad warriors bearing wooden swords. Some of the defenders the warfather had promised them.

"There are *seven* of them!" moaned Rax, as they peered up the road from cover.

"There are ten of us," Yeatin pointed out.

"Nine," corrected Dolwyn scornfully. "Look at the size of them!"

"Regardless, we outnumber them," Yeatin said. "And we need not engage them. We can always go around."

"That doesn't look practical," Walven suggested. "Not unless we want to backtrack up river and try to go through the swamps. That could take hours, and the fortress is just beyond them."

"Then what do we do?"

"Let's attack," Rondal decided.

He was elected leader again the night before, after the successful raid on the manor. "I'm tired of skulking around. And we don't have to kill them," he reminded, "we just have to get past them."

"Attack?" asked Walven, curious. "I didn't think you were the aggressive type. Why not use some spell?"

"I've had occasion to learn, recently," Rondal said, dryly. "And while I'm sure there's some clever magical device I could use to achieve our goal, the truth is I'm sick and tired of skulking about.

"Our camp is right over there, and I need a hot meal and a warm blanket more than the breath of life itself. There are only seven of them. And how many times have we been told that a sudden, all-out attack with no regard for our personal safety was often the best tactic to take in an engagement?"

"I thought that was just bluster!" Yeatin whined.

"It was good advice," Orphil agreed. "But I still don't want to get creamed the moment we stick our heads out there."

"We won't," Rondal assured. "Remember, we only have to get past them, we don't have to defeat them."

"And how do you propose to do that?"

Rondal looked around. "Someone needs to steal some rope."

It took almost half an hour for the boys to round up what they needed by raiding a peasant's shed, under Rondal's direction, and if they were skeptical about the plan, they couldn't conceive of a better one.

It began with the smallest of the squad, Verd, apparently blundering out into the road in front of the guards without his helm, shield, or sword. He looked for all the world like a cadet who got separated from his unit.

The yellow-clad guards grinned and gave chase, most of them, leaving only two guarding the entry to Relan Cor.

While Verd led his heavily-armored pursuers on a merry chase through the village, the other boys surprised the remaining guards.

To keep from getting bogged down in a protracted engagement, Rondal had the largest two boys pick up the small punt and rush the defenders with it, using it as a giant shield against their blows. Immediately behind it ran four more boys, who sprung out against the bowled-over guards and bashed their helmets with their wooden swords while the others passed by.

Meanwhile, Verd rounded a corner of the road and ducked into an alley between two hovels, and nimbly leapt over the rope they'd stretched between. In their cumbersome helmets, their attention on Verd, the warriors didn't see the rope until it was too late. By the time they untangled themselves from it, Verd had sprinted away to follow his mates.

"All right!" Rondal bellowed, as the gate of Relan Cor came into sight. "Let's form up, marching formation! Banner-bearer to the front!"

"We did it!" Rax chortled in delight. "I can't *believe* that worked!"

"We're not there yet," Rondal said, grimly. "Somehow I don't think that will be the last obstacle in our path. Not a good time to get complacent."

As if he was prophesying, five more knights in yellow and black tabards sprang out from the brush beside the causeway and challenged the squad on its way back to camp.

Much to Rondal's surprise, he recognized one of the men under his helmet.

"Tyndal!" he spat, angrily, for no real reason.

He hadn't seen his fellow apprentice in almost a full moon, and apart from some general resentment over what happened at Inrion, he hadn't spared him much thought.

But the sight of his grinning face under the visor of the helmet enraged Rondal for some reason. He had originally planned on trying to skirt the causeway, but as soon as he saw Tyndal, he changed his plan.

"Ishi's tits! All *right*," he called out, "Shields to the front, spears behind, wedge formation with Rax and Verd on reurguard, Scorpion's

195

Tail team, Yeatin keep the banner in the center, right behind Jofard. We hit them hard and keep going. Watch for magic, that one on the end is a warmage, and I'll take care of him. The rest of you barrel on through and don't stop until you're on the practice field. We've *got* to be at least fourth or fifth place, at this point."

"*Maybe* fifth," Gurandor said, dejectedly.

"It doesn't matter if we're last; we go in there like we're the *first*," he insisted.

"Take your positions; make ready to charge . . . he shouted, as the boys quickly re-formed according to his direction. He took a deep breath, surveying the backs of the helmets of his squad.

He didn't care if they got the snot beat out of them, he realized. They were *going through* that causeway.

". . . And . . . STRIKE!"

They marched along at quick order, without calling a cadence. It only took moments for the defenders to recognize an attack and arm themselves – but Rondal didn't care. They set up a defensive shield wall, but it was ragged and undisciplined.

When they arrived within twenty feet of the most forward-positioned defender, Rondal ordered the charge.

The front two squadmates, Jofard and Orphil, kept their shields locked together as they appeared in force and used their big shields to bully their way through the first two defenders, both armed with wooden greatswords. The spearmen behind them growled and entangled the defenders' blades just long enough to allow the boys on either side to beat their helmets soundly as they passed.

"DEAD!" Jofard bellowed with each resounding slap of wood against metal.

Walven leapt out and assailed two defenders on their flanks, armed with wooden cavalry swords and shields. Gurandor slipped in behind him to support his ferocious assault, and between the two the left flank was secure.

Rondal kept to the right flank, and when the front shields pushed passed the others, he found himself shield-to-shield with his fellow apprentice. He felt Walven float quietly behind him, spear ready to support his attack. Tyndal couldn't see that, but . . .

Tyndal grinned broadly through the bars, his shaggy blond hair hanging out of the borrowed practice helmet like too much hay in a barn.

"Hey, Ron!" he began to say. "I saw—"

Rondal didn't hesitate. As Dolwyn, in front of him and on his left, pushed Tyndal's cavalry shield slightly out of line, Rondal threw his elbow up as if he was feinting for a head strike.

Tyndal reflexively raised his shield . . . but did not cant it enough to avoid the hard snap Rondal's increasingly strong wrist brought to bear, when he snapped it back over the shield. There was a mighty thud of wood on steel, and Tyndal was reeling from the blow. Rondal didn't spare him another glance.

"KEEP MOVING!" he ordered, as the Scorpion's Tail moved in behind. That was a formation that put most of the spears in the rear, allowing them to rove to the left, right, or over the heads of the front shieldmen. As they passed by the shattered line of defenders, the spears were able to strike swiftly at the disorganized defenders, keeping them from regrouping . . . or even rising.

Rondal heard another hard clunk behind him, and knew that Handol's fake spear had smashed against Tyndal's helmet, hard.

"Racquiels, *form up!* To the practice field!" Rondal ordered. "*Double time!*" They re-formed into a better-dressed line and began to trot, a difficult thing to do with a full pack and arrayed for battle.

But the boys were no longer unused to such burdens, and the prospect of food and rest and sleep so close at hand was too alluring for them to let weariness interfere. Rax began to sing a particularly dirty marching song concerning the proclivities of the whores of Barrowbell that finished up scandalously just as the squad marched boldly into the practice field.

There were already some cadets there, and Rondal's heart fell – he *almost* thought that they would be the first. It was a foolish hope, but it had kept him going for a few miles.

But then he realized that the boys milling around were there in singles and doubles – four was the most he saw standing together around their shredded banner, and it looked like it took all four of them to keep it aright. But nothing close to a full squad.

The Third Squad, Second Company was, as the Warbrother at the gate informed them, the first *complete* squadron to make it back. The others had not been permitted to sound the great horn at the reviewing stand, not until the largest squad had been determined.

"You mean . . . we *won?*" asked Jofard, in a girlish whisper.

"Indeed, by Duin's grace," chuckled the pleased warrior monk. "You may sound the horn at will."

"Let's do this right," Rondal said, like a man suddenly possessed. "Form up, parade block, Yeatin on the banner, ready . . . MARCH. Walven, call the cadence!" he grinned.

The bystanders broke into applause and shouts of praise. Instead of tearing after the prize like they were attacking it, Rondal brought them in as a disciplined unit. As the Racquiel Squad marched into the field and took up their parade position, it felt like every instructor, monk, and Ancient in Relan Cor had come out to watch.

"Squadron . . . HALT!" ordered Rondal. His fellows obligingly came to a stop and rested their spears in one disciplined movement, as Ancient Feslyn approached, grinning.

"Third Squadron, Second Company, reporting as ordered, SIR!" Rondal said, saluting with his spear and shield after calling his squad to attention.

Their Ancient stood at attention and returned the salute, then formally bowed. "Well done, Neophytes!" he boomed. "Racquiel Squad! You just won me a beefsteak dinner! Not that I'm complaining, but . . . how *did* you get back here so quickly?" he asked, amused but mystified.

"We took to the river and by-passed the road entirely, Sir!" Rondal called.

"And the defenders at the gate?"

"The squadron conducted a surprise attack using distraction, concocted an ambush, and *kicked their asses* . . . SIR!" Rondal said, proudly.

"Then you *have* won," he pronounced. "Squadleader, please blow the horn of victory, and then dismiss your men. You have three hours before your feast will be ready at the Warbrother's Chapel," he said, his wrinkled and scarred face breaking into a grin. "I would recommend you spend at least *some* of that time productively in the bathhouse."

"Squadron . . . DISMISSED!" Rondal called, and then the boys followed him over to the stand after stacking their arms neatly in place.

He took up the great ox horn, looked around at his excited fellows, and held it to his lips, blowing a mighty blast. It was a low, deep, rumbling sound that seemed to make his very bones vibrate. He didn't know why, but when he handed it to Walven he felt . . . *changed.*

He was watching with excitement as each of the squad, including frail Yeatin, who had borne every burden asked and had done so without serious complaint, blew a blast on the horn. It was while the weakest member of his squad was celebrating that Tyndal approached, still wearing his yellow and black tabard.

"Ron!" he called as he crossed the field. "Ron, that was *amazing!"*

"What?" Rondal asked, confused.

"How you just plowed through us like that!" the senior apprentice laughed. "We were ready to take you apart, and you just didn't give us a chance! Why didn't you stick around to duel?" he asked, sounding a little . . . hurt? "I wanted to see how good you've gotten."

"That wasn't part of our mission," the junior apprentice said, coolly. "Our mission was to get past you, not defeat you."

Tyndal snorted. "Like you could *ever* defeat me—!"

Before Rondal could mount a defense, his squadmates beat him to it. Walven was in Tyndal's face instantly.

"You fight him, you fight the whole *fucking* squad!" the young man said in a serious voice. "I don't know what your problem with him is, but Striker is an *outstanding* soldier," he continued, aggressively, "and he got us through this trial without a hiccup! It was his idea to take the river!"

"Striker?" asked Tyndal, confused.

"That's his war name," Verd insisted, the little bantam just as aggressive in Rondal's defense as the larger lad. "We just decided on the way up the causeway. Striker . . . for how hard he struck *you,*" he added, with a sneer.

"Struck *me?*" Tyndal asked, confused.

"Why don't you just scamper back to the fortress with the rest of the knights?" Jofard asked, his hands on his hips. "This field is for the Mysteries. Neophytes *only.* Your service as a target is appreciated, but you are dismissed. We need no interlopers here."

Tyndal looked at Rondal thoughtfully, almost respectfully. Rondal didn't mind the change.

"Well, it looks like you have your own little band now, Ron," he said, reluctantly. "I guess you don't need me keeping an eye on you."

"I never *did,*" Rondal said, his jaw clenched. "Now please excuse me . . . my squad and I have some celebrating to do." He watched as Tyndal left without another word. And when he was gone, he felt as if yet-another burden had been suddenly lifted from him.

He had felt as if he was in Tyndal's shadow for the last few years, ever since he became Master Minalan's apprentice by default. It hadn't mattered that he was a better mage than Tyndal; the younger boy was more like their master than he was by nature and temperament.

But now he found he didn't care as much. After Tyndal left, Rondal looked around at his celebrating squadmates and was glad that the other boy wasn't involved in this victory. It was something he had done on his own – earned on his own – without even *his witchstone* to rely on.

He slowly started to grin as he realized that. He and his team had triumphed over everyone else not because he was a High Mage, or a Mage Knight, or a Magelord . . . apart from a few fires and a little scrying, he'd done precious little magic at all.

What he saw around him was the result of his *own personal efforts.* He hadn't borrowed anything, hadn't gotten any help from his master to win through the challenges of the Mysteries. He had done this, he and his squad, on their own.

For no particular reason, Rondal suddenly felt at ease, peaceful in a way that had eluded him most of his life.

"Let's get back to camp," he ordered, when the squad's enthusiasm had banked. "A couple of hours of napping, a hot bath, and we can attack the banquet table."

*　　　　*　　　　*

The feast was laid out in the Warbrother's Chapel, a long tent that served as the commanders' lounge during the day when it wasn't being employed for instruction or services.

The feast itself was a simple affair, but artfully prepared, and included all the food they could eat. Bread, fish, vegetables cooked in broth, and an entire goat was roasted for their meal, and another small barrel of ale was made available. The ten boys were thoroughly elated, stuffing their faces like they were starving and drinking heavily after their grueling march.

During the feast each one was called upon to tell his part in the trial to the three Warbrothers and two Ancients who attended. As they were now twice victorious in their contests, they were given a far more private rite than the mass of their fellow Neophytes, who were still trickling in. The final rite could only be performed for the full squad, so many ended up waiting on stragglers, their whole squads paying for the individual soldier's failure.

The rite was solemn, with Warbrother Thurgar lighting the sacred torches that called Duin's attention and giving to them the instruction in the Mystery:

"For twenty generations men have performed the Mysteries," he said, quietly, "to be initiated into a career of arms. The skills taught in the Mysteries are valuable," he said, looking around at each of them in the torchlight, "but it is not the skills that elevate a man from being a mere soldier to being an Initiate. The skills can be taught to anyone – even women, aye, in the defense of their homes, at pressing need.

"But the men who complete the Mysteries are bound together by bonds of sweat and blood. Duin's rites grant you his grace, in your transformation. Less than a moon ago you were competitors and strangers. You were boys who bore the names of your fathers or your homelands and looked forward to a life with a sword in your hand.

"Now," he said, enthusiastically, "now you are *brothers*, your bonds forged from the toil and effort you have put into the Mysteries. You have been made kin by your mutual suffering, your mutual dependence, and your loyalty to the Mysteries.

"Are they difficult? Aye. Unfair? Aye. Brutal? Of necessity. *A boy doesn't become a man over a cozy cup of tea.* It takes fire, sweat, blood, effort, two hands, two feet, a head and a heart, and that must be heated and beaten in the Mysteries, overseen by older men and initiates. Else the blade that results will be weak when it most needs to be strong.

"But Duin grants to all who complete his Mysteries an especial boon. Each squadron who completes the Mysteries stands together in the sight of Duin, after death, for the Mysteries stay with the soul long after the body has grown cold. In the sight of Duin your comrades will answer for you, sing of your deeds, testify to your valor, and share in Duin's judgment with you.

"For that is one of the Mysteries: for he who picks up a sword in accordance with sacred law, to defend their homes or to attack another in conquest, he is blessed by the Red God.

"A man who is willing to lay down his life for his family, his people, his nation, that man is blessed in his sight, and his death shall be a time of great mourning and celebration.

"Be it for gold or for honor or for duty, the man who dies an initiate *never* dies alone. For each of you are now obligated to attend the funeral of your fellow initiates, speak words over their grave, and help pray their souls to the halls of Duin the Destroyer."

Rondal looked up at the warrior-monk with a new appreciation for what the warfather had been doing. He looked around the low table they were gathered around.

From Rax, who would complain the gold you gave him was too shiny, to Jofard, who could inspire with his presence yet took orders with soldierly grace, to Walven, whose scheming mind and keen insight had allowed them to out-think their challenges, each of them had given something of themselves on this journey. He could have less stalwart squadmates, he decided. He had been fortunate. As rough as they had been coming into the Mysteries, now they knew how to work as a unit.

"Duin's Gift is death in battle," the Warbrother continued. "While the priestesses of Ishi and Trygg and Briga champion the force of Life, as they should, the gifts of the goddesses are for times of peace, and are there to bring comfort and growth. They are given to women, first and foremost, for women bear the future of Man.

"Duin's Gift is granted to menfolk, and his Mysteries reserved for us, for while we can serve the force of Life, as Huin does, the ability to slay and conquer is the responsibility of men alone. When invaders pour over the frontier, and women and children are safely within stone walls, it is the men of the domain who take up arms and give their lives to defend them.

"On women, the gift of life is bestowed, and they are reminded of this in blood every month. On men is the gift of death bestowed. We are reminded of this by the blood that stains your blade."

They were all silent for a few moments as they reflected on this. Rondal knew women fought – during the siege of Boval, plenty had taken up arms or supported the militia manning the walls. And he knew there were some militant orders of priestesses, even warsisters.

But he also knew that it was men who were the first in battle, and men who died first when invaders came. It was a heavy burden, knowing that to be a man meant dicing with death every time he picked up a sword.

"You all have been called to the Mysteries. You are learning the brotherhood of arms, the rites of war, the secret, sacred Mysteries of attack, defense, obedience, and duty.

"For when you all fight together, united in purpose, giving up your autonomy as warriors in exchange for the glory of a unified purpose. The honor of service to your fellow soldiers. Valor, my sons, is its own reward. Beyond domains and lands, titles and riches, to take up a sword and shield with stout comrades at your side . . . that, my sons, that is Duin's true gift to men!" the sermon concluded.

Eventually the time came to choose their War Names, an important part of the Mysteries. Now that they had been in – mock – battle together, the rite required that their comrades grant them the name by which they would someday face the War God.

Warbrother Thurgar oversaw the ritual, and called out the War Name when it was presented to him with a loud "Thus shall Duin greet thee as . . ."

Rondal became *Striker,* by unanimous acclamation.

Jofard became *Giant*, even though he wasn't exactly a giant.

Handol became *Hardhead*, for how poorly he picked up on advice. And for how well he could take a blow to the head.

Verd was called *Fleet*, because of his lightness and speed.

Rax was to be known as *Bloody*, after the practice skirmish in which his helmet had torn his scalp and he'd had to fight the rest of the day with a gruesome, bloody visage.

Dolwyn became known as *Fixer,* for his facility with trading and arranging deals with other units.

Orphil was called *Crusher*, for his fondness of the overhead stroke and preference for mass weapons.

Walven was given the name *Ace,* for his ability to lay out an opponent with one quick shot.

Gurandor was called *Snake,* for how stealthy he could be at need.

And Yeatin, whom none suspected would persevere this far, or even live through the Mysteries, was given the name of *Shatter* . . . mostly because he looked like he could shatter any time someone hit him.

The scrawny mage grinned proudly when it was bestowed to him, though. "Shatter" had a lot more style than "Yeatin", Rondal had to agree.

The Warbrother solemnly officiated the giving of names, and allowed each cadet the opportunity to speak a few words about his experience. When the last name had been given, he gave Duin's Blessing to them all, led them in a few hymns to the War God, and drank a cup of strong red wine with each of them before dismissing them for the night.

They walked back to camp slowly, thinking about the warrior-monk's sermon and its meaning. As most of the cadets had yet to return from their mission, the camp was quiet for once. Rondal called a final formation, in which he thanked them all for their service and valor, and called them each by their War Name. Then he oversaw the election of the next day's leader, and crawled gratefully into his blanket.

For two days the Third Squad had light duty as one by one the other squads wandered in. By the time the rest day dawned, almost all of the cadets had returned. Warbrothers rode through the countryside looking for a few stragglers, but the rest of the cadets were back at work. Thankfully, most of that work was mere instruction in the Laws of War from the sacred Book of Duin.

They learned the laws and rites devoted to siege warfare. They learned how a mercenary who was hired for garrison duty could not be used to fight in a conquest, without his leave. They learned the structure of rank in the new Royal Army and in various mercenary armies.

They learned a soldier's duty to a civilian, a noncombatant, and an insurgent. They learned the penalties for insubordination and disobedience, for being drunk on duty and for falling asleep on guard. They learned the rites and hymns sung at a brother's funeral, the proper greetings and salutations for a fellow initiate, and the law regarding prisoners, razing, pillaging, looting and rape.

It was a lot to remember. The laws handed down by Duin the Destroyer so long ago covered many elements of warfare, and the Imperial war gods, Gobarba and the others, were just as particular about how they were served.

When training commenced anew the following day, they put their new knowledge of siege warfare to work as they were instructed on how to build a field redoubt. Then, after every squad's efforts were judged, for the next two days they learned how to *attack* a field redoubt.

Then they learned how to dig a ditch, and spent two days doing nothing but digging a trench around a redoubt.

Then they learned the art of the ambush. Then how to move quietly through the swamps, responding to their squadleader's hand gestures as they had been instructed. They learned how to scout, how to report, and how to interrogate a prisoner.

All week they practiced. A few different types of artillery were assembled at one end of the field, and the redoubts the cadets had so painstakingly built were smashed to bits as the boys learned how to run a siege engine. The rubble that resulted was made into a huge bonfire.

The last two days of the Mysteries focused on unarmed combat: wrestling, punching, and maneuvers to use against an armed opponent. Rondal, who had always considered himself somewhat weak and puny, surprised himself by toppling Jofard the Giant within moments, using some clever leverage.

That's when Rondal realized that his long labor at the Mysteries had taken his puny body away and replaced it with a wiry, well-muscled one. When he drew back and pummeled the boy from First Squad, he was amazed at just how much power his shoulder and arms gave him. The boy from First Squad had to be led away to the warbrothers for tending his shattered nose.

Then one day dawned without them being awoken before the sun rose. Instead they were called from their blankets by a simple horn call for assembly. The units struggled into formation and were finally addressed by the swaggering commandant.

"Well, Neophytes, you have truly impressed all of us," he smiled. "Only four deaths this time, which makes this one of the more peaceful Mysteries. But those brothers will be granted Duin's grace posthumously and be considered initiates.

"As for the rest of you . . ." he said, grinning. There was a murmur of expectation among the ranks.

"When you came here, you were children. Now you are men. When you complete this rite, I will be glad to hail you as my brother-in-arms. Regardless of what side we fight on, we have all labored through the Mystery, and taken from it the blessings of strength."

The final ritual involved marching in formation through the gates of Relan Cor, parading past a throng of well-wishers from the citadel, and trading their wooden swords for the plain steel leaf-shaped infantry swords and steel bracelets that symbolized their completion of the Mystery.

Then they marched back to the practice ground for the last time, solemnly turned in their banners, and then each of them solemnly drank with wine to the health of them all from ewers borne by congratulatory warbrothers.

Then there was more drinking, of a far less religious nature.

"Ishi's *tits*, I never thought we'd make it through!" Rax said, his voice full of relief as he dipped his cup back into the ewer of wine. "If I never see the sun rise again, I'll count myself fortunate!"

"What are you going to do now?" asked Handol, looking relaxed for the first time in six weeks.

"Back home, to finish up my squirehood," Rax admitted. "But I might secure a place among the Baron's guard, with a Relan Cor certificate in my kit!"

"I'm for home, too," Jofard agreed with a smile. "If I take just a little too long getting upriver, I might just miss out on the end of plowing season."

"You *plow?*" asked Walven, surprised.

"He's big enough to pull one!" Dolwyn remarked.

"I don't plow," Jofard said, indignantly. "But my father makes me follow the reeves around to make them nervous. It's supposed to teach me how to run the estate. How about you, Ace?"

"I'm staying on to take advance classes," the Remeran informed them. "Siege warfare, in particular. I've already paid my tuition," Walven said, proudly.

"*Siege* warfare?" asked Dolwyn, surprised. "Isn't that hideously boring?"

"No more boring than garrison duty," Walven said. "Siege engineers are always in demand. But that's just my next lesson. I plan on getting plenty more after that. I'm for the Free Companies," he said, the closest thing to a boast that Rondal had heard from the boy.

"I am, too . . . just a little more directly," Orphil said, chuckling. "If I passed the Mysteries, I have a billet with the Bloody River Company. In Gilmora," he added, with a certain amount of relish.

"You're going to fight goblins!" Dolwyn said, enthusiastically. Last year's goblin invasion of the rich agricultural country had attracted mercenaries from all over, fighting at the king's expense. "I'm for the Free Companies, too, but I have no billet yet."

"I'm to go home and train the peasants," Rax said, discouraged. "All this beautiful lore about warfare, and I'm going to be making a bunch of clodfoots try to fight!"

"What about you sparks?" asked Walven, curious. "Where are you heading, Sir Striker?"

"I'm staying on," Rondal said. "For a while, at least. All three of us are. Warmage training. It's supposed to take another four weeks. Or more."

"Aw!" Orphil complained. "I was hoping you would come with me to the Bloody River."

"I've been to Gilmora," Rondal reminded him. "And I've seen enough goblins to last a bloody lifetime. But I expect I'll be back there before long. Uh, watch yourself. Those gurvani are nasty fighters."

"They won't be so bad," Orphil dismissed. "The Bloody River is three-thousand strong infantry and cavalry."

"You've never faced the goblins before," Rondal said to his squadmate, simply.

"I'll be fine. Hells, after the Mysteries, I feel like I could take on the Goblin King himself!"

Rondal let the brag pass – they had worked hard, they had achieved much, and they deserved a little over-enthusiasm, he reasoned. He had to admit, he was happy that the Mysteries were behind him, now. He felt strong, he felt dangerous, and he felt as if he had become something more than when he'd started.

In fact . . . he didn't even feel like a mage. He wasn't Sir Rondal, Knight Magi, or even Magelord Rondal of Sevendor, he was *Striker* now. He looked around at his comrades and smiled. He had liked few of them when the trials began, but now he couldn't think of any of them – even annoying Yeatin – with anything but fondness.

"My lord?" came a timid voice from the front of their camp. "My lord? Sir Rondal of Sevendor?" It was a young page, no more than eleven, wearing a yellow tabard with the arms of Relan Cor on them in black.

"Yes?" Rondal asked, almost not recognizing his name.

"My lord, you are bidden to come to the Master of Warmagic's office," he explained, nervously. "Then I'm to take you to your assigned quarters. At your convenience," the lad added, when the celebrating cadets looked at him harshly for interrupting their reverie.

"All right," sighed Rondal. "There you go, fellas. Duty calls. I've got to go play magelord, now."

There was a chorus of groans from them, and for the next ten minutes the initiates – the soldiers – said their farewells. There were more than a few tears, and declarations of admiration abounded. Rondal finally tore himself away, hefted his pack, tucked his new – plain and serviceable – infantry sword into his belt, and followed the page.

*   *   *

It was odd to be inside Relan Cor after camping in its shadow for six weeks, but while he had sweated and bled and struggled the business of the War College went on. He passed pages and soldiers and advanced students and masters as he found Master Valwyn in his office. For all he knew, the man hadn't moved from the spot since he left him, more than a moon ago.

"Ah! Well done, Initiate!" he said warmly, rising when he recognized Rondal. "Well done! I've had several good reports of you during your training. And your squad went on to win the bivouac competition -- that's outstanding!" He made a note on a piece of parchment in front of him.

"Thank you, Sir," Rondal said, coming to attention automatically.

"At ease," Master Valwyn dismissed. "I'm looking forward to your warmage classes," he added, as he got up and retrieved Rondal's witchstone from the box on the book shelf. "I've been talking to your fellow apprentice, and he speaks very highly of you."

"*Really?*" snorted Rondal, surprised. "Tyndal? Sir?" he added, belatedly.

Master Valwyn chuckled. "Quite so," he agreed, setting the box down on the desk. "He's had nothing but praise for you, although he considers you somewhat . . . bookish."

Rondal snorted again. "I'll keep my opinions about him to myself, if you don't mind, Sir," he said ruefully.

"I *thought* I detected a little acrimony there," Valwyn said, as he dispelled his spellbinding.

Rondal did the same, which was difficult after six weeks of using very little magic. He had to apply himself far more than he anticipated to finish the work. But soon the glittering field around the small box fell.

Holding his breath, he worried for no good reason that his stone would not be in the box, he opened it. Much to his relief it was, indeed, still there, and his mind rushed to contact it the moment the lid was open.

"Ahhhh!" Rondal said, as the first waves of power washed through him. "I'd forgotten how much I missed that!"

"I'm envious," chuckled Valwyn. "Oh, I'll get one eventually – they already want me to ship to Gilmora and lead a troop of cavalry – but I can't help but covet that kind of power."

"It's a heady thing," Rondal agreed. He eagerly examined his stone, inside and out, until he was satisfied that it was still the powerful shard he'd left there. "But it's dangerous, too. I probably shouldn't have been given one, but . . . well, necessity is a bitch who drives us all, Sir."

"Look not on it as misplaced in your hands, Son," suggested Master Valwyn. "Just . . . *early*. I was serious, Sir Rondal. The warbrothers were keeping a *very* close eye on you and your squad. By all accounts, you are an excellent soldier.

"From what I understand, after your camp was attacked instead of pursuing bloody vengeance your squad focused on the mission. That's admirable . . . and rare. And I also heard how you led the charge through the defenders in the village. Whatever your master was thinking when he gave you that stone, his confidence has *not* been misplaced."

Rondal wasn't sure what to say to that. "Well, thank you, Sir. When do classes begin?"

"Three days from now," the master of warmagic informed him. "We're still awaiting six students. We have twenty from the Mysteries, but there are several more already arrived and waiting. But . . . you have three days, if you want to get some leave and celebrate a bit."

Rondal thanked the mage and then followed the page deep into the recesses of the fortress, where he was given a room.

A double room.

There were two cots inside, one on each side of the room. As it was designed for four soldiers, there was almost enough room for two, following standard military logic. But Rondal didn't have to guess who his roommate was. He recognized Tyndal's baggage and the trademark disheveled state of his side of the room.

"Ishi's tits!" he swore, angrily. "Was there no more room elsewhere?"

212

"I was informed that you were to bunk together," the page said, diplomatically. "By your master's orders."

"We'll see about that!" Rondal said. He tipped the boy a penny after he'd carried his baggage inside the room and set it on the press at the end of his bed. Then he sat on the straw tick, closed his eyes, and reached out with his mind. It had been awhile, but the spell came back to him easily enough.

Master, it is Rondal, he announced, when Master Minalan deigned to answer his call.

Rondal! How fared you in camp?

My squad excelled, Master. Thank you for the opportunity.

That's amazing! Well done, lad! How are you holding up after . . . after Inrion? he asked, concerned.

I'm fine, Master, Rondal assured him. *The Mysteries were a great distraction. But I am speaking with you because I've been told that Tyndal and I have to bunk together, per your orders.*

That is correct, Minalan said, simply.

But . . . why? Rondal demanded.

Because I know you two have some business to finish, the Spellmonger told him. *And avoiding it and avoiding each other isn't going to make it go away. Quite the contrary.*

Master, he blames me—

I don't want to hear it, Minalan snapped. *Figure it out, Rondal. There are . . . there's a lot going on right now, and I need both of you trained, fit, and ready to do my bidding. Soon.*

Master, are we not always doing your bidding?

Do my bidding better, the magelord corrected. *You still have a few weeks of warmagic school. Try to work out whatever it is between you before you return to Sevendor.*

But Master—

Do it! insisted the Spellmonger. *I know Tyndal is kind of an ass. But I still need him. And you. And I need you to be able to work together. Anything else?* he asked, impatiently.

No, Master, admitted Rondal, sourly.

Then take a day or so to relax and then prepare for your studies. If I recall correctly, warmage school was only slightly better than infantry training.

Yes, Master, Rondal said, and ended the connection.

"Damn," he said, out loud.

*   *   *

For two days, Rondal avoided Tyndal mostly by being elsewhere.

At first he spent his time in the village tavern, saying a more thorough good-bye to his squadmates as they took barges or horses toward their destinations one by one. Gurandor and Yeatin, who were scheduled to continue to Warmagic classes, were housed in the barracks in the fortress, but spent plenty of time in the tavern – the *Iron Gate,* named for the device of Relan Cor.

The village inn was a busy place, thrice the size of a normal inn, with two additional bays and a side house. With soldiers, warriors, knights and mercenaries constantly coming and going, the inn had a lot of business . . . and a lot of fights.

The public room at the *Iron Gate's* heart was the haunt of old soldiers, mercenaries, and students in the art of warfare who lingered near the War College. The décor reflected its use, with souvenirs of campaigns, banners of defeated enemies, ancient swords notched with battle, and battered pieces of armor hanging from the rafters and walls.

Tyndal seemed to be avoiding Rondal as much as Rondal was avoiding him. He seemed to spend an awful lot of time working with various masters-of-arms in the practice yard, honing his swordplay. Sometimes he worked with a mock mageblade, sometimes with a cavalry sword, sometimes with an infantry sword. But he was getting better and better, Rondal could see from afar, even though he still made a lot of mistakes.

Rondal tried his best to put him out of his mind.

He had a somewhat different perspective, after the Mysteries. He knew it was unfair of Tyndal to blame him for Estasia's death, but that did not deter his guilt over the matter. While the sting of it had faded, the burden of it had only grown. He imagined what she might say to him several times, but each time he found himself thinking such maudlin thoughts he found something physical and punishing to do.

When he got back to his room, if he was first, he tried to get to sleep before Tyndal got in. Tyndal, he noticed, always seemed to be asleep when he came in. They spoke barely five words to each other in three days.

Finally, they were called to the Assembly Hall on the first floor for their first classes of Warmagic school, and he was able to let the volume of work occupy his mind instead.

There were thirty-seven pupils for the class, most of them young magi with the ink still wet on their charters. A few were older and had sought out the training because they wanted to go to the Penumbra and try their luck to find a stone. Compared to Infantry Training, it was almost as studious and civilized as Inrion Academy.

Master Valwyn was the one who addressed them first, giving a long rambling speech on the history of Warmagic, its current utility, and the importance of the Magical Corps in the defense of the kingdom. He referenced the goblin invasion several times, but did not dwell on it.

Valwyn instead spoke about the Mad Mage of Farise and the threat he posed, and the gallant attack by the best warmagi in the Duchies that defeated him. He spoke of great Warmagi of old, told of their achievements, and praised the brave men and women fighting in the new Arcane Orders.

215

Rondal listened but did not pay attention; he was just grateful for the warm clothes, dry bed, and full belly his now-muscular body seemed to cherish. As much as he had come to appreciate the brutal efficiency of the soldier's life, he still felt more at home around the smell of dust and parchment than he did leather and steel.

A few other prominent magi spoke, both militant and civilian, and Magelord Hartarian, the new Royal Court Mage and former Censor General, addressed them with a plea for more recruits for duty in the Penumbra, and a commendation for the nascent Iron Ring order that was beginning to police its frontier. Then there was a light reception, allowing the students and the faculty to casually discuss the curriculum and readings, of which there were many.

Master Valwyn would be lecturing them in the Philosophy of Warmagic, he knew, as well as Defensive Combat Spells. The compact warmage was a veteran of Farise and several years' honorable service on the frontier with Alshar. He wore a smart little red cap – Rondal found out later it was the traditional cap of a professional warmage seeking employment, in some quarters – had a lively manner about him. A good choice for the job, Rondal decided.

Beside him, Master Sirisan would be teaching them everything he knew about war wands, Master Renando of Cormeer would discuss the basics of using a mageblade, as well as running several practical drills, and Master Loiko himself would be teaching them Offensive Combat Magic. There were other teachers and lecturers on other subjects, but those were the ones Rondal was most interested in.

He gravitated toward one side of the trestle table where Gurandor was hovering over a plate of tiny sausages and a stack of buns. Rondal grabbed one of both and started nibbling.

Rondal looked around the room. "A bit of a stuffy crowd, for warmagi," he murmured to his former squadmate.

"The real tough ones are at the front," the other mage pointed out. "That's probably where I'm going, eventually."

216

"Wait long enough, the front will come here," he remarked sourly, between bites. "Some of these fellows are rather good," Rondal pointed out.

Gurandor ceded the point. "You don't go up against Orril Pratt with a couple of cantrips and a winning attitude. Master Valwyn is famous for some of the spells he oversaw at the conquest of Farise. And Master Loiko . . . he's the best." The mention of the war made him think again of Kaffin of Gyre, and how much Rondal hated the boy. Now that he understood what a sword could do, he looked forward to the day where he could use one on Kaffin.

Or a wand. Or a rock. Rondal wasn't picky.

As if to add to his sour mood, Tyndal picked that moment to blunder by.

"My lords," he said, with slight exaggeration. He was wearing a green velvet tunic, suitable for formal occasions, and Rondal was loath to admit he looked quite regal in it. "I hope that lecture didn't keep you awake."

"After Infantry Training," Gurandor said, with a sneer, "there's not much that could keep me awake. My bones still ache! So what have they been keeping you busy with while we've been at the Mysteries?"

"Mostly swordplay," Tyndal admitted. "There are some outstanding swordsmen here. Masters of the mageblade. I've been sparring as much as possible. And occasionally hitting the Warmagic Library."

"I didn't know there was a Warmagic Library," Rondal said, thoughtfully. "And I'm twice as surprised that you knew of it."

"I like to take the opportunity to improve myself," Tyndal said, vainly. "There are whole tomes of nastiness in there. Some of it is even proscribed, marked with a big FOR EDUCATIONAL PURPOSES ONLY – PENALTY FOR USE letter attached. But . . . *fascinating.*"

"I look forward to taking a run at it," Rondal said, cordially.

"You'll love it, Ron," Tyndal assured. "And . . . I actually passed a few examinations after you left Inrion," he added, proudly. "Mathematics, Geometry, Basic Elemental Theory, Practical Cantrips, a couple of others."

"I'm delighted," Rondal said through clenched teeth.

Tyndal finally caught that Rondal was behaving coolly toward him, and a look of confusion crossed his face. "Uh . . ." he said, looking at Gurandor, "can we have a moment's privacy?"

Gurandor sized up Tyndal. "Let me know if you need help, Striker," he said, and headed for the other end of the table.

"What is wrong with you?" Tyndal demanded in a whisper, when they were out of earshot.

"Whatever do you mean?" Rondal asked, sarcastically as he bit into a sausage.

"I mean you've been acting like I took a dump in your hat since the moment I got here!" he said, harshly.

"I have been occupied with my studies," the older boy said, irritated. "Did you need me to brush your hair or something?"

"You've been avoiding me," Tyndal accused. "Like I have the pox."

"How do I know you don't?" Rondal challenged.

"See?" Tyndal pointed out. "That's just not like you!"

"What isn't like me?"

"You . . . acting like a . . . a . . ."

Thankfully, they were interrupted by the imposing figure of Master Hartarian. A High Mage like them, he carried his shard of irionite in a golden cage around his neck. He towered over them both. The former head of the Royal Censorate of Magic, he looked less at-ease in civilian life than he had as head of the order. Here he fit in admirably.

"Hail, good knights magi!" he said, smiling just a little too broadly. "I am pleased to see you both here. I've been speaking with your master frequently, of late, and he asked me to check on your condition.

So . . . still have all your limbs, I see," he chuckled.

"The night is still young, Master," Tyndal said, slyly. "But we appreciate your oversight. Don't we, Rondal?"

"Of course," Rondal agreed, politely. "And we look forward to the opportunity to improve our skills."

"That's encouraging to hear," Hartarian sighed, filling his wine cup from the table. "As busy as things are at the capital, now, we're going to need all the warriors we can field in Gilmora this summer. I expect you two will be prominent?"

"That depends entirely on the mood of our master," Rondal said, before Tyndal could say anything. "He has yet to disclose what tasks he has in mind for us."

"I'm sure fighting goblins will be mentioned," Tyndal grinned.

"Sir Tyndal was just telling me how proud he was at passing his recent examinations at Inrion, Master Hartarian," Rondal said, conversationally. "Didn't your niece attend Inrion?"

"Only for six months," he sighed. "She did most of her schooling at Alar. Although I dare say she has picked up a few things at court," he said.

Rondal could guess there was a story there, but he didn't feel confident to ask of the mysterious Lady Isily. She had been a close aide to their master during the Battle of Timberwatch, but apparently they'd had a falling out. Tyndal knew something about it, but he had yet to share the intelligence with Rondal due to its sensitive nature, and it remained a mystery.

"So what subjects did you complete, then, Sir Tyndal?"

"Uh . . . Mathematics. Lesser Elemental Theory. Geometry," he said, each admission of success in the basic levels of knowledge making the boy squirm in front of the most senior mage in the kingdom.

"Don't forget 'Practical Cantrips'," Rondal reminded him with just a hair too much enthusiasm.

"Yes," Tyndal said, slowly. "Practical Cantrips."

Master Hartarian looked at the boys thoughtfully. "Well done," he said, without much eagerness. "And how about you, Sir Rondal?"

"I am well into my intermediate course of study in Thaumaturgy, Master," he answered, ignoring Tyndal's embarrassment. "I'm hoping to pursue some Enchantment, if I have the opportunity."

"Thaumaturgy and Enchantment?" Hartarian said, impressed. "Those are difficult subjects."

"You'll find Sir Rondal excels at the difficult," Tyndal said, recovering somewhat. "It's rare you find a book without his nose somewhere in the vicinity."

"One must put them somewhere," Rondal said, smoothly.

"The kingdom will be full of opportunities for a couple of bright young lads like yourself," Hartarian assured them, ignoring their blatant rivalry. "I look forward to reporting to your master how diligent you've been."

When the court mage had wandered off to speak to some more senior warmagi, Tyndal stepped uncomfortably close to Rondal. "What the hells was *that?*"

"What?" Rondal asked, innocently.

"Mentioning my examinations!" he said angrily, his nostrils flaring.

"I thought you were *proud* of your examinations," Rondal shrugged.

"Not in my *remedial* classes!" Tyndal said. "Nor was that news for Master Hartarian's ears! He's the Royal Court Wizard!"

"You said it plainly enough for mine and Gurandor's!" Rondal countered.

"You know *exactly* what I mean!" Tyndal said, his face burning.

"Do I?" Rondal said, pushing past him. "You mean, how I pointed out that you are *years* behind me in study? Or how you actually passed a few – remedial – examinations, finally?"

"Well . . . both! Neither! Bah! You are infuriating!" Tyndal fumed as he stomped off.

Gurandor came back the moment Tyndal left the reception. "What was that about?"

"A difference of opinion," Rondal said, tight-lipped. "It's nothing. What do you say we leave this lovely and utterly uninteresting reception and walk down to the village? I'll buy," he added. Among his other belongings he'd made the re-acquaintance of, his purse was one of the dearest. And while he rarely indulged in drink to any great degree, Rondal was suddenly feeling like doing so.

"You're buying?" Gurandor, who had arrived at Relan Cor with little coin in his purse, asked excitedly. "Then let's go. I'm suddenly finding myself quite thirsty."

"Me, too," Rondal said, his eyes narrowing. Perhaps, just perhaps, Tyndal would have the same idea, and they would chance to meet on the way down or back.

*   *   *

Classes began in earnest the next day, and despite drinking far more than he was accustomed to, Rondal managed to make it back to bed in good order. Interestingly enough, Tyndal had been in his bunk neither when he arrived nor later, when he awoke. Rondal was concerned for a moment, and thought about calling him mind-to-mind, but then decided against it. Instead he wandered down to the mess hall, grabbed a mug of ale and a sweet roll, and headed for class.

It was warwands, today, taught by Master Sirisan, a veteran warmage long retired, and it was in an auxiliary dining hall that had been converted to use as a classroom by the expedient of placing twenty long benches in front of the main table.

Master Sirisan was situated behind the lectern. He looked five years older than dirt to Rondal, with a long flowing beard and voluminous red robes. Rondal quickly realized that Master Sirisan was enamored of the sound of his own voice.

Tyndal was there, too – sitting to the right, and all the way in the back. Rondal made his way to the left, and moved all the way down to the front. Master Sirisan had just begun the meat of his lecture.

". . . the warwand, along with the mageblade, is the basic weapon of the warmagi," the old instructor said, demonstrating with an eighteen-inch plain wooden wand. "Why use a wand? First we should ask . . . what *is* a wand? Anyone?"

"A stick," answered someone from behind Rondal. There was a titter of giggles.

"Yes, a stick. A wand is a *stick*. A humble piece of wood, usually no longer than your forearm and no thicker than your wrist. As such, it is the basis of many other weapons. Put a rock at the end, it is a mace. Put a thick piece of metal at the end, it becomes a hammer. Sharpen it, it is an axe. A thin piece of pointy metal at the end, a spear. A wire or rope, it becomes a whip.

"But a warwand is not a mere haft or handle," he continued, beginning to pace slowly in front of the class. "The purpose of the warwand is not to become other weapons, but to become a weapon itself. So . . . why use a wand?"

"It's free!" came another mage's answer. That inspired some giggles, too.

"Sometimes," conceded Master Sirisan. "But that is not why; it is merely a contributing factor. No, we use a stick for our warmagic because first and foremost, it *points*." He indicated the function by pointing at various things around the room.

"As I'm sure we all remember from Geometry, any two points connected will form a straight line . . . and by extension, a ray. From the tip of the wand," he said, demonstrating with his inert model, "extending in a ray from base and point, the line will continue to be straight right off into infinity.

"But it only points to one direction. Direction is very important for many warmagic spells. One does not want to hit one's friend, after all, but the foe. Sticks *excel* at pointing." More chuckles. The old man smiled at the response and continued.

"Secondly, we use a wand for our warmagic in many cases because the effect of the spell we choose to bring down our enemies may be too potent to discharge in close proximity to our persons without injury.

"The warwand has the advantage of keeping the magical death you have conjured at least a span away from your delicate fingers. Indeed, a protective element is often a component of the enchantments used for warwands. It also helps preserve the device for multiple uses." He walked in front of the lectern, and suddenly threw the stick to the floor.

"Thirdly, we use warwands because, unlike our mageblades, they are *disposable*. That is, any given piece of wood will only hold so much enchantment before the arcane pressures overcome its natural resiliency. Usually no more than one type of spell, and with limited energy. Once those charges are discharged . . . well, your warwand may make a lovely conversation piece, but *don't* try to re-enchant one. Only a few specialized woods, such as weirwood, or socohol, can safely be used more than once. Which is why weirwood is so precious." He picked another stick out of a basket of them next to the lectern.

"A warwand, once exhausted, can be safely discarded without regret. Indeed, carrying a variety of warwands can be a decided advantage for the warmage, as not every permutation of magical expression is going to be unchallenged. Finding your only means of attack is pointless because of counterspells is disappointing. Being able to switch from, say, a direct physical attack to a more subtle magical one gives the warmage a powerful advantage."

Rondal knew the pragmatic use of that rule himself – twice during the siege at Boval he had tried to discharge a wand at a goblin shaman, only to have the spell negated by some arcane defense. Being able to switch to another wand with a different profile quickly had saved his life.

"The basic theory is simple: after proper preparation, the wand is invested with energy, directed, shaped, and tuned by the warmage, that can be converted into a useful – and by that I mean deadly – purpose. These spells can cause fire, plasma, lightning, pure physical force, sound, and far more subtle and insidious effects.

"Today we are going to use a very basic enchantment to create a simple Cisguyine Wand. These were once very popular in antiquity, and were even provided to guardsmen in the great cities of the Magocracy to break up fights."

"Are we just going to learn about stunning wands?" asked a young mage Rondal didn't know.

"There are over three hundred varieties of warwand cataloged here in Relan Cor's library – some haven't been used since the Magocracy. And practicing warmagi have been adding their own variations for centuries. While we are using the Cisguyine Wand as an example I encourage you to explore the other varieties available to you. You should have plenty of opportunity to find the wand enchantments that work best for you.

"We have provided a sufficiency of wand blanks for your use. None of them are what I would call 'superior' for such duty, but all are adequate for simple use. Today we will be learning the basics of the craft, and over the next several days we will be expanding that knowledge to include the basic permutations of force one can manifest through a warwand."

After that he invited everyone up to select a blank upon which to practice the craft, while he began sketching the runes used in the process on the slate behind him.

What kind did you get? Tyndal asked, when Rondal answered his call mind-to-mind.

What does it matter? Rondal asked, annoyed. *Is it really important?*

I was just wondering. I like wand work.

I know. Big hero of Boval Castle. I remember.

I was just curious. I got an oak.

Birch, Rondal replied with a mental grunt. *Happy?*

Blissful. Why are you so mad at me?

Go play with your wand.

Rondal ended the connection abruptly, and focused on the lecture. Master Sirisan outlined the process for proper vetting and examination of the piece before serious enchantment began, and went over the signs that a wand was unworthy of use. Rondal did his best to ignore the seething he felt when he even thought of his fellow apprentice, right up to the point of charging the wand.

"Now, the advantage of the Cisguyine wand is its relative ease of enchantment. Once you have done the proper preparation, it is time to charge it, using the filter of your emotions to determine the strength of the charge.

"Don't be discouraged if your first attempts lack luster. Some warmagi who build deadly wands with ease still find the Cisguyine unwilling to be bridled by their Talent. But using the Nekarth Rune as a conduit allows you to add emotional energy to filter the magical. The more intense the emotion you can generate, the more powerful the result.

Rondal understood that – the Nekarth Rune had a strong emotional component, which kept it from being useful for many sophisticated magics. But for such simplistic things as stunning a man unconscious, it was of good utility.

As he poured power into the rune, after inscribing it lightly on the wand, Tyndal tried yet again to speak mind-to-mind. Rondal did not answer . . . but the resulting surge in emotion almost made him lose focus and wreck the enchantment.

Angrily, he maintained control, and poured the anger into the enchantment. When he had completed the charge, Master Sirisan instructed them in creating the mnemonic trigger that would release the

225

effect.

"Theoretically," the old warmage continued, when the final stage of the ritual was complete, "a Cisguyine should have a potent effect on the target within fifty feet. Further than that and the effect diffuses quickly. While that may not seem helpful in a battle, it does make Cisguyine an excellent alternative to a deadlier device. And many higher-level warmagi stupidly forget to cast counterspells. I have seen contests where the Cisguyine Wand settled the matter.

"The stunning effect lasts no more than ten minutes, which is why this wand is favored by footwizards well-read enough to have mastered it. That is, apparently, enough time to get away from a bandit . . . or an angry customer," he chuckled, as did several of the magi in the class. "It will also stun a horse of decent size for at least five minutes or a hound for an hour, based on the strength of the charge, which often puts a cavalryman at a disadvantage."

They continued through the rest of the exercise until they had finished with a binding rune. When they were done, the lightly-etched wand felt pleasantly warm in his hands. That was a bit of an illusion – most of the heat had been absorbed by his own hands. But he was satisfied with the result. Not the most complicated wand in the world, but he was glad he had learned the craft to make it.

"Now we are going to test our devices," Master Sirisan said with a twinkle in his eye. "To do that, let us pair up. I trust none of these are so powerful that we must fear injury, but I have had a room prepared with additional rushes to cushion any falls." He led them all to another room across the corridor, smaller than the lecture hall. Then he invited the class to square off against each other two at a time.

The first few bouts were exciting, due to the novelty. A tall man in green went up against a shorter, stockier man in yellow. The man in yellow prevailed, sending the man in green crumbling to the floor.

"Drag him into the corner until he wakes," Master Sirisan instructed. "I'd like to make the observation that if one wishes to use a warwand, then one should consider carefully when pointing. As good as wands

226

are at pointing, they are only as good as the eye of the master who wields them.

"The secret," he confided, "is to forget *aiming*, as you would do with a bow or arbalest, and simply . . . *point*," he said. "Imagine the wand as a finger. When you point with your finger, you never miss. Point with your wand and have faith that your hand and eye know better together than you do."

The next bout was between a slender young woman with an unfortunate face and a well-muscled mage from the south. The man from the south was slower, and joined the man in green snoring in the corner.

"Alacrity is frequently a component in successfully using a wand," Master Sirisan lectured. "The young man made the mistake of a six-syllable mnemonic, whereas the young lady's was but three. You can see the difference three syllables can make," he said, as the southern mage was dragged away.

Two by two the class tried their wands. Gurandor was taken down by a Gilmoran mage who in turn was taken down by Rondal's comrade Yeatin. Both were dragged to the corner just as the man in green was waking. Then it was Rondal's turn. He walked to the other end of the chamber and waited for an opponent.

Of course Tyndal had to be the one to face him.

You sure you want to do this? Rondal asked, mind-to-mind.

Are you kidding? This is fun! Usually when I blast someone, they stay blasted. This way we get to see who the better wand maker is!

Rondal didn't reply. He was busy fuming over Tyndal's arrogance and competitive nature. The big stupid puppy thought this was a *game* . . . another chance for him to score an easy victory.

Rondal planned on disabusing him of that notion. He waited until Master Sirisan dropped his arm and told them to begin . . . and while Tyndal was still raising his arm, Rondal merely bent his wrist and elbow.

"Pen-ol!" he said, as quickly as he could as he willed the wand to discharge. He'd chosen the word – the old Narasi term for 'ass' – because of its brevity. He felt the surge of power through the stick as it fired. Tyndal crumpled to the floor before his wand was half-way raised.

"Impressive," Master Sirisan nodded, approvingly. "Very efficiently played, Sir Rondal."

Instead of ten minutes, however, Sir Tyndal was still snoring more than thirty minutes later, when Master Sirisan finally used a waking charm on him to rouse him from consciousness.

"Where is everyone?" he asked, confused. Rondal watched from just outside of the corridor, where his fellow apprentice could not spot him.

"Gone, already," the old man chuckled. "An excellent display of wand work."

"Thank you, Master," Tyndal said as he struggled to his feet.

"Oh, I didn't mean you," the master warmage laughed. "No, Sir Tyndal, you never even uttered the command. Your fellow Sir Rondal took the bout. And . . . from the length of your slumber, I'd say he put a fair sum of emotional energy into the device. To look at him, you wouldn't think he'd be capable. But his effect lasted the longest of any of them."

"Really?" Tyndal asked, sitting up. "Here I thought I was better at warwands."

"It seems Sir Rondal has improved," the master said diplomatically as he helped the mage knight to his feet.

"Yes," Tyndal said, shaking his head. "He's full of surprises."

Smiling smugly to himself, Rondal left without seeing Tyndal, heading down to the library to begin research on new wand types. He was suddenly feeling *quite* competitive.

*   *   *

The next day found them both in the spacious indoor practice yard Relan Cor boasted. A few permanent magelights hung from the vaulted ceilings and wooden swords and blunted steel ones lined the walls. The thick pile of rushes had been well-trod, and here and there one might encounter bloodstains.

That day their topic was mageblades, and the man who taught the subject was a master of the art of magical swordplay: Master Renando of Cormeer.

Master Renando was a slender man with dark hair and a sharply-cut Imperial beard, and he looked, at first glance, more like a coinbrother or a shoemaker than a warmage.

But Rondal knew Renando was an acknowledged master warmage, and one of the best swordsmen in or out of the trade. He considered it a privilege to learn from him, and found a spot near to him on the man's left. Tyndal filed in late and went to the right.

Master Renando shot Tyndal an irritated glance but did not comment. The master of the mageblade sat utterly still on a stool in front of a wall upon which were hung several swords. He addressed the students in a loud, clear voice with a manner and Cormeeran accent that seemed perpetually amused.

"A sword," he began, "is a blade, a sharpened edge used to puncture or slash. Within that definition, ladies and gentlemen," he said, rising smoothly, "there are hundreds, if not thousands, of variations. Length. Width. Shape. Material. A sword can be made out of copper, bronze, iron, steel, or metals more exotic. It can be whittled out of bone or chipped out of stone. It can be straight, curved, pointed, blunted, one-sided, two-sided, one-handed, two-handed, heavy, light, pretty, ugly, mundane, or magical.

"But at the core, a blade is a sharpened edge. Swung with force. Sufficient to cut the intended target . . . or block a cut meant for you.

"For a sword is not merely an offensive weapon, as a bow, an arbalest, or even most wands; a sword is an offensive and a defensive weapon. It can prevent harm, as well as inflict it.

"More, it is a tool; a tool whose primary purpose is violent, but which can be employed in non-violent ways, by those skilled in its use."

He walked over to the wall, and began gesturing to weapons, naming them as he did. He began with one Rondal had become intimately familiar with in the Mysteries.

"First, we have the short infantry sword. This example is from the barbarians on the steppes, a horse-loving people. Yet the first weapon a boy is given in manhood is an infantry sword. The idea is that a warrior's first duty is to protect his village or encampment from enemies. A defensive role. For this he was given a blade no longer than his arm, double edged with a point. With it, he could stand and fight toe-to-toe with any who invaded. Across the centuries, the short infantry sword has proven the most efficient of weapons." He crossed to the next example, familiar by sight but not use. Rondal was an unenthusiastic horseman at best.

"When a man climbs on horseback, he seeks to extend his reach, and therefore extends his blade. The double-sided cavalry longsword, as favored by the Narasi cavalry in this day and age, is a highly effective way of projecting force against the heads of your foes. Combined with the lance and shield, it makes heavy cavalry virtually invulnerable. Combined with bow and axe, it makes light cavalry extremely effective. The cavalry of the Farisi, such as they were, used a curved version of the sword, which actually provides greater cutting leverage."

He turned to face them, as he stood in front of another example Rondal was familiar with.

"What, then, of the mageblade?" he asked. "Longer than an infantry blade, shorter than a cavalry blade, not much guard to speak of in most cases, a hilt long enough for two hands but a blade that needs but one to lift it. It was crafted originally by the great magi of Lost Perwyn, who sought to give it what neither the cavalry blade nor the infantry sword possessed.

"Versatility."

He took the blade off the wall and turned to show it to them, holding it up in profile. "The mageblade is not designed to decapitate from horseback. But it can. Nor is it made exclusively to defend on foot, but it is well suited for that purpose. The ideal mageblade was forged from the finest steel, and enchanted throughout the process, to build for the warmage the perfect extension of his arm and his Talent. The perfect tool for killing. The perfect vessel for wielding magic."

He pulled the sword suddenly to guard, and then saluted. "The mageblade is not merely a blade; it is also, in its way, a wand. It can direct magical force, convey magical power, and respond to arcane command, once properly enchanted. The steel is strong enough to keep it from snapping, and when it is finished the spells improving its strength also allow it to be used in a variety of ways. As a ladder, to get over a wall," he said, leaning the sword up against the bench and then using its guard as a step.

"As a balance," he said, using his feet to shift his weight on the sword until it was balanced perfectly over the bench, his slender slippers on hilt and point. "As a lever," he said, shifting his feet again, which shot the sword upward. He caught it deftly in one hand just as his feet hit the floor. "The mageblade is not merely a tool of war; it is a tool of magic."

"But the ones we're issuing you lot," he added, "are crappy, rusty old practice pieces with nary a spell upon them. Because long before you learn to use the powers and versatility of the mageblade's full arcane potential . . . you're going to learn how to use it as a sword. Just a sword. But the right kind of sword . . . for just about anything."

Rondal looked at his 'new' mageblade, a cold steel blunted sword that had seen hundreds of sparring matches. He had his real mageblade of course, a serviceable but simple sword, a gift from Master Minalan, back in his quarters, but he was forbidden to use it. Not that it would have given him much advantage – it had only a few basic enchantments on it. But it was a real mageblade, not a practice blade.

231

"Feel the grip in your hands," the Master urged, "feel the length and balance of the sword. A master warmage knows his mageblade better than his pecker. Just to ensure that you do understand the depth of that knowledge, one of the first spells I'm going to teach you is known in the trade as the Bladelore spell, or more properly Gurther's Exploration. In this meditation you will extend your consciousness into the steel of your blade and get to know it, layer by layer, inch by inch, until you know it the way your tongue knows the back of your teeth. Let's begin . . ."

Rondal threw himself into the meditation without much native enthusiasm . . . but he knew how to study a spell. Under Master Renando's patient instruction he – along with the rest of his troop – crawled through their blades, mentally speaking, from hilt to point.

Rondal could tell his particular sword had been broken and mended twice, and was particularly strong along the forte of the blade. It was balanced too blade-heavily in his hand, and the leather that wrapped the hilt was soaked with the sweat of dozens of other students.

"Once you know the blade," Master Renando continued, when they had completed the two-hour long meditation, "then you can begin to understand how to use it. And using it in combat is different than other sorts of swordplay. So you will learn the basic postures and positions our tradition brings us: the Sword Dance of the Magi."

They spent the rest of the afternoon learning the rudiments of the positions and the transitions. Thanks to Master Minalan's insistence, Rondal was already fairly familiar with the Sword Dance, up to the first eight movements. Master Renando complimented him on his stance when he came by, even.

When the time came to pair off with sparring partners, Rondal made certain that he found Gurandor before Tyndal found him. No need for another awkward confrontation.

They hacked at each other in slow motion as Master Renando instructed the class in swordplay at half-speed. He almost forgot his fellow apprentice was there until the last few minutes of the class, when the master instructed everyone to switch partners. Tyndal tried to get to Rondal, he saw, but Rondal was able to snag a short hairy Remeran instead.

"That was a lot of fun," Gurandor said as the class broke up. "A lot more fun than infantry drills."

"It's a whole different style," agreed Rondal, who had not minded learning shield work. Few warmagi used shields. "Fighting with a mageblade makes you a lot more vulnerable."

"But a lot more deadly," Gurandor countered. "Once you add in the spellwork—uh oh. The Haystack is heading this way, Striker."

"The Haystack" was what Gurandor had taken to calling Tyndal, after the shaggy mop on his head that seemed to turn brighter and more golden every day.

"You want a quick bout, Ron?" he asked, invitingly . . . as if it was a privilege.

"I'm done for the day," he answered, coolly. "You should able to find a pick-up match though."

"All right," Tyndal said, though he didn't look intrigued by the prospect. "Is something wrong?"

"What do you mean?" Rondal asked as he folded his equipment.

"You know damn well what I mean!" Tyndal said in a low voice.

Rondal looked around. He didn't want to make a scene.

What are you talking about? He demanded of Tyndal, mind-to-mind.

You've been acting strange since I got here, Tyndal accused.

In what way?

"*I . . . well, you aren't being your old friendly self,*" Tyndal began.

You mean I'm standing up for myself and not taking your abuse?

What abuse? Tyndal asked. *I've been nothing but nice!*

Rondal didn't have an answer for that. Tyndal had been nothing but nice. In a condescending and arrogant way. He decided to try another approach.

"Do you really think that what happened at Inrion I'm just going to . . . to . . ."

"To what?" Tyndal asked. *"And a lot happened at Inrion. For both of us."*

"You know damn well what I mean!" Rondal replied, hotly.

"You mean . . . Estasia?"

"Of course I mean Estasia! Or were you worried I was pissed over your examinations?"

"What about Estasia? It was a tragic misadventure. Kaffin will get what's coming to him – I'll see to that."

"You'll see to that? That's mighty gracious of you, fixing my *mistake!"* Rondal blasted back, and then walked away hurriedly.

"Ron, wait!" Tyndal said aloud. "*What* mistake? Wait!"

"That's enough," Gurandor said evenly, stepping between Tyndal and his squadmate. "Let him be. He's obviously not—"

"You have *no idea* what he's thinking!" snarled Tyndal, trying to break free. Gurandor pushed back just enough to show Tyndal he wasn't going to chase after Rondal without getting through him.

Rondal stomped down to the main hall, where people were beginning to gather for the evening meal. "What was that all about?" Gurandor asked, concerned. "I thought you were going to draw on him!"

"That's why I left," Rondal said, disgusted. "He doesn't even . . . no, don't trouble yourself," he sighed in resignation. "If he's going to be as thick as an anvil, I'm not going to worry about it. Let's just eat . . . and then find a bottle someplace. I suddenly feel the need for a drink."

Gurandor grinned. "We can go into the village to the inn, tonight. A few pints will make you feel better."

"Or make me bawl like a baby," grumbled Rondal. "Can he really be that stupid? She's *dead*, and he blamed me, and now I'm supposed to just pretend like it didn't happen?"

"Let it not trouble you," Gurandor soothed. "You have to work with him. You don't have to like him."

"True," Rondal sighed. "I guess if we could work with Yeatin in the squad, I can work with anyone."

*   *   *

The one-eyed barman at the *Iron Gate* was dealing with five tables of customers, but there were plenty empty at this time of day. Rondal paid a penny for two pints poured out of an earthenware jug and handed one to his squadmate.

They talked of the day's lesson and argued over what the best-designed mageblade would be enchanted with. Rondal had a slight advantage over Gurandor, as he already had acquired one.

It was as sturdy and as functional as the common blades distributed for practice, but it had been made by Master Cormoran in Tudrytown. Rondal had barely added enchantments himself, but now that he understood the process better, he had several he was considering.

They were in a debate argument over whether a focus on offensive or defensive spells was more prudent when Tyndal and two other magi from the class came in. Gurandor was immediately on his feet.

"Sit down," Rondal casually commanded. "He's not here for trouble. He's just thirsty." His squadmate took his seat, but never took his eyes off of Tyndal. Tyndal, for his part, spared the two a long glance, but then promptly ignored them, focusing instead on his two companions and a barmaid.

Rondal appreciated his friend's loyalty, but he knew that what was between he and Tyndal would have to be dealt with alone. "If he just wasn't so damned arrogant!" he fumed aloud.

"Has he always been that way?"

"Well . . . I guess it's been since . . . well, since we came to Sevendor, but it's always been there. Headstrong, proud, and impulsive, certainly. And then we went to Inrion, and he had to be the biggest dog in the kennel. Even as he was failing."

Gurandor shook his head. "My father always said that the gods built up such men to make them fall all the harder as an example to the rest of us," he said sagely, and took another sip of the rich ale.

"He wasn't the one who fell," Rondal said quietly, but bitterly. "Estasia did. That would have solved a lot, actually . . . "

"And you say this . . . Kaffin of Gyre is to blame?"

"Or Relin Pratt. Orril Pratt's beloved nephew himself, to hear him tell it," Rondal scoffed. "Shadowmage. Family trained. And he wants vengeance."

"On who?"

"On everyone. But Tyndal and I are probably at the top of the list, now. We . . . well, we stopped him from stealing a witchstone."

Gurandor looked shocked. "Someone tried to steal your witchstone?"

"Someone – Kaffin – *did* steal Tyndal's for a day or so. If we hadn't . . . anyway, we retrieved it. But only after Estasia was thrown from the roof by one of Pratt's mates. I liked her. A lot," he said.

"Did she like you?" Gurandor asked.

"Well . . . not as much as she liked Tyndal," Rondal admitted. As he did so, he recognized part of the burden he'd been carrying. "She *really* liked him, even though we had more in common, and I liked her. So . . . well, Tyndal liked her some, I suppose, but not like I did."

"So when she died, and he blamed you . . . oh," Gurandor said, finally understanding. "So he thought it was *your fault* that the girl *you liked* died."

"So did I," agreed Rondal. "But to hear it coming from him, after all we had been through . . . Ishi's stinking rose," he swore, bitterly, "he didn't even *really* like her! I swear he only showed an interest because I did."

"You think you're angry at him . . . because he blamed you, or because she liked him more than you?" Gurandor asked, quietly.

Rondal wanted to dispute it – violently. If it had been anyone but one of his squadmates, he might have. But Gurandor wasn't goading him, he was just being a good squadmate, trying to help him out.

"Probably," he whispered after a long silence. "Damn it, everywhere he goes, he has girls follow him around like they're a bunch of cats and he's covered in cream! And it's only gotten worse since we were knighted, and his head grew nine sizes too big for his hat. They . . . they won't leave him alone. Me," he sighed, "I could glow like a magelight and they'd walk right past me."

"And Estasia walked right past you," Gurandor supplied.

"In a matter of speaking," agreed Rondal, dully. "I was the smart one, the educated one, but she only had eyes for that big Haystack. Why *wasn't* she interested in me?" he asked, feeling the effect of the ale a bit.

Gurandor sympathetically laid a hand on his arm. "There's no accounting for girls' tastes," he said, shaking his head. "They say they like one thing when they mean the exact opposite. They expect you to know what they're thinking when they don't even know what *they're* thinking."

"Well, I knew what Estasia was thinking, and it wasn't about me," Rondal said, sullenly, draining his tankard. "And yes, I was angry about that. I still am. And twice so because I can't even tell her because . . . because . . . I *killed* her!"

"You did *not* kill her!" Gurandor insisted. "She was pushed off a roof by an enemy. You just made a mistake."

"A mistake that cost her life," Rondal pointed out. "A mistake I should have avoided."

"But you didn't, and now she's dead, and you can't ask her to the Spring Dance," Gurandor said, rolling his eyes. "Look, Striker, I'm sympathetic . . . I *am*," he assured him. "But unless you want to find a necromancer and have him call up her spirit, I think your chances with this girl are gone."

"I *know!*" Rondal said, angrily.

"So . . . *forget about her*," the other mage encouraged. "If she liked the Haystack more than you, well, that was her error, not yours. Or even his. And that had *nothing* to do with how she died. So think about that while I get the next round," he said, scooping up both mugs.

Rondal stared at the fire and brooded, thinking of Estasia's beautiful face, her shapely figure, her sparkling eyes and her wide smile . . . and then thinking of it all being reserved for Tyndal's appreciation. It made him *burn* – burn at Tyndal for blaming him and burn at Estasia for being more interested in Tyndal.

"Screw 'em both," he muttered to himself.

Unfortunately, he said it just as Tyndal was headed to the bar himself to refill the drinks of he and his new friends.

"Both?" he asked, merrily. "Somehow I don't think you have it in you to even do one," he said, and danced past.

Rondal seethed – and without thinking about it, his toe lashed out and caught the tip of Tyndal's heel. The force of the tap was enough to push Tyndal off-balance . . . and then sent him sailing across the public house's wooden floor.

The rest of the patrons erupted into unintentional laughter as the boy skidded painfully to a stop. The expression on Tyndal's face, however, was anything but humorous.

"*Ishi's tits!*" he snarled. "You *meant* to do that!"

Rondal stared at the other boy intently. "Are you sure? *I doubt that I have it in me*," he said, coolly.

Tyndal bounded to his feet in an instant, and Rondal stood just as fast.

Both boys squared off as the crowd suddenly scattered from between them.

"No knives!" the barman ordered. "You spill blood, you clean it up!"

"I don't need a knife for this!" Tyndal spat.

"You wouldn't know which end to hold, anyway," Rondal shot back.

"You wanna take this out to the Luck Tree, churl?" Tyndal drawled in his thickest Alshari accent.

Rondal's eyes narrowed. That was a special kind of challenge, back home in Boval Vale, and the rest of the Wilderlands, where nearly every village tavern had a Luck Tree just outside its door. Fights around them were common, and an invitation to the Luck Tree was a challenge to a fight. It was how two village men at a public house settled their differences, man to drunken man, under the eyes of the gods, their ancestors, and fellow tavern patrons.

"What's a Luck Tree?" asked Gurandor, confused.

As it was an Alshari Wilderlands custom, he was unaware of the significance. But there would be no knives, no magic, and no rocks. It was just the two combatants hammering at each other until someone surrendered or they were pulled apart by the crowd. It wasn't a formal challenge to a duel . . . it was a rustic come-uppance between village men.

"I would be *delighted!*" Rondal said, his nostrils flaring and his fists clenched.

"Oh, I'm comfortable here… *why wait?"* Tyndal said, and leapt at his fellow apprentice with a savage growl.

Rondal was prepared for the spring. Tyndal was predictable, even if he was impulsive.

Rondal lowered his shoulder and kicked back his right leg, lowering the point until it was in-line with Tyndal's midsection. As he made contact, he quickly pivoted and re-directed the larger boy's weight. Tyndal went flying, landing on the edge of a trestle table that upended spectacularly, sending crockery and drinks flying.

239

Tyndal struggled to his feet, his face showing signs of the impact. "Looks like *someone* thinks he learned to fight!" he chuckled, nastily.

"He'd be right, Haystack," Gurandor said, darkly, as he took Rondal's flank. The other mage gestured for him to stay back, however.

"This is my quarrel, Snake," Rondal murmured.

"You sure you don't need the help?" Tyndal called, squaring off again.

"Certain!" agreed Rondal, as the two lunged for each other again, fists flying.

Rondal felt the other apprentice's closed fist hammer down on his face and head and the explosion of pain that resulted with each impact . . . but his willingness to endure the pain, so minor in comparison to what he'd suffered in the Mysteries, kept him on the offensive. His own fists pounded into Tyndal's midsection as fast as he could manage, and his feet kept him moving forward.

Before he knew it, Tyndal had swept one of his legs and sent him sprawling – but Rondal pulled his rival down with him. They fell still punching and hitting like a couple of drunks at a harvest festival.

Rondal found himself in a superior position for too brief a moment. He drove his fist into Tyndal's face as hard as he could, his rage and resentment from all the months being disrespected fueling his fight. For Tyndal's part, the snarl of anger on his face told Rondal that Tyndal was similarly frustrated, which accounted for the blow to Rondal's chin which landed with such force.

At some point the two were dragged away from each other, bruised and bleeding, and hustled off to separate corners of the inn by their compatriots. Rondal watched Tyndal leave, limping in the company of his new friends, as Gurandor tended his own bleeding scalp. Tyndal spared him one intense and thoughtful look before he left, then was gone.

"That was harsh," Gurandor commented as he wiped away blood with an ale-soaked cloth. "Good form, though. Solid delivery."

"And solid receipt," Rondal agreed, shaking his spinning head. "He hits hard!"

"You might want to avoid looking glasses and placid pools for a few days," Gurandor winced. "That's going to give you some lovely bruises."

"He had it coming," Rondal insisted.

"I think he learned that lesson," Gurandor nodded. "I didn't see any victorious handsprings on the way out."

"Maybe he'll leave me alone now," Rondal groaned, his face beginning to hurt in earnest.

"What did he say to you, anyway?"

Rondal had a hard time articulating exactly what Tyndal had done – after all, it was a mild enough jibe. He'd traded far worse with his squadmates and not come to blows.

With Tyndal it was different, though. He had been there since the beginning, almost. He had seen . . . well, more than even Rondal had seen. He was the one in the best place to judge him, and by his actions that judgment had been, up to now, poor enough.

For him to question Rondal's ability – unproven though it might be – in any capacity got him fighting mad. How dare he? How did his adventures give him any right to criticize? It had felt good to hit back at the boy for his arrogance, his insults, his . . . his success, Rondal admitted to himself.

"He didn't respect my strength," Rondal finally answered. "He's been strutting around since Timberwatch like he shits gold and his cock makes stallions jealous, acting like I'm some sort of dorky sidekick. He used a facility with swordplay and an arrogant attitude to try to push me around, and . . . well, he learned differently today."

"I'd say he did," Gurandor agreed. "I'm just glad you didn't draw. That might have been awkward."

241

"It was a matter for the Luck Tree," Rondal explained, dismissing the concern. "Under the Luck Tree, in the Mindens, you don't use anything but your bare hands. It's not like a formal duel."

"What the hell is a Luck Tree?" Gurandor repeated.

"Oh. It's a . . . a kind of miniature shrine to Herus or Huin, or even Pram the Blessed, outside of an inn or tavern," he explained. "It's usually just a big old dead tree, but sometimes it's a post or a pillar. It's where you go to take a piss, pray for luck, or beat the piss out of someone. That happens a lot, and what happens under the Luck Tree is not the affair of the reeves or magistrates. But it's not designed to be . . . well, permanent," he decided. "Just a violent settlement of differences."

"Good," Gurandor decided. "Because if either one of you came at me with an expression like that on your face, I'd fall on my sword."

"Did it really get that fierce?"

"Like a dogfight," Gurandor nodded. "Some of the old veterans were even approving."

"Good," Rondal sighed. "Maybe I beat some sense into him."

*   *   *

That evening, after the portcullis bell had rung and the gate had shut for the night, Rondal limped back to his room, dreading meeting his fellow apprentice once again. Part of that was guilt from fighting with someone who was supposed to be as a brother to him. Part of that was reluctance to sustain any further damage to his face. As it was his face was beginning to resemble the inside of a sausage.

He opened the heavy wooden door to their mutual chamber and found Tyndal in bed, reading by magelight.

"Good evening," he grunted, without emotion.

"Evening," Rondal replied, stiffly. He went immediately to the ceramic basin and poured water from the ewer to bathe his eye. As he was patting it dry gingerly with the rough woolen towel, he glanced at Tyndal, whose face nearly glowed in the arcane light. "Ran into a door, I see," he noted.

"A very, very heavy door," agreed Tyndal, after a pause. "Clumsy of me."

"You should be more careful in the future," Rondal said, after he considered the situation. "Doors can be dangerous."

"Especially when you don't expect them to be. I shall take note for future reference."

"That is wise of you. Good night."

"Good night." Tyndal extinguished his magelight, putting the scroll he was reading next to his bed.

Rondal stripped and crawled into his own bed. He winced involuntarily as his damaged head brushed his bedding. His roommate took notice.

"Try ice," suggested Tyndal. "Soak the towel in the water and then freeze it. It numbs the pain and helps the swelling."

"Oh . . . thanks. Yes, I forgot about that," he admitted. It took only a few moments to tap into his stone and remove the energy from the water in the towel, rendering the cloth stiff and cold. His burning face immediately felt better. "Thanks," he repeated, as he began to feel drowsy.

"Don't mention it," Tyndal dismissed. "It's easily one of the better things about being a mage."

"Almost makes up for the . . . the number of wayward doors," Rondal said, dreamily.

"What?" Tyndal asked, confused.

"Forget about it," Rondal insisted. "We have to get up early tomorrow. Mageblades, remember?"

"Oh, yeah," Tyndal recalled. "That's going to be brutal. Uh . . . what are you going to tell people about your face?"

"Since you've already claimed the aggressive door excuse? I had a haystack fall on me," Rondal decided. "If they have any questions after that, I'll just look at them in stony silence and dare them to ask."

"Uh . . . *haystack?*"

"That's what we call you behind your back."

"Oh." Tyndal was quiet for a long time, so long Rondal thought he might have gone to sleep. Suddenly an amused chuckle filled the darkness. "I guess that fits, then."

"I thought so," agreed Rondal, grinning to himself in the dark. "Good night, Haystack."

"Good night . . . *Striker,*" Tyndal added with a snort.

Rondal let him live.

*   *   *

The next day's lessons began early, and involved learning coupling the art of the mageblade with the augmentation spells a mage could throw on his own body, altering his perceptions, his reactions, his strength and speed.

Crafted for use without witchstones, the spells consumed the significant natural reserves of power most magi managed quickly, allowing them to be employed only for very limited periods of time – usually seconds. Of course, to an augmented warmage seconds could be as helpful as hours.

Such spells also took a toll on the body, to a greater or lesser extent. You could push human muscle fiber to do incredible things . . . for a while. Then the toxins built up and the exhaustion set in, taxing your efforts. Even killing you, if you persisted in using the augmentations past your well-understood limits.

But combining a mageblade cunningly employed with the power and speed the combat spells granted made a warmage one of the most deadly foes on the battlefield. Even in short bursts a warmage could inflict tremendous damage on an enemy. Rondal had done it himself. Not artfully, but he'd done it. You could stab a lot of goblins when you moved thrice as fast as they did.

He could also see how quickly the other magi tired when they employed the spells. He had, too, when he had been separated from his stone for the Mysteries. Now he summoned power through it, leaving his natural reserves alone. It was still tiring, but not exhausting. Some of the other magi looked like they'd been through a fifty-mile march.

Rondal wasn't the only one to notice. Master Renando approached him in the afternoon, ignoring his tender face, and asked him how he was faring.

"Well enough, Master," he admitted.

"So I see," the old man nodded. "This is the first I have had experience with High Magi, much less High Warmagi. Knights Magi, I believe the popular term is. I wish to conduct an experiment, if you are able."

"What would you like, Master?"

"I would like to see just how long a . . . knight mage can sustain the augmentations through the agency of the irionite."

"I've done it for four or five minutes, Master," Rondal provided. That provoked a gasp from some of the warmagi.

"And a minute is about all most can manage," he nodded. "So let us see the limits of your power."

"Very well, Master," Rondal said, used to people poking and prodding him about his abilities. "Shall I . . . run around the fortress until I drop?"

"I figured a more practical demonstration would be in order. I'd like you to fight – to spar – while augmented. And fight as long as you can."

"Master, I'll do it," he said, confused. "But I'll defeat anyone I fight who can't keep up with me."

"Exactly," the swordmaster grinned. "So we'll pair you to your fellow, and see which of you drops first."

Rondal's heart hit the floor. Him? Fight *Tyndal?* Tyndal outclassed him as a swordsman any way you looked at it. Longer reach, more strength, faster, better reaction time. Rondal could stand and fight just about anyone else, but Tyndal? *Augmented?* He groaned.

"I thought you might enjoy it," Master Renando smiled. "I heard about you two dancing at the pub last night. I like to see that kind of energy. Let's see if you can make it useful."

Rondal slowly walked to the center of the circle chalked out for demonstrations, trying to loosen up his arms before the contest.

I'm not any happier about it than you, he heard Tyndal say mind-to-mind, as he entered the ring. He swung his mock mageblade around a few times.

I'd wager otherwise, Rondal sent back. *Why would it bother you?*

Because now they'll all think I'm taking advantage of you after I already beat your face in last night.

Who beat whose face in? Rondal quit worrying about Tyndal's strength, reach, and aptitude. He suddenly wanted to fight him very much.

"Gentlemen," Master Renando said, serenely, "prepare your spells. Take your guards. Salute . . . and begin!"

Rondal felt the effect of the augmentations take hold of his body and mind just before Tyndal did, but he did not attack until he was sure both of them were affected. He didn't want to be seen taking unfair advantage. He didn't have long to wait. Once Tyndal heard the command to begin, he aggressively began his approach.

246

Fighting against another augmented warmage was tricky; in many ways it was similar to regular sparring. But Rondal's spell worked a little faster, he noted with satisfaction, and therefore his was the first strike to fly.

Tyndal neatly caught it on his wooden blade and spun another in response, and for the next several moments they traded parries like their first day of swordplay. Then Tyndal apparently grew weary of the monotony and began varying his attacks. His footwork kept him coming in on three main approaches, Rondal noted as he did his best to block the flurry of blows. He couldn't fault Tyndal for his footwork – it was flawless – but it also lacked imagination. It was swordplay. It wasn't close combat.

That was his advantage, he realized, as he bore the impact of the well-placed blows. Tyndal knew swordplay, and he knew a lot of it. But this wasn't – technically – swordplay. This was warmagic. Combat magic. The mageblade was the focus, but it was by no means the only weapon at his disposal.

He doubted Tyndal realized that. He was too busy showing off what a good swordsman he was

When Tyndal made his next attack, instead of parrying Rondal allowed the other boy's momentum to carry him forward a few steps, nearly into the slowly chanting crowd. Rondal turned to strike from behind, only to find Tyndal's mock blade already blocking the blow in anticipation, even as he fell.

That was fine – and it confirmed his theory. Rondal would have tried to move out of the way to avoid the strike instead of blocking it. Tyndal was thinking of this as a *sword fight*.

Rondal spun back around, pivoting on his heels and turning his shoulders to snap a second attack at Tyndal's exposed legs. Once again the Haystack twisted and parried an artful block . . . when he *could* have just moved an inch and allowed the sword to miss him altogether.

It was what his masters in the Mysteries had called a *'failure to*

247

appreciate the outcome.' Thinking you were in one kind of a fight, working for one goal, when in actuality you were fighting a different way for a different goal than you started with.

If he was an adept swordsman, Rondal knew, he would have tried a complex combination of blows designed to try to push his opponent out of his rhythm and make a mistake. That's what the swordmasters he'd heard, including Master Renando, usually counseled.

But here he was with a *perfectly good* opportunity to kick Tyndal in the padded shoulder with his boot . . . so he did.

Rondal had timed it well. Tyndal was slightly off-balance and moving in that direction anyway. Rondal's augmented foot pushed against the other boy's shoulder, hard. Tyndal skidded to a halt almost fifteen feet back. The moment he stopped he was right back on his feet again, rushing Rondal hard. He had enough sense to avoid a full tackle, which Rondal could have thrown, and instead hammer at him with his blade in increasingly sophisticated ways.

And not just his blade. Once Tyndal understood the fight and the goal, he threw himself into it. Rondal was not just blocking sword blows; he was now dodging elbows, knees, and fists. They weren't always well-thrown, but any of them had the potential to knock him back if he let them land fully. He had to focus mightily on keeping his body out of the way of Tyndal's onslaught.

Tyndal had the initiative, Rondal knew. He had the momentum, and he had sufficient motivation, apparently, to fuel a powerful attack. Rondal found himself merely able to defend for a while. He did an adequate job, prohibiting anything solid from hitting, but he was nowhere close to winning.

Then he realized . . . just by *not getting hit*, he was winning.

He didn't have to knock Tyndal out. All he had to do was keep Tyndal from knocking him out. If he could patiently keep up the parries, not extend himself recklessly or foolishly, conserve his energies and momentum and wait for the big haystack to make a mistake . . .

And soon enough, it happened. Tyndal put a little too much power into a chopping overhand blow. Instead of parrying it, Rondal slipped into the swing, grabbed Tyndal's arm . . . and threw him over his hip in a move he'd learned in the Mystery's unarmed combat class. Once again the boy skidded to a stop, and once again he was on his feet and fighting in moments.

Only this time it was Rondal advancing, pushing his advantage against the taller boy while he was still rising. He swung his mock blade with a furious motion from the top and sides, and even attempted a quick thrust.

Tyndal, frustratingly enough, managed to avoid them all. Soon enough he was back to pounding away at Rondal's defense and slowly pushing him back across the room. Rondal could see by the look in his eye that he wasn't about to over-extend himself again. At least, that's what Tyndal was telling himself.

Rondal knew his opponent better than just about anyone, and as he kept up his desperate defense against him he figured that if he gave Tyndal enough bait, he could coax him into making another serious mistake.

His opportunity took a while to come, but once again he was ready for it. One of the senior apprentice's blows came in short and underpowered, and Rondal used the chance to push back – hard. The blow was hard enough, in fact, to push the blade out of line. Rondal had a great opening – which Tyndal could have blocked or avoided. Instead, Rondal leaned in and punched Tyndal in the stomach, hard. Hard enough to double him over, and as his practice helmet swam below Rondal's field of vision, he brought the pommel of his practice sword down on it. Tyndal went down like an anvil off a bridge.

"Victor!" Master Renando said, when Rondal dropped the augmentation and could hear properly again. "Well done, lads! That was more than *eight minutes* – I've *never* seen an augmentation held so long before!"

Rondal was panting for breath as he slid his helmet off. "Can someone check on his head?" he asked, his arms tingling after such effort. "I hit him kind of hard."

Tyndal was fine, of course, but it took a few moments for him to return to consciousness. He rubbed the back of his neck confusedly as he sat on the floor, a warbrother tending to his head. It wasn't bleeding, but it was hard to discern under the brilliant bruises he still wore.

"An excellent job, Sir Rondal," murmured Master Valwyn, who had elected to sit in on the class. "It appears you have discovered something, something you needed here at Relan Cor."

"Skill?"

"Strength," corrected the old warmage. "Skill is respectable, but strength is *respected*, even if you lose. When you arrived here, I was anxious that you would not find that strength in yourself. Once again I was gratified that the gods saw fit to see you through the Mysteries. Many a man has discovered his strength there."

"I am a lot stronger than I was when I got here," he agreed, as he stripped off his padded armor.

"Not just in your body," agreed Master Valwyn. "Your Master's letter gave me some hint of your difficulties when it asked for your inclusion in the Mysteries. He told me of your . . . rivalry with Sir Tyndal. He suggested that your greatest deficit lay not with your lack of skill in war – although he did address that – but in your lack of confidence in your own strength."

"But I didn't beat him because I was strong," he pointed out. "I . . . sucker-punched him."

"You took unorthodox action which ended the engagement," Master Valwyn corrected, helping him with his armor. "And you wouldn't have done it if you were afraid of him."

"I was never afraid of him!" Rondal said, viciously.

"Weren't you? Not of him, personally. But the *idea* of him. Sir Tyndal the Golden Warrior. He's handsome, he's tall, his blonde hair flows like water, his shoulders are broad and so is his smile. He's skilled in swordplay – even if he lost, he still bears more skill with a blade than you.

"But you won the bout because you were confident of your own strength, and you stopped being scared of the shadow of the man and confronted the man himself."

"I . . . I *sucker-punched* him," Rondal repeated, dazed.

"Yes, yes you did," smiled Master Valwyn. "And no doubt part of you thinks he deserved it. Part of your face, in any case."

"Uh, yeah," Rondal grunted, touching the lingering bruises. "But . . . I guess I was afraid. But not of him. Of his reputation. I've spent so much time trying to measure myself against him that I was working against myself."

"Exactly," nodded the old warmage. "You have demonstrated your strength. Even if you had lost the contest, you would have demonstrated your strength today."

"Thank you, Master," Rondal said, gratefully, once he realized what the man was saying. "I guess I did let . . . my own expectations fight half my battle for me, before I even drew my blade." He looked down at where Tyndal was still being encouraged to sit. "Are we . . . are we ever going to *not* want to kill each other?"

Valwyn shrugged. "Only Duin knows. But regardless of whether or not he'll kill you, or you he, there is one thing that he will never do again. Disrespect you."

Rondal shook his head. "And I had to hit him in the head . . . a lot . . . to get him to realize it."

"That's the only way you get a sixteen-year-old boy to realize *anything*," laughed Master Valwyn. "Rondal, don't dismiss the importance of this lesson. And it isn't about Tyndal, it's about yourself."

Rondal scowled. "Shall I prepare myself for a lecture?" he asked.

"It seems appropriate," Valwyn agreed. "The metaphorical scroll in your metaphorical saddlebag you should ride away from Relan Cor with is this: *being weak makes you despised*. It isn't malice, on the part of the strong; it is reaction to the nature of weakness by strength."

"I . . . can't seem to understand this metaphorical scroll, Master," Rondal said, tactfully.

"Let me put it another way," the man said, walking with the young apprentice, "Nature, as you know, constantly seeks equilibrium. That means it seeks balance, even in human affairs. You and your fellow apprentice share a burden and a responsibility, but if you share it unequally that will force the strong one to compensate – over-compensate – in some other area, in order to seek equilibrium.

"You came here . . . if not weak, certainly not strong."

"I'll never be as strong as him, I fear," Rondal admitted, quietly.

"You needn't be," Master Valwyn said, leading him to an alcove. "You must merely be as strong as *you* can be. That will be sufficient. Standing up to him like that, after being in the weaker position, you will be tempted to take revenge, or otherwise find redress against him.

"But he could no more avoid his behavior than the water can avoid filling the mill's wheel. I encourage you not to blame him for it, just as you did not blame another squadron for the theft of your food in the Mysteries. In avoiding that you found a quicker and more beneficial answer to the problem, one that motivated you all to fill your bellies."

"You . . . you *know* about that?" Rondal said, embarrassed.

"I'm an initiate myself – I sit upon the Initiate's Council," chuckled Valwyn. "The Officer's mysteries, no less, held in the autumn. Believe me, all of us keep an eye on the young men who make it to the Mysteries. In them we find the leaders of tomorrow, the marshals and knights and commanders who will see our kingdom to future victories. You were one of the favorites, though I should not tell you so. Your special relationship with the Spellmonger, of course, merited the observation, but then you displayed enough native talents and determination to draw eyes of your own accord."

"That seems unlikely," sighed Rondal. "We did fairly well, but we were hardly a model unit."

"And that is precisely the point," argued Valwyn. "You weren't a model unit. Yet you did 'fairly well,' regularly performing ahead of the other units in some key contests. Some you never knew you were competing in. Oh, we watched you *carefully*, Sir Rondal."

"So why wasn't Tyndal invited to the Mysteries?" asked Rondal.

"He did not need them – not yet. Sir Tyndal has much promise on his own, do not mistake me, but it was thought that your talents needed the Mysteries more, for now.

"Sir Tyndal is bold, brave, forceful and arrogant. You are cool, calculating, thoughtful, and cautious. Sir Tyndal is adept at improvisation, whereas you see and can execute a plan to its successful conclusion. Sir Tyndal is charismatic and inspiring because of his personality . . . but you, Sir Rondal, are inspiring because of your *competence*. And that is far more compelling, in a military officer."

"How so? I always thought valor belonged to the bold."

"Valor belongs to the *winner*," countered Valwyn. "Valor becomes vainglory when it serves no purpose. Valor in a losing cause might be noble, but it will not be rewarded. As we were discussing your entrance into the Mysteries, it was pointed out repeatedly that you have the mind to plan and plot and lead and figure in ways Sir Tyndal never will."

"In all fairness, Master Valwyn, Sir Tyndal is not incompetent," Rondal found himself saying. "In fact he can be quite surprising about his competencies, sometimes."

"It's not a matter of competence versus incompetence. It's a matter of degrees. Don't mistake me, Sir Tyndal's style of valor is noble, and it makes him a worthy warrior. But if he did not have men of determined character and clear mind to point him at the foe, could he be trusted to find him on his own? Or do what needed to be done when he did?"

"No. But you think I do?"

"So we believe," the warmage nodded. "And believe more strongly now than before."

"Because I didn't get myself killed at the Mysteries?"

"Because you went into the Mysteries without vocation, and yet passed through them and became initiated as one of the top candidates in your cohort. You went in a boy of average strength and flexible character. You came out harder, stronger, and more resilient than before. You have confidence in how you walk and speak and act, now, because you have a better understand of the outcomes. And once you understand how things are going to turn out, you can act with confidence, and from confidence comes authority."

"I don't particularly *want* authority," protested Rondal.

"I didn't particularly want my *rajira*, when my Talent emerged," Valwyn pointed out, "but the gods are rarely cooperative with such whims. You will have authority because you are intelligent, talented, and you *know how to learn*. Most importantly – now – you have strength.

"You will not stand for a weaker force to assail you. And you are willing to test that strength in conflict. Such is the warrior's way. Such is the way of the Mysteries. And such is the way of every successful warlord and general in history."

"So that confidence is going to make Tyndal respect me? Leave me alone?"

"Respect you, yes," agreed Valwyn. "Leave you alone, likely not."

Rondal frowned. "Why the hells not? Why does he have to—?"

"You haven't figured it out?" chuckled Valwyn. "He *likes* you, boy. Despite your antipathy, he genuinely likes you. More, now that you have shown him your strength, he can admit to liking you and not feel ashamed of the emotion. You have far more in common than you have differences, even taking your different characters into account."

"I'm *nothing* like him!" Rondal said, proudly defiant to the notion.

"How many other brave, resolute spellmonger's apprentices from a rustic mountain hamlet currently occupied by goblins do you know?"

Rondal grimaced. "Give me a moment to think . . ."

"You two don't have much family. Not outside your master's household. Your loyalties are the same, your ages are near enough alike, and your preferences in battle are even well-matched."

"So why does he have to be such a—?"

"Because he is a sixteen-year-old boy being forced to do a man's job, and he hasn't mastered the task yet."

"Then why do I—?"

"Because you are a sixteen-year-old boy being forced to do a man's job, and we'll be mindful that *you* haven't mastered the task yet."

Rondal looked subdued. "He still . . ."

"Your feuds are destined to be frequent, I have no doubt, and many will stick to memory. But you will overcome them. You can, now, because compared to the other things you have overcome, they are minor. Inconsequential. Unless you allow them to be consequential. You are strong, now, Rondal.

"The Mysteries gave you purpose, meaning, form and order to build your manhood upon. They open us up to tearing down the men we were and building the men we wish to be. It is a portal to honor, glory, achievement, and most of all strength. Strength of body, of mind, of character. That's something he can't take away from you – it's part of you – and that is something you have now forced him to respect."

"So what if he keeps challenging me? Baiting me?"

"Then you will – once again – have to choose how to respond. And if he needs another lesson in your strength to keep him from despising you, I think you are well-prepared for the task."

Rondal was silent for a time, considering everything that had been said about his fellow. He didn't hate Tyndal, exactly, but he still felt wounded about Inrion, and he still resented the younger boy's blaming him for it. That still stuck in Rondal's stomach like a bloodworm, every time he thought of him, regardless of how reasonable it was to think otherwise.

"So how do I keep from wanting to stick his head in the nearest convenient bucket and hold it there until he stops wiggling?" Rondal asked.

"You exercise your control. You choose *not* to. You consider the consequences and plan accordingly. You rise above the petty discomforts of your life and take solace in the pursuit of your goal."

"So . . . I should just ignore him when he acts like an idiot?"

"Essentially, yes," Valwyn agreed with a chuckle. "I suppose that is exactly what I'm saying. Ignore it until you can't. Then intervene forcefully. He respects you, now. He isn't going to do anything to lose that respect without cause."

"It's a lot to let go of . . ."

"For your own good, I urge you to find a way. Such rivalries take time and energy away from your mission. And they sap your strength when it could be used to more noble purposes."

"And if I can't?"

"Then you have three more weeks of intensive training in a wide variety of subjects, many of which will allow you further opportunities to test your strength against your fellow, if you'd like."

"Are any of them painful or humiliating?" Rondal asked, after chewing his lip in thought.

"Oh, gods yes," snorted Valwyn.

"Then let's just see how I measure against him," Rondal decided.

"And if he gets his nose bloodied along the way . . . well, we can just rationalize it as an opportunity to better himself."

"Yes," smiled Master Valwyn indulgently, "you do have wit. And intelligence. Say . . . have you ever considered aspiring to the *officer's mysteries* . . . ?"

Part III:

ERRANTRY

Bontali Riverlands, Summer

Tyndal

After the boys returned to Sevendor from Relan Cor early that summer, their wounds mostly healed, there was a tangible change in their relationship. Far from contesting territory around the castle with innumerable petty fights, they stayed far away from each other when they could.

That wasn't too hard – though the spring plowing season was over, and vegetable planting was under way, there was still plenty of military work for them to do. And with Lady Alya's belly growing ever greater with the Spellmonger's new baby, the mysterious machinations of the Alka Alon in their new tower of Laesgathal, Karshak work crews seemed to be everywhere and the approaching autumn Magic Fair, Master Minalan did not have much time to spare for them. And he had an abundant list for them.

Rondal worked with the militia groups at Brestal Tower, using his newfound knowledge to drill he rudiments of infantry into the heads of Bovali and Brestali lads. Tyndal was on duty at the expanding Diketower complex, seeding the place with fresh enchantments while he watched Master Olmeg and his company of River Folk plant yet more trees in Sevendor's outer Enchanted Forest. At night they bunked in different parts of the domain.

Even when both boys were at Sevendor castle, they avoided each other. Tyndal was still wary of how furious Rondal had been their last few days at Relan Cor, and while their mutual injuries were healed, their feelings were apparently not. There was something still bothering Rondal, Tyndal knew, something that kept the boy glaring at him whenever they saw each other.

So Tyndal just avoided the glare. He found a way to be elsewhere.

It wasn't like he didn't have plenty to distract him other than trees. The girls from Boval Hall, across the road from the Diketower, where he claimed a bed, never failed to stop by and chat with him, flirting outrageously as he improved the arcane defenses of the place. He did not try to deter them, despite the fact that some of their fathers would not let his knighthood or his youth keep them from beating him to within an inch of his life.

Tyndal just liked girls, and liked their attention. Pretty ones, ugly ones, dumb ones, smart ones, he liked girls. And he liked how they scrambled over themselves to try to impress him. It was amusing, most days.

He was being amused by two of the young ladies from Boval Hall who were supposed to be planting cabbages when he was called up to the castle with a mind-to-mind summons from his Master. He sadly bid the girls farewell, turned over his duties to the Ancient on duty, saddled up a nag and rode up to Sevendor Castle.

Just as he was leaving the Diketower, Rondal rode up next to him, late from Brestal Tower.

"So he summoned you, too, eh?" Rondal grunted. "Must be important."

"Apparently," Tyndal grunted back. "I won't complain of a change of duty."

"Yes, enduring adoring girls and watching trees grow is *so* arduous," Rondal said, dryly.

"True, but I wouldn't mind stretching my legs a bit. I felt for certain that Master Min would have deployed us by now. Things are bad in North Gilmora, I hear."

"Maybe that's what's happening now," Rondal pointed out.

"Might be," Tyndal considered. "Only one way to find out."

259

The castle doors were thrown open to let the cool spring breezes air it out. Even so, a fire burned on the hearth. The days were warming, but the white snowstone castle seemed to take a long time to realize it.

Master Minalan and Sire Cei were waiting for them in the Great Hall, at the big stone table Sire Cei once broke with his fist and Rondal had had to meld back together.

Tyndal was instantly anxious. He admired Sire Cei, but he always had the feeling that the older knight was looking to catch him in something. Probably just residual guilty conscience from his youth in Boval, he reasoned, but that did not curb his anxiety.

"Well, gentlemen," Master Minalan said, his big green sphere bobbing merrily over his shoulder like a faithful hawk, "you have learned magic, and you have learned warfare. But you have yet to learn how to be knights."

Both of them groaned.

"Is there some diabolical camp where they beat such things into you?" moaned Rondal.

"If I read another scroll, Master," Tyndal assured him, "my head may well explode!"

"Nonsense, both of you," Minalan said, cheerfully. "You now have the skills of a warmage, the abilities of a soldier, but to be a knight . . . that is beyond the scope of either scroll or drill instructor. For that you need instruction in *chivalry*."

"So who's going to teach us?" Tyndal asked, fearful of the answer.

"I am," Sire Cei said, firmly. "I was squired for nine years before I won my spurs," he said, proudly. "Squired to one of the most honorable knights in all of Alshar, a Wilderlord of renown. He inspired in me a love of chivalry that speeds my every action. And I feel compelled to extend those valuable lessons to the two of you."

"Sire Cei is teaching us chivalry?" Rondal asked, suspiciously.

"There is no one better," Master Minalan said, a challenge to name one implicit in his answer. "He is regarded among the local knights as a most well-trained gentleman, for all his foreign ways. He's highly admired for his devotion to the vocation and his knowledge of its good and proper practice.

"Therefore, I am turning your education over to him for a few weeks, this summer, so that he might pour the finer points of chivalry into your brains. With a *hammer,* if need be," Minalan added, with good-natured menace.

"But . . . do we have to learn to *joust?*" Rondal asked, anxiously. "I'd hate that!"

"I'd love that!" Tyndal said, thrilled at the idea. He could fight from horseback, he knew, but the manipulation of horse, knight, shield, and lance on the field of battle was a highly specialized skill, one that drew honor, glory, and acclaim.

"There is more to being a knight than tilting," Sire Cei affirmed, without humor. "More than tilting, swordplay, horsemanship, and all of the other traditional duties of the knight. Any man-at-arms can master those.

"No, gentlemen, to be a *true* knight – to honor and value the codes of chivalry – is to transform the warrior into the nobleman, the soldier into the statesman. Within the institution of knighthood," he pronounced, "lies the very best aspirations of mortal man and the gods desires, alike."

"As if we didn't have enough to live up to," Rondal sighed, rolling his eyes.

"Master, is this really necessary?" Tyndal said, shaking his head. "It feels as if we've spent a year in training!"

"Not even close, although I'd welcome the chance to have given you a full year," Master Minalan said, eyeing them both thoughtfully. "You have both done well at what I have tasked you with – apart from a little friction – but fighting and magic are not the totality of how you are to be of use to me.

"You are two of the first Knights Magi. Others will be looking to you for guidance. It would be helpful to me if you had some inkling of what was expected of you, in terms of chivalry."

"So we're just going to stay here and . . . and train?" Tyndal asked, miserably. "I thought for sure we'd be deployed to Gilmora!"

"Gilmora doesn't need you yet," Minalan said, shaking his head. "Things are bad there, but they're static. The goblins have not tried to advance beyond where they were last year. Unfortunately, that means that they're picking the region clean. Every human they capture goes

261

north, up the Timber Road and into the Penumbra. They don't come back.

"But they aren't moving forward, either," continued the Spellmonger. "That gives us time to build strength, prepare a defense, and determine what their goals are.

"None of which requires the two of you. So for the next few weeks, until Midsummer, at least, you will be in Sire Cei's charge. But you won't be staying here," he added. "My newest apprentice finds you . . . *distracting.* No, don't worry, I'll deal with her, but for now it would be more convenient if you were away from Sevendor Castle while you learned knighthood."

"So where?"

"My estate," Sire Cei said, dreamily. "Cargwenyn. We leave in the morning."

They made the peaceful journey back to the tiny estate Sire Cei had won at last year's tournament at the Chepstan Spring Fair on horseback, three gentlemen riding. They spent the time discussing chivalry in general, the older knight using the opportunity to lecture them about the noble codes of ethics and warfare that were the basis of the military class. Once they were at Cargwenyn, however, his manner changed from lecturer to administrator.

Tyndal was impressed with the man's versatility – one of the qualities of the well-trained knight, Sire Cei insisted. The Wilderlord seemed to fit in the small Riverlands estate perfectly. Tyndal reflected that he seemed as natural in the role of a country knight of a small estate as he was the castellan of a busy castle.

First, he greeted his pregnant wife, Lady Estret – whom he had *also* won in the tournament – in the yard of the small manor with a gentle grace and obvious affection that was so vulnerable that it made Tyndal blush to watch. He inquired after her health, and the state of her pregnancy, listening to every detail with uncommon eagerness. Then he greeted his step-daughter, little eight-year-old Lady Faresa and her puppies, before sparing any attention to business.

Then the knight tended to his estate's affairs immediately afterward, however, quickly consulting with his steward about important matters of business with the alacrity of a merchant, and delivering instruction about village affairs with the confidence of a captain, before returning his attention to his two young charges. He had done all of it without seeming overwhelmed by the varied nature of his duties or the import of hid decisions. Indeed, he made that very matter the subject of one of their first official lessons in chivalry.

"The role of a knight in our society is manifold," Sire Cei explained to them after luncheon in the manor's "great" hall, no larger than a small tavern. "With him lies the responsibility to defend and protect the people, to act with authority of ordering their affairs, to defend the weak against the oppressive, yet to enforce the lawful orders of our liege and his administration.

"Any man can be knighted, at cause. But to be a knight is a commitment to that manifold responsibility. At once a warrior and a landowner, an administrator and leader of men, devoted to an ideal but committed to a society replete with custom, knighthood requires a tremendous amount of responsibility to do well. And much training and observation of good chivalric examples . . . which the two of you, unfortunately, lack."

"We have you, and Sire Koucey," Tyndal reminded him.

"We're quick studies," Rondal assured him.

"There are some things that cannot be learned from a book, Sir Tyndal," the older knight said, pouring wine for each of them. "Ten thousand rules of social behavior and responsibility, mostly unwritten, which you are required by your new station to know and enforce. Usually a squire picks them up in service to a knight over the course of years. The Magelord has invested me with the responsibility of . . . shortening that period for you. Considerably."

"And just what does that entail?" asked Rondal, suspiciously.

"Whatever I decide it entails," Sire Cei replied, dryly. "Everything a knight does, and how he does it, has meaning and purpose. For instance, the fact that I am serving you wine has meaning."

"It means I need a drink!" Tyndal agreed.

"It means . . . that this is a serious discussion," Rondal guessed.

"More," Sire Cei explained as he swirled the wine around in the opaque glass goblet. "Wine is a luxury, which requires a sophisticated and well-run estate to cultivate, produce, ship, and sell it. It only grows better with age and the older the vintage, the higher the quality - a suitable symbol for a hereditary class. A stable, prosperous hereditary class whose holdings span generations.

"Ale, mead and spirits have different meanings," he explained, gesturing with his goblet, "but when a senior gentleman pours wine for two juniors in rank, it indicates that he is giving them instruction or orders, and that especial note should be taken."

"That's what wine means?" Tyndal frowned. That seemed . . . complicated for a mere beverage.

"Not just the wine . . . the wine *in context* of the situation. If I was your peer, instead of senior, then the nature and tone of the discussion would change. This is the way our society has determined a senior noble instruct junior nobles. If there were oaths of fealty involved, then the context changes . . . and so does the meaning of the service."

"But . . . why?" Tyndal asked, confused. "Why should wine signify . . . well, anything?"

"Something must," Sire Cei explained. "Such social cues enrich our conversation, as they are invested in meaning. The meaning supplies the context for us without the need for further explanation. Our agreement on the meaning of wine in this context marks us as fellow members in our culture of understanding. And wine is a pleasant enough drink for the meaning.

"If we were having ale, however, then the context changes. Our social ranks are removed with ale, not emphasized. As it is more common and less expensive, so does the context of our conversation change to subjects of a less-formal nature.

"It would not be proper to discuss weighty matters over ale," he lectured. "A couple of comrades from the wars, however, can reminisce about old campaigns over ales. We can talk about our wives, our children, our homes . . . but rarely about our definite plans, money, or property. Nor would I give you serious instruction or command over ale. These customs are understood among all men of the Duchies. From duke to cowherd, we share a common understanding of their meanings."

"How about mead?" Tyndal asked with a grin. "Or spirits?"

"Mead is for celebrations, thank goodness," Sire Cei said, looking up toward the honeycomb heraldry he had won with his tiny fief. As the owner and patron of an apiary, a great deal of his revenue came from those who brewed mead, Tyndal knew. He also knew that, soon after taking possession of both land and wife, Sire Cei had invested greatly in building a meadery on his fief in fulfillment of his charter.

"A bride and groom are supposed to take seven bottles on their honeymoon, and not return until they are all but one empty, if the union is to be fruitful. A man toasts his love with mead, or a dear friend – an intimate friend. He drinks to the health of a babe or a marriage. To a maid it implies friendly seduction or at least flirtation. In death, mead is signifies mourning and sorrow. A girl's first bleeding or a boy's entrance into a trade or profession is celebrated with mead and hydromel. Blessing a new home is also appropriate for mead."

"And spirits?" asked Rondal, curious.

"Business, mostly," Sire Cei said. He knew the knight was not partial to spirits, himself. "And some men do not hesitate to use the courage from the flask to make bold propositions. And foolish ones," the knight reminded. "Domains have been lost due to a man being too overcome with spirits and making a rash decision over his life. And in battle, a sip of spirits in the company of gentlemen is considered fortifying, a sign of mutual respect. Or a way to raise morale, particularly if a senior ranked officer does so with his juniors."

"I remember some at Timberwatch who . . . respected each other a lot," snorted Tyndal.

"In some cases spirits can drive away the pain and grief of war," admitted Sire Cei, sadly. "My own father sought such refuge, and paid the price. But we were discussing the customs of wine."

"What about tea?" Ronald asked.

Tyndal looked disgusted. "Tea? Who the hells cares about tea?"

"Your brother knight makes a point," Sire Cei agreed. "Offering tea is a sign of hospitality and warmth, accepting it a sign of friendship. That is true in peasant's hut or king's castle. And offering milk to a grown man would be an insult, lest he requested it. It would be appropriate to a maid of sufficient youth."

"This . . . is confusing," Tyndal said.

"No, it's not," Rondal grumbled. "It's not just what is being shared, but by whom. And where and when. The drink is secondary to the meaning," he ventured.

"Of course, it's all so clear to me know," Tyndal said, sarcastically.

"Exactly, Sir Rondal," Sire Cei approved. "They are all part of a knight's understanding of the world."

"So drinking wine in the afternoon would be a different meaning than drinking wine at night?"

"Yes. The context changes depending upon whether food is involved, and what kind. On feast days, wine is celebratory, a complement to the food. On ordinary days, drinking wine is a way to honor a guest. And while either wine or mead can be drunk as the stirrup cup in parting, wine signifies a more formal character, while mead a more personal.

"The rules change if the drink is between a man and a woman, too, and their relationships of course must be taken into account. If a member of the clergy is present, the rules change again as does the context. Discussing gentleman's humor in the presence of a priestess of Trygg while drinking wine would be improper, especially before sundown. Drinking spirits with the same birthsister at midnight, however, would be an appropriate time to share such jests. And hear a few in return."

"So why must a knight know all of this?" Rondal asked.

"It is part of his station . . . not because he drinks wine when he is supposed to, but because he does so and *understands why*. Hospitality is a noble virtue that all knights should exhibit. Whether to his liege or lord, to his vassals and yeomen, or to his brother knights. Knowing those . . . ciphers helps smooth relations between gentlemen, and allows much of import to go unsaid."

"It seems to be no more than a method for someone to find offense," Rondal said, suspiciously.

"Such things have happened," admitted Cei. "A wise man – and wisdom is another chivalric virtue – knows how to avoid such things by applying yet other social rules. Also context-dependent. A good knight will be adept at avoiding them in the first place. But if circumstance and fortune place him in such a position, he will do what needs to be done. Remember, a knight is a warrior, first and foremost."

"A warrior with wine," Tyndal snickered.

"There are many kinds of battles, and wine is but another arrow in your quiver. What a man might gain by the sword he may well lose by the cup, if he is incautious."

"About . . . gaining by the sword," Tyndal began, slowly. "Just what are a knight's duties, responsibilities . . . and liabilities in *conquering* someone?"

Sire Cei smirked. "Ambitiously planning your empire, are you?"

"Well, is that not the right of any knight?" asked Rondal. "The right to challenge possession in combat?"

"Ambition is good in a young knight, but without support from a good liege, going around and randomly attacking someone else's property is rarely a wise idea. Such errantry exists, as some lords feel that if a man can conquer, he is strong enough to hold it and will be therefore a better vassal than his predecessor.

"Other times they take great offense. Often with hundreds of men-at-arms. If you plan on conquering a domain, Sir Tyndal, you had best be prepared to fight to *keep* it. If your neighbors do not attack you, your predecessor nearly always has relatives. And even if you should prevail, you may well find your new lands very difficult to rule."

"Like the troubles Master Minalan is having," Rondal observed.

"In that context, it is *Magelord* Minalan," reminded Sire Cei. "He holds those lands and rules them on the basis of his nobility, not his profession."

"I see," Tyndal frowned. "But if I wanted to raise an army and take them away from him – theoretically –"

"Then I prophesize that Magelord Minalan would kick your arse until your nose bled . . . *theoretically* speaking," pronounced Rondal.

"Raising an army is not as easy as it sounds. Many a knight has beggared himself hiring men for conquest, and afterward ended up a sellsword himself to pay off the debt. Raising an army of peasants is possible, of course . . . but doing so is rarely seen in a favorable light by your peers."

"Peasant uprisings," nodded Rondal, sagely.

"Dead peasants," corrected Sire Cei. "A man who falls to a sword cannot plow a field or clip a sheep. A knight who is not capable of conquering a domain by attracting real fighting men to his cause is rarely worthy of such rule, history shows. Oft the best conquerors make the poorest rulers. Such men are better suited to selling their swords in service of more powerful men, rather than inflict their poor rule on some poor peasantry.

"And of course there is the legality – if a proper Writ of Conquest is not submitted to the Kingdom, then the King can order you deposed and the original owner or his heirs restored. If you wish to contend with a Royal Army the likes of the one Count Salgo is building, I wish you luck. And I pray we meet again in the afterlife."

"I . . . see," Tyndal said, scratching his chin.

"I hope you do," Sire Cei said, sternly. "Such conquests should never be entered into lightly, for the cost of war is dear to all. A knight should be prepared for battle, always, but never lust for it so much that he destroys more than he gains. His honor most of all. "

"And a domain that can be easily conquered is likely not worth the price," Rondal observed. "No offense, Sire Cei, but should someone wish to conquer it . . ."

"Then they will face the wrath of my liege . . . and kin to my lady wife," Sire Cei grinned. "As his son holds one of my neighboring domains, and his son-in-law another, I feel secure enough not to invest in fortifying my tiny fief. Besides," he chuckled, "whomever would risk such retribution would win a poor prize. It may be a lovely place, but it is hardly lucrative. Bees make poor tenants."

"But not all knights are landholders," Rondal pointed out. "You weren't, until you won the Chepstan Fair tournament."

"True, Sir Rondal," agreed Sire Cei. "The difference between 'sir' and 'sire.' There are many landless knights, oft younger sons of poorer houses who have the training and skills to rule a domain, in theory, but lack the patrimony to do so. Usually they take honorable service with a higher-ranked lord, for as you know there is much involved with the management of estates.

"I served as deputy castellan for Lord Mieyor, in Ganz, before Sire

Koucey took me to service under old Sir Gindon. When the old knight took ill, Sire Koucey gave me the opportunity, and then found little reason to change."

"What happens if you can't find a lord to serve?" asked Tyndal, looking amused for some reason.

"Then one has three honorable recourses," Sire Cei said, refilling the glasses for a second time. "To take service with one of the Free Companies, to take holy orders, or . . . errantry."

"Errantry," Rondal repeated. "Doesn't that just mean . . ."

"It means a number of things to a number of people," explained the knight with a smile. "Usually it means wandering from place to place, looking for a position . . . but horses must eat and knights cannot graze by the side of the road. So a knight errant will fast, pray, and seek what opportunity the gods see fit to send to him. At need a knight might work for wages, but only when starvation beckons.

"When no honorable means is available to sustain him, then traditionally the knight seeks to live on his honor. Finding a cause to support, a widow to defend, a tournament to enter, a shrine to protect, a rogue to be slain."

"Or a fair lady to be rescued from a horrible marriage," grinned Tyndal.

"Those are far fewer than the stories would suggest," chuckled Cei. "But I cannot say such things do not happen – not after how I met my good Estret," he said, glancing out the window fondly at his pregnant beloved, who was tending the flower garden with her daughter and a crone from the village. "Errantry can prove its own reward, and every knight should undertake it, at some point in his career."

"That seems like a haphazard way to pursue one's livelihood," Rondal said, doubtfully. "I prefer a roof over my head and a good meal every now and again."

"A knight must have faith that the gods will reward his honor and support his chivalry through their providence," Sire Cei pointed out. "If a knight did not throw his fate into the wind without fear from time to time, then the gods have little opportunity to blow the chaff of his life to the wind, leaving only the kernel of his honor."

"That's . . . a complicated metaphor," Tyndal said, slowly, struggling to understand the meaning.

"But apt, I promise you," Sire Cei assured with confidence. "Choose another, if you like. Consider steel: it must be tested and tried by fire and hammer, heated red-hot, beaten and beaten—"

"Wheat is a fine metaphor," Rondal interrupted. "For Huin is a mighty god and Trygg his wife is the mother of all."

"Every knight should have the faith in his skills and the blessings of the gods in his life to test himself. In tournaments against his worthy peers, in battle against a fell enemy, in the world against injustice and disorder. In so doing he not only seeks to improve himself and his fortunes, but test his peers and give them good challenge of their own honor and chivalry."

"And enrich himself, should the chance occur," Tyndal added, cagily.

"Strong faith is oft well-rewarded by fortune," conceded Sire Cei, unapolgetically. "But when the fickle hand of Ifnia is involved, such faith can lead to glorious death or utter ignominy as easily as fortune and glory. Such are the caprices of the goddess of luck.

"But by Fortune's fires our faith and virtue into our honor is forged. The chaff blown away by challenge. Only by attempting the difficult or rising to the harder challenge can we exceed the frontiers we, ourselves, set for ourselves. Ever does the knight seek to improve himself, for honor is a cup never filled.

"Which brings me to my *final* point about wine," Sire Cei said, draining his glass. "One cup for courtesy, two for orders, three for instruction. But no more in one sitting, if you want to get anything else done in the day.

"And while quiet reflection feeds a man's soul, we have much work to be done and precious little time to do it. Tomorrow, gentlemen, we embark on your abbreviated squirehood. Warriors and magi you might be, but tomorrow you learn the sublime art of chivalry."

*   *   *

The next morning saw them in a familiar situation, if an unfamiliar place. The practice yard of Cargwenyn was just off of the main yard, a well-tended sand-pit that had seen decades of moderate use. It was more garden than guard's den, with planters of flowers and herbs around the edges and a wide paved stone pergola at one end. Spring's bounty had caused hundreds of blooms to decorate the place, a living multicolored tapestry of flowers surrounding them . . . and providing nectar for the bees the estate relied upon.

"This is lovely!" he declared, chuckling as he strapped on his armor. "I feel so . . . *dainty!*" It certainly smelled better than any practice yard he'd fought it, Tyndal decided. It was a decided change from both the practical mud pit at Sevendor castle and the gloomy, expansive facilities of Relan Cor. It was far more pleasant in form than the little sandyard at Inrion that had played such a significant role in his recent history.

"You'll feel less so, if one of Noapis' children chances to join you under your gambeson," Sire Cei chuckled, as he strapped his thick leather gorget around his neck. It sounded as if he knew from experience. "As pretty as it is, it suits our purposes. I want to see how you two rogues have improved your swordplay, since last we crossed swords."

"I think we might surprise you," Tyndal smirked, eager for the challenge. He had trained hard at Relan Cor, spending hours and hours in the yards and learning all he could from whomever he could get to teach him. He felt his skills had vastly improved – and were well able to prevail over such a mature man as Sire Cei.

"I hope you do," Sire Cei said, settling his battered helm on his head. "You and I first, Sir Tyndal."

Tyndal had been anticipating this contest for weeks. Apart from their master, they both had sparred with the castellan as their instructor for most of the last year. It had been his yelling, sarcastic insults, and discipline to which they had been subjected, and he was as close a thing to a swordplay master as Tyndal had. They saluted solemnly, the gods, the ancestors, and each other, and began.

Both were using single practice swords. Tyndal had the wooden double of Slasher he used for practice, less blade and more hilt than the traditional greatsword Sire Cei's weapon mimicked. It was lighter, and presumably more maneuverable.

"No augmentation spells," Rondal called from the side. "That would be cheating."

"I *know!*" Tyndal said, annoyed. It was just like Rondal, trying to

271

bring him down before a bout. He was trying to *enjoy* this.

They circled and sized each other up as if they were meeting him for the first time. Tyndal saw a large warrior with a very big sword, but he also noted how close together Sire Cei's footwork was. He had learned that such steps usually signaled an overly cautious nature, and a willingness to only attack when the advantage was clear.

Tyndal, on the other hand, took much wider steps. He crossed a lot of ground, compared to Cei, and soon he was circling the Dragonslayer instead of the movement being mutual.

That suited him fine. He took two quick steps and threw a strike at Sire Cei's right shoulder – only to have it blocked when the man twisted and parried. That surprised Tyndal. He thought the move would have gotten past Sire Cei's guard.

Tyndal threw a fast combination from the Sword Dance, but the knight managed to deflect all of his strikes without so much as twitching his mustache. He switched to a leg-and-shoulder-targeting flurry of blows that departed wildly from what he was used to, only to have Sire Cei sidestep the first one, block the second, and catch the third on the tip of his blade . . . before powering back so hard that Tyndal nearly lost his footing.

That was frustrating, he realized, as his boots skidded him to a halt in the sand. Tyndal had fully expected to have first blood by now.

He shook off his disappointment and launched a sophisticated combination that involved half-steps in one direction and then a change-up to the other, then a sudden dart back. Ordinarily, he should have bisected his opponent. Sire Cei was too fast. When his fake mageblade swept back, Cei's long blade was inexplicably in the way . . . held at an angle behind him, over his shoulder.

Tyndal was so surprised he didn't realized that he had been set up for a nasty spin attack that drove the sweet spot of the blade so hard against his helm that his ears rung.

"First blood!" Rondal called. He sounded pleased with it.

"All right," Tyndal sighed. "What did I do wrong?"

"Nothing," Sire Cei said, taking a step back and raising his helmet. "You did it flawlessly."

"Then how come you got first blood?" complained Tyndal.

"Because while you performed flawlessly, that doesn't always mean you prevail. There is a lesson there. *Again.*"

Sire Cei and Tyndal sparred for five or six bouts before Tyndal finally scored a solid hit on the man. He became more and more impressed by Cei – and realized just how much he had babied them before they had gone to the War College. At first he resented it, and then he just felt a little embarrassed. But he started trying a little harder, and just when he was starting to get exasperated, he finally saw an opening and struck.

"Well done," Cei said, approvingly. "You really have improved, Sir Tyndal. I can see a definite refinement in your technique. You have true talent at this. Now you," he said, pointing at Rondal, barely breathing heavy.

Rondal nodded grimly and pulled the practice helmet over his face. Rondal's practice blade was slightly shorter, and he had a tendency to use it one-handed more than Tyndal did. Tyndal expected Sire Cei to make short work of him.

To Tyndal's surprise, Rondal took a defensive position and waited for Cei to engage. As a result he was able to block two blows from the greatsword before pushing back, dropping his two-handed grip to use his arm to counterbalance. Not as hard as he could, but enough to push Cei slightly out of line. His wooden blade tapped the older knight lightly on his unprotected forehead.

"Strike!" Cei said, surprised and impressed. "First blood! *Well done,* Sir Rondal!"

Tyndal's mouth was open. He had laid into Cei with as serious an attack as he was able to muster without magic, and the man had defended nearly every one. Then this bookworm gets in the ring and scores a point in moments. Despite his effort to control himself, he sucked in air through his teeth.

Rondal spent ten minutes showing off the skills he'd developed at Relan Cor, and while he lacked the sophistication of Tyndal or Sire Cei, even Tyndal had to admit that his footwork was solid, his positioning was well-formed, and his strikes were clear and hard.

They took a water break and discussed their performance before Sire Cei instructed them both to attack him at the same time.

"Uh, Sire Cei, do you really think that's fair?" Tyndal asked, skeptically.

"Probably not," the knight conceded. "But I'll take it easy on you." He lowered his visor.

Tyndal looked at Rondal, who shrugged. Tyndal sighed and pulled his own helm back on.

Rondal was on his left, so Tyndal moved quickly to Cei's right side. He threw a quick blow at his thighs, which Cei side-stepped without deigning to watch, and then pivoted and threw another blow across his shoulders. To his dismay, his blade got entangled with Rondal's. Enough so that he heard the dull thunk of wood on steel a moment before he heard it much louder – and much more painfully.

When the ringing in his ears stopped, he heard Cei chuckling wickedly. "That, gentlemen, is what happens when you *don't* work together. *Again.*"

They continued trying to defeat Cei for another twenty minutes, stopping here and there to discuss the fighting. In the last bout of the day, they both tried much harder, but to no avail. The faster and harder they attacked, the faster Sire Cei seemed to defend . . . although Tyndal was gratified to see the older knight start to get rushed.

Just when he thought they had worn the man down and could start beating on his helmet like a drum, Cei grunted, twisted, and sent his sword singing across Tyndal's chest. Too late they all realized that there was magic involved. As the blade hit Tyndal's armor, Cei's talent unexpectedly engaged. The wooden sword shattered. Tyndal was thrown back twenty feet across the yard, to land on his back, looking up at the treetops.

"Owwwww," he groaned, his chest throbbing.

"Ishi's tits!" Rondal said. "Are you *dead?*"

"Sir Tyndal!" Cei said, throwing his helmet off and rushing to the boy's side anxiously. "Pray the gods you are all right!"

"Owwww," Tyndal reprised. He felt like he had been kicked by a charger. With both hooves. "I don't think . . . I broke . . . anything." He pulled himself slowly to a seated position with their help. "Duin's . . . *axe*, Sire Cei . . . I hope I didn't get you riled!"

"Apparently you did," Rondal said, thoughtfully. "It looks like his Wild Talent activated. Magical force transformed to concussive force at the point of impact. There are similar effects from spells in the libraries at Relan Cor. They take a lot of power," he added.

"I remember," Tyndal said, rubbing his chest where the wooden sword had struck. "I read them too. I just never thought I'd be on the other end of one."

"My apologies, Sir Tyndal," Sire Cei said, helping him to his feet. "I cannot always control this . . . 'talent'. Perhaps it would be best if we called the end of practice."

"I would hesitate to argue with that," Rondal agreed. "Does that happen often, Sire Cei?"

"Only when I get roused," he admitted. "If I hold my temper and control myself, I can keep it from happening." He sounded anxious about it.

"Of all the gifts you could have gotten from the gods, there are many far worse," Tyndal pointed out, still gasping for air. "For a knight to be able to deliver such a blow . . . "

"In battle, yes," Sire Cei said, helping Tyndal strip off his armor. "But on the practice field . . . well, I would hesitate to send home only half of the apprentices the Magelord entrusted to me. It wouldn't reflect well."

That afternoon they studied the lineages of the great houses, particularly the ducal houses and powerful counts and other dynasties. Tyndal was in the middle of reciting perfectly all of the dukes of Remere in order when he got the tingle of sensation that indicated a request for mind-to-mind communication.

Tyndal, how is your tutoring going? asked his Master.

Fine, Master. I now know more about the ducal houses than I ever wanted to know.

Bunch of inbred buggers aren't they? Look, I've got a problem. I need your help.

How may I be of service, Master? Tyndal asked, using his best court manners. Sire Cei had required them to use such formal address as much as possible.

Impressive.

275

Thank you, Master! Tyndal said, pleased.

Not you, Sire Cei. I didn't think he could teach you and Rondal manners. The Westwoodmen brought a report to me today. It seems one of their hunters was ranging southwest of Sevendor and came across something troubling. Someone in the next domain over seems to be secretly mining snowstone.

Snowstone? Are you certain?

No, which is why I am speaking to you. Whatever I did to create it in the first place wasn't concerned with my property rights. From what I can tell, there are outcroppings of snowstone in at least two other domains. The larger of the two is this one. Taragwen. The lord of Taragwen is a vassal of the Lord of Sashtalia, so he's not going to be pleasantly disposed to an embassy from Sevendor. Not after what we did to his ally, the Warbird. But he might not take too much notice of a small hunting party or such. The estate is supposed to be great hawking and fox hunting territory.

I don't know how to hunt, Master, Tyndal confessed.

I'm sure you'll get around to it. But you don't need to hunt. I want you and Sire Cei and Rondal to take a gentleman's stroll down there and see what is actually happening. The last thing we need is for the Dead God to get his nonexistent hands on it. You're more than a day closer than I am, and I think between the three of you I can get a good report.

I shall inform Sire Cei of your orders, Master. Is there any other service I might do for you?

How are things between you and Ron? he asked quietly.

We're . . . civil, master, Tyndal replied cautiously. *No more incidents.*

See that there aren't, he ordered. *I've got enough going on without the two of you clawing at each other's eyes like a couple of five-year-old girls. The war is heating up in Gilmora again. A lot of raids, and always where we expect them least. No dragons yet, but it's early in the season. We might be making another quick trip back there, if things don't quiet down.*

Yes, Master. Tyndal didn't feel comfortable revealing to Master Minalan the issue at the root of the animosity – his botched handling of

276

the Inrion Affair. He was just going to have to be on his guard with his fellow apprentice, and hope the usually mild-mannered boy did not snap. There was something dangerous in his eyes now, something Tyndal was wary of.

Tyndal outlined the orders to Sire Cei and Rondal over dinner that evening. Cargwenyn Manor was much smaller than the great hall at Sevendor Castle, much more intimate, but with the hivesister and her two apprentices dining along with Lady Estret and her daughter, the two old servants who brought their meal had to dodge and weave quite a bit around the trestle.

"Taragwen, eh?" Sire Cei said, stroking his chin as he glanced over at a map on the wall, in place of a tapestry. The map was at least a generation out of date, Tyndal could see, but the essential features hadn't changed. "Part of Sashtalia's domain now. A marginal estate, if I recall, though better off than Sevendor. But it does extend into the Uwarris a-ways behind the ridge."

"And we can just walk right in, introduce ourselves as fellow nobles, ask to take a look around, and maybe get invited to lunch?"

"Nearly," conceded Sire Cei. "Only we'll ride. We are gentlemen of some means. Arriving on foot would belie that."

"But they will just let us wander in?" Rondal repeated skeptically. Peasants who did that sort of thing often got a beating for their trouble, or worse.

"The rules of hospitality demand it," agreed Sire Cei. "To refuse such a reasonable request to a fellow knight without cause would cause talk amongst the lord's peers."

"For just *any* wandering knight who happens by?" Tyndal asked in disbelief.

"If he is of gentle birth and begs the boon," Sire Cei said, cutting a rind of cheese to lay between he and Estret on their common trencher, "then it would be a failure of hospitality to refuse it, and call the lord's honor into question. A knight could request to spend a full day there, perhaps several, without note."

"Free of charge?"

"It would be inhospitable to charge for a mere night's board. Longer than a night and the guest may be asked to assist in some minor chore as a service – which he likewise could not refuse, after accepting

277

hospitality."

"So a knight could, theoretically, just go skipping from castle to castle, getting free meals and a fire . . ." Tyndal began.

". . . and drink for free, and stable his horse . . . just because he's a knight," Rondal said, shaking his head in disbelief.

"Exactly," Sire Cei said, satisfied. "Further, asking leave to hunt or fish is a common practice, and the lord is almost obligated, save under special circumstances."

"I think I just understood a *lot* more about knights," Rondal said, his eyes wide.

Tyndal knew what he meant. Such rights were sold to the commoners for dear coin; to have them granted to a fellow knight as a matter of course was a huge economic boon to the class. It also explained all the spare chivalry he'd seen clogging up some castles.

"At least about errantry," agreed Tyndal. "It's like a free meal under every manor!"

"Gentlemen, you make it sound so *sordid!*" Lady Estret chuckled. "Knights travel for many reasons, and being able to count on the hospitality of their peers allows them to do so without fear of the perils of the public house. Under the codes of chivalric hospitality, a landed knight who turned away a fellow without good cause would himself lose honor by forcing an errant into an inn, or worse. When you have been riding for days, the last thing you want to do is fight with some bandit over your dinner."

"But . . . couldn't you just keep traveling like that, from manor to manor . . . forever?"

"Some do," Estret admitted. "There are always 'gentlemen of the road' who cannot seem to find a lord to serve. If they stay in any region long enough, their reputation spreads. There are ways to take care of such presumptions."

"Like what?"

"Like requiring him to assist in some noble but tedious task – like collecting rents, or evicting a tenant. In a time of war, his sword is put to use. And he *must* comply . . . or expect the accommodations to become less gracious. Hospitality demands food and drink and shelter

. . . it does not specify what *kind*."

"I . . . see," Tyndal said, calculating just how long he thought he could keep up such a pleasant-sounding lifestyle.

"Errantry is no feast day," Lady Estret said, shaking her head. "Many a knight has found himself between castles at sundown . . . and he is more of a target on the road, due to his station alone. Some errants turn to banditry or pillage to survive, if they become unwelcome and will not move on. Others are content to stretch whatever stipend they have as a legacy until they can secure a position."

"So is this mission considered . . . errantry?" asked Rondal.

"Yes," agreed Sire Cei. "We are specifically on an errand for our lord. But we are also on an errand to further the noble pursuit of hunting. It would not be uncommon for three good friends to take to the road with a few bottles and scout good hunting grounds . . . particularly if they had harridans for wives." He smiled good-naturedly at his bride. "Something I have no experience with, I'm afraid."

"So a knight doing anything that is not actually riding to battle or managing an estate . . . any knight on the road is an errant?"

"Essentially," agreed Sire Cei.

"It sounds like a recipe for trouble," Rondal said, his brows knit.

Tyndal smiled. "I was thinking the very same thing."

*　　　　*　　　　*

The three set out the next day, with food for a few days prepared by the staff. Lady Estret bade them a formal farewell . . . to help the boys practice. Her belly was starting to show, and Sire Cei seemed genuinely loath to leave her, but she assured him that she was safe and in good hands. It would be a few months yet before the baby was due. He deserved a few days relaxing on the road, she insisted. Reluctantly, and only because their master bid him so, did Sire Cei take his leave.

The three road south, stopping that afternoon at Fulanor Manor. The lord, a tenant knight in his twenties called Sir Merendol, was a friend of Sire Cei's and a cousin of Lady Estret. He leapt at the chance to avoid the laborsome chore of overseeing the summer hayfields.

Leaving the matter in the hands of the manor reeve, he wasted no time in packing a bag and having his horse saddled. He brought along a brace of brown hunting dogs as well.

Sir Merendol proved a boon as a traveling companion. He was Master Minalan's age, or thereabouts, a good country knight of noble lineage but modest station. He had welcomed Sire Cei warmly when he learned that his cousin had wed the Alshari knight, and the two had become friends and good neighbors as Sire Cei had consulted him about the running of the estate.

Tyndal found Merendol a welcome companion largely because of the large sack of wine he brought. Tyndal was quite fond of wine, and counted it as one of the better benefits of the life of a noble. They toasted each other's health for miles before they settled into a good traveling pace.

Sir Merendol was full of news of the region, and was happy to share it with the boys. He oversaw Fulanor Manor as a vassal of the Baron's son, paying for the privilege of running the lucrative estate. He had yet to take a wife, and seemed in no hurry to, although he discussed his prospects at length.

That evening they came to the frontiers of Sendaria, the domain of Birchroot. Just as twilight was setting in, Rondal grinned widely and rode ahead, stopping at a small building just shy of the river. A woman outside greeted him warmly . . . and from the shape of her belly, she was just a few months ahead of Lady Estret.

"Dear Ishi!" he swore, without mentioning the goddess of love's breasts for once in deference to Sire Cei, "did Sir Rondal go and put a foal in some maid's stable when we weren't looking?"

"It appears there are indeed things about him we don't know," agreed Sire Cei, as he watched the young knight greet the woman. "He does seem quite familiar with her."

"She's comely enough," agreed Sir Merendol. "But where in seven hells did that *bridge* come from? It's been two years since I've been this way, but I could have sworn—"

"Ah! *That* explains the riddle," Sire Cei said, snapping his fingers. "Sir Rondal was tasked with building a bridge in Birchroot, as part of a bargain of Magelord Minalan's with the Baron last year. This must be the famous bridge."

"Famous?" asked Merendol. "How, famous? I didn't even know it was *here!*"

"Famous because the mage knight enchanted it," explained Sire Cei. "Note the pure white snowstone used in its construction, imported from Sevendor. He ran into some trouble while building it, from what I understand. So he used magic to repair the problem. Now it is said that when regarded from Sashtalia, all one sees is a menacing-looking fortress. From here, a pleasant little inn."

The *Birchroot Inn* was pleasant, though crude and under construction. Apparently Rondal did know the proprietor and his family, and made a point of introducing them like old friends.

Even more impressive, the innkeeper, Baston, insisted on treating them all to bed and board that night at his own expense, saying that Rondal's coin would never spend there. Baston was a stout fellow, a former highwayman, from what he said, although Tyndal doubted it – the man was far too congenial to be a bandit. But he knew his way around a crock of ale.

It was odd, though, seeing Rondal as the object of gratitude and respect of others, like that. Not that he wasn't worthy of it, Tyndal reasoned as he grew sleepy by the fire, but he had rarely seen his fellow apprentice so animated and social. After the cool demeanor of the last few weeks, it was a startling change.

"At least you know it was not he who tupped the innkeeper's wife," Sir Merendol murmured, watching the three of them talk around a table. "She only has eyes for her husband. A rogue, perhaps, but an entertaining one."

"He brews well enough, too," admitted Tyndal, draining his glass. "And the stew was good." He couldn't bring himself to voice suspicions of the friendly man, but anyone who treated Rondal *that* respectfully had to be up to something. He fell asleep near the fire considering just what the innkeeper was plotting with his fellow apprentice.

The next morning he woke unmolested, un-ravaged and un-robbed, to the smell of biscuits and hot tea. They left with fond well-wishes and blown kisses. Tyndal did have to admit, when they'd crossed the bridge and he'd looked back at it, that the enchantment his fellow had crafted was impressive, and grudgingly told Rondal so. He thanked Tyndal graciously, which made it all the more irritating.

They approached their goal before he realized it. Taragwen was a
sliver of an estate that stood on the other side of the southwestern ridge
of Sevendor. Part of the Lord of Sashtalia's domain, Taragwen, like
Sevendor, had been passed from one henchman to another over the
years. Unlike Sevendor, it had not suffered neglect. It was just
remote, small, and had little arable land.

It was not a particularly healthy estate. With only two hundred odd
acres under cultivation – mostly rye and barley, with some wheat – it
grew enough to support the village of Taragwen and the small fortress
there . . . but little more.

Sir Merendol informed them of its scant history as they rode toward
the squat tower-and-keep on the hillside. Once part of the great
Lensely landholding empire, Taragwen had been calved off of larger
domains, mostly to reward loyal retainers with some sort of estate for
their upkeep.

The castle was little more than a modest three-story shell keep and
four-story round tower, with a thick wooden palisade surrounding. On
parchment, Sir Merendol told them, the estate had twenty hearths and
owed service for four lances. In actuality there were three or four
hundred souls within its bounds, most of them living in near-poverty.
But the village boasted a soapmaker and a small trade in apothecarial
herbs.

"I recall visiting a few years back," Baron Arathanial's vassal told
them. "I was on duty at Chepstan, at the time. The Baron wanted to
buy hardwoods, and Taragwen has more wood than field. The village
is no prize, not even a proper manor, as it is proximate to the castle.
Just a common hall for moots and such. No inn. No mill. No proper
smithy. But the countryside is wild and fair. I stayed three days, and
went hunting one of them with Sir Corvyan, the castellan at the time, a
most hospitable fellow."

"So who rules Taragwen now?" Tyndal asked, curious.

"From what I understand Sir Corvyan was transferred to a richer
estate by Sashtalia. The present castellan is Sir Pangine. A local man,
long a trusted man-at-arms of the Lord of Sashtalia, and rewarded with
the estate when he remarried. His wife died a few months after he took
office, but that doesn't seem to have affected him much, from what
tales the road tells. He has a circle of fellow knights and men-at-arms

he relies on."

"Let us go see this Sir Pangine," Sire Cei said, evenly, "and discover to whom he is selling the snowstone."

The village of Taragwen was a small affair, a circle of round huts clustered around a single longhouse. There were four stone granaries behind it, but little else of note in the un-walled, un-diked hamlet. The peasants were well into the spring plowing, and Tyndal could see three teams of plowmen trudging across the poor soil, their teams of horses and oxen struggling in the mud. They did not look as wretched as the Sevendori had once been, but they were by no means affluent.

They rode to the gatehouse where a single bored-looking guard in an iron cap asked their names and business before sending a boy up to the keep for instruction. He came back soon enough following a middle-aged man well-dressed.

"Hail," Sire Cei said with a slight bow. "I am Sire Cei of Cargwenyn and these are my friends, Sir Tyndal, Sir Merendol and Sir Rondal. Are you the lord of this estate?"

"I have that honor," the knight said, bowing in turn. "I am Sir Pangine, and I hold this estate in the name of the Lord of Sashtalia. To what do I owe the honor of your visit?" he asked, politely, but a bit nervously.

"We merely seek permission to range through your woodlands," Sire Cei said, serenely. "We have been told that the hawking and hunting in Taragwen are superior, and we have tired of the grounds around our own domain. Yet I would be loath to make such a journey without the leave of the lawful lord."

It was a reasonable enough request. Sire Cei had explained the subterfuge, pointing out that it was not, exactly, a lie. A knight valued truthfulness and honesty, he had taught them. That didn't mean he had to be so forthcoming he inadvertently betrayed his master.

The knight considered. "Cargwenyn? That's north, in Lensely territory, is it not?"

"It is," conceded Sire Cei. "I am but new to the region, and recently introduced to the lands. As you can tell from my accent, I am a Wilderlord, and miss the mighty Mindens. I thought to visit the Uwarris to ease my longing. And I am passionate about the hunt. Tell me, are there moose in these mountains?"

"Moose? Aye, as big as bulls," bragged the knight. "I take three or four every autumn myself. Yet it is not an appropriate season for such game," he said, curious.

"For my part," Sir Rondal said, lazily, "I seek better hawking grounds. I can barely get my bird to take wing before we've reached the limits of the wood and field."

"Taragwen has long held a reputation for good hawking," conceded Sir Pangine.

"And I seek to find a different view after a long winter," Sir Merendol said. "Could we beg permission to scout the fields for the day? I promise we brought enough wine to keep us entertained," he said, patting the wineskin on his saddle.

Sir Pangine eyed the sack thoughtfully. "I see no trouble with that, my lords. Could I persuade you to come warm yourself by the fire inside? It is but a humble keep, but the fire is hot and I have maps you may find helpful."

The keep was, indeed, humble, and the four travelers were invited to take a seat at the lone permanent table in front of the fireplace.

As Sir Pangine summoned glasses and food from his castellan, Sire Cei took the lead in fleshing out their story: four knights, comrades, ready to escape the busy plowing season under the pretext of an errand about hunting. Sire Cei mentioned his new bride and then mentioned broadly how as much as he was enjoying the comforts of marriage, he had found the need to see less of her face for a while. Sir Pangine, twice a widower, nodded understandingly.

Little was learned in the great hall from Pangine himself; the man was a glorified caretaker, an older knight being rewarded for stalwart service with running a marginal estate. But there were few other warriors about, Tyndal noted. He counted one common guard on look-out in the tower, another at the gate. That was it. Not that Taragwen was likely to be attacked – but Tyndal found himself finding fault with its state as a fortress, and imagined how he would conquer the place if he had a mind.

When the gentlemen departed an hour later, Sire Cei warmly thanked Sire Pangine and quietly passed him a few coins "in earnest of our desire to hunt these lands" later in the season. As noble and ostensibly gracious a knight as Pangine was, he was also of common enough means to appreciate such largess.

"He will look forward to the next time he sees us," Sire Cei explained as they rode back down the road toward the village. "It cost us but a few silver and a glass or two of wine, and we have learned a great deal for the price."

"We did?" Tyndal asked, curious. "I thought he was an old boor."

"Who is careless with how he speaks," Sire Cei reminded him. "If one knows which questions to ask, and how, and if one pays attention to the answer and how it is delivered, then a man might say a few words in passing that give you what you desire to know."

"So what did we learn?" Sir Merendol asked, chuckling.

"Sir Rondal, how many armed men in the keep?"

"Three, Sire Cei," the apprentice answered. "Top of the tower, at the gate, and one inspecting the back wall." Tyndal swore to himself. He'd missed that last one.

"Sir Tyndal, what is the most defensible place in the castle?"

"The tower," he answered. "One entrance in, with a portcullis and door."

"We also learned that Sir Pangine is the only knight, that his closest neighbor is six miles north, that he and his neighbor are not amicable, and that he has not laid eyes on his liege in two years."

"Why is that important?" Tyndal asked.

"A man is loyal to his liege in proportion to his proximity and his acquaintance. Sir Pangine served honorably as a mercenary for the Lord of Sashtalia's castellan and was taken on as caretaker – not liegeman – of Taragwen. While he collects the rents and pays tribute to Sashtalia, Taragwen is not, strictly speaking, his own."

"Why is that important?" Rondal asked. "He looks pretty comfortable to me."

"It's important because a man who watches another man's property fights differently than one who defends his own," agreed Sir Merendol.

"Exactly," agreed Sire Cei. "Taragwen is not well defended, it is not in great repair, and it is poorly provisioned. Ten men, at most, could garrison it at once, and there are half that number there."

"So it's a dump," conceded Tyndal. "So what?"

"Did you see any sign of riches? Of new wealth?" inquired the knight.

"No," Rondal answered. "So . . . if someone is mining snowstone, Sir Pangine hasn't been involved. He wouldn't let that kind of revenue go without claiming a share."

"Correct," agreed Sire Cei. "So let us discover who has."

Rondal was able to lead them to the outcropping, using a spell that pointed the direction toward the lowest etheric density in the area. The trail led into a wood and up into the higher reaches of the mountainside. From here they could see the white peaks of the mountains that had been affected by the spell, but the ridge closest at hand was gray and brown.

They had climbed three hundred feet up the trail before they discovered the mine. The perimeter of the snowstone spell cut through the southernmost edge of the mountain, and a large expanse of stone had been transformed – as had a shallow valley of soil, home to a small grove of cedars and hickories and ash trees.

The mine itself was on the edge of the hollow. An area three rods wide had been excavated, the soil removed and the dead vegetation laid aside. A pile of rocks had also been gathered.

"Luin damn them!" Rondal swore. "They've probably taken half a ton of it already!"

"Why is this white stone so important?" asked Sir Merendol.

"It is unique," answered Tyndal. "And highly treasured among the magi. Our master the Spellmonger created it. It makes magic easier to do. Unfortunately, it also makes magic easier to do for goblins. Or unscrupulous magi."

"The soil also has some interesting properties," Rondal agreed. "We're growing a couple of enchanted forests in Sevendor with it. But Master Minalan is worried that it could be misappropriated."

"Having a bit of snowstone outside of his control is vexing him," agreed Sire Cei. "Is there any sign—?"

"Of a camp?" Tyndal asked, as he discovered a cache concealed behind some brush. "I think so. Tarpaulin, a bit of food, some firewood, and a lantern."

"There's a fire pit over here," Sir Merendol called. "Looks to be at least three or four days old."

"How did they get it down?" asked Tyndal, looking around. "The trail is too narrow for a wain."

"They carried it down in sacks," explained Rondal. "You can see the impressions in the dirt over here."

"This *is* troubling," murmured Sire Cei. "If you wouldn't mind reporting to your master, Sir Rondal, I want to take a more thorough look around."

They spent nearly an hour searching the outcropping but found little else to indicate just who had been working the mine, despite their magical inquiries. Rondal spoke with Master Minalan mind-to-mind and received instructions about how to proceed.

"Hey, Tyndal," he said, after he broke contact and opened his eyes. "How much Blue Magic do you know?"

"Everything I read," he admitted. "Why?"

"Because Master Min wants us to do what I did with the Birchroot Bridge, only he wants it a little more subtle." He outlined the nature of the spell. "Since putting harmful spells on someone else's lands would be an act of war, Master Min thinks we can figure out who is doing this that way. He wants to know that as much as he wants the mining stopped."

Tyndal agreed to help, and the two boys proceeded to tap into their witchstones and erect a sophisticated spell that would not merely indicate who was doing the mining, but that would act upon their minds without them realizing it. Tyndal was impressed with the plan – he would have just lain in wait for the miner to return.

Sire Cei insisted on stopping at the cottage closest to the mine and politely questioning the fawning widow who lived there, learning that some men had been going up the mountain and bringing back sacks after he'd paid her a copper.

They had claimed that it was merely clay for sweetening the soil, but they were led by an armored man with a long tattered cloak, the hood of which was always pulled low over his face. Sire Cei noted that with interest, and then paid the old woman a few more pennies for her time.

They made a point of stopping back by Taragwen Castle to thank Sir

Pangine, who welcomed them to return at any time, before they struck back for the road north. They discussed the implications of the mine for the greater war, along the way, and the challenge of it existing outside of the Spellmonger's control.

"That *will* be a problem," agreed Sire Cei. "It is no secret that my liege Baron Arathanial has aspirations of re-taking the former Lensely lands. He has made a proud start after the conquest of last summer, and now the Lord of Sashtalia has lost his most powerful ally in the region. Had we been tarrying in a more important domain, mayhap we would have called too much attention to ourselves being from Sendaria. But you can wager that the Lord of Sashtalia and his men will be increasingly on their guard against any scouting of their fortifications."

"This mysterious hooded figure is intriguing," Sir Merendol said, engagingly. "If that is not some sort of spy . . ."

"Aye, but from who?" asked Rondal. "The Censorate? Someone from the Royal Court? The Brotherhood of the Rat? Or just some enterprising hedgemage who realized what a find he had?"

"We'll know more after the next time they arrive to mine," Tyndal said with a smirk.

They pushed on and made the Birchroot Bridge by dusk, just in time to enjoy a dinner of pork and pie. The inn was a little busier that night than before, as a few pack traders had stopped for the night, but it was still roomy.

After dinner and the production of a flask of local spirits, the former highwayman-turned innkeeper, Baston, broke out a battered lute and favored the half-dozen patrons with a song. Then Sir Merendol led them in a bawdy song after that, which got everyone feeling festive. After that Sire Cei, to Tyndal's surprise, sang a lovely melody about love in the springtime that did not challenge the limited range of his deep voice.

But it was well-sung, and totally at-odds with the man's appearance as a warrior. Tyndal was almost speechless. He had never considered the older knight a musician, but he did a passable job.

"Now *you*, Sir Rondal," the castellan prompted, gesturing at his fellow apprentice.

"Me?" the boy asked, horrified at the prospect. Tyndal couldn't help feel a thrill of pleasure at Rondal's embarrassment. It served him right for being such an introvert.

"You must remember that being a knight also carries a *social* obligation," Sire Cei prompted. "You are expected to ever be a good companion and cheerful company, to liege, comrade, and vassal. At any time you may be asked by your superiors to provide entertainment."

"The ancient order of professional knighthood, the Narasi Red Branch, would allow no initiate entrance unless he could prove a wholesome companion and also that he was an educated man," Sir Merendol added, pouring more of the strong ale into Rondal's glass to prime him for the trial. "Of course, back then, the knights were all illiterate, so the only way to prove their knowledge was to recite poems thousands of lines long without a single mistake. Consider yourself blessed by the gods to be born in a more enlightened time."

"You should always have at least one or two good songs and stories and poems you know you can recite," Sire Cei lectured, "and do so entertainingly. Now, in an empty inn among good friends is an excellent time to practice," he said, taking some obvious pleasure in Rondal's discomfort as he tried to squirm his way out of the command.

"Sire Cei, I think—"

"I think it would be best if you began with something light and humorous, owing to the occasion," Sir Merendol suggested, laughing. "Leave the sad ballads for another time."

Rondal looked like he had accidentally drank vinegar. But there was no escaping the ordeal, he finally realized. He sighed heavily and struggled to his feet.

"That's the spirit, lad!" Baston the innkeeper said, grinning enthusiastically. His wife seemed just as encouraging. "What shall you sing?"

"A dirge, by the look of him!" called one of the patrons, a pack trader getting deep in his cups.

"How about . . . *Rosafel?*" he asked, hesitantly.

"Aye, I know that one," Baston agreed, picking the popular tune out on his lute, repeating the chorus, and then nodding to the young knight to begin at his leisure.

Rondal opened his mouth, a look of terror on his face . . . and he began to sing. Tyndal held his breath in anticipation, half-expecting his rival to bellow like a donkey. But when he began singing about the maiden Rosafel and her lover, lost in battle, after a hesitant start Tyndal was surprised to hear a strong, clear voice that sang with a certain passion, if not confidence.

Once again, Rondal had surpassed Tyndal's expectations. For some reason, that soured Tyndal's disposition.

It was bad enough that they were sitting near to one of the classier pieces of enchantment Tyndal had ever seen – that bridge *was* impressive, especially as it was done long before Rondal went to Inrion and learned to do such things properly – but to have him be put on the spot like that and . . . do *really well*, despite his fear of public attention, that was nearly insufferable. To make matters worse, there were approving nods and smiles from the strangers in the crowd. Strangers who didn't know how irritating Rondal could be.

"Well done, lad!" Baston boomed enthusiastically as the crowd applauded. "I didn't know you had a voice!"

"It's only recently settled," Rondal admitted sheepishly. "I'm glad I remembered the words. I nearly considered singing a marching cadence."

"Perhaps not the best choice for this venue," Sire Cei nodded. "You picked wisely. Short, sweet, and well-delivered. *Your* turn, Sir Tyndal," he added, casually.

Tyndal stared at the knight, his mouth agape. He had been so focused on Rondal's potential failure that he had forgotten that he, too, might be expected to perform for the hall. He scrambled desperately for something, *anything*, but for the life of him he couldn't remember any song he knew well . . . or completely.

"Well? What shall I play, young master?" the innkeeper asked, smiling.

"Uh . . ." he searched his mind for inspiration . . . and with Briga's blessing it came. "Just an accompaniment," he directed. "For a poem."

It was Rondal's turn to look startled. Tyndal knew he had a passable voice, and it seemed to be growing deeper by the day. But he couldn't think of a single song that would not embarrass him for not knowing it all the way through.

Poetry, on the other hand, need not be sung. And he happened to have a bit on store.

"First a little lighting," he said, stepping into the role of a performer. Unlike Rondal, he not only was not fearful of a crowd, he enjoyed the attention. He cast a pale magelight overhead, bathing him in an unearthly glow. He could see Rondal squirm at the showmanship.

"I wish to recite to you tonight the *Lay of Gessa and Lukando*," he said, referencing an old Remeran ballad of unrequited love. It was in a complicated verse form, and had some intricate wording. It was not an easy thing to do from memory, even if one had studied it.

Tyndal had not studied it, but he had *read* it, finding an old copy in the Manciple's Library at Inrion. He had taken a break from his studies and read the old scroll in the hopes that it had some dirty parts. While he had been disappointed that the lyrics were, alas, wholesome and virtuous, he had also had the foresight to employ the memory spells he knew to bring the scroll instantly to his recall.

"*'I tell to you a tale of love and loss,'*" he began, "*'of hearts and lives torn asunder; for in the wake of war and strife, a lady's heart oft lies ripe for plunder . . .'*"

He continued to recite, reading from the conjured page and speaking slowly and deliberately, while Baston plinked out a complementary melody in the background.

He told the tale of Lukando the Remeran mercenary who conquered a rebellious castle on the coast for his liege and was ordered to put all to the sword, and how Lady Gessa's feminine charms and persuasion kept his wrath at bay until the old duke died, but how when the new duke came to power she changed her tune and rejected Lukando. The mercenary then put the castle to the sack in revenge, finally taking his own life in the light of the flames that consumed it in his despair at her betrayal of his heart.

It was a sad and poignant tale, and the complex rhythms in the words made it all the more difficult to deliver without becoming confused. But he had it right there in front of him, he was reading it right from the page. He made no mistakes. When he finished with a lowered voice, and faded his magelight from existence, the crowd was enrapt, and exploded in shouts and applause.

"Well done, Sir Tyndal!" Baston boomed. "Give me a week and I could make a jongleur of you!"

That . . . wasn't bad, Rondal admitted to him, mind-to-mind.

Thanks, Tyndal said, grudgingly. *You, too. I had no idea you could sing like that.*

I'm just figuring it out. But how did you . . . oh! The memory spell! Why did you bother to enchant that one?

Honestly? Because it's a skirt-flipper. If you can recite that to a girl on a moonlit night, you'll be up her skirts in a flash.

Rondal didn't respond . . . but he could nearly feel his fellow apprentice blush. That made Tyndal feel better, for some reason.

*   *   *

They tarried back at Cargwenyn for a week, with Sire Cei lecturing them on the finer points of chivalry while they helped him with the work of getting new hives ready for the bees and filtering last year's honey.

But then they left again, this time for a stay at Chepstan Castle, where Sire Cei paid a call on his liege, Baron Arathanial. He had much to report to the old baron in private concerning his journey into Sashtalia. Tyndal considered using the Long Ears spell to overhear their counsel, but Chepstan Castle's fair ladies kept him too distracted for such a blatant violation of his trust.

The boys had both met the distinguished baron several times but had rarely had the opportunity to speak with him alone. But when Sire Cei asked his leave to impart some of his wisdom on the art of chivalry on the boys, the man was eager for the chance. He spared much of the day for them, allowing them to accompany him as he toured one of his outlying estates for a surprise inspection.

The knight in charge of the manor was pleased to be able to show off for his overlord, and provided as delightful a feast as his holding could command that evening. If being an errant was a ticket to regular meals, Tyndal observed, the upper nobility were even more richly treated. Of course, since it was Arathanial's estate, it was technically his own food he was eating, he reasoned.

"That is interesting news about the snowstone," Arathanial agreed at table, after Sire Cei informed him of the illicit mine. "Twice so that Sashtalia does not know what he owns in it."

"Yet it is only a matter of time before he does realize it, and seeks to put a guard on it," Sire Cei pointed out.

"That is not insurmountable," the baron demurred as he worked his way through a bowl of beans and salt pork. "What makes it difficult is how many leagues lie between Taragwen and Sendari lands."

"Not so many between Taragwen and Sevendor," Rondal pointed out. "Merely a three-thousand foot ridge."

"That may be more insurmountable," grunted the baron. "What is this snowstone worth, do you think?"

"It's weight in silver, at least," Rondal said, just before Tyndal could say the same thing. "Perhaps as much as gold, once its full capabilities are realized."

"I would not have my rival keep access to a mountain of gold in his domain," pronounced Arathanial. "Nor silver. Currently I have the upper hand in lances, thanks to last year's conquests. Even with the loss of the men in Gilmora, I have edged out that pretender. But should he suddenly be able to hire mercenaries in large quantities . . ."

"I see your point, Excellency," agreed Sire Cei. "I will confer with the Spellmonger and see what can be done about this . . . before Sashtalia realizes what it has."

Sire Cei took the opportunity that evening to tutor the boys in how to properly serve their betters at table, among other tasks.

"It is an honor for a knight to be asked to serve his liege at the board," Cei instructed them. "It is both a sign of humility and a sign of pride that you would submit so graciously to your master. Even counts see it as an honor to serve a duke his dinner."

Baron Arathanial indulgently welcomed the lessons, offering his own opinion and perspective of their service. It was not difficult, Tyndal quickly realized, but there were certain rules you had to follow, lest you accidentally slop soup on someone who could send you to the battlefield someday.

On the ride back to Chepstan the next morning, the Baron continued to expound on chivalry. "You must always endeavor to treat your inferiors as equals, your equals as superiors, and your superiors as beyond reproach."

"What if your superiors are . . . *un*worthy, Excellency?" asked Rondal.

"They often are, but that does not mean they are not superiors. Honorable service is honorable service; it matters not, in most cases, to *whom* it is rendered."

"Why would a good knight serve an unworthy master?" Tyndal asked. "Excellency?" he added, belatedly, when Sire Cei caught his eye.

"Any number of reasons," shrugged the baron. "Heredity, among them. Oft a knight inherits a liege from his father. Men die and produce heirs. Agreements made between two men in one generation may lose their value in the next, as situations change. That does not lift the burden of such agreements, however, and an honorable knight will see them through to the letter, if need be."

"And a less-than-honorable knight?" Tyndal asked.

"If a man finds his honor challenged by such agreements," suggested the baron thoughtfully, "then he is often intelligent enough to discover an honorable way out of it. Appeal to the gods, for instance, or a competing agreement. A wise knight seeks not to place himself in such straits to begin with."

While at Chepstan Castle they spent a day with the squires at practice in the yard. Many were near their own age, near to winning their spurs themselves.

In a way Tyndal envied them – they were learning the trade by the more tedious route than he, but the expectations of them were lower. They were still struggling with letters and estate management, for instance, but they were already adept horsemen.

Seeing what a squire had to endure to win his spurs was instructive, Tyndal found. Running laps around the castle in a full mail hauberk, for example, or bearing a shield while your comrades rammed logs into it to "toughen" you seemed unnecessarily brutal. After consideration, Tyndal decided he much preferred the honored-on-the-battlefield path to knighthood.

At Chepstan they focused on horsemanship. Tyndal knew plenty of horseflesh, as any former stable boy does. He was even a passable rider, compared to Rondal.

But when it came to the art of fighting from horseback, and controlling an animal in a chaotic situation on a battlefield, he discovered he knew far less than he thought. The old knight who was Chepstan's Master of Horse, charged with overseeing their horsemanship, was replete with criticism for his riding, and some of it was even constructive.

At least he was at ease with horses. Rondal seemed perpetually nervous around the animals. The horse master had to speak with him repeatedly in hushed conferences, no doubt unpleasant affairs. As bad as it was being called a sack of potatoes for how he rode, he could only imagine the vitriol reserved for such discussions that Rondal endured. He had to admit, his rival's riding improved significantly afterward, so he couldn't fault their utility.

But then there was tilting, something he was extremely intrigued by. He took a few turns at jousting himself, and while he did a passable job at the quoits, when it came to running a perfectly good horse into another perfectly good horse, he found he lacked enough basic skill in the matter to find himself painfully thrown from his mount thrice.

Rondal, he was gratified to see, had even less skill at the art.

They both fared better at swordplay from horseback, employing their mageblades as skillfully in a charge as the squires were able to. Both of them neatly sliced the targets on either side of their mounts in the drill, once they got the trick of balancing in the stirrups for leverage. With magical augmentation they were particularly effective, though there was little they could do to extend their spells to their mounts. That was Brown Magic, and they knew very little of it.

What Tyndal enjoyed most about Chepstan wasn't the listfield, however. It was the bounty of young ladies within its walls.

Baronial castles were big, draughty, uncomfortable places, for the most part, but they were also secure. More, they served in peacetime as centers of social activity, where the mid-level nobility served and courted the baron's household.

It was also a popular place to send younger daughters or sisters to the baron's castle "for safe keeping" as the baron's wards. That such associations with the squires and young knights of the land often led to beneficial matches was also well-known, and most noble families sought to send their daughters to the castle for the refinement of society. Chepstan had a large crop of these, more so when you added in the students at the nearby temple to Trygg, where noble daughters were taught their letters and the arts until they were married-off, apprenticed a trade or took holy orders.

There were over two dozen young noblewomen at Chepstan, and each one of them seemed eager to make his acquaintance. Teaching the boys the rudiments of courtly dance provided plenty of opportunity for discourse and flirtation, and the Midsummer Feast allowed them an opportunity to practice with the gaggle of giggling maidens. Tyndal was studying more than pavannes and courtly manners, however. Tyndal was studying the maidens.

Tyndal found it an ideal opportunity to hone his knowledge of the Sixteen Laws of Love and their application. He was careful never to engage any one maiden overmuch, as the Laws bid. At a feast of femininity as lush as Chepstan he was content to indulge his appetites within the bounds of propriety (and, twice, just outside those bounds).

But the maidens of Chepstan were hardly a challenge. He even caught Rondal kissing a girl once. When it was time to leave, he was grateful. A few of the maids had started to get territorial.

Sire Cei led them back to Cargwenyn by a circuitous route, and Tyndal could tell the Dragonslayer was searching for something in particular, though he would give little clue what it might be. Instead of the direct route, they traversed the domains of Grendor and Taricil, prosperous lands with tidy, well-kept Riverlands villages and neatly laid-out fields sprouting wheat, rye, oats and maize. But then they entered a dark and twisted wood.

"The forest known as Herus' Grove. For the bands of thieves who are purported to haunt it."

"That sounds to me like you chose this route apurpose," Rondal observed, a little anxiously.

"At the request of the Baron, actually," corrected Sire Cei. "He invited me to tour the domain of Lormyr. This grove marks its frontier with Tarcil."

"And why should we tour the domain of Lormyr?" asked Tyndal, suspiciously. "Particularly when it lies on the other side of a wood so ominously named?"

"Do you fear a name, Sir Tyndal?" asked Sire Cei with a chuckle.

"It is but a name," he agreed. "and I fear neither thief nor wood. But still . . . it seems imprudent," he pronounced, bringing his horse to a halt.

"From time to time, a lord may wish to investigate a matter in his lands, but knows that an official inquiry may not be the best way to discover the truth of the matter. So he asks the gentlemen of his court to quietly look into it, without troubling the lord overmuch with their inspection."

"He has his vassals spy upon each other," answered Rondal, sourly.

"He uses the resources at his disposal to ensure accountability," corrected Sire Cei. "He has a responsibility to the people of his barony, and depending on officials who can be bribed and corrupted is not necessarily the best way to safeguard their security. Lormyr is ruled by one Lord Galenulan, whose line has been loyal Lensely vassals for three hundred years."

"But there is a problem now," Tyndal guess

"It has reached the Baron's ears that Lord Galenulan has been lax on his response to the banner call last autumn, informing Baron Arathanial that he could supply but a dozen lances when his lands should be able to produce more than a score. He sent only six, and they did not volunteer for duty in Gilmora."

"So Lord Galenulan is holding out, for some reason," supplied Rondal.

"I am to discover the reason for the deficit," Sire Cei answered. "It is possible that there are many good, reasonable reasons for it. I am to determine what those are, preferably without alerting Lord Galenulan as to my purpose. Our purpose," he amended.

"And to what could such a deficiency be blamed upon, Sire Cei?" Rondal asked, thoughtfully.

"Any number of legitimate reasons," reasoned the older knight, as he nudged his horse forward. "Plague and poverty are the usual reasons cited. Anything less than that is not usually taken seriously as a reason by your liege. That doesn't mean he can necessarily do anything about it. But if he's conspiring somehow, or merely wishes to avoid the expense . . . well, a good overlord seeks to know these things."

The village of Lentry was on the outskirts of Lormyr, but as it lay on the southern road through the barony it was a large village. At least a thousand souls called Lentry home, and if there was sickness or poverty there, there was no sign that Tyndal could see.

The peasants looked happy, or at least not miserable, as they chopped at the weeds around the furrows of wheat and beans, or listlessly worked at mowing the meadows. The village was large enough to boast two inns, a tavern, a blacksmith, a barber, and a twice-a-week market. A brightly-painted green shrine to Trygg Allmother was popular, he noted. But there seemed no overt reason why the men carrying hoes between fields could not just as easily carried spears in Gilmora last year.

"Interesting," murmured Sire Cei as they rode to the tavern's rail.

"I don't see anything out of the ordinary," declared Rondal.

"That is precisely what is interesting," agreed Sire Cei. "Perhaps a pint or two to clear the road dust from your throats, gentlemen?"

As they were tying off their horses and Sire Cei paid a boy a penny to watch them, the older knight made a point of whispering to both of his charges.

"Say little and listen much," he counseled. "A casual word in a public house can oft tell the wise man volumes. If questioned, we're three knights on the way back from Sendaria to our estates in the south. Say little more, if you are able."

Tyndal reached out mind-to-mind to Rondal as they entered the tavern. *Do you find this at all like spying?*

This is precisely like spying, Rondal answered.

Well, isn't that . . . unchivalrous?

You'd have to ask Sire Cei, but . . . well, considering that a knight's first duty is to his liege, in particular the rendering of military service, and reconnaissance lies within that field, then from his perspective he is jus performing honorable service. And it is a liege's duty to police his vassals. So . . . it might be technically unchivalrous, but in the grander scheme of things . . . wow, she's pretty.

Tyndal quickly turned around and saw who Rondal had spotted. A young woman, only a few years older than them both, was sitting with in the company of two much older women, all wearing traveling cloaks.

She was, indeed, quite pretty, under her wimple. An angular face, high cheekbones, and striking brown eyes. Her hair was dark under the headcloth, braided into two neat plaits. From her clothing and her jewelry she was decidedly not a peasant. The pewter rings in her hair were well-made, the sort of thing a burgher's daughter might wear.

The women were deep in conversation, each nursing an earthenware mug of ale, three empty dishes of stew on the table in front of them, a few crusts of bread the only thing left of their lunch.

Too bad she's headed for an abbey, Tyndal replied.

And not a fun goddess like Ishi, from the severe look of those two guard dogs, Rondal agreed. While not every order required celibacy for its clergy, most discouraged such things as distractions from devotion, at best. More than likely the maiden was looking forward to a few long, lonely years in meditation and contemplation.

Such a waste, Tyndal sighed.

Sire Cei led them past the women, and Tyndal was gratified when the pretty one looked up and caught his glance. He gave her a friendly smile. She looked away just as quickly.

That wasn't a bad sign, Tyndal had learned. In fact, it could be a good sign.

"Three ales," the knight ordered from the portly barman, who filled up three more cups from a huge jug he carried on his shoulder and passed them over when Sire Cei pushed him a few pennies. "What village might this be, Master?" he asked, conversationally.

"That would be the village of Lentry, chief settlement of the domain of Lormyr, gentlemen," the man said, a little loudly. "By your cloaks you're gentry – what brings you to our fair little hamlet?"

"Just passing through from Sendaria," Sire Cei admitted, handing the ales to Rondal and Tyndal. "On our way to inspect an estate. Tell me, what tolls lie on the road ahead?"

"Southward? You should bear east, first, and avoid Darnevron. That's the domain of Sire Oskellet, a harsh and cruel banneret. Lordly folk like yourself will suffer a silver penny each to cross his lands," he predicted.

"A *silver* penny?" Tyndal burst out. "That's . . ."

"An *excellent* way to raise revenue," Sire Cei finished. "Has this knight banneret found other ways to line his purse at your expense?" It seemed an innocent enough question, and Tyndal did not expect such a profound reaction. But the barman immediately began complaining bitterly.

"By Trygg's holy womb, he has!" the proprietor said, setting his jug down on a table with a thud. "He purchased the estate of Rena's Run, near to the river, and then had the stones to levy a tax on every fish taken from it on either side of the stream! When the good folk of Lormyr have fished there at the lord's sufferance without fee for generations! There's many a cottager who would have no flesh at all, if they did not take fish from the stream!"

"And what has your lord done about this?" Sire Cei asked, sipping the ale appreciatively. "Surely he is not standing for such an imposition on his realm."

"He . . . I cannot say," the barman said, suddenly realizing he may have been talking too much. He looked around guiltily. "But you might notice cheese is a bit expensive in the market," he muttered.

"I see," Sire Cei said, smiling quietly. "Good luck to you then, my friend. Have one for yourself," he said, pushing a third penny to the man.

"Trygg's blessing on you, milord!" the barman said, beaming. "I'm feeling thirsty, now that you mention it."

As he bustled off to pour himself an ale, Sire Cei took a seat with the two young knights and nodded, satisfied.

"There you have it, gentlemen. The answer to our question, and it took but three copper pennies and the right questions."

"Uh . . . what do you mean? I heard a man complaining about fish. And the price of cheese," Tyndal pointed out.

"Sir Rondal? Any other insights?"

"The folk of Lormyr don't like the lord of Darnevron," he decided. "And the banneret is feeling in an expansive mood."

"What . . . is a banneret?" asked Tyndal, a bit embarrassed for his ignorance.

"A kind of senior knight," Sire Cei answered. "It is not a title used much in the Wilderlands but is more common in the Riverlands. A banneret traditionally can raise two dozen lances, and usually has two or three domains as vassals. A bit above a sire, a bit below a baron, a banneret knight is oft looked-to by his peers for advice, counsel, and wisdom."

"Only this one seems to want to encroach on his neighbor's territory," Rondal pointed out. "Increasing revenues, putting pressure on the population . . . ah! Now I see why cheese was the key!"

"Exactly," nodded Sire Cei.

"Exactly . . . what?" Tyndal asked. "What has cheese to do with anything?"

"If a lord suspects that the crops of his folk will be disturbed, or that there may be a siege in the future, one of the first things he does is start buying cheese," Rondal answered, authoritatively. "High protein, high fat, and it keeps for months and months. Cheese, ham, bacon, eggs, sausage, any food that can be put in stores usually rises in price directly before hostilities," he finished, proudly. "Next will be grain, and then vegetables and fodder. But cheese takes time, so you start buying it up as soon as you think there might be war."

"So . . . the lord of Lormyr is anticipating a war with this knight banneret," reasoned Tyndal.

"Which explains why he sent only a token force to the banner call," agreed Sire Cei. "It is not uncommon for an aggressive lord to use such an occasion to infringe on a neighbor's unguarded territory. Raiding the hen house while the dog is hunting, so to speak."

"But . . . aren't both of them vassals of the baron?" asked Rondal.

"They are," Sire Cei agreed. "But a wise lord is careful not to interfere overmuch in the affairs of his vassals. From the baron's perspective, this is a contest to see who is stronger. Regardless of how it plays out, he will have the strongest lord in command of these lands."

"But what about justice?" Tyndal asked, concerned. "Is it not a liege's duty to ensure justice among his vassals?"

"If the banneret proceeds with his encroachment, it may well become such a matter," acknowledged Sire Cei. "But if the lord of Lormyr goes to Arathanial with a petty matter, it will be a sign of his weakness. A lord who cannot defend his territory without recourse to lawbrothers is weak."

"But how does it serve the baron to have two of his men spend the lives of their troops on each other?" Rondal prompted.

"Again, it is a matter of scale. If war does break out, there will be an attempt to negotiate between the two, under the auspices of the clergy or of their mutual liege. Such as there was between West Fleria and Sevendor," he reminded them. "But such contests rarely go that route. It is usually a matter of a few weeks' skirmishes and raids, then a parley.

"In this case, I foresee that Lormyr will begin pushing back against these fees. Some warden may find himself on the wrong side of the stream, for instance, and be sent back to Darnevron in chains. Or a few discouraging arrows from guards on this side of the bank will being the feud. A wise knight should always be wary of such skirmishes, however," he added, "for they can quickly become more involved, as emotions run high and retribution is demanded."

"So you're just going to report that there's about to be a war in southern Sendaria," reasoned Rondal, "even though you don't think the baron will do anything about it?"

"That was the extent of my commission," Sire Cei said, finishing his ale. "I will ask a few other questions, listen to a few other conversations, but I think our assessment of events is clear enough. A contest amongst vassals, nothing more."

Tyndal looked around. "It might be more to *these* folk," he said, quietly.

"In truth," nodded Sire Cei, gravely. "They will be the ones to suffer most while their lords argue. Thus should every good lord understand the gravity with which he makes war. It is the curse of our time that rash words and bellicose attitudes lead to suffering and devastation of the innocent."

"So how would you handle such a neighbor? If someone was encroaching on your domain like that?"

Sire Cei considered. "In this case, I would challenge the man to single combat. As a knight banneret, leading other knights by example, he would be honor-bound to answer such a challenge under most situations. If a man is willing to put an army in the field to achieve his objectives, he should be willing to face danger himself. And that would force him to choose his course.

"But I am not the lord of this land, and this is not my fight. My duty is to my liege. Now that I understand the situation better, I should report back to him of what I have found."

Rondal groaned. "So we're headed back to Chepstan Castle?"

"Nay," Sire Cei said with a small grin. "I shall return to Chepstan, alone. You, gentlemen, I gift with a commission: as part of your errantry, I ask that you attempt to collect a debt on my behalf. Or, on behalf of my domain, I should say."

"Is chivalry to be used in such a manner?" Tyndal asked, nostrils flaring. "I thought lawbrothers and paid collectors did such work?"

"And should the matter descend to that," agreed Sire Cei, "then those will be the avenues of approach I shall take. But the situation is thus: long before I won Cargwenyn, the estate has several outstanding payments for honey and wax which were made in good faith but, alas, have not been paid by other estates.

"Before I became its lord, Cargwenyn had to depend on the good faith of those estates, and Lady Estret did what she could to collect through messages and letters requesting payment. Since I have come into power, many of those have suddenly been paid. It is one thing when your creditor is a sweet noblewoman. It is another when it is a man who is called Dragonslayer." Both boys laughed at that, appreciating the humor.

"But there are two estates with large balances that have resisted Lady Estret's best efforts to collect. As it happens, both lie nearby: the estates of Ramoth's Wood and Lufhorn Manor, which lie in the next domain south, Durandor."

"So you want us to go shake down these debtors?" Rondal asked.

"I would put it more delicately," Sire Cei said. "I merely wish for you two gentlemen to pay a call to the estates, speak with their castellans or reeves, and remind them of their debt and the honor of paying it promptly and in full. If you find extenuating circumstances, then I trust you to contend with them chivalrously.

"And you needn't hold the folk at swordpoint – we are not bandits," he reminded them, sternly. "But a personal visit from my armed representatives – especially two such formidable young knights – could well speed payment. And while I am not suffering," he smiled – he was well-paid by their master for his service as Sevendor's castellan, and had received gifts from duke and king for his valor – "I find such outstanding balances . . . *untidy*. A man who cannot collect his debts displays his weakness as much as when he allows his walls to fall into disrepair. Note that I would be open to trade, as much as coin," he added. "I just wish these matters to be gone from my accounts."

"It still seems . . . un-knightly," grumbled Tyndal. Knights were supposed to be fighting or dancing or off being brave against unfair odds, or such. Acting as a collection agent just didn't seem to fit the vocation.

"Faithfully executing the instructions of your liege in the running of his estate is honorable service," Sire Cei disagreed. "Nothing could be more chivalrous than a knight performing his duty.

"Remember, we are not merely military officers, we hold a social rank as well – and most aspire to commercial success to the extent that we can perform our duties and support our horses and arms properly. Being openhanded and generous is a sign of grace in a gentleman. Allowing his estate to be cheated out of fairly-owed debt is not chivalrous, it is a sign of weakness."

"But would you have us draw swords over a fifty-weight of honey?" Rondal asked in disbelief.

"You need not draw swords at all," Sire Cei explained. "Just . . . *appear*. Introduce yourselves as emissaries of the House of Cargwenyn, and bring the debt to their attention. Somehow I doubt they are willing to draw swords over fifty-weight of honey either, but . . . in truth, I know not the names or characters of the debtors in the slightest, merely the names and amounts and dates of their purchases and deliveries."

He stood, after handing a sheet of parchment to Rondal containing the specifics of the accounts. "Is that within your capabilities gentlemen?" he challenged.

"Of course, Sire Cei," Tyndal said, rising and bowing. Rondal followed suit. "It would be our honor to hound your debtors on your behalf."

"And we shall endeavor to be a credit to your estate," added Rondal. "Of course . . . we know not the way, nor do we have the resources to make an extended journey . . ." he mentioned, expectedly.

"Ah," Sire Cei said, philosophically, "life is replete with such challenges, and the brave errant accepts them gladly as an opportunity to demonstrate his resourcefulness.

"You have been given your charge, gentlemen. I look forward to hearing of your adventures in a week's time, in my hall at Cargwenyn. But do not tarry – I know your master has a much more important errand on your horizon, and I would not have you be late."

"So . . . you want us to go forth without a penny?" Tyndal asked, mentally calculating the weight of his own purse.

"Of course not," Sire Cei said, tossing a small – a *very* small – purse on the table. "There must be at least nine, ten copper pennies in there, and perhaps a few silver bits as well. I trust in your ability to use it wisely, or add to it as you see fit."

"A pouch of copper?" Tyndal asked in disbelief. "We—"

"—gratefully accept your assistance and will be steadfast in completing our commission, Sire Cei," Rondal finished smoothly, after quietly kicking Tyndal's shins enough to interrupt him.

Sire Cei nodded. "Good luck, then, gentlemen." And without another word he left.

"Why in four hells did you do *that?*" complained Tyndal. Not that the kick had hurt, but he resented being interrupted like that.

"For your own good, idiot," Rondal murmured as they watched the Dragonslayer mount his horse through the window. "I learned back at the Mysteries that complaints about resources usually led to a *reduction* in resources. He gave us all he was going to give us. That's part of the exercise."

"It sounds more like an excuse to get some free service done on his behalf."

"Now you're starting to understand the glorious subtleties of feudalism," Rondal said, sarcastically, motioning to the barman for two more pints. "And I have considerably more than that in my pouch, if we need it."

Tyndal remembered he, too, had a half-dozen silver pennies in his pocket, the remains of what Master Minalan had given them . . . but he still resented being used like a common bill collector.

Rondal saw his discomfort. "This is a test, Sir Haystack. It matters less if we actually secure payment and more how we conduct ourselves. We've just been handed our first solo errand."

"But . . . there are two of us," Tyndal pointed out.

Rondal looked at him like he was an idiot. "Oh," Tyndal realized. "I see what you are saying. First errand without . . . adult supervision."

"Right," Rondal agreed as the barman brought two more rounds. "And it's a simple task. Like . . . building a bridge was," he groaned. "But it's one that's unlikely to result in bloodshed. Sure, we won't be staying at the finest inns, but this is rural Sendaria – there *aren't* any fine inns. And that other place is in rural Sashtalia. So we're going to be begging room and board from manors the whole way. That's what this is about. *Errantry*."

Tyndal sipped his ale and thought about what his fellow apprentice said. Sometimes he felt utterly intimidated by Rondal's keen insights and quick wits. Tyndal wasn't stupid, not by any measure. But sometimes it took him longer to recognize important details and realize what seemed to spring to Rondal's mind naturally. It was easily one of Rondal's more annoying traits.

"All right," he said with a sigh. "We'll go do this trial. I suppose a little light errantry *is* good practice. Besides," he said, cagily, "just about all of those manors have dewy-eyed maidens who like the look of a brave young knight. And I do so enjoy meeting new people," he decided.

"That's . . . whatever keeps you motivated," Rondal said, sighing with resignation.

Tyndal watched the young woman and her two older companions get up, pay the shot, and leave, making the room a bit quieter, if less fair. He watched her go and saw her glance over her shoulder at him. He smiled, she blushed, she left.

It felt odd taking their ease in the afternoon with a pint without a lesson, lecture, or exercise threatening them, he realized. He forced himself to relax. This was the first time in a long time that he'd been left to his own devices, more or less – only now he was saddled with Rondal, who was sure to keep this outing from being as much fun as it *could* be.

That wasn't completely fair, he chided himself. Rondal had come a long way in a short time, and was far from the insufferable snot he'd been last year.

Tyndal looked over to his fellow apprentice and noted that he wasn't even the scrawny bookworm he'd been at Yule. The Mysteries and the grace of the gods had filled out Rondal impressively. He was still of smaller stature than Tyndal, but his shoulders and arms seemed to have doubled in size, and instead of being hesitant when he walked he strode with confidence now.

Unless there was a girl around.

Rondal realized he was being stared at. "So what do you think about all of this chivalry stuff?" Tyndal asked, a little awkwardly, to deflect the attention.

"How do you mean?" Rondal replied cautiously, as they finished their ales and left money on the table. Whichever direction they were headed, if they did not get on the road soon it would be dark before they got there.

"I mean . . . it has some benefits, I can see, but . . . does it have to be this demanding?"

"Well, every profession has it's tough parts," Rondal said as he untied his mount.

"I feel as if I've been put through a millwork," Tyndal admitted to his rival, despite himself, as they mounted their horses. "Inrion, Relan Cor, now this errantry . . . forget the metaphors, I really do feel like I've been beaten betwixt hammer and anvil!"

"Me, too," agreed Rondal as he turned his horse southward. "And you didn't have to endure the Mysteries. But why the sudden concern? I thought you liked being a knight?"

Tyndal watched the young maiden and her two escorts start down the road in a light carriage pulled by a pair of rouncies. She barely acknowledged him as she rode by. Tyndal tried to imagine a different outcome of their chanced meeting, one in which she was desperate for one last moment of passion before she was cloistered in whichever abbey or temple she was destined for. It was a pleasant distraction to the talk of hammers and anvils.

"Since Yule, there haven't been many days that weren't crammed full of learning something vitally important about which our fate and perhaps all of Callidore's might someday depend. I know we're lucky to be where we are, but *Ishi's itching twat*, I feel like I've been pushed around and told what to do for so long . . . well, I guess I was just wondering if I was just feeling sorry for myself, or if the gods *do* seem to be kicking our arses daily."

"I . . . I'd favor the divine in that debate," Rondal agreed with a sigh. He still rode like a sack of meal, despite some improvement. But he was far more confident in the saddle, "Ever since . . . well, Yule, but especially ever since Inrion, I've felt like my life was one long tragically comedic epic."

"Like being sent home through country you've never heard of without a guide, on a mission of vague importance, and being judged by Duin-only-knows what standards by our masters?" Tyndal snorted. "The tale would be worth a drink, at any rate.

"But I was asking, I suppose, what do you think of all of this . . . *knights magi* business?"

"You're reconsidering your profession?" asked Rondal, surprised. "Seems a little late for that now."

"No, no," Tyndal said with another snort. "I've got ambition, and the gods have given me a worthy path. But . . . all of these *rules*. All of these expectations . . . about a job no one has really had before."

"Well, that's the thing," Rondal said with a shrug. "They can't really say we're fouling it up, without anyone to compare us to."

"And yet . . . I get the distinct impression that we're just on this side of utter failure," Tyndal pointed out, speaking his true feelings for the first time. "If we're the first, or among the first, shouldn't *we* get a say in just what a knight mage is? What he does? What he doesn't do?"

"If you are attempting to institutionalize your way out of guard duty and other shit work, Ifnia's luck be with you," Rondal chuckled. "Not that I'm unsympathetic, mind you, but I don't see a way for us to avoid it."

"Well, at least *this* part isn't so bad," Tyndal admitted, as they rode

out of the village along the southern road. "But all of that other stuff . .
. the social obligations, the legal obligations, the arcane obligations,
and all of it wrapped up with chivalry, which has precious little to do
with magic. The magelords of old didn't have to contend with
chivalry."

"And see what happened to them? Really, I thought you, of all
people, would be eager to don the mantle of chivalry," Rondal said,
surprised. "Most days you can't be pried out of the practice yard."

"If it was just fighting and swordplay, I'd be fine – better, perhaps.
But everything else . . . well, it makes me wonder how knights have
any fun."

"Are we supposed to have fun?" Rondal countered.

"I damn sure am!" Tyndal said, sullenly. "I'm due some fun.
Without someone looking over my shoulder." He looked at Rondal
warily.

"Why are you looking at *me?*" snorted the other apprentice. "I'm not
your bloody warden! Go bugger virgin goats, if you'd like. I'll refrain
from judgment," he said, unconvincingly.

Tyndal snorted back. "What? You'd really not tell Master Min or
Sire Cei if I, ah, took some creative liberties with their carefully laid
plans?"

"You're your own idiot," Rondal assured him. Then he paused a
moment. "Why? What did you have in mind?"

"Nothing felonious," Tyndal assured him. "I think. I hadn't any
particular crime in mind. I'm just proposing that we be open to
adventure."

Rondal shrugged, which surprised Tyndal. "Isn't that the nature of
errantry, supposedly? So you just want to follow the road and see what
kind of trouble you can get into?"

"*We* can get into," Tyndal reminded him. "And I'm not saying we
ignore our errand. Merely that we enjoy it as much as we can. If that
means risking a little trouble . . ."

"I just said I wouldn't tell and I wouldn't judge," Rondal said,
quickly. "By all means, do what you please. I'm sure it will be
instructive to watch. But . . . well, don't expect me to hold the down
the goat while you do it."

*   *   *

As fortune favored them they had little in the way of adventure for the rest of that day as they rode south. They came to a prosperous manor late in the day and – for the first time – traded on their knighthood for a night of room and board.

Despite Tyndal's dreams of luxury, the matron of the manor asked that he split some wood for the fire, as her servant had injured his shoulder. He did it with axe and maul, not magic, just to stretch muscles cramped by hours of riding. Rondal was tasked with bringing in water from the well, which he likewise did without revealing his arcane skills.

Dinner was adequate, a hot stew of beans and chicken served on day-old trenchers. There was no cheese with their meal, but some butter that was not quite yet rancid.

At supper, they shared a table with the cream of the manor's ladyhood. None were younger than thirty, and all seemed to have the sort of face that Sire Cei graciously called "unfortunate."

So where are the dewy-eyed maidens? Rondal teased his fellow apprentice.

I think they must be in the stew, grumbled Tyndal. *I'd figure there would be at least a maid or two about. This lot looks like a crone's wake.*

The next morning they thanked their hostess, received a stirrup cup after praising her hospitality, and accepted a modest lunch for the road. Biscuits and the leftover stew from the night before.

"So where is this first manor we're to find?" Tyndal asked, as they discovered the fare was better after a night's rest. "Ramoth's Wood?"

"From what I understand, it is one of the estates belonging to the lord of Lormyr," Rondal supplied. "Which you would know if you had listened to half of what our hostess said at dinner last night."

"I was paying attention," protested Tyndal, annoyed. Rondal seemed to pick the most inane things to reprove him over. "I didn't ask who owned it; I asked where to find it."

310

"Oh," Rondal said, taken aback. "It should be down this road, then west at the next crossroad. That will take us into Lormyr, and Ramoth's Wood should be on the east side of the road. From what Sire Cei told me, the tenant lord is Sir Gamman the Red."

"That . . . is a foreboding sounding name," admitted Tyndal. "So . . . any points of interest between here and Lormyr?"

"I think there's an inn at the next village," Ron answered. "But I think we really should—"

"Be pursuing an errant's life of adventure?" Tyndal interrupted. "I couldn't agree more. All of this study . . . training . . . practice . . . don't you want to use some of that great store of knowledge in the field?" he teased.

Rondal looked uncomfortable – a common expression on the boy's face – but shrugged. "I suppose," he admitted. "But . . . I don't want any trouble."

"That's your problem," Tyndal said, shaking his head sadly, "you *never* want any trouble."

"Trouble gets people killed," Rondal pointed out. "And imprisoned. And fined. And captured. And—"

"And experienced," he soothed. "That's why Sire Cei sent us out here. *Seasoning.*"

"And if I do not feel the need to be seasoned?"

"Then you are working against your liege's orders," pronounced Tyndal. "Didn't Master Min say he wanted us to be independent and self-reliant?"

"I thought his emphasis was more on training and instruction," Rondal said, as they clopped along.

"This is training and instruction in self-reliance and independence," Tyndal rationalized. "It's just an inn. Two dashing young errants having an ale on the road. What could happen?"

Rondal's groan was a pleasing sound in Tyndal's ear.

*   *   *

It being market day, the inn was crowded and bustling with traffic when they arrived. The boys tied their horses and paid a lad an iron penny to watch them. They followed the trail of peasants and merchants within.

The inn was called the *Rampant Rabbit,* and featured a colorful sign over the door: a buffoonish, somewhat effeminate rabbit in a jousting helm and scarlet shirt threatening a powerfully muscled bull with a limp carrot. Behind the rodent was a pretty lady rabbit, elegantly gowned, who seemed far more interested in the bull than her erstwhile protector. Tyndal found the sign highly entertaining, and wondered who had painted it.

As busy as the trade was on a market day, their mantles and swords told them out as gentlemen, and that got them some attention quickly. Before long their host, Goodman Rogal (who seemed far too skinny to be a real innkeeper) ushered them to a good table near to the window, and soon ale and bread and game pies were put before them, along with a plate of the local cheese.

"Now this is living properly," Tyndal said with a sigh as he sipped the rich, nutty ale. Far better than the last tavern's. "No pressures, no worries, just a couple of mates in an inn, enjoying a meal."

"This does seem to be the first time we've been without our masters and betters around, in a while" Rondal agreed, almost sounding enthusiastic about it. "And this is truly excellent ale. Strong, too," he said, sipping it slowly.

"I sometimes wonder if this is truly all a man needs," Tyndal said, philosophically, as he looked around the friendly hall.

"A woman's favor would be nice," Rondal murmured, as he watched a trio of local village girls burst into the place. One of them might even be pretty, Tyndal decided with an expert eye, at least for another few years yet. They were not the type of maidens Tyndal found himself drawn to, but Rondal's attention had been captivated.

Tyndal considered. He had no understanding of why his fellow apprentice resented him so. It was a mystery to Tyndal, but clearly there was still some secret issue between them. Perhaps, he reasoned, if he endeavored to assist his comrade with one of his largest deficits – understanding the mysteries of femininity – then he would see that Tyndal was not inherently antagonistic.

And if he failed, well, at least that would be entertaining.

After what they had been through, he felt he at least owed Rondal the attempt at correcting his presentation, when it came to girls. Although the lad was sullen, moody, and oftentimes cranky, he was still a fellow apprentice under the same master, and he was still Bovali.

If Tyndal found him irritating and plodding, he had to admit that Rondal had never resorted to the sorts of bullying or underhanded behavior that some apprentices had to fear from their fellows. In fact, most of the time Tyndal didn't mind Rondal's company at all, when he wasn't being aggressively sullen.

"What would you say if I told you how to seduce yon maiden that your eyes suddenly can't seem to leave alone?"

"What?" Rondal asked, struck out of his reverie. "What? Who? *Her?* Me? *What?*"

"Let us begin with your appalling lack of eloquence," Tyndal said, smoothly.

"Wait!" Rondal sputtered. "Why do I need *your* help to seduce her? And who said I wanted to seduce her at all?"

"Perhaps the gentlemen with the portly figure is more to your liking?" suggested Tyndal.

"No, you idiot, I like girls plenty. And . . . yes, that one is fair," he admitted, embarrassingly. "But I don't need *your* help to woo her."

"Then by all means, have at it," Tyndal approved, sipping his ale. "Go ahead. I shall observe your stunning victory."

"Who said I *wanted* to pursue such a dalliance?" demanded Rondal quietly. His eyes flashed angrily, and he held his drink in front of his lips protectively.

"Your eyes, for one, and the way you have your jaw clenched up, like you did around . . . around . . . around girls you like," he said, not able to mention that it was Estasia's presence that had brought the signal to his attention the first time. "Then there's the uncomfortably awkward way you are shifting in your seat, as if you suddenly have a hot coal in your lap. But no, they are all liars. I'm sure you're just considering taking holy orders," he teased.

"That doesn't mean that we have the time or—" Rondal sputtered.

"I'm not saying *marry* the girl – Ishi's twat, no! But she's . . . *almost* comely, particularly when she's standing in such forgiving light and so near to her unfortunately-faced friends, so . . . at least go get *her name*," Tyndal demanded. "Put a word with the breasts and face the memory of which you will be consoling yourself to sleep by tonight."

"It's not that simple!" Rondal hissed, his eyes darting around.

"Boy," Tyndal said, gesturing toward Rondal with one long finger, before turning it on the maiden. *"Girl.* It's really no more complicated than that. You cannot finish the hunt you never start," he said, quoting from one of the many commentaries on Sire Rose's Laws.

"So why do you have to learn how to hunt women like game?" asked Rondal, sourly.

"Because they don't just fall into your bed of their own accord," Tyndal countered, amused at his fellow's naiveté. "At least not usually, and rarely the worthy ones. *They* need to be persuaded. Coaxed. Charmed." He grinned wolfishly. "Pursued. *Hunted.* But gently, ever so gently."

"Lied to, you mean," Rondal accused. "That's all that 'Sire Rose' is counseling: how to lie creatively to women."

"Not at all!" Tyndal objected. "That's a gross misstatement of the Laws! And the hunt is a perfectly apt metaphor for the pursuit of love.

"He speaks of the many arrows in a man's quiver, each one a means to allure a maid's attention and keep it. Lying is rarely necessary, if a man knows the proper way to pursue a maid's heart. Indeed, Sire Rose is merely instructing the young gentleman in how best to achieve no less than the noble aim of Love."

Rondal snorted. "His aim tends to be a bit lower than a lady's heart, I recall."

"Oft has an impassioned embrace led to a lifetime of love," objected Tyndal.

"And even more often a full belly or an unpleasant pox," Rondal grumbled.

"We know the spells to ward against such things," reminded Tyndal, who had shared them with his fellow as soon as he'd learned them.

"You have the desire for a lady's favor in your heart – and no doubt for more intimacy than holding hands."

"That doesn't mean I need to hunt down everything in a skirt!"

"You are not a child any more, Ron. Why is this troubling you, so?" Tyndal asked.

"Because love should happen naturally, as guided by Ishi's hands," Rondal said, stubbornly. "It should not be practiced as a craft!"

Tyndal sighed and studied his fellow determinedly. He had to alter his approach.

"Craft? More art than craft. Attend: a man spends his life married to one woman, gods willing," Tyndal reasoned. "In its way, it is a decision that affects his life as greatly as going to battle. Or more. Agreed?"

"Well, yes," Rondal said, sullenly, finishing his drink. "Who one marries is, perhaps, as profound a decision for a man as picking up a sword."

"And would it be wise to go into battle with *no idea how to use a sword?*" challenged Tyndal. "No," he answered himself. "A warrior trains, he practices, he learns how to use a sword. How to kill. How to defend himself. He learns how an enemy attacks and how he doesn't."

"I'm familiar with the process," Ron said, dryly.

"Yet for choice as important to a man as his fate in battle, you suggest he go into the affair without the *slightest* idea of how to conduct himself? What the rules of engagement and ordinances of propriety are? How one can expect a lady to respond? Why would you cripple yourself so with ignorance?"

Rondal was silent for a while, as the question hung in the air. "Love is supposed to be *natural*," Rondal repeated. "If a man weds for love, as the bridesisters advise, then it is because Ishi's will has guided it thus," he said, reverently. "A man need but be his natural self, and be of gentle demeanor, and--"

"And he will enjoy many a long, *lonely* night as celibate as a deathsister, or married to a shrew of impressive quality," finished Tyndal, matter-of-factly. How could his fellow apprentice be so stupid? "Really, Rondal, do you really believe that Ishi decides who beds whom? Or do you think a maid decides herself?"

"Well *of course* the maiden decides!" Rondal snapped. "It is *always* a lady's choice!"

"And upon what merits does she decide to give her head . . . or other parts . . . to a man?"

"Why, on whatever merits she wishes!" Rondal snorted again. "If she has a fancy for a man, and class and duty allow, then she may decide on whatever merits she likes. That is the Ishi's command."

"Agreed!" Tyndal smiled. The goddess had decreed that all free, unwed women enjoy the right to govern their favors as they alone saw fit, before they wed.

Of course, if a maid enjoyed Ishi's Blessing with every lad in town, there would likely not *be* a wedding. Many a bridesister had succumbed to the allure of her own desires, and had been forced to take orders when no honest husband would support her. "And, as Ishi wills, every woman will have her own personal preferences, will she not?"

"Of course," Rondal said, clearly annoyed with Tyndal's patronizing tone.

"But when one examines the personal preferences of *all* women, or even of a number of women, would you not find *some* commonalities? Some elements of a man's character and bearing that many, if not most, would find desirable?"

"Well, yes," Rondal said, warily. "A preference for men who are not ugly, deformed, infirm, cruel, mad, bound by law or sacred oath, or of low estate would seem reasonable."

"And lucky for you that you fulfill at least most of those requirements," Tyndal said, sarcastically. "But you can agree that there are some things that women -- in general -- prefer over others. Height, for instance. Women enjoy a tall man."

"It seems to be Ishi's design that you are taller than me," Rondal observed, dryly. "And I have no means to correct her error. Height is not one of my arrows."

"So I am," Tyndal continued with a smile. "But then you can wear boots. Perhaps a hat. It matters not how tall you are, really, as long as you are taller than the *maiden*.

"And your quiver is far from empty. You are *strong*. Women tend to value strength in a man. And courage. Bravery. Decisiveness. Being fair of face," he grinned suddenly, "certainly helps, and understanding how to speak intelligently to a lady is an asset. But there is one thing above all others that women desire when they see it in a man. And for it they will forgive much, if not all."

"A dazed expression and a purse the size of a pumpkin? I seem to have left those back home."

"No, the expression is correct. But do not despair. Despite your lack of a boyishly fair face, muscles the size of chargers, or a purse the size of a pumpkin, even a man such as yourself may attract a woman of quality. Rondal, you merely lack *confidence*."

Rondal snorted. "You say that as if all I had to do was conjure it up! You don't perhaps have a spell for that, do you?"

"No, it's not magical in nature. It's merely a feeling," he said, pleased that his knowledge of Blue Magic allowed him to speak so confidently on the subject. "Confidence, you ass, is nothing more elaborate than the *feeling of assuredness you have in the outcome of events*. That is all."

"It's more than . . . It can't be . . ." Rondal faltered, as he considered the subject.

"It *is*," Tyndal assured him. "Nothing more. When you feel as if you know what is going to happen, you *act* confidently. When you are unsure of the outcome of events . . . you *lack* confidence."

"So if I bloody well know in advance that some lady will offer me nothing more than polite discussion about the weather . . ." he said, sourly.

"That would work," agreed Tyndal.

"I was joking!"

"I wasn't," Tyndal insisted. "That's my point. Ladies are attracted to men who act confidently. *That is all.* They care not why a man is confident, or in what he is confident, or in whom his confidence might rely. They merely sense that he is at ease because *he* is assured of the outcome in his own mind and acts accordingly."

"*What* outcome? Whether or not a maid will bed you? One can hardly be assured of that. Unless she's a whore," he amended.

"The nature of the outcome is not at issue," Tyndal instructed, feeling pleased with himself. "One must only be certain of *some* outcome.

"For instance, while I may not be assured of enjoying the favors of a particular lady, I *can* be assured that I will have a hot breakfast the next morning. I am *utterly* confident in it.

"Therefore, when I speak to a lady, I think not about the obstacles between me and Ishi's Blessing, about which I am almost never assured, and dwell instead over the certainty of breakfast. With that pleasant thought in mind, I can proceed to discourse at length with a lady and appear utterly confident. Which I am," he said, pleased with himself.

"About breakfast," Rondal repeated, dully. "*That's* your secret?"

"It gives me confidence. That is just the largest arrow in the quiver of the paramour," Tyndal said, airily. "Another is jealousy."

"Jealousy?"

"Indeed. A maid may have only a tepid interest in you, if she spies you alone and lonely. You may only arouse a passing interest . . . until *another* maiden declares her interest. Then the first lady suddenly sees you far, *far* more intriguing."

"That, indeed, is true," Rondal admitted. "It has never happened to me, of course, but I have witnessed it."

"It *could* happen to you, right now, should you wish. Go speak to them," he urged. "Only speak not to the fairest one. Speak to the *second*-fairest first. She will be flattered that a lord should deign to speak to her first, and your possible ladylove will be far more receptive to your courting once she sees that interest."

"Do you truly think so?" Rondal asked, doubtfully.

"And let us not forget our purse, position, and power," Tyndal continued, grinning. He enjoyed lecturing about a subject so dear to his heart. "You are a *lord*, a man of means. She is a village girl, perhaps even a villein. A man of means is *always* more attractive than a pauper. And a man of high position always more attractive than a villein."

"Obviously," dismissed Rondal. "And a gulf that purse will not bridge, position may." That was a common saying back in Alshar.

"Power is more alluring than either," Tyndal said, quoting Sire Rose

318

again without attribution. "A man with power needs neither position nor purse. He may have either at a word. Women flock to him like bees to honey. When you have it, you will see. Do you not see all of the doe-eyed maidens who follow our master, since his ascension? Power may be relative, but a little is often enough to encourage a kiss or even hike a skirt."

"I do have position," Rondal pointed out.

"You do," Tyndal agreed. "You are a knight and a magelord. The agent of a rich and powerful man. *Use* that," he urged. "Is it a lie to say it?"

"No," Rondal agreed. "But . . ."

"But you think your jests and cow eyes are going to convince her to hike her skirt? Or even get her name, of her own accord? Women are attracted to achievement and success. Concealing such things from them in the name of humility is a monk's game, not an errant's. It matters not *how* you impress her, you must merely impress her."

"I would not have a woman like me only for my title or position," Rondal objected. "Or because she saw me as a rung on a ladder to higher position."

"Such a woman would be unworthy to wed," Tyndal agreed. "But quite easy to bed, if you follow the Laws of Love. And perhaps even worth the trouble. But there is one more arrow you could loose at a maiden's heart. One easier than wealth, position, or power to manage: *notoriety.*"

"Reputation, you mean," Rondal corrected.

"I chose the word carefully," Tyndal demurred. "Reputation may attract some women, but notoriety . . . whether for treason or triumph, a man whose name is on everyone's lips oft finds maidens aplenty on his own."

"That, too, I will admit," Rondal agreed. They had both seen just how potent notoriety had been during the Coronation festivities in Castabriel, and after the Dragonfall in Barrowbell. One maiden after another had done whatever they could to attract their attention, and some of them had been very, *very* committed. Tyndal could recall his comrade faring poorly even then, due to his inexperience and unwillingness to act.

Tyndal had been less cautious in enjoying the rewards of his notoriety. In Barrowbell in particular he had indulged in dalliances with a number of ladies, noble and common. Lady Pentandra had encouraged and advised him, seeming amused by his enthusiasm, and he had faithfully followed her instruction. Indeed, much of what he was saying to Rondal with such sagacity he had heard first from Lady Pentandra, or read from books she'd recommended.

"But no one here knows who I am or what I've done. My notoriety is a broken arrow."

"True," Tyndal admitted. "So one should take advantage of it when one can. But," he added, "you have many other things in your favor. Youth. Vigor. Position. Bearing. And the sword helps," he pointed out.

"It does?" Rondal asked, surprised.

"Women enjoy the attention of dangerous men, when they have a mind," Tyndal assured him. "Some find it . . . quite compelling. A man of arms can always find a maiden to comfort him willingly, if he looks for her. In addition, you are a traveler, a stranger, an exotic foreigner with tales to tell and adventures to relate."

"I . . . I suppose that is true," Rondal conceded, eyeing the girl with a more hopeful expression.

"See?" Tyndal encouraged. "You have many arrows in your quiver. All you lack now is a bow."

"How do I lack a bow?" demanded Rondal.

"Simple," countered Tyndal. "You have all the weapons you need . . . save the *will to act*. Initiative. You have to go *talk* to them," he emphasized. "Your bow is your willingness to pursue a lady." He looked over at the peasant maiden. "Or a girl," he added.

"So if I lose my position, my looks, my strength, my wit—"

"Such as it is," Tyndal interrupted. Rondal ignored him.

"—the fact that I am a stranger and the fact that I am a warrior, all of those will be enough to woo her, if I have but the will to pursue the affair with the zeal of a hunter pursuing a wounded hart," he concluded, skeptically.

"I count your chances far better than dancing with that mug and staring at her all day," Tyndal observed. "But . . . there is one more thing you must – *must!* – understand about the esoteric nature of Ishi's Blessing."

"Instruct me, oh sagacious master!" Rondal mocked.

"It is actually quite . . . profound," Tyndal murmured, looking around as if he feared being overheard. "Once you first understand the nature of a woman's cycles—"

"Oh, *Trygg's hairy armpit!*" objected Rondal. "Is there *nothing* you hold sacred in your quest for girls?"

"Listen!" insisted Tyndal, seriously. "A woman's cycle is the key to her heart. Or at least to her skirts. You know of a woman's monthly courses . . ."

"Yes," affirmed Rondal, uncomfortably.

"Well, near to two weeks prior or after, a woman's desires are most inflammable, to a man who understands the mystery. It's as if she becomes . . . *warm*. She bares her neck, sometimes, or wears more revealing gowns. So Lady Pentandra assures me," he added, to lend credibility to his statement. "A woman will be far more intrigued with feats of arms or displays of largess during this critical moment.

"More, she is oft so moved by her desires that her resistance to a thoughtful persuasion is lowest. Pentandra also says that this is a woman's best time to conceive a child."

Rondal groaned. "Of course, it *would* be. The gods have a nasty sense of humor."

"You're not the first to note that."

"So I should quietly inquire as to when their monthlies last came, before I decide to pitch my woo?" asked Rondal, amused. "Another round!" he called to the innkeeper, who nodded happily.

"I would advise against it," Tyndal insisted. "You have to *guess*, based on her state and demeanor. Something else to amuse the gods, I suppose. But even then, you can begin to track her heart. If you know the *other* mystery."

"And that is . . . ?"

"Simple: Ishi has ordained that the path to a woman's heart – and between her legs – lies in her *reactive nature*."

"Reactive nature?" Rondal asked, confused.

"A woman's desire is *reactive* in nature," explained Tyndal, "both in the words of the ancients and in my experience. Perhaps one in three, one in four will be more . . . aggressive," he chuckled, "or lack desire entirely. But the other three or four . . . they require something to react *to*, to engage their desires."

"What, precisely, do you mean?" asked Rondal, warily.

"Women require a man to be provocative before they feel able to surrender their hearts to a man," Tyndal said, as if he was relaying the deepest secrets of magic. "They need a man to be strong, take a stand, and take the initiative . . . before they can decide whether or not they will follow."

"You sound like a mad man," snorted Rondal. "Honestly, Tyn, women do not merely respond. They take *plenty* of initiative . . ."

"In affairs of the heart? Forget for a moment those . . . ladies in Castabriel, who wanted to bed us to get closer to Master Min, and the noble maidens of Barrowbell whose hearts were inflamed by our victory over the dragon. When a man and a woman entertain to spark, the woman tends to react to what the man does, not the other way around. Not if he's smart," he added, ruefully.

"That's rubbish!" snorted Rondal, as the innkeeper set down two more mugs.

"Have you ever waited for a girl to kiss you?" Tyndal challenged. "Have you been alone with her, the moment seemed right, and you looked at her and waited for her to do something . . . and she didn't?"

"Well . . . yes," Rondal admitted quietly. "I always thought it was just because they didn't really want to be with me."

"Idiot!" Tyndal snorted in return. "She was waiting for you to *take the initiative*. For you to 'loose your arrow,' so to speak. Because you didn't hazard an action, she was not, therefore, in a place in which she could naturally *respond*."

"What if she's not really excited about being with you?" Rondal countered. "What if she really does just prefer your company, as a brother?"

"Then the taint of your rejection will lie on your brow like a sigil for all to see," predicted Tyndal dramatically. "Everyone will know what a craven buffoon you are. At worst she will slap you," Tyndal continued, less sarcastically. "As long as she is not above you in station, or particularly naïve, she will forgive the attempt, if it was sincerely made and properly executed. If not . . . well, there are worse reputations to gather than that of a lad who likes to kiss," he offered.

"Are you gentlemen perhaps referring to the maidens?" asked the innkeeper, who had chanced to linger after delivering their drinks.

"Maidens in general," Tyndal replied, "but they were the ones to inspire our discourse."

"I'd advise against it," warned the innkeeper. "Fali is filthy, Carsa is like to drag you to a bridesister after getting you drunk, and Dindra . . . well, she's a fair one, and agreeable . . . but a bit *too* agreeable, if you take my meaning."

"Your candor is appreciated," nodded Tyndal with a smirk. He'd figured as much, but Rondal had to start *somewhere*. "We weren't seriously considering paying court, just admiring their form. We seek the lord of the domain, one Sir Gamman, with whom we have business."

"Sir Gamman?" asked the innkeeper in surprise. "Then you'll be better off passing up these common skirts; Lady Kresdine is as fair a lady as one could hope to see."

"Sir Gamman's wife?"

"Aye," the man said, pleased to be able to share the local gossip. In Tyndal's experience, innkeepers and stableboys knew more than captains and commanders. "She's a fair one. As is their daughter, Lady Thena. If you are considering paying court, she would be a better prospect than these," he said, gesturing toward the giggling girls disdainfully.

"And where might we find Sir Gamman's manor?"

"Ramothwood? Take the west road a half mile, and then turn north. You'll see the gate: the sign of a hare on a field of white, under a scarlet chevron."

"A *rabbit?*" snorted Tyndal. "Hardly a beast to inspire terror in the hearts of one's enemies."

"Sir Gamman inherited the device from his forebears," recounted the innkeeper. "Nice enough folk, I suppose, but . . ."

"But what?" asked Rondal, curious.

The innkeeper shook his head. "'Tis not wise to talk idly about your betters. If you have business with my lord, then you gentlemen can make your own judgments." Tyndal was about to ask for details when an ear-splitting call from the upper room cut through the chatter.

"*Astin!*" it called, hoarsely and viciously. "Astin, get up here! I need you to bring more hot water!"

The innkeeper closed his eyes as if he'd born a hard blow. "That's the other reason why you need to avoid the village girls," he sighed. "I had my head turned by a pretty ankle and a shy smile once. When you do go to court a maid," he said, with sudden intensity, "by all the gods *choose wisely!*"

"ASTIN!" repeated the call. The innkeeper sighed again, and went to fetch a kettle of water from the fire.

Tyndal glanced back at the village girls, who were starting to take more notice of Rondal's attention. He could suddenly imagine all of them aged, worn, and rotund after years of comfortable marriage. He suppressed a shudder. He supposed that sort of thing was all right for some, but he was a man of action. No common woman would lure him from a life of adventure.

"Let's go," he said, quietly, as he dug for his purse and drank the last of his ale. "I'm suddenly anxious to go lay eyes on this highborn lady."

*   *   *

Ramothwood Manor was far grander in appearance than its size would indicate – the number of ostentatious decorations, mostly featuring the hare-and-chevron of Sir Gamman, belied the actual modest nature of the hall. It was a two-story building, with impressive peaks and dainty spires overlooking a tidy, well-kept yard. But it was not large, Tyndal could see. It was half the size of Jurlor's Hold, back in Sevendor, if half as shabby.

The manor folk were hard at work when the two knights magi arrived. Though it was high summer, there was still much to prepare for the summer mowing and autumn's harvest. Only a few looked up to watch the strangers dismount and chase down the hall's steward.

Once the man was convinced that they were gentlefolk and had legitimate business with Sir Gamman his brusque manner was replaced with one of surpassing obsequiousness. Sir Gamman was inspecting the far end of the estate, they were informed, and was not expected to return before nightfall. Lady Kresdine and her daughter, however, were at leisure in the garden, and the man ran off to see if they would deign to meet the knights.

Does this place seem a little . . . odd to you? Rondal asked him, mind-to-mind, as they stabled their horses.

A little, Tyndal agreed. *Like it's trying a little too hard to convince us of something. Let's play this on the mundane side, shall we?*

Huh?

Don't mention magic. We're just a couple of young errants. Mention magic and that might . . . complicate things.

How so?

Just trust me, all right? Tyndal insisted.

The steward returned in a short time to inform them that after they'd had an opportunity to refresh themselves, the lady of the manor would enjoy conversing with them in the garden. Tyndal may have been imagining it, but there was a devilish look in the man's otherwise supplicant eye.

They were shown to the hall, where they were granted water and a towel to wash the road dust from their faces and a sip of wine in front of the tiny fire. The interior of the hall was even more ostentatious than the exterior, filled with tapestries, paintings, statues, steles, and other noble regalia . . . all featuring rabbits.

By the time they finished refreshing themselves and were ready to meet the lady, Tyndal felt that the motif had been entirely overdone. He was not sophisticated In matters of taste, but even his humble aesthetic was disturbed by so many rabbits so proudly displayed.

It's like someone is fiercely proud of being an herbivore, Rondal agreed with him as they were led through a gallery to an enclosed garden. *It's . . . creepy.*

The garden was meticulously kept, with shrubs and herbs and flowers bursting forth from well-made stone risers. The season and the weather seemed to conspire to push out as many blossoms as each plant could bear. It had as its central point a bathing pool, no more than ten feet on a side.

While it looked cool and inviting in the heat of the day, the effect was lessened, Tyndal thought, by the twelve-foot tall topiary rabbit that loomed benevolently over it. Tyndal supposed that the vaguely rabbit-shaped bush (he could tell where the ears and head were supposed to be, at any rate) was designed to look fearsome, but like his friend he just found the decoration . . . *creepy*.

Fortunately, there were more attractive things to stare at, namely Lady Kresdine, who was escaping the heat of the day by plunging into the cool water and then lounging in her soaked shift so that the summer breeze could keep her cool. The wet garment left little of Trygg's gifts to speculation. Lady Kresdine was a well-formed, mature woman.

Her daughter lounged nearby, a light summer mantle cast over her shift for modesty's sake. She had merry eyes and a pretty face, even prettier than her mother's, and both mother and daughter seemed utterly at ease at the sight of two young errants. The servant announced them formally.

"Presenting my lords Sir Tyndal and Sir Rondal, knights of Sevendor, who beg a word from Lady Kresdine of Ramoth's Wood. The Lady Thena, in attendance!" he called, as if in front of a court full of people.

"My lords," the woman's soft, warm voice said as she wrapped her mantle about her shoulders. Such a gesture would have been modest in most women, but Lady Kresdine managed to make it into a seductive dance. Her eyes sparkled as they lighted on the two young knights. "We bid you welcome to Ramothwood, and pray your business is not so dire that you cannot spare a few hours of this glorious day to converse with two ladies near to overcome by boredom."

"While our errand is pressing," Tyndal replied smoothly while Rondal's jaw gaped, "it is not so pressing that we would ignore the rules of hospitality, my lady. Should our business be concluded positively, I see no reason why we should not enjoy a few hours of idle amusement with two such gracious noblewomen."

Tyn! Rondal said, mind-to-mind. *She's damn near naked!*

It's a hot day, Tyndal observed. *Shut up. I'm working.*

There were only a few reasons why a woman would abandon

propriety in such a way, Tyndal knew, and few of them involved her naiveté about such things. A lady of the manor had certain social expectations.

Meeting guests, particularly strangers, required a level of presentation that Lady Kresdine had not indulged in. While it could merely be a mark of her casual nature, Tyndal reasoned, as Lady Pentandra was wont to say, you rarely see boobs unintentionally.

Tyndal was on his guard. He could understand why Rondal was standing there like the village idiot in the face of Kresdine's sensual display. He'd likely only seen a handful of boobs in his life and that included his mother's when he nursed. But Tyndal had attracted attention from unlikely quarters, and he was wise enough now to know when a woman was using her charms to influence, more than to allure. Lady Kresdine was up to something.

"Then pray state your business, Sir Knight, and let us dispense with it," Kresdine said, as she toweled her dark blonde hair dry, her light blue summer mantle peeking open. "My husband is away inspecting his estates and is not due until eventide, so you will have to contend with my poor management in his stead, if the matter cannot wait."

Tyndal knew then that the matter was not naiveté, which he had doubted to begin with. That meant her purpose was either business or pleasure. Tyndal found himself prepared for either eventuality, or a combination of the two. While he enjoyed the spectacle she granted, he wasn't going to let this woman gain the upper hand in negotiations through the pretense of immodesty.

"My colleague and I represent the Castellan of Sevendor, Sire Cei of Cargwenyn, known far and wide as The Dragonslayer," he began. "Perhaps you have heard of him, milady? The Wilderlands knight who bested the field at Chepstan Spring Fair a year ago, to win the hand of a lady and an estate?"

"Such news has reached me in this remote manor," she admitted, smiling. It was a pretty smile. The name of Sire Cei sparked Lady Thena's interest as well, and she sat up on her bench attentively. "What business does our humble estate have with such a worthy knight?" She pushed a stray lock of hair behind her ear, exposing her slender neck. Tyndal could hear Rondal swallow. Amateur.

"In the assumption of his new estate, Sire Cei wishes to clear the accounts. It is stated in the estate's book that Ramothwood owes a sum

327

to Cargwenyn for the purchase of a hundredweight of honey. As we were passing by, he imposed on us to stop and inquire after the bill."

"Such things oft escape my husband's attention," she said with a girlish giggle. "He is a very important man, you know, the head of the Council of Seffwan." Tyndal had no idea what that was, but she sounded like he should be impressed. He made a point not to be.

"Surely he has an attendant who sees to such things, my lady?" reproved Tyndal.

"We did. Alas, old Gilmar died last year of a wasting cough. Our new man is . . . learning the job, but he has yet had the chance to clear some of our accounts. I sincerely apologize for the oversight, gentlemen. *Bamar!*" she called in a harsh voice that belied her previous gentle tone.

A few moments later a thin, pasty-faced man with a scraggly beard appeared, breathless, his eyes wide with fear.

"Yes, milady?" he asked with a shaky bow.

"These gentlemen are here inquiring as to an account on behalf of a friend of theirs. They say we owe for a hundredweight of honey, more than two years ago. The estate's name is Cargwenyn. "

"Cargwenyn, milady?" Bamar asked, confused.

"It appears that your father clearly bungled yet another matter, Bamar, and it falls to you to set it right. Investigate the book and verify the debt, and report back here immediately!

"In the meantime, I think we will have wine here in the garden to enjoy the coolness of the water on such a hot day. Have it delivered, and then ensure we are not disturbed unless I send for you. Is that understood?"

"Y-yes, milady," he said, bowing even lower. "I shall see to it at once."

She turned back to Tyndal while he scurried off. "His father was just as weak," she confided with disgust. "An ineffectual man who couldn't do the simplest thing without guidance. I do not know why my husband persists in keeping Bamar in his sire's place; if anything, he is even worse. But he *can* read," she admitted, "and he does know his place.

"Now," she said, gesturing to the pleasant poolside garden under the looming eye of the verdant rabbit, "would you perhaps like to doff those mantles and lay aside your swords for an afternoon, gentlemen?" she asked, sweetly. "My daughter and I have been confined here for days by the heat, and it is two weeks yet until the next ball of any consequence. Without distraction, we may soon succumb to hysteria."

"Well, we wouldn't want *that*," agreed Tyndal, smiling, as he unfastened his cloak pin.

What the hell are you doing? Rondal screamed in his mind.

I'm getting comfortable, Tyndal replied. *You should, too. This is going to take awhile.*

Why?

I don't know yet, but she's up to something. Just follow my lead, for once.

Rondal didn't reply, but he did remove his summer mantle and lay it on a stone bench with Tyndal's. Next they removed their mageblades and laid them on top.

"So what have you ladies been filling your time with today?" Tyndal asked as Lady Kresdine led him by the hand to a larger bench . . . large enough for two, and sporting a long, soft pillow of down.

"Idle gossip," Lady Thena said, "vicious, brutal, scandalous gossip. A common weakness of our sex, I'm afraid," she added with a coquettish smile.

"How delightful!" Tyndal said with a grin as he settled into the great stone seat. Lady Kresdine settled in beside him, an intoxicating cloud of floral scent following her. Rondal just stood there, looking awkwardly around, as if purposefully avoiding the seat next to Lady Thena.

Sit down, idiot! Tyndal shot. *And don't mention magic!*

Where do I sit?

Next to the pretty girl, maybe? Tyndal shot back sarcastically. *I said follow my lead. I'm smiling, you be smiling. I'm sitting down, you sit down. And then keep your mouth shut.*

I . . . I can do that, Rondal said, and then plastered a smile on his face before sitting down next to Thena.

Tyn, she's . . . she's kind of young, isn't she?

Only a year or two younger than we are, Tyndal pointed out. *She's getting to sit next to a handsome young knight errant. Some girls go their whole lives without getting a chance like that. It's what they dream about, or didn't you figure that out at Chepstan? So shut up and let her enjoy the moment.*

I'm not handsome, was all Rondal could respond.

Try not to let her know that, Tyndal advised, and turned his attention to the woman sitting so alluringly next to him.

"Now," he began, settling in, "as we are strangers in your land, we are curious about its history and the reputation of your noble lord. Is he a puissant gentleman?"

"Daddy?" Thena burst out with a giggle.

"My daughter is impolitic," Lady Kresdine said, smoothly. "Her father is of noble lineage and distinguished house. Sir Gamman was properly squired and belted, but his skill lies far more in oratory than action. He has never drawn his blade in anger," she admitted. "When he serves out his duty to his liege, he oversees the garrison at Garsby Castle, protecting our land from invasion from Bocaraton."

Tyndal was surprised. "I was not aware of the danger of invasion from Bocaraton," he admitted.

"There isn't one," agreed Lady Kresdine, who seemed disappointed in the political situation. "My husband spends a month watching the wheat grow outside of the castle walls. Every autumn," she said with some deliberation, "betwixt the equinox and the Feast of Huin. We ladies are left in solitude at that time . . . and are *always* welcome of diversion."

Tyndal almost swallowed nervously, before he caught himself. Her meaning was unmistakable. One thing he had learned from the patient tutelage of Lady Pentandra in the arts of love was knowing the subtle ways a woman indicated how desirous she was . . . often in ways she herself was unaware of. Tyndal had a suspicion that Lady Kresdine knew precisely what she was doing, and what she was saying. He responded as he knew she wished.

"Mayhap if we are near Ramoth's Wood we could stop by to alleviate your inactivity," he said, diplomatically. "But if your lord is not renowned for his skill at arms, of what use is his oratory?"

"Oh, my lord has a gift with speech," she said, with quiet humor. "He can expound at length upon *whatever* topic comes to mind . . . endlessly."

"Do his words have such value, milady?" asked Tyndal. It was clear that Lady Kresdine had mixed emotions about her husband's talents.

"Apparently his entourage believes so," she admitted with a sigh. "He is considered a troubadour of some repute . . . by some. A small but . . . small band of knights and admirers who follow him incessantly, eager for whatever spittles of wisdom or thick, steaming piles of verse might fall from his lips."

"My lord sounds . . . charismatic," offered Rondal, looking uncomfortable with Lady Thena's proximity and casual attire. For her part, the young noblewoman was eyeing his fellow like a kitten eyes a mouse that might or might not be too large for its abilities . . . but who was daring enough to make the attempt.

Poor Rondal . . . he had no idea what a voracious young woman absent the frontiers of propriety was capable of. And from her attitude and demeanor, Lady Kresdine was not discouraging of her daughter's attentions. On the contrary.

"Charismatic?" she asked, amused. "Mayhap. Our marriage was arranged by my father and seemed a well-suited one, at the time. He was charismatic," she disclosed. "I had hopes of . . . well, let us not speak of that.

"Our union is pleasant enough. My lord's business and his philosophies keep him away frequently, and my daughter and I have found amusement and distraction in society. We attend what functions we're able, and entertain ourselves at need.

"Ah! My servant returns. Let me pour us some cool wine, gentlemen," she insisted, leaving the bench and her mantle behind. Clad only in her swimming shift, still damp from the pool, there was little Trygg had given her that Tyndal did not gain a glimpse of.

That confirmed it enough in his mind. Tyndal had no doubt just in what form that entertainment occurred. Regardless of her other motivations, here was clearly a woman who exercised her frustrations by supplementing her marital fulfillment with . . . well, with passing knights errant, he reasoned. Like himself. He could not help but feel excited by that thought.

Rondal was, too. But not in a positive way. *Tyndal, what are we doing?*

At least it's we now, Tyndal said, as he watched Lady Thena straighten Rondal's baldric unnecessarily. *You're being seduced,* he observed. *See how she's touching you when she doesn't need to? And how she's looking at you and looking away? She admires you. In a moment she's going to ask you to tell her how manly you are, somehow. Don't disappoint the lady. Brag a little.*

But that's hardly chivalrous—

It's completely *chivalrous. You are entertaining a lady. That's what a good knight does. She just wants details, so she knows who she's seducing.*

She's not seducing me!

Not if you stick with that attitude, agreed Tyndal. *Ishi's glorious holy twat, Ron, when the universe decides to grant you a boon, dare to take it, won't you? Bravery on the field is hollow if a man is a coward in the bedchamber.*

We're not in a bloody bedchamber! he said as Lady Kresdine brought a tray of silver goblets around to his bench. *We're in a bloody garden in the middle of the bloody afternoon!*

Which means that we can actually see their faces without the glamour of candlelight, Tyndal pointed out. *They might not be the fairest ladies in the land, but they are comely enough. Pretty ladies in a beautiful garden with a creepy giant rabbit . . . this is an errant's dream!*

Those sorts of dreams usually end with an angry husband and father with a band of fanatical followers with swords chasing the hero out of the domain.

Relax, Tyndal soothed. *He's far from here, we have legitimate business, and believe me, this is not milady's first such entertainment. She's of the kind who treats love the way some knights treat tournaments, and she's grooming her daughter for the same. You are merely an exercise,* he pointed out. *So enjoy the examination for once.*

"To Ishi's lips," Lady Thena said, dipping her finger in the sweet white wine and letting a single drop fall from her lip to the ground in solemn libation. It was a maiden's blessing. It required a response. Tyndal watched in amused sympathy as his horrified fellow was forced to complete the rite or humiliate his hostess. He knew which course propriety and chivalry required.

Rondal swallowed, dipped his own finger into the wine, and touched his mouth.

"From Ishi's lips springs the font of love," he mumbled. Lady Thena looked utterly pleased with herself. She leaned forward and planted a soft, sweet kiss of surpassing elegance on Rondal's startled lips.

Kiss her back, you idiot, Tyndal growled into his mind. *This is a sacred rite.*

Rondal didn't reply, but he found it within himself to respond with some cautious enthusiasm. Lady Thena broke the kiss and relaxed, looking quite pleased with herself.

The rite was supposed to ensure a maiden's future happiness, under the pretense that the holy lips of Ishi fell best on lips oft-kissed. The rite could be as chaste as a peck or . . . not, depending on the maiden, the lad, and the circumstances. But to decline even a peck was considered a bit of an insult, once she had begun the rite.

It was a coquette's game, but one that frequently led to even deeper rites of the goddess of Love. Even respectable girls from conservative families performed the rite. It did not necessarily indicate that a lass was interested in a lad . . . but that was certainly the case in this instance.

"Thank you, my lord," Thena said, sweetly, sipping her wine. "May I inquire as to your position and station? Surely a knight so young has yet to bare his blade," she added, suggestively.

It's a challenge, Tyndal counseled, amused, as Lady Kresdine returned to settle beside him. *Do not fail it. Charge ahead with valor.*

Despite the encouragement, Rondal stammered and stumbled to the point where Tyndal was forced to rescue him.

"Actually, milady, Sir Rondal was born a commoner, as was I. Simple mountain lads from the vales of the Mindens, apprenticed to a common trade. But then the goblin invasion occurred," he said, gravely, "and our homeland was overrun."

"Duin protect us!" Lady Kresdine said, her eyes wide in genuine fear.

"We have heard of the invasion, but . . ."

"We were there at the beginning," affirmed Rondal.

Finally. Rondal had, at least, learned enough of warfare to be able to discourse on it with some authority and confidence. He almost didn't sound like an idiot. "At Boval Vale, which now lies at the heart of the Dead God's dark empire. We were besieged, and both of us were required to take up arms in defense. We were rescued from certain death only by the intervention of Minalan the Spellmonger," he said, keeping their relationship with the man a secret for the moment.

So the boy wasn't a *complete* idiot.

"That sounds . . . awful!" Lady Thena said, enrapt.

"It was worse than you can possibly imagine," Tyndal agreed. "Only what came after was worse. Once rescued, we followed Master Minalan into battle, as did many Bovali. For our service on the field at the Battle of Timberwatch, we were knighted by the hands of two dukes – the night before Duke Lenguin died from his wounds." It never hurt to drop a few names, and naming a recently-deceased Duke could not help but elevate their status.

"Surely many fought in that battle," Lady Kresdine observed. "Yet not all came away ennobled and knighted."

"There were dark deeds done that day," Rondal said, with sincere gravity. "I pray you ladies not ask us our parts, for they were fell. So many did not return from that fiery field that I would not sully their memory with a casual account."

Oh, well played! Tyndal encouraged. *You completely avoided the fact that you were stuck safely in a tower for the entire battle while I repeatedly risked my ass!*

I've been practicing for that one, admitted Rondal. *It's kind of embarrassing to note that you got your knighthood for accurate field observations.*

You've more than made up for it since, reminded Tyndal.

"That was even more treacherous a day than the Battle of Cambrian Castle, the day that Sire Cei and Lady Lenodara the Hawkmaiden slew the dragon," added Tyndal, out loud. Nothing could top that boast, lest it was he who had wielded the lance. "In truth we are still recovering from that battle. Sire Cei, whom we serve, has mandated a period of rest and repose before we return to battle."

"I do hope you have found sufficient comfort and support, Sir Tyndal," Lady Kresdine said, licking her lips. Her eyes held new respect for her guests. And they didn't even know that they were magi, he reminded himself. Just a couple of knights errant out erring.

"Well, save to further our studies," reminded Rondal. "We took part in the War College at Relan Cor this spring. And we have of late been practicing tilting and other noble arts at Chepstan Castle. That was hardly . . . restful."

"Such busy, strong young knights," Kresdine smiled. "We are so favored to have you here to entertain us today—*what is it?*" she demanded, as her obsequious steward reappeared.

Lady Thena, who had arrayed herself quite comfortably against Sir Rondal, made no move to add distance between them in front of the servants, which told Tyndal much. He knew who ruled at Ramoth's Wood, and it wasn't the knight with the fondness for rabbits.

"Begging your pardon, milady," said the man, "but I searched the accounts until I found the record. We do, indeed, owe a sum to Cargwenyn for the purchase of honey. It is . . . a substantial sum," he said.

"So substantial we cannot settle it at present?" she asked, warningly.

"If my lady will inspect the listing," he said, with a trace of warning in his voice, "she may make her own determination."

Lady Kresdine looked momentarily taken aback, but she recovered quickly. "So I shall, and we will get to the bottom of this. I will ask my gentlemen to bide a moment while I do, and then perhaps they will entertain us further at a picnic out in the meadow?" She looked at her daughter pointedly. "Why don't you go change into something suitable, my dear," she instructed. "We will return anon with our luncheon."

When the ladies had left, Rondal bolted up out of his seat. "What are we doing here?"

"Being seduced," reminded Tyndal, casually. "I told you that. Is there something wrong with Lady Thena?"

"She's pretty," agreed Rondal, sullenly. "But she's young!"

"Old enough to ask for Ishi's Kiss. And perhaps more. She'll be wed within a year, if her mother can find a right match. Until then, she wants to practice."

"Her mother is *right there!*" Rondal whispered harshly, ignoring the mind-to-mind link that would keep them from being overheard.

"Her mother is all but holding her skirt," Tyndal pointed out. "Look, she's a coquette. She's being groomed for such a life, as much as we are in our chosen profession. No one is asking for your hand in marriage, Ron, she just wants to enjoy an afternoon with a lusty young knight. If it bothers you so, stop short of assaulting her virtue, if you must."

"And are you like to do the same with her mother?" Rondal asked, accusingly.

"I'm uncertain as to just how much virtue Lady Kresdine has left," joked Tyndal. "But do try to hold yourself in check from saying anything *too* stupid. In fact, if you have any doubts, use the Long Ears to overhear what they're saying. I'm sure we will find it instructive."

"That would be . . . impolite!" Rondal said, when he couldn't think of a more damning condemnation.

"Intelligence gathering often is," reminded Tyndal. "But in a way we are on a mission, and if you doubt my summary of the situation, I invite you to listen to what the ladies say between themselves. You need not act on any information you so discover," he promised.

"All right," Rondal said, after a few moments of struggle. He sat down next to Tyndal and they both cast the spell. Finding Kresdine and her daughter within the manor by voice was not difficult – indeed, the lady of the manor was being quite loud as she argued with her cowering servant.

"What do you mean, we owe them nine ounces of silver?" she was demanding.

"Nine ounces and one half ounce, and three silver pennies, when interest on the debt is calculated," the man corrected. *"My lady, the honeys of Cargwenyn are of surpassing quality, and are blessed by Noapis. My lord prefers a godly honey with which to sweeten his porridge—"*

"If you had any idea what your lord actually *preferred,"* Kresdine

reproved angrily, *"you would look upon me with pity and revulsion. What is the state of the treasury?"*

"My lord has four ounces of silver and thirteen half-ounces, as well as some copper coin. We should be receiving nearly double that, this market, but we just paid—"

"Shut it!" Kresdine said, angrily. *"I have two hot-blooded young knights down there who are demanding payment – and my idiot husband left me nothing! Typical! Thena, how much coin do you have?"*

"Mother, I—" she protested.

"Don't you start with me, little lady!" Kresdine exploded. *"I spent a ransom on your introduction party, and I know you received at least some token from those no-account uncles of yours! How much?"* she demanded.

"I have but three ounces of silver left," the young woman admitted.

"What did you do with the rest of it?" her mother shrieked.

"A girl has expenses, Mother," the younger noblewoman shot back. *"Did you not teach me that?"*

"Oh, shut it! We have to do something to mollify them – your father is already near to being the laughingstock of the Bontal Vales, the last thing we need is for it to be said he does not pay his debts! Damn him and his lackluster poetry! And these are no mere country knights, Thena, these are men of position. They serve Sire Cei the Dragonslayer, who himself is the castellan to the Spellmonger."

"Mother, are not spellmongers mere bourgeoisie?" asked Thena, disdainfully. *"Why do we care—?"*

"You little idiot!" snarled Kresdine. *"This has naught to do with class, this is about power! The Spellmonger is the talk of the entire Bontal, along with his Dragonslayer and his Hawkmaiden. Now he has knights wandering around collecting his debts . . . this is a disaster! If we fall from favor now, when we are searching for a good match for you, all of our work will be undone."*

"Mother, I hardly think a little honey—" Lady Thena began.

"You hardly think, let's leave it at that. It's not about the damn honey. It's about our reputation. It's bad enough we have those stupid rabbits all over everything, if we send these men away empty-handed,

we will be the talk of the Bontal. We must mollify them. A token now, and a pledge of the balance . . . yes, I think we can manage this situation. Thena, go change into the blue riding gown, boots, and . . . don't bother with the undergown. It's a hot day."

"Mother! Without the undergown, they'll see—"

"Ah, my sweet, this is you hardly thinking again," she said with sarcastic sympathy. *"I know full well what they'll see. Why do you think I gave you the instruction? Now off with you, and do not scrimp on the cosmetics. You are about to see what a lady does when her idiot husband leaves her no choice in the matter! And you! Have the team hitched to the carriage. We will be taking our lunch in the meadow by the river. Ensure no one disturbs us,"* she said with particular force, *"or I shall see you cleaning out pigsties until you're in your dotage!"*

"That," Tyndal said, as they let the spell drop, "is what is *actually* going through milady's mind. Not issues of propriety and chivalry. She's just like any wife with a debt collector."

"But we weren't sent here to demand payment," reminded Rondal, "we were sent to merely inquire about it!"

"And so we have," Tyndal pointed out. "But milady Kresdine is apparently unaware of the distinction."

"I don't know," Rondal said, uneasily, "it seems unchivalrous to take advantage of them like this . . ."

"Are we not faithfully serving our master? Are we not advocating on his behalf? Are we not undertaking a mission?"

"This is errantry," corrected Rondal, "not a real military mission."

"All the better," Tyndal insisted. "Without errantry, chivalry is mere military service and social obligation. We aren't doing anything wrong. We haven't even done anything . . . *yet.* Just bide a moment, then they'll return, we'll have a pleasant afternoon in their company, and be on our way."

Rondal was thoughtfully silent as he contemplated Tyndal's words, so Tyndal took the opportunity to contact Lady Pentandra, mind-to-mind.

What is it? Pentandra asked, brusquely.

My pardon, my lady, is this a bad time?

No, I'm just on my way from one meeting to another. What is it, Tyndal? Trouble?

Of a sort. Rondal and I are on an errand for Sire Cei in the Bontal. We're inquiring about an account to a local manor on his behalf, where the lord is out and the lady of the manor and her daughter wish to entertain us.

When you say entertain . . .

My lady understands exactly. I am well-disposed to the idea, but Rondal . . .

I see. Tyndal could hear quiet amusement in Pentandra's mental voice. *Are the ladies objectionable?*

Quite comely and well-mannered. Rondal has misgivings over the propriety of the situation. But the daughter offered him Ishi's Kiss, so I don't think there's much to worry about.

And the mother?

Lovelier than her lord deserves and in a poor marriage to a bore. A knight jongleur, with a flattering following of admirers and a fetish for rabbits. She endures it while grooming her daughter for higher station.

That sounds suspiciously like my mother. Then her sins are her own to bear. I trust you aren't as concerned with propriety?

I find myself strangely ambivalent on the matter at the moment, he said diplomatically.

And the inspiration for this ambivalence?

The hungry way in which the lady gazed upon me. Like a starving dog looking at a bone.

Then assuage your conscience, Sir Knight. You are likely not the first bone she's gnawed.

That was my feeling as well.

So tell your dull companion to attend to the higher matters of chivalry: coaxing a young lady into womanhood is a sophisticated process, and he is called upon by the goddess to play but one small part. He should embrace the opportunity to feature so boldly in this young woman's dreams. Soon enough she will be married to some boorish old knight herself and be looking for distraction among her own errants. He should give her a fond memory to recall on future lonely nights.

I shall relay your counsel, Lady Pentandra. Thank you for your wisdom.

There was a mental snort. *Wisdom? It sounds like the ladies are damn near panting. And if he can't handle a simple seduction like this, they're going to eat him alive once he gets to court.*

"Lady Pentandra counsels that you accept your destiny boldly," Tyndal informed his fellow apprentice quietly, "and without concern. She says also that this is training for your future political service. She's correct, you know. From what I've seen of the court, seduction and flattery are as common as daggers and poison."

He thought guiltily of his knowledge of Master Minalan's dalliance with the shadowmage Lady Isily, back during the Battle of Timberwatch. That had been something to do with court politics, he knew, although the details were sketchy. It was a point of pride to him that he had never revealed his knowledge of the affair, especially to Lady Alya or Lady Pentandra. The last thing he wanted to do was see Alya hurt. And he suspected that if Master Min wished to tell her, he would have done so.

Rondal stared at him in disbelief. "She thinks I need to *seduce a knight's daughter?*"

"She thinks that you should allow yourself to be seduced to the extent that the lady is willing," countered Tyndal. "As they are returning now, I suggest you plaster your warmest, most charming smile on your face and start thinking of poor jests to force her to laugh at."

Rondal swallowed, a little pale faced, and nodded. Both knights stood when the ladies returned, now clad in more demure traveling clothes. Once they assured them that they looked absolutely beautiful, using the courtly language they'd learned, they escorted the noblewomen to the yard where a small carriage waited. Rondal took the reins, with Lady Thena next to him, Kresdine and Tyndal behind.

From the moment Kresdine sat next to him, her hands proved what her intentions were even as she calmly gave directions to Rondal. He found his blood racing with excitement as she quietly caressed him, beginning innocently enough on his knee but progressing quickly northward. He chanced a caress or two of his own that was met with

340

her favor.

One of the advantages of the sideless surcoat, Tyndal reflected as his fingers traced the outline of her left nipple, was its discreet accessibility. He was gratified to see the lady close her eyes for a moment of quiet reflection as she enjoyed his attentions. Lady Thena proved more demure, although she hooked her arm around Rondal's as he drove.

The meadow the ladies suggested was at the crest of a hill overlooking the ripening fields of wheat and rye. On such a glorious summer's day finding shade was their biggest concern, but a big elm tree near the side of the meadow proved ideal, and they spread their afternoon meal under its shady boughs. Bread, cheese, wine, fruit, a pot of preserves and a half-dozen boiled eggs made up their luncheon while they talked about the weather, the village, the crops, and the news of the wider world.

It was a pleasant meal, made better by the excellent weather and the attentive company. Tyndal found his foot, once his boots were removed, caressing Lady Kresdine's ankle under her skirt, out of sight of the others. He exchanged several meaningful glances with her as they watched Rondal struggle with Lady Thena's suggestive banter. Finally, the older noblewoman caught his eye and something, he knew, was settled in her mind.

Don't be surprised when Lady Kresdine finds some excuse to leave you alone with Thena, Tyndal prepared Rondal, mind-to-mind.

What? Why would she do that?

She needs to isolate you to give her daughter the chance to seduce you. She can't do it in front of us, now can she? That might be much for even these ladies. I doubt her mother's tutelage extends to that end . . . but then again . . .

So what am I supposed to do? Rondal whimpered, as Lady Thena suggestively ate an apple in front of him.

Once you're alone . . . kiss her, you idiot. And then enjoy yourself, though I'd advise stopping short of her virtue. Unless you like the maid enough to wed her, I'd advise caution in that regard.

Now *you advise caution,* grumbled Rondal.

"Sir Tyndal, you said you had an understanding of horses?" asked Lady Kresdine innocently. "This mead overlooks a pasture where

341

there is a glorious chestnut mare I covet. She belongs to one of our reeves, but I am considering purchasing her. I would delight in having your counsel on the matter."

"And where lies this pasture?"

"Just through that copse of trees," she said innocently, indicating the rough-grown barrier that divided one field from the other.

"Then lead the way, my lady. I am always eager to see new horseflesh." He rose and assisted Kresdine daintily to her feet, and then led her boldly toward the copse. He didn't need to look back to know that there was a panicked look on Rondal's face.

"Your daughter is quite lovely," he said, quietly, when they were out of earshot. "But you must have been twice as beautiful in your maidenhood."

"She does, unfortunately, favor her father in some ways," agreed Kresdine. "But I was a pretty maid, by all accounts. My father thought so . . . to the point where he married me off as soon as he was able to keep me out of trouble. He sent me to this backwater to live with the Rabbit Lord in his dingy little manor. He said he had to, to keep the peace in his house. I had many suitors, at Thena's age," she bragged.

"Are you so unhappy here at Ramoth's Wood, then?" Tyndal asked, as he held a branch out of her way.

"It is a good life," she admitted. "I have my child and my dalliances. I have friends, here. And my husband, as dull as he may be, does provide for us, in his fashion. But . . . it drains me," she confessed. "Every day is like a heavy fog, and I crave the slightest breeze to blow it away."

She stopped, once they were a few rods into the wood and out of sight of their companions, and she turned to face him. He could see she was breathing far heavier than her exertions should warrant. He expected her to be demure, but she surprised him with her directness. "You are a handsome lord, Sir Tyndal. Young, robust, and eager. I admire that passion."

"And you, my lady, are beautiful." It was a simple statement, but one which caught Kresdine by surprise – and was not unwelcome.

He could have praised her for any number of things – her wisdom, her daughter, the beauty of her home, her management of the estate – but it was flattery of her own beauty she craved. And he was not lying. Tyndal did find her beautiful, even if the blush of maidenhood had long fled her face. He pushed a lock of hair out of her eyes unnecessarily. "I envy the Rabbit Lord in this one thing."

"You flatter me, my lord," she said in a low voice. "And yet I cannot help but wonder at your sincerity. My daughter—"

"Is a *girl*," Tyndal finished. "A kitten who needs to sharpen her claws on the dull wood of my companion. You, my lady, are a *woman*, and for all of your propriety," he said, without a trace of irony in his voice, "you are just as much in need of honing your claws as she, if not more."

She chuckled and kissed him. "An old cat with but one kitten," she mused, "what need have I for claws?"

"When a cat must lie with a rabbit every night, no doubt her claws get restless," countered Tyndal, kissing her in return. His arms wrapped around her mature hips as he stared her in the eye. "My lady, do we really need to banter so?"

She sighed and smiled. "It is refreshing to have a young knight who understands the Game, Sir Tyndal, and thus relieve me of the burden of being a coquette."

Kresdine moved closer and he embraced her ever more tightly, feeling every inch of her womanly curves cleave to him. Her hands felt his back and shoulders as she pressed her breasts full into his chest.

He found her lips in earnest now. They were full and warm and inviting, lacking the hesitation and self-consciousness of a younger maid but also lacking the sophistication of a more worldly woman. He gave her high marks for enthusiasm, however – she kissed him hungrily, her mouth communicating her need and desire and accepting his passion in return. He felt himself grow ever more aroused by her ardor. Finally, he broke the kiss.

"I take it my lady knows of some leafy bower nearby where we are unlikely to be disturbed?"

"I know just the place," she nodded, impishly, as she shrugged out of her sideless surcoat. Her soft cotton shift revealed she had neglected underclothing, no doubt due to the heat of the day. Tyndal measured her breasts with his hands without much interference, now, and he appreciated their weight and firmness. Lady Kresdine appreciated the attention, arching her back and pressing them more firmly into his palms.

"And have you shown many young knights this bower?" he asked in a low voice as he allowed her breasts to go free.

"Not all were as fortunate as you, Sir Tyndal," she said, leading him by the hand deeper into the grove. "I might be free with my favors, but I am choosy about to whom I grant them."

Tyndal kept his doubts about her choosiness to himself. She led him to a dense cluster of cedar trees clustered around a single low boulder. From within, he could see, there would be little chance of them being spied upon. Kresdine nearly skipped over to the boulder.

"My shrine to Ishi," Kresdine giggled, turning to face him again. She looked ten years younger, now, her hair unbound and her formal bearing dropped with her outer clothes. He kissed her again and felt her busy hands. "Now, just how does this catch work?"

Their coupling was passionate, gentle and fierce at the same time. Tyndal had rarely had the opportunity to explore a woman of such mature charms, compared to the young girls who threw themselves at him. He found he admired them greatly, once he had removed Kresdine's shift and saw her naked under the trees.

He did not speak as he pushed her gently back on the boulder, making a pillow of her shift under her. He kissed his way down her body, as he'd been taught, leaving a trail of lips from her ear to the vale between her breasts, and thence to her quivering belly.

"My lord!" she sighed, happily, as she guessed his destination. "Few men of your age are so attentive to a lady's needs!"

"And few ladies are willing to judge a man not on height or length or width, but by his appetite," he said, and began to pleasure his hostess.

"Too true," she groaned, laying her hand on the back of his head. When he had taken her to the brink of ecstasy, he disengaged and stood.

"My lord?" she asked, breathlessly. "Is there a . . . ah," she said, understanding his need as he pulled off his jerkin and hose. "I do so enjoy a bold knight." She examined him thoroughly with her eyes, once he had doffed his clothes entirely. "And one with such a rampant lance . . ."

Tyndal said little else as he climbed between her knees. He found her perch on the boulder sturdy enough so that he could entertain the lady's lust with proper devotion. He labored at the task fitfully, doing what he could to continue his hostess' pursuit of pleasure while enjoying it himself. Soon he tired of the position, and encouraged Kresdine to turn herself over.

"Like the peasants do it!" she agreed, lustfully, as she did as he bid. "Like the animals do it!"

"Does your husband not enjoy such diversions, milady?" he asked, unsure whether mentioning him would cool her desire.

"Bah! He knows but one manner of pleasure, and is deaf to suggestions of another," she said, looking over her shoulder. "But I revel in the primal nature of such positioning – surely Ishi intended her gifts to be enjoyed in every manner they can be!"

Tyndal seated himself firmly within her, causing her to gasp. He paused his actions – until she protested.

"Is the rock uncomfortable my lady?" he asked, as he grabbed a hold of her naked hips.

"I . . . I cannot . . . I cannot even feel it," she confessed, breathlessly. "Indeed, I can feel but one thing, and I feel it from my head to my toes!" Tyndal was glad she was not situated so that she could see the grin that spread across his face at the admission. No man tires of hearing his manhood praised, he decided.

Nearly an hour later, the chestnut mare long forgotten, the two returned to Rondal and Thena. The young noblewoman was lying with her head contentedly on Rondal's stomach, and the young knight was looking both unbearably guilty and unmistakably pleased with himself.

Tyndal was likewise pleased with himself. Lady Kresdine had been a passionate woman and an adept lover – a woman wasted on the tepid Rabbit Lord, he knew. He counted himself well satisfied, and had satisfied Kresdine repeatedly . . . and a little loudly, according to Rondal, when he spoke mind-to-mind.

I nearly came after you, when I heard the scream, Rondal admitted. *Thankfully Thena persuaded me to stay. She can be very persuasive,* he added.

I'm very pleased that you resisted the urge to rescue her, Tyndal answered. *Though I daresay the lady would have found something creative to do with another knight around. She seems very resourceful.*

Rondal didn't say anything for a moment. *What could she possibly do with . . . oh. Dear Trygg's tender ears, Tyndal, do these women have no* shame?

I inspected Lady Kresdine fairly thoroughly, Tyndal reported. *If she has some, she must hoard it like a miser. How about her daughter?*

Lady Thena will make some lord a very passionate wife some day, gods willing, Rondal said, as the two lovers approached the blanket.

It sounds like you had a good time, Tyndal said, reluctant to get any more details. As curious as he might be, it was still *Rondal* . . . and the thought of him engaged in such sport was not appealing to Tyndal's mind.

I . . . I did, Rondal agreed, guiltily. *I think she did, too.*

From the look on her face, that would be a safe wager, Tyndal guessed.

After quickly cleaning up the picnic, packing it away and mounting the carriage again, the party rode back to the manor as the late summer afternoon unfolded around them.

"About your debt to Cargwenyn," Tyndal brought up, casually, as they finally entered the overly ornate gates of Ramothwood. "My lady, if your estate could pay but a token of one or two ounces of silver," he proposed, "I am certain I could persuade my master to wait on the balance . . . until, say, sometime after the Equinox? Then we can return for the full amount, perhaps, when you have had long notice of it."

Kresdine quietly smiled. "That is a gracious and generous offer, Sir Tyndal. I think that would be an appropriate course of action, until I can consult with my lord." And it neatly side-stepped the embarrassing issue of the state of her treasury . . . as well as promising her a return visit, he noted to himself. "And I do hope we can encounter one another again, perhaps at a baronial function."

"I'm afraid my companion and I are men of action," protested Tyndal. "We have little time for such social affairs. We expect to be deployed to Gilmora soon, to face the goblin hordes. Not all knights,

I'm afraid, have time to wax poetic at the sight of sunsets and the antics of rabbits. Some must make their fortune with their swords, not their quills."

Apparently Sir Gamman's works tended to dwell on simple pleasures and natural beauty, subjects with which Lady Kresdine had quickly tired of. His one long martial work, she had confided between sorties, was a saga of the War of the Ancient Knights.

It had been somewhat popular for awhile, in parts of Sendaria, but the verses were considered hopelessly derivative of the great Golden Age poets of the later Magocracy by those who fancied themselves critics. Tyndal vowed to procure a copy just so that he could witness the dull wit of the Rabbit Lord himself.

"When must you depart for such dangers, good knights?" asked Lady Thena, pouting prettily. She had apparently grown fond of Sir Rondal, and from the blushes and sidelong glances the lad cast in her direction, the feeling was mutual. Mere shallow infatuation, in Tyndal's opinion, hardly more than the tryst he and Kresdine had shared.

But Thena's attention was also something his fellow apprentice needed more than the breath of life itself, after his difficult year. Also in Tyndal's opinion.

"We could be deployed any time, now," Rondal said, slowly. "And likely will, by the Equinox. We await word on our precise orders, but our deployment is not in doubt."

"Are you afraid?" asked Thena, quietly.

Rondal tried to console her. "No more afraid than your father is, no doubt, when he goes to serve his liege in war."

Thena snorted derisively. *"Daddy?* Daddy couldn't hurt a . . . a *rabbit.* You should see how mother orders him about—"

"Thena!" Kresdine reproved. "Be respectful of your sire!"

"As *you* are, mother?" she shot back, challenging, over her shoulder. "If Father ever had to face a real goblin, he'd soil himself . . . and you know it! He is a parchment knight, Sir Rondal, hardly better than a manor reeve. Proud of his lineage and his lore, but he is not a man of action like you brave knights."

There was no disguising the contempt Thena held for her father, to the point where Tyndal began to feel uncomfortable on the cuckolded lord's behalf. Indeed, he found himself defending the ineffectual man.

"Now, Lady Thena," Tyndal said, shaking his head, "there is more to being a knight than mere vainglory. It is position, as well as station. Not all are blessed by Duin with great skill at arms, yet that does not lessen their fervor or their devotion to their duty. Not all knights are fortunate enough to have to heed Duin's horn and defend their homes. I pray your sire never finds the need."

"I am certain he would defend his home and his family as gallantly as any knight," agreed Rondal.

"In his terrifying armor," agreed Lady Thena, giggling, "with his helm crested with his dire . . . rabbit ears."

"What?" asked Rondal, surprised.

"*Rabbit ears?*" asked Tyndal, amused. "My lady, you jest!"

"I fear she does not, my lords," Lady Kresdine said, quietly. "My dear lord Gamman is so proud of his illustrious house and its principals: *'Fairness, Reverence, Modesty,'* qualities lore dictates are shared by the rabbit. He therefore had twin silver rabbit ears added to his war helmet as a crest." There was little doubt in Tyndal's mind how his new lover viewed the ornaments.

"What a fearsome visage he presents," Lady Thena said sarcastically, her disgust obvious. "At my introduction tournament he had the audacity to enter into the lists – with the sword, as he gets dizzy on horseback. He strode into the lists with that ridiculous helmet and I nearly died on the spot of embarrassment."

"He did cut a comical figure," added Lady Kresdine with a bitter chuckle. "By the grace of Trygg, I maintained my composure as a good wife should. Sir Dorix of Masran gallantly fought my lord, but in the end Sir Gamman prevailed."

"Honestly, Mother, Sir Dorix *let* Daddy win that bout to spare you the shame of dishonor, as well as the ridicule the crowd developed for those preposterous ears. Sir Dorix is ten times the man my father is."

Kresdine did little to defend her husband. "Sir Dorix is a gallant knight," she agreed, evenly. "And I assure you, my daughter, he was properly consoled for his gracious loss."

"Did you not favor your lord husband on his victory, milady?" asked

Tyndal, surprised. Had he a wife, he would expect at least *some* affectionate return in the wake of a victory.

"Of course I did, as any good wife would on such a magnificent triumph. But my lord's admiration for rabbits, unfortunately, extends not to their lusty nature . . . but their penchant for quickness. I had *plenty* of time to reward my lord *and* console his victim." She smiled fondly at the memory. "Twice."

"*Mother!*" squealed Thena wickedly. "*You* and Sir Dorix? And to think that at the same time I was . . . never mind," she said, blushing.

"What?" demanded Lady Kresdine. "Say not that you gave away your virtue that evening! *Thena!* You know-"

"No, Mother," the younger woman said, rolling her eyes, "I am as pure as the day you bore me into this world. Where it *matters*," she added with a naughty grin. "But while the manor door reserved for my future lord husband, Ishi willing, remains sealed, perhaps the tradesman's entrance was unlocked that night for the first time," she said with especial relish.

"THENA!" her mother shrieked. "Gentlemen, I *must* apologize for my brazen daughter: she is but newly come to the mysteries of Ishi, and has not learned yet how to deport herself *discreetly* in polite company!"

"And *I* apologize for my mother, gentlemen, who is far more concerned with how to marry me off to a rich lord than to seeing to my future happiness," Thena pouted. "Did you know she's considering sending me to a *temple school*? A *maiden's* school? An abbey?"

"A man often enjoys a wife who has her letters, and has been instructed in the rites of the home," Rondal said, diplomatically.

"It's a temple on a river island," Thena said, her displeasure clear, "were no men are allowed to go. Or boys. There I am to be trained to be some man's wife. I will likely be condemned to some union with some simple country knight who idolizes ferrets and writes them poetry, bearing his brats and watching myself age into ugliness." She stole a bitter glance at her mother, as if she was accusing her dame of such poor taste.

"Is that not the lot of any woman?" countered Tyndal. "Just as it is for a man to see his strength fade with the years?"

"I am a maiden, my lord," Thena riposted. "I am rising in my glory.

I wish a worthy man to be my husband, and marry me on the temple steps in front of the entire barony, my dress the most beautiful of the age. I deserve a strong, vibrant lord, a husband rich in spirit and coin, and one who will not let me order him about like a servant, timidly accepting what favors I deign to grant him. And certainly not some rodent-obsessed, obsequious lap dog who barks at *whatever* he sees and belches forth verse daily in small, pellet-sized piles." Thena's ire with her father was palpable.

"How, *deserve?*" asked Rondal. Tyndal's heart immediately began to sink. The idiot didn't know enough to keep his mouth shut. "What entitles you to such a husband, my lady?"

"Am I not fair?" demanded Thena, arrogantly. "Am I not of noble house? Am I not deserved of a mate worthy of my station?"

"You are a fair maiden," agreed Rondal, awkwardly, "and exceptionally pleasant company, but . . . why would you make a good *wife?*"

"Does not every man want a fair wife?" asked Lady Kresdine, confused.

"It does not harm a marriage, in my estimation," Tyndal observed. "If one must wed, then marrying a fair woman is preferable to marrying a plain one."

"But neither makes a woman a wife," pointed out Rondal. "If comeliness was a guarantee of virtue, then the whores of Barrowbell would make the finest wives in the world."

"They would at least know the business," Tyndal joked. "On what basis does one judge a wife?"

"If she is committed to the health and happiness of her husband, that is a blessing," offered Rondal.

"I do wish my lord good health and a long life," agreed Lady Kresdine. "Yet if I was not fair, he would eventually lose interest in me. What interest he has. By Ishi's nips, he cares more for pen and parchment than for me, or the needs of my body. A good wife, Sir Rondal? Had he ambition and talent, I could have been the *best* of wives, I assure you, and the most loyal. Had he been but worthy of me, I could have made Trygg Allmother herself jealous of my fidelity.

"But when a man is too weak to bend my will or too deferential of my wrath, and sees more value in the mindless praise of strangers than the earnest praise of a loving wife, even the *best* of wives will turn bitter, my lords. Pray take heed of that counsel, before you take your own brides."

"You would your husband countermanded your will, my lady?" asked Rondal in surprise. "That seems an odd wish for a wife!"

"It would be a refreshingly novel change, my lord. If it is advice on marriage you wish, then heed this: grow not content and complacent after your nuptials, my young lords, nor stray too long from your blades."

"That is good advice," agreed Tyndal, wondering if there would be time to get Kresdine alone again before they departed.

"Further," she continued, "be ever stronger than your wives, and let them prosper in the wake of your ambition, lest they grow impatient and seek to find their own. Keep them sated and interested and intrigued and inspired. If you desire their respect, then endeavor to earn it in some manly fashion . . . not by absent praise and the repetition of the flattery of your admirers. If you desire a worthy wife, then you must *earn* her respect and devotion afresh daily."

"That seems too akin to labor, my lady," Tyndal said, disdainfully. "I'm afraid I will die a bachelor knight. Likely in a duel with a jealous husband."

Lady Thena giggled. "There are worse deaths for a brave knight, my lord. How about yourself, Sir Rondal? Are *you* destined for a lonely dotage?" she asked expectantly.

"I shall wed, I feel," Rondal said, dreamily. "At least, that is my desire."

"Is it, Sir Rondal?" asked Lady Kresdine, suddenly interested.

"Not before my term of service at arms is finished," he added hurriedly. "But when the war is over, I can see taking comfort in hearth and home. Perhaps a small country estate, like Sire Cei's."

"Or Ramoth's Wood," offered Lady Kresdine. "With no male heirs, Thena's husband is destined to gain the manor upon his death."

"I . . . I will bear that in mind, my lady," Rondal said, blushing.

By the time the carriage returned to the manor Tyndal was already growing anxious to leave. Their time at Ramothwood had been productive and entertaining, but as dusk neared so too did the prospect of encountering the Rabbit Lord.

He tarried at the manor just long enough to collect the promised token payment and spend a few stolen moments bidding his lusty hostess farewell. Rondal had been likewise occupied with Lady Thena, who went so far as to gift him with a kerchief she had embroidered to remember her by.

"A most educational bit of errantry," Tyndal remarked as they rode from the rabbit-ridden manor at a brisk pace. "All in all, a delightful afternoon."

"I'm still shaking with nerves," confessed Rondal. "I feel as if I have erred, somehow."

"Erred? Not against propriety, unless you stole her virtue—"

"I did not!" insisted Rondal, panicked. "I merely . . . *inspected* it. Closely."

"Then you have naught to worry about," soothed Tyndal. "If there is no breach, then what could her father possibly say about it? Even if he did know?"

"And you? You who abetted an *adultery?*"

"If I had been the first to venture down that path, I might feel a pang of conscience," agreed Tyndal, after a moment's thought. "But that path was well-trod ere I arrived . . . likely before I was born."

"Yet her marriage is a holy sacrament," countered Rondal, as they rode down the long slope. "Have you not enticed her to break her vow, indebting her to Trygg's grace?"

"That is between her and the goddess," pointed out Tyndal. "It is not a knight's job to police the virtue of anyone but himself. To offer guidance to a fellow knight, at need or request, perhaps, and to lead the people by example, certainly.

"But to hold a wife to her vow, who has broken it so often it leans in the wind like a broken fence? Let a bridesister preach her the virtues of fidelity and chastity. As the gods did not see fit to call me to their service, I shall not deliver a sermon on their behalf. Save perhaps for Ishi," he chuckled.

Rondal made a sour face. "Ishi did not call you, you hang upon her like a lovesick suitor. I'll grant you this: you play in her realm far better than I ever will." He sounded dejected about the subject – too dejected for a lad who had just enjoyed a dalliance.

"It is not a matter of luck or fortune," he explained. "I see love as a worthy pursuit, and just as I pursue magic and swordplay, I seek to divine its rules and practice it as a craft instead of sitting back and waiting for Ishi's favor to bring her blessing. What crime is there in that?"

"It is a sport beyond my talents," Rondal said, shaking his head. "You have the face and the heart for it. I . . . I do not."

"Argue not in favor of your weaknesses," counseled Tyndal, reasonably. Rondal blushed.

"It's not a weakness! I . . . I want *love* in my life. Aye, and a bit of lust," he admitted, self-consciously. "But I am just not the type of man most maidens are drawn to. Not the ones I prefer, at any rate."

"You weren't the type of man who could lead a squad through the countryside, either," Tyndal pointed out. "Or build a bridge out of rocks, magic and spit. But you learned."

"That's different. I *had* to learn those things."

"And now I'm saying you *have* to learn this, too."

"But why?" his fellow asked, miserably.

"Because . . . because it's the great game, Rondal, the duel eternal betwixt man and maid! And the study need not be arduous. You needn't become a tournament champion in order to learn the basics of swordplay."

Rondal sighed, and slumped in his saddle. "You aren't going to shut up about this," he reasoned, "so go ahead and instruct me, oh sagacious master."

"Pray attend," Tyndal instructed, as the Inrion masters had always begun their lectures. "It's actually quite simple. Stripped of all superstition and fluff, women – *most* women – want the most desirable man in the village as a husband. That is, the man with the most wealth, fame, position, power, fair looks, charisma, muscles, cows, just . . . the most. And men – *most* men – prefer pretty women for wives. Pretty and young."

"True enough," grunted Rondal with a heavy sigh. "Go on."

"Nearly all of the women will compete for the attentions of the most powerful of men, and accept those of lesser status as their beauty, skills, and guile dictate. Men, on the other hand, tend to compete for the fairest and warmest ladies within their class and station. And sometimes outside it."

"It occurs to me that you have a low opinion of womenfolk, Sir Tyndal," Rondal said, sarcastically.

"Not at all," Tyndal replied, a little hurt. "I don't blame women for competing for the best of men. Nor men for the fairest of maids. They but follow their natural interests. If men value youth and beauty and warmth, then the women who present those most excellent qualities in the best manner will win the attention of the best of men," he reasoned.

"Yet whole *trades* exist to cheat that market," Rondal pointed out. "The cosmeticians and seamstresses of Barrowbell, for example. And the perfumers."

"And do not goldsmiths practice the trade of gilding to make a man seem wealthy beyond his station?" Tyndal pointed out. "And jongleurs would starve if there were no knights wishing to boast of their achievements. Why? To make themselves look far more successful, to advance their reputation among their peers and ideally to secure as sweet a marriage as Sir Gamman managed to procure. A man might rent a fine horse, for instance, or use a rich cloak to cover modest dress." He looked at his fellow thoughtfully. "And there are even a few who have been known to be less than fastidious with the truth when speaking to a maid."

"I will not lie to bed a woman," Rondal said, flatly. "That's dishonorable!"

"Nor need you," Tyndal stressed. "But the truth your lips speak may not be the truth your ladylove hears. For example, ask me what kind of horse I ride."

"What? I can plainly see what kind of horse you ride!"

"No," Tyndal said, patiently, "ask me, *as a lady might*, what horse I might ride."

" 'Sir Tyndal, what kind of mount do you ride?' " Rondal asked, batting his eyelashes exaggeratedly.

"Today I rode the courser," Tyndal explained.

"But that's the only horse you *have*," protested Rondal. That was not, technically, true, but this was the only horse he'd been riding this summer.

"But the answer presumes that I have *many* horses," Tyndal pointed out. "Without actually admitting that I have but the one. Horses represent wealth," he reminded his fellow. "They're expensive to keep and care for. To own one is to be a man of means, by definition.

"To have *more* than one . . . well, that's enough for country maids, of course, but in the cities, like Castabriel and Barrowbell, a man's position and presentation account for more. And his fame," he reminded himself. "You saw how the ladies responded when we admitted we were in battle. When we dropped Master Minalan's name—"

"About that," Rondal interrupted, "why didn't you want them to know we were magi? I thought we were *trying* to impress them."

Tyndal scowled. "And get caught up in a magic show? I had more important business in mind. And we were already impressing them. As mere errants, we were attractive enough. And they were remote and lonely enough. Magic would have just complicated matters. When entertaining ladies, be a knight first, a mage second."

"Who made up *that* rule?" demanded Rondal.

"I did. Just now," Tyndal said, smugly.

Tyndal felt good. It was a lovely day; he had just enjoyed an exciting and relaxing afternoon with a charming and skilled lady, quite sating the itch for feminine companionship he'd been nursing for some time. More importantly, despite his fellow's misgivings about their dalliance, Rondal was clearly the better man for it. He rode more proudly, now, less like a sack of potatoes and more like a proper knight.

It was amazing what the attentions of an eager young woman could do to fortify a young man, Tyndal reflected. He knew some fellows only felt the pull of their hearts (and other regions) infrequently, and could sate their needs quickly in the back room of a tavern for a few coins. That was not his preference, though he did not eschew it at need. He preferred the eternal dance of seduction, even with its dangers, to the cold certainty of a whore's embrace.

But he also knew its potential costs. The possibility of rejection, loss of reputation (or the earning of an unsavory one), the possibility of scandal, jealous lovers, cuckolded husbands, irate fathers, angry nuns, demanding mothers . . . and that didn't even count the myriad of disasters that stalked a man when he courted a woman's heart. There was always a chance a child could result. That was one fortune Tyndal had been spared, to his knowledge, but Trygg's hands sometimes reaped what was sown by Ishi's desires.

There were some women who would cling to you as if they'd paid for you in the market, others who were passionate to the point of obsession, still others who sought no more than to use your seduction to further their own conspiracies. Many could confuse lusty indulgence for love, and tender hearts sometimes resulted.

Tyndal disliked being in that position, but he had been, a few times now. A certain innkeeper's daughter continued to dote on him, to the extent of paying for a letter to be sent to him upriver to Sevendor last summer, mentioning her lack of a proper husband no less than four times in two pages.

He had penned a short but sympathetic response, citing the nature of his new duties were such that precluded, alas, any commitments of the heart, but how he looked forward fondly to visiting her magnificent inn the next time he was in the vicinity. He hoped he'd satisfied the maid's honor even if he'd frustrated her designs.

Then there had been that moon-eyed girl in Barrowbell, some courtier's youngest daughter. Pila or Pilsa or something like that, she had followed Tyndal around from occasion to occasion, trying to attract his attention. After briefly flirting with the idea of a liaison after a few heated moments in a Barrowbell garden one night, Tyndal had tried to avoid her.

While she was a fair enough maid, she was rather dim and unintelligent. Worse, she was uninteresting and annoying. She had mentioned marriage within two hours of meeting him, and had been so obsequiously adamant about her intrusion into his sphere that he had done his best to ensure he had other companionship when she was around.

That hadn't helped, in the end. Every pretty new coquette who vied for his attention only seemed to inflame her passion and make her more resolute. She started weeping when she saw him, which just made him dread her presence all the more. By the time he'd boarded the barge to

Sevendor, he was thankful to leave the wretched girl behind.

Still, the experience had been valuable. Had he been captivated by her allure – and her demonstrated willingness to dally – it would have been easy enough to wake up and find himself wedded, doomed to a long, unhappy marriage. Had she set her cap on Rondal, the poor boy would have been conquered in short order.

That was one very good reason why he had to teach his fellow apprentice the rudiments of the Laws of Love. Else he'd find himself condemned to a lifetime of matrimony to a woman of low quality.

And as annoying as Rondal, himself was, there was no way he would wish such a fate even on an annoying acquaintance. A man who settled for such deserved the miserable result, in Tyndal's estimation. While he was ruminating on the subject, Rondal spoke again.

"I just wonder the fairness and propriety of pursuing such pleasures so casually," confessed Rondal. "It seems like a lot of work for such a tenuous reward."

Tyndal smirked. "Then perhaps you're doing it incorrectly."

"I assure you, I am not!" Rondal snorted. "I enjoy such interludes. I *like* girls. They're just . . ." he said, trailing off wordlessly.

"Aren't they, though?" agreed Tyndal, dreamily. "I like girls, too. So why not study how they *like* to be liked? If it makes you feel better, understand that while every girl has the potential to grant you Ishi's Blessing, not every girl wants to drag you before a bridesister's altar. They're all looking for a good match as much as you are."

"And if we are not a good match?"

"Many are willing to explore an unpromising line of interest in the name of experience. As long as you understand what a maid desires – *really* – and not what is likely to fall out of her mouth in her banter, honing your own experience with one maid prepares you for when those skills will matter most to you."

"Would not a maid be troubled to know that a lad she fancies has 'honed' himself with several other girls?" Rondal countered.

"Quite the contrary," Tyndal explained, "in my experience – and according to the noble sages of the Crimson Arts of Castle Heart – the more a lad is known to keep the company of women, the more women desire to keep *his* company."

357

"Yet would not a woman who did likewise—" Rondal began. Tyndal stopped him. He knew where this line of inquiry led.

"Nay, rather say a woman who was *known* to have done likewise," he amended. "Reputation is vitally important to both men and women. Discretion is an essential part of successful dalliance. There are many – *many* – wives and women of high station who enjoy a pristine reputation, but who discreetly are as randy as a dockside whore.

"When one becomes conversant with the codes and ciphers of desire, one can discern the subtle hints and clues that tell such women out from those who merely seek a good match. Or no match at all.

"But for a lad, the more maidens who take your company, the more maidens will *desire* to take your company. It is as simple as that. They seem to desire what the others have, simply *because* it is desired. Jewelry, estates, or men, women seem particularly intrigued with what each other possess," he said, thoughtfully.

Rondal considered. "Not everyone. Lady Pentandra."

"Oh, she pays attention," Tyndal said, with especial knowledge. "She's just very subtle about it. And she doesn't feel as if she's in the same domain as most women, so she doesn't heed the allure of coveting that which she doesn't have. She measures herself arcanely, and finds most women wanting. But she is a special case," he admitted.

"Do you think she pines for Master Min?" asked Rondal, hesitantly.

"No," Tyndal said, after considering the matter for a moment. "Not really. I think she's got the part of him she really wants, and has no issue sharing the remainder with Lady Alya."

"I wonder if Lady Alya feels the same way," Rondal said, quietly.

"*You* ask her," dismissed Tyndal. "That's not the sort of question that you're going to get an answer to. Not a useful one."

"I'd rather not," agreed his companion. "I hope our next call is not so fraught with excitement. Please tell me that Lufhorn Manor doesn't have any nubile young maidens lurking to spring on a poor fellow."

Tyndal chuckled. "I don't think you have to worry. Lord Dewine of Lufhorn is a well-known devotee to Andrus, according to Lady Kresdine. He has taken the Oath of Andrus never to enjoy the Blessing of Ishi. Indeed, he has established a small cloister of his cult's order in Lufhorn, where he has gathered a congregation of his coreligionists."

"Oh . . ." Rondal said, quietly.

Andrus was a minor but colorful Imperial deity of music, poetry, and discourse who had survived the Narasi Conquest relatively intact. His followers were ascetics, of a sort, but not like the humble monks of Ludris or the wandering priests of Herus.

Andrus' devotees were exclusively male, and all forswore enjoying the touch of a woman. By denying themselves Ishi's Blessing, their sect taught, their suffering and unfulfilled longing honored the god and fueled their devotion.

While that seemed like an innocuous enough religion, to Tyndal's mind, in practice most of the followers of Andrus seemed little inclined to ever seek the comfort of a woman's touch to begin with.

Her seamstress, perhaps, but not her *touch*.

While the Oath of Andrus prohibited sexual contact with women, it tacitly endorsed initiates seeking comfort in the arms of their fellow devotees. Or passing knights errant. Or handsome farm boys.

The priests of Andrus were not always particular.

"You aren't concerned with your virtue amongst such men?" asked Tyndal, amused, but surprised by his companion's agreeability.

"After dealing with those two . . . *ladies*," Rondal said, carefully, "I think I can manage dodging a lusty, drunken Andrusine better than I could another randy noblewoman."

"It *would* be more straightforward," Tyndal admitted. "I have heard tales of their inner rites. They are reputed to be quite . . . lurid." Whispers of all-male orgies and other outlandish behavior were frequently associated with some of the Andrusines. The order did little to dispel their reputation.

"So have I," nodded Rondal, warily. "Which explains what they do with that much honey . . ."

"Oh . . . yes, I suppose it does," Tyndal said, his mind swimming. He wished Rondal hadn't mentioned that.

"Besides," added Rondal, mildly, "with your pretty face and muscular buttocks around to distract them, I doubt *I'll* have much trouble."

Tyndal winced – but he couldn't deny the truth of it. He'd had adherents of Andrus – both formal and informal – admire him, sometimes in ways that made him quite uncomfortable. But he did find the attention flattering, he had to admit. So far his own virtue in such matters had been secure, but he was wary about strong drink in such circumstances.

He was about to deliver a classy retort when he felt the beginnings of mind-to-mind contact.

Tyndal, are you busy? asked the no-nonsense tones of Master Minalan's mental voice.

We're on the road at the moment. What service can I do for you, Master?

You can cut short your itinerary and return to Sevendor at your soonest convenience.

Master? Why?

Because Commander Terleman has finally come up with an important assignment for you two, he answered. *He's got a mission that he thinks would benefit from the attention of a High Mage. Or a Knight Mage. Or two.*

May I ask the nature of the mission, Master?

You may, but I don't have many details yet. Just that it's highly dangerous, behind enemy lines, and somewhere in Gilmora.

And the Lord Commander wants both of us, Master?

He wants someone, and I'm sending both of you. You won't be alone. But you are going to have to suspend your errantry for a while. Duty calls. Don't delay. I won't have much time to brief you before you go, and soon I'll have less. Alya is in labor, and she'll bear the child before you arrive. His master was trying to sound business-like, but Tyndal could tell how excited he was.

That's wonderful news, Master!

Yes, but the Alka Alon are buzzing like bees, for some reason, and it has a lot of us concerned. There have been . . . well, we'll have time to talk later. For now, wrap up your business and get back here as fast as your horses can bear you.

I'll tell Rondal, Tyndal responded with a heavy sigh. Oh, well. It was fun while it lasted.

Do that, agreed Master Minalan. *In truth, I almost wish you weren't going. I could use your help. I'm going to have my hands full with the new baby, the Alka Alon embassy, giant hawks, stumbling apprentices, a moody wife, sneaky queens, weird happenings in the forest, riotous River Folk, and stubborn Karshak. Just wait until you see who won the Spellmonger's Trial this year, too. But once you get back from Gilmora – assuming for the moment that you will come back from Gilmora – then we'll sit down and discuss your progress. Both of your progress. And your future in Sevendor.*

That . . . that sounds ominous, Master, Tyndal observed.

It was meant to, growled Master Minalan. *Don't think that just because you've managed to get through your basic training that you've progressed beyond my criticism.*

Tyndal swallowed. *Never, Master!*

Good to hear it. Now finish up what you were doing and make haste for Sevendor. You depart from here in five days. You should be back in Barrowbell within two weeks. From there on, you are Terleman's problem.

Master Minalan ended the discussion and Tyndal opened his eyes. Rondal hadn't even realized he'd been communicating.

"It looks like your virtue is spared a challenge from Andrus," he said, "Master Minalan just recalled us to Sevendor."

"Why?"

"We're being deployed. To Gilmora. So I hope you enjoyed Lady Thena's charms, because somehow I think it will be awhile before you get the opportunity again."

What was worse, Tyndal realized, was that now that they were deployed, they were unlikely to be around Ramoth's Wood come the equinox. It was unlikely that he'd be able to collect on Lady Kresdine's debt. Well . . . perhaps he'd visit her on his return.

If not, he realized, there were hundreds of castles and thousands of manors across the Kingdom stuffed with ladies as fair or fairer than those of Ramoth's Wood. It would be a shame not to investigate such places, he reasoned.

Errantry truly was its own reward, as Sire Cei had told him. And Tyndal planned on getting as much reward as he could.

PART IV:

MISSION

Gilmora, early Autumn

Rondal

"The gurvani have stopped advancing from last year's positions," Commander Terleman said as he displayed the magemap of the region in front of them. "After the Dragonfall, they went into cantonments scattered across northern and western Gilmora. Captured castles and manors, mostly, but some caves and woods, as well. We thought they were resting up for a fresh push this spring, but . . . well, instead they've looted bare what they've captured."

"And sent raiders against the surrounding settlements," added Marshal Brendal, the new military commander of the campaign. He was a local man, a baron whose lands lay in the eastern part of the war zone. Count Salgo had appointed him and he seemed an able commander.

Of course, anyone could seem an able commander in a tent, Rondal thought.

"We didn't think anything of it at the time. Just stirring up trouble, picking off some easy rations. But they weren't just stealing chickens. Those scrugs were taking inventory."

"As soon as the ground thawed this spring," Terleman continued, "the expected offensive south didn't come. Instead they began to systematically loot the country bare. Horses, cows, sheep, even some grain, but . . . mostly they came for people. Wherever there was a large settlement, they attacked in force. And then forced a surrender. One of their dark priests, or one of their human lackeys—"

"They're using humans as messengers now?" asked Tyndal, surprised.

"They're using humans in the *field*, now," Brendal said, darkly. "Light cavalry, mostly. But they're also using them to process the slaves, as they come in. A whole . . . evil syndicate."

"The Soulless," sneered Tyndal.

"Not all," countered Marshal Brendal. "The Goblin King's banner attracts those with evil in their hearts. Not all of his servants have survived the sacrifice pits. Some seek power or wealth or release of their debts. Who knows what such folk find alluring? But they coffle their fellow men together like cattle and lead them up the Timber Road. The Murder Road, they call it, now," the Marshal said, grimly.

"And some warmagi among them," agreed Terleman. "There are those who are impatient for how the Arcane Orders distribute witchstones. The rangers of the Iron Band have discovered several such renegades in the Penumbra, seeking to slay a shaman and take his tainted stone. Or willing to offer themselves in service directly for the chance of being gifted with one. Thankfully we've seen only a few of them in Gilmora.

"The Dead God's priests cast spells on whole villages, then capture them without slaying them. They fall asleep and awaken in chains. Or they are surrounded, and offered a bargain," Terleman said, shaking his head. "An emissary will approach under a flag of truce and propose that *half* of the people will be allowed to flee if the other half are surrendered to them."

"Of course, the second half rarely sees freedom, nor should they," Marshal Brendal said, nastily. He clearly thought ill of such victims, seeing them as traitors to their race. "But thanks to their games and the constant skirmishes and raids, most of northern Gilmora is now depopulated. The people are dead, fled, or taken. The fields lie fallow, the castles empty or occupied. A few remote locations still stand, but only at the goblins' sufferance."

"Probably securing the most prosperous estates for later," Rondal observed.

"That's what we figure," agreed Terleman. "In the Penumbra, we understand, the survivors are put under some token human lord, usually Soulless. Or enslaved by some gurvan who speaks the language, with a garrison of gurvani to keep everyone peaceful. The sheer number of people they've . . . harvested is appalling. Our estimates are in the tens of thousands. Over a hundred thousand," he corrected.

"And the ones they haven't gotten or slain are crowding into the rest of Gilmora," added Brendal. "Where they'll be nice and ready for next year's harvest."

"That's assuming they continue their advance," Tyndal said, looking at the map thoughtfully. "What if their goal is merely to keep Gilmora depopulated?"

"And do what?" Rondal scoffed. "Extend the Penumbra?"

"Essentially," Tyndal agreed. "Extend their area of influence. We've beaten them at several key engagements, and their dragons aren't as effective as they thought. Maybe they're getting over-extended."

"That's one theory, and a popular one," Terleman said as he closed the map. "They've sent hundreds of thousands of troops into the field, now. And they have been extending their supply chains through foraging and pillaging. There have even been reports of different tribes fighting each other, may they gods bless their efforts.

"But another theory is that they are preparing for a more concentrated thrust south next year, now that the resistance in the area has been led away in chains. They won't be able to continue without confronting more serious fortifications than the moated manors of northern Gilmora. And a few rivers where we hold the bridges."

"So what can we do?" asked Rondal. That was the big question. Why did a master warmage like Terleman need a couple of half-trained runts like him and Tyndal?

"We need to establish an outpost deep in their rear," answered Terleman, tapping on the map with his finger. "Someplace quiet, where we can scout, perhaps launch attacks from. Actually, we need several, but I want you lads to scout the first one.

"We need to find out what the gurvani are up to in their largest cantonments. Find out who is still holding out behind their lines, how secure they are, what help they need and what we can expect from them.

"We want you two to lead a force to do just that. Establish a secure base in Northern Gilmora, begin gathering intelligence, and help the survivors plot a strategy for resistance.

"But most importantly . . . find out what the scrugs are *really* up to. See what we have to look forward to, next spring."

"And you need both of us to do it?" Tyndal asked, eyeing Rondal. Rondal felt disgusted with his fellow. It was clear to him what the utility of the mission was, and why they had been chosen to lead it.

"It's an important mission," Terleman reasoned. "And dangerous. There's not going to be much hope of support, once you're out there. Odds are, one of you is likely to get killed."

Tyndal looked puzzled. "Well, it's a warzone. I still don't see why you're sending both of us."

"I like having a spare."

Rondal almost gloated at Tyndal over that. Almost.

"Sir Tyndal, I want you to take a cavalry squad up through Dendara to Castle Hathyn. Gather intelligence along the way and make daily dispatches.

"At Hathyn, you'll pick up another squad of cavalry and a baggage train – the supplies will be waiting. Then you'll escort them west through goblin country all the way to here . . . the barony of Losara. There are several manors in the vicinity that might serve our need as a base – we have a list to choose from. But it is far enough away from their larger cantonments in Murai and Daronel to avoid notice, yet close enough to spy upon them."

"And while Sir Tyndal leads his expedition of horse," Marshal Brendal said, clearing his throat, "Sir Rondal will be awaiting him with a contingent of foot. A squad of medium infantry, plus a few rangers. You'll go with pack horses overland and establish the base."

"Me?" Rondal asked, surprised. "I get to go in first?"

"Isn't that the more glorious place in battle?" Tyndal smirked

"We're trying to *avoid* open battle," Terleman said. "Remember, we're there to scout, not to raid. Or at least not yet. We need someone competent on the ground who can see to the establishment of a base of operations. From what your masters at Relan Cor said, Sir Rondal, you're just the man for the job."

"They did?" he asked, surprised.

"They *did?* " Tyndal asked, confused.

"They did," Terleman assured them both. "Rondal's report listed outstanding leadership and tactical abilities, good command instincts, adept at logistics and fortifications. And an excellent grasp of intelligence and strategy."

"And what did they say about me?" asked Tyndal, his nostrils flaring.

"That it would be handy to have a spare," shot Terleman, annoyed. "You *both* bring value to the operation. We're going to need a secure base and we're going to need a small, deadly mobile force for future intelligence and resistance operations.

"You're to establish that base, secure some secondary outposts, and begin relaying field intelligence. Including assisting any surviving refugees in escaping south. Eventually, we can use the outposts for offensive operations against their cantonments, but right now we only have a vague idea where they are."

"Just how long are you anticipating us being deployed?" Rondal asked. The scope of what the commander desired from them was more open-ended than he preferred. He did not see the task as insurmountable, but he did not particularly want to winter in a secret base, even in Gilmora's mild clime.

"Don't worry, you won't be there forever, but we need you to set it up," soothed the head of the Kingdom's magical corps. "But that's why we need you, specifically. You two are among the few who understand how the gurvani fight, and how they use magic.

"Once you get the outpost set up, you can be relieved by a non-magical commander, but having your eyes in the field will be more valuable than most."

The warmage didn't sound pleased by making the admission. He was a young man, around the same age as their master, but he had been given responsibility almost as great as Master Minalan. And far more oversight.

"So when can we expect reinforcements?" asked Rondal, suspiciously.

"In three or four weeks," Brendal offered. "Assuming that we find the place useful, we can get the men, and you aren't all wiped out to the last man."

"It's us!" Tyndal boasted. "What's the likelihood of *that* happening?"

"That's what happened last time we tried this tactic," Terleman pointed out. "We lost contact, and the next ranger patrol found the whole company slaughtered in their beds."

"Oh," Rondal said in a daze.

"I'm sure it was just bad luck," dismissed Tyndal, after a reflective pause in the conversation grew uncomfortable.

*   *   *

Maramor Manor was a stately, prosperous home, once, Rondal decided, but that had been before the goblin invasion had swept over it, the defense had swept back, and then back over it again. It was a proud lady, harshly-used, and the secluded estate showed its distress appallingly.

The once-meticulously maintained greenery along the roadway was hacked and chewed or overgrown. Grass had begun to sprout along the dirt path leading to its brown stone walls. There was no stock in sight, not a sheep or pig or cow. The fields were empty, unplowed and unplanted, and the village a burnt-out ruin.

No one challenged them as they cautiously approached. Rondal's scrying had revealed little evidence of goblins within, although he could not be certain. That they had been here in the past there was no doubt.

The big wooden gate had been rent away. The house had been sacked, and sacked again, until all that was left was debris and the remains of once-hidden camps of refugees within. Broken furniture and empty grain sacks littered the grounds, and carcasses - human, animal, and goblin - rotted into tangled parcels of skin and bones.

The rangers who were in the vanguard found plenty of broken goblin darts, vicious little arrows with jagged cast iron points, and other signs of raiding. But little signs of a heated defense. Though the place had been looted, it was intact. It had two compelling reasons for being a good forward base, to Rondal's estimation.

The manor house was attached to two defensible towers within the stout stone wall. While it was far from a true castle, they had provided refuge for the lords of Maramor against their bellicose neighbors at

369

various times. Neither one seemed to have been breached, although the manor that connected them had fallen into disrepair. Sixty feet tall and forty feet thick at each base, the two stone-faced spires were as sound as anyone could expect in northern Gilmora.

Rondal reached Maramor first, at the head of a squadron of seven mounted infantry and two keen-eyed rangers, as well as a portly corporal who drove the two-wheeled cart and had some facility with tools and carpentry.

Their goal was to secure the manor, fortify it as much as possible, and use it as a base to scout the surrounding territory, so the stout fellow was perhaps the most important of them at the moment. Rondal made certain the corporal could wield a sword as well as a hammer before he included him in the expedition.

Maramor was deep behind the rough "line" that stretched across northern and western Gilmora, now, only seventy miles from the official frontier with the Wilderlands to the north.

Theoretically this was goblin territory, but they had seen no recent signs of activity the entire cautious way north. They had passed through almost a dozen burned-out villages on the way out here. But they had not seen so much as a gurvani scout during that lonely ride.

Twice they had found manor houses still occupied, albeit lightly, their owners or tenants too stubborn to give up their land. Rondal and his men had taken shelter there, gotten news, and established protocols for staying in touch as a part of a potential escape route. The locals were grateful for the help, but suspicious, too. Apparently there were turncloak humans working with the gurvani, now, men and women who would weep and beg entrance, only to unlock gates and open doors in the night.

That did not bode well; Rondal knew that the Soulless, the Dead God's pet humans, were enthralled to his dark power, but he did not think that they had the wit to behave with such guile. Most were shattered shells of human beings, or so twisted and warped by their time in the Dark Vale that they were barely human.

It didn't take long for his team to secure the place. It was not a huge manor, one of the reasons it was chosen for consideration. The unbreeched walls would keep trouble reasonably at bay, and the gates could be repaired, he reasoned. Until then . . . well, he was a knight mage. He could enchant a gate with his witchstone, using magic to fortify it, if need be.

The interior of the manor was atrocious. Rondal himself investigated the upper rooms of the place, a warwand in hand and a magelight floating above him. He had scryed for signs of life, but the results had been spotty for some reason, indicating the presence of . . . someone. Or something. He proceeded with caution, ready to blast any stray goblins to bits.

It was Rondal who discovered that Maramor was not –quite – as deserted as expected. He heard what he thought was a muffled cough.

When he heard the noise he whirled and peered with magesight. The battered tapestry before him, torn in several places and starting to mildew, revealed a space behind it under arcane vision. And within that space there was . . . *someone.*

"Come out with your hands where I can see them!" he ordered, raising his wand in a mailed fist.

The tapestry moved. No one was forthcoming.

"This is your last warning," Rondal said in his best military voice. "Reveal yourself now in the name of the King—"

"Who are you?" came a voice from behind the tapestry. It was female, and sounded young. He almost relaxed. It wasn't a goblin's harsh voice.

"I am Sir Rondal of Sevendor," he began, "In service to the Marshal of Castal, Magelord Minalan. Who the hells are you?" he demanded.

The tapestry parted. The threatening end of an arbalest poked through, pointing in his direction, the barbed dart looming ominously less than ten feet in front of his heart.

"I am Lady Arsella of Maramor," the woman – girl – said haughtily,

371

"and this is *my* home you are invading!"

That made Rondal snort despite himself. "I wouldn't be the first, apparently."

"It's been a while since the maids have come," the girl admitted in a shaky voice, her grip on the crossbow steady as she advanced, "and I've been forced to see to my own security. Tell me, Sir Knight, have I your word that I may come and go in my own home unmolested?"

"My lady," Rondal said with a grunt as he put the warwand away, sure she was little threat, "as long as you are taller than five feet and not covered with black hair, I have no quarrel with you."

"Four inches over the limit," she smirked, anxiously, and lowered the crossbow an inch - but no more. "Gods be praised. And as you can see, my hair is golden, not black."

"Brown, more like," Rondal said, ignoring the crossbow that was still pointed at him.

"It's golden when I have the chance to *wash it* properly!" The crossbow quivered mere inches from Rondal's nose.

"Put that thing down," growled Rondal, looking around. "Are there any more?"

"Any more what?" the girl asked, mystified.

"Any more refugees?" Rondal demanded. "Is there anyone else who is going to pop out with an arbalest and make my day interesting? And perhaps get themselves killed?"

Finally, the girl let the crossbow fall. "No, Sir Knight," Lady Arsella said, reluctantly, "I am all that is left of my line, if my brothers and father are dead as I believe."

"So what happened?" Rondal asked, not seeing any other sign of life.

"I was here with my maids," she said, carefully, "when the first news of the invasion came. My father and brothers were called to their banners. I stayed here with six men-at-arms and a few servants.

"We were here for days, with no news . . . but when it came, it was all bad. Goblins. Hundreds of them, swept over the countryside. Some raided Maramor, and one night some ferocious beast banged on our gates with its fists until they collapsed."

"A troll," Rondal nodded. "Then what happened?"

"They captured or killed the others," she said, her face growing pale. "Mostly captured. They wanted them alive, I think."

"Why weren't *you* taken?" Rondal asked, suspiciously.

"Me? Why, I had a place to hide. My family has been in Maramor for seventy years. There are hidden places of refuge in times of attack. I hid myself there while my . . . my servants were taken away."

"When was that?"

"Two months ago," she said, weakly. "Two months of hunting and running and hiding and eating . . . well, let's not discuss what I have eaten. But Maramor is still held," she said, hefting the crossbow over her shoulder. "And as long as Maramor is held, then we have not lost. I take it my father sent you?" she asked expectantly.

"Who was your father?"

"Sir Hagun of Maramor," she asked, holding her breath. "My brother was Sir Hagarath. House Maramor, of course," she added, as if she might forget.

"I've heard no tale of them, dead or alive," Rondal said, reluctantly. "We're not exactly a rescue party," Rondal admitted. "We're here to establish an outpost. To observe," he emphasized. "We're not here to drive the goblins back, yet."

"When does that happen?" she demanded.

"Not soon enough," Rondal said. "I have but seven men with me, and I expect a like number in a few days, gods willing. But we are here to scout out the scrugs, not rout them. Have you seen any recently?"

"I go look in the daytime, at the top of the tower," she said, biting her lip. "It's scary, but I've spotted them before. I just don't want to be seen myself. But I haven't seen anyone in days. At least a week," she decided. "And then it was but two scouts. And one of those horrible dogs of theirs."

"Dogs?" Rondal asked, curious.

"Some beastly mastiff, I think. More wolf than dog," Arsella decided. "Though I've never seen a wolf so fearsome."

"Some devilry of the Dead God's priests, I'd wager," Rondal decided, setting a stool to rights in the ruin. "But that does not bode well, if he is using our own beasts against us. They rode hound-drawn chariots, at Castle Cambrian," he recalled. "I'll have to report that."

"See?" she said, almost smiling. "I've proven useful already."

"Why should that matter?" Rondal asked.

"Because I am one woman in a ruined manor, surrounded by men who can defend her . . . or defile her."

Rondal realized why she was fearful. "If you are the lady of the manor," he said, carefully, "then as a knight it is my duty to defend you in a time of war. My men will not defile you. You have my word."

Arsella caught her breath. "And . . . *you?*"

"I'm not in the mood to defile anyone," Rondal said, wearily. "I'll let you know if that changes. Right now, I want to know if you think it's safe to light a fire in the great hall. If the gate is guarded, that is."

"I've chanced small fires a few times," she admitted. "Just enough to boil some water, make some porridge. If the gate is guarded, then I don't see the harm. In fact," she said, straightening, "if you are to be so valiant as to offer he lady of the manor protection, Sir Knight, then it is my gracious duty to see to your men as best as the hospitality of this poor hall can allow."

Rondal smiled in return. "Then we have an agreement. As to supplies . . . we have a small store, and more to come, but we expect to forage. "

"I can tell you where you might find a cache or two, laid in against such times or overlooked," she agreed. "And I will be happy to cook for you and your men while you are my guests. As soon as a proper fire is laid on the hearth." She suddenly looked very thin and terribly hungry.

When the rest of the compound was secured, and proper wards were set, Rondal detailed one of his men to duty on watch in the northern tower, and put another two on the gate. The balance he allowed a chance to rest and eat, after their beasts were tended.

The fire in the grand old hearth in the great hall was rekindled by the lady of the manor, and after it was fed with the shards of a broken trestle that had been used as a shield, she began to boil water in a copper kettle she produced. The company's store of beans and salt pork was raided and soon the smell of savory soup filled the desolate hall.

While the soup was cooking, Lady Arsella excused herself upstairs. She returned soon after wearing a gown of dark gold and black, a bronze noble's circlet tying back her hair which she had freshly brushed and banded.

It may have been golden, Rondal conceded, if it was clean and the light bright enough. She devoured the soup wolfishly, after serving his men and himself, her eyes darting around the door they had turned into a table in the main hall. She asked for news, and they gave her what they could.

"Most of northern Gilmora is deserted, now," Rondal explained. "Most of the peasants have either fled south or been taken north in chains. The warriors have either died defending their homes or are in a strange castle hundreds of miles south. Barrowbell is the last great defended city."

"Barrowbell? They've gotten all the way to *Barrowbell?*" Arsella asked, her mouth agape in a most unladylike way.

"Nearly," Rondal agreed, sadly. "We've managed to hold them. Only . . . they aren't actually pushing any further. They aren't holding

375

castles like they did in the Penumbra. They raid, they enslave, they slaughter, they pillage . . . but then they move on. They are looting it bare, but they are not trying to hold Gilmora."

"That's strange," she agreed. "But the gods alone know what drives the minds of the goblins," she said, distastefully.

"They have minds like any man, and they make war better than most," admitted one of the men-at-arms at the far end of the table. "You don't raid a country bare. Not like that."

"So why?" she asked, pouring another bowl of soup.

"That's one of the things we're here to find out," Rondal nodded. "You don't happen to have a map of the area, do you?"

"I believe there were some maps in my father's chamber," Arsella nodded, "but I don't know if they survived the pillage." Rondal knew that most lords and castellans kept such maps to keep property rights straight. Often a manor's maps were quite extensive.

"If you don't mind looking for them, they would be a great help. We have a well inside, and the walls are stout, once we repair that gate. But we'll soon run out of this . . . bounty," he said, distastefully eyeing the soup. "Where might we find more? Surely not every inch of Gilmora is scoured."

"I . . . I have a few ideas," she admitted. "Places to go where I was afraid to go myself. With you and your stalwart men," she said, smiling warmly, "perhaps we can risk it. By day."

"I'll not fight goblins in the dark, if I can help it," agreed Rondal. "We have another caravan arriving soon, and another beyond that. But we will have to exist on forage as much or more than our baggage trains. The gurvani have proved adept at raiding our caravans," he said, annoyed. "We also intend on stopping the flow of prisoners into the Penumbra. Both from here and from the other end of the Timber Road."

"Why are they taking so many prisoners?" she asked, anxiously.

"What are they doing with them all?"

"Slaves," one of the men told her. "Sacrifice. And . . . rations."

"Rations—oh!" Arsella said, horrified. "They . . . eat *people?*"

"After the sacrifice part," agreed Rondal. "They dry the flesh and distribute it to their armies. Never eat a goblin's lunch," he said, disparagingly. "It might just be someone you know."

"That's . . . that's *revolting!*" she gasped, looking ill. "I thought they would just hold them for ransom."

"Goblins aren't Gilmoran gentlemen playing at dynastic feuds," Rondal said, darkly. "They intend to exterminate every human being on Callidore. They may keep a few alive to help the process along, but I have no doubt as to their goal."

"Dear gods," Arsella said, her eyes dazed. "All those *people.*"

"That's why we're here," Rondal assured her. "We're looking at how we can stop them from continuing. The northern third of Gilmora is the most sparsely people region. What happens when they turn to the more populated south? We think they were just getting started with their invasion last summer.

"This year, they're setting up their structures. Next year . . . well, imagine a hundred trolls, all in a row, knocking over every castle in sight. Or dragons digging through the ruins of our strongest fortresses to get at the yummy parts inside."

"All those people," she repeated, her face ashen. "My lords, I think . . . I think I will retire for the evening." With that she got up and left, a taper in her hand.

Rondal felt badly about telling her the truth, but there was no escaping the horror of the gurvani invasion.

If anything, he had spared her the worst of what he'd heard went on within the Penumbra: the makeshift torture camps, the sacrifice pits turned into butcheries, the sadistic and cruel contests the goblins forced the humans into, pitting them against each other in contests designed to maim and hurt, but only rarely kill. That privilege was reserved for the priests of the Dead God.

Rondal listened to the girl's footsteps as she mounted the stairs, crossed to her chamber, and locked the heavy door from within. Then silence. Then, just barely in the range of his hearing, he heard sobs of despair.

*   *   *

Rondal's first priority was securing the perimeter of their new home. Repairing the gate was a big job, and though the portly corporal had some skill with wood, Rondal could do little more than prop one of the doors up and wedge it into place, push the cart in front of it that first night and ward the opening as tightly as he could. Thinking of the poor noblewoman within, he warded the entire manor compound heavily, placing sigils, wards, and active spells wherever they might do the most good to take the place of guards he did not have yet.

Lady Arsella set to making herself useful, for which Rondal was grateful. The last thing he needed was an idle body around while he and his men toiled. Arsella seemed quite capable for a noblewoman, willing and able to carry water, build a fire, and cook with greater facility than he would have expected.

She was also quite friendly, smiling at the men as they came on and off duty, and always willing to pitch in to help with some project where nimble hands were better suited.

Despite the ruined condition of the hall and the manor in general, the girl was surprisingly able to locate several key items in the rubbish, from shears to rope, when asked. She was also instrumental in setting the place to rights, more or less, indicating exactly what sheds and cots had been used for what purpose.

She was replete with knowledge on the habits of the various servants, the manor officials, and even her own family. Rondal wrote it off as a nervous girl in a bad situation babbling, but he learned a bit about her past life at Maramor during her ranting, and he soon felt sorry for Arsella.

Rondal took the former Castellan's chamber in the northern tower as his own, as it had a good view and most of a bed and there were a few maps and such rolled up and tucked away in the rafters.

Many were years out of date, but the rivers and bridges had not moved, even if the domains and their owners had. He spread the largest map out over one wall and attached it with a spell so he could imagine the countryside around him. He transferred most of the physical features to a magemap he was building, allowing him to see where potential allies, enemies, and un-looted provision might be hidden.

He kept in contact with both Terleman and Tyndal, who was taking a different route, but was bringing twenty men and a wain of supplies with him. They helped fill in details about specific areas and sightings of the foe from rangers skulking through the deserted fiefs of Gilmora.

Terleman had news about Arsella's family the third day at Maramor.

They brought nine lances to Cantinal, and thence to Dormorar. That's one of the places where the dragons attacked, a week after they probably arrived. Right after the attack when the survivors were regrouping, the place was sacked by two legions of hobgoblin infantry. There weren't many survivors. I will check, but in all likelihood the girl really is the last of her line.

So what do I do about her?

It's her manor, legally, Terleman advised. *We can use it under order of the King, and even compensate her. But since her father and his liege – and his liege above him – are all dead, I'd say she'd be better off abandoning the place and moving south with the rest of the refugees.*

I'll suggest it, Rondal replied, doubtfully. *But I don't think she'll go.*

Then let her stay – but she's living in an active war zone. You could

be ordered to abandon that manor at any time, and withdraw all
protection. Make certain she understands that. If she still wants to
stay, that's between her and the gods.

Tyndal was less severe, when Rondal solicited his advice after
reporting their success, mind-to-mind.

Is she comely? was the first thing he asked.

When Rondal assured him that under the dirt she was likely a lovely
girl, his fellow apprentice was convinced.

Then keep her around. It keeps a certain element of class to the
place.

You haven't even seen the place.

If it's at all like the last three manors we've seen, it needs all the
class it can get. Besides, what else can you do? Until someone is
headed south, you're stuck with her. And we're going to be there a
while. So it's a good thing she's not bad to look at.

Rondal didn't have much to say in response to that. In truth, he had
begun to notice Lady Arsella as a woman, and he felt guilty about it.

After all, this was her home. If Sire Cei has taught them anything, he
had taught them the demands of hospitality, and feeling lustfully
toward your hostess was never appropriate, particularly if a knight had
her at a disadvantage. It was the duty of a knight to defend the
defenseless, he reasoned. Not annoy them with unwanted suits.

He explained Commander Terleman's position and proposal to her
that afternoon, during their first real meal in the great hall. She
tearfully took the news of her family's probable demise, then agreed to
let the patrol set up their outpost at Maramor.

She had very, very pretty eyes, he noted. Eyes like . . . well, eyes he
found alluring. Warm and friendly, despite her condition. Rondal
suppressed a desire to be forward with the defenseless girl anyway, and
chided himself from such thoughts. He could be stalwart about it, his
brain insisted. He was, he kept reminding himself, a professional. A

knight mage.

He didn't exactly avoid Arsella after that, but he didn't seek her out, either. Instead he busied himself with restoring the manor's limited defenses.

He spent the next day directing earth elementals he conjured to clear out a trench and build a short, five-foot tall earthen dike around the manor to improve its profile; good, easy magical work. A lot like directing trained dogs, he often thought. Good work a man could get lost in.

Only it was difficult to keep his mind away from his hostess when she sought him out on purpose. A few hours after noon she appeared with a basket, dressed in a red gown and a black mantle. She'd even donned a wimple.

"I thought you might be hungry," she said, smiling as he allowed the spell to fade, the piles of dirt falling into place where they'd fallen out of existence. "I brought a few things . . . there wasn't much. I'm just grateful for you sharing." She spread a cloth over a boulder his excavations had revealed and sat the basket upon it.

"You're right, it wasn't much," he agreed. "But it looks like you've lived on less."

"A lady learns to be resourceful," she said, biting her lip. "I found a ham in the rafters of the smoke shed, the second week. It felt like a feast. It only lasted a week. Then I boiled the bone. Most of the food in the kitchens is long gone, but I'm wondering if the village—"

"There's not much left to the village," Rondal said, gently, as she removed a parcel of griddle cakes from the basket. "I don't know the last time you were there—"

"Not since the . . . the men marched away," she said, guiltily, pulling some cold grilled sausages out of the hamper. "I went to see them off. The castellan and th— my father. And all the men in the village went, and all the men at the manor. Only a few were spared. The others left to go to Castle Dormorar where the baron and his men were holding out."

"So why didn't *you* go?" he asked, curiously.

"They wanted me to, of course," she said, looking away. "I should have. But I couldn't bear to leave Maramor all alone. Alone and undefended."

"So . . . how is your valiant defense going?" Rondal asked with a chuckle as he took a griddle cake. "The last time I checked, you had but three quarrels left in your quiver and had slain but one goblin."

"It was a *big* goblin!" she assured him, a little irritated. "Hiding from goblins is a perfectly acceptable tactic, for a lady!"

"And so is shooting it in the back!" Rondal laughed. She had regaled the squadron of her one brush with combat, a few weeks prior. She had taken a lone goblin scout who was looking for loot in her manor hall by surprise, shooting it in the back of the neck from a hiding place. She even proudly showed them the body, which she had dragged out to the midden pile.

"But what would have happened if I'd followed the rest of the folk of Maramor?" she asked. "I'd be as dead as they are," she said, sadly.

"It's a war," he said, trying to comfort her. "People die. Not just soldiers. Not in this war."

"What do you know about it?" she demanded crossly, a tear in her eye. "Was your home destroyed by goblins?"

"Yes," he said, sharply. "Mine was one of the first. Away in the Mindens, in a tiny valley called Boval Vale. Hundreds of my friends perished. I barely escaped with my life." He hadn't meant to sound bitter about it – he rarely thought about the home of his boyhood, now. But her bitterness made him angry – she wasn't the only one suffering in the war.

"I apologize," she said, wiping away a tear. "I'm . . . I'm new to this. Being the Lady of the Manor and all."

"I've just recently been made a knight," he admitted. "Just over a year. I'm not very good at it, either."

"You seem to do well," she said, handing him an apple. They hadn't brought any apples. It must have been from her private store. "Your men look to you like . . . like my father's men did to him."

"That's not the same as knowing what you're doing," he said, shaking his head. "Most of these men are older than me. But they are all regular soldiers, not militia, and they know how to follow orders. Good orders," he added.

"Well, I think you do it well," she said, sincerely. "And I cannot thank you enough for your assistance, here, Sir Rondal."

"It's just . . . a bit of errantry," he dismissed, blushing a little. She seemed a little too grateful.

"It's gracious of you to think so," she said, brushing a lock of hair behind her ear. She was right, Rondal realized. In the sunlight, her hair was kind of golden. "I know that you are just on a mission. But . . . . I'm happy that your mission brought you to Maramor," she said, softly. Her hand reached out and touched his.

Rondal was very self-conscious, but he found his hand caressing hers. It was soft, softer than his by far. Her fingers seemed long and thin and almost childlike next to his. Once the hands of a scholar, they now had sword calluses, and his wrists were far thicker than they'd been a year ago. They seemed to dwarf hers.

"Lady Arsella," he began softly, but uneasily. "It would not be proper . . ."

"Let's leave proprietary to the bridesisters," she said, rolling her eyes. "I have been here in this manor alone for weeks. Now a handsome young knight arrives – with *food* – and protects me. Propriety is for formal balls, not war zones."

"Still," Rondal said, reluctantly pulling his hand away, "while I admire you, my lady, and feel . . . well, it would not be proper for me to discuss how I feel under any circumstances I can think of, it would complicate matters with my command. For now," he said, deliberately pushing her hand back into her lap, "I think it best if we keep to a professional relationship. Perhaps later . . ."

"I am at your disposal, Sir Knight," she said, a little awkwardly. "I suppose if we were to become intimate, your men would, indeed, grow—"

"Restless," Rondal finished for her. "In a war zone, at a deserted outpost, propriety is sometimes all that keeps a soldier's baser nature at bay. If I do not live by it and keep discipline here and now . . ."

"I understand," she smiled. "I like you, Sir Rondal. You are a gentle man, for a soldier."

"Knight mage," he said, his throat dry. "Actually, I'm a knight mage."

"I've never heard of that," she said, leaning uncomfortably close to him.

"We're new," he said, absently. She was so close. So close he could smell her breath. It was sweet. Like an apple.

"We . . . we should get back," he said, reluctantly. "It's late afternoon. I have to inspect the pickets and change the guard. And tomorrow we go into the village and see what's left of it. "

Arsella nodded, looking a little ashamed as she packed up the picnic. But when she walked back with him, he carried the basket . . . and she held his hand the whole way.

*   *   *

Maramor village was actually two villages – Maramor Village proper, and then a hamlet a half-mile down the road called Argun. The former was devoted to the cotton fields and corn fields that were the heart of Maramor's demesne, while Argun was devoted to growing tobacco. Both were deserted, and Maramor Village was largely burned to the ground.

Lady Arsella accompanied Rondal and two of the men on the short expedition, and from the moment she saw the circles of stumps where once peasant cots had stood she burst into tears. She ran from hovel to hovel in the former village, naming the people who once lived there. Rondal only half-heard what she was saying, as it came out half a mumble, but he could tell she was terribly distressed.

"Most left with . . . with Mother," she said, sadly. "Some stayed, at least for a while. But then . . . then the goblins came. They fought, but I hid."

"It's what you were supposed to do," soothed Rondal, looking around anxiously. There hadn't been any sign of goblins nearby since they arrived, but with the girl making so much noise . . .

"I know, I know," she sobbed. "But . . . it's not fair! It's not fair that they're d-d-dead and I'm, I'm . . ."

"Calm yourself, Lady Arsella," Rondal said, dismounting and pulling her to him by the shoulders. "Lady Arsella," he repeated, two or three times, as he looked into her eyes. It was as if she couldn't remember her own name. Finally, she caught his eye, and was brought back into the present.

"Oh, dear Ishi and Trygg!" she said, tears in her eyes. "What a sight I must look . . . but . . ."

"You said you might know where some food was overlooked," Rondal reminded her.

"Food," she repeated, dumbly, then took possession of herself again. "Yes," she assured him. "I believe I do.

"Aunt Gi always kept some back from the reeve," she explained, as she kicked the dirt aside from the edge of a burned-out hovel. "She died a few days before the first reports came in, and they were going to settle her will, but then everyone got called to their banners.

"I don't think anyone remembered . . ." she said, reaching down and pulling up the edge of a doorway hidden in the dirt. "She had this root cellar," Arsella explained triumphantly. "And she always kept some extra." She reached down into the hole she had revealed and began pulling up food.

"Cheese," she said, pulling out two small wheels of peasant-made cheese, "a sack of wheat flour, a half-sack of barley, half-sack of oats . . . look!" she said, grinning, as she struggled to pull a jar from the ground. "Pickled eggs!"

There was actually a fair amount of food stashed within the old root cellar. Enough to feed his men for a week or more, if they were careful, he guessed.

The last jar Arsella pulled from the pit was the most promising, though. It was a large crock with a wooden lid, and when he pulled it off, Arsella wrinkled her nose.

"Ale!" Rondal grinned. "And quite far gone, if poor Aunt Gi made it before she died. A few month's worth. This should be a proper drink!" The other men were pleased by the find, too. "I wonder if there are any more caches around . . ." he said, summoning power from his stone.

He shaped a spell that would tell him of any hidden chambers and cast it. To his pleasure he found two more, neither as large as Aunt Gi's, but yielding several more days' worth of food.

"Let's scout the hamlet, too," he suggested, once the provisions were stored on the horses. "While we're here. I at least want to ensure there aren't any gurvani lurking about."

His fears were unfounded; Argun was even more burnt-out than Maramor Village. The lonely row of huts and cots near the road looked desolate without thatch on them, and the burnt stumps of the walls sometimes concealed human remains. Only one cache was discovered there, a mere sack of potatoes and a measure of rye flour. The expedition proved fruitful in other ways, however.

"Look, Sir Rondal," one of his rangers, Fursar, said as he examined the rough track that bisected the hamlet. "Tracks. Fresh. Some human and some . . . not."

Rondal came over to examine the impressions. "I'm no tracker, Fursar. What do they tell you?"

"Four gurvani came this way, probably four, five nights ago," he pronounced. "They had two humans with 'em. A woman and a man, looks like."

"Are you sure they were here at the same time?" Rondal asked in a low voice.

"Positive, milord," the soldier grunted. "See how that gurvani print overshadows the human . . . and then this human print overshadows the gurvani? They were here at the same time, no doubt," he assured.

"Slavers, then," Rondal said, his eyes narrowing. "Picking up the remnants. You are lucky they strayed no further from the road, Lady Arsella," he called.

"Can . . . can we go back to Maramor, now?" she asked, shivering under her mantle.

"I think we've found enough," Rondal agreed. "We know there have been goblins here. We know there have been people here. Let's hope we can avoid both . . . at least until our relief arrives."

Dinner was a merry feast, as not only had the stores been replenished by the foraging expedition, but also one of the men had had luck with his arbalest. A fat goose was waiting for Arsella to dress when they returned.

Rondal expected the noblewoman to blanch at the idea of plucking and cleaning the fowl, but Arsella pitched in excitedly. She found the prospect of goose tempting. Rondal had a large fire in the main hall and oversaw the roasting himself. Some roasted potatoes, cheese, some biscuits baked in the fire, and a few more sausages from their original stores filled their bellies. Aunt Gi's final brew filled their hearts.

Rondal sat at the opposite end of the trestle-door table from Lady Arsella, as if they were lord and lady in a hall, surrounded by their knights. Their "knights" being rough peasant infantrymen, their hall draughty and bare, and their fare of the commonest sort, at least the ale was fit for a king, he decided. Rondal found himself feeling almost lordly, and caught himself smiling at Arsella in the magelight several times.

Is this what it's like? he wondered. *Is this what Sire Cei and Master Min are so enraptured of?*

He studied Arsella when she wasn't looking at him, catching her in mid-laugh. She was comely, he decided. And very warm. Intelligent and friendly. She teased with the men without being disrespectful or inviting rude jests, he noted, and carried herself proudly . . . mostly.

Every now and then he caught her off-guard, just being a girl, and not the lady of the manor. It was at those times he found her most appealing.

His attention was noted by Fursar, the Gilmoran ranger from the south.

"Watch that one, lad," he warned in a fatherly tone. "She's a quick wit and a pretty face, but there's something amiss about her. More than meets the eye," he said, tapping his cheek meaningfully.

"Oh, I don't have an eye for her," Rondal said, unconvincingly. "She's just a poor girl in a rough spot. Scared and desperate."

"And that's not cause enough for caution?" Fursar asked, amused. "I'll not call fair foul without cause, milord, but . . . just watch yourself. She's the sort who always wants to stay on top and will do what she must to stay there. A survivor," he admitted, approvingly. "But that's not the best sort for a man such as yourself, milord. A lot can happen in a war zone."

Rondal tried to dismiss the man's warning as misplaced, that Arsella was just being friendly and grateful . . . until she tapped at the door to his chamber that evening.

"Is there something amiss, milady?" he asked, tiredly, as he checked the wards.

"No, not really," Arsella said, biting her lip. "I was just . . . I wanted to know if milord would be interested in a game of dice and a cup of cheer before bed?" she asked, hesitantly. "I found this stashed away in

. . . Father's things," she admitted, offering a small, ornate cut-glass bottle filled with some honey-colored spirit. "And I quite enjoy a game of Chasers, if you've a mood to pass the time."

"A lady alone with a man in his chambers?" he clucked. "How improper!"

"Consider it a military consultation with the civilian leadership, then," she said, pushing past him. Her hair smelled delicious to him, and kept him from mounting a credible defense. "Besides," she rationalized, "who is going to know? Or care?"

"I . . . I don't have a good argument for that, save that we will," Rondal stumbled.

"Good . . . because I trust me, and I trust you implicitly," she said, gamely as she pulled a stool over to the small table. "Find some glasses, Sir Rondal," she said as she opened the board. "I feel like a game."

Reluctantly, but eagerly, Rondal found two small earthenware cups and poured the spirits while Arsella set up the board. It was a simple game, a peasant's game, a child's game. She won handily the first time, teasing Rondal into mounting a spirited second game.

He laughed with her easily, finding speaking to her something that came naturally. She put him at ease. And she smiled at him. A lot.

"So what do you think is going to happen to Maramor?" she asked, after he barely managed to win the second game. The spirits were almost gone.

"It's in the middle of a war zone," Rondal said, after some thought. "As much as I'd like to, I can't see us re-taking this region in force any time soon. As fast as troops are arriving in the garrisons south of here, they're going into a defensive posture. Preparing to receive another advance. Not make one of their own."

"So . . . Maramor will be lost," she said, sadly.

"Mayhap," Rondal shrugged. "It's a pretty place, or was once. But without the village, it's just a big house. Without the peasants to plant the cotton and the tobacco crops, it's . . . useless. It's useful to us now because it's remote, relatively defensible and . . . disposable," he said, apologetically. "If the goblins advance, we leave it behind."

"And . . . me?"

"That would be unchivalrous," he said, swallowing. Something about her vulnerability was playing on him like a sweet, sorrowful tune. "I'm sure we can find some room for you. And there's always the possibility that the goblins will all just go home." He smiled. She gave him a smile for courtesy, but she was not happy.

"Oh, Rondal, what am I going to do?" she said, tearfully. "I . . . I'm alone. My family is dead. I have a manor that no one wants, lands that are useless, and no hope of much else."

"You seem very resourceful," Rondal said, knowing how awful that sounded the moment he said it. "Something will come along."

"Like what? What use am I? A scullion for rangers at the edge of ruin. With no hope."

"Some hope," Rondal said, insistently. "Surely there is something that could be salvaged from this," he said, gesturing around. "Every lord keeps secret treasuries."

"If my father had such, he neglected to inform me," she sighed. "I think he took most of it with him."

"Something will turn up," Rondal said, without much enthusiasm. "Don't worry, we'll take care of you. I'm supposed to help survivors, after all. But we're a long way from pulling out, and for now Maramor is my headquarters. Once the rest of my men arrive, we'll begin our work in earnest. Who knows," he added, hopefully, "maybe I can secure some funds for you for the use of the place."

"That would be . . . helpful," she agreed. "I don't have much, but if I did have to flee, some money would be helpful. Oh, thank you, Rondal!! You gave me hope, when I didn't have any. And a game of Chasers." Before he knew what was happening, she kissed him. Not long, and not insistently, but gratefully. "Thank you," she repeated, and kissed him again before leaving.

"You're welcome," Rondal said to the back of the door after she left.

With the immediate issue of supplies at bay, Rondal ordered the men to stay close to Maramor and see to its repair for the next few days. He kept scrying the surrounding country, but no gurvani came within miles of the place. Without a reason to leave the outpost, Rondal focused on the defenses.

"It would never stand to a real siege," he remarked at breakfast the next morning. "One battering ram and that door would come apart. The towers, too. More decorative than functional." It was an observation, not a judgment – but Arsella took it personally.

"Hey!" she protested, as she brought the big pot of tea to the table, "Maramor has withstood dozens of attacks!"

"Bandits," grunted one of the men, "or petty feuds between lordlings. Not a proper siege. It'll keep out a pissed-off knight, mayhap, but a troll? Not bloody likely!"

"It has so!" she insisted. "It's as good as a proper castle!"

"It's our outpost," Rondal said, firmly, "and regardless of what it was, we are living in it as it is. And as it is . . . it leaves much to be desired. As soon as the cavalry contingent arrives, we're going to start scouting the nearby manors. Which ones would those be, milady?"

"Huh? Oh!" Arsella said, startled. "You should probably start with Ketral Manor, and then Farune Manor. They're both nearby, I believe," she said. She didn't sound too sure. "But there's no telling what's happening there, is there?"

"That's why we're going," Rondal reminded her. "To find out."

She was quiet, after that, but he could tell she was not happy with the idea of exploration. He supposed he could see her perspective: after weeks on her own, having a bunch of soldiers around with sharp swords made her feel safe. Thinking about them running off and attracting trouble back to her manor probably worried her.

That afternoon she joined him again as he finished the dike-and-ditch around the manor wall. She brought lunch again, and she also brought her arbalest.

"I want you to teach me to shoot properly," she proposed. "I got lucky with that one goblin. Next time, I don't want to depend on luck."

"It's not very ladylike," he teased.

"Either is dying for a soup pot," she retorted. "Are you going to teach me, milord?"

So he taught her. The mechanism was a bit different than the ones he'd used at Relan Cor, and far more complex than the simple crossbows made in the Wilderlands. It was also more ornate, to the point where it barely looked like a tool of war.

But the bow was strong, the catch was easy to operate, and teaching her to use the slide windlass wasn't difficult. In two hours she was hitting the target – her wimple, laid upon a pile of dirt – from thirty paces, reloading and hitting it again within the span of twenty heartbeats.

"You're very good at this," he remarked, as she put a third quarrel inside the circle. "I'm surprised your father never taught you."

"Sir Hagun felt that such pursuits were better left to his fosterling sons, not his daughters," she sniffed. "Needlework, now, that was a craft for a lady!" She sounded rueful about it. She was far from the only noblewoman who disliked needlework – it was a common complaint.

"Probably a good thing," Rondal decided, "with your temperament."

"My temperament?" she asked, mockingly, as she loaded a fresh quarrel into the slot. "Whatever do you mean?" She let fly a little too quickly, and missed the mark . . . by less than an inch.

"You seem to like to act rashly," he pointed out.

"How so?" she asked, halting her practice and staring at him.

"Well, the decision to leave the evacuation and return to Maramor, for one thing," he pointed out.

"Sir Hagun left good people behind!" she protested. "It wasn't right that they were here without protection!"

"And you protected them . . . how?" Rondal asked, patiently. Arsella blushed.

"They should have at least had some representation from House Maramor," she said, proudly. "It is the least the family could do after abandoning them like that!"

"Yet your father felt otherwise, and you disobeyed him."

"I'm alive, aren't I?" she asked, defensively.

"And yet the people you came to protect . . ."

"You think I wanted that?" she objected. "So, I acted rashly. When I heard that, that *thing* breaking down the big gates, I ran and hid. One of my servants, the brave girl, *insisted* on it. Only . . . there was only room for one," she said, tearfully.

Rondal felt awful – he had been having a reasonable discussion, he hadn't meant to invoke such a painful memory. But something in the way Arsella spoke told him she was desperate to talk about it.

"It was a horrible night," she said, setting down the bow and sinking to the ground. Rondal stooped closer to listen. "They came just after midnight. They had already burned the village, after taking the few people left there. There were only a score of us here, then, all that was left. We thought we were safe. The gate was shut and locked. We thought they'd passed us by. But we were wrong.

"They howled," she said, her face streaked with tears. "A terrible noise, like a . . . a. . ."

"A goblin's war cry," supplied Rondal with a faint, sympathetic smile. "I'm familiar with the sound."

"They chanted. A few could speak our language, in a way. It sounded horrible in their foul voices! They called for us to open the gate, even as they started a fire. Then that troll came, and bashed down the gates, instead. The men, the men fired at it, but it barely noticed their bolts."

"They're dumb that way," agreed Rondal. "It takes a lot to kill a troll. Hard to do, even with a crossbow. Mostly, it just pisses them off."

"This one wasn't happy," she agreed, nodding her head with tears in her eyes. "But after it bashed the gate down, they just . . . swarmed in. The goblins. The men drew swords, and the goblins only had clubs, but they . . . there were just *too many*," she whispered.

"That's when the servant girl insisted I go to my hiding place. She closed it just as the goblins pushed the manor hall doors open. I heard them come for her. I heard her screaming right outside as they took her. I heard . . . oh, dear gods, Sir Rondal, I heard her beg for mercy and then she just . . . *stopped*."

"Probably fainted, or was knocked unconscious," Rondal said, weakly. "We didn't see much sign of blood."

"I hope . . . I hope . . ."

"I *know*," Rondal said, comfortingly. "I know that feeling. You can't dwell on it, though, or it will eat you alive. I *know*," he repeated, with emphasis. "Trust me, you can't . . . you can't wish someone alive again. Not even with magic."

"Of course you can't," she agreed, absently. "But it was horrible."

"I'm sorry," he said, taking her hand. Without realizing it, he was suddenly embracing her, and she was sobbing into his neck.

He felt awkward and helpless. He had no idea what to do. Rondal decided to just hold her, and let her sob, because he didn't have any better plan. He knew Tyndal would – he'd know *exactly* what to do to appear sophisticated, cocky, and charming. Rondal felt like a manure-smeared rustic half-wit.

As if in response to his thoughts, Tyndal chose that moment to contact him mind-to-mind. Rondal wasn't nearly as appreciative of his advice as he thought he'd be.

What?! Rondal responded to Tyndal's overture.

What's wrong? Tyndal asked, anxiously. *Are you under attack?*

No, just – what do you want?

We're about a day from you, now. We just hit that big village you went through. We didn't see any sign of gurvani, but I didn't expect to.

Oh. All right. I guess we'll get ready for you, then. Um . . .

What is it? Tyndal asked.

Um . . . I have a girl on me.

Congratulations! Tyndal said. If Rondal didn't know better, he would have thought his fellow apprentice was being genuine. That idea disturbed him more than the thought of him being sarcastic. *What's the problem?*

She's crying.

That's not a problem, Tyndal assured. *Hells, that's great.*

You're really not helping this situation.

Just kiss her, tell her everything will be okay, and change the subject. Trust me.

But . . . things aren't going to be okay, Rondal said, evenly.

Of course not. We're all swimming in the Dead God's chamberpot, now. But that's the last thing she wants to hear.

So I should lie to her? Rondal asked, hesitantly.

Well, yes! Tyndal replied. Rondal could imagine his eyes rolling. *Believe it or not it would not be the first time a man has lied to a woman. Don't let it worry you. It's not an important thing. You're just trying to get her to feel better. And you're not lying to her, if you want to be technical. You just have a broader vision of what 'okay' is,* he said, philosophically.

But . . . she's sobbing hysterically now, Rondal said. *I can feel it on my shoulder.*

That's excellent. Let her get it out. That's all she wants to do for now. Let her get it out, lie to her, change the subject.

This is really not sounding like the kind of advice Lady Alya would give.

Lady Alya doesn't know much about courting women, Tyndal retorted. *I'm not saying ravish her, you idiot. Just give her a kiss. A comforting kiss. Give her a place of stability in a wild and chaotic world.*

What if . . . what if she doesn't want to kiss me? asked Rondal worriedly as Arsella seemed to break down even further.

Don't give her the option, Tyndal recommended. *Really, just take the matter out of her hands. It's a kiss, not a marriage proposal. If she doesn't want it, she'll let you know.*

This is really making me uncomfortable, Rondal said, as he shifted uncomfortably.

It's kissing, Tyndal dismissed. *That's what it's supposed to do. Just . . . get her calmed down. When I get there, we're going to have a lot of work to do, and the last thing we need are any distractions. Hysterically sobbing women count as distractions.*

Rondal agreed and ended the contact. Arsella must have felt the change in his demeanor, or had just reached the end of her mood, and looked up at him, bleary-eyed.

"It's . . . it's going to be okay," Rondal said, awkwardly.

"P-promise?" Arsella asked.

"Yes," Rondal said, with far more assurance than he felt. He couldn't think of any compelling reasons to support his promise, and he started to panic when he imagined her asking him to explain just why everything would be okay.

So he kissed her.

Much to his surprise, she kissed him back. It was . . . it was wet, what with her tears, and clumsy. She had not practiced the art much herself, not nearly as much as Lady Thena had, perhaps less than even he, but she was enthusiastic . . . and then a little desperate.

Be the rock, he reminded himself as he kissed her, trying to breathe and kiss and think all at the same time. *Be her point of stability.*

"Let's head back to the hall," he suggested, when they finally broke apart. He had to change the subject. "Our reinforcements arrive tomorrow, and we need to get ready for them." He gave her one last embrace, and caught one last kiss she insisted upon, and then they walked back to the manor, hand in hand.

I can't believe that worked! Be the rock, he reminded himself again, when he suppressed the urge to grin like a fool when she looked at him. *Be the rock.*

Although, he reflected as he stumbled, being the rock wasn't hard to imagine at the moment.

*   *   *

Everything changed the next day, when at midmorning a warning whistle from the tower announced the arrival of Tyndal's detachment.

Tyndal was at the head of the column, of course, riding a midnight-black charger and wearing a dashing green mantle over his armor. Except for the mageblade on his back and the lack of helmet he looked all the world like a handsome knight errant. That, Rondal discovered all too quickly, was readily apparent to Lady Arsella, too.

"About time you got here," Rondal said casually as his fellow dismounted. "I expected you at breakfast."

"The goblins made us breakfast," Tyndal retorted. "A patrol stumbled on us last night and clearly wasn't expecting to. Ten of them," he said, dismissively. "It was hardly a fight. As soon as they crossed my wards, I was awake. Didn't even disturb the horses," he said, proudly.

"That's the first sign of goblin activity we've seen," Rondal said, shaking his head. "Figures that you'd bring trouble along with you."

"Bring it? I dispensed with it," Tyndal countered. "None of them will be reporting our whereabouts. We hid the bodies well."

"Hopefully they won't be missed," Rondal sighed. "I'd hate to have to leave this place just as we're getting settled."

"So show me around this magnificent manor," Tyndal said, just a shade sarcastically. "And introduce me to the lady in charge." As Arsella was near to hand, that wasn't hard.

But the moment Rondal did so, he regretted it.

Suddenly, Rondal stopped being the focus of Arsella's attention.

As the Ancients ordered the new men to their billets and led their horses to the abandoned stables, Rondal realized that Lady Arsella could not take her eyes off of his fellow apprentice. He even tried testing her focus by asking her where the tanning shed was, which elicited a vague and dismissive response. Arsella was suddenly very formal and polite, and made a show of welcoming Sir Tyndal and his brave troopers to Maramor.

Rondal recalled that when she had first met him, she had almost shot him.

"So why don't you give me a tour?" Tyndal asked, as her welcome ended. "As I'm going to be staying here, getting to know my hostess is demanded by the laws of hospitality."

"And I would be remiss in my duties as a lady if I failed to do so," Arsella said, beaming. She slid her arm into Tyndal's offered elbow, and without a word or even a look back at him, she left the yard and went inside.

"Orders, Captain?" asked a familiar voice, breaking Rondal's brooding. He looked up . . . and into the face of his squadmate Walven.

"Walven!" he burst. "What are you doing here?"

"I told you I was headed for the front," he reminded Rondal after they had embraced. "I got in with a mercenary outfit just in time for it to be hired permanently by the Crown. I'm a corporal in the Third Royal Commando, now."

"Third Royal Commando?" Rondal asked, confused.

"It's supposed to be an elite unit – all the Royal Commando units are. But right now it's mostly just the best of the mercenaries coming upriver to Barrowbell. The first two are deployed in other advanced regions near the front. Having completed the Mysteries got me in. One nasty battle in Gilmora got me promoted."

"But . . . the cavalry?" asked Rondal, skeptically. "You always struck me as more of an infantryman. Or artillery."

"Versatility," chuckled his squadmate. "That's supposed to be our watch-word. Part ranger, part knight, part soldier, part spy. And the Commando is a mobile unit, in theory, so that's why I'm mounted. I hadn't planned that, but they had a spot available for a corporal and I wasn't going to turn down the pay increase just because my arse hurts when I ride."

"I don't blame you," nodded Rondal. "You know, I don't even know if I'm being paid," he grumbled.

"So what is the local situation like?" Walven asked, returning to business. "I like this place – remote. If we hadn't known where to turn, we might have missed it."

"Not with Sir Haystack with you," Rondal reminded him. "But that is one reason I like it. You have that long stretch of nowhere to get through before you get here. And now that the entire region is depopulated, we can let it grow up over the road, if we need to conceal ourselves."

"Which we will," Walven agreed. "There are apparently one or two manors and castles that have been turned into cantonments in this barony. We're to find them and scout them. That patrol this morning told us we're close."

"We set out tomorrow," Rondal promised. He glanced suddenly up at the tower above, where he heard the sound of Lady Arsella laughing – too hard – at something witty Sir Tyndal had said. "And let's hope there are some goblins around. I suddenly feel like stabbing someone."

*   *   *

The next morning Rondal awoke before dawn and detailed a five-man squad to accompany him, including Walven and the rangers. Lady Arsella, who had stayed up late into the evening around the fire in the great hall, meeting and laughing and drinking with the new arrivals – especially Sir Tyndal. He found her barely awake, stirring porridge in the kitchen around dawn, and she was able to provide him vague directions to Ketral Manor, only eight miles away. Farune was just to the north of that, she said, but she wasn't certain.

Rondal had his maps from the castellan's room, so he wasn't operating blindly – but he had anticipated Arsella being more help than she was. She didn't know much at all about either place, or what he could expect.

Worse, she treated him cordially, but distantly. The warmth he'd come to expect from her wasn't there, and she barely paid attention to him. She did ask him to keep an eye open for bacon and lard while he was scouting, as they had not been included in the inventory in the wagons.

He gruffly took his leave with Walven and the men. He didn't say when he would be back. She did not ask.

He felt better as soon as they passed beyond Maramor Village and into open country. They rode along the deserted road, almost daring an attack. Frequent stops to scry, particularly at crossroads, told Rondal there was little chance of that, but he almost hoped he'd overlooked a goblin.

The countryside was ruined. The cottages were either burnt or broken or both. Unlike the round huts the peasants in Sevendor lived in, these were more rough poled sheds of wattle-and-daub. It didn't take much to break the walls. None were occupied. It looked as if a giant burglar had broken them open, searching for coins.

The fields were unplowed since last season, and the crops either growing wild or absent. As they came to a hamlet four miles from Maramor, they saw one of the gurvani's grisly tributes, a man and a woman flayed alive and displayed in an obscene position in the ruins of the town's shrine. Swearing angrily, Rondal used the power of his witchstone to incinerate the unfortunate couple's corpses, giving their deaths at least a modicum of dignity.

"Ishi's tits, that's awful," Walven swore.

"They do that constantly," Rondal complained. "Just to taunt and terrify us. We do it back to them, too – after battle we spike their heads. But we usually burn the bodies. Not . . . entertain ourselves with them."

"This Goblin King is a nasty fellow," Walven said, appraisingly.

"He's not a goblin king," Rondal said, shaking his head. "He's an unearthly undead magical construct. He's not even alive. All he wants is us dead. And things like this," he said, gesturing to the smoldering corpses now mercifully at rest, "*delight* him."

"How old were they?" Walven asked, looking away.

"You can't really tell, when you find them in that state, but – oh." Rondal swallowed. " Uh, probably six, seven weeks?"

"A while, then," Walven nodded. "Good."

They turned left at the next crossroad, a ghost village called Ricoy on the maps, and proceeded down a narrow dirt track that led through a swampy area before spreading out into what once had been rich cotton fields. By noon they were riding through Ketral Village, which had once enjoyed a sophisticated prosperity due to its use as a market town. Now the houses lining the high street were empty or gutted, the smell of ashes still lingering in the air.

Rondal stopped to scry while the rangers scouted ahead, and when he pronounced the manor clear, they rode cautiously through its twisted gates.

The folk of Ketral Manor had put up a fight, those who had been left at the grisly end.

There were huge bales of last year's cotton piled in a barricade in front of the manor house, peppered with gurvani darts and javelins and black with dried blood; one had been hurled through the upper story of the manor, creating a large crater in the masonry and exposing the interior. Two rotting horse carcasses and piles of debris from the hastily-looted hall littered the once-tidy yard. In the worsening heat, the stench was overwhelming.

Particularly when you accounted for the defenders who had been honored for their heroics by being flung from the second story with their intestines nailed to the wall. Their bodies were still where they had suffered their excruciating deaths, their extended guts covered with flies.

In the end it was easy to see who the victors had been. Crude gurvani symbols had been painted in blood across the face of the manor. Carrion birds still sported in the horrific decorations. Apart from a few stray goats gone feral, there was little sign of life here.

"Search it for food and whatever might be helpful," Rondal ordered, his stomach in knots. "And weapons. Anything we can scavenge and keep out of goblin hands is a good thing."

Their efforts yielded a few sacks of rye flour, some preserves in earthenware, a few pounds of salt, and a sack of maize. They found a sheaf of spears and a battle axe that had been an heirloom, but little else of value. There were other good supplies left in the stable, and

Walven had them gathered and protected. He was about to cut the offending entrails off of the manor house, but Rondal stopped him.

"Leave them. That way whatever goblin patrol happens by might not realize we've been here. And those weapons, hide them in the stable. We need to start caching weapons when we can't carry them off."

'Why not just destroy them?" asked Walven, curious.

"Because it's likely that we'll have a human insurgency here, even if it's just irregulars, if the goblins are planning on staying. It would be nice to be able to direct them to weapons and not have to worry about supplying them."

Once they had packed all they could carry, they set out for the second manor, Farune.

Farune was smaller but better fortified than Ketral. It had a small, sturdy keep within its walls, almost invisible behind the tall, narrow manor, and thought the gate was open, it was undamaged. After scrying it thoroughly, Rondal led his men inside. The whole countryside smelled of death and decay now, he reflected, but the difference from the stench of Ketral was striking. It wasn't quite as bad here.

A grain farm, not a cotton plantation, Farune was nonetheless every bit as prosperous as Ketral had been. The village outside the walls would have been charming, had it not been deserted.

The goblins had been here, it seemed, but had found no one when they arrived. Farune seemed to have been abandoned in anticipation of the attack, and abandoned in an orderly fashion. When the goblins arrived, Rondal reasoned, they did not find the humans they were hunting . . . so they moved on after a token looting.

While the interior of Farune Hall had been trashed it had not been destroyed. Better yet, the kitchens were still well-stocked even after the withdrawal, and there was both food and firewood. Rondal ordered two big slabs of bacon to be brought along, and selected some roots and a wheel of cheese before he ordered everything else loaded into the keep.

"So we have a place to retreat to, if Maramor gets hit," Walven nodded.

"Exactly," he nodded as they opened up the thick wooden door to the keep. "This is the most secure place I've seen in Gilmora. It's intact. If well-supplied, we could hold out for weeks in here."

"While no one comes to our rescue," Walven nodded.

"Well, maybe the goblins would get bored," suggested Rondal as he sent a magelight ahead. "Look, this place has weapons," he said, pointing to a rack of pikes and shields, "it has water, it has food . . . and it has walls that are two bloody feet thick. Even a troll would have to take his time with that. And if we could strengthen them with spells, they'd be good enough to keep them busy a long time."

"You're such an optimist, Striker," Walven chuckled. "At least it doesn't smell of death in here."

"No," agreed Rondal, "just chickens. Someone left that window un-shuttered and a couple of hens got in."

"Lovely. Oh, well. Just leave them there. We'll enjoy the eggs."

Darkness was still a few hours away when they quit Farune Hall, leaving behind a tidy amount of provisions and a possible second refuge. Rondal had even spellbound the door before they left to keep it that way. On the way back he felt noticeably better, now that he and his men had an escape route. As comfortable as Maramor had been, it was disposable.

"No sign of refugees or insurgents, yet," Walven pointed out as they re-crossed a stream. "Otherwise those manors would have been looted bare."

"I think the attacks came too quickly and were too thorough for anyone to just slink away undetected. Especially once the goblins started hunting in earnest. From what Arsella has said, they were very thorough about it."

"Still, you'd expect to see . . . someone. *One* girl. That's it."

"I expect there are some about. But if the gurvani are using human confederates, I'm sure they don't want to assume that everyone over six feet tall is a good guy."

"Good point," conceded Walven. "You're pretty good at this command thing."

"Don't spread that around," Rondal told him. "It's a royal pain in the arse."

They arrived back at Maramor Manor an hour shy of dusk. Rondal found the place bustling with activity as the new men settled in. Both towers sported sentries, now, and Tyndal had spent the day improving the wards and other defenses around the place . . . including repairing the great wooden gate. It was intact with a guard behind it when they arrived, to Rondal's pleasure.

Tyndal was in the hall and the evening meal was almost ready to be served. Rondal saw that Arsella had excused herself from cooking duty, as one of the drovers fancied himself an army cook, and was instead near to Tyndal's elbow at a table when he came in.

"Here's the bacon you requested, milady," Rondal said in a toneless voice as he flopped half a slab on the table in front of her. "Sir Tyndal, if you'll meet with me in the castellan's room, I'll go over what we saw today."

Tyndal looked up at him, clearly not eager to leave cup and fire for military intelligence. But the knight mage knew his duty. He heaved a heavy sigh.

"All right, all right. My arse was just starting to heal, after all that riding, but I suppose I can take a look."

Rondal led the way upstairs to the old castellan's solar, stripping his armor off his body wearily as he did so.

"So what's the news? Any gurvani?"

"No signs," admitted Rondal. "But they're out there. Both manors had been visited. Farune was abandoned and might make a good refuge. Ketral . . . Ketral tried to fight. Its ruined. No survivors."

"So much for my dreams of a native army to rally around me," grumbled Tyndal good-naturedly as he sat in one of the chairs . . . the same spot Arsella had sat that first night they had kissed. "But no goblins . . . don't you find that strange?"

"In a relaxing, soothing sort of way, yes," Rondal said, shrugging out of his hauberk. "But I take your meaning. Where are they, then?"

"They didn't head back to the Wilderlands," Tyndal agreed. "In fact, I checked in with Terleman earlier, and he said that most of the traffic going north is human . . . in chains, but human."

"So where are they?" Rondal repeated, unrolling the parchment map he'd been using in addition to his magemaps. He drew a circle around Farune and put an X through Ketral. He paused. "Well, it only looks like there are . . . nine more manors in a ten-mile radius to check?" he said, in disbelief. "Luin's staff, that's a lot of people in one place!"

"It's nothing like the Mindens," agreed Tyndal, helping himself to some wine from the bottle on the table. "In the Wilderlands, you could go twenty miles between settlements. In most of the Riverlands you'd have three or four every ten miles or so.

"But Gilmora was densely settled, thanks to the fertile soil. Easy to plow, mostly flat, rivers everywhere . . . the climate is warm enough for three crops a year, in some places. And it takes a lot of people to produce cotton. Thank Huin you can feed a lot of people on beans, maize and potatoes."

"That's a lot of people," agreed Rondal, still staring at the map. "The villages we went through were big – bigger than those around Sevendor. In the Wilderlands we'd call them towns. But now it's about empty. So where did they all go? Some fled south, or are castled, but the rest . . . how many went north into the Umbra?"

"Tens of thousands, at least," Tyndal said, taking a big sip of wine. "Maybe a hundred thousand?"

"At least," nodded Rondal, imagining the horror of the long lines of Gilmoran peasants being escorted along the trade roads into the perilous north. "I'd say closer to two. The problem is, we have no way of knowing how many were killed, how many fled, and how many were taken."

"Which is why they get brave, stupid young lads such as ourselves to go out and see," nodded Tyndal.

"But it does answer the question, 'why Gilmora?'. It's the largest, most densely populated part of the Duchies."

"The kingdom," Tyndal reminded him.

"If the Dead God is pushing the horizon of the Umbra through sacrifice, then he just took a bumper crop. Processing," he said, wincing at the heartless term, "that many people is going to take time and organization to . . . process."

"You really have a sick way of thinking about things," Tyndal said, admiringly.

Rondal ignored him. It was getting easier.

"That's why they stopped their advance. Not because we were beating them. Not because we killed a dragon. They . . . they probably had already stopped by the time of the battle of Cambrian Castle. They stopped because they simply didn't need to go on any longer. Their organizational structure was full."

"That's probably why they're using human confederates now, too," agreed Tyndal. "Let's face it: as impressive as Sheruel and his priests are, and as fierce as some of the gurvani are, they aren't exactly masters of organization. They're operating mostly from a tribal culture, and they just don't think in those terms. Humans would. And we're terribly corruptible."

"That's a good point," admitted Rondal thoughtfully. "And just think of the looting possibilities. You've seen how wealthy these Gilmoran aristocrats are. Goblins don't appreciate the really valuable stuff that's just sitting around unguarded, now."

"Oh, I've been thinking about it," nodded Tyndal with a grin. "As I said, we're terribly corruptible."

It niggled at Rondal's nascent sense of honor that such looting was morally wrong, at some level. But he had also learned in the Mysteries that the fortunes of war were ephemeral, and a smart soldier knew when to take clear advantage. Looting might not be, strictly speaking, chivalrous, but it was part of the military economy. And most considered such gains as a sign of Duin's Favor.

Besides, he'd proven he wasn't above doing a little looting himself, at Birchroot.

"So we understand their strategy, now that we know their goals: the efficient processing of sacrificial victims. Disrupt that and we disrupt the pursuit of their goal."

"Reasoned like a general," nodded Tyndal. "And we also know what they'll be after in the next phase of the campaign. There's probably half a million extra people crammed into southern and eastern Gilmora, and that's before you get to the heart of the Riverlands. Now that they've set up their . . . organization, they'll be able to process them a lot faster."

"But they're protected," countered Rondal. "I admit, most of the castles in this part of Gilmora are built to impress, not to resist. But there are some tough ones in the south. That was the border between Castal and Alshar for awhile, remember. Those are big castles, and the fortified towns down there are nothing to yawn about."

"And they attract dragons," Rondal said.

"Which are terribly hard to control and difficult to deploy," Tyndal pointed out, finishing his cup. "Not to mention hard on the very thing they want to collect: people. If you want to . . . harvest people, then why dash them to bits and scatter them when you have them all contained?"

"Because you don't have adequate supply train for siege work," Rondal said.

"You're thinking about this like a human," Tyndal said, frowning.

"It's one of my strong points," Rondal shot back.

"My point is, you're thinking in terms of human warfare. But humans don't use dragons. Or trolls to rip the gates off of castles. They built siege towers at Boval, but they were crude, crude enough so that a couple of spellmongers could knock them apart."

"And they have magic," Rondal admitted. "That adds an unpredictable element."

"Thank the gods," nodded Tyndal.

"But that still doesn't mean they can besiege a castle successfully. Not one that is well-defended and provisioned. Even with trolls, it would take a whole lot of them put together to take down a walled-town."

"So it remains an interesting question," dismissed Tyndal, "but it doesn't answer the one we asked. Where to next?"

Rondal studied the map. "I'm thinking . . . a little three-day expedition up through Randure. It borders the Cotton Road. Hefany Castle is supposed to be a big one, and it's connected to seven other domains by road. If I were a goblin bureaucrat, that's where I'd put my . . . depot."

"Three days," nodded Tyndal. "A dozen men. The rangers, maybe a squadron of cavalry—"

"Take Walven," Rondal recommended. Tyndal shrugged. He had an ambivalent relationship with Rondal's former squadmate.

"So who is leading?" Tyndal asked. "You or me?"

"I figured since I went out this morning, you could take this one," suggested Rondal. It was a perfectly reasonable suggestion. It was also, he knew in the back of his mind, a perfect way to get Tyndal out of the manor and away from Arsella for a few days. "You can keep contact mind-to-mind, and if anything goes amiss, we can come rescue you."

Tyndal snorted, as if that wasn't a realistic possibility. "I think I'll hit these three manors along the way," he said, tapping the map in a way that told Rondal he was committing it to a magemap. "Lorwyn, Asgal, and Heem. If possible, I'll scrounge a cache of provisions along the way to cover a potentially hasty retreat."

"That sounds like a good plan," Rondal decided. "While you're gone I'll continue to survey the local country and fortify this place. And I'm going to send a small party south along this road to find a good place where we can hide another cache, in case we have to retreat from here in a hurry, too. I like knowing which way is the best way out."

"Whereas I like to know which way is the best way in," conceded Tyndal. "See? We can work well together."

"If you mean you get into trouble, and I get you out, I cannot disagree," Rondal said, flatly.

Tyndal ignored the jab, and instead he clapped his fellow apprentice on the shoulder. "I'll save you some choice loot, too," he assured him.

Rondal was about to rebuke him for his arrogance . . . but then he realized that he would be turning his nose up at Duin's Blessing. That was asking for bad luck, at best.

"I trust your judgment," Rondal said, unconvincingly.

*   *   *

Tyndal announced the expedition at supper that evening, a roasted goat that had wandered too close to the range of the gatekeeper's arbalest. He announced the roster, gave orders, and outlined the itinerary for the mission. Rondal watched carefully as he delivered the orders. The men were unconcerned about it – they were just orders.

But the look on Lady Arsella's face satisfied him. She looked stricken, when she realized that Tyndal would be leaving Maramor. As soon as dinner was over, he watched her approach his rival and began speaking in urgent tones. Rondal was considering casting a Long Ears spell when she suddenly left, mounting the stairs toward her chambers, looking back over her shoulder once before she hurried upstairs.

Tyndal glanced over at Rondal, and caught his eye.

Relax, he told him, mind-to-mind, *she just wanted to be sure we took enough bandages and such. She's just trying to be helpful.*

I didn't say anything, Rondal returned, sullenly.

Your face did. Like I said, relax. You've got three days with her. Cozy.

Rondal didn't reply. Instead he went to his own room after checking the guards and warding the manor for the night. There was just enough wine left to give him a taste for more. That was something he could request the expedition scavenge. The local vineyards produced a gods-awful sweet-sour vintage, he recalled from his time in Barrowbell, but the Cotton Lords were wealthy enough to keep good cellars from far-off lands. He reached out to Tyndal mind-to-mind.

Wine, he said, as he made contact.

What?!

Wine, Rondal repeated. *While you're out skulking. Find some damn decent wine.* He paused. *What are you doing? You sound distracted.*

Oh. Nothing. From his mental tone, he sounded guilty. *Wine. I got it.*

What's the problem? Rondal demanded.

Uh . . . Arsella came to say goodbye to me. Sorry. I'll send her away.

Rondal's heart sank. *No, don't bother,* he said after a few moments of anguish. *She's the lady of the manor. She's entitled to demonstrate her affections toward anyone she likes. And that's you, apparently.*

I'm sorry, Tyndal repeated. He truly did sound sorry. That made it worse, somehow.

Don't be. I'm getting used to it, Rondal said, doing his best to cloak his emotion.

You know, it's not like I ask for it, Tyndal said defensively. *Sometimes it's a real pain in the arse.*

Yes, you sound like you're suffering.

She's just . . . kissing me a little, Tyndal defended. *It's almost sisterly.*

No, it's really not, Rondal replied, disgusted. *You enjoy yourself. I'm going to sleep. Don't wake me in the morning, I'm tired. And . . . forget about the wine.*

Really? Are you sure?

Yeah. Bring me back some spirits, instead.

That's the commander's prerogative, chuckled Tyndal.

Rondal went to sleep eventually. But it was no respite from his cares. His dreams were filled with a nauseating combination of the horrors he'd witnessed and the women he had been interested in. At various points wise-cracking goblins and sadistic Ancients got involved, and when he awoke at mid-morning he was covered in a sheen of sweat.

It was still hot enough in the steamy cotton lands, even in early autumn, but his sweat wasn't due to the heat. Blearily he bathed his face in the basin and stumbled down stairs to the great hall, where two of his men were finishing their porridge. When he asked, he found out that Tyndal had departed at dawn, on schedule and in good order.

The place was almost quiet without the extra men around. Rondal spent the day inspecting the walls and the stores, figuring out how long their supplies would last and how much more they would need. It was good, productive work. At mid-day he sent two troopers out to scout the roads and villages along the southern road to ensure that they were not leaving a foe behind them. Lady Arsella was nowhere to be seen.

That afternoon, while he was staring at the map in his room again, Tyndal checked in.

Well, scratch Lorwyn off the list. Burned to the ground, along with the village and the mill. Caught a goblin scout, too. Shot him before

412

he could get away.

I'll inform the minstrels of your victory, Rondal replied, dryly.

We also found the first survivors. A couple of peasants hiding in the bush. They told us about some resistance further up the road. Might be promising.

Send them back our way, suggested Rondal, *assuming you think they're uncorrupted.*

They're starving and scared. But I used a truthtell spell on them just to be sure. It's not impossible to lie under such a strong magical compulsion, but it would took great skill and effort.

Then send them back. We can put spears in their hands for a few days, get them fed, and prepare to send them south.

That night, just as the cook was serving the last of the leftover goat, Rondal got another message.

Remember that resistance the refugees were speaking of? We met them. It's more like a real insurgency.

Insurgents? Really? How? How many? Where?

We came across a large goblin patrol encamped in a village. About twenty. So of course we had to attack. Just as we began, they got attacked from the other side by a band of irregulars. Turns out they're holed up in Asgal Hall with some others. That's where we are, now. We're the first sign of help they've seen in six weeks. They've escaped two slaving expeditions so far, attacked a couple of patrols when the opportunity was right, and they even freed a column they found lightly guarded. But they've been talking about moving locations because they're starting to get noticed. I suggested they go to Maramor Manor to await a convoy south.

We don't have a convoy going south.

We will if we get a few dozen refugees together, reasoned Tyndal. *But they've been a wealth of information about local activities. We might get a few of them to stay on as scouts, perhaps.*

413

Are they armed?

Decently. Bows and spears and a few swords. Not much armor, but then they're insurgents, not infantry.

We'll get them outfitted, those who want to enlist. Any luck on those spirits? he asked, casually.

Around this lot? Not bloody likely. They look half-starved. They drank the place dry long ago. But they told me which way to approach Heem Manor, and where the next-closes goblin cantonment is. And apparently Sire Rath of Heem had a reputation as a drinking man, so that's encouraging.

Rondal finally saw Lady Arsella when she came down to dinner later. She was wearing a somber green gown that didn't quite fit her anymore, and a stoic expression that put Rondal on his guard. She spoke rarely, during the meal, and seemed subdued and withdrawn. Rondal was almost ready to go speak to her, when she caught his eye and looked away guiltily.

She knew. She knew he had feelings for her, he realized, and she'd chosen Tyndal over him. Her look told him everything.

A surge of rage flirted with Rondal's mind, but he pushed it down, embracing a cool, logical approach to the problem instead. When your emotions raged out of control, Sire Cei had told them often enough, taking refuge in the cool, safe confines of duty and custom could spare you the poor consequences of rash action. And no initiate of the Mysteries respected a commander who could not control his temper. That kind of man invited disaster in the field.

So Rondal inquired from his men the state of the manor's defenses and their supply, although he knew the tallies well by now, and he took a report from the two riders who'd returned at dusk from their errand. The roads had been empty, they said, and the villages deserted, but their scavenging had brought in a few sacks of oats overlooked in a barn.

Lady Arsella retreated to her room the moment dinner was over.

The next morning the two refugees Tyndal had sent along arrived at the gates of Maramor. Rondal welcomed them cautiously, and after giving the men as much as they could eat from their meager stores, he listened to their tale.

They were from a village in the north that had been among the first to be raided. They escaped and had traveled from one hamlet to another, avoiding goblin patrols and slaver crews by hiding. They'd fought when they had to, they admitted, but they'd never had proper training in arms, not even militia training. It wasn't encouraged in Gilmora, where peasant rebellions were uncommon but typically bloody.

The time for such distinctions was over. Rondal ordered the two to report for elementary training on the morrow, then went to fill in the information he got from them on the abandoned manors and towns they'd been in. They looked frightened at the prospect, but as this was the first sign of organized human activity the two had seen in weeks, they agreed to do their part.

Rondal was just rolling up the map when Tyndal contacted him again.

Rondal, remember those insurgents? They're on their way, most of them. We're going to keep a half-dozen with us as we scout, but in about three, four days you can expect almost two dozen.

We'll have to go get more supplies, he said, after some calculations. *Fast.*

That's your problem, Tyndal said. *But here's a bit of bright news: you can tell Lady Arsella that one of the men from Maramor village was among the slaves that the insurgents freed. A lad named Alwer, former hayward of Maramor. He's a good fighter,* Tyndal praised. *He's going to stay with us awhile and help us with the scouting. He was shocked to hear that Arsella survived.*

I'll tell her, he promised. Maybe delivering such news would get him some notice, Rondal reasoned. It was at least an excuse to compel her to speak to him.

We're going to escort the insurgents to the crossroads before we split up, so add an extra day to our mission. I think it will be worth it, though. They seem pretty excited about showing us the camps around Hefany.

Good luck. Let me know how it turns out.

He was surprised by Lady Arsella's reaction to the news of fellow survivors, and of Alwer, in particular. Instead of being pleased, she looked troubled. Almost anguished. She asked several times if he was certain, and Rondal assured her that the message was clear.

Again she disappeared into her chamber. Rondal was busy making preparations for the arrival of the refugees. He couldn't spare the time to seek her out and asked her about her strange behavior. The issue of supply was becoming critical.

With twenty-odd new mouths to feed, they'd have to forage quickly. He sent out three two-man scouting missions of his remaining rangers to other villages and manors in the area, and prepared the great hall and the lower rooms of the towers as best he could.

The next morning, he made a full report to Terleman, mind-to-mind, and got encouragement for his works. The Knight Commander

He was watching the two new men go clumsily through the basic drill under the eyes of a watchful guard from the top of a tower when Lady Arsella appeared. She looked even more troubled than before, but more resolute.

"Sir Rondal," she began, formally, "I have been thinking about what you have said about survivors. I did not think that was possible, of course, but . . . well, there is one way in which it might be. When the attack came, there was a man . . . I think he was from the village . . . who was working with the goblins. He's the one who led them here, I think. And he pointed out where people were hiding."

Rondal looked at her in surprise. "A collaborator?"

She nodded. "I only caught a few glimpses before . . . before I hid, but I can clearly recall that Alwer was the one who led them here and helped them capture everyone."

"Are you certain?" he asked, skeptically. "Alwer of Maramor?"

"He was the village's hayward," she nodded. "A man of devious nature, from what little I can recall. I would hesitate to trust him with anything."

"He was liberated from slavers," Rondal said, calmly, his mind racing. *Had Tyndal walked into a trap? Was he about to be betrayed?*

"Then they betrayed him as much as he betrayed us," she said, her eyes narrowing. "Would that he had died, instead."

"Sir Tyndal sent word that he has been most helpful in scouting the region," Rondal said, calmly.

"He is *with* Sir Tyndal?" she asked, alarmed. "Oh, Sir Rondal, you must send him a message at once – the man is *not* to be trusted, and if possible he should be . . . be . . ."

"What?"

"Do you not *execute* such traitors in war time?" she asked, coolly.

"It is the custom, yes," he admitted. "But—"

"Sir Rondal, I urge you to send word to poor Sir Tyndal and his brave men at once," she declared. "I fear for his safety!"

"I . . . I will consider it," he promised. "I don't want there to be any mistakes on this mission, and allowing a traitor in our midst would count as a big one. Thank you for your intelligence, Lady Arsella," he said, gravely.

"Thank you for your honorable service and loyalty, Sir Rondal," she said, bowing formally. "I do hope we can avoid another tragedy. This war has given us too many as it is."

She turned to look at him plaintively. He felt himself start to move in her direction . . . but then his discipline intervened.

He recalled how she had abandoned him the moment Tyndal appeared, and he stopped himself. She was *expecting* him to react favorably to her attention, he realized. He did not feel like giving her that satisfaction.

"Of course, milady. Is there anything else?" he asked, stiffly. Arsella looked at him, a hint of surprise on her face. She seemed confused for a moment, then withdrew.

"Just look to the safety of your men, Sir Rondal," she said. "I'm wary of the two vagabonds you've taken in as it is. I don't much like the look of them," she added, suspiciously.

"They are welcome here," Rondal said, firmly. "They are refugees. More, they're helping with chopping wood and keeping the horses, tasks my men would otherwise have to devote their time to. And they have – grudgingly – taken up arms in our defense. Their billeting is within our mission."

"Just keep them away from my chambers," she said, a bit haughtily. "I don't trust peasants I don't know."

He agreed to keep an eye on them, and then left the tower. Something about Arsella's accusation bothered him, but he couldn't figure out what.

But he had a duty to warn Tyndal. He contacted him mind-to-mind immediately.

I told Arsella about your man from Maramor, he told him. *She was cool to the idea, when I mentioned he might be coming back to the manor . . . and then today called him out as a collaborator.*

Is she sure? Alwer of Maramor? A former hayward?

She says so, but . . . well, I'm not going to hang a man without more proof than that. Just keep an eye on him. Has he shown any signs of treachery?

Unless you count the breakfast he served this morning, no. He's been as stalwart as any of these lads. Good with a bow, too. But I'll watch him. And maybe ask him a few questions on the sly.

You do that. I'm going to try to see what else Arsella knows. How goes the reconnoiter?

Well. We've taken Heem Hall, and you will be happy to know that

418

there are three bottles of very expensive brandy from Cormeer living in my saddle bags. We had capture a wine skin, but I regret to inform you that it didn't survive the night.

It didn't survive the knight, you mean. All right, that is good news. No short-and-hairies yet?

Not yet, but soon, we hope. We're coming up on an encampment, now.

Good luck. And let me know if you get yourself killed.

*   *   *

"We're going to make a quick supply run," Rondal told his duty officers the next morning at breakfast. "We need food, and we need it quick. We have people incoming in two or three days, and I don't want anyone to go hungry. The one place where we know there is a stash is at Farune, and it's not that far away. We know it's probably still clear of goblins.

"So, we're going to take all three carts down the road, load them up with whatever we can carry back, and get it done by sundown. With that many more men, we should be able to do a more thorough job of foraging."

"*Looting,* you mean," Arsella said, disapprovingly.

"The former owners are not around to compensate," Rondal reminded her. "When civilians do it, it's looting. When military do it, it's *foraging.* And you'll get a first-hand look. You're going with us."

Her eyes widened. "I *am?*"

"Yes. Your knowledge of the local country will be invaluable. And perhaps you can give us information on Farune Hall we aren't aware of. You *have* been there, haven't you?"

She bit her lip. "Just the one time, for a dance. I was in a carriage the whole way. I don't remember much beyond the food and the music. I

419

wouldn't be much use."

"We'll just enjoy your company then," Rondal said, coolly.

Arsella's jaw jutted out defiantly. "I believe I informed you I wished to *stay!*"

"And I regret to inform you that you are going, for military necessity," he returned. He couldn't believe she was getting so tense about a field trip.

"I am . . . indisposed," she said, retreating behind a veil of femininity.

"You are . . . *going,*" he said in a tone that indicated he was confident of that. It surprised him that he was capable of it. "Prepare yourself. We leave in an hour."

Her jaw jutted out, but she gave no more argument. Instead she switched tactics.

"I cannot help but notice that no messenger has departed from here," she said, even more coolly. "Is it your intention to *not* warn Sir Tyndal of his danger?"

Rondal smiled. "Sir Tyndal is a big boy, milady. I trust he can handle himself against a single hayward."

"A treacherous hayward," she reminded, warningly.

"So noted," Rondal said. "I shall have a horse saddled for you. "

"You . . ." she said, irritated.

"Yes, milady?" Rondal asked, innocently.

She glared at him, but did not say anything else.

An hour later, when the party was getting assembled in the yard, she did join them, wearing a traveling wimple and a mantle of gray. She had thrown it back defiantly over her shoulder, revealing a simple tunic and hose, with tall, high-heeled riding boots of rich brown leather. Her crossbow was slung over one shoulder, a long knife in her belt.

Rondal didn't think a woman could look even more feminine when she was armed, but he suddenly found himself even more attracted to the girl as she strode boldly across the yard, a glare plastered on her face. She really was quite well-formed, he thought admirably. Then she stumbled, and some of the glamour was broken.

"It's been awhile. My boots don't quite fit anymore. I suppose I've grown," she explained, apologetically. But her tone reminded him that he was still upset with her over her fickle attentions.

She tied two small bags on the back of the gray mare that had been saddled for her. She was a bit nervous around the beast, but Tyndal had chosen a well-tempered horse with calm demeanor for her, when Rondal had asked him his opinion, mind-to-mind. The mare stood patiently while the girl mounted the saddle. Rondal had no idea how one could tell such a thing in a horse, but he was willing to concede to his fellow's expertise.

Rondal left the manor with only a few men to guard it. Arsella looked at them skeptically as they left through the makeshift gate.

"Are you quite certain that they can keep out a horde of goblins?" she asked, an urgent tone to her voice.

"I'm quite certain that they couldn't, milady, nor would I expect them to. I have given them appropriate orders," he added.

"Well. I *suppose* you know your business, then," she said dismissively.

Suppressing a flash of irritation over her manner, Rondal sent a scout ahead and led the carts down the road, his troopers fanning out to cover the flanks. A rearguard of three stood ready with bows, and the drovers each carried arbalest and sword. They were raiding a pantry, after all, not storming a castle.

"Let us hope I do know my business. I'm going forth to confer with the van, please stay near to the carts."

"I can quite take care of myself, thank you!" she said, indignantly.

"I wasn't asking you to do that so that they could protect you. I asked you to do that so that you could protect *them*. You should ready your weapon."

He knew with fair certainty that there wasn't a goblin in a mile, probably two. He'd scryed the route ahead while they'd waited, and it was clear, to his determination. But he enjoyed the anxious look that immediately haunted Arsella's face. He knew it was petty, beneath the dignity of a knight and unworthy of his pursuit of chivalry. He didn't care.

The day was turning warm quickly. The Gilmoran sun was famous for its intensity and brightness, even in autumn, and it didn't take long for his helmet to start catching the heat. He knew there was even a temple to the old Imperial sun god, Reas, at Cigny Town which sheltered the victims of sunstroke from the cotton fields. His steel helmet quickly became hot to the touch. Despite his better judgment he removed it and tied it to his saddle horn, donning his apprentice cap instead.

Other than the heat, it was a pretty day. There was just enough cloud to obscure the sun every so often, and the breeze from the north kept the sweat to a minimum. The crickets chirped all morning, and when they came to the swampy thickets that dotted this part of the Riverlands they were joined by deep-throated bullfrogs and whining oyags.

"Not so much as a doe or a hen scratching," Fursar, the southern ranger noted when Rondal checked with him. "I've ranged almost a half-mile out. Nothing larger than a dog hiding out."

"There are plenty of rats," Rondal observed as they came to the ruins of Maramor Village, where a few of the vermin were slinking around the edges of the sunken holes that used to be homes. "I hear the gurvani like a good rat, when they can't find better."

"I suppose a man might do the same," the veteran noted, dispassionately. "Why bring *her,* milord?" he asked, casually.

"To keep an eye on her, more than anything else," Rondal confided, quietly. "She's been awfully moody lately. Jumpy. I want her where I can see her."

"She's not so fond of you, anymore, I noticed."

"I hadn't. I've been running a military expedition and don't have time for such frivolities."

"Glad to hear it, milord. But . . ."

"Yes?"

"Begging your pardon, milord, but is it *wise* to have a woman with an arbalest and a poor disposition toward you riding *behind* you? Ishi preserve you from such a fate, but . . ."

"She is fickle," Rondal agreed. He wasn't sure if he was speaking of the goddess of love or the troublesome noblewoman, but the man had a point. He halted until the column passed him. Lady Arsella gave him a cool glance and proudly let her mantle fall away in the heat just as she rode by.

Rondal fell in with the rearguard until they came within a few hundred feet of the crossroads, then rode ahead to scout the other directions himself. He rejoined the wains for a few moments as the rode through the next village.

"I trust there are no goblins about, Sir Rondal?" she asked, almost accusingly.

"Not yet, milady. But they do enjoy surprises."

"I'm getting thirsty," she complained as she fanned her face. "We should stop at the next well and cool the horses."

"No, we will push on to the manor as planned."

She snorted. "You seem awfully sure of yourself Sir Rondal."

"When it comes to giving orders to my men, I am. Stopping would put us at risk, or at least make concealing our presence difficult. If you're thirsty, drink from your water bottle."

"I don't *have* a water bottle," she said, sounding accusing again. Like it was *his* fault.

"That was very shortsighted of you," he snickered. He waited, but continued riding alongside her in silence.

"Well?" she asked, expectantly.

"Well what, milady?"

"Aren't you going to offer me *your* water bottle, Sir Rondal? It would be the courteous thing to do," she reproved.

"Milady, your own father was a knight," he reminded her. "Do you know of chivalry?"

"Of course," she snorted prettily, tossing her head.

"Then you should know that true chivalry must spring from a place of strength. Part of that strength in a man lies in his foresight and preparation. It was reasonable to expect to get thirsty on a hot day in Gilmora. It was therefore reasonable to pack a water bottle."

She looked away, embarrassed, then looked back even more annoyed. "You must forgive me, as I am unused to the needs of the open road! I lack the knowledge and wisdom of an experienced campaigner such as yourself, Sir Knight!"

He stared at her. "You've never been . . . *thirsty* before?"

She glared back. "I just think it is rude of you to have not offered me your water."

"And I think it rude for you to presume that I am obligated to."

"You are not a very honorable knight!"

"On the contrary," Rondal chuckled, as she got more upset with him. "I am a *very* honorable knight. Chivalry is born of strength, the windfall harvested when a warrior chooses honorable service to an ideal, rather than use his might to bully and do violence maliciously."

"And depriving a thirsty maiden of water is not malicious?" she demanded.

"It is not dishonorable," he countered. "For chivalry must be employed by grace, not obligation, or a knight is a mere soldier to be ordered and commanded."

424

"So . . . you're saying that by not giving me water, you're being *more* chivalrous?" she asked, scornfully.

"I'm saying that denying you the consequences of your ill-reasoned actions would be unfair to your instruction, and therefore it would be dishonorable of me to facilitate such a thing. If you do not learn to pack water when you leave camp, then you will be a burden on your mates. That's a valuable lesson to learn."

"Fine!" she said, with a sneer. "I will suffer, then, until we make the manor. I hope you enjoy my anguish!"

"No more than you enjoyed mine," he said, the first hint of speaking of her lack of attention since Tyndal had been around.

"*What do you mean?*" she demanded.

"Contemplate it," he suggested. "Perhaps something will come to you. I ride ahead to scout, again. Keep your wits about you, though. We could be ambushed at any moment. When you enter your destination and when you leave are the two best times to be attacked."

She frowned, but looked around anxiously again while he rode ahead.

"Are you trying to get that one in a lather, milord?" asked Fursar, when he approached the man at point. "I could hear her all the way up here."

"She forgot her water bottle," Rondal said. "Now she's complaining about it."

"So you *do* want her riled," Fursar said, contemplatively.

"I . . . I suppose I do," he admitted, feeling a little guilty. "She has . . . I . . . oh, forget I spoke," he sighed.

"Oh, I have eyes, milord," the ranger chuckled. "You had her favor until Sir Tyndal arrived, and then she only had eyes for him."

"That's . . . not . . . untrue," he said, quietly choking out the words from between clenched teeth.

"Don't let it worry you none," Fursar dismissed. "A doe like that is bound to follow after the biggest carrot in the sack, if you take my meaning, milord."

"I'm used to Sir Tyndal getting attention," he explained, some tension in his voice . . . but also some resignation. "If she would prefer to keep his company that is her business. I'm here on a military mission, not to pay court to some country knight's daughter!"

"Aye, milord," Fursar grunted. "I am utterly convinced. And acting like you *don't* care about her now is sure to drive her mad, or at least that has been my experience. We're only a few miles away from the manor, now . . . perhaps you'd want to scout the village ahead?" he asked, expectantly.

"You know, I think I would," Rondal said as he blushed. He suddenly found that he did want solitude. He nudged his mount ahead and was musing darkly on the mysteries of femininity when something caught his attention. He drew a warwand and rode forward, cautiously scanning every corner of the darkened and abandoned village as he prepared to scry it more thoroughly.

He was just bringing the spell into play when his eyes caught something moving – and moving with deliberate purpose.

He didn't hesitate. He let his arm follow his eye as he screamed the command word, and a powerful bolt of magical plasma shot forth from the wand on a path of his desire. The shot was true, sending a furry black shape cartwheeling into the road, its limbs aflame.

Even as the goblin shrieked in pain and rolled across the road, the hum of a bowstring jerked Rondal's head around and kept him from having his nose pierced by a vicious-looking black dart.

He pointed the wand again without looking, waiting for his eye to catch up, his mouth ready with the mnemonic. When he saw the gurvani archer clearly, the wand spat again at his command and the beastly little warrior squealed and burst into flame as it caught the bolt in the chest.

"Gurvani!" he shouted over his shoulder, finally getting around to completing his scrying spell. As his vision grew to encompass the

426

region in his mind he saw a third form appear. Gurvani were distinctive from humans when scrying in combat, and the little bugger shone like a candle in a darkened temple. There was one . . .

"Over there!" he directed as Fursar's horse skidded to a halt nearby. Quick as lighting the man turned, nocked an arrow and his bowstring snapped. A second arrow followed the first, and both hit home. A squeal and a moan told the tale.

"Is that all, milord?" asked the ranger anxiously.

"At the moment," Rondal assured him, nervously, as he re-scryed to be certain. "But if they were scouts, you can wager there are more around. Get everyone moving toward that manor, fast!" he ordered as he looked around, scanning the rest of the horizon. The shouts went down the line, and the rumble of the carts picked up in pitch as they increased their speed.

"I *told* you leaving and entering was the best place to get ambushed," Rondal said, as Arsella passed by him. "Keep your eyes open, I might have missed one!" She looked appalled at the smoldering corpse her horse stepped around, and then looked afraid, trying to look at everywhere at once.

Farune Hall was just as they had left it, Rondal was gratified to see. After dismantling the spellbinding on the gate, the carts went through, and he re-sealed it behind them. The laborious process of loading them began, as the men spread out and began systematically foraging.

Rondal threw some cursory wards up to alert him of any further goblins and posted one man as lookout before helping the others load the grain and other foodstuffs.

Arsella made a point to draw water from the well and drink it thirstily and noisily, shooting him dark looks between draughts.

Rondal rolled his eyes. "Find an empty water bottle for the way back," he advised. She glared at him even more.

As the men made a more careful exploration of the abandoned manor, they discovered two other storerooms with provisions that had been overlooked. That was as good as a supply convoy arriving, in Rondal's estimation. He was in charge of feeding everyone, now, and finding a smokehouse full of hams and bacon was like finding gold. The twenty sacks of wheat they discovered could feed them for *months*.

Even after packing three carts full there was still an abundance left. Rondal had the carts leave with two-horse escorts, one after the other, rather than go in a large group and risk all of them not making it back to Maramor.

Arsella did not like that plan, but he did not bother to answer her objections. He detailed himself out to leave with the last cart . . . and ordered Arsella to do likewise.

He gave her some credit – after complaining for the first few minutes, she pitched in and helped carry and sort and stack the supplies despite her noble lineage and generally irritable demeanor. She knew how to work, at least. Rondal knew plenty of common girls who had a hard time with that.

He was loading up the last few sundries by late afternoon when he got the call.

Ron! Tyndal called to him mind-to-mind. The tone was frantic.

What is it?

We're under attack! he said, excitedly. *We got too close to one of their encampments and one of the sentries got wind of us. After . . . well, let's just say we're riding for our lives and we have about a hundred goblins pursuing us!*

That's not good, Rondal said, uneasily. *Tyndal, what the hells have you done?*

We're heading down the south road toward Danharp, but I don't know what's there. I don't want to lead them back to Maramor, but we have to go somewhere!

I understand, Rondal said. *Bide.*

He sounded calm, but his mind was racing. This was *his*

responsibility. He was in charge of Tyndal and the other men in his command. A hundred goblins was nothing to take lightly, either. And Tyndal was right. They didn't need to lead them back to Maramor. A company of goblins was more than their feeble defenses could manage.

That was the nature of the problem. Separating Tyndal and his insurgent allies from the goblins and then making the goblins go away. Rondal had precious little at his disposal in terms of resources, though, and what he did have was vulnerable.

But then he remembered a War College lecture on the importance geography in battle, and realized that he had, perhaps, more resources than he'd thought.

Tell me where you are, exactly, he began, when he resumed contact.

I'm in the saddle dodging – dodging arrows! Ishi's tits, that was close!

How are they keeping up? Rondal asked, mystified.

You know those dog cart chariots they used last summer? Well, the puppies grew up big enough to allow a small goblin to ride it. And while they are terrible shots while mounted, they seem to have grasped the basic idea of cavalry.

Dog cavalry?

Calling them dogs is a kindness, Tyndal assured him. *These things may have started out as dogs, but they aren't the typical hound any more. Dread hounds, is more like. Fell hounds, maybe. They – hey! Sorry. They nip at the horses' heels and chase us in bursts. I've killed three or four myself, but there's a whole howling pack on our tail.*

When I asked where you were, Rondal said, patiently, *I meant where were you* located?

Huh? Oh. We're getting close to that big crossroads.

You are? Good. Instead of continuing south, go west. Then go south on the next major crossroad, it will be a half-mile down the road.

Why?

Because that will lead you toward me, he explained, *and I can get ready for them.*

With what? You don't have but a few men with you. You're on a supply *mission, remember?*

I have what I need, Rondal assured him. *You just stay alive, stay ahead of them, and be prepared to do what I tell you.*

You're the commander, Tyndal conceded. *Just get us out of here!*

I'm working on it, Rondal said, and cut contact.

"Milord?" asked the ranger when he opened his eyes.

"Change in plans," Rondal said, abruptly. "Tell the last cart to push fast and catch up with the second cart, because we'll need the guards. I want them in that tower," he said, waving toward their refuge. "Tell them to get inside and close it up. You and I will be taking a little trip down the road."

"Aye, milord," he agreed, and bustled off to give orders.

"What about *me?*" asked Arsella in an almost demanding tone.

"You stay here in the tower," he ordered. "We'll be back soon enough."

"I most certainly will *not!*" she bristled. "Escort me back to Maramor, at once!"

"I don't have time to argue," Rondal said, almost to himself. "As far as I am concerned you're a combatant, now. Find some more quarrels, climb up those stairs to the top of the tower, and make yourself cozy. If you see a goblin, shoot it. Other than that, stay out of our way."

"Sir Rondal!" she almost shrieked when he turned to prepare his mission, "I *insist* you take me back to Maramor!"

"And I insist you stop acting like a spoiled child," he said, evenly. "We are in the middle of a warzone and you are imperiling our mission. You can try to catch up with the cart on your own or you can stay here, shut up, and be a good soldier. Which is it?"

She grimaced. "I'll stay," she said, finally.

"I'm enchanted," he said, rolling his eyes. "Now leave me alone. I have work to do."

*　　　　*　　　　*

Farune Hall was a defensible place to run to. But that's why Rondal wanted to lead the gurvani party *away* from it. The tower was secure, but without hope of reinforcement a prolonged siege would inevitably fall in the goblin's favor.

But Farune Hall wasn't the only manor in the area. He and Fursar galloped a few miles down the road to the ruined Ketral Manor. As it was already ruined, he didn't mind messing it up a bit more. That made it the perfect place to set an ambush for the goblins.

He studied the grounds for almost five minutes before he did anything, but when he did move, he moved quickly. He sketched out what he wanted done to the ranger and then set to work on his spellcraft.

He used the power of the irionite liberally, and utilized spells he'd learned in War College and thought he'd never had the chance to try.

Mindful of the foe's new mounts, he cast some spells aimed specifically at canines and set them in sigils across the yard of the manor. He entrapped doors and windows and enchanted various items around the yard as quickly as he could. Then he prepared a potent suite of offensive spells for himself, before finally reclining behind a bale of cotton with the tired ranger and calling Tyndal again.

How goes the pursuit? he asked, when contact was finally established.

They seem to be doing splendidly, growled Tyndal. *We've lost two of our insurgents, damn them! We just made that turn you told us to make. Now what?*

431

Rondal explained the plan to him, including a few contingencies. He tried to keep it as short as possible.

You think this will work?

We can at least thin them down a bit, reasoned Rondal. *Being chased by fifty goblins seems a lot more manageable than being chased by a hundred.*

More like eighty, now, Tyndal corrected. *We've been busy.*

Even better. Just let me know when you're ready . . .

It only took an hour before the sound of hoof beats rumbled through the ground . . . followed by the high peal of barking dogs. But the howls, whines and barks did not sound like those of dogs Rondal was used to, like the Westwoodmen's hounds that his master was so fond of. These canines were . . . different, somehow, and not in a friendly puppy sort of way.

Ron . . . Tyndal said, mind-to-mind, *I hope you're ready. We're ready to drop. If we don't rest the horses soon –*

I know! Relax, just stick to the plan. Remember to go around anything marked with a tuft of cotton. Those are the bad spells. Just ride into the yard, circle around the manor house, and return to the front of the yard. I'll be there waiting, and hopefully we can settle this then.

Here we come! Tyndal shouted in his mind, just as the first of five horsemen thundered through the gate. The horses were visibly lathered, flecks of foam on their lips. Their riders were not much better. Two carried wounds from the pursuit, the darts still protruding from their bodies.

Care to announce us? Tyndal cracked, mind-to-mind.

It would be my pleasure, Rondal agreed, and activated the first of his spells as soon as the first fell hound appeared, a screaming goblin clinging to its back. The gurvan bore a long, thin blade he waved clumsily as his mount sped through the gate. Rondal grinned to himself and whispered the mnemonic.

As the horses ran around the building to the north, the first pack of goblin cavalry bounded past . . . and directly into the thickest field of sigils, each one marked with a small tuft of white cotton on the ground.

Whenever they passed, they bore the brunt of his spell, which usually threw down rider or hound or both. He'd used high-profile explosives and brilliant flares, as well as spells that shredded internal organs or otherwise incapacitated the target. Fursar the ranger was gleefully shooting at those who missed the field of combat magic. His deft archery landed more often than missed.

When Tyndal indicated that he was directly behind the building, Rondal activated his next spell . . . and the bulk of the pack that howled into the gate was caught in a sudden firestorm that appeared out of nowhere, engulfing the yard in flame and setting alight the fur of rider and mount alike. Dozens of fell hounds writhed in the dirt and gurvani screamed and rolled to stop the flames.

Rondal didn't pause to watch the carnage he'd wrought; he had plenty of other goblins to contend with. He launched spell after spell from his nest behind the cotton bales.

Each was targeted on a different section of the yard, which was already dotted with individual goblins or dogs who had blundered into his static spells. Now he unleashed the powerful assault spells he'd recently learned.

The first was a pain-causing sheet of magic that did little real damage, but left its victims with about five minutes of uncontrolled, unbearable agony that could prove quite distracting. He followed it quickly with a second, a cone of force that blasted a dozen goblins clean off of their mounts and sent their dogs spinning into disarray.

The final spell was composed of three well-placed piles of the sharpest rocks he could find. They concealed spells that caused them to explode when the dogs came too close, sending shrapnel shredding everything around it. Rondal liked that one. After the three quick bangs, there was as much blood as there was fur and smoke.

We're coming around the building, Tyndal advised him. *I hope you got them ready!*

Go straight for the gate, Rondal ordered. *We'll be right behind you.*

He drew his mageblade and encouraged the ranger to draw his sword. As soon as Tyndal and his band rode out, swords flashing, they sprinted into the chaos of the yard, slashing at everything in their way.

What a difference a year makes, Rondal reflected as he triggered his warmagic augmentations and began plying his mageblade. At last year's battle at Cambrian Castle he'd been terrified and unsure of himself. Now he surveyed the battlefield of Ketral Manor with a more experienced and learned eye.

He saw the majority of the foe still clumped toward the north where they had halted pursuit after the first magical attack. Most were not paying any attention to him or his comrades. The gurvani and dogs between him and the gate were scattered. As imposing as they appeared to be, his now well-trained eye understood the battlefield as zones of threat, each step forward changing the gradient of peril and offering him options in response.

That goblin, there, with his back turned – a flick of his wrist and his mageblade sliced through his arm at the elbow. It wouldn't kill him, but he wouldn't be fighting for a while, and that was sufficient. His boots trod on.

The canine on his right four steps beyond that was turning to face him, albeit slowly, with a rider on his back. If he charged, he would intercept Rondal in his path. The warwand in his left hand blasted the goblin cavalryman and his dog with a concussive wave strong enough to snap the dog's neck and throw the goblin into the air. It was the big brother to the stunning wands they'd practiced with at Relan Cor, and it packed a punch.

Five steps beyond that two gurvani had dismounted – smoldering – and had drawn blades. He plunged his mageblade through the chest of one, then shifted his position to put the skewered goblin in the path of his fellow before yanking the blade free and decapitating him as he spun back around.

A third was leaping toward him, a dagger in each hand and a wicked grimace on its fanged face, when an arrow blossomed in his throat – Fursar the ranger had gotten off a shot before using his bow to knock a few goblins off of their feet.

He considered stopping long enough to slit their throats or otherwise finish them off, but he stopped himself. The goal, he reminded himself, was not to kill the enemy. It was to escape. He could have turned and given battle and slain a dozen or more, but that wasn't the plan. And a good commander stuck with his plan unless there was a compelling reason to change it.

They made the gate in good order, leaving a trail of dead and wounded gurvani behind them, and as the ranger ran past him Rondal turned and magically pulled as much debris as he could into the wooden doorway before sealing it with a spellbinding. It wouldn't last long, under concentrated attack, but it should slow down their pursuers enough for them to get away.

Their horses were tied off fifty feet off the main road, behind the ruins of a peasant's cot. The two of them made it to their mounts without incident, and caught up with Tyndal and his men before they got to the ruined village.

"Ron, damn it's good to see you!" Tyndal said, gratefully, as he gulped water and walked his lathered horse. "That was great work! Are they preoccupied?"

"We have at least ten minutes' head start," Rondal agreed. "Plenty of time. We can obscure the crossroads and they'll not know which way we left."

"That was some impressively destructive spellcraft," Tyndal repeated, admirably. Rondal blushed – he wasn't used to getting compliments from his rival. "Looked nasty as nine hells, coming around the corner like that. How many do you think we left behind us?"

"Fifty or sixty, mayhap," Rondal shrugged. "I was too busy to call the role."

"Still enough to give us problems," nodded Tyndal, "but not so many we can't handle."

Rondal shook his head. He knew his fellow was correct, but it amazed him that between the two of them they now felt capable of dealing with *sixty* goblins.

"How far away is this hidey hole of yours?"

"Six miles. But they're easy miles. We can hole up there overnight. Once we're sure the gurvani have lost interest, we can head back to Maramor without fear of being followed."

"Any wine there?" Walven asked, from behind them. "I'd kill for a cup. Indeed, I think I just did."

"Enough," agreed Rondal. "The lord of Farune had a decent cellar. And the tower is secure. If we enchant the exterior, we can have a snug and secure evening." He took a moment to catch his breath, then continued. "So tell me, what got the goblins so riled up?"

"Probably what we saw," Tyndal said, meaningfully. He took a parcel from his pouch and handed it over.

It was a rag, a scrap of someone's tunic, wrapped around what looked like some sort of clay. Rondal touched it. It was cold and a little wet, and it had a pungent aroma. When he felt it between his fingers it seemed to flake apart. "What is it?" he asked, as he held some up to the sunlight.

He was about to smell it more carefully when Tyndal snorted.

"Some sort of poop."

Rondal glared as he looked at the substance in a new light. "Were you going to let me *taste* it?"

"I was curious to see if you'd try," admitted Tyndal, grinning.

"So you discovered *poop*," Rondal said, disgusted. "This is the goblins secret weapon?"

"No, it's poop *from* the goblins' secret weapon," corrected Tyndal. "And there was a lot of it."

"So you discovered the goblins had a lot of poop," Rondal said, annoyed.

"No, I said there was a lot of this . . . *particular* . . . poop," he enunciated. Rondal sighed. Clearly Tyndal thought that the poop was important.

"I concede to your expertise on poop," he said, referring to Tyndal's former job as a stableboy. "Why is *this* poop important?"

"Because this particular poop was *three feet wide*."

"Three feet? That *is* a lot of poop."

"Not three feet long, three feet . . . *wide*. Rondal, what kind of animal has a butt hole *three feet wide?*"

"I . . . have no idea. Dragon?"

"That's what I thought, too," Tyndal nodded. "But it's not . . . dragony."

"What do you mean?"

"I'm not exactly sure," Tyndal admitted. "But as you so tactlessly pointed out, I'm kind of an expert on poop. And in my 'expert' poop opinion, that *particular* poop didn't originate from a saurian butt hole," he said, authoritatively.

"I hope you realize how stupid you sound," Rondal said, earning a chuckle from the men behind. He wrapped up the poop and returned it to Tyndal. "So this was a really big non-dragon poop."

"From a source unknown," agreed Tyndal. "And we got too close. We saw it on the road, and first I thought it was . . . well, it was poop. And then I realized just how big a creature would have to be to take such a giant dump. And that got me speculating about all sorts of unlikely and increasingly unpleasant images.

"So I had our insurgent friends take us to the manor they're using as a base to get a closer look . . . only that's when the patrol was alerted to our presence. Since then it's been a lovely ride through a tranquil Gilmoran countryside, being chased by bloodthirsty beasts."

"You're right," Rondal admitted after some thought. "That's a significant poop. All right, we know where they *don't* want us to look, so we should look there. Meanwhile, we should be where they don't know to look for us."

They stopped briefly at the crossroads in the village to properly obscure the direction they headed, adding a few arcane measures that would further cloud the issue, and then proceeded to Farune Hall. Rondal went ahead with Walven, to prepare for their arrival and alert the sentries, leaving the ranger to guide the rest of the party.

"Sir Haystack had more mettle than I'd thought," Walven admitted, when they were alone. "He's actually not as dumb as he looks. And he does take an aggressive approach to warfare."

"He's not so bad," conceded Rondal, and quickly changed the subject. "But just from your perspective: this poop. Is it something to worry about?"

Walven shrugged. "I'm worried, Striker. And I think he's right. That didn't look like dragon droppings, though I've never seen a dragon. And we found tracks, too, big, big tracks. No animal I've seen makes tracks like that."

"Then we'll have to investigate," decided Rondal. "After we shake these gurvani off. So they have cavalry now. Not terribly effective."

"Not in a charge, perhaps," agreed Walven, "but they did a fine job of screening and pursuit, let me assure you. We lost a few men along the way. And those foul dogs may not have the endurance of a horse, but with a pack of them they don't have to. They'll never be able to stand up to proper lancers.

"But if they ever learn to shoot from the saddle they might be something to contend with. I could see how they would be pretty intimidating to the average Gilmoran peasant family."

"I'll report it," Rondal agreed, dutifully. "Now . . . what is your opinion of this insurgent, this man Alwer of Maramor, the hayward?"

"He's a hayward?" asked Walven, surprised. "He's a demon with a spear. Good fighter, on foot at least. He rides like a peasant. But he's as stalwart as any of them. Why?"

"I . . . it's complicated. But I have a potential security problem." He thought a moment in silence. He reviewed the situation as objectively as possible in his head. He hadn't spoken to Alwer himself on purpose. He wanted the man's story, but he didn't want it just yet. He had to be certain of Arsella, first, regardless of what the hayward said.

Farune Hall looked deserted as they rode in, but there was a man concealed by the gate with an arbalest. They told him of the newcomers arriving behind them, and then took their horses to the stable before retiring to the tower.

Lady Arsella was where he had bid her to go, in the topmost chamber. Her arbalest was cocked and loaded, and she was pacing back and forth nervously when Rondal mounted the stairs, after checking on the guards he'd left behind.

"You're back!" she said, anxiously. "What happened?"

"Goblins," he said, without elaborating. "We ambushed them at Ketral Manor. There are a score less, now. And a score less of their damned dogs."

"Were you hurt?" she asked, concerned. Rondal looked down at himself. He had splashes of goblin blood and singed fur on his surcoat, but no blade had touched him.

"No," he said, carefully. "I am fine. But we won't be headed back to Maramor just yet."

"What?" she asked, her eyes wide.

"There are more goblins in the neighborhood," explained Rondal. "We still have some men out there. We've laid some false trails, but just to be safe we're going to stay the night here."

"Oh," she said, her eyes shifting. "I suppose that's prudent."

"So glad to get your approval," snorted Rondal.

"I just meant that it sounded like a good idea," she said, softening. "Sir Rondal, I hope you don't mistake my worry over our situation for animosity. I meant no disrespect."

That seemed an abrupt change of mood, Rondal observed to himself. He knew some women had the capacity to go from joy to distress and back with frightening regularity. He was not overly fond of that type of girl. But there was something more to Arsella's presentation that bothered Rondal, something disingenuous.

"Milady," he began, formally, "Since I have come to Maramor I have been nothing but polite, courteous, and respectful to you and your home, though I was not required to under these circumstances. We have developed a friendship of which I am quite fond. But your manner toward me has lately been unfavorable, when I do not see where I may have given you offense."

"I . . . I have been hard put, of late," she said, looking away guiltily. "I have lost all I know, and have no idea what the gods hold in store for me. Please understand," she said, tears in her eyes, "I am just trying to exist in a home turned hellish."

"I am giving you all the courtesy and grace due your station in this situation," Rondal pointed out. "But when the matter of Alwer arose . . ."

"The traitor?" she asked, suddenly. "Of course my heart turned hard – if you had been there that day, yours would have, too. The screaming, the crying, the murders in the yard . . . oh, if only you'd been there, Sir Rondal, mayhap the day would have fallen differently!" Suddenly she was in his arms.

"So you still wish me to put this man to the question for his crimes, and hang him if he is a collaborator?" he asked, swallowing hard. He hadn't expected the embrace.

"Take no such chances!" she urged. "Slay him at once, and spare us all the burden! He is a wicked man, a liar who gave over his own people to the goblins. Surely it is no crime to slay a foe in battle."

"No, it is no crime," Rondal said, firmly, as he pushed Arsella away. "But I would not slay a man for a crime before he has a chance to speak of it."

"Why are men so obsessed with the rules when lives are at stake?" she snarled, looking at him angrily, suddenly. "Is the word of a lady not sufficient?"

"To have a man brought to trial, perhaps," Rondal said, sternly. "But for the gallows? Nay, not if you were a duchess."

"You don't know what danger you put your comrades in," she said, accusingly. "Sir Tyndal would know how to deal with such a vile traitor! At any time Alwer could slay brave Sir Tyndal from behind, and yet you have sent *no* word or warning! Is it because you are jealous of him? Of my attentions and . . . and affections? Do you hate him so? So much that you wish him *dead?"*

That accusation caught Rondal short. For there was a time when his animosity toward his rival was so great that he wished harm to him, at some place in his mind.

But now he felt proper guilt at such feelings. As tumultuous as his relationship with Tyndal had been over the years, the other boy had not been unfair to him, had not betrayed him or his secrets, had not done him any serious harm when he had had the chance. Tyndal might be an annoyance, even a rival, but he was not an *enemy.*

"Jealous?" asked Rondal quietly. "I think not. Yet your words are curious, milady. And telling. We will determine the guilt of Alwer and the truth of the attack on Maramor."

"Sir Tyndal might well be dead by then!" she argued, shrilly.

"I doubt it," Rondal dismissed. "He should be riding through the gate any time now. Then we will speak of this vile hayward of yours . . . who apparently slew a number of his supposed confederates while convincingly playing that he was fleeing for his life from them."

He did not mention Alwer would be with Sir Tyndal. He kept back that surprise. He was wary of Arsella, now.

"W-what?" snapped Arsella.

"I went out to assist Sir Tyndal and his band as they were fleeing goblin riders," explained Rondal slowly and deliberately. "After our victory, he is now on his way up the manor's drive as we speak with a few of his men. They will be joining us for the evening.

"Sir Tyndal has had time to make Alwer's acquaintance and take the measure of the man – we will see if his assessment of his character matches yours. We will have plenty of time to discuss Alwer's guilt or innocence. Among other matters."

Arsella's eyes filled with tears and her shoulders shook with sobs. "You know not what danger you lead your comrade into by keeping this from him," she said, softly. "Alwer is a monster. He will destroy . . . he will destroy us all!"

"He is but one hayward, milady," Rondal reminded her, firmly. "We faced a dragon last year, I think we can manage. But *clearly* you are distressed milady. Pray take a moment to rest and compose yourself while I see to the men and prepare to ward us in for the night. Then we can discuss this matter more fully."

He left her there, weeping, his heart aching and growing more indelicate with every step he took. Whatever misgivings he had about slaying Alwer out of hand were well-placed, he knew now.

When the rest of the company arrived a while later, Rondal ordered the gate closed and he and Tyndal both warded it with as strong of a defensive suite as they could, with Tyndal adding some charms of his own he'd picked up in Inrion.

"They're going to keep searching for us," he predicted. "They have lost too many gurvani now, and they still have not brought us in or slain us. This will help convince them that they've already checked out this manor and found nothing."

"Blue magic," nodded Rondal.

"It's surprisingly useful," agreed Tyndal. "If subtle. And harder to work on gurvani minds, of course."

"But it does work on human minds," he affirmed. "That might come in handy. We have a certain matter to discuss."

"What? Oh, the girl," Tyndal reminded himself, looking troubled. "That is going to be problematic. I spoke to Alwer at length, and there are some holes in Arsella's story. And according to Alwer, he was as much a victim of the raid on Maramor as anyone else. He never collaborated."

"Are you sure?" demanded Rondal, his heart sinking.

"Absolutely," assured Tyndal. "He described the fight. He's not stupid, but he's not smart enough to lie convincingly about something like that. Not if you know what to ask him."

"Still, anyone can be fooled," Rondal pointed out, lamely.

"I know. Just to be sure . . . while he wasn't paying attention I cast a truthtelling on him. I could have asked him about his first tumble, and he would have told me all about it. He didn't collaborate."

"Then why in seven hells would she *lie* about that?" Rondal asked, mystified.

"There's only one person who can answer that," Tyndal pronounced. "Let's get washed up and have a drink . . . and then we'll go see just why Lady Arsella was so anxious to put this man's neck in a noose."

Rondal asked Tyndal to request that Alwer take his meal in the stables, and gave him some instruction and explanation while he saw to the men's evening meal in the abandoned great hall. They would sleep in the tower, but until night fell there was little reason not to use the more comfortable great hall to sup.

Lady Arsella was sullen and silent throughout the meal, answering questions with one-word responses or nods of her head. She barely looked up from her food, and only long days between meals compelled her to do more than pick at the traveler's stew they'd made. When Sir Tyndal came in, Rondal watched her carefully.

She looked longingly at him at first, but then her expression changed to guilt. Then fear. Then anxiety. Then hopelessness. Then desperation. Then contemplation. Then despair.

Ishi's tits, Rondal remarked to himself, *how can one girl's head contain so many emotions in such a short time?* Her eyes darted between he and Sir Tyndal several times, and Rondal could swear he could hear the mill gears of her mind grinding away at some idea.

"I'm going to go stroke the Luck Tree," Rondal said, stretching and yawning. "We can get secured when we're done eating. Everyone take a dump before we close up the tower, unless you want to smell your own chamberpot all night." He gave Arsella a crude grin. She didn't make a face, as he would have expected at his boyish behavior. Instead she looked away.

Rondal relieved himself in the yard and then went to the stables, where Alwer was dining with the horses.

"I'm sorry I deprived you of the comfort of the hall," Rondal began, "but under the circumstances . . ."

"This is the best hall I've supped within in weeks, milord," the hayward assured him, leaping to his feet. "No apologies necessary. I owe you, after how you saved us from those scrugs!"

"My pleasure," Rondal said automatically. "And if you truly feel indebted to me, then do me this boon: when we retire to the tower for the evening, I want you to come speak with Sir Tyndal and me about Lady Arsella. But I bid you not to discuss the matter with anyone, before or after, save as I bid. Sir Tyndal assures me of your character and your innocence, but the accusation before me is severe enough that I feel obligated to see it spoken of openly. Can you do this for me?"

"Aye, milord, anything to clear my name," the man assured him, earnestly. "I've no truck with the scrugs, and I'll fight any man who says otherwise!" There was no mistaking the sincerity of his tone. This man hated goblins. He was not a collaborator.

As dusk fell, Tyndal secured the stables with additional spells to confound the olfactory senses – if the goblins had not discovered a canine's facility with tracking by smell, they were sure to do so soon – before sealing the tower from the inside for the night.

"Even if they do get past the walls and the spells on the gate," he announced to the six men in the snug room at the base of the tower, "they'll spend hours running around this place trying to find the door. There's an enchantment on it that makes it always seem to be on the other side." That made them all laugh.

Rondal grabbed a bottle of wine from the cellar and left Tyndal to see to ordering the men for the night. The men were to stay in the base of the tower near to the door. Rondal and Tyndal would keep watch – mostly by magic – allowing everyone to get a much-needed night's sleep.

In the third-story room above Lady Arsella was curled up under her mantle, her crossbow at hand, when Rondal came in. She started, then settled back into her make-shift bed.

"My lady, please tell me again, from the beginning, what happened on the night of the attack on Maramor."

"Why? I've *told* you—"

"Humor me," he ordered, flatly. She sighed in frustration, then began speaking in a very deliberate voice, as if she had practiced it.

"We had snuck away from Sir Hagun's party, my maid and I, and gone back to Maramor to hold it in his absence. Foolish, perhaps, but . . . well, the manor was filled with the village folk. For a week things were . . . fine. A little chaotic, with the yard filled with villeins camping out, hiding from the goblins, but nothing bad. Folk went out to the village or the fields by day and came home to the safety of Maramor at night.

"Then one night someone knocked on the gate and begged permission to come in. The steward let them in, curse him. I *swear* it was Alwer the Hayward. An hour later the gate was attacked. That . . . *thing* tore it right apart, and then there were goblins everywhere.

"My maid rushed me to the hiding place Sir Hagun had prepared and pushed me inside just as the goblins were coming up the stairs. I can still hear her screaming," she said, her face locked in horror and regret, as tears fell down it. "And if it hadn't been for Alwer . . ."

"But what did Alwer *do?*" asked Rondal, his arms crossed. "What exactly did he do that was treacherous?"

"He . . . he must have sabotaged the gate!" Arsella insisted. "Gotten word to his damnable confederates that . . . that . . ."

"That there were people barricaded inside?" finished Rondal. "I doubt they needed his help for that. He didn't even let them in, if there was a troll breaking down the gate," he said, accusingly.

"But he was *there!*" she insisted, tearfully. "He came in, then they attacked, and everyone got led away in chains! Everyone they didn't kill on the spot! He sabotaged the gate, he must have, he betrayed the guards, he . . . he . . ."

"If he had sabotaged the gate, milady," Rondal said, quietly, "then the goblins would not have had recourse to a troll. But your gates were decidedly removed by a troll. Yet you still insist on Alwer's treachery . . ."

"I do!" she pleaded. "You *must* kill him!"

"Thank you, milady," Rondal said, bowing. "Sir Tyndal, did you hear all of that?"

"Every word," Tyndal said, as he mounted the narrow stairs, a magelight floating ahead of him. "The Long Ears spell. And . . . so did Goodman Alwer," he continued, as the hayward followed behind him.

"So what do you have to say to the accusations of your treachery made by Lady Arsella, Alwer of Maramor?"

The peasant looked troubled as he stared at Rondal, then Tyndal, and then at the girl.

"Well, milords, as far as treachery goes, I will swear on Trygg's holy womb that I have never betrayed anyone, ever, as I am an honest man. Not even if my own life was at risk." He sounded indignant and angry, but still cautious. "And as far as Lady Arsella is concerned, I know not what she says, if she still breathes at all. For that girl is *not* Lady Arsella."

Rondal and Tyndal stared at him, mouths agape. When they both looked back at the weeping woman, she had her face buried in her hands, sobbing.

"What do you mean, Goodman?" asked Tyndal, slowly. Rondal was afraid to breathe.

"I mean that girl is not Lady Arsella. Lady Arsella is younger, has truly blonde hair, and is more shapely about the face. Favors her mother, she does. This woman here is Maid Belsi. She's Lady Arsella's lady's maid. Or at least she was."

"What?" Rondal and Tyndal asked, in shocked unison.

"Do you want to tell the tale, lass, or should I?" Alwer asked, accusingly. When she didn't answer, he shrugged and continued.

"Tale was that old Sir Hagun's older brother, Sir Hagbel, sired a bastard on a common village maiden in his youth, and then got himself killed at tournament. Sir Hagun took the child in when she were old enough to foster, as a kindness and in honor of his brother. He had his own daughter, Arsella, just a year younger so it was a good fit.

"'Tis true enough the girls slipped back to Maramor, and it's true as well that the attack happened. Even that I came late to the gate. But I had tarried in the village to avoid a patrol, not collaborate with them.

"When they attacked it had nothing to do with me, that I swear. The girls ran into the manor when the attack came. We fought – by Duin's sack, we fought, milords. Killed a few of them, too, but there wasn't no getting around that troll. Then the evil men came and tied us up. All twenty-odd of us. *Including* Lady Arsella."

"So she was taken captive with you," repeated Tyndal. "She didn't escape into some hiding place."

"No," Alwer agreed, slowly. "And that first night they had us, she said that her maid Belsi got to the hiding place, first. That she had locked her out from inside. That she had screamed and cried for her to open it and let her in, but she did not." His voice was filled with condemnation.

"So what happened to Lady Arsella?" asked Rondal in a hushed voice.

"I know not, milord. After that first night, we were separated out, men from women. So the . . . the evil men could have some sport before they took us north. I heard them. We all heard them. They screamed all night long, poor girls, but we were tied and could do naught.

"We were marched out at dawn the next day, but the women were still in camp. We got rescued that day, thank Duin, but none of the womenfolk were ever seen again."

Belsi broke down in sobs anew at this news. Tyndal thanked the peasant man. "Go on down and have a cup or two . . . but do not speak of this to anyone, yet, Alwer. For now, she is still 'Lady Arsella,' is that clear?"

"Aye, milord," the peasant said, his eyes hard against the girl. "For now."

When he had gone, and Tyndal had shut the door behind him, Rondal took a seat on a stool near the window. "So . . . do you deny anything that Alwer said?"

She would not look up or speak to them. Rondal repeated the question, but she still would not speak.

Tyndal finally boomed, "Belsi of Maramor, you now stand accused of bearing false witness in a capital crime in a time of war. Will you not speak in your own defense?"

The commanding tone brought the girl upright almost against her will . . . but soon she was kneeling in front of them both, her hands clasped, tears streaming down her face.

"I . . . I . . ."

"Do you deny the truth of what Alwer said?" repeated Rondal. He waited again for her to speak, and was about to accuse her again when she finally found words.

"Do you have *any idea* what it was like, growing up here?" she spat, angrily, instead. "Do you have any idea what it was like knowing that but for a few words said in temple all of that . . . all of Maramor should have been mine? I was the *older* brother's daughter!" she bellowed. "*I was the older daughter!*"

"It all makes sense now," Rondal said, almost to himself. "The way you knew your way around a kitchen better than most noble girls. How your clothes – *her* clothes – never quite fit. How you rarely referred to Sir Hagun as 'father,' he was always 'Sir Hagun'."

"Why waste good coin on finery for a bastard servant girl?" she asked angrily. "They put *her* in silks while I was in cotton rags! When *she* wanted to slip away and come back to Maramor, she was trying to come back for *more clothes*, the stupid snot!

"Oh, I was the loyal little maid, doing everything she asked, everything she demanded, knowing all the time it should have been *me* giving the orders! You have no idea, you damned knights, knowing what it's like to grow up a bastard and a commoner!"

"Actually," Rondal said, quietly, "Tyndal and I are both. We didn't let it spoil our aspirations."

"What did you hope to gain from this deception, anyway?" asked Tyndal.

"My birthright," she said, hotly. "My legacy. But mostly my life. That day when they came, I was the faster one. I was the one who thought about the refuge first. I was the faster one up the stairs. She was always a little dim, a little slow, Arsella was. But bossy. I got there first, and there was only room for one. Why should I yield my security and doom us both? Damn right I shut her out! I saw her, I heard her. Then I closed it and hid, and *I'd do it again!*"

"All of which might be forgiven. But then you misrepresented yourself," Tyndal continued, relentlessly. "You told yourself off as a noblewoman to our company, claiming by deceit what was not yours by birth."

"I was fearful of the soldiers invading my home," she said, indignantly. "Would your men have been as deferent to a servant girl as they were Lady Arsella of Maramor?" she accused.

Rondal pursed his lips in thought as he considered what she said. Yes, he had to admit, her pretense to social status had, indeed, ensured her security at the outpost. There was no telling what would have happened if Belsi had revealed herself as a common serving girl, even around disciplined men.

But what kind of man did she think Rondal was? He would not have allowed them to molest her. He had picked them on good recommendations from their commanders, and none had a reputation for such sport.

While he understood her fear in a chaotic situation, he and his men had given no sign that they meant her ill. They treated her with the courtesy and respect any man who knew Ishi's laws would.

"Why did you persist, then, when it was clear that my men and I were well-behaved?"

"Would you have extended me the treatment that you did if I hadn't?" she demanded tearfully. "Would you have looked upon me as a peer, not as a hindrance? Would you have taken me seriously as common old Belsi, and not the noble Arsella?"

"Now we shall never know," Tyndal said, unprompted. His eyes were flashing angrily. "Because of your lies, Maiden Belsi, you have inherited the legacy of their consequences. Pretending to be a noble, pretending to own Maramor, pretending to a name not your own. All are punishable offenses, in Castal, under civil law

"All that," he said, waving it away with a hand, "could be overlooked, under the circumstances. But," he continued, his voice as sharp as a mageblade, "when you tried to murder a good man, an innocent man, by bearing false witness . . . that, Maiden Belsi, is too much for an honorable man to ignore!"

"I . . . I had no *choice!*" she insisted, her voice a pitiful wail. "If he told you what really happened that night, if he told you who I really was . . . I would have lost my only chance at Maramor!"

"Maramor is *lost*," Rondal said, his voice aching as he spoke. "I told you that when I arrived. Maramor is an abandoned estate behind enemy lines in a war zone. It has temporary utility as a military outpost, but until this land is recovered, it is lost. What would you have done had my men moved on the day after we arrived?"

"Begged to go with you," she admitted. "But as the gods delivered to me a chance, I took it. Would you have done otherwise in my place?"

"*Yes*," both boys said in unison.

Tyndal continued. "We have done . . . less-than-honorable deeds in our lives, Maiden Belsi," he said, his contempt for her deeds obvious. "But we have *never* tried to murder in defense of our dishonor. You tried not merely to murder Alwer, but tried to do so by proxy, implicating other men in your crime. Through a sworn soldier of the King. Under the banner of war."

Each fact was spoken like an indictment. "According to the Laws of Duin, such actions are tantamount to looting and treason," Rondal agreed, slowly.

"Each are capital offenses, subject to battlefield justice," Tyndal pronounced. "What say you in defense of your actions?"

Her eyes grew wide, and her face turned white. Her tears did not cease, but she stopped making noise. For some reason Rondal found that even harder to bear.

"I beg you, Sir Tyndal, be merciful!" she said, finally, breaking the awful silence. "I knew not what I was doing! I was merely trying to survive!"

She looked around desperately, seeking some means of escape. Rondal could see it in her eyes – like a trapped animal, watching frantically as its doom closed in.

Suddenly her eyes alighted on him . . . and to his shock so did her ire.

"If you seek a traitor, look to *Sir Rondal,* my lord! Regardless of his guilt or innocence, when I told him of the danger Alwer presented to you, he was reluctant to inform you. Reluctant enough that he sent out no messenger -- *I checked!* Every day I checked! He had hopes that Alwer would be the assassin that would put an end to you! Can you not *see* how jealous he is of you?" she asked, as if it was the most apparent thing in the world.

"Now why would Sir Rondal wish ill of me?" demanded Tyndal, scornfully.

"Is it not *obvious?*" she snorted. "He has ambition of taking your position, once you are dead! And, no doubt, my affections! Trust me, my lord, I have heard him say as much, though he speaks subtly. Once you were gone he—"

"Would have *twice* as much work to do," laughed Tyndal, derisively.

Despite how distraught he felt over Arsella's – Belsi's – deception, the thought of being solely responsible for all that Master Min had in store for them was, indeed, terrifying. At least with Tyndal around, he did not have to bear it alone. On that basis alone he would have fought through a legion of goblins to rescue Tyndal right then, despite whatever ill-feelings might still stand between them.

He looked at Belsi with a new light. Anyone who might mistake his feelings toward Tyndal for hate, hate enough to arrange his murder, truly did not understand him.

"I assure you, my lord, he did nothing to alert you to the potential of danger—"

"Which turned out not to be dangerous," Tyndal pointed out.

"Nor did he look forward to your arrival as a good comrade should," she continued, ignoring his jibes. "He all but cursed the news!"

"I don't doubt it," Tyndal said, "I'm quite the asshole, most of the time."

It amazed Rondal to hear him say it, although he wasn't surprised at how perversely proud of the fact he seemed to be.

"Sir Rondal and I have always had a rivalry," he continued, thoughtfully. "But, in fact, he *did* send word to me, by arcane methods . . . about *all* of his concerns," he said, turning to her accusingly. "*After* he managed to save my life. Curious behavior for a backstabbing traitor, don't you think? We discussed them in detail."

"If you think this man is your friend, Sir Tyndal," she said, her eyes dark and desperate, "then you mistake yourself!"

"Friend?" Tyndal asked, as if the word was strange in his mouth. "We are fellow apprentices. Comrades at arms. We grew up in the same village, near-enough. And we're both knights magi, whatever that may come to mean.

"But I do not doubt he was not eager for my arrival, the same way I do not doubt for a moment that the idea of putting me in harm's way unnecessarily never crossed his mind. Ishi's tits, I do enough of that on my own!

"But most of all you are mistaken, Maid Belsi, because Sir Rondal has no ambition to take my position. Why would he? *He is my commanding officer.*"

Belsi gasped, her head turning to stare at Rondal. "*You* . . . are the commander?"

"I am," Rondal admitted, looking at her coolly. "In charge of the entire mission. Including the man you would have me put a dagger in."

She looked from one of them to the other, her mouth open in shock and surprise. "My lords . . ." she said, but nothing else was forthcoming as she struggled to reassess her position. "I admit my mistake," she said, finally, her eyes tearful and downcast. "I abjure my falsehoods, and I . . . I appeal to your chivalry and your grace."

That last pleas seemed to make Tyndal even angrier.

"My *chivalry?* You invoke that honor after you sought to use that institution as a weapon to protect your stolen position? How are you then entitled to its protection? Nay, chivalry flows from grace, and you have *not* earned that grace, in my eyes. You are *false*, Maiden," he said, condemningly.

"I am not!" she insisted. "I'm not! Please! If you bear me any love at all—"

"And now she speaks of *love*," Tyndal sneered harshly. "Your love is as inconstant as the sands, Maid Belsi! First you made eyes at brave Sir Rondal," he said, scornfully. "Your admiration for him was clear to all – until *I* arrived. Then his heart was a phantom to you. Thinking I was his commander, you flashed your skirts at me instead to further your ambitions. Love? What cause have we to love you, madame? You who have conspired against us?"

"I have not, I have not! I just wanted . . . wanted . . ."

"Will we not have the truth?" Rondal growled.

"I have *told* you the truth!" she pleaded.

"I don't think you have," Tyndal said, conversationally, as he knelt in front of her. "And a knight mage must *always* seek the truth. So let us ensure that the truth is, indeed, spoken this night, before anything permanent is decided. I would not have your pretty neck stretched for a lie," he said, darkly.

"And how do you propose to do that?" Rondal asked, crossly.

He felt miserable. He *did* like Belsi. He could understand her fear and her trepidations. But her aspirations to what did not belong to her disturbed him, and her willingness to use others so callously offended him.

He remembered the few days they had enjoyed together, before

Tyndal had arrived, when he felt as her protector. She had seemed so vulnerable, then.

She seemed vulnerable now, but not in a delicate way. She was wretched, sobbing as she struggled for some response that might save her. It disgusted Rondal that someone he had respected had fallen so far in his estimation. As much as part of him still wanted to spare her any further humiliation, he knew his duty.

"Blue magic," Tyndal reminded him. "Ilsar's Truthtelling. I know it well. A very potent version."

"Doesn't that risk leaving her an idiot?" he asked. He wasn't certain – he'd heard of such misfirings of spells before. It happened, with Blue Magic, from what he understood.

"I'm not certain we'd know the difference, after this," he smirked. "Let's cast this and see what the little . . . maiden *really* thinks."

The threat was delivered calmly, but as soon as Belsi heard it her eyes opened even wider. "No! No, milords, I have spoken the truth to you I swear—!"

"Then we shouldn't hear any surprises then, should we?" asked Rondal, his nostrils flaring. "Go ahead, Sir Tyndal. On *my* authority." He was angry, and he knew a commander shouldn't make decisions based on his emotions. He was trying to be fair. How could this be unfair? "Let's hear the truth. Then we'll decide what shall be done with you."

Tyndal closed his eyes and made a few movements with his hands, but then he seemed finished with his casting. There was no visible effect on the woman.

"If she utters a falsehood, now," Tyndal assured him, "that could well make her the most dangerous woman alive. But let's test it. What's your name?"

She barely hesitated. "Belsi of Maramor, daughter of Sir Hagbel, rightful heir of Maramor Manor."

"Who was your mistress?"

"Lady Arsella of Maramor," she said, her tear-stained cheeks flushing.

"Who was your first kiss?" Tyndal continued.

"Roric of Regsiway," she said, staring at him angrily. "I was *twelve*."

"Sounds like it worked," nodded Tyndal. "Your prisoner to interrogate, Commander."

Rondal made himself comfortable in front of her. "Tell me about the night the goblins came for the folk of Maramor," he ordered her.

"We . . . we were inside, in Arsella's chamber," she began after heaving a great sigh. "We were trying to decide where to try to find some supplies, as ours were running low. The . . . the other servants were waiting for orders, and they were not happy we came back. We were scared. We weren't supposed to be there, and I didn't want to go back in the first place, but Arsella insisted – she was always bossy," she said, almost fondly . . . but with a tinge of resentment.

"Then we heard the noise at the gate. We went to the window to look, and it sounded like a wolf pack was outside. But Arsella just laughed and bragged how strong the walls of Maramor were.

"Then something, a troll, ripped the gate off of its hinges, as we were headed downstairs. By the time we got to the door they were already in the yard. The troll punched Gythar so hard his head snapped back. The goblins were howling and laughing and stabbing at everyone.

"I saw Arsella freeze. She was fascinated. She wanted to watch, the stupid girl. I realized that the hiding place her father had prepared for her was open . . . I had been entrusted with its location and access by her father, as her 'loyal' maid. I realized she wasn't going to move unless I prompted her, and when I saw Bukkal fall to those bloodthirsty animals I knew we were lost.

"So I ran. I ran to the stairs, and it wasn't until I made the landing that Arsella figured out what I was doing. She followed me, screaming – stupid thing to do, when the goblins were everywhere.

"I didn't scream. I ran. I got to the chamber and rolled myself into the space. It was cramped. Only meant for one. It's even warded against magic. I closed it just as she came in. She was . . . she was pounding on the outside with her little fists," she said, sobbing uncontrollably now.

"I could hear them, too, just little girl fists making soft little bangs on the wood. She was screaming. She was screaming . . . my name. Begging me to let her in. It was awful. It was pitiful.

"But . . . I didn't let her in. It would have meant both of us would be captured. I didn't think she deserved to survive, stupid girl. I was faster. I was older. I should have been the lord's daughter, not her. I . . . loved her, the foolish girl, but . . . but it was her or me, and I was faster."

"So when did you decide you would become your cousin?" asked Tyndal, unsympathetically.

"When I heard horses. When I saw they were soldiers and not goblins, I thought maybe I was saved. Then I thought what . . . what else might happen if a bunch of soldiers happened on a servant girl. Then I thought that they wouldn't dare do that to Lady Arsella. So I became Lady Arsella."

"And so you condemned poor Alwer because he threatened to expose your lie," Rondal said, flatly.

"Yes," she agreed without prompting, much to her dismay. "I barely knew the man. I felt bad about it, very bad. But I did not know him well."

"And he had nothing to do with the attack," repeated Rondal.

"No, he was as scared as anyone," she recalled, sadly. That was enough to satisfy Rondal. He was about to dismiss her when Tyndal continued the interrogation in an unpleasant direction.

"So when you first saw Sir Rondal, what did you think of him?"

"He seemed kind of plain," she answered. "Not too tall, not too strong. I thought I might be able to gain his sympathy, if I was pleasant enough to him."

"Were you grateful for his presence?"

"After I was done being fearful, yes. I felt protected by him and his men."

"And did you bear Sir Rondal any legitimate affection?" asked Tyndal with an impish glance at Rondal. Rondal glared back at him. He didn't think he wanted to know the answer to that.

"A little," she admitted guiltily. "He was nice enough, but he seemed a dull fellow. Not dashing, like . . ."

"Like Sir Tyndal," finished Rondal, when it was clear the girl did not want to finish the sentence.

"Aye, like Sir Tyndal," she said, hanging her head. Rondal's face burned and he stared daggers at Tyndal, who didn't seem to be bothered. In fact, he continued his interrogation.

"So when you . . . were affectionate with Sir Rondal, what was your motivation?"

"I had aspirations of keeping Maramor. He seemed like a decent man who might consider backing my claim."

"He was . . . persuadable, then," Tyndal continued. Rondal resisted the urge to blast him into pieces.

"He was gullible," she said, shocked at the words even as she spoke them. "Naïve. He was willing to believe whatever I said, provided the same lips kissed him after."

"Remember, Ron, she's only speaking the truth of her perceptions," Tyndal reminded, uneasily. "Not the absolute truth."

"That's not terribly comforting!" Rondal shot back. His hands were clenched in fists.

"It should be – you told me your suspicions of her almost the moment you met her," he pointed out. "Not so naïve and gullible as milady would suggest, apparently."

"Tyn, stop this—"

"Ron, indulge me," Tyndal said, turning to face his fellow apprentice. "Please. There is purpose in this."

Ron wanted to scream, but he knew better. Besides, when Tyndal had an idea in his head, you couldn't drive it out with a mace. "Continue," he said, rolling his eyes.

"Trust me," he said, catching Rondal's eye. "Maid Belsi, what were your ambitions, once the outpost was established?"

"At first it was escape, but when it seemed as if Maramor might be saved, I contrived to take it as my own," she confessed. "I saw Sir Rondal as a means to do that. If I had to trade my virtue for the manor that was not too high a price to pay," she said, and blushed deeply.

"In the name of chivalry I'll spare asking you whether it was intact and yours to give," Tyndal said with a chuckle. "But you had no greater feelings for Sir Rondal than that? A means to claim your property?"

"That is true," she said, hanging her head.

"And then when I arrived . . ."

"I thought you were the new commander. I didn't think anyone as aggressive and flamboyant as you would settle for being anything less than the commander." It was Rondal's turn to enjoy the truthtelling, and Tyndal's turn to blush. But he didn't blush much.

"You were certainly forward enough," he reminded her. "When you came to my chambers, I thought it was *my* virtue under siege."

"It was," she agreed. "When I saw you I felt . . . possessed of a fire. You excited my blood and made me dizzy. If I could have both Maramor and a handsome young knight to protect it, well, it seemed a gift from Ishi."

"I suppose it would have," conceded Rondal.

"This is not the time to be sympathetic, Ron," snapped Tyndal.

"Tyn, in her position would you have done any different?"

"Mayhap!" he protested. "I would not have imperiled an innocent man to steal a worthless estate!"

"You are not a woman," Belsi said, angrily. "Subject to the whims of men who have no consideration for your feelings or even your fate. To be ordered around, bartered off, or discarded when you grow tired of them . . . were you women, gentlemen, you would have *no* trouble mustering the courage to use the weapons Ishi gifted you with to save your life!"

"Yet honor has no sex," Tyndal spat. "You were a victim here, madam; right up until you traded your honor for position. Now you have neither. Were I a woman, I would at least have clung to my honor. That can never be taken from you. You have to discard it yourself."

"What use is honor if you are raped and killed?" she snarled.

"You were in no danger of that," reminded Rondal. "I gave you my word."

"You gave *Lady Arsella* your word!" she snarled. "But deceitful Belsi you would have punished, used, and discarded!"

"No, he would not have," Tyndal said, unexpectedly. "For Sir Rondal *never* forgot his honor. Once he gave his word, he would have kept it. Even if you broke yours. He's just like that, it's quite annoying.

"But whatever excuse you give us, it will never serve as more than a rationalization of your dishonorable conduct. There was a time at which the good and proper choice was presented to you. And you did not take it. You relied on your affections instead."

"You seemed happy enough with my affections when they were freely given!" she shouted at Tyndal, tearfully.

"They were genuine affections," Tyndal shrugged. "Why would I spurn them?"

"Because your comrade had eyes for me," she said, accusingly. "You *knew* he fancied me, and yet you did not stop yourself!"

460

"No, Maid Belsi, I did not stop *you*. I stopped *myself* aplenty. Rondal was well-aware of your disloyalty to his affections at that time. Being an honorable man, he ceded the field." He dismissed the matter, which both stung Rondal's pride and flattered his honor. Being told how much you deserve second place was harsh medicine.

"And being an honorable man," Tyndal continued, pacing in front of her, "I would not snatch a prize I did not covet merely to keep another from having it. It would take long acquaintance and ample proof of your worth before I would have felt affection for you sufficient to contend for your virtue with a comrade. As it appears, Maid Belsi, my caution was well-founded."

"A noble title is not proof of a woman's worth!" she said, defiantly.

"It was not your common status to which I was referring," Sir Tyndal said. "You have revealed your character, and it is not worthy of my attention – for love or for sport.

"My fellow here does not have the experience with women that I do, through no fault of his own, but more he does not understand how quickly their affections can be given if they see it to their profit. Not *all* women," he cautioned. "There are plenty of ladies worthy the title by birth or nature who would never dabble dishonestly with a gentleman's affections, finding other, more honest means to achieve their ends.

"But a certain *type* of woman," he said, shaking his head sadly, "will turn her affection like a sail in the wind, tacking against fortune and circumstance on one strong breeze or another. Mayhap it is a phase, or a failing of youth, or a product of her fortunes – but we have the proof of her deceit by her own lips. That's admission of a crime, if one wanted to be technical," he said.

"Please, my lords," she wailed, reminded again of her plight, "I beg you not to try me for this!"

"You attempted to murder someone in order to steal an empty manor," Rondal said, flatly. "How do you expect to do that and *not* be held accountable?"

"I . . . I was only trying to survive!" she pleaded.

"You know, we could send her back to headquarters for trial," Tyndal pointed out, casually. "Let one of the line officers oversee her case. Eventually. They're a little busy, back at headquarters. And they tend to take a simplistic approach to battlefield justice." The implication was enough to make Belsi moan in horror. "Or we could just convene a tribunal right here to judge her ourselves," he said, menacingly.

"Oh, stop it," chided Rondal. "You're scaring her!"

"She *should* be scared!" Tyndal shot back. "She tried to kill a man just as certain as if she had shot a bolt at him!"

"She made a ham-handed attempt to manipulate the situation," countered Rondal. "I don't think . . . Would you have allowed us to kill Alwer?" he asked, suddenly curious.

It was apparent from the struggle in her eyes that Belsi did not want to answer. "Y-yes," she finally admitted, tears pouring down her cheeks. "As long as I did not have to watch it," she added.

"Even worse," sneered Tyndal contemptuously. "She's not even content to kill a man – she wants someone else to do it, off stage. No dirty hands for her!"

"I just wanted the problem to go away!" she explained, tearfully. "I didn't really want to hurt anyone!"

"And now you just want to pretend it didn't happen!" accused Tyndal. "But it did happen. And there are consequences to our actions," he added menacingly. "As soldiers of the king it is our duty—"

"That's *enough!*" repeated Rondal, more loudly. "Don't make this any more difficult than it already is!"

"Please don't hang me!" she begged. "I didn't mean . . ."

"You, too!" Rondal ordered. "Enough! " He issued a frustrated sigh, and slumped his shoulders. "Luin's staff, what are we going to do?" he asked, looked to Tyndal for some hint of support.

"*You're* the commanding officer," Tyndal reminded him, almost gratefully. "I'm just the spare. This is your decision. I'm not holding this goat."

Damn him! Rondal was hoping for some sort of guidance, but Tyndal – rightly – was insisting that he decide what was to be done about the murderous maid.

At the same time he was disgusted with his fellow for dumping the problem at his boots, he was also more satisfied that he had some control over the decaying situation. While that might imperil his honor or his duty or his soul, at least he had some influence.

But . . . just how *did* he wish to influence the situation? As angry as he was with Arsella – Belsi – he still did not feel her crimes warranted hanging.

Traditionally, that was the only punishment meted out in such cases in a war zone. There was just not enough time or resources to give the accused the benefit of Luin's blessing, and officers resorted instead to the swift and severe justice of Duin.

He had hated to see such things come to pass in the field, in his limited experience, but he knew that they did. He had usually felt some sympathy for the accused, as a minor crime brought to justice was enough to see a man's neck stretched.

Now the terrible decision was his to make. And this was no mere looting or banditry. This was a civilian conspiring to gain property through the expediency of attempted murder of an irregular in a war zone. Tyndal was right. That was too serious an issue to allow to pass without judgment.

But as he watched the girl cower before them, weeping inconsolably about her self-wrought plight, the last thing Rondal wanted to do was prolong her misery. Despite her crime and her lies he still felt a terrible pang at the thought of harm coming to her.

He still thought about the first time he saw her, the terrified eyes and disheveled hair peeking out at him above a crossbow. She had been vulnerable and afraid and all he'd wanted to do was protect her.

She had taken that protection and sullied it. She had accepted his affections and then spurned them, when a better-seeming situation – no, he cursed himself, admit it, a better-seeming *man* – had caught her attention. She had taken his desire to protect and cherish him and traded it. The feeling of that betrayal also surged through his mind.

Yet there was a third voice that spoke to him, the calm, cool voice that had been growing since it had manifested at the Mysteries: the voice of his honor. Not the vainglorious urging to prove his position and demonstrate that he could coldly order a traitor executed, at need, but the more compelling voice that spoke from his very soul. His honor was the voice of his conscience, writ large, and it was less concerned with achievement and victory than it was doing what was right. What he could live with.

It was the voice that had been born after Estasia's death, he realized. And it was telling him not to be hasty. There was nothing compelling him to act in the moment. While he felt Tyndal's anger and resentment for the girl, and shared it somewhat, that was also tempered with some understanding of her motivations. While that understanding did not excuse what she had done, it did make him sympathetic.

And she was so pretty . . . which was all the more reason not to make a hasty decision. If he acted out of either affection and saved her or petty revenge and condemned her, that would be unacceptable, his honor spoke to him. If he was given Luin's judgment over her, then he would do as fair and impartial job as possible. Which meant, right then, to investigate further.

"Nothing will be decided tonight," he pronounced, finally. Belsi gasped with relief, and her eyes swam with gratitude. It made Rondal highly uncomfortable. "It is stupid to debate such things while goblins sniff for us. And once they are gone, our primary duty," he said, emphasizing the word, "is to the mission."

"Mission?" Belsi asked.

"We're going to wait out the pursuit and then we're going to go on a little jaunt through the scenic Gilmoran countryside: to visit that manor they were so keen to keep you from seeing. And find out the source of that massive dump."

"You think *now* is a good time to go gathering intelligence?" Tyndal asked, curiously.

"That's why we're here," he reminded his fellow. "*Not* to banter with deceitful servant girls. This is a distraction from what is important, and what is important is whatever they don't want us to see that badly. So tomorrow, should the way be clear, you, me, Alwer, and Belsi, here, are going to take some horses and head back up the road. Everyone else will return to Maramor and continue to fortify it until we return."

"In the meantime," he said, crossing the room to retrieve Belsi's arbalest, "you will stay here, secure and alone, where you may reflect on what you have done. The fact that no actual harm was done will figure in your judgment, but so will your conduct from here on. Can I count on your good conduct?"

"Yes, yes," she agreed, truthfully, "I promise, I will serve you faithfully, my lords. I am so sorry," she wept.

"You're a *distraction*," Rondal reminded both her and himself through clenched teeth. "One I don't need. And one I cannot afford to indulge. Right now I am too close to this matter to give it a fair hearing, and in the light of more pressing matters, I will defer it."

"Ron, I'm not arguing with you," Tyndal said, with a smirk, "but isn't bringing along a weeping, treacherous woman on a spying mission a poor idea? Alwer can handle himself – he's a fair fighter, no mistake. But . . . her?" he asked, thumbing in her direction. "Is that wise?"

"Possibly not," admitted Rondal. "But I can't very well send her back to Maramor and let her honeyed tongue and dewy eye convince one of our men to let her go free. If she is with us we can watch her. If she becomes a liability," he shrugged, "well, we can handle that."

"Let's find out," Tyndal said, and turned to Belsi. "So, madame, if you accompany us tomorrow, do we have to worry about a crossbow quarrel in our backs?"

"N-no," she said. "I might try to run away."

"I wouldn't attempt it," Tyndal continued, conversationally. "The new breed of fell hound the gurvani are employing might not be as fast or have the endurance of a horse, but they can sniff out a scent like a hunting dog."

"And they have razor sharp fangs," added Rondal.

"I promise if I go with you," she said, after searching their eyes, "I will serve you faithfully and not try to run away."

"Hold on," Tyndal said, fingering his chin. "Something occurs to me. Belsi, was there anything else you didn't want us to discover?"

"Y-yes," she admitted, against her will.

"And what was that?"

She swallowed. "The treasure of Maramor Manor. Sir Hagun and the family always kept some coin and such stashed away for emergencies. He took most of his wealth with him, but he left behind . . . some."

"How much?" Rondal demanded.

"Seventy . . . or eighty ounces of gold. And nearly four hundred of silver. Plus some jewelry."

"Oh ho!" Tyndal grinned. "So you wanted to get away with a new name, a new title, a new estate . . . and literally steal the family jewels!"

"If you are aware of a better claimant, Sir Knight, I would be happy to hear of them," she said, contemptuously. "That money belonged to my . . . *my* father. My *real* father. If I am the only one of the blood left . . ."

"We shall deal with that when we get back. If we get back," he added, rising. "But Tyndal is correct: you must face accountability for what you have done. That cannot be avoided. And we shall use our journey into danger as a means of discovering your true character, now that you have given your parole. Good night . . . *my lady,*" he added, harshly, and left.

*   *   *

The next morning, they awoke before dawn, and while they had broken their fast and armed themselves, Rondal scryed the area. Once he was sure there were no goblins still in the neighborhood, he sent most of the men back to Maramor. He kept behind only Tyndal, Alwer, and Belsi – whom he continued to refer to as Lady Arsella. No need to explain more than he had to of the mission to his men.

Tyndal had selected their mounts and saw to their saddles. He had chosen good coursers, as opposed to chargers, horses with good endurance and good speed. They were not going into battle, but they might end up fleeing for their lives. A horse that was winded after half a mile was an invitation to death.

Each of the knights magi armed themselves with bow, quiver and sword. Rondal added a wooden roundshield to complement his mageblade and traded his chainmail hauberk for a lighter leather coat of plates. He had a dagger and a few warwands in his belt. He kept his infantryman's helmet.

Tyndal carried his mageblade Slasher, of course, kept his heavier armor, and took a horseman's javelin as a secondary weapon. Alwer was apparently adept as a bowman and carried an eighteen-inch long dagger at his belt. He had eagerly traded his ragged tunic for a heavy gambeson from the manor's armory and covered it with an archer's waxed leather curiass. To that he'd added a steel helmet. He looked far more confident in the armor, and grateful for the chance to help.

Belsi carried her crossbow, and now had a full complement of darts for the weapon and her a long, heavy dagger. She, too, had taken a padded gambeson and an archer's jerkin. She looked less confident. In fact, she looked at the brink of anguish.

"Hardly the stuff of legends," Rondal frowned.

"We write our own legends," Tyndal shot back. "Come on, let's go before this goat wakes up."

The two parties split up, the smaller heading cross-country over fields to save time and avoid the roads. They stopped repeatedly to scry ahead and check their bearings, and did not talk much in the saddle. Rondal could tell Alwer kept casting suspicious glances in Belsi's direction, and for her part the lass was doing her best at avoiding discussion of any sort.

They made good time. At noon they stopped in an abandoned village and ate some hard tack and smoked beef before they got back in the saddle. By early afternoon they started to see signs of goblin activity.

They stopped at a crossroads where the unmistakable litter of goblin troops was thrown casually within the ruins of a burned-out hovel next to the road. A couple of rotted skeletons lay in heaps nearby.

"This is where we first saw them," Tyndal explained in a near whisper as they examined a fork in the road. "The left hand path heads to that manor or castle they've taken over. This is where I found that poop."

"The poop is gone," Rondal observed.

"Count yourself fortunate," Tyndal said. "As impressive a poop as it was . . ."

Rondal studied the road. "Is this the only way to the manor?"

"No, there's another road that comes from the south-west," he said, shaking his head as he deployed his magemap. "But I'd bet they have both ways guarded." He studied the map for a moment. "But . . . you know, those scrugs don't think about rivers the same way we do."

"What do you mean?" asked Alwer. He was an intelligent peasant, Rondal had found, but unimaginative.

"I mean that they think of roads as means of transit . . . but they don't think that way about rivers. They are not fond of boats. There's this stream that runs right into the village and past the manor. I'm thinking that they won't be watching that as closely. And that will make it harder for those damn dogs of theirs to track us."

"I can see that," agreed Rondal. "But . . . I don't think all four of us are going to be able to make it without detection," he said, skeptically. "And the water will slow us down."

"So we leave our assistants back here with the horses, ready to come get us if things get hairy," reasoned Tyndal.

"You mean leave Alwer the insurgent fighter together alone with the woman who conspired to murder him?" asked Rondal, skeptically.

Tyndal grinned. "Exactly. What could possibly go wrong? I know why you did this," he added, unexpectedly.

"What?"

"Brought Lady Baggage along on a combat mission."

"What? Oh. Why *did* I do that?" Rondal asked, genuinely curious.

"Because she might die. Or Alwer might die. Or they might both die. Or best yet, *you* might die, and then you would be spared the task of deciding her fate."

"You seem awfully cheerful about such a dangerous mission on which you might die as well."

"Me?" Tyndal dismissed. "Not likely. I'm a survivor. Besides, someone is going to have to tell this sordid tale."

"I'd appreciate this sordid tale dying a quiet death," Rondal said, shaking his head. "But let's put the lady aside for a moment. You ready to wade up that creek?"

"As hot as it is, and as long as it's been since I've had a bath," Tyndal said as the early autumn sun pounded down on them, "I'm rather looking forward to it."

They explained their plan to the other two, but neither was happy about it.

"Milord, I'll follow orders," Alwer said to Tyndal, "but she's done tried to slay me once . . ."

"By proxy," soothed Tyndal, "and her plot was exposed. She has given her parole."

"And if a goblin patrol happens by?" asked the big peasant, as he nocked an arrow.

"Hide," suggested Tyndal. "Failing that, run. Failing that, fight."

"I'm honored milord has favored us with his brilliant martial guidance," grumbled Alwer, looking around nervously. "I'm not going to hang with my arse out at this crossroad, though. Too open and exposed. I'll make for that grove over there," he decided. "Should give us good cover, but enough to still see the road and screen us from scouts. In case we have to employ any of that stunning military strategy milord has gifted us with."

"I knew you'd understand, Alwer," Tyndal said, cheerfully. He glanced up at Belsi. "And there is one advantage of having her with you," he added. "If the goblins find you, you just need to be faster than she is."

"You are the epitome of chivalry, Sir Tyndal," Belsi said, sarcastically.

"There is nothing unchivalrous about giving good counsel," he chuckled. "And the same could be said for you: be faster than he is. Now you two play nicely," he chided, playfully, as the two commoners exchanged disgusted looks with each other. He handed the reins of his horse over to them, first removing several weapons and adjusting the armor he wore.

Rondal did the same. This was a scouting mission, not a combat mission. Metal armor made noise, and while it could save your life it could also endanger it. Wading through a stream made it doubly foolish.

He debated taking his shield. It was bulky, but he was reluctant to leave it behind. He'd looted the roundshield from Farune's great hall.

It was an aberration among the finery, a genuine tool of war instead of a ceremonial trophy weapon. He had found it hung high and out of sight in the rafters.

It was not a tournament shield, with some lord's device barely scuffed from use. It had seen battle. It was well-made, the planks fitting cunningly together in a well-crafted concave design, thirty inches across and banded with iron. The thick leather strap and solid wooden handle were worn from use, but only somewhat brittle with age. It was light, weighing only fifteen pounds – he barely felt it on his arm. There were notches and gouges in the face, but no weapon had ever pierced it.

A good, solid infantry shield, as much a weapon as armor in the right hands. Rondal had no idea how it had gotten there, but he took it knowing he could discard it at need. It was heavy to port such a ways, but he felt safer with it, and more able with sword and shield than just a mageblade.

Their bows were short, utilitarian weapons taken from the armory of Farune, and each bore a score of arrows. Tyndal had abandoned his steel cap and had tied a band around his forehead instead to keep his hair out of his eyes. Rondal kept his.

After seeing their uncomfortable comrades to the grove Alwer had chosen, the two magi cautiously walked their horses up the road before turning aside and cutting across the open fields. Once they got to the creek, they tied the horses and scryed the area heavily.

"They've got it warded up tight," Rondal said, warily.

"You don't think you can handle it?" Tyndal asked, part challenge and part question.

"Of course I can handle it," Rondal snapped. "The Magredal will slice right through them."

The Magredal was the traditional countermeasure against wardings on the battlefield. It wasn't sophisticated, but it was effective. Once employed, the wardings it targeted would be nullified. Walking through them would not alert the shaman or priest who had strung them

. . . theoretically.

"The Magredal?" asked Tyndal, skeptically. "Don't you think they've found a counter by now?"

"So what do you suggest?" Rondal challenged. You didn't disagree with a command decision unless you had an alternative.

"I'd say . . . Rarwin's Helm."

"Rarwin's . . . I don't even know that one!"

"I do," Tyndal said, smugly. "Picked it up in Relan Cor, while you were off camping." That burned.

"And what, precisely, is Rarwin's Helm?"

"You know how the Magredal and the other counterspells are designed to drop the wards or cancel them? Rarwin's Helm doesn't disturb the wards, it just shields the mage from their effects. You don't register as a human being," he emphasized. "To the shamans, you're just a squirrel or a bird or something."

"How does it do that?" Rondal asked, skeptically.

"It temporarily changes your Shroud," he explained. "That's what most wardings are tuned to detect. But most are also designed not to make you come running every time a robin builds a nest. So . . . we look like birds," he said, matter-of-factly.

Rondal considered. He'd heard of the spell. And the thaumaturgy was sound. But . . .

"Have you ever cast it before?"

"Me? No!" snorted Tyndal. "Haven't had the need to. Until now."

"And you think a reconnaissance mission into a heavily armed and fortified enemy installation is the perfect time to do so?" asked Rondal patiently.

"If one has the courage," challenged Tyndal. Rondal stared at him. That burned, too.

"All right," conceded Rondal. "Do it."

"What?"

"Cast the spell. On both of us," he reminded. "If you say it's a better spell, I'll yield to your judgment."

"Why?" Tyndal asked, as if he was mystified by Rondal's behavior.

"Because a good commander learns to trust the advice of his counselors," explained Rondal. "If you think it's such a good spell . . . let's stake both of our lives on it."

"Ron?" Tyndal asked, cautiously, as he studied him. "Are you . . . well?"

"Because I took one of your suggestions?" he asked, angrily.

"Well . . . yeah," admitted the taller boy as he prepared to cast the spell. "You *hate* taking my suggestions."

"Sometimes they aren't bad. I'm not going to insist I have the only answer to a problem," he declared. "I'm here to get a job done. If I let my personal feelings get in the way of that, I've left the path of wisdom. And will probably get us both killed."

"So . . . why is it such a problem to . . . to let your personal feelings get in the way? Do you really hate me that much?"

Rondal was silent. This was not the conversation he wanted to be having now.

"What did I ever do to you?" Tyndal asked.

It was such a simple statement. And it had been delivered in such a heartfelt way that Rondal knew there was no duplicity or cynicism behind the question. It wasn't an accusation, he realized. It was an actual earnest question.

Rondal looked at him, his jaw slack. "You . . . you don't *know?*"

"What? Know what?"

"Well, since you essentially blamed me for Estasia's death," Rondal said, much more quietly than he intended, "I figured that we had an issue between us. "

"Blamed YOU for Estasia's death?" Tyndal asked, amazed. He stopped and faced Rondal, his mouth still open. "You think I blamed *you* for her death?"

"Well, that's the meaning that matches the words that fell out of your mouth," Rondal reasoned, angrily, "so yes, I was under that impression!"

"And all this time . . . you thought I . . . *meant* that?"

"You seemed pretty serious about it at the time!"

"Duin's hairy sack, Ron! I just watched the girl *die!* And then killed the man who did it!" he said, angrily. "After losing my stone and getting reamed in my exams! I wasn't exactly thinking clearly!"

"You didn't exactly apologize!"

"You didn't exactly stick around long enough for me to!"

"What in nine hells was I supposed to do?" Ron demanded in a harsh whisper. "Beg your forgiveness? Wait for you to remove your head from your arse long enough to discuss it? Or did you mope and stomp around like . . . like . . ."

"Oh, forget it!" Tyndal said, in a hoarse whisper. "I can't *believe* you . . . all this time . . . Listen," he said, staring into Rondal's eye with such intensity that it made him uncomfortable.

"I know full well that there are only two people to blame for Estasia's death, and neither one of them are us! I put one in the ground," he said, viciously, "and I am conspiring to do the same to Pratt! If anything, I owe you a debt for all you did to recover my stone. I don't blame you for her death *at all.*"

"Really?" Rondal asked. It was as if a great weight was lifted from his chest. "You don't?"

"Hells, no! It was an accident. Well, it wasn't, but it certainly wasn't your fault. Who could have thought that Galdan was in league with

Pratt? That took me utterly by surprise. Alas, it did poor Estasia, as well. If I said I blamed you . . . I'm sorry! Damn, I'm sorry! Ishi's tits, that's what's been bothering you this whole time?" he repeated in disbelief.

"It was a pretty serious accusation," Rondal said, simply.

"Why didn't you . . ."

"Just . . . drop it, now," Rondal ordered. "Right before we sneak up on a bunch of sleepy goblins is not the time for a heartfelt discussion."

Once Tyndal finished casting the spell, Rondal followed with a spell of silence and another one of un-noticeability. He slung his shield on his back and drew his bow. Tyndal did likewise. They traveled in silence for two hundred yards, following the creek upstream towards the castle.

As castles went, it was modest, from a distance. Only the tallest of the towers along the wall could be seen over the trees as they approached. As they came closer, they saw that the walls were manned – or goblined, as the case was. Squint-eyed sentries peered uncomfortably into the sun-filled daylight, repeatedly shading their eyes and staving off yawns.

Their spells held, Rondal was happy to note, as none of the sentries on the walls noticed them, though some he felt had looked right at them. They finally climbed down the embankment and waded through the center of the creek until they came to within a bowshot of the wall, where a rickety bridge crossed the creek.

There was no sentry on the bridge, they were happy to see, but they also noted that the bridge itself was heavily warded. Had they crossed over it, instead of under it, they would have quickly alerted their foe if they hadn't been protected. Instead of lingering near the bridge they went another fifty feet and then crawled up the other bank, using the side of the ditch as cover as they tried to peer inside.

Do you think we could scry inside the walls? Tyndal asked, mind-to-mind.

Not one bit. They have it protected. Besides, I want to put eyes on whatever it is they don't want seen.

The gatehouse to the fortified manor - technically a castle, Rondal decided - was occupied by a band of gurvani, decked out in captured Gilmoran finery and gilded armor more suited to jousting than guarding. Most of them were asleep, sprawled out all over the cool stones of the gatehouse. Two actually leaned on spears, and one almost seemed awake.

Kefney Castle is under new management. So, do we just come up to them and tell them we're collecting for Trygg's temple houses for crippled children and ask for a donation?

Rondal wasn't paying attention to the guards, not really. He wanted to avoid the guards, asleep or not. He could tell his fellow wanted to fight, but that's not what this mission was about. Instead he scanned the walls. There were sentries there, but they seemed more concerned with looking inside, not outside.

And there was one section of the castle that seemed abandoned. On the far east side, Rondal observed, an outrigger square tower, part of an older section of the castle, had been unoccupied due to its ruined condition. The top of the tower was missing and the side gaped open, the result of some calamity.

Tyndal, wouldn't you say that was a Lord's Refuge? He asked, mind-to-mind.

That? An old one, maybe, he conceded. Back when this place was really about defense and not topiary. Why?

One important feature of a Lord's Refuge is usually the escape route it provides the lord's family, explained Rondal. *The point was you could escape to it from several points in the castle. Or escape from it to several points in the castle. Usually by an underground tunnel.*

Don't you think the gurvani know about that sort of thing?

No, not really. They've only been around our fortifications for a year or two. I'm guessing if you weren't aware of that, after attending Relan Cor, most of them might be ignorant as well.

You really can be an ass sometimes, Tyndal complained. Rondal smiled as he moved quietly toward the ruined tower. He considered it a compliment, coming from someone in the profession.

The tower had apparently been abandoned long before the goblins took residence, from the empty state of its interior. But the section of wall that connected it to the rest of the castle was still intact. A few boards were nailed over the big wooden door to keep anyone from wandering inside. No doubt the door at the other end was likewise secured, if not bricked over entirely.

Tyndal began doing a simple scanning of the stone floor of the tower without being asked, and they soon found a stairwell down to the basement. Once used for storing a little bit of everything, the litter and debris of a century of castle life had been scattered haphazardly around.

"Here!" Tyndal whispered harshly, outlining a section of stone wall under the staircase. "The stones all around this section aren't really mortared in. It's just for show."

"How do we open it?"

"I thought you were the expert with stone?"

Sighing, Rondal took a thoughtful look at the possible doorway and had to agree. There was a passageway concealed there. Sending his consciousness through the rock he could detect the great iron hinge that hung the heavy door. In a few moments, the great piece of iron had rusted away to nothing under his spellwork.

The door fell into the passageway behind it by six inches. With both of their shoulders on it, they were able to force it open enough to admit them into the stale-smelling tunnel.

"Magelight?" Tyndal asked.

"Cat's Eye," ordered Rondal, and both of them cast the spell that allowed them to see in the dark. A magelight might shine through and reveal them somehow. They slung their bows and drew their swords, Rondal and his shield in front as they went single file down the ancient tunnel.

Along the way they came to a chamber off to the side – not much, but enough of a space to harbor a sheaf of spears and a few iron helms. Just beyond it was a heavy and defendable door which, luckily, stood open. They moved carefully through and continued up a narrow flight of stairs. At the top, the passageway led right, left, and forward.

Which way?

Straight, Rondal decided. No particular reason why.

As luck would have it, the passageway Rondal had chosen led into the base of one of the towers that ringed the inner bailey of the structure, and into a hidden chamber. There were three separate doors, each concealed from the other side.

These Gilmoran lords dearly love their hidden passageways, Rondal chuckled.

They're for all the whores and mistresses, remarked Tyndal. *Hey, can you see out of that one?*

The door that led to the bailey did, indeed, have a gap next to it that allowed them to see out. Whatever decorative feature on the other side was so deeply cut that it could not be discerned as a fissure. As a result, they could see a great deal of what was going on inside the castle.

The sight was horrific.

Clustered in groups of a score were human slaves, bound neck and hands together, men, women and children. Almost all lacked shoes, and many had only a few scraps of clothing left. Everyone was sporting wicked-looking whip scars on their backs, arms, and faces. Among them toiled a few who brought water around to them, giving each but a few sips before they continued to the next.

They're almost dead of dehydration! Rondal told Tyndal, when he used his magesight to get a better look. *Look at them, the way they watch the slave with water. That's how they keep them docile. Give them just enough water to keep them cowed.*

There were guards among them, too. Mostly mangy-looking gurvani, many of them in tribal gear or captured armor, carrying clubs and whips. A few had spears, and all carried knives or short swords. Among them were a few humans who walked freely, if deferent to the goblins. Collaborators. Slavers. Traitors.

I think the whippings and summary executions might play a role, too, Tyndal pointed out sarcastically. *Dehydration keeps them weak. Fear and pain keep them docile.*

How many are out there?

They each counted, and then counted again. Over two hundred within their sight alone.

It seems a shame to leave them there, all tied up like that, Tyndal said.

We're not here to rescue them, we're here to observe, reminded Rondal. *I'd like to save them too, but there are just two of us.*

So?

There's a lot more of them. They taught us at War College that's a bad move.

So is this what the goblins were trying to hide? Slaves? We knew about their slaving operations. None of them looks capable of dropping a load as big as the one I saw. Maybe that plump burgher on the end, but . . .

We need a better view, sighed Rondal, turning away from the hole. *Where do these other doors lead?*

This one . . . likely to the chamber beyond, answered Tyndal, crossing to peer through its hidden viewport. *The place is filled with sleeping slaves. It looks like a banquet hall they're using as a pen.*

How many?

Another hundred, maybe. Tied hand-to-hand. The main door looks locked from the outside. This one is behind a tapestry, I think.

Rondal was peering through the third door. *This one is more stairs – going down. I think it leads to another tunnel. Probably into the keep,* he reasoned.

That sounds like an excellent vantage point, Tyndal agreed. *You know, this sneaking around stuff is kind of fun!*

It's one of the reasons warmagi make such expensive but useful mercenaries.

They followed the stairs back down, and then through a tunnel at least fifty feet long, narrow and close on all sides. Rondal eventually had to sling his shield and move sidewise, it narrowed so much. At last it came to a narrow passageway straight up, accessed by a stout wooden ladder.

They must have designed this as the lord's escape route, Rondal said excitedly as he began to climb the ladder. *Like Arsella's hidey-hole.*

Belsi, reminded Tyndal.

I knew her for weeks as Arsella, Rondal shot back. *Give me some time to adjust.*

Touchy . . .

You really shouldn't irritate the man climbing the ladder above you, Rondal pointed out. *Gravity is a cruel mistress.*

Just don't fart and nobody will get hurt.

Rondal didn't respond. He kept climbing.

Three stories of ladder led to the summit of the keep. The topmost rooms were reserved as the chamber of the lord and lady, as well as the living quarters of the senior servants. It was deserted now, the bedchamber thoroughly looted and destroyed.

But it was empty.

Rondal pushed the hidden door open from the inside, and a section of wall gave way. The top floor was deserted. There was no sign of goblin encampment here.

They don't particularly like heights, Tyndal reminded him. *The watchtower over in the outer bailey is taller, so they'll have their lookout there. You can't see much beyond the walls from here. But you can see just about – good gods eternal, what the hells is that?*

He pointed out of one of the arrow slits in the ruined chamber at what Rondal first thought was a rickety redoubt on a hill of dirt.

Then it moved.

It was a beast – a gigantic beast, easily fifty feet long from blunted snout to thick tail. Six giant, squat legs, as thick as the thickest tree Rondal had ever seen, supported the beast. The redoubt Rondal had seen was in fact a kind of saddle-fortress, a covered platform that could be filled with warriors in battle, creating a walking castle.

The redoubt was situated just behind the second pair of legs and secured with broad straps and ropes. Empty at the moment, Rondal was appalled to see. in addition to the platform for archers, some sort of cunning mechanism on the roof he guessed was a compact sort of ballistae or catapult.

That thing . . . that thing is a walking siege! Tyndal finally said.

What the hell is it? I've never even heard of something like this before!

It's like a leggy worm, only . . . that snout. It's got a thick plate of horn or bone or something on it.

Like a living battering ram, agreed Rondal. *How long would it take to go through a castle gatehouse with that?*

A lot less time that it would take to attack with trolls or scrugs, agreed Tyndal, darkly. *Shit, Ron, what does that thing eat?*

I don't see any fodder around, Rondal said, scanning the courtyard below. Then he realized the awful truth when the great beast yawned

Oh. Never mind. Look at those teeth, he said. Its head was like a huge alien tortoise. The teeth it revealed were sharp, pointed, and numerous. *I'm guessing its carnivorous. And I bet it eats people.*

That's why they haven't moved these poor bastards north yet! They're supplying their siege worms!

That's . . . that's horrible, Rondal said, shaking his head.

Tyndal looked at him. *Feel different about a rescue mission, now?*

Rondal stared at him. His mission was accomplished. They knew what the goblins were hiding, and why. It would only take a moment to alert Commander Terleman, mind-to-mind, and then they could return.

Only that would leave the hundreds of people below to die in the jaws of that hideous beast.

Gods, I hate you sometimes, Rondal said, shaking his head.

Just keeping you on the path of chivalry.

How do you propose we take on . . . Trygg only knows how many goblins, at least a shaman, possibly more, there could always be a couple of trolls hiding out in the cellar, and at least a dozen vile remnants of humanity who are collaborating with the enemy? Oh, yes, a fifty-foot long death machine that seems to eat people?

Easy, Tyndal smiled. *Remember, there are two of us.*

Every castle and manor house had a cistern, and most had many. As much as a castle relied upon a well within the walls of the bailey to slake the thirst of the besieged, in dire circumstances, when a retreat to a tower or keep was necessary, it became important to ensure a temporary supply.

Kefney Castle was no different. In fact the third-tallest tower overlooking the inner bailey had a large one, at least a thousand gallons, fed by rainwater and magically protected from stagnation. It was at the center of the top-most floor of the tower, a chamber of rock lined with clay. But cisterns needed to be emptied and repaired from time to time, and a drain a foot wide led to the inner bailey for that purpose.

Rondal had let himself be persuaded to approve of Tyndal's plan mostly because of the profound distraction the sudden appearance of that much water to that many people so close to being mad with thirst would produce.

There were guards enough to handle a few isolated incidence of resistance among the humans huddled around their knees. If several hundred of them all went into action at once, they would be hard-pressed to keep control of the situation.

And once an angry siege worm was loosed on the scene, well, Rondal couldn't deny that whatever mayhem and destruction it wrought was no less than the goblins deserved. While he knew that some people would inevitably get killed in the fight that was a better fate for them than being wormfodder.

Tyndal had volunteered to make his way quietly across the rooftops of the manor over to the tower, which was taking enough time so that Rondal was able to make a brief report, mind-to-mind, to Terleman while he waited. The military commander was surprised and disheartened by the news of the siege worms, but he took the news coolly. When he was done with the conversation, Rondal checked in with Tyndal, who was still slowly creeping across the rooftops trying not to be seen.

It's going to be at least another half-hour, he reported. *There are more sentries on the back side of the keep, and I'm trying to avoid them. See if you can keep yourself busy until I get there.*

By doing what? I left my embroidery back at the manor, he replied sourly.

What about contacting those other prisoners, the ones in the banquet hall, and arming them with those siege spears we saw in the tunnel? And maybe getting the women and children out through the secret passage? That might be a better use of your time than needlepoint. Just do it quietly.

That's . . . that's not a bad idea, actually, Rondal admitted. He hated when Tyndal was right.

He looked through the squint hole into the banquet hall-turned-prison, and with his Cat's Eye spell he was able to see dozens of bodies crammed into the room. A few were pressed up against the wall, so when he did finally release the catch on the concealed door, two poor souls spilled into the hidden compartment, squeaking in surprise.

"Shhh!" Rondal said, insistently. "I'm here to help rescue you, but you must be silent!"

"Wha—?" asked one dull-witted fellow. "Is it my turn for the beasty, now?"

"I'm here to *rescue* you!" Rondal repeated, looking to the other man – a younger, scrawny fellow who looked like he'd been beaten a few times – where he found more wit looking back.

"I'm Sir Rondal of Sevendor. I'm under the command of King Rard," he said, hoping invoking the new monarch's name would grant him some authority with the half-mad prisoners. "Is there a leader among you?" he asked, hopefully.

"Aye, milord!" the skinny man nodded, "I'll go fetch him!"

"Silently!" Rondal insisted. He waited patiently with the thicker fellow, shushing his every attempt to make a sound.

Soon three more men stumbled back through the darkness and into the hidden chamber. One was a tall bearded man of noble bearing, the other a shrewd-looking hawk-nosed fellow in sturdy garments. Neither looked as distressed as the first two prisoners he'd encountered.

"I am Sir Rondal of Sevendor," he said in a whisper. "I've come to try to help."

"I am Sire Darduin of Romm," said the bearded man, "this is Master Gil the Weaver. We . . . we keep things in order," he said. "How many are you?"

"Not many," Tyndal admitted. "But they know not that we are here. There is a passageway leading out of the castle. I want you to quietly –

silently! – gather the women, children, old and sick and file them down into the passage.

"Have them gather in the ruined tower, but they should make no move out of it until our diversion occurs. Then they should run south for their lives. I'm afraid I don't have any advice beyond that – we're too few to give you any aid. But we can give you a chance at escape."

"Duin's axe, that's all we have prayed for!" Sire Darduin said, fervently.

"The guards check on us every hour," reported Master Gil. "They made their last check only ten minutes ago. But some of our fellows are half-mad with hunger and thirst. We must be careful lest they alert our jailors."

"What about the wounded?" Rondal asked.

"There are few," admitted Sire Darduin, grimly. "When someone gets hurt, they become the next meal for that horror out there."

"We saw it," nodded Rondal. "Children?"

"Only a few. They took . . . they took most of them away when we first arrived. But we will get the non-combatants to safety first. I just fear discovery, if we make too much noise . . ."

"I can cure that," Rondal said. "Lead me to this door."

Making their way gingerly through the crowded hall, around moaning and wretched bodies who watched him with the dazed expression that told him they knew not whether he was real or phantom, he came to the great wooden double doors that in better days had made a jolly and homey entrance to this hall. Now the polished wood was hacked and pitted and bloodied, barred from the outside.

Rondal first cast a silencing spell that would permit no noise to pass beyond the door. Then he spellbound it with a simple cantrip. Not enough to stand up to a counterspell, but easily enough to prevent someone opening the door without one.

"All right, let's get them moving," Rondal said in a louder voice, once he was done. "Sire Darduin, there is a cache of siege spears down that passageway. Can I trust you to select the twenty men best able to use them, and return to this hall?"

"To what purpose? And what did you do to the door?"

"I am a knight mage," Rondal explained, dismissively. "I spellbound it and proofed it against sound. We have a little time and freedom, now. "

He realized something was bothering him. He took his water bottle from his pack and handed it to the knight, who gratefully took a swallow – but only one – and passed it to the weaver, who did likewise.

"If we can get a few stalwarts with spears here to act as a rear-guard, we can ensure your people have the best chance at escape. In addition," he said, cagily, "once our diversion begins, it may be helpful to suddenly have an organized force to deploy against them." He looked at the knight and the weaver appraisingly. "Can I count on you gentlemen to lead that force?"

They conferred quietly, but quickly. "I will lead the spears," declared Darduin, "while Master Gil will lead the prisoners away, if that be permitted."

"I know a village nearby where we might hide through the night," he explained.

"Good," nodded Rondal. "After that, make for the southern horizon. We have a hidden outpost at Maramor Manor, and we have a cache at Farune Hall, so if you can make it to one of those places we might be able to speed you further, but . . ."

"A chance is all we ask for," the weaver assured him.

It took nearly twenty minutes to pass the word and get the prisoners sorted out, but things went more efficiently than Rondal had anticipated.

Sire Darduin brooked no resistance to his authority, and Master Gil was persuasive and insistent. Between the two men and a few lieutenants, they had ushered the majority of the frightened people out of the wretched hall and into the escape prepared for them, without detection.

Meanwhile some had been sent back for arms, and in addition to the spears had brought out a few helmets, a few axes, knives, and other weapons they'd found roaming the other hidden passages. Rondal feared that one of them would inadvertently alert the foe, but that was an increasingly moot point: Tyndal was almost in position.

This is a lot harder than I thought it would be, he complained.

I'm trying to keep a hundred thirst-crazed prisoners from rioting and organizing an escape, Rondal shot back. *So glad that I gave you the difficult task.*

The men who were remained, willing to fight, were a mixed collection of peasants, tradesmen, and a few men-at-arms, many with some militia training or war experience. Sire Duin detailed an older man to organize the makeshift squad while Master Gil bid Rondal good-bye.

"Can you use a bow?" he asked, suddenly. "Take mine," he offered, pushing it and his quiver into the weaver's hands.

"I've plucked a few strings in my life," the man said with amusement as he accepted the weapon. "Thank you, Sir Rondal, and the blessing of Duin go with you!"

To Sire Darduin he gave his roundshield, and the knight armed himself with a short axe someone had uncovered in the passageways. He looked valiant and grim as he swung the axe through the air a few times.

"I thank you for giving me a chance to die on my feet like a man," he said quietly. "Those scrugs killed my wife in front of me and led me and my people away in chains. Would that I had died in that attack. Many a time I have prayed to Duin for one last opportunity to strike at them, and lo! The Destroyer has heard my prayer!"

Rondal wasn't terribly comfortable being viewed as an agent of

487

divine will, so he returned to more practical matters. He drew his mageblade and sketched out the situation on the other side of the door under a dim magelight, until the men felt they had a good grasp of what they faced. None looked particularly hale, but they all seemed enthusiastic.

Since they were all probably about to die, that was probably fortunate, if foolish.

I'm in position, Tyndal finally reported. *As soon as I catch my breath, I'll start. How are things looking down there?*

While you were gaily skipping across rooftops, I made a couple of squads of light infantry. After you soak the courtyard, we'll wait until things get nasty. Then these fellows will attack whatever organized response they put together from an unexpected direction.

And . . . then what?

That was a good question. What happened after they stirred this chamberpot of horrors into deadly chaos? A good plan usually has a point, he chided himself.

I'll look toward the prisoners, Rondal decided. *You tackle that siege worm.*

Me? There's just one of me!

And there's only the one siege worm. What could be more glorious? Rondal shot back, amused. *You wanted a challenge—*

I didn't want a bloody suicide mission!

Don't be such a baby. I don't expect you to slay it. Just test it. See what it responds to, what its weaknesses are, what it is resistant to. Stuff that would be useful to know the next time we face one.

That's a pretty big order.

That's the only kind knights magi get. Just try not to get yourself killed. Challenge it, test it, but don't try to kill it, if it's too much problem. Or do you want to trade positions and have me go after the worm? he challenged.

I can only guess that this is part of your elaborate plan to become senior apprentice, Tyndal said. *All right, I've caught my breath. I'm in position. I've got a wand pointed right at the wooden drain. The water . . . well, it's cistern water.*

I'm guessing the dying prisoners won't be picky. Wait for my order.

Yes, Commander.

Damn. Rondal thought he almost sounded serious in his response.

"Prepare your men for action, Sire," he told the axe-wielding knight. "When I give the word, charge out that door and slay every goblin in sight. Free other prisoners, arm them, and keep fighting until you're free."

"Duin's blessing go with you, Sir Rondal!" the big knight called as Rondal went back into the secret chamber, after lifting the spellbinding from the banquet hall. He wanted to be able to provide better direction, and as much fun as leading a ragtag infantry squad into battle against desperate odds would be, he had other responsibilities.

He took position behind the door that led to the bailey and peered out of the peep hole. He could see the rump of the six-legged siege worm, huddled prisoners, sleepy goblins, sinister-looking human collaborators.

He watched one of the cutthroats who had taken the Dead God's coin to war against his own kind look appraisingly over one knot of prisoners, mostly women, tied up in front of what was once the castle's herb house. A nasty, rat-like man with a hooked nose looked over the prisoners before selecting one, a young woman who looked so dazed with thirst she did not know what was happening. With a leering eye he forced her to her feet, his intentions clear.

Now, Rondal said to Tyndal, without thinking, *do it now!*

It seemed to take hours for anything to happen – the rat-like man was almost out of sight, the poor girl he'd taken as his prize led away like a dog – when a rumble and geyser from the drain way began spilling a torrent of water down into the bailey, over the heads of some surprised prisoners . . . and within sight of all the rest.

There, he heard Tyndal report. *If that's all you require of me . . .*

Go fight your worm, Rondal ordered. *As soon as you're able to get free, cut out. I'll meet you back where we left the horses.*

The sudden appearance of life-giving water had the desired effect. Already there was a riot brewing in the bailey, he could see through the port. The prisoners who were not directly under the spout saw the water and went mad. Ignoring the guards, the goblins, the worm, even their own bonds, they surged toward the unexpected blessing with incredible force and speed. People were shouting with joy and terror as the bewildered guards frantically tried to keep order.

The human confederates shrank back against so many of their fellows, and a few of the prisoners took advantage of the chaos to strike down their captors. But most continued toward the water, even as it splashed across the bailey toward them.

It only took moments for the goblin guards to wake their sleeping comrades, and soon fresh troops were pouring in from the gatehouse and various dens around the castle. A line of them formed behind the crowd – directly in front of the door where the newly-armed former prisoners awaited.

"Attack!" Rondal shouted at the men. They opened the door and charged out, spears held ready, and crashed into the back of the goblin line with a savage growl. The freed prisoners fought ferociously, stabbing and slashing with their spears like fanatics. More came behind them, arming themselves and other prisoners from the fallen goblins. As the gurvani turned to face this unexpected threat, Rondal realized that he was in a very good position to attack their flank. All by himself.

He pushed the concealed door open. It had been so long since it had been used he had to put his shoulder behind it, hard, but it soon swung open, spilling him into the bright courtyard. All around him there was screams and tumult, and the smell of blood was starting to linger in the air as the battle to his left matured. There were over a score of freed prisoners armed well enough to give fight to the confused and increasingly panicked goblins.

Rondal pointed his mageblade at the goblins lined up before him and threw a solid sheet of painful magical force from it. The invisible spell lanced out from his sword point and suddenly the bulk of them began to stumble and scream.

While that was gratifying, it did little real damage. The damage was being done by thirst-crazed prisoners who were freeing and arming themselves – and throwing themselves at their captors with vengeance in their eyes. Writhing in pain was a poor defensive posture, even against such poorly armed foes, and the goblins died quickly.

Rondal continued to walk steadily through the tumult, his mageblade in one hand, a warwand in the other, doing what he could to help the prisoner uprising. A blast from a wand or a timely slice with his blade settled many contests, and the grateful victors were quick to distribute looted weapons to other prisoners.

Twice he fought in protracted duels, once with a grim-faced human collaborator with an axe and once with a snarling goblin warrior wielding a short stabbing sword with impressive ferocity. In each case he used an unexpected blast from wand or blade to end the contest.

Just as he was wondering where Tyndal was, he heard a bravado-filled cry, and watched in horror as his fellow apprentice repelled down the tower he'd been safely in and leap onto the back of the siege beast.

The great worm did not notice him in the slightest, thanks to the distraction of a riot in front of it. The animal was dull-witted, either naturally or from domesticated service, but it wasn't unresponsive. Tyndal fell onto the upper torso of the thing, ahead of the empty wooden castle saddled on its back, and began firing at the goblin attendants desperately attempting to keep the creature from bolting.

Then another knot of goblins charged, attempting to restore order with spear hafts and clubs against unarmed, starving, and weakened prisoners. Rondal gave them a fully-armed and armored, well-fed and well-rested knight mage to contend with instead.

When the last body slipped from his blade he looked up to see that his foes were getting themselves better organized. The thin, reedy horns the gurvani favored bellowed, summoning more reinforcements, and someone was gathering a force of them in front of the great hall. There were a score there already, and more were fleeing from individual engagements with the enraged prisoners to find safety in regrouping.

Tyndal, quit messing around! Rondal sent through their link. *They're going to have those fell hounds in here shortly, and then they'll all be torn to shreds!*

What do you think I'm trying to do! Do they still hold the gatehouse?

Rondal spared a quick glance. The nearest organized – if that term could be used – band of prisoners was still hundreds of feet from the gatehouse, and it seemed to be held in force. The portcullis was down, and the drawbridge seemed to be up. Rondal could see dozens of little black furry figures inside, frantically trying to secure their station.

They still hold it, Rondal agreed. *It's going to take a lot to get through that, too,* he added. *And we have fresh resistance pouring out from the great hall.*

Lovely. Well, I have an idea.

I'm terrified, Rondal said, parrying a quick blow that would have taken his knee, and then slicing neatly and efficiently through the goblin's neck. *What is it?*

It occurs to me, Tyndal began, quoting a signature Sire Cei line, *that we happen to have a fully-operational siege beast here.*

Which you cannot control, Rondal pointed out.

I won't need to, Tyndal explained. Rondal watched as he ran up the beasts neck toward its head, where a goblin drover had managed to find a perch. A flash of light sent the goblin flying to his doom. *I just need to get it moving. If it can break into a castle, it can break out of one.*

Rondal was about to object to the possibility of such mass carnage when he heard the baying of those foul hounds from behind the great hall. *Whatever you're going to do, do it quick! Or we're looking at a really furry bloodbath!*

As you wish, Commander, Tyndal said. Rondal could almost hear the cocky grin. A few moments later there was a pop, another flash . . . and a monstrous bellow that stopped the entire battle for a brief moment of terror.

I think I pissed it off, Tyndal said quietly in Rondal's mind.

You tend to have that affect, agreed Rondal. *Is it moving?*

Before Tyndal could answer, the ground shook, and then shook again. The great beast strained against the chains that held it . . . until Tyndal helpfully blasted them. Then the huge, lizard-like animal began pushing toward the front entrance of the castle, anxious to escape whatever it was that irritated it.

It's moving, Tyndal agreed. *Headed your way. I'd move, if I were you.*

"EVERYONE CLEAR THE WAY!" Rondal bellowed in his best battlefield voice. "NOW!"

Only a few of the prisoners heeded his warning, at first, but the moment the siege beast's gigantic head loomed overhead, everyone – goblin and human alike – fled its path. Not all were lucky enough to do so, and the hideous monster left red-smeared footprints all the way across the courtyard.

"Follow the beast out!" commanded Rondal. He looked over to the battered and bloodied knight, Sir Darduin, who had lost his axe but kept his shield and had liberated a cavalry sword from somewhere. "Sire! You are the rear-guard! Get your men to keep the goblins from hindering our escape!" The knight wordlessly saluted to acknowledge the order and turned to give some of his own.

That was about the best Rondal could do, as he moved himself out of the way of the huge creature. Tyndal was still riding atop it, grinning maniacally and successfully keeping the goblin drovers from recapturing the worm. He waved from its back as he passed by Rondal, as if he was in a parade.

You had better get off that thing before it hits the gate, warned Rondal as he directed more prisoners to follow the beast, not flee from it.

I want to see what it does, protested Tyndal.

We know what it does, countered Rondal. *It smashes, crashes, and destroys. Or were you planning on seducing it, too? Tired of goats already?*

All right, all right, grumbled the other wizard. *I'm off of it now, about ten yards from the gatehouse on the left. Join me?*

I'll be there momentarily, he said, and turned back to Sir Darduin. "Lead them out through the breach," he instructed. "Keep the goblins off of them until they're clear of the gate, then run for your lives south."

"Thank you for the opportunity to avenge my kin," the knight said, gravely. "I shall never forget you, Sir Rondal!"

"Duin's blessing, Sire Darduin!" Rondal said, clasping the older man's shoulder before he moved on.

Tyndal was standing next to the gate as the beast demolished it in a blind, animalistic rage.

"I've been irritating its hindquarters with magic," he explained. "I kept thinking about that poop, and what would irritate a three-feet wide butt-hole. I figured that the tender parts wouldn't be armored, and I was right. I gave it a nasty case of magically stinging rectum."

"Well, if anyone knows how to be a pain in the ass, it's you," Rondal agreed.

Tyndal ignored the jibe. "I think we've done everything we can here. We should be going." The siege worm lunged aggressively against the gatehouse one final time, toppling the masonry and creating a breach large enough to escape through. A flood of terrified prisoners trailed behind, some stopping to finish off the gurvani trapped by the rubble.

"As soon as the gate is clear," Tyndal agreed. "You lost your shield," he observed.

"Someone else needed it more than I," dismissed Rondal. "And we'll travel faster without it. We bolt for the horses, then make our way back to Maramor. We need to make a full report of this to Commander Terleman."

"This might help," Tyndal said, hefting an odd-looking contraption of beads, ropes, leather and bone. "This was the magical device controlling the beast, I think. We can learn a lot from it."

"That . . . was actually a really good idea," Rondal admitted, as he looked around. The baying of the hounds was coming closer. "Stow it away, and help me think of a way to keep these curs off of our people."

Tyndal nodded, and obediently did as he asked. Rondal was amazed. No argument, no banter, no discourse on his shortcomings . . . Tyndal just did as he was ordered.

Rondal struggled with that a moment. A year ago, that just would not have happened. He couldn't have said the sky was blue without getting an argument. Now . . . now he wasn't sure if the change had been wrought in Tyndal, or in himself, but he was sure he liked it. Even if he was uncomfortable with it.

They elected to do a quick field of sigils, a variation of a simple spellmonger's enchantment to keep stray dogs out of chicken coops. With the power of two witchstones at their command the effect was far more severe. When the squadron of gurvani cavalry loped around the corner of the hall, they ran into the field and their canine mounts immediately began whining and howling, not chasing their prey with eagerness.

"Let's get out of here," Tyndal said. "It won't take long for them to find a way around that."

They climbed through the breach, dispensing advice and encouragement to the half-starved prisoners until they had cleared the debris-filled moat in the wake of the beast. The worm was plodding across country now, moving slowly but irresistibly east across the barren fields, trailing a few screaming gurvani drovers who were desperately trying to bring their charge under control.

The two young knights made good time, once they reached the road. Most of the prisoners had fanned out and taken off cross-country, now, so there was little to slow them down. Using warmagic to improve their endurance and speed, they had made it back to where their horses were hidden without incident . . . when the baying of the fell hounds sounded again.

"Looks like the bad puppy spell wasn't that effective," Tyndal said, discouraged, as he mounted.

"We're here, aren't we? And if it's any consolation, I doubt they pooped in the area of effect. The spell was a complete success. It was just not the best spell for the job."

"Let's not dally with experimentation today, all right?" asked Tyndal as they spurred their horses. "I used the last charge on my last wand attacking that beast, and I lost Slasher."

"Ouch!" Rondal winced. "That's not going to please Master Min!"

"Either would my corpse, I'm guessing. I picked up a sword on the way out from one of the collaborators," he said, gesturing to the plain-hilted blade at his side. They wasted no more words as they sped toward where their friends were hidden, waiting for them.

Unfortunately, before they could arrive there the first of their pursuers were after them. The large dogs that made up the gurvani cavalry were fast, and they moved in packs through terrain a horse would avoid. Each one had a small, vicious-looking goblin with a slashing spear or sword on its back, as well as being well armed with tooth and claw. As they raced with his courser he spared them quick glances to size up his foes.

Tyndal noted with professional interest that they had a feral cunning in their small black eyes, unlike any dog or wolf he'd had ever seen. Their fur was thick and matted, black and gray and brown, and their faces were squatter than the hounds of Sevendor. Thick, sharp teeth protruded from their shaggy muzzles, fangs as cruel as daggers.

And they were fast. Before they knew it, there was one dogging Rondal's left stirrup, trying to slash at his mount's legs with his spear. Rondal kicked him in the face with his boot and sent the goblin flying. The hound, however, kept up his pursuit until a quick thrust with his mageblade ended the chase. Another replaced him almost at once, weaving between them and going after Tyndal.

Rondal tossed Tyndal a warwand and mentally told him the command word and mentioned it only had a single charge, and Tyndal blasted it and then threw the empty stick at the next mutt. There were a half-dozen canines keeping pace behind them, snarling and baying. For a terrified moment he was very sympathetic to the fox who was victim to the hunt.

We're not going to be able to keep this up forever, Rondal sent to Tyndal as they rode for their lives. Mind-to-mind communication was actually easier than shouting over the hoof beats and pounding of his heart.

That's what they're counting on, Tyndal realized. *Horses can run a long way, but a dog pack can run in relays. You remember how the mountain wolves could chase a cow down . . .*

They must have bred wolves with those Minden's farm dogs, Rondal suggested. *They have the same bone structure and coloration. But those legs and tail, that's all wolf.*

I hadn't noticed, Tyndal said, dryly. *If we don't lose them soon, then the horses will lather. Then they'll slow, and then . . .*

I know. We need to break their chase. Any ideas?

Magic?

Anything more specific? asked Rondal, patiently as he spurred his mount even faster.

Magic that works against dogs?

Well . . . don't we know a few spells like that? Rondal pointed out.

Tyndal's smile told him he realized that his commander was right. They had learned plenty of spells concerning canines . . . not at Relan Cor or even at Inrion Academy, but back in Boval Vale when they were both spellmongers' apprentices.

One of the mainstays of the rural spellmonger were enchantments to keep various types of livestock safely in their enclosures and pastures and not wandering off to get eaten or poached or impounded by the stockwarden.

Among the arsenal of common spells every spellmonger knew were plenty to keep dogs from barking, keep them in their yards and lots, keep them from harassing the chickens or horses or goats, spells to keep them alert at night, spells to keep them pooping in convenient places, spells to make their noses better in the hunt . . . and spells to ward against strays, trespassers and feral dogs.

In fact, Tyndal realized, he had learned more about battling canines in his first six months as a mage than he'd learned in the two years since. And dog spells were relatively simple, because dogs were relatively simple. But which one to cast . . .

He settled on a nameless spell used to distract and misdirect dogs away from areas they weren't allowed. Its mechanism involved convincing the dog in question that they were seeing something far more interesting elsewhere. Tyndal liked it because it was a nice blend of Blue and Brown magic, and elegant in its simplicity. Using a phantom rabbit to lure their pursuers from their trail seemed deliciously poetic for some reason.

He summoned the power from his stone while he rode, which was simple, and then projected the symbols he needed to focus and tune the energy. An irresistible squirrel, it would seem to the dogs, just to the side of the pursuit. With a devilish grin Tyndal glanced over his shoulder, targeted the largest of the hounds to focus the center of his spell upon, and then he activated the illusion.

The effect was almost instantaneous. Suddenly the three dogs on their heels, their riders preparing to slash at their mounts' legs, veered crazily to the east, almost ninety degrees from the road. The gurvani squealed in protest, but the hounds were relentless. They abandoned the pursuit of the horses in favor of the juiciest rodent their minds could conceive of.

How's that? Tyndal asked with a grin.

I'm impressed, Rondal grudgingly admitted. *How long do you think it will take for them to regain control?*

Not long, agreed Tyndal, reluctantly. *I wouldn't slow down the horses just yet.*

Good idea, agreed Rondal, looking over his shoulder at the misdirected dogs.

They continued galloping for another five minutes, covering a lot of road. They didn't slow until they came to a small bridge, unguarded, just before the turn toward the crossroad where they had left Belsi and Alwer. Tyndal hurriedly cast some protective spells to foul their pursuit while Rondal watered the horses.

"Not much longer now," he observed when he led both steeds back to the bank.

"Until we die a gruesome death?" Tyndal remarked. "Probably. But we still have half a day's ride over hostile country before we get back to Maramor. If, that is, we've kept them off our trail."

"Let's go overland," suggested Rondal. "If we take the horses across and then skirt the other bank a few hundred yards, we should keep them guessing. We can cut through the fields and get to the crossroads without leaving much of a trail."

They moved quickly, jumping the horses over ditches and the low stone walls that separated the fields here. They came to the road just a few hundred feet from the crossroads. The burned-out hovel that may have once been an inn was familiar, but there was no sign of their companions. When they got to the crossroad Rondal dismounted and began scrying to locate them.

"They were going to hide in that grove," Tyndal reminded him, helpfully.

"I know," Rondal said, sullenly. "Only they aren't there now."

"What?"

"Scry for yourself," shrugged Rondal. "They aren't there."

"Then where are they?" Tyndal asked, anxiously. "They were supposed to be at the grove!"

"I don't know!" snapped Rondal. "Let me . . . oh. All right, I think they moved further up the road. Maybe a hundred, two hundred yards."

"Why?" demanded Tyndal.

"Maybe the area got too crowded?" Rondal suggested, as he knelt in the dust of the crossroad. "I'm a lousy tracker, but these . . . these are fresh." He suddenly stood, his eyes wide in alarm as he searched the brush and ruins surrounding the crossroad. If he recalled correctly there was fresh litter strewn about the place, and the dusty in the road did look freshly trod. He suddenly felt dozens of eyes on the back of his neck.

"Ron . . ." Tyndal began, nervously, his hand moving to the hilt of his captured blade.

"I can feel it," Rondal confirmed, "probably an infantry patrol with a shaman covering for—"

He was interrupted by the twang of a bowstring and the woosh of a black-fletched arrow with a jagged iron point whizzing within inches of his ear. Both knights turned to face their attackers, drawing their blades as they did so. More arrows flew, but thankfully in the light of day most goblins were poor shots with their short bows and their shafts fell short.

The gurvani were starting to charge out of the brush next to the road, a half-dozen with spears and bows – an infantry patrol, as Rondal had guessed. But there was indeed a shaman – one of the lowlier types – in the back, waving his hands and conspiring to do them harm. Tyndal spurred his horse to ride the gurvan down as Rondal invoked his combat magic and began slicing goblins apart.

The moment his awareness stretched to take in the entire scene, he understood just how much trouble they were facing. Not just the shaman, but more than two dozen goblins were springing from their hidden positions and rushing at them.

He slashed adeptly through the throats of the first two who charged him, their spears lowered to skewer, then spun with enough force to bisect the spine of the third. Before his body hit the ground the point of Rondal's mageblade was buried in the chest of a fourth . . . but there were more coming.

He looked frantically around for his mount, which was beginning to shy away from the attack demonstrating good sense. Rondal sprang back with an augmented leap and clambered into the saddle just as Tyndal was ceremoniously leaping from his own saddle to tackle the shaman, sword in hand.

Of course the idiot was oblivious of the six or seven other goblins rapidly closing in behind him. His horse was kicking at them, but defensively, not aggressively, and they were ignoring it in favor of the foolhardy knight. If Rondal didn't do something, the lad would be overwhelmed. While he briefly considered hanging back and watching how his fellow responded to the challenge, he also knew that would not be good leadership. This was a fight, not a sparring match, and Tyndal was his rival, not his enemy.

His stock of hung spells was dangerously low, but there were a few left. He recalled one from Relan Cor that might break the foe's momentum, one developed for use in dispersing crowds during riots or peasant uprisings: an obnoxiously loud and sudden blast of sound, pressure, light, and magic that caused disorientation and loss of balance temporarily. It was called the Castigatix and it didn't take much power, preparation time, or focus to release. He called the spell's mnemonic, targeted the knot of knight and goblins in his mind, and spoke the command word.

The effect was startling. The sudden noise and wave of chaotic sensory data caused all affected to spin around drunkenly as they lost their balance and flinched. Tyndal was in the thick of it, but was spared the brunt by the bodies of his foes. Still, he careened crazily as he slashed at the body of the shaman with his sword, something clutched in his fist.

Rondal rode quickly to where his fellow was and started taking apart disoriented gurvani skulls with meticulous precision while Tyndal struggled to get his boot in the stirrup. Rondal finally had to tuck his sword under his arm and steady his companion as he tried to right himself.

"What in the name of Ishi's twat was that?" demanded Tyndal. "Castigatix?"

"First time I've used it," Rondal said as he kicked at a goblin that was vomiting profusely on the corpse of his shaman. Castigatix was a nasty spell. "I like it."

"Try being on the other side!" Tyndal complained. It looked like his eyes were having a hard time focusing. "Let's go, they're regrouping!"

"Why did you tackle him like that?" Rondal asked, a note of criticism in his voice.

"The glass," Tyndal grinned, holding up a bloody green stone between the fingertips of his riding gloves. "One more High Mage for our side!"

"If we get back alive and intact," conceded Rondal gruffly. He had to admit that acquiring irionite was worth the risk. Every warmage and knight mage they could put on the field was a victory. He looked back at a few gurvani archers preparing to fire. "Can you gallop?"

"No, but my horse can," Tyndal said, lamely, as he blinked his eyes.

"Just go, and he'll follow you!"

They spurred their mounts and outpaced the feeble bowshots that tracked them, moving so fast they almost missed the copse of trees that Alwer and Belsi had taken refuge in. The two stumbled out after the knights had passed them, calling for them to wait.

The reunion was brief – neither commoner had killed the other while they were gone.

"We had to move, my lord," Alwer explained to him, as they continued down the road. "The land is filled with those damned dogs of theirs, and they can smell a trail as well as any bloodhound. We shot two or three and escaped."

"You did well," agreed Rondal. He glanced at Belsi, who looked pale and frightened, her crossbow cocked and loaded. "You are unhurt?" She nodded, but didn't say anything else. She was trembling.

Rondal's heart lurched for a moment, when she would not meet his eye, but he pushed the feeling away. He had a mission to accomplish. "Back to Farune. I don't want to lead them back to Maramor."

"Farune?" Belsi asked, her eyes wide with concern. "Then . . .?"

"One godsdamned thing at a time!" Rondal burst. She finally met his eye . . . but only when it was her fate in jeopardy, he noted. He hardened his heart a bit, part of him disgusted at her self-interest. They may not be alive by dusk, and she was wondering about her inheritance? Or even her charges?

The foursome spurred their horses as fast as they could, pounding down the road until they had to slow to rest them. Alwer related a more detailed version of their fight and retreat, and Rondal assured him that he had done well. Tyndal was right: the man was a good irregular fighter.

Dusk fell as they neared Farune, and Rondal was beginning to feel hopeful that they might elude pursuit. Those hopes were dashed the moment he scryed the area. There were clearly several goblins about, moving quickly. More quickly than a gurvan on foot. Fell hound cavalry, it had to be. They must want the boys awfully bad, after what they had done to Kefney Castle.

"Back on the horses," he ordered, only moments after they stopped. "We have pursuit . . . the closest is less than a quarter-mile away, to the southwest. We need to get going and we do not stop moving until—"

One of the tinny-sounding horns the gurvani used as an alarm sounded to the south, and another answered from the west.

"Oh, three bloody hells!" Tyndal said, his face almost looking normal now. He drew his captured sword again. "That *was* close!"

"Ride!" Rondal yelled, as he jumped back in the saddle, slapping Belsi's mount on the hock as he did to encourage it along. The baying of the fell hounds could be heard echoing across the land. They continued to ride as fast as they could make the horses, already tired.

They found new inspiration when another group of goblin cavalry spilled out onto the road only a hundred yards behind them and began tearing after them. Arrows and javelin whizzed past them. Most were wild shots fired in haste, but no less deadly if they found their mark.

I've got an idea, Tyndal sent to him as he brought up the rear, *if they can chase us in relays, we can defend in relays!*

What? What do you mean? Rondal replied, his hands holding the reins tightly.

I'll ride forward and prepare a defense, you ride past me while I hold them off, just throw them a bit, and give you a chance to ride ahead and prepare the next defense while the others ride past.

That's . . . that's a decent plan, Rondal agreed. *Go ahead, I'll tell the others.*

Rondal watched as Tyndal stood in the saddle, another goblin arrow passing harmlessly overhead, and urge his horse into an even faster gait. He spared a glance backwards, seeing the lead hound only thirty feet behind, and three more just behind him. Their vicious little riders were continuing to lob missiles at the horses, but they hadn't closed enough to employ their nasty blades.

He really hoped this would work. He didn't think their mounts could handle much more of this pace before one of them faltered. He said as much to Alwer and Belsi, as he watched Tyndal pull his reins and wheel his courser around, his hands instantly moving to draw forth a spell.

As he passed by he could feel the spell his comrade had built release – something sharp seemed to cut the air. A blast of sound exploded at his back, making his ears ring and his head hurt. He could only imagine what it did to the sensitive ears of the hounds.

Oh, well cast! he sent to Tyndal, without thinking about it.

Thanks! Tyndal said, a note of surprise in his voice. *I figured that dogs don't like squeaky wagons and other high-pitched noises. They probably wouldn't like a soundstrike spell.*

How did they react?

It bought us another hundred feet, Tyndal said, *but those bastards are still back there. I did my bit – your turn!*

Rondal sighed and spurred his horse on with determination – determination not to look bad in front of Tyndal. As his horse outpaced the others, he began thinking furiously about what he could do that would be effective against a pack of dogs. Sound, of course, as Tyndal had pointed out . . . but what other weaknesses did canines have?

He had found a spot in the road at the top of a rise he felt would make a good stand, and he pulled his horse to a halt. The beast was grateful for the rest, but it wasn't unaware of the baying hounds that pursued, and it was reluctant to turn and face the threat.

Rondal's mind raced through a variety of esoteric attacks, discarding one after the other until he came to one that seemed appropriate. Rondal began calling power and weaving the foundations of the spell the moment he decided, creating a swirling vortex of concentrated magical energy between his hands as his comrades thundered toward him.

The goblins were almost fifty paces behind their prey at this point, thanks to Tyndal's spell. If Rondal could peel off another fifty with this attack, perhaps they could slip down some side track and elude them. The ball of power grew, and when it reached a reasonable size Rondal began shifting the mode of energy expressed within into something very specific. Ordinarily this was a runic sigil, but the principal was easy enough to transfer to an area effect spell.

As Alwer, bringing up the rear, galloped by him Rondal stood in the stirrups and waited until the baying hounds and their wicked riders were only a few dozen feet away before he cast the spell. Suddenly, all five hounds skidded to a stop. Others were coming up behind, but the five closest were suddenly staring intently at Rondal and the sphere of power in his hand.

That was how the spell began. The ball was designed to attract and keep someone's attention. Sometimes used as a defensive sigil to slow down infiltrators, in this iteration the spell instead compelled the animals that saw it to watch the thing as if were the most fascinating thing in the world.

Rondal had often seen a dog drop everything to stare at an object in a man's hand.

He was about to play the world's most dangerous game of fetch.

To ensure he the spell was fully effective, he shifted the ball to his left hand, and then to his right. Five beady pairs of eyes followed it with intent interest.

"Where's the ball?" Rondal asked, gamely, while the goblin riders screamed and tugged on the fur of their mounts ineffectively. "Where's the ball, fellas?" He threw it back and forth, and the five hounds all began wagging their tails like puppies. He shifted it from his right hand back to his left, and when it returned he hurled the sphere far to the left, down a gentle embankment and over a small drainage ditch.

The five hounds took off after the phantom ball like it was an errant squirrel. It continued to captivate their attention in preference to all else, compelling them to chase after the phantom and completely ignore the commands of their riders. Even as he grinned at their outraged howls the next batch of pursuers was closing. Rondal turn and spurred his horse on.

Five of them will be chasing their tails for a while, he sent to Tyndal. *How is our progress?*

The next crossroad is ahead, he answered. *The left fork leads back to Farune Hall. I'm going to put a confounding spell to foil their tracking, and we can slink back to safety – Ron!* screamed Tyndal in his mind a moment later, just when he considered slowing his horse again. *Shit! We're under attack! A damned patrol! Seven or eight of them!*

Rondal screamed and spurred his horse faster and faster. Every foot of distance was vital, and seemed to take forever to cross.

A patrol appearing like that was unlucky, at best. At worst it demonstrated the gurvani's improving ability to coordinate. An infantry patrol appearing to shore up a cavalry chase suggested the latter. He could hear the yelps and barks of their comrades to both left and right of the road. If they didn't deal with the infantry patrol, they would be caught between them. Every second that passed could mean their deaths.

When he arrived at the crossroads a moment later, Tyndal was slashing from horseback, Belsi was desperately trying to reload her crossbow, and Alwer was on foot, his horse down and screaming in pain. The animal had been dropped by one of those vicious bolos the goblins had been employing against human cavalry. This one was made of iron chain, nastily barbed, and had taken the beast's hind legs down hard.

Alwer had his long dagger in one hand and an axe in the other, and was giving good account of himself. Two bodies already lay at his feet, and he was dueling two more warriors. Ringing the crossroads were five or six other gurvani tossing spears and shooting arrows while a like number tried to attack the humans hand-to-hand.

Rondal took the head of one of Alwer's attackers with his sword as he passed, and then for good measure he plowed into the knot that Tyndal was fighting with his horse, his blade slashing with precision. As they were bowled over both mounts began kicking and stomping on the aggressive little creatures. Horses, unlike dogs, were not particularly fond of gurvani.

Rondal heard a bowstring snap and saw Alwer's other attacker drop to Belsi's quarrel, and he shot her a grateful glance. Unfortunately, when he turned to face the next foe another bowstring snapped.

When he turned back a moment later, a black-fletched arrow was protruding from Alwer's left eye socket, and a blank expression appeared in the other. Wordlessly the big peasant collapsed to the ground, dead on the spot. Somewhere to his left a goblin cheered at his good aim.

That angered Tyndal. Before Rondal could react, the younger apprentice howled in fury and began waving his hands. A moment later a wild devastating blast of flame erupted among the scattered goblin archers, and most fell down screaming, their black fur afire.

"Damn them!" Tyndal screamed. "*Alwer!*"

"He's *dead!*" Rondal called back, sadly, as he examined the body from horseback. The shaft was just too deep. That point had to be far behind the man's eyeball and deep into his brain. Even if he was alive, he was in shock, and likely would not be for long. Nor would Rondal wish the kind of life he'd have left on an enemy. When the sight and smell of his bowels and bladder relaxing came, Rondal knew it was too late for the brave man. Alwer was dead.

Tyndal was angrily slaying the last of the goblins, impaling one through the chest with a captured javelin, when Rondal looked back up at the sound of their cavalry's horns. "They're still behind us! What happened?"

"Their infantry got an ambush set up behind us," Tyndal said, angrily.

"I didn't see it. Not until it was too late. They had those damn bolos! Alwer's horse was the only one they got, but . . ."

"Understood. Are you hurt, Arsella?" he asked, automatically, forgetting the girl's actual name in the moment.

"N-no!" she answered, tearfully, staring down at Alwer's still-quivering body.

"Then let's head for Farune Hall and hope they don't figure it out."

"Hold," Tyndal said, wrinkling his nose. He carefully raised the point of his captured blade and quickly ended the wounded horse's suffering. "Now we can go," he said, heavily, taking one last look at Alwer's body.

Belsi nodded, ashen-faced, and started to turn her horse when she stopped. "Wait! They're just . . . just dogs, right?"

Rondal shrugged. "Yes, but I wouldn't want to take one of those puppies home to the kids."

"I have an idea," she said, digging around in her saddlebag. It was the same one she'd packed from Farune just a few days before. "Demon pepper powder," she explained, carefully unwrapping the small bag. "It's as expensive as jewels, but every regal manor kitchen in Gilmora has some. That's why I took it," she confessed. "It's very, very powerful. Get some in your eye, and you're blind." She scattered the dust all around her feet. "Any dog who sticks his nose in that won't be smelling anything else for a while."

The pungent, spicy aroma was potent enough so that Rondal's eyes were already watering. "That was clever," he acknowledged with a bow of his head, nostrils flaring as he tried to avoid a sneeze. "Now let's get the hells out of here!"

The last leg to Farune Hall was frantic, as the three humans tried to outdistance their pursuers while keeping watch for additional patrols. While they continued to hear baying hounds and tinny horns in the distance, scrying and scouting kept them from encountering any more searchers, and they made it to the roadway leading to their refuge without further incident.

They slipped through Farune Hall's warded doors just as dusk fell, stabling the horses as quietly as they could in the deserted manor and warding the gate tightly before they retired. They deprived themselves of light until they were secured inside of the refuge tower, behind three sets of locked doors and fresh wards

"We'll stay here tonight," Rondal ordered, when the last bolt was thrown. "We can scry the route to Maramor tomorrow."

Tyndal nodded and went upstairs. Belsi, her eyes streaming with tears, went to the little garderobe on the first floor, where she began sobbing. Rondal stripped off his sweat-soaked, blood-splattered armor and left it in a heap by the thick wooden door in case of need, then ascended the staircase as much to get away from the sound of the miserable girl's crying as to seek a basin in which to wash away the filth of a filthy day.

Tyndal was on the second floor, helping himself to a pint of grog from the tower's stores before tending to his wounds or the dirt on his face. Rondal was about to pass by and leave his fellow to his own thoughts when Tyndal looked up . . . and set a second glass down beside the first.

Rondal was reluctant, at first. The adrenaline that coursed through his blood had left him exhausted, now that they were safe. While the refuge at Farune was well-warded and secure, he still didn't feel as if he could relax.

But then he saw the glint in Tyndal's eyes, and he realized that his fellow knight needed company, not solitude, to fight away the memory of the day. He couldn't turn away from a comrade in need like that, not even Tyndal. Only one drink, he promised himself . . . but he could not deny that he looked forward to the liquor washing away the taste of blood, dust and bile from his mouth.

Wordlessly, Tyndal poured the clear liquid into the two small earthenware cups. Without libation or salute, both lads drained them.

Only when the drink burned a trail of warmth down his gullet did he feel able to break the silence.

"Good work, today," he said, sincerely, if hoarsely. "The siege worm, especially, but . . . all of it. The attack. The retreat. The spellcraft. The swordplay . . . you proved yourself a worthy mage knight today," he admitted, grudgingly. "Sire Cei and Master Min could not have done better."

Tyndal looked surprised but troubled by the praise. "Me? You carried off that evacuation like you were Luin leading the sacred herds!" He paused a moment and winced at the memory. "Too bad about Alwer, though," he said, quietly.

"We were so close," agreed Rondal sadly. Tyndal filled their glasses again and Rondal found it at his lips before he remembered his resolution to stick with one. "To Alwer," he said, a moment before he drained his glass. "May he find his way to his ancestors in peace."

Tyndal nodded in agreement and they drank. Two drinks on an empty stomach, no matter how gratifying, made Rondal's head spin a bit, particularly after the exertions of the day.

"I'm going to go upstairs and clean up. You want to start supper? I don't think . . . I don't think Belsi is going to be up for it."

"I saw a smoked pork shoulder in the larder when I was rooting around for this," Tyndal nodded. "I'll hack some off. I don't think we should chance a fire, though," he added. "Wood smoke would be too difficult to disguise."

"Cook it by magic, then," Rondal agreed, dully. "I don't care if we have to gnaw it off the bone. I . . . I need to wash my face," he said, lamely, and headed upstairs.

A glance outside an arrow slit on the landing showed him that it had begun to rain. That was good – the rain would obscure their track further by washing away their scent. It would also discourage too many goblin patrols. The furry buggers didn't particularly like the rain. Besides, he reasoned, they would have their hands full with the new bands of escaped slaves and the rampant siege worm roaming the countryside. Surely they would abandon their search, he reasoned.

On the third floor, he found an ewer, basin and a slip of soap, so he indulged in sponging himself clean. But if there were tears in the water he discarded through the arrow-slit, not even Rondal could tell. He was drained, exhausted and spent. As much as they'd gained in the day for the mission as a whole, losing Alwer had made the whole thing seem like a defeat.

He came down the stairs, cleansed and resolute, if no less tired. Tyndal was smoking a pipe and absently stirred an iron kettle of pork and potatoes that he'd heated near to boiling by magic. Belsi was sitting quietly under the magelight, stiffly stripping down her crossbow the way Rondal had shown her. She barely glanced up at him when he came in. Tyndal spooned out the stew into wooden bowls and added a strip of hardtack to each.

The meal passed in near silence. The question of Belsi's disposition loomed over all three of them. Rondal found both of his companions stealing guilty glances toward him, then looking away before he could catch their eye. It made him uncomfortable, more uncomfortable than he already was. But if there was anything to be said that hadn't been already, he couldn't think of it.

"I'm going to turn in," he announced, finally. "I think we all need some sleep. I think we can dispense with a watch. We've warded the place. We'll awaken if anything tries to get inside the walls," he reasoned to himself as much as anyone.

He dragged himself upstairs without waiting for a response, and then made up a bed for himself in one corner of the tower out of his cloak and a few dusty blankets.

But once he laid his head down, despite how much his body ached with exhaustion, sleep refused to come.

It was Belsi's fate that weighed on him, he realized. Losing Alwer so suddenly and violently had been a shock, but that was not what was tormenting him. Knowing he would have to . . . do *something* about the girl on the morrow was the demon that chased sleep away.

He stared into the darkness above his head and toyed with the idea of calling Master Minalan mind-to-mind, or even Lady Pentandra – this sort of thing was well within her domain.

But he knew doing that would be pushing the burden onto someone else's shoulders. No matter how dreadful it was to bear himself, the idea of forcing someone else to bear it for him was abhorrent. He could not ask Minalan or Pentandra – or even Tyndal – for advice on this. *He* was the commander, and this was an issue – she was an issue – within his command. It was his responsibility, and he alone had to live with the consequences. He and Belsi.

He felt the beginnings of mind-to-mind contact and desperately hoped it was Pentandra or Minalan, but it was just Tyndal.

What?

I've been thinking about Belsi.

I'll contain my shock.

What if she just . . . slipped away? If somehow she—

No, Tyndal, Rondal said with a mental sigh. *You aren't holding this goat, remember?* There was a long pause.

Just thought I'd call it to your attention, Tyndal finished glumly as he climbed the stairs and made himself a bed in the opposite corner. He rolled up a spare blanket for a pillow and pulled his cloak over him. The cool Gilmoran autumn wasn't nearly as bad as Sevendor's – and in Boval they'd have snow by now – but it still required a bit of wool against the night.

Rondal did his best to ignore Tyndal and go to sleep. Instead, tortured thoughts of all he had seen and all he had felt churned in his mind . . . until they were all banished by a creak on the stairs.

Belsi. He'd thought that she would take advantage of the more-comfortable second floor the boys had yielded to her. It was less draughty. But he listened as she walked across the creaky floor and paused. He automatically invoked magesight to watch her. She hovered at the top of the stairs.

For a terrified moment Rondal thought she might want to speak to him again, perhaps plead with him about her fate. He nearly called a Cat's Eye spell, which would have revealed much more detail to him. But he didn't, for once appreciative of the concealing darkness. He let magesight drop, too, and then closed his eyes altogether.

He listened as the steps moved in another direction – and Rondal realized that Belsi was headed toward where Tyndal was bedded down.

Part of him was relieved, another part of him became cold, his heart hardening at the thought. He could hear whispers, almost audible (and well-within the range of the Long Ears) but he made no effort to discern them. He didn't want to know what they were talking about. He could guess.

Feeling humiliated and rejected, he tried to calm his angry mind by reciting various brutal hymns to Duin in his head. Better than spells, he decided. He might accidentally cast something nasty, the way he felt.

He had nearly drifted off to sleep when he heard another creek, and then a shadow loomed over him in the darkness. A feminine shadow.

"Sir Rondal?" she whispered hesitantly. "Are you awake?"

"What is it, Belsi?" he asked, tiredly, with exaggerated patience.

She didn't answer. Or rather, she answered by crouching down and sliding into his bedding beside him. She wore nothing, he discovered. Her bare skin smelled of fresh soap and dried herbs.

"What are you doing?" he whispered.

"Say nothing, my lord," she pleaded in the darkness. "Ask no questions, speak no words," she commanded. Before he could consider responding, her mouth was on his.

Tyndal? He squeaked, mind-to-mind, in a panic. *What—?*

Shut up and be a goddamn knight, came the harsh reply. It was a command, not a suggestion.

Rondal had a hard time doing that with Belsi's soft, compliant body plastered against his own. It was the fulfillment of weeks of fantasies and dreams, and his body rejoiced with every fresh kiss.

Yet Rondal's mind was in turmoil, still reeling from the rejection and anger she'd inspired. The entanglement of her deceit tainted the first of her kisses, but soon Rondal's resolve crumbled, allured by the soft promise of her femininity.

Her hands were soft and cool and very busy as she undressed him in the darkness. At first he just lay there passively and let her work at the laces, so dazed was he by confusion over her actions. Why was she there? Because she felt obligated? Because she wished to sway judgment? Because she felt scared and alone and wanted comfort? Because she honestly liked him? He was grateful for her admonition not to speak – he had a thousand questions, and he feared the answer to every one.

But then some part of his mind rejected his rejection, citing the soft, warm, intoxicating creature removing his tunic and quietly asking him to move over as a compelling reason to do so.

He'd nearly been killed today, as had she, and her lips were like a glass of honey-rimmed mead. A knight knew that mead was for celebrations, he remembered dully. That seemed like enough reason for him to abandon his misgivings and cooperate with Ishi's blessing.

Belsi was hesitant but determined when she began, penitent and apologetic; but as he began to respond to her actions she renewed her efforts and her kisses with enthusiasm, particularly her attack on his neck. She crawled on top of him, just to lay there with her breasts pressed against his hairy chest, and nuzzled her nose into his neck below his ear.

"I feel so safe right now," she sighed, her body going limp on top of his..

Rondal didn't respond – he wasn't sure what to say, and now really wasn't the time for conversation. But it seemed to banish some of the lingering doubt about whether she truly wanted to be with him, and why.

He knew she did not love him. He knew she favored Tyndal more. He knew that her giving herself to him might be a bribe, or an attempt to maneuver.

But that is not what his instincts told him as she twisted and turned in his arms. Here was a very, very frightened girl who had suffered and brush with death and was desperate for comfort and security. He was not her jailor, here, nor her commander, nor her lord to her common blood. He was a merely a strong man who could make the vulnerable girl feel safe, and her actions were, in part at least, inspired by the pure gratitude she bore him, and her desire to reward and indulge it.

That he understood. That he could accomplish. He didn't have to be cute or wealthy or brave or handsome, he just had to be here and be her protector for a little while. He considered what Tyndal had said about confidence, during their errantry, about it being the feeling of assuredness you got when you knew what was going to happen. Regardless of anything else, he knew he could give this poor, mixed-up girl a sense of protection to cling to.

He considered saying something stupid and funny to break the tension, like he would after an awkwardly stolen kiss. Instead he kissed her back, feeling his accumulated rage and anger mingle with his feelings of victory and success and all of that transformed with the touch of her lips into passion.

Overwhelming passion. His heart thudded like he was in battle, and his hands traced her lines as he delighted in her reaction. The fear, the rejection, the suspicion, the sense of betrayal he'd felt for her evaporated in the face of the inundation of pure, animalistic passion he felt now that he had he in his arms.

In moments, he was as naked as she was, the cool of the night forgotten as he began to explore her body with his hands. His fingers felt in the dark all that he had dreamed of about the girl. Her rounded arse, her perfectly curving back, the nape of her neck, the firm, resilient and utterly soft skin of her breasts. He was gentle, if firm, and he noted with pleasure that his hands had her quivering with excitement as they sought to commit her body to memory.

She, too, became caught up in passion when his hands found her most sacred parts, just before her hands found his. Eagerly, their hands sped the connection they both sought. Their mutual passion became a cleansing wave, scouring away the encrustations of doubt and confusion he'd borne so long.

Regardless of everything else, there was something right, something pure in this. He understood Ishi's Blessing, now, he realized in part of his mind. He understood the magnificent restorative power a woman's touch could have on a man – not just his body, but to his soul.

They coupled feverishly, at first, with a terrible intensity that threatened to overwhelm them. But Rondal realized the danger of such a precipitous course and eased her pace instead into one of consistent, but compelling desire. He chanced magesight a few times to monitor how Belsi was enjoying herself, and she seemed just as engaged and excited as he was. He relaxed and allowed his body to enjoy itself. And hers.

He did not know when Tyndal joined them, but after they had sated their desires a first time and were beginning a second, his fellow knight and apprentice quietly appeared over them in the darkness.

Rondal was confused - was the Haystack actually jealous? Until Tyndal also slid into the impromptu nest – helpfully bringing another blanket. "Scoot over," he whispered to Belsi.

Rondal struggled a moment with a surge of emotions so strong and vicious they threatened to accidently be expressed magically. He felt a sense of possessiveness and territoriality with Belsi after such an intimate moment. But felt her heart quicken under his breast and he saw the gleam in her eye by magesight and he knew that she favored the inclusion. She was not *his*, after all. She had shared herself with no promise or expectation. With barely any words.

Rondal tensed as his fellow joined them, but he let the tension dissipate. He decided he cared not if she favored Tyndal the more, or if she was posturing for escape or angling for favor in his decision. As sweet and attractive as Belsi was, she had proven herself unworthy of his permanent affections. This was not a woman he would wed, he knew, nor did he care to give her his heart any more than he had already.

Other parts, he decided, he was far more willing to share.

"Scoot over," repeated a half-naked Tyndal. "It's cold! But I brought a bottle of spirits."

Belsi giggled and did just that, making Rondal move, too. He started to get resentful again when her hand stayed him.

"No maiden was ever so fortunate as to have the favor of two such magnificent knights," she announced in a contended voice after she took a sip of the small bottle. "Thank you, gentlemen, for your bravery today. And all the days before. Whatever may come, you have my respect, admiration, and gratitude for that."

It was a speech Lady Arsella would have made, Rondal realized. It sounded natural coming out of her mouth. He looked across her naked breasts at Tyndal's grinning face. He was willing to take her declaration at face value. Rondal sighed and decided he would do the same. It just kept things less complicated.

Rondal watched, idly, for a few moments as Belsi mounted Tyndal as she had him, and he enjoyed the vicarious thrill of observing her passion from a different perspective. In magesight he saw the wild, untamed look on her face as she found Tyndal's manhood and seated herself on it, a moan of satisfaction escaping her lips. He watched them couple for awhile, appreciating the act from a spectator's vantage until it began to have an effect on him.

He rose, silently, and both of the lovers looked up, confused, momentarily stopping their lovemaking to look at him. Belsi looked more fearful, Tyndal looked more curious. Rondal had a brief desire to let his suppressed anger and rage overtake him . . . but that was not his first or strongest inclination.

Wordlessly he bent to kiss Belsi, who continued her gyrations atop of Tyndal. Indeed, her movements became more excited the longer he held the kiss, until he felt her hands once more wander to his body, her skin nearly aglow with excitement.

Her desires had gone from apologetic to grateful to enthusiastically eager, and she demonstrated that by her willingness to entertain both of the lads at the same time. Indeed, Rondal noted, she seemed to enjoy that most of all.

Rondal almost reached out to Tyndal, mind-to-mind, during their long, lusty night, but something held him back. This moment was to be shared without magic, he decided. He could feel Tyndal's participation in the tryst, and he even reacted when his rival counseled a change of positions and manner of fulfillment.

But the feelings and emotions were too intense for mere words. Ishi's blessing, Rondal decided, was to sand away such rough emotions under the relentless refreshment of the pleasures she ordained.

They lay together late into the night, enjoying the safety and security and the intense intimacy of each other. But in the morning, the three were quiet as they dressed in the chill and prepared to return to Maramor to reunite with the rest of the unit.

That was fun, last night, Tyndal sent to Rondal as they saddled the horses.

Yeah, Rondal replied, noncommittally. Then he had to grin despite himself. It had been a whole lot of fun, he admitted to himself. He felt . . . renewed. *I enjoyed it. I think Belsi did, too.*

I know she did, agreed Tyndal, confidently.

So why did she go to your bed first? Rondal asked, hating himself for feeling compelled to.

You want to know the truth? Tyndal asked, after a pause.

Rondal considered. He wished he was the kind of man who could just accept convenient fictions, but he wasn't. *Yes, I want to know the truth.*

Well, she said she didn't come to plead for her life, Tyndal said. *She said she was just scared, she felt rejected and depressed after Alwer's death, and she was looking for comfort.*

With you, Rondal finished, dully.

Tyndal paused and considered. *Yes, with me,* he admitted. *I'm sorry, but that's how it happened. I didn't ask her to.*

So why didn't she stay with you? Why did she come to my bed?

Because I told her I wouldn't even consider such a thing with her after she had treated you so cruelly. She knows you have feelings for her, but she stepped all over them the moment I showed up. That touched my sense of honor.

You have a sense of honor? But wait, you told her no . . . because of how she treated me?

I told her that I wouldn't so much as speak with her intimately until she was square with you. I won't favor a girl who treats my friends like that. It's disloyal.

I . . . thanks, Rondal replied, for want of anything else he could think of.

And she does *like you, you idiot,* Tyndal insisted. *She just likes me more.*

Asshole!

"Lady Arsella, your mount is saddled and waiting," Tyndal called formally. He turned to Rondal. "You scryed the route?"

"It's deserted," he said, taking the saddle. "We should be back at Maramor in a few hours. Less, if we have to run for our lives."

They walked the horses, keeping them on the dry edges of the road and not the muddy channel in the center, and barely spoke in the cool autumn morning. Rondal welcomed the silence. As pleasant as the previous evening was, he had a major decision to make about the girl who had been so giving of herself. And he realized how he had complicated his decision even further.

The short journey back to Maramor passed without incident, until they came to Maramor Village. There they were challenged by a sentry, an armored man with a crossbow hiding in a blind made from a burned-out hovel. He accepted their passwords and blew a very short single note on the horn he carried before letting them pass.

Maramor looked almost like home, when they saw it appear in the distance. But once they passed the gate, it looked less like home and a lot more like a military camp.

While the lads were on their mission, an unexpected party arrived from the south: Marshal Brendal, on a surprise inspection and re-supply tour. The guard at the gate informed them of his presence. He had arrived with a hundred commandos, part of the Third, who would be temporarily based at Maramor before spreading out to other outposts in Gilmora.

Rondal looked around in amazement. The courtyard bustled with activity, and the stables were beyond capacity. And with Marshal Brendal here . . .

"Take . . . Lady Arsella to her quarters," Rondal ordered Tyndal in a low voice. "Keep her there, for now."

"But I—" Belsi began, her eyes open wide at the press of activity.

"I have to brief the Marshal," Rondal explained quickly, in a low voice. "I have a lot of briefing to do, actually, after that raid. It might be awhile before we discuss your case. Just . . . stay in your room and stay quiet while I handle this."

"Listen to him, Belsi," Tyndal urged, just above a whisper. "He's smarter than you and me put together, and he knows what to do."

Rondal tried to look confident at the compliment – he was surprised at Tyndal's assessment – but then he realized he was just trying to make *her* feel better. He wasn't trying to encourage Rondal.

That was almost a relief. If Tyndal started being respectful and conciliatory to him, it might serve as proof of madness. He relaxed, handed his reins to a stableboy – when the hell did they get a *stableboy?* – and entered the re-inhabited great hall of the manor.

With the additional men, the place was crowded. Rondal wondered how the suddenly over-taxed kitchen would struggle to feed them all. Walven was standing near the fireplace, speaking with a group of men who Rondal assumed were his comrades from the Third Commando. His squadmate saw him and beamed.

"This is Commander Sir Rondal of Sevendor, gentlemen," he introduced Rondal, pulling him forward by his hand. "Sir Rondal is the knight mage in command of this outpost for the moment. My lord, it pleases me to present Ancient Oskad, and sergeants Reithe and Drafan." Rondal found himself bowing to three men much older than he. The point was noticed.

"Begging your pardon, milord," Oskad – a large, well-muscled balding man in his early thirties –said with only a token trace of apology in his voice, "but aren't you more of an age to be tending the horses, not commanding them?"

Rondal could appreciate why the man was skeptical: there were plenty of young snots whose pedigree got them a command, he knew, not their experience. It would be easy enough to assume that's how Rondal got his. But if Oskad didn't know who Rondal was, then he must have just arrived.

There was a time for modesty and a time for boldness, as Sire Cei was fond of saying, and meeting a military subordinate you may command was a time for the latter. Timidity earned you no respect, when meeting a man for the first time. If he was a good Ancient – and Rondal could only assume he was, based on what he knew of the new Royal Commandos – then he was right to be skeptical.

"I've done my time with shit-work," Rondal dismissed. "I'm just an up-jumped bastard warmage, so don't kiss my ass too hard. I *work* for a living."

"You've seen battle?" asked Reithe in such a conversational tone that it subtextually implied a challenge. Rondal responded coolly, as he knew he should.

"Today? No. But my second and I just eliminated an enemy depot a half-day's ride north of here yesterday. And we destroyed a few patrols a few days before. It's been a quiet week." He was just as casual. It seemed to impress the men – but it didn't end the challenge.

"So you've only seen fights with gurvani, then?" asked Drafan, a slender, dark-haired man in his late twenties. A veteran campaigner, if Rondal was a judge. "Never against humans?"

Rondal fixed the man with a steely stare. *Only* gurvani? "Humans? A few times. And I understand why you might not think a few scrugs are very noteworthy. But they're just part of this war. Soldier, may I ask how many *dragons* you've faced? Or shall we limit our count to trolls?"

Drafan looked startled and had no reply – but his mates laughed uproariously. Drafan joined in, after a moment. He might be seen as merely a liar of the first order, but Rondal knew his presentation had been convincing even if the man doubted the truth of his deeds.

"No offense meant, Commander," Oskad assured him with a grin. "Just getting to know our officers. Walven has mentioned you've run a model operation, here, he just didn't mention your . . . lack of experience."

He meant his age, Rondal knew. "Ancient, I've been fighting goblins on and off for almost three years," Rondal explained, "when I wasn't learning magic on the fly or cramming my skull full of useful stuff. I daresay I've seen more blood than most men twice my age. But that doesn't mean I know what the hells I'm doing."

"If you and your mate destroyed an enemy installation yesterday," Drafan observed, "you must be faking it pretty well."

That caught Rondal short. The last two days had felt like a running disaster. But when viewed like that . . .

"I'll catch up with you gentlemen after I've spoken with the Marshal," he promised, "and if there's a keg of beer or a bottle of spirits in this dump, we'll drain it."

"One more thing, before you go, begging your pardon," Oskad said, catching his elbow and speaking earnestly. "Rumor has it that the scrugs are using mutts, now, in force. Any truth to that?" That was something Ron felt he could speak with with some authority, owing to his last encounter with them.

"All too true, and they are bigger than any cur you've laid eyes on," Rondal assured. "Fast, too. Riders carry bows, javelins, swords, and bolos. They work in packs. We faced one yesterday."

"Any advice?" the Ancient asked, thoughtfully. Rondal appreciated that. Here was a man of his craft.

"Remember," he said, after considering a moment, "They're big mean dogs, but they're just dogs. They act like dogs. Apart from using magic, you can distract them or confuse them. They hate high-pitched sounds, like dogs. And even though they're vicious, they have their weaknesses. When they're attacking in relays, you defend in relays. Attack the mutts, not the riders. Don't let them get on either side of you. Oh, and get your hands on all the demon pepper powder you can – they *hate* that stuff. It burns their eyes and confuses their noses."

He hoped the advice was helpful, he thought to himself as he tiredly mounted the stairs toward his office, where he'd been told the Marshal awaited him. It had been dearly won, but perhaps if it saved some of his comrades, poor Alwer's sacrifice might mean something after all.

The rest of the day was filled with meetings and briefings with the Marshal and the officers of the 3rd Commando, as well as a walking inspection of Maramor and an in-depth discussion about the local situation over maps. By midnight, Marshal Brendal was satisfied that this advanced base was well-chosen and well-maintained, and he retired after commending Rondal on it.

But that did not end his day. Then he had to make further detailed reports, mind-to-mind, to Commander Terleman and Master Minalan about the raid and its results, especially in regard to the siege worms and their capabilities. By the time finished and he stumbled into his bed it was the darkest part of the night.

He did not wake until midmorning, when Tyndal brought him a plate and a bottle of ale.

"You've got the whole manor abuzz," he confided in his fellow knight as Rondal gratefully ate breakfast. "I don't know what you said to those commandos when you came in, but everyone is talking about you like you're a genius."

"Me? How so?"

"According to that big bald ancient, you had a detailed set of tactics for evading pursuit and combating the new enemy cavalry," Tyndal chuckled. "He was so impressed that he had me describe the whole procedure to the men at dinner last night while you and Brendal were in conference. Now everyone thinks you're a military prodigy."

"Everyone must have been drinking heavily," dismissed Rondal. "Any sign of patrols still searching for us?"

"Falyar returned this morning from a sweep along the main road, but not one scrug. I've scryed the area, too. I think we lost them. Brendal wants to send a squad of rangers to permanently occupy Farune, though, and find another such decoy refuge to the east. And a place further south for a line-of-retreat, in case Maramor is endangered."

"I know," sighed Rondal tiredly as he sipped his ale. "I'm the one who suggested it to him. The idea is to set up a network of clandestine outposts of Royal Commandos all across northern Gilmora. Decentralized, small, and easy-to-abandon little bases. Using them for intelligence gathering, civilian rescue, and counter-insurgency – more or less what we've been doing the last few days."

"That doesn't sound like a very decisive measure," Tyndal said, making a face. He preferred an old-fashioned charge to all of this thoughtful consideration.

"It isn't meant to be," agreed Rondal. "The gurvani are preparing for a push south into the rest of Gilmora next year, and the only castle big enough to stop them flat is Darkfaller, away to the south. With those siege worms at their disposal, they'll be able to open up anything smaller than a baronial castle like a chamber pot lid."

"And a bunch of lightly-armed commandos hiding in the bushes is supposed to stop them?" asked Tyndal with a snort.

"No," Rondal agreed. "The commandos are to clear the way. Discover their routes. Disrupt their slaving operations and mostly to observe and report. Prepare the battlefield against next spring's offensive. If you are destined to fight a foe," he said, quoting some ancient general he'd read about at Relan Cor, "then preparing the battlefield ahead of time is just good sense. The Commandos will disrupt and observe, but they'll also be learning how to fight the gurvani. You have to admit, those fell hound riders weren't like the gurvani we saw in Boval."

Tyndal shook his head in agreement. "They're changing. Three years, and they're changing. First the hairless ones, then the hobgoblins, now these little brutes . . ."

"And they have men working for them, now," Rondal reminded him. "That presents some ugly problems . . . but it also presents some lovely opportunities."

"Now you're making my head hurt," Tyndal said. "How are human collaborators a good thing?"

"Because up to now we haven't had a hope of infiltrating them. We can't exactly disguise ourselves as goblins. But if they have men working for them, freely, then we can turn some of those men.

"You've studied Blue Magic a bit – you know it doesn't work as well on goblins and other non-humans. But a truthtelling on a collaborator would be a lot easier. And getting a spy into their councils will be much, much simpler."

"I doubt the Dead God is going to be sharing pillow talk with any of us big folk," Tyndal said, sourly.

"That doesn't mean that they won't overhear things. Intelligence is about taking seemingly unrelated facts and weaving them together. Those facts may not seem important on their own, but . . ."

Tyndal looked at him, impressed. "You really did learn a lot at Relan Cor."

It was Rondal's turn to make a face. "I got my ass kicked a lot at Relan Cor. But intelligence is easy, compared to other areas of warfare. Command, for instance," he sighed.

"Oh, come on!" Tyndal protested. "I've been on my best behavior! Mostly!" he added.

"Actually," Rondal agreed, "you haven't been nearly the pain in my ass I thought you would be. But everything else . . . being responsible for the unit . . . making sure everyone gets fed . . . keeping the roads clear . . . dear Ishi's rosy nips, it's added a year to me in a month."

"And then there is the matter of . . . Belsi," Tyndal reminded him. "I made her show me the hidey-hole she hid in when the goblins came. She's right, there was room for just one person. I couldn't even get both of us in there, and I tried. But there was also that hoard she mentioned. A fair bit of silver and some gold.

"Just what are we going to do about her? We could have her hung, for what she did to Alwer, not to mention impersonating a noble. But now that Alwer is dead, the only ones who know the truth are the three of us."

"You mean, the three of us who happened to share a bed, the night before last?" Rondal shot back.

"It wasn't much of a bed," Tyndal chuckled mirthlessly. "Are you regretting what we did?"

"I'm still wondering *why* we did it."

"Why?" Tyndal asked, his eyes wide. "Ron, we escaped with our *lives*. Barely. We freed a bunch of people from certain death and likely gave them an uncertain one. We are only human. Ishi grants her blessing to us to help us bear such burdens. Belsi *needed* us, Ron. *I* needed it. And I'd bet the tip of my wand that you found it somewhat relieving and not entirely unpleasant."

"So the question now is, are you willing to put a noose around the neck of a maid you've bedded?" he asked, accusingly.

"I . . . Ron, it's not my call. You are the commander, here, not me."

"It's *my* goat," he reflected, bitterly. "It sounds like you're enjoying that, for once."

"It's not enjoyment," Tyndal corrected, "it's relief that I'm not the one who has to decide what to do with her. I wouldn't want to be in your boots for anything."

"So what would *you* do?" Rondal challenged, rising and dressing. "If this was your goat?"

"Me? I'd . . . I'd likely allow the maid to slip away while I was otherwise occupied," Tyndal suggested, slyly. "Maybe with a purse to help her on her way. But I'd spare her the gallows."

"You'd let her go without being held accountable?" Rondal asked. He was pretty certain that was what Tyn would do.

"It's a war zone," Tyndal reminded him. "She was desperate. So yeah, that's what I would do." He stared at Rondal a moment while he pulled his mantle over his shoulders. "Is that what you would do?" he asked, expectantly.

"I'm not you," Rondal sighed. "Sometimes, honestly, I wish I was. Life would be easier. Bring her by this afternoon, at the third bell. I'll make my decision then. And Tyn," he added, casually, "make sure she's here. This is my goat. Not yours."

Tyndal swallowed. "Yes, Commander," he said. And for once, Rondal didn't detect a hint of sarcasm.

*　　　　*　　　　*

By the time the third bell after noon had tolled, Rondal had already accomplished much. He had communicated repeatedly mind-to-mind with various high magi, and he had consulted with Marshal Brendal about the new commander at Maramor.

One of the things he'd learned that morning was that he was being replaced almost immediately, and he and Tyndal were being reassigned. Another officer would take command here and continue to prosecute the war.

That made disposing of Belsi's case all the more pressing. In a matter of hours, it would no longer be his duty or his prerogative. His replacement, a captain from the Third, had arrived and would take command on the morrow.

He had prepared the room, after his consultations, and he did so mindful that this was once her uncle's room. And that this would likely be the last time she would see it – or Maramor – in her life.

We're on our way, Tyndal sent him, mind-to-mind, just after the third bell rung. Rondal thanked him and took a seat behind the small table, where he had prepared two silver goblets and a bottle of wine. The best wine he could scrounge.

In front of him were two chairs, each with a bag at its feet. One was a campaign bag, tough, durable leather, suitable for traveling on the open road. The other was a lady's traveling bag, of finer leather and elaborately embroidered.

Tyndal knocked, and then opened the door, escorting the frightened-looking girl into the chamber. Rondal swallowed but forced his face into a mask of impassivity. Tyndal closed the door behind them, and stood in front of it. Belsi walked hesitantly between the chairs, her shoulders trembling.

"You have put me in a difficult position," he began, not inviting her to sit in either chair. "You have misrepresented yourself, for whatever reason, impersonated a noble and attempted through subterfuge to even attempt murder – and yes, I use the term – to procure an estate not

529

rightfully yours.

"You have also committed acts of bravery and cleverness that have aided our stay here, and aided the war effort. I cannot consider the former acts without also considering the latter.

"The key to what I must decide is just whom I am addressing: Maid Belsi, or Lady Arsella of Maramor."

"Does my name matter so?" she asked, bitterly.

"It does," Rondal nodded. "For what name you are called will decide your fate. If you are Belsi . . . then even if I were to forget your crimes in consideration of your service and bravery, you would be sent forth from Maramor with the next caravan south. Whence you go from there would be your own choosing, as a free woman. But so would your protection become your own responsibility. You would be free to live what life you could make for yourself.

"But if you are Arsella, last scion of Maramor, then the matter shifts dramatically. If you are a noblewoman, then you would be escorted safely out of the warzone in the company and under the guard of the next caravan south, thence to Barrowbell.

"You would be entitled to protection and even succor, at the expense of your father's liege or his liege, if necessary. And you would be entitled to the hoard secreted by your . . . sire for that purpose, as well as any title or interest in Maramor.

"Further, you would be entitled to certain compensation from the Crown for our use of Maramor as an outpost – a modest amount, but one which, perhaps, would support you for a time."

"So, which am I?" she asked, eyeing him intently. "Belsi or Arsella?" There was a lot in that question: doubt, anxiety, fear, greed, and emotions so subtle Rondal could not begin to imagine them.

"That's the question," agreed Rondal. "Who better to answer it than . . . *you?*"

"What?" she asked.

"What?" Tyndal asked, startled.

"Who are you? Belsi or Arsella? Justice says you must face accountability for what you have done, mercy dictates that you be spared your life, after your assistance. If I am to be the one responsible for solving this problem, then I leave the responsibility for how I solve it to you. That is only fair."

"To me? You want *me* to decide?" she asked, puzzled.

"It isn't as easy as you might think," Rondal continued, evenly. "On the one hand, you can be poor, common and free. On the other hand, you could be wealthy – relatively – noble, but constrained by the rules of that nobility. You would lose your freedom, in other words. Perhaps a minor thing for you, or perhaps it means everything. That will depend entirely on just whom you are: Belsi or Arsella."

"So you want me to choose," she repeated, dully, as she considered the possibility.

"Not at an instant," conceded Rondal. "I am going to take my friend here downstairs for a drink before the fire, to toast the last night of my command – for we have been reassigned. Sir Varigon, Captain of the Royal Third, arrived this morning from the south. He shall be in charge of this province at dawn tomorrow. Indeed, I shall be escorting he and Marshal Brendal to this office after our farewell toast to give over to him the notes of my command.

"When I do, I shall pour wine and either introduce Maid Belsi, or Lady Arsella, depending upon which chair you are seated in. Once I make that introduction," he said, warningly, "forever thus shall you be known."

"You have . . . you have . . ."

"He has given you a *choice*," Tyndal said, sharply, "far more of one than you would have given poor Alwer. Noble or common, lady or maiden: you decide. But you must live with the consequences of that choice. *Forever.*"

The girl's eyes were stricken as she realized what a profound decision she had ahead of her. Rondal smiled, calmly. "I think that, under the circumstances, I am being more than fair to you."

"But . . . but you *laid* with me!" she whispered.

"It would be indiscreet of me to consider whether such a fact influenced my decision – and in which way," Rondal said, idly.

"A good knight is never indiscreet," Tyndal agreed.

"But . . . you loved me!" she said, her eyes wide.

"Did I?" Rondal asked, his eyes narrowing the smallest bit. "If I did, that love was not returned. I will not extend my hand indefinitely, my lady, and not to a maid who has her eyes on another. I deserve *better*. Nor one of . . . dubious character." She blushed at that, but could not answer. "You have much to discuss with your conscience and the gods. We shall leave you to it." He nodded to Tyndal, who opened the door for him dutifully, then closed it behind them.

Lock it, commanded Rondal, mind-to-mind.

Tyndal looked at him, and then looked at the key in the lock. He made no move to lock it. If he was to do it, Rondal realized, Ron would have to voice the order out loud. Leaving the door unlocked gave Belsi – Arsella – a third option, Tyndal's option: To slip away and forge a life apart from either identity.

"Oh, Ishi's tits," he swore, rolling his eyes in resignation. "Let's get a drink."

It was nearly two hours before Tyndal and Rondal returned with Marshal Brendal and Sir Varigon.

Varigon was not alone - he had come with Master Denga of the Horkan Order. Denga had been recently granted one of Horka's Seven, one of the seven Alka Alon-crafted spheres of irionite that not only provided incredible power, but superior mastery of those arcane forces as well.

As Sir Varigon looked every inch the professional military commander, Master Denga appeared as the epitome of the master warmage, able to handle that level of power with no trouble. He was a tall man, broad-shouldered with a clean-shaven jaw like an anvil. He had a permanent scowl on his face and appraised everything and everyone he saw in tactical terms.

They may have been knights magi, but he was a warrior-mage. He may have sprung from noble birth and taken a knighthood for his actions on the field of Cambrian, but he was a man of battle, not a "gentleman of action" like many of these Gilmoran knights. He was more than a little intimidating. They both were, and Marshal Brendal didn't help. If it hadn't been for Rondal's relative rank and the fact that he was retiring his post, he might have been intimidated.

Instead he graciously briefed the men on the magical and mundane defenses of his outpost, and delivered a succinct overview on the situation in the countryside. When in doubt, Rondal always felt he could fall back on the reliability of facts. When the time came to give over operations of the post, Rondal led Varigon, Brendal, Denga and Tyndal back up to the former lord's solar . . . where the girl was waiting.

Where *Lady Arsella* was waiting.

The girl born as Belsi was seated in the right-hand chair, dressed in a richly-embroidered green velvet surcoat, her sleeves tied against the chill and her mantle pulled around her. A silver noble's circlet held down a demure white wimple.

"Gentlemen, may I present Lady Arsella of Maramor, last surviving scion of this distinguished house," Rondal said smoothly. "You may find this remarkable: she slipped away from her family's retreat on the basis that her house should be represented at Maramor, regardless of the unfriendly new neighbors. Unfortunately, they perished during the Dragonfall, leaving her behind unbeknownst to anyone. When we arrived, she was all alone, ready to impale me with an arbalest, thinking I was a goblin!"

"You have to admit, the resemblance is uncanny," Tyndal shot.

"My lady," Marshal Brendal said, with a respectable bow. "Your courage does you credit . . . though perhaps not your wisdom."

"She yet lives," grunted Varigon, "while her kin are dead. 'Tis difficult to fault such fortune."

"My lords," she said, curtseying prettily. "I fear the hospitality of my house suffers of late, but please feel welcome."

"Your house no more, I'm afraid," Marshal Brendal said, pouring himself a glass of wine and then one for Arsella. "It has been rendered to the Crown for military use – not that you'll find the estate that productive these days," he said, laughing at his own pale joke.

"So I am to be sent away?" Arsella asked, her eyes flashing toward Rondal and Tyndal.

"Better," Rondal said, pouring more wine from the bottle. "I had Commander Terleman look into the matter as a personal favor to me, in recognition of all you have done for the war effort here at Maramor," he said, smoothly. "And it seems you are not entirely alone in this world after all."

Arsella stopped her cup before it touched her lip. "I am not?" she asked, alarmed.

"Nay, my lady," Rondal said, smiling. "I bear good news: you have an aunt: Lady Yesta. The eldest half-sister of your father, from his sire's first wife, long married to Lord Shand of Longmarsh, a Coastlord of some means." Rondal sounded pleased with himself as he sipped the wine and watched the expression on Arsella's face as he revealed the good tidings.

"An . . . aunt?"

"A half-aunt, if you want to be technical," Tyndal pointed out. "But a blood relative. And one in line to inherit your sire's holdings and estates . . . and you."

"Me?"

"Of course, my dear!" Marshal Brendal said, warmly. "Your wardship falls to your nearest living relative, upon your sire's demise.

In this case, that would be your Aunt Yesta. It will be her duty to take you in, protect you, finish your education and find you a suitable marriage."

"A *what?*"

"It's her duty," soothed Rondal. "Well, technically it is the duty of your sire's liege, but since he is probably dead—"

"Oh, no, he's *very* dead," Tyndal assured him.

"—since he's very dead, Lady Yesta is now responsible for arranging a marriage worthy of your rank and station."

"A marriage," Arsella repeated, dully.

"Indeed. Of course the reparation the Crown pays you for its use of Maramor, in addition to whatever assets the estate may hold in the south, plus the hoard your father left you, all together it should provide a handsome dowry. And there are plenty of poor country knights willing to take a young girl off a busy household's hands for the right price."

Arsella looked tormented by the idea. But she also realized that making a scene in front of the military commander of the region would do her no favors. She swallowed grimly and managed a meek smile.

"I do look forward to meeting my aunt," she said, formally. "Thank you, gentlemen, for discovering her. I feel much safer knowing I have kin with whom I might take refuge."

"Well spoken!" approved Marshal Brendal. "My lady, why don't you go ready your baggage – we depart at noon, tomorrow, to meet with a patrol headed south near Kiplan. From there it is but a week to Barrowbell, and then downriver by barge to the Coastlands . . . you could be in your family's bosom within a month, and wed by Yule, Ishi willing!"

"Ishi willing," agreed Tyndal, as he watched Arsella struggle with the idea. "May she favor you with a giant of a man for a husband who will give you many, many children!"

You are such an asshole, Rondal said to Tyndal, mind-to-mind, as

Arsella's eyes bulged.

She broke your heart, Tyndal pointed out. *I don't mind watching her squirm a little.*

Clearly.

After finishing a single cup of wine, as propriety dictated, Lady Arsella excused herself. The boys let a few off-color comments about her nubile status by their new comrades pass. Rondal did not feel that defending the honor of a woman like Arsella would be a credit to his own.

"So where are you being stationed, Commander?" asked the Marshal, moving from wine to spirits.

"Yes, just where are we being stationed? Commander?" asked Tyndal, happily accepting a cup.

"Master Minalan has had Commander Terleman pull us from the front for a mission," Rondal reported. "A secret mission. I have no idea what, just that we're supposed to meet up with Sir Festaran at Fillisby with a caravan, proceed south overland to some place in the lower Riverlands, and then return to Sevendor."

"A secret mission," repeated Tyndal. "In the Riverlands? With Sir Fes?"

"He's a knight mage, of sorts," explained Rondal to Brendal and Varigon. "A sport, not a true mage. But he has a few talents that are useful, and he is well-trained. A good, solid fellow. What he has to do with the task, I know not, but then the Spellmonger keeps secrets like barons keep mistresses."

"Your master has quite a reputation in many matters," agreed Marshal Brendal. "I've yet to meet the man, yet by all accounts all hope for victory in this war lies upon his shoulders. I've seen what you folk," he said, indicating the three magi, "can do on the battlefield – you won't hear of me charging a dragon – but is he up to the task? Can he find a way to slay the Goblin King?"

Rondal looked at Tyndal, and while he hoped some soothing and reassuring words would flow from him, mind-to-mind, his fellow was just as challenged to answer the question as he.

"If he is not, my lord Marshal," Rondal finally said, "then no other man is better suited. And it will not be because he did not try everything in his power. Our master is committed to the cause of Sheruel's destruction. And we are committed to aiding him, however we may," he answered.

"Well spoken," murmured Varigon, taking a third sip of liquor.

"Indeed," agreed Brendal. "Then let us drink to the health of the Spellmonger, before we retire, and pray the gods that he has the stones to see this through."

Tyndal went to bed shortly thereafter, citing exhaustion. Rondal found he had trouble sleeping, and after seeing Varigon and Brendal to proper quarters, instead of finding his own bed he found himself walking through the manor's courtyard, going in no particular direction.

"Sir Rondal," came a quiet, insistent – and female – voice from the shadows. "I had hoped to see you here before you slept."

"Arsella," he answered, invoking magesight to find her in the darkness. "What do you want to speak with me about?"

"What do I want to speak with you about? You spared my life and gave me station today . . . you don't feel that merits a word or two?"

"Mayhap," conceded Rondal, uncomfortably. "I didn't do it for you, really. It was just . . . it was just the best thing for everyone."

"You didn't have to do it at all," Arsella said, taking his arm.

"I'm not certain I did you any favors," he warned. "I wasn't joking about your aunt. She has six daughters and four sons. She's not going to like a spare fosterling around. She's going to want to marry you off quickly."

"That is my battle to fight," she shrugged. "I could have been dead by nightfall. If the price of that is some fat, hairy old knight heaving his pasty body on top of mine every night for the next twenty years, then it is not too dear a price to pay."

"So you say now," chuckled Rondal. "You have yet to meet the man."

"Goddess willing, he's handsome, rich, and kind," she sighed. "But if not . . . well, I know how to use an arbalest," she reminded him. "Accidents happen . . ."

Rondal suppressed a shudder at how casually she said it – he told himself she was joking, but he wasn't quite convinced. "So you really aren't that upset about it?"

She shrugged. "I lost Maramor, but it wasn't ever really mine, save for a few weeks when no one else was around. I gained a name and a title. And wealth, even, after a fashion. My . . . others in my family were not as lucky."

"But you could have had freedom," Rondal pointed out.

"Freedom? To what, starve?" she snorted. "Do you have any idea what I would have to do to survive in the southlands?"

"Well, no," Rondal admitted.

"Neither do I, but I can't imagine it would be pleasant. Just how many young girls of common blood from northern Gilmora are begging in the streets of Barrowbell? Or worse? How many are on the road, fleeing for their lives with only what they have on their backs? You gave me a chance, Rondal. Not a good one, but a chance. As hard as the consequences might be to bear, you gave me a chance at a life. Maybe even a good life."

Rondal waved at the sentry beginning his patrol of the grounds as he walked by – his last night as commander here, he realized. Arsella smiled. "In a way, I'm glad things worked out this way. I . . . I know you probably don't think much of me, but I do admire you very much, Rondal. You have my respect, even if I could not give you my heart."

"Don't—"

"I wanted to," she interrupted. "I did, I swear to Ishi, I did. I wanted to be rescued by a handsome knight and taken away, or have Maramor restored to me by him. And then you showed up, the answer to my prayer . . . and for a while, I almost loved you. I really wanted to. But . . ."

"But then Tyndal showed up," Rondal said, sourly.

"It was more than that," Arsella insisted. "I was terrified you'd find out my secret and have me thrown out of the gate. Or worse. I feared you were going to be replaced, and then when he and his men showed up, I thought you had been."

"So you never had real feelings for me," Rondal said, bitterly.

"I had great feelings for you," corrected Arsella. "But I had to do what I felt was best for me. That wasn't you. Or at least that's what my heart told me."

"And now your heart is leading you to some smelly, hairy, fat old country knight who gets to rut with you," Rondal said, sourly. "How is that better than . . . than me?"

"It's not," laughed Arsella. "But if that is to be my fate . . . will you at least grant me a few sordid memories to carry with me into my marriage bed?" she asked, pulling him to her, tightly.

He glanced around, but they were alone, save for the guards. "I thought you didn't love me?"

"I do not," she agreed. "But I am not ungrateful. And you have proven a far fairer friend than I deserve. While you may not move my heart, Sir Rondal, I cannot fault you as a gentleman of great honor. Honor that should be rewarded by a noble lady."

"From what I understand, high-born women are not wont to share their favors so lightly," he murmured into her ear as they walked through the autumn mist.

"Lucky for you, I wasn't high-born," she said, pulling him into an embrace. "And don't think I do share my favors lightly. You are the worthiest knight I have ever met, my lord, and you honored me with your attention. I was . . . I was a fool to dismiss it so lightly." She kissed him.

He almost asked how she felt about him now – but his lips were busy and in truth he feared the answer. He knew she was not for him – as much as he liked her, as much as she aroused his ardor, she had failed to gain and keep his respect. The woman he gave his heart to would have to be worthy, far worthier than Arsella.

But that did not mean Arsella was broken. She just wasn't for him.

At least, not after tonight.

He broke the kiss. "It occurs to me that no one has inspected the secluded cotton shed at the far end of the manor for goblins in the last day or so. I would be remiss in my duty if I allowed an infiltrator to escape notice by hiding there. Would milady wish to go with me to investigate? I promise to protect you."

Lady Arsella of Maramor smiled contentedly and took his arm. "Sir Rondal, I am *ever* at your service."

Epilogue
Taragwen Domain, Winter

My heart sank when I saw the front gate of the castle.

Well, "castle" might be too generous, it was a fortified tower and a small, hardened shell keep, but this far up in the mountains it was perfectly adequate. The castle wasn't the problem. The banner that hung from the top of the gatehouse was crude, an old un-dyed wool blanket painted with a design I couldn't quite make out. There was a mage's star, and a shield, and some kind of animal, but the whole thing was off-center, poorly done, and indistinct at best.

It had my apprentices' touch all over it.

"It occurs to me, Sire," Sire Cei said, in an almost amused voice, "that perhaps we were not specific enough in our instructions in this matter."

"It didn't seem like a job that required a lot of detailed thought," I growled. There was someone on the battlement of the gatehouse. I used magesight to call the image closer. Sir Festaran, his helmet looking more like stovepipe than armor. He had a big goofy grin splitting his face. I relaxed a touch – Sir Fes has a good head on his shoulders, and he's as loyal as they come, so if he wasn't upset, it couldn't be all bad.

From his perspective. From mine . . .

"It was a simple enough commission," I muttered as the horses walked up the incline toward the gatehouse. "Stop by and see if poachers were still mining the snowstone here on their way back to Sevendor. But they were to deliver our guest as quickly and expediently as possible."

"Perhaps they merely *misinterpreted* the command, Sire," Cei soothed.

"This is one hell of a misinterpretation," I said. "Dara, for future reference, if you don't understand an order I give you, please ask for clarification to avoid these sorts of . . . misinterpretations."

My youngest apprentice looked amused, which was better than anxious, I suppose.

"Master, I don't think I would be stupid enough to screw up an order this badly," she smirked. "To do that, I believe I would have to change my gender."

"I cannot argue that point," I conceded. "And I appreciate your good sense more than you know. And after I speak to those three . . . gentlemen, I predict I'll appreciate it all the more."

"Hail, Spellmonger!" called Festaran from the battlement, waving his gauntlet at us in the cold air. "Welcome to Estasi Hall."

I did a double-take. "*Estasi* Hall? This is Taragwen Hall." The name was familiar . . . and it didn't belong to this place. It belonged to . . . *oh.*

Oh. Now I had a glimmer of why my instructions had been "misinterpreted". We rode under that homemade banner and into the yard, the chill winter breeze picking up at twilight. Sir Festaran came down the stairs from the battlement, his grin even wider.

"And who may I ask rules Estasi Hall, Sir Festaran?" Sire Cei asked as he got down from his horse. A churl had scurried out and held the heads of all four of our mounts for us. He wore no livery, but he seemed properly cowed by us.

"Why, that would be the Steward of the Order, Sire Minalan," the young knight mage said as he descended the ladder to greet us. "All will be made clear in time. If you gentlefolk would accompany me into the hall, explanations will sound better with fire and cup."

I nodded warily, and then spotted Joppo the Root lounging by the kitchen shed, eating an ear of corn. If Joppo wasn't upset, that was telling. The peasant was not one to linger near danger or disaster. That, more than Festaran's smiling face, made me relax a bit. Whatever my two young idiots had done, it presented no immediate danger.

"Lead on, Sir Festaran," I nodded. Whatever it was he was concealing, he seemed rather pleased with himself.

He took us on into keep's small great hall, where a fire was roaring on the over-sized hearth at the far end. Magelights floated above the three tables in the room, but most were concentrated over the table nearest the fire where my two apprentices were sitting. In comfort - though Tyndal's right arm was in a sling, and Rondal sported a fresh bandage over his left eye. They were smoking and drinking at table like they were two gentlemen taking their ease at an inn.

Both rose when we entered, and bowed from the shoulders in unison until we had arrived near them and the fire.

"May I present Sire Minalan, the Spellmonger of Sevendor," Sir Festaran announced," Sire Cei of Cargwenyn, the Dragonslayer; Lady Lenodara of Westwood, the Hawkmaid, and Lady Ithalia of . . . the Alka Alon!" He stumbled over that last bit, presumably because he was unfamiliar of her exact title – for that matter, so was I – but more likely because Ithalia's presence just has that effect on men. Dara snorted in a most unladylike way at the young knight's difficulty.

Tyndal was the first to speak. He stood up from his bow a full two inches taller than I remembered him being. Some of that could be accounted for the new riding boots he wore, but not all. Not even most. His shoulders were broader under his mantle than I remembered, too, and his face had lost all but a hint of that boyish sharpness in the last year. And grown some fuzz.

"My lords, my ladies, we bid you welcome to our humble hall."

"'Our' humble hall?" Sire Cei asked in my stead. My sphere hovered overhead among the magelights and bobbled at my growing frustration. "To my knowledge, gentlemen, Taragwen domain is ruled by Sir Pangine, tenant-in-chief to the Lord of Sashtalia. In fact, I was here in your company not two seasons ago and enjoyed a cup with the man myself."

"Your information is no longer current, I'm afraid, Sire Cei," grinned Rondal impishly. "There has been a change in ownership."

"And just how did this change occur?" I asked, my teeth clenched. "And to whom does the honor of 'sire' of this domain now belong?"

"Ah, as to that," Rondal said, with enough grace to sound a little guilty, "you may find the tale humorous, Master. And as to the new lord, that would fall to the Chief of the Order."

"What order?"

"It would be improper to begin at the ending," Sir Rondal said. "It might be better if we told you what happened from the beginning. And . . . perhaps a glass is in order," he said, looking even more guilty.

"Yes, by all means, let us tell you the tale over a glass of wine," Tyndal encouraged, waving at the table where glasses and bottle were waiting.

I took a seat, but could not tear my eyes from the two truants as my senior apprentice poured. "If I recall correctly, I asked you to return to Taragwen on the way back from your mission to *quietly* check on the snowstone smuggling here," I reminded them. "Assuming you and your charge had safely eluded your pursuers, I had thought that an order so simply delivered could be as simply carried out."

"One would think, Master," agreed Rondal.

"We were overtaken by events," Tyndal sighed.

"Things were . . . more complicated than we had assumed, Magelord," Sir Festaran said, apologetically.

"*So* complicated," I said, doing my best not to lose my temper, "that you figured the best answer to the situation was to take it upon yourselves to *conquer the domain* and potentially start a war between Sevendor and Sashtalia?" I asked, letting more and more anger sound in my voice.

The three young knights looked at each other. For all I know, there was some mind-to-mind communication going on. But they turned to me shaking their heads in unison.

"Yes, Magelord," Sir Festaran said, with some hesitation.

"That is exactly what happened," agreed Tyndal, confidently.

I picked up the wine cup and sipped, not tasting the vintage at all. "I did not ride for two days to take a few long tales by the fire," I said, darkly. "As succinctly as you can, describe to me the actions that led to this . . . situation."

The three exchanged glances again. Then Rondal spoke, perhaps by previous determination.

"Magelord," he began formally, "As you know, you instructed us to meet up with the Gobarbine Order and receive from them their charge, to avoid detection and capture by any and all parties—"

"Some of whom, I might add, did indeed try to relieve us of our duty," interrupted Tyndal, holding up his sling as testimony to the strength of their defense.

"—and bring said charge to the safety of Sevendor," continued Rondal.

Sir Rondal, I reminded myself. He spoke like a grown man, now, not a mere apprentice. If he was hesitant in his speech it was due to thoughtfulness, I realized, not insecurity.

"Once we checked in with you at Talry, where you ordered us to change our route," he continued, "once we were assured we were no longer being chased, you ordered us to reconnoiter Taragwen.

"If you recall, Magelord," Rondal said, carefully, "when I asked what we were to do if we discovered that the clandestine mining was continuing, you told me – your exact words, in fact – were *'I'm sure you'll think of something'*."

"So?" I asked, warily. *Had I said that?*

"So we thought of something," Rondal explained. "It's actually quite an elegant solution, once you know the story," he said, engagingly.

"I beg you before the thrones of all the gods to explain that to me as quickly as possible," I replied, impatiently.

"In short, then," Rondal said, quickly, "Upon arriving here with our charge safely in the carriage, we begged shelter for the night from Sir Pangine. The gentleman happened to be in conference with . . . a *business associate* when we arrived, and so he declined to see us."

"Custom does not require him to do so," reminded Sire Cei, looking at the lads thoughtfully. Lady Ithalia and Dara were enjoying the show, and Tyndal was enjoying the attention of the ladies. With a start I realized that it had been nearly a year since either of them had enjoyed the company of my youngest apprentice. She had grown more toward womanhood herself, and if she had yet to reach maturity, her infectious attitude gave her a charisma beyond her years. I'd have to watch that.

"Alas, too true," Tyndal nodded. "Yet hospitality, while it must be dispensed by grace alone, should not be spared for the sake of mere trade," he declared.

"Well spoken," Sire Cei agreed.

"Seeing how reluctant Sir Pangine was to entertain us, and being curious as to what would alter the esteem in which he previously held us, we decided to investigate the matter," Rondal continued, patiently. "Using certain spells, Sir Tyndal and I ascertained that the knight was, indeed, discussing the mining of the snowstone deposit on his domain.

545

And knowing our master might be curious about just who was involved in this enterprise, we decided to act in his best interest."

"My best interest?" I demanded. "So what makes you think you know enough to act in *my* best interest?"

"When the Magelord said *'I'm sure you'll think of something'* he was *clearly* investing us with that authority," explained Rondal, confidently. "Else he would have given us better instruction. As you did not, Magelord, we took you at your word."

"And that gave you license to conquer a domain?" I asked, a pained note in my voice.

"Since Sir Pangine had not invited us inside, clearly we were not covered by the laws of hospitality. As such, we were as any band of errants, potential foes to any weak-willed lord who does not look too closely to his security. If we were not Sir Pangine's friends, then, by the gods, we elected to be his foes."

"And just how did that translate into conquest?" asked Sire Cei, not nearly as angry as he should have been. In fact, he seemed to be admiring their chivalric handiwork.

"Actually securing the castle proved easy enough," bragged Tyndal. "It may be stout, but the stoutest walls can be overcome if not properly guarded. Since we had not adequate artillery for a prolonged siege, we elected to focus our efforts on the staff, instead. After consulting and agreeing to a plan, we caused a distraction to be made that drew every fighting man in the fortress."

"A fire outside?" I asked, coolly. Despite myself, I was finding myself interested in the tale.

"Nay, Master," Rondal said, grinning. "We considered that, but it seemed so . . . mundane. Instead I went back to the gatehouse of the castle and begged to buy a loaf of bread and a wheel of cheese for our supper, showing a fair amount of silver. While the lord was closeted in chambers, the castellan's assistant was eager enough for the trade and had gone to fetch the food . . . when the hue and cry went up from the top of the tower."

"I had climbed the exterior and caused a few select cantrips to activate," the taller apprentice said, smugly. "A bit difficult in a sling, but I managed well enough. I used a few Blue Magic charms to agitate the guards on duty into a panic over things they thought they saw and heard. It only took a moment or two to convince them all that they were being robbed."

Rondal took up the tale again. "The cry aroused most of the men – of course I was immediately suspected, being so near to the hall and a stranger.

"Alas, I was taken into custody. My blade was taken from me and I was told to stand in the hall against the capture of my supposed confederate. Being a gentleman," he said, a gleam in his eye, "I of course surrendered my sword to the lord upon request, and rightly denied being a party to any petty theft. They left a single man to watch me while the rest charged up the tower stairs, certain they had cornered a thief caught in the act.

"Once I was certain nearly all of the fighting men in the castle had gone into the tower . . . I easily overpowered my guard and closed the door to it. With only one way in or out, it was simple to turn a refuge into a jailhouse. A quick spellbinding, and they were effectively imprisoned."

"I subdued the guard at the gate," Sir Festaran said, proudly. "I used that sleeping charm I can just barely manage," he added, proudly. "He went down like a pregnant sow Once he was in captivity, we had effectively taken the castle, as there were no more defenders."

"And the domain," Rondal reminded him. "Taragwen was ours."

"And . . . the . . . domain," I repeated, my head spinning. "You just figured you would do something *utterly* stupid and impetuous and get me involved in a war with Sashtalia. You *know* the Lord of Sashtalia is not going to appreciate losing a domain, even a pissant little estate like this, to a couple of up-jumped ruffians."

"On the contrary, Magelord," Rondal said, smoothly, "we were *quite* straightforward in our execution, and obeyed all of the applicable rules of warfare. Indeed, not a drop of blood was spilled. It was a most gentle conquest. Sashtalia's men surrendered to us the next day, once it was clear they could not escape the tower without our leave, nor eat more than bread or water without our permission."

"And where might they be now?" asked Sire Cei.

"They pledged token ransoms, to be paid by next spring, and we allowed them to take their personal weapons and belongings and quit the fief on parole against those ransoms. Even Sir Pangine, though he made many empty threats about the lord of Sashtalia's willingness to commit to total war to retain this pissant domain. The others, however, were happy to find other employment, considering the alternative to ransom. I do believe they will be gentlemen of their word," Rondal said, thoughtfully.

"The mage stars on their brows will help ensure that," Sir Festaran said, smugly.

"And why will the Lord of Sashtalia *not* immediately answer your rash act with a full-scale invasion of Sevendor?" I asked, patiently.

"Two reasons, Magelord," Sir Festaran said, with the others' permission. "Firstly, there is the matter of his preoccupation with the antics of Baron Arathanial, who it is well known is toying with the idea of invading Sashtalia himself, from the north in the future. Now that there is a good and secure bridge through Birchroot, he could march a host through into the heart of Sashtalia directly," he said, as if he was lecturing.

"Which is why Sashtalia would not entertain so much as a skirmish with Sevendor - it had nothing to do with the conquest. The Sire of Sashtalia knows that if his banners are involved with an internal war," Tyndal added, "Sendaria could not pass up such an opportunity to fish in troubled waters."

"But the main reason he will not go to war with Sevendor is because Taragwen was not, in fact, conquered *by* Sevendor," Rondal picked up, smoothly. "As will be plain to any and all who read the *utterly*-legal Writ of Conquest filed with the Duchy, you had nothing to do with this at all, Master Minalan. The conquest was executed and the domain was claimed by the Estasi Order of Arcane Knights," he said, with a certain sense of theater.

"The Order – quite recently constituted," Tyndal added, slyly looking at his fellow knights, "is a small but select band of knights magi dedicated to furthering the ideals of chivalry and enlightened magic through productive errantry.

"Accepted members of the Order are required to conduct themselves according to the highest standards of chivalry, pledge themselves to at least one act of errantry a year, one week in residence at Estasi Hall as Day Steward, and to defend the lands of the Order to the best of their ability. They are to gather once a year, as their duties allow, and give tale to their errantry and renew their pledge to the ideals of the Order . . . and we'll also have a really good party," he added.

"The Rule of the Order grants members wide latitude in the performance of their duties, but the hall shall be open to any member at any time, in perpetuity," Sir Fes said. "And in addition to the Knights, there is provision for a certain number of sworn sergeants and men-at-arms who may aspire to the ideals of the order, but lack noble birth or chivalrous recognition. We didn't want to leave out a worthy candidate, just because they hadn't been knighted . . . yet."

"Upkeep of the Order's lands, specifically the Domain of Taragwen and the keep known now as Estasi Hall, will be paid by the Order through payment of dues, rents from the village, and other regular business of the estate," Rondal recited. "Tribute is likewise to be paid from that treasury. In addition, a permanent castellan – preferably a member knight of the Order – shall be hired to oversee the operations of the estate and maintain its defense. At the direction of the Head of the Order and its Council—"

"Which," Tyndal interrupted, "currently is comprised of the three founding members and the Head, each having an equal vote in the affairs of the Order."

"—the castellan of which shall be in residence, or his designated assistant, for the entire year. To him would fall the responsibility of overseeing the watch on the snowstone outcropping."

"We'll probably have to build a fortified installation at the site," Sir Festaran remarked, apologetically, "and man the tower constantly. And ward it tighter than a baron's daughter."

"But that's just the *public* mission of the Order," Rondal continued, before I could speak. "*Secretly* it will be dedicated to pursuing and destroying Pratt the Rat and his slimy brethren," he said with a surprisingly severe sneer of contempt. "After what he did to Estasia, and Tyndal, and then to the rest of us on the way here, it's clear he has a vendetta against us, regardless of what we do, what we did, or what we might do. So we use the Order as a cover to hunt him. *Relentlessly.*"

"No one else is dedicating themselves to that," Tyndal pointed out. "Your contacts at Court are only mildly interested in what the Brotherhood does. They certainly don't have an interest in hunting

Pratt. The Brotherhood is a minor inconvenience, politically, mostly active in a province outside of the control of the Crown.

"Yet Pratt and his rat-folk have an enmity against us that should – that must – be challenged. The Order gives us the tool with which to challenge it, and Taragwen gives us the resources."

I stared at the three of them slack-jawed for a moment, my head spinning. Thankfully Sire Cei was thoughtful enough to speak before I could once again.

"So, *you* gentlemen," he began, without a trace of irony in the term, "have taken it upon yourselves to not just insert yourselves into a delicate regional political situation, but have decided to take your interests beyond the borders of the Kingdom, itself."

Again the three knights looked at each other, seemed to confer by expression alone, and turned back to face their elders.

"Yes," Rondal said, as the other two nodded.

My head had yet to stop spinning. The implications of what these youngsters had done were impressive. In one stroke, they had . . . they had accomplished a lot.

I stood. The three young knights stood as well.

"Sir Rondal," I began, "Sir Tyndal . . . *surrender your witchstones to me.*"

They both went pale as death. They hesitated, but their hands were already moving toward the silk pouches around their necks as their eyes flashed in panic.

Both stones eventually appeared, and with shaking hands they gave them over to me. Both boys had bowed heads. Both looked terrified. As well they should.

"I entrusted the two of you with responsibilities," I began, my voice low. Only the crackle of the fire joined me. "I have invested tremendous energy, resources, and money in training you for my service. I have armed you with both knowledge and weapons unseen since the Magocracy, and provided for you as you were raised in your station. I gave you a home," I pointed out, pleadingly, "I tried to give you a family. By all the gods, I tried to give you the guidance you needed to become, gods willing . . . men.

"Not just men, but knights of the realm. Men of *honor*," I said, sharply, turning on my heel in front of them. "Men who know how to do their duties. Knowing that it means surrendering your witchstones, gentlemen, are you still ready to answer for what you have done . . . here and elsewhere?" I asked, pointedly.

In truth I had very little idea of what my apprentices had been up to in the last year while I had kept Sevendor from falling apart, help raise my children, held the hand of the King, and dealt with the increasingly-complicated Alka Alon situation.

But I was sure they had done *something* they should feel guilty about. I expected them to look at each other, at least, before they answered. Instead they stared straight ahead.

"Yes, Master," Tyndal said.

"Yes, Magelord," Rondal said, at nearly the same moment. Both had a stubborn gleam in their eye and a resolute set to their jaw. "Even if it means our stones," Rondal added. "We did what was right . . . if not perhaps what was expected of us."

That brought a snort from Cei and a giggle from Dara. I thought Sir Festaran would cower a bit, but he stood as well.

"You are not my apprentice, Sir Festaran, you are my *vassal*. As such I will address your actions in a moment."

Festaran did not budge. "I shall stand with the other members of my Order, Magelord," he said, quietly.

Interesting.

"I suppose one could argue that you only half fouled this up," I sighed. "After all, you did deliver your charge from the Gobarbans, did you not?"

"He sleeps in the cellar below," agreed Rondal. "Safe and hale."

"I sincerely hope so, or this *would* be a total disaster. So one could argue that you failed half of your mission. Should I return one stone, then?" I asked, a bit sarcastically. "And if so, which of you is the more deserving?"

Again I expected to see them look at each other for support. Again they stared stubbornly ahead. But Tyndal spoke first.

"Master, Sir Rondal deserves the stone far more than I," he said, quickly. "His mastery of warfare and strategy make him a far more valuable asset in the war than I am."

"Magelord, I must disagree," Rondal said, finally looking at his fellow. "Sir Tyndal has demonstrated uncommon valor and a unique approach to situations that make him a profound asset in the field. His daring and willingness to take initiative has proven to be a decisive element in several of our encounters. Sir Tyndal should take the stone," he pleaded.

I tried to keep my face expressionless. Instead of handing a stone to either of them, I opened the pouch at my belt where I keep such precious things and set them gently inside. I closed the pouch with a bit of ceremony.

"By your actions you clearly have demonstrated your unsuitability for a shard of irionite," I said, as both boys blushed with embarrassment. "Gentlemen, when I sent you out of Sevendor a year ago, it was with the intention of forging you into useful tools and potent weapons.

"You learned magic at Inrion, warcraft at Relan Cor, and knightcraft at Cargwenyn. Trygg only knows what you learned in Gilmora, but even Marshal Brendal was impressed with you, so you must have learned *something*. I sought to see you transformed into knights of the realm, warrior magi who could lead as well as follow.

"Yet when I give you a simple order – the *simplest* of orders – you take it upon yourselves to . . . to seize the initiative and conquer a domain I distinctly *do not* recall telling you to conquer. You founded a chivalric order that for the life of me I don't recall asking you to found. You decided – on your own – to cultivate a deadly enemy when, Trygg knows, we have a gracious plenty already."

I looked at them but they were no longer looking at me like guilty boys, they were looking at me like men being harshly criticized . . . and ready to respond. Powerfully.

Time to end their suspense. No use torturing them too long.

"In other words, you have both exceeded my wildest expectations. And Sir Festaran, I commend you as well for your assistance and loyal support of these two miscreants. It does you all credit."

"Does . . . does that mean you *aren't* mad at us?" Rondal asked, confused.

"Does that mean we get our stones back?" asked Tyndal, excitedly.

"Yes . . . mostly. And no."

That took them by surprise. So did what I did next. I held out my hand and Lenodara placed two small wooden boxes I'd had prepared for the occasion into my palm. I handed one to each of them.

They opened them hesitantly, and then I got the pleasure of seeing their eyes open wider than ever before. In each box was a perfectly smooth sphere of irionite, crafted and enchanted by the Alka Alon. They were each twice the size of their previous shards, and they were further soaked in the arcane sophistications of Tree Folk magic. These were far more powerful tools than the shards they had borne.

But then these were no longer boys. Tyndal and Rondal had become men in the last year, men deserving of my respect. The stunt with their new chivalrous order was ingenious, and saved me a lot of time and energy – as they had known it would. With the boys watching the outcropping in Taragwen, I felt it was as secure as it could be if anyone else was watching it without political risk to Sevendor.

And this new order might have its uses, too. I couldn't fault them for their antipathy toward the Brotherhood of the Rat – they had taken a very active hand in politics lately, and a couple of vengeful, scheming, terribly-powerful knights magi on their collective ass might turn out to be a good thing.

The boys looked at their new prizes in wonder, as well they should. The two spheres were part of a set known as The Spellmonger's Seven, and they were unlike most of the other witchstones among the various Arcane Orders in that they had never been associated with the Dead God. They were also laced with such a beautiful magical architecture that doing magic with them was almost intuitive. Plus their extra mass gave them far more power than they were used to with their old stones.

"I put those stones in your hands because you have proven yourselves worthy of them," I continued lecturing them as they began to appreciate the power at their command. It would take a few days for them to get attuned to them, but if the recent overhaul on the Witchsphere – have to find a better name for it now – was any indication, the Spellmonger's Stones would be as easy to uses as a glove.

"Master, we . . ." Tyndal said, and trailed off wordlessly as he began to explore his new stone.

"Thank you, Magelord," Rondal said, more formally . . . but no less distracted by the power in his hands. "But surely there are more worthy—"

He stopped when Tyndal's elbow dug him in the ribs. I grinned.

"Perhaps more powerful, perhaps more effective, perhaps more . . . *intelligent,*" I jibed. "But no more loyal. You have proven yourselves as knights magi. From now on, you will be partially in charge of magical enforcement, too – part of the burden of the Spellmonger's Seven. But I think that you will be more than up to the task. Indeed, I cannot think of a task I could set for you that you couldn't accomplish, short of slaying the Dead God."

Tyndal shrugged. "Give us time, Master," he said, casually. "I'm working on a few things."

The idea of Tyndal, of all magi, discovering the way to slay the unslayable almost made me laugh uncharitably. Dara wasn't so fortunate, earning her a look from my senior apprentice.

"Well, put those toys away until later," I said, warmly, "fetch another bottle and tell me about this plot to smuggle snowstone. To whom was Pangine selling it?"

The boys were relieved, and they imposed on Sir Festaran to bring more wine under the pretense that it was part of the job of the Day Steward, a point about which Fes promised to address at the next meeting. But he good-naturedly headed out to the buttery while his fellows told their tale.

"It seems that a local bandit – of noble birth but fallen estate – discovered the value of snowstone somehow and recognized the outcropping in Taragwen. He was quietly mining and shipping small quantities westward, through Sashtalia and as far as Lasserport, where his partner would take delivery. From thence . . . he did not know. But he was very helpful in giving us the name of that partner, and the shop to which the deliveries are made."

"Good, good," I nodded. "We'll track that down and trace it back to its source. Let's pray it's just an unscrupulous enchanter, and not agents of the Dead God. That might prove be disastrous."

"And just who was this local bandit?" Sire Cei asked, picking up on something I missed.

Tyndal grinned. "I believe you know the gentleman . . . and he well knows you. You were a defining event in his life. Our old acquaintance, Sir Ganulan, son of Gimbal. He still bears the magemark on his face in token of his unpaid ransom, and he hates us all bitterly. We gave him a few additional marks before we let him go—"

"Let him go?" I asked, astonished. "Why in Luin's name would you do that?!"

Rondal looked confused. "Master, he wasn't doing anything *illegal."*

"He . . . *what?"* my turn to look confused.

"Master, he was mining snowstone – *which isn't illegal.* The Crown has not seen fit to regulate its trade, since you were nearly the only source, and he had secured permission from the rightful lord of the domain so . . . he wasn't doing anything wrong. That's one reason why we had to conquer Taragwen, not just spy on it. We could not *legally* stop the mining any other way."

"But his magemark—"

"Makes him an outlaw . . . in *Sevendor.* Or in the domains sworn to Sevendor. But this is Sashtalia, Magelord, so he is free to come and go as any honorable gentleman would."

"So now he's just . . . down the river, somewhere, in hiding!"

"Yes, Master," Tyndal said, innocently. "And wherever he hides, he will be taking his magemarks with him . . . and the tracking spell we placed upon them. If Ganulan is involved in more mischief, I figured it would be best if we could discover where he was at our convenience."

"An excellent plan," Lady Ithalia said, nodding. "He knows far too much about snowstone, now, this knight, and if he has an antipathy for the Spellmonger, then he will likely lead you to your enemies. Knowing where he goes and who they are is strategically sound. You reason like an Alon," she approved.

"Thank you, my lady," Tyndal said with a shy smile, bowing as he poured her more wine. If I didn't know better, I'd swear he was trying to charm her.

Of course, the transgenically-enchanted Alka Alon, male and female, were beings of surpassing beauty in human eyes, I'd learned. But few humans would have the temerity to even consider such a liaison. Tyndal apparently had a secret temerity mine somewhere I didn't know about.

"What news of the war, Sire?" Rondal asked, trying to break Tyndal's attention away from her.

"Thanks to your helpful reconnoitering," I said, after trying to decide just which parts to tell them, "we will be much more prepared for the offensive this spring. The gurvani have spent most of the winter gathering forces in the Penumbra, so we're anticipating a very big push in Gilmora and preparing accordingly. It will be a bloodbath, but they want Gilmora and we don't want them to have it.

"Are we going to be part of that?" asked Tyndal, eagerly.

"Mayhap," I shrugged. "But you'll start the campaign year on detached duty." That was the big piece of news they needed to hear. "Lady Ithalia bears news from a council of the Alka Alon, and they have asked us to participate in a . . . conference? Moot? Gathering? Party?" I asked, unsure of what the proper term was. I looked to Ithalia for help.

"The council of high lords in this region merely desires an opportunity to discuss the Abomination, snowstone, and other issues of mutual importance to our peoples," she said, her voice like bells. "The events of the past few years have attracted the attention of some long-sundered from the affairs of this world, among my people. They wish to know what is happening, and more importantly who this brave new humani leader is who has rallied his own folk to war so quickly and adeptly."

"Which is polite Alka Alon language for *we're in trouble*," interjected Dara. I shot her a look. She had overheard far too much and had guessed far more in the last few months, particularly since she had begun working directly with the Alon on her hawk project.

While that gave her some insight into their affairs that I found valuable, I also wished she had a better sense of discretion. Lady

556

Ithalia, at least, seemed to be acting in humanity's interest, but some of the things Dara had passed on to me had given me some doubts about other Alka Alon. I looked forward to the Springtime moot with the Tree Folk as much as I did my next audience with Her Majesty.

"We are not *'in trouble'*, my lady," Lady Ithalia corrected with as much of an impudent grin her breathtaking face was capable of making. "Far from it. The elders just wish to know more about snowstone, and about the mage who crafted it. It is the first novel thing that they have seen since your people fell from the Void. They are curious, and they are as worried about the Abomination as you. There are two large Alkan settlements that will be endangered soon, if the gurvani continued their advance."

"Alkan settlements?" asked Tyndal, curiously. "In the Wilderlands? Like the one in Boval Vale?"

"These are much larger, and much more important," she said, shaking her head. "Ancient cities of great power, once, but now they are but shadows of their former glories. Some are but half-empty with our folk. They remain all but hidden behind veils of magic so thick even our own kind have difficulty seeing them . . . but the evil horizon of the Umbra threatens to strike away those protections. If that happens . . . well, this war will begin to look very different."

I wasn't sure what to make of that statement, but that's what the proposed council was ostensibly for. "We're not the only ones going," I pointed out. "The Karshak and some of the other Alon have been invited."

"In an *advisory* capacity," stressed the beautiful nonhuman woman. "This remains a council of the Alka Alon of this region. Six lords from four kindreds will be represented, leaders of might and power."

"Well, good," grumbled Rondal. "Maybe they can help us fight this war!"

"Their priest-kings are not exactly the rough-and-tumble kind," I warned. "The Alka Alon are deadly fighters, but from what the ambassadors have been telling me, their numbers have dwindled. And not all of them are eager to take on the Dead God."

"As they are neither priests nor kings," Ithalia said, amusedly, "I would hesitate to characterize them thus. And many bear humani almost as much antipathy as the gurvani do. But some are much more in favor of close relations to your people, particularly among my

557

kindred. There have been hundreds who have volunteered to take up arms and join your fight."

"*Our* fight," I corrected her.

"Our fight," she agreed, reluctantly. "So many, in fact, that the few songmasters who know the old transgenic enchantments are growing weary with the transformation songs."

"You mean . . . there will be *more* Alka Alon around like you?" Tyndal asked, excitedly. He was so obvious about his interest I wanted to cringe. Is there anything more relentless than the libido of a seventeen year old?

"Yes, Sir Tyndal," she smiled and giggled, which made me think of sugarcakes for some reason. "So many that some of our lords grow fearful of the movement and seek to prohibit it. Already more than a hundred have taken on new, taller, stronger bodies. While we lose a bit of our power in doing so, I cannot argue that the strength and vitality in a human-cast body is exhilarating!" she said, her eyes flashing.

I cleared my throat to regain the lads' attention.

"The upshot is that we will be departing from Sevendor just after the Equinox to . . . well, parts unknown. They're still figuring which magical tree city in which to hold the council, but they at least agreed on a time that won't interfere with the campaign too much. After that, we'll have a lot better idea of exactly where to deploy you two new . . . tools.

"But that's next year, and this is this year. We're going to escort you and your charge back to Sevendor, have a truly drunken Yuletide, and then get ready for the battles ahead. Assuming the head of your new order sees fit to release you from your duties," I added, dryly.

"Well, that is a good question," Rondal agreed.

"We probably *should* ask him," Tyndal nodded.

"Yes, you are released from your new duties long enough to go to Yule at Sevendor and fight a few battles before you get back to the important job of guarding a pile of rocks," I said, rolling my eyes.

Rondal blinked. "I beg your pardon, Master, but you seem to be under the impression that *you* are the head of the Estasi Order."

"I'm *not?*" I asked, confused. "You mean one of *you* snotlings is the head?"

Rondal looked appalled. "Magelord! We are but new-made knights, still learning the trade. For one of us to make ourselves head of the order would be to invite ridicule, when we dearly wish to see this institution taken seriously."

"So when my friend and I were planning this," Tyndal nodded, "we concluded that only the *finest* example of chivalry and errantry would be of sufficient stature as to allure the kind of idealistic young warmagi who aspire to our company.

"So we decided that the Dragonslayer was clearly the best choice."

"Sire Cei?" guffawed Dara.

"Me?" Sire Cei asked in surprise.

"My castellan?" I asked, absently. I didn't mind, really, as I was certain the post would be largely ceremonial, and Cei truthfully had enough on his hands, with the new baby. But I wasn't thinking about the potential imposition on one of my most important vassals without them having the least bit of courtesy in asking me about it first. I was focused on something else Tyndal had said.

He called Rondal "friend." For the first time I could remember.

I smiled, despite myself. With all the other chaos we were suffering with, I realized I had one less thing to worry about.

The End

Thank you for reading! Remember, you can always contact the author directly at tmancour@gmail.com!

Made in the USA
Monee, IL
10 July 2024

61619714R00329